THE KILLING

Also by David Hewson

Nic Costa series

A Season for the Dead

The Villa of Mysteries

The Sacred Cut

The Lizard's Bite

The Seventh Sacrament

The Garden of Evil

Dante's Numbers

The Blue Demon

The Fallen Angel

Carnival for the Dead

Other titles

The Promised Land

The Cemetery of Secrets
(previously published as *Lucifer's Shadow*)

Death in Seville
(previously published as *Semana Santa*)

DAVID HEWSON

THE KILLING

BASED ON THE BAFTA AWARD-WINNING TV SERIES

WRITTEN BY SØREN SVEISTRUP

MACMILLAN

First published 2012 by Macmillan
an imprint of Pan Macmillan, a division of Macmillan Publishers Limited
Pan Macmillan, 20 New Wharf Road, London N1 9RR
Basingstoke and Oxford
Associated companies throughout the world
www.panmacmillan.com

ISBN 978-1-4472-1395-6 HB
ISBN 978-0-230-76174-2 TPB

Based on Søren Sveistrup's *Forbrydelsen* (*The Killing*)
– an original Danish Broadcasting Corporation TV series
co-written by Torleif Hoppe, Michael W. Horsten and Per Daumiller.

1 3 5 7 9 8 6 4 2

A CIP catalogue record for this book is available from
the British Library.

Typeset by SetSystems Ltd, Saffron Walden, Essex
Printed and bound by CPI Group (UK) Ltd, Croydon, CR0 4YY

Visit **www.panmacmillan.com** to read more about all our books
and to buy them. You will also find features, author interviews and
news of any author events, and you can sign up for e-newsletters
so that you're always first to hear about our new releases.

Non nobis solum nati sumus.

We are not born for ourselves alone.

Cicero, *De Officiis* (Book I, sec. 22)

Acknowledgements

Trying to turn an epic television crime tragedy into an epic crime book is no easy feat, especially with a story set in a country I'd never visited before, one that is a million miles from the warm, outgoing climate of Italy where most of my work is located. I couldn't have embarked on this journey without a lot of selfless, dedicated work from people close to this project both in Denmark and the United Kingdom.

Søren Sveistrup, the creator of the original series, very kindly made time from shooting the third *Killing* series to brief me on his thoughts, and then generously advise me to make up my own mind when it came to moving the story from screen to page. Susanne Bent Andersen of my Danish publisher, Engstrom, helped me enormously with local insight into the city and culture of Copenhagen, as did Søren's ever-obliging agent Lars Ringhof. I was also assisted by countless individuals, too many to name, inside Copenhagen Police Headquarters, the city Rådhus, and other local institutions.

In the UK, my editor Trisha Jackson and her colleagues at Pan Macmillan – all dedicated Sarah Lund fans to a man and woman – were a constant source of advice, opinion and encouragement, as were many 'civilian' *Killing* fans. Among the latter I'm especially grateful to Keith Blount, not only for his own insights into this story, but also for writing a piece of writing software, Scrivener, that allowed me to capture and control the three threads of the narrative from beginning to end (without which I can't imagine how this major project could have been undertaken).

That said, this reimagining of the original story – and it is necessarily a different take since books and TV are not the same – is mine and mine alone.

Tak.

David Hewson

Principal Characters

Copenhagen Police

Sarah Lund – *Vicekriminalkommissær, Homicide*

Jan Meyer – *Vicekriminalkommissær, Homicide*

Hans Buchard – *Chief Inspector, Homicide*

Lennart Brix – *Deputy/Acting Chief, Homicide*

Svendsen – *Detective, Homicide*

Jansen – *Forensic Officer*

Bülow – *Investigations Officer*

Birk Larsen family

Theis Birk Larsen – *father*

Pernille Birk Larsen – *mother*

Nanna Birk Larsen – *Theis and Pernille's daughter*

Anton Birk Larsen – *Theis and Pernille's son*

Emil Birk Larsen – *Theis and Pernille's son*

Lotte Holst – *Pernille's younger sister*

Rådhus (City Hall) politicians and employees

Troels Hartmann – *leader of the Liberal Group and Mayor of Education*

Rie Skovgaard – *Hartmann's political adviser*

Morten Weber – *Hartmann's campaign manager*

Poul Bremer – *Lord Mayor of Copenhagen*

Kirsten Eller – *Leader of the Centre Group*

Jens Holck – *Leader of the Moderate Group*

Mai Juhl – *Leader of the Environment Party Group*

Knud Padde – *chair of the Liberal Group*

Henrik Bigum – *committee member of the Liberal Group*

Olav Christensen – *a civil servant in the Education Department*

Gert Stokke – *a civil servant heading Holck's Environment Department*

Frederiksholm High School

Oliver Schandorff – *a pupil, Nanna's former boyfriend*

Jeppe Hald – *a pupil*

Lisa Rasmussen – *a pupil*

Rektor Koch – *the headmistress*

Rahman Al Kemal – *a teacher, popularly known as Rama*

Henning Kofoed – *a teacher*

Others

Hanne Meyer – *Jan Meyer's wife*

Carsten – *Lund's former husband*

Bengt Rosling – *a criminal psychologist, Lund's current boyfriend*

Mark – *Lund's son*

Vagn Skærbæk – *Birk Larsen family friend and long-term employee*

Leon Frevert – *taxi driver and part-time Birk Larsen employee*

Amir El' Namen – *son of an Indian restaurant owner, Nanna's childhood friend*

John Lynge – *a driver for Troels Hartmann*

One

Friday, 31st October

Through the dark wood where the dead trees give no shelter Nanna Birk Larsen runs.

Nineteen, breathless, shivering in her skimpy torn slip, bare feet stumbling in the clinging mud.

Cruel roots snag her ankles, snarling branches tear her pale and flailing arms. She falls, she clambers, she struggles out of vile dank gullies, trying to still her chattering teeth, to think, to hope, to hide.

There is a bright monocular eye that follows, like a hunter after a wounded deer. It moves in a slow approaching zigzag, marching through the Pinseskoven wasteland, through the Pentecost Forest.

Bare silver trunks rise from barren soil like limbs of ancient corpses frozen in their final throes.

Another fall, the worst. The ground beneath her vanishes and with it her legs. Hands windmilling, crying out in pain and despair, the girl crashes into the filthy, ice-cold ditch, collides with rocks and logs, paddles through sharp and cutting gravel, feels her head and hands, her elbows, her knees, graze the hard invisible terrain that lurks below.

The chill water, the fear, his presence not so far away . . .

She staggers, gasping, out of the mire, clambers up the bank, splays her naked, torn and bleeding feet against the swampy ground to gain some purchase from the sludge between her toes.

At the ridge ahead she finds a tree. Some last few leaves of autumn brush against her face. The trunk is larger than its peers and as her arms fall round it she thinks of Theis her father, a giant of a

1

man, silent, morose, a staunch and stoic bulwark against the world outside.

She grips the tree, clutches at it as once she clutched him. His strength with hers, hers with his. Nothing more was ever needed, ever would be.

From the limitless sky falls a low-pitched whine. The bright, all-seeing lights of a jet escaping the bounds of gravity, fleeing Kastrup, fleeing Denmark. Its fugitive presence dazzles and blinds. In the unforgiving brilliance Nanna Birk Larsen's fingers stray to her face. Feel the wound running from her left eye to her cheek, vicious, open, bleeding.

She can smell him, feel him. On her. In her.

Through all the pain, amidst the fear, rises a hot and sudden flame of fury.

You're Theis Birk Larsen's daughter.

They all said that when she gave them reason.

You're Nanna Birk Larsen, Theis's child, Pernille's too, and you shall escape the monster in the night, chasing through the Pentecost Forest on the fringes of the city where, a few long miles away, lies that warm safe place called home.

She stands and grips the trunk as once she gripped her father, arms round the splintering silver bark, shiny slip stained with dirt and blood, shivering, quiet, convincing herself salvation lies ahead, beyond the dark wood and the dead trees that give no shelter.

A white beam ranges over her again. It is not the flood of illumination falling from the belly of a plane that flies above this wasteland like a vast mechanical angel idly looking for a stray lost soul to save.

Run, Nanna, run, a voice cries.

Run, Nanna, run, she thinks.

There is one torchlight on her now, the single blazing eye. And it is here.

Two

'Around the back,' the cop said. 'Some homeless guy found her.'

Seven thirty in the morning. Still dark with the rain coming down in straight and icy lines. Vicekriminalkommissær Sarah Lund stood in the lee of the dirty brick building near the docks, watching the uniform men lay out the Don't Cross lines.

The last crime scene she'd ever see in Copenhagen. It had to be a murder. A woman too.

'The building's empty. We're checking the block of flats opposite.'

'How old is she?' Lund asked.

The cop, a man she barely knew, shrugged his shoulders then wiped the rain from his face with his arm.

'Why'd you ask?'

A nightmare she wanted to say. One that woke her at six thirty that morning, screaming bolt upright in an empty bed. When she got up Bengt, kind, thoughtful, calm Bengt, was padding round the place finishing the packing. Mark, her son, lay fast asleep in front of the TV in his room, didn't even stir when, very quietly, she peeked in. That night the three of them would catch the flight to Stockholm. A new life in another country. Corners turned. Bridges burned.

Sarah Lund was thirty-eight, a serious woman, staring endlessly at the world around her, never once herself. She was starting her final day in the Copenhagen police. Women like her didn't have nightmares, terrors in the dark, fleeting glimpses of a frightened young face that might, once upon a time, have been hers.

They were fantasies for others.

'No need for an answer,' the cop said, scowling at her silence as he lifted up the tape and walked her to the sliding metal door. 'I'll tell you something. I've never seen one like this.'

He passed her a pair of blue forensic gloves, watched as she put them on, then put his shoulder to the rusting metal. It opened squealing like a tortured cat.

'I'll be with you in a minute,' he said.

She didn't wait, just walked ahead the way she always did, alone, staring, this way then that, bright eyes wide open, always looking.

For some reason he rolled the sliding door shut the moment she was inside, so rapidly the cat squealed an octave higher than before. Then fell silent with the metallic clatter of the heavy iron slamming out the grey day behind.

Ahead lay a central corridor and a chamber like a meat store hung with hooks at intervals along the rafters. A single set of bulbs in the ceiling.

The concrete floor was damp and shining. Something moved in the shadows at the end, swinging slowly like a gigantic pendulum.

There was the clatter of an unseen switch and then the place was as dark as the bedroom that morning when a savage unwanted dream shook her awake.

'Lights!' Lund called.

Her voice echoed round the black and empty belly of the building.

'Lights, please.'

Not a sound. She was an experienced cop, remembered everything she was supposed to carry, except for the gun which always seemed an afterthought.

She had the torch though, safe in her right pocket, took it out and held it the way cops did: right hand upright, wrist cocked back, beam ahead, searching, peering into places others didn't look.

The light and Lund went hunting. Blankets, discarded clothes, two crushed Coke cans, an empty packet of condoms.

Three steps and then she stopped. By the right wall, visible at the point it met the floor was a puddle of liquid, scarlet and sticky, two horizontal lines along the peeling plaster, the way blood smeared when a body was dragged along the floor.

Lund reached into her pocket, took out the packet of nicotine gum, popped a piece in her mouth.

It wasn't just Copenhagen getting left behind. Tobacco was on the hit list too.

She bent down and placed a blue gloved finger in the sticky puddle, lifted it to her nose and sniffed.

Three more steps and she came upon a woodman's axe, the handle clean and shiny as if it had been bought from a store the day before. She placed two fingers in the pool of red liquid that ran around the blade, tested it, sniffed and thought.

She'd never learn to like the taste of Nicotinell. Lund walked on.

The thing ahead was getting clearer. It swung from side to side. An industrial tarpaulin so smeared with red it looked like the shroud of a slaughtered beast.

What lay inside had a familiar, human shape.

Lund changed the position of the torch, held it close to her waist, beam upwards, checking the fabric, looking for something to grip.

The material came away in one swift movement and what lay beneath swung slowly in the beam. The frozen face the light caught was male, mouth open in a perpetual O. Black hair, pink flesh, a monstrous plastic penis erect and winking. And over its head a vivid blue Viking helmet with silver horns and gold braids running down.

Lund cocked her head and, for their sake, smiled.

Tied to the chest of the sex toy was a notice: *Thanks boss, for seven great years. The boys.*

Laughter from the shadows.

The boys.

A good prank. Though they might have got real blood.

The Politigården was a grey labyrinth on reclaimed land near the waterfront. Bleak and square on the outside, the interior of the police headquarters opened up to a round courtyard. Classical pillars stood in a shadowy arcade around the edge. Inside spiral staircases led to winding corridors lined with striated black marble running round the perfect circle like calcified veins. It had taken her three months to find her way around this dark and maze-like complex. Even now, sometimes, she had to think hard to work out where she was.

Homicide was on the second floor, north-east. She was in Buchard's room, wearing the Viking helmet, listening to their jokes, opening their presents, smiling, keeping quiet beneath the cardboard horns and the golden braids.

Then she thanked them and went to her office, began to clear her belongings. No time for fuss. She smiled at the photo of Mark she kept in a frame on the desk. Three years before, back when he was nine, long before he came home with the ridiculous earring. Before – just – the divorce. Then along came Bengt to tempt her to Sweden and a life across the bleak, cold waters of the Øresund.

Young Mark, unsmiling then as now. That would change in Sweden. Along with everything else.

Lund swept the rest of the desk, her three-month supply of Nicotinell, the pens, the pencil sharpener in the shape of a London bus, into a flimsy cardboard box then placed the photo of Mark on top.

The door opened and a man walked in.

She looked, she judged, the way she always did. A cigarette hung from the corner of his mouth. His hair was short, his face severe. Big eyes, big ears. Clothes cheap and a little too young for a man who wasn't far off her own age. He was carrying a box much like hers. She could see a map of Copenhagen, a kid's basketball net for the wall, a toy police car and a pair of headphones.

'I'm looking for Lund's office,' he said, staring at the Viking helmet perched on the new pair of skis they'd given her at breakfast.

'That's me.'

'Jan Meyer. Is that uniform around here?'

'I'm going to Sweden.'

Lund picked up her belongings and the two of them did a little dance around each other as she struggled to the door.

'For the love of God . . . why?' Meyer asked.

She put down the box, swept back her long brown wayward hair, tried to think if there was anything left that mattered.

He took out the basketball net, looked at the wall.

'My sister did something like that,' Meyer said.

'Like what?'

'Couldn't keep her life in one piece here so she moved to Bornholm with a guy.' Meyer stuck the net above the filing cabinets. 'Nice guy. Didn't work.'

6

Lund got sick of her hair, pulled an elastic band from her pocket and tied it in a ponytail.

'Why not?'

'Too remote. They went mad listening to cows fart all day long.' He took out a pewter beer tankard and turned it in his hands. 'Where are you going?'

'Sigtuna.'

Meyer stood stock still and stared at her in silence.

'It's very remote too,' Lund added.

He took a long draw on his cigarette and pulled a small child's football out of the box. Then he put the toy police car on the desk and started running it up and down. When the wheels moved the blue light burst into life and a tiny siren wailed.

He was still playing with it when Buchard walked in, a piece of paper in his hand.

'You've met,' the chief said. It wasn't a question.

The bespectacled uncle figure she'd sat next to at breakfast had vanished.

'We had the pleasure—' Lund began.

'This just came in.' Buchard handed her the report slip. 'If you're too busy clearing up . . .'

'I've got time,' Lund told him. 'All day . . .'

'Good,' Buchard said. 'Why not take Meyer with you?'

The man with the box stubbed out his cigarette and shrugged.

'He's unpacking,' Lund said.

Meyer let go of the car, picked up the football and bounced it in his hand.

He grinned. Looked different, more human, more rounded that way.

'Never too busy for work.'

'A good start,' Buchard said. There was an edge to his voice. 'I'd like that, Meyer, and so would you.'

Window down, looking round from the passenger seat, Lund scanned the Kalvebod Fælled. Thirteen kilometres south of the city, near the water. It was a bright clear morning after a couple of days of rain. Probably wouldn't stay fine for long. Flat marshland, yellow grass and ditches, stretched to the horizon, with a bare dark wood to the right. Faint smell of sea, closer stink of dank decaying vegetation. Moisture in the air, not far from freezing. A hard cold winter stirring.

'You can't carry a gun? You can't make arrests? What about parking tickets?'

An early morning dog walker had found some girl's clothes on wasteland near a patch of silver birch woodland known as the Pinseskoven. The Pentecost Forest.

'You've got to be Swedish to arrest people. It's a . . .' Lund wished she'd never answered his questions. 'It's how it works.'

Meyer shoved a handful of potato crisps into his mouth then balled the bag into the footwell. He drove like a teenager, too fast, with little thought for others.

'What does your boy think?'

She got out, didn't check to see him follow.

There was a plain-clothes detective by the find, a uniform man wandering through the hummocks of grass, kicking at the dying clumps. This was all they had: a flowery cotton top, the kind a teenager might wear. A card for a video rental store. Both inside plastic evidence bags. The top had bloodstains on it.

Lund turned three hundred and sixty degrees, her large and lustrous eyes looking for something the way they always did.

'Who comes here?' she asked the uniform man.

'During the day nursery school kids on nature trips. At night hookers from the city.'

'Some place to turn a trick,' Meyer said. 'Where's the romance these days? I ask you.'

Lund was still going round slowly on her heels.

'When was this stuff left here?'

'Yesterday. Not Friday. There was a school trip then. They'd have seen it.'

'No calls? No hospital reports?'

'Nothing.'

'No idea who she is?'

He showed her the bag with the top.

'Size eight,' the detective said. 'That's all we know.'

It looked cheap, the flowers so garish and childlike they might be ironic. A teenager's joke: childish and sexy too.

Lund got the second bag and examined the video rental card.

It had a name: Theis Birk Larsen.

'We found that near the track,' the cop added. 'The top here. Maybe they had a fight and he threw her out of the car. And then . . .'

'And then,' Meyer said, 'she found her shoes and coat and purse and pack of condoms and walked all the way home to watch TV.'

Lund found she couldn't stop looking at the woods.

'You want me to talk to this Birk Larsen guy?' the uniform asked.

'Do that,' she said and glanced at her watch.

Eight hours and it was over. Copenhagen and the life that went before.

Meyer came round and she found herself swamped in smoke.

'We can talk to him, Lund. Leaving a hooker out here. Beating her up. My kind of customer.'

'Well it's not our kind of work.'

The cigarette went into the nearest ditch.

'I know. I just . . .' A pack of gum came out of his pocket. This man seemed to live on crisps and sweets and cigarettes. 'I just want to have a little talk with him.'

'About what? There's no case. The hooker never complained.'

Meyer leaned forward and spoke to her the way a teacher might address a child.

'I'm good at talking.'

He had prominent, almost comical ears and a good day's stubble. He'd do well undercover, she thought. And maybe had. She remembered the way Buchard spoke to him. Street thug. Cop. Meyer could play either.

'I said . . .'

'You should see me, Lund. Truly. Before you go. My gift to the Swedes.'

He took the card from her fingers. Read it.

'Theis Birk Larsen.'

Sarah Lund turned one more circle and took in the yellow grass, the ditches and the woods.

'I'll drive,' she said.

Pernille perched above his big chest laughing like a child.

Half-dressed on the kitchen floor in the middle of a working morning. That was Theis's idea, like most things.

'Get dressed,' she ordered and rolled off him, rose to her feet. 'Go to work, you beast.'

He grinned like the tearaway teenager she still remembered. Then climbed back into his bright-red bib overalls. Forty-four, ginger hair turning grey, mutton-chop sideburns reaching down to his broad chin, face ready to switch from hot to cold then back to its usual immobile in an instant.

Pernille was one year younger, a busy woman, still in shape after three children, enough to catch his eye as easily as she had twenty years before when they first met.

She watched him clamber into his heavy uniform then looked around the little apartment.

Nanna had been in her belly when they moved to Vesterbro. In her belly when they married. Here, in this bright, colourful room, pot plants in the window, photographs on the wall, full of the mess of family life, they raised her. From squawking baby to beautiful teen, joined, after too long an interval, by Emil and Anton, now seven and six.

Their quarters stood above the busy depot of the Birk Larsen transport company. The place downstairs was more ordered than the cramped rooms in which they lived, five of them, forever in each other's way. A jumbled mess of mementoes, drawings, toys and clutter.

Pernille looked at the herbs on the window, the way the green light shone through them.

Full of life.

'Nanna's going to need an apartment soon,' she said, straightening her long chestnut hair. 'We can put down a deposit, can't we?'

He grunted with laughter.

'You choose your moments. She can choose hers. Let Nanna finish school first.'

'Theis . . .'

She wound herself back into his burly arms, looked into his face. Some people were scared of Theis Birk Larsen. Not her.

'Maybe it won't be needed,' he said.

His rough face creased in a crafty, teasing grin.

'Why?'

'Secret.'

'Tell me!' Pernille cried and punched his chest with her clenched fist.

'Then it wouldn't be a secret.'

He walked down the stairs into the depot. She followed.

Trucks and men, pallets and shrink-wrapped goods, inventory lists and timetables.

The floorboards always creaked. Maybe she'd cried out. They'd heard. She could see it in their grinning faces. Vagn Skærbæk, Theis's oldest friend, who pre-dated even her, tipped an imaginary hat.

'Tell me!' she ordered, taking his old black leather coat from the hook.

Birk Larsen put on the jacket, pulled out the familiar black woollen cap, set it on his head. Red on the inside, black on the out. He seemed to live inside this uniform. It made him look like a truculent red-chested bull seal, happy with his territory, ready to fight off all intruders.

A glance at the clipboard, a tick against a destination, then he called Vagn Skærbæk to the nearest van. Scarlet too, and like the uniforms it had the name Birk Larsen on the side. Like the red Christiania tricycle with the box on it that Skærbæk kept running eighteen years after they bought it to ferry Nanna round the city.

Birk Larsen. Patriarch of a modest, happy dynasty. King of his small quarter in Vesterbro.

One clap of his giant hands, barked orders. Then he left.

Pernille Birk Larsen stood there till the men went back to work. There was a tax return to finish. Money to be paid and that was never welcome. Money to be hidden too. No one gave the government everything if they could help it.

We need no more secrets, Theis, she thought.

Beneath Absalon's golden statue, beneath the bell-tower turret and castellated roofline, against the red-brick, turreted fortress that was the Rådhus, Copenhagen City Hall, stood three posters.

Kirsten Eller, Troels Hartmann, Poul Bremer. Smiling as only politicians can.

Eller, the woman, thin lips tight together in something close to a smirk. The Centre Party, forever stuck in a philosophical no man's land, hoping to cling to one side or the other then catch the crumbs that slip from the master's table.

Below her Poul Bremer beamed out at the city he owned. Lord Mayor of Copenhagen for twelve years, a plump and comfortable statesman, close to the Parliamentarians who held the purse strings, attuned to the fickle opinions of his shiftless party troops, familiar with the scattered network of backers and supporters who followed his every word. Black jacket, white shirt, subtle grey silk tie, business-like black spectacles, Bremer at sixty-five wore the friendly disposition of everyone's favourite uncle, the generous bringer of gifts and favours, the clever relative with all the secrets, all the knowledge.

Then Troels Hartmann.

The young one. The handsome one. The politician women looked at and secretly admired.

He wore the Liberal colours. Blue suit, blue shirt, open at the neck. Hartmann, forty-two, boyish with his Nordic good looks, though in his clear cobalt eyes a hint of pain escaped the photographer's lens. A good man, the picture said. A new generation vigorously chasing out the old, bringing with it fresh ideas, the promise of change. Part way there since, thanks to the voting system, he ran with energy and vision the city's Education Department. Mayor already, if only of its schools and colleges.

Three politicians about to fight each other for the crown of Copenhagen, the capital city, a sprawling metropolis where more than a fifth of Denmark's five and a half million natives lived and worked, bickered and fought. Young and old, Danish-born and recent, sometimes half-welcome, immigrant. Honest and diligent, idle and corrupt. A city like any other.

Eller the outsider whose only chance was to cut the best deal she could. Hartmann young, idealistic. Naive his foes would say, bravely hoping to knock Poul Bremer, the grandee of city politics, from the perch the old man called his own.

In the chill November afternoon their faces beamed at the camera, for the press, for the people in the street. Past the smoke-stained ornamental windows of the red-brick castle called the Rådhus, in the galleried corridors and cell-like chambers where politicians gathered to whisper and plot, life was different.

Behind the fixed and artificial smiles a war was under way.

Shining wood. Long slender leaded windows. Leather furniture. Gilt and mosaics and paintings. The smell of polished mahogany.

Posters of Hartmann stood everywhere, leaning against walls, ready to go out to the city. On the desk, in a wooden frame, a portrait of his wife on her hospital bed, placid, brave and beautiful a month before she died. Next to it a photograph of John F. Kennedy and a doe-eyed Jackie in the White House. A band played in the background admiring them. She was smiling in a beautiful silk evening dress. Kennedy was talking to her, saying something private in her ear.

The White House, days before Dallas.

In his private office Troels Hartmann looked at the photos, then the desk calendar.

Monday morning. Three of the longest weeks of his political life ahead. The first of an endless succession of meetings.

Hartmann's two closest aides sat on the other side of the desk, laptops before them, going through the day's agenda. Morten Weber, campaign manager, friend since college. Committed, quiet, solitary, intense. Forty-four, unruly curly hair beneath a growing bald patch, a kind, intense and neglected face, roving eyes behind cheap gold-rimmed glasses. Never knew what he looked like or cared. For the last week he'd seemed to live in the same shabby creased jacket that didn't match his trousers. Happiest in the minutiae of committee paper and cutting deals in smoke-filled rooms.

Sometimes he'd roll his office chair away from the table, propel himself into a quiet corner, take out his needle and insulin, pull his shirt from his waistband and jab a shot into his flabby white belly. Then slide back into the argument, tucking himself back in without losing a single thread.

Rie Skovgaard, the political adviser, always pretended not to notice.

Hartmann's mind wandered from Weber's tally of the appointments. He found himself torn from the world of politics for a moment. Thirty-two, angular, intense face, attractive more than beautiful. Combative, strident, always elegant. Today she wore a tightly cut green suit. Expensive. Her dark hair she seemed to take from that photo on Hartmann's desk. Jackie Kennedy around 1963, long and curving into her slender neck, seemingly casual though not a strand was ever out of place.

The 'presidential-funeral cut' Weber called it, but only behind her back. Rie Skovgaard hadn't looked that way when she arrived.

Morten Weber was the son of a schoolteacher from Aarhus. Skovgaard came with better connections. Her father was an influential backbench MP. Before she moved to the Liberals she was an account executive with the Copenhagen office of a New York-based advertising agency. Now she pitched him, his image, his ideas, much the way she once sold life insurance and supermarket chains.

An unlikely team, awkward sometimes. Did she envy Weber? The fact that he preceded her by two decades, working his way up the Liberal Party secretariat, the backroom man while Hartmann's handsome smile and fetching ways brought in the publicity and votes?

Rie Skovgaard was a newcomer, scenting opportunity, bored by ideology.

'The debate this lunchtime. We need posters at the school,' she said in a calm, clear professional voice. 'We need—'

'It's done,' Weber replied, waving his fingers at the computer.

It was a dull day. Rain and cloud. The office gave out onto the front of the Palace Hotel. At night its blue neon sign cast an odd light on the room.

'I sent a car out there first thing.'

She folded her skinny arms.

'You think of everything, Morten.'

'I need to.'

'What's that supposed to mean?'

'Bremer.' Weber muttered the name as if it were an expletive. 'He didn't own this city by accident.'

Hartmann came back to the conversation.

'He won't own it for much longer.'

'Did you see the latest poll numbers?' Skovgaard asked.

'They look good,' Hartmann answered with a nod. 'Better than we hoped for.'

Morten Weber shook his head.

'Bremer's seen them too. He won't sit on his comfy arse and let his kingdom slip through his fingers. This debate at lunchtime, Troels. It's a school. Home ground. The media will be there.'

'Talk education,' Skovgaard cut in. 'We've asked for extra funds to put in more computers. Better access to the net. Bremer blocked the allocation. Now absenteeism's up twenty per cent. We can throw that at him . . .'

'Blocked it personally?' Hartmann asked. 'You know that?'

A subtle, teasing smile.

'I managed to get hold of some confidential minutes.'

14

Like a guilty schoolgirl Skovgaard waved her delicate hands over the documents in front of her.

'It's there in black and white. I can leak this if I have to. I'm finding lots we can throw at him.'

'Can we avoid this kind of crap, please?' Weber asked with an ill-disguised peevishness. 'People expect better of us.'

'People expect us to lose, Morten,' Skovgaard replied straight away. 'I'm trying to change that.'

'Rie . . .'

'We'll get there,' Hartmann interrupted. 'And we'll do it properly. I had a meeting with Kirsten Eller over breakfast. I think they want to play.'

The two of them went silent. Then Skovgaard asked, 'They're interested in an alliance?'

'With Kirsten Eller?' Weber grumbled. 'Jesus. Talk about a deal with the devil . . .'

Hartmann leaned back in his chair, closed his eyes, felt happier than he had in days.

'These are different times, Morten. Poul Bremer's starting to lose support. If Kirsten throws her not inconsiderable weight behind us . . .'

'We've got a coalition that holds the majority,' Skovgaard added brightly.

'We need to think this through,' Weber said.

His phone rang. He walked to the window to take the call.

Troels Hartmann skimmed the papers she'd prepared for him, a briefing for the debate.

Skovgaard moved her chair next to his so they could read them together.

'You don't need my help, do you? You came up with these ideas. We're just reminding you what you think.'

'I need reminding. I lost my watch! A good watch. A . . .'

Skovgaard nudged him. The silver Rolex was in her hand, held discreetly beneath the table so no one else could see.

She opened his fingers and pressed it into his palm.

'I found it under my bed. I can't imagine how it got there. Can you?'

Hartmann slipped the Rolex onto his wrist.

Weber came back from the window, phone in hand, looking worried.

'It's the mayor's secretary. Bremer wants to see you.'

'About what?'

'I don't know. He wants to see you now.'

'Fifteen minutes,' Hartmann said, checking the time. 'I'm not at his beck and call.'

Weber looked puzzled.

'You told me you'd lost your watch.'

'Fifteen minutes,' Hartmann repeated.

The hallways ran everywhere, long and gleaming, frescoes of battles and ceremonies above them, grand figures in armour staring down at the figures beetling along beneath.

'You don't look happy,' Hartmann said as they walked to the Lord Mayor's quarters.

'Happy? I'm your campaign manager. We're three weeks from an election. You're forming alliances without even telling me. What do you want? A song, a dance and a joke?'

'You think Bremer knows? About Kirsten Eller?'

'Poul Bremer can hear you mumbling in your sleep. Besides, if you're Kirsten Eller trying to cut a deal . . . do you only offer it to one side?'

Hartmann stood outside the council chamber door.

'Leave this to me, Morten. I'll find out.'

Poul Bremer was in shirtsleeves standing on the podium by the ceremonial chair he'd occupied these past twelve years. Jovial on the phone.

Hartmann walked ahead and picked up the book on the table by the mike. A biography of Cicero. And listened, as he was meant to.

'Yes, yes. Hear me out.' That deep and generous laugh, Bremer's breathy blessing on those he favoured. 'You'll be in the government next. A minister. I predict it and I'm never wrong.' A glance at his visitor. 'Sorry . . . I must go.'

Bremer took the deputy's seat. Not the Lord Mayor's.

'You've read the book, Troels?'

'No. Sorry.'

'Take it. An instructive gift. It reminds us the one thing we learn from history is . . . we learn nothing from history.' He had the voice and manner of a genial schoolmaster, honed across the years. 'Cicero was a fine man. Would have gone far if he'd bided his time.'

'It looks heavy going.'

'Come and sit with me.' Bremer beckoned to the seat beside him. The Lord Mayor's. The throne. 'Try it for size. It doesn't belong to anyone. Not even me, whatever you think.'

Hartmann went along with the joke. Fell onto the hard polished wood. Smelled the mahogany, the scent of power. Looked around the chamber with its semicircle of empty councillors' seats, flat-screen monitors and voting buttons in front of them.

'It's just a chair, Troels,' Bremer said, grinning at him.

He always spoke and moved like a younger man. That was part of the image.

'Rome liked Cicero, appreciated his ideas. Ideas make pretty rhetoric. Not much more. Caesar was a dictator but a rogue the Romans knew and loved. Cicero was impatient. Pushy. An upstart. You know what happened to him?'

'He went into TV?'

'Very funny. They slaughtered him. Put his hands and head on show in the Forum for everyone to laugh at. We serve an ungrateful bunch of bastards sometimes.'

'You wanted to see me?'

'I saw the polls. Did you?'

'I did.'

'You'll make a fine Lord Mayor. You'll run this city well.' Bremer smoothed down the sleeves of his black silk jacket, pulled out the cuffs of his smart white shirt, took off his glasses and checked they were clean, ran a hand through his silver hair. 'Just not this time around.'

Hartmann sighed and looked at his silver Rolex.

'I retire in four years. What's the hurry?'

'I believe it's called an election. Third Tuesday in November. Every four years.'

'I've an offer for you. A seat around my table. Running more than schools. There are seven mayors. Lord Mayor and six for the departments. You'll get any of the six you want. You'll learn how this city runs. When the time comes you'll be ready for the job and I'll happily hand it on.'

Bremer turned that swift smile on him.

17

'I guarantee no one will stand against you. But you can't have it now. You're not ready.'

'That's not your decision, is it?'

The smile was gone.

'I'm just trying to be friendly. There's no need for us to be enemies . . .'

Hartmann got up to leave. Poul Bremer strode in front, stopped him with an outstretched hand. He was a burly man, still fit. There were stories about how he'd strong-arm for support when he was young. No one knew whether they were true. No one had the courage to ask.

'Troels.'

'You've outstayed your welcome,' Hartmann said curtly. 'Go quietly. With dignity. Maybe I could find you a job somewhere.'

The suave old man stared at him, amused.

'Does one tiny promise from the Centre Party inspire such confidence? Oh please. They're the house pets. That fat bitch Eller will suck the cock of anyone then let you piss on her. So long as she gets a subcommittee after. Still . . .' He straightened his gold cufflinks.

'They know their place. A wise politician does.'

Bremer picked up the book, held it out to him and said, 'Read about Cicero. You might learn something. No one wants to end up torn to pieces for the public to gloat over. It's best these transitions are managed. Quietly. Efficiently. With some—'

'You're going to lose,' Hartmann cut in.

The old man chuckled.

'Poor Troels. You look so impressive on the posters. But in the flesh . . .'

He reached out and touched the collar of Hartmann's silk suit.

'What's under here, I wonder? Do you even know yourself?'

Meyer was out before she'd time to kill the engine, flashing his ID at a woman packing the boot of an estate car.

Red.

Everything here seemed a vivid shade of scarlet. The workmen in their bib overalls. The vans. Even a shiny Christiania trike with a box on the front for taking kids to school, bringing back the shopping, riding a lazy dog around town.

All the same colour, all with the name Birk Larsen on them.

Lund walked over, half-listening to Meyer, mostly looking around.

Two sliding doors opened to a depot-cum-garage. Beyond the crates and cases and machinery she could see an office behind glass windows in the corner, stairs at the back with a sign that read 'Private'. This was Birk Larsen's home address. He had to live above the job.

'Where's Theis Birk Larsen?' Meyer asked.

'My husband's working. And I'm going to the accountants.'

A woman in her forties, smart, good-looking with chestnut hair just a touch better tended than Lund's own. She wore a fawn gaberdine coat and a harassed, preoccupied air. Kids, Lund thought. She owned the badge. And she didn't like the police. Who did?

'You live here?' Lund asked.

'Yes.'

'Is he upstairs?'

The woman walked back into the garage.

'Is this about the vans again? We're a transport company. We get in the way.'

'It's not about the vans,' Lund said as she followed a couple of steps behind. More scarlet and uniforms. Hefty men heaving around crates, checking clipboards, looking her up and down. 'We just want to know what he did at the weekend.'

'We went to the seaside. With our two boys. Friday to Sunday. Took a cottage. Why?'

Tarpaulins and ropes. Wooden chests and commercial pallets. Lund wondered what she'd meet as a not-quite-cop in Sweden. She'd never really asked herself that question. Bengt wanted to go. She wanted to follow.

'Maybe he came back to town on business?' Meyer said.

The woman picked up an accounts ledger. She was getting sick of this.

'But he didn't. First weekend off we've had in two years. Why would he?'

Untidy office. Papers everywhere. Big companies didn't work this way. They had systems. Organization. Money.

Lund walked outside and looked in the woman's boot. Papers and folders. Kids' toys. A small football, much like the one Meyer had left in the office. A battered Nintendo. She wandered back into the office.

'What did he do when you got home?' Meyer was saying.

'We went to bed.'

'You're sure.'

She laughed at him.

'I'm sure.'

While they talked Lund strolled around the office, looking at the mess, searching for something personal in all the bills and receipts and invoices.

'I don't know what you think he did . . . and I don't care either,' the woman was saying. 'We were at the seaside. Then we came home. That's it.'

Meyer sniffed, looked in Lund's direction.

'Maybe we'll come back another time.'

Then he went outside, lit a cigarette, leaned against one of the scarlet trucks and stared at the starkly pallid sky.

At the back of the office, behind some rickety, old-fashioned filing trays, was a set of photographs. A beautiful teenage girl smiling with her arms round two young boys. The same girl close up, bubbly blonde hair, bright eyes, a little too much make-up. Trying to look older than she was.

Lund took out her packet of nicotine gum and popped a piece in her mouth.

'You've got a daughter?' she asked, still looking at the girl, the fetching smile. Both photos, alone, too old, and with the young boys when she played big sister.

The mother was walking out of the office. She stopped. Turned, looked at her and said, her voice quiet and small, 'Yes. And two boys. Six and seven.'

'Does she borrow her dad's video rental card sometimes?'

The Birk Larsen woman was changing as Lund watched. Face falling, getting older. Mouth open. Eyelids twitching as if they had a life of their own.

'Maybe. Why?'

'Was she here last night?'

Meyer was back inside, listening.

The woman put down the papers. She looked troubled now, and scared.

'Nanna spent the weekend at a friend's house. Lisa. I thought . . .' Her hand went up to her chestnut hair for no real reason. 'I thought she might phone us. But she hasn't.'

Lund couldn't take her eyes off the photographs, the face there, happy, staring out at the camera without a care.

'I think you should ring her now.'

Frederiksholm High School in the city centre. Where the money was. Not Vesterbro. Morning break. Lisa Rasmussen phoned again.

'This is Nanna. I'm doing my homework. Leave me a message. Bye!'

Lisa Rasmussen took a deep breath and said, 'Nanna. Please call me.'

Stupid, she thought. Third time that morning she'd left the same message. Now she was sitting in school, listening to Rama the teacher talk about citizenship and the coming election. No one knew where Nanna was. No one had seen her since the Halloween party downstairs in the school hall the previous Friday.

'Today,' Rama said, 'you'll have the opportunity to decide who to vote for.'

There was a photo on the whiteboard. The semicircle of seats in the Rådhus. Three politicians, one good-looking, an old man, a smug fat-faced woman. She couldn't care less.

Out came the phone again and she typed one more message. *Nanna, where the hell are you?*

'We're lucky to live in a country where we have the right to vote,' the teacher went on. 'To decide our own future. To control our destiny.'

He was thirty or so, from the Middle East somewhere, not that it showed in his voice. Some of the girls fancied him. Tall and handsome. Nice body, cool smart clothes. Always helpful. Always had time for them.

Lisa didn't like foreigners much. Even when they smiled and looked good.

'So let's hear the questions you've prepared for the debate,' Rama said.

Class full, the rest of them seemed interested.

'Lisa.' He had to pick her. 'Your three questions. Are they on your phone?'

'No.'

She sounded like a petulant kid and knew it. Rama cocked his head and waited.

'I can't remember them. I can't . . .'

The door opened and Rektor Koch walked in. Scary Koch, the stocky middle-aged woman who used to teach German before she rose to run the school.

'Excuse me,' Koch said. 'Is Nanna Birk Larsen here?'

No answer.

Koch walked to the front of the class.

'Has anyone seen Nanna today?'

Nothing. She walked over to talk to the teacher. Lisa Rasmussen knew what was coming next.

One minute later Lisa was outside with the pair of them, Koch glaring at her with those fierce black eyes and asking, 'Where's Nanna? The police are looking for her.'

'I haven't seen Nanna since Friday. Why ask me?'

Koch gave her that 'you're lying' look.

'Her mother told the police she spent the weekend at your house.'

Lisa Rasmussen laughed. People used to think she and Nanna were sisters sometimes. Same height, same clothes, blonde hair too though Nanna's looked better. And Lisa was always heavier around the middle.

'What? She didn't stay with me.'

'You don't know where she is?' Rama asked a little more gently.

'No! How could I?'

'If she calls tell her to ring home,' Koch said. 'It's important.' She glanced at Rama. 'They need your classroom for the debate. Be out of there by eleven.'

When she was gone Rama turned, took Lisa Rasmussen's arm and said, 'If you've any idea where she is you must say so.'

'You're not supposed to touch me.'

'I'm sorry.' He took his hand away. 'If you know—'

'I don't know anything,' Lisa said. 'Leave me alone.'

Lund and Meyer were upstairs in the Birk Larsen flat. It was as cluttered as the office but in a pleasant way. Photos, paintings, plants and flowers. Vases and mementoes from holidays. *Decorated*, Lund thought. She never got round to that herself. The woman she now knew to be Pernille Birk Larsen worked at being a mother. Seemed good at it. As far as Lund could judge.

'She's not at school,' Lund said.

Pernille still wore her raincoat as if none of this was happening.

'She must be at Lisa's. They're friends. Lisa rents a flat with a couple of boys. Nanna's always there.'

'Lisa's at school. She says Nanna never stayed with her.'

Pernille's mouth hung half open. Her eyes were wide and blank. On the kitchen wall Lund saw the same two photos from the office: Nanna with the boys, Nanna on her own looking beautiful and too old for nineteen. Fixed to a cork-board alongside a timetable for school sports events. The easy, casual air of domesticity hung around this place. Like the smell of a dog, unnoticed by the owner, apparent to a stranger from the outset.

'What's happened to her? Where is she?' Pernille asked.

'Probably nothing. We'll do our best to find her.'

Lund walked into the tiny hall and phoned headquarters.

Meyer took Pernille out of earshot and began asking about photos.

Through to Buchard, Lund said, 'I need everyone we can spare on this.' The old man didn't even ask a question, just listened. 'Tell them we're looking for nineteen-year-old Nanna Birk Larsen. Missing since Friday. Send someone here for the photos.'

'And you?'

'We're going to her school.'

Hartmann and Rie Skovgaard had an empty classroom to prepare. She went through the numbers about the education allocation again. He paced round nervously. Finally she closed the laptop, came and checked his clothes. No tie, blue shirt. He looked good. But still she fiddled with his collar, came close enough so he had to hold her.

Hartmann's hands slipped round her back. He pulled Skovgaard to him, kissed her. A sudden passion. Unexpected. She wanted to laugh. He wanted more.

'Move in with me,' he said and pushed her against the desk. She fell on it, giggling, wrapped her long legs round him.

'Aren't you too busy?'

'Not for you.'

'After the election.'

His face changed. The politician returned.

'Why the big secret?'

'Because I've got a job to do, Troels. And so have you. We want no complications.' Her voice fell a tone. Smart eyes flashing. 'And we don't want Morten jealous.'

'Morten's the most experienced political aide we have. He knows what he's doing.'

'So I don't?'

'I didn't say that. I don't want to talk about Morten . . .'

Her hands were on his jacket again.

'Let's deal with this when you've won, shall we?'

Hartmann was reaching for her again.

The door opened. Rektor Koch was there. She looked embarrassed.

'The Lord Mayor's arrived,' she said. A confidential smile. 'If you're ready.'

Hartmann buttoned his jacket and walked out into the corridor.

Poul Bremer was beaming beneath a poster of a half-naked pop singer. Skovgaard left them alone and went to check out the room.

'I hope the Centre Party likes your ideas, Troels. A lot of them are good. Very like your father's.'

'Is that so?'

'They have his vigorous energy. His optimism.'

'Conviction,' Hartmann said. 'They came from what he believed. Not what he thought might win a few votes.'

Bremer nodded at that.

'It's a shame he was never quite good enough to see them through.'

'I'll think of him. When I've got your job.'

'I believe you will. One day.' Bremer pulled out a handkerchief and cleaned his spectacles. 'You're more robust than he was. Your father was always . . . How should I put it?' The glasses went back on, those icy eyes looked him up and down. 'Fragile. Like porcelain.'

Bremer held up his right hand. A big fist. A fighter's, in spite of all outward appearances.

'He was always going to snap.'

The click of his strong fingers was so loud it seemed to echo off the peeling walls.

'If I hadn't broken him he'd have broken himself. Believe me. It was a kindness in a way. It's best not to allow one's delusions to linger too long.'

'Let's get to this debate,' Hartmann said. 'It's time . . .'

When they turned to go Rektor Koch was walking towards them. She looked worried. With her was a woman in a blue cagoule, an odd black and white patterned sweater visible beneath it, hair swept back from her face like a teenager too busy to think about boyfriends.

A woman who thought nothing of her own appearance. Which was odd since she was striking and attractive.

Now she was looking straight ahead, at them, nowhere else. She had very large and staring eyes.

Somehow Hartmann wasn't surprised when she pulled out a police ID card. It read: *Vicekriminalkommissær Sarah Lund.*

Bremer had retreated to the back of the corridor the moment he saw the cop approaching.

'You have to cancel the debate,' Lund said.

'Why?'

'There's a missing girl. I need to talk to people here. People in her class. Teachers. I need . . .'

Rektor Koch was ushering them into a side room, out of the corridor. Bremer stayed where he was.

Hartmann listened to the cop.

'You want me to cancel a debate because a pupil's skipping school?'

'It's important I talk to everyone,' Lund insisted.

'Everyone?'

'Everyone I want to talk to.'

She didn't move. Didn't stop looking at him. Nothing else.

'We could put back the debate an hour,' Hartmann suggested.

'Not for me,' Bremer cut in. 'I have appointments. This was your invitation, Troels. If you can't make it . . .'

Hartmann took a step towards Sarah Lund and said, 'How serious is it?'

'I hope nothing's happened.'

'I asked how serious it was.'

'That's what I'm trying to find out,' Lund replied then put her hands on her hips and waited for an answer. 'So . . .'

She looked round, checking the rooms.

'That's agreed then,' Lund added.

Bremer took out his phone, checked some messages.

'Call my secretary. I'll try to fit you in. Oh!' A sudden flash of geniality. 'I've got good news for your inner-city schools. It seems absenteeism is up by twenty per cent.' He laughed. 'We can't have that, can we? So I've allocated funds for extra facilities. More computers. Children love those things. That'll fix it.'

Hartmann stared at him, speechless.

Bremer shrugged.

'I would have told you in there. But now . . . We'll put out a release straight away. Good news. I trust you'll welcome it.'

A long moment of silence.

'You're happy, I see,' Bremer said, then, with a wave, walked off.

Half past three in the afternoon. They were still in the room where the debate was supposed to happen, getting nowhere. Nanna had been to the Halloween party in the school hall the previous Friday, dressed in a black witch's hat and garish blue wig. No one had seen her since.

Now it was the teacher's turn.

'What's Nanna like?'

They all called him Rama. He stood out and not just because of his dark, striking Middle Eastern looks. He was one of Troels Hartmann's role models, part of an initiative to bring immigrant groups more closely into the fabric of the community. An articulate, intelligent, convincing man.

'Nanna's a clever kid,' he said. 'Always full of energy. Always wanting to do something.'

'I saw the photo. She looks older than nineteen.'

He nodded.

'They all want that, don't they? Desperate to grow up. Or to feel they have. Nanna's top of her class in most things. Bright kid. Doesn't stop her wanting what the rest do.'

'Which is?'

The teacher looked at her.

'They're teenagers. Are you serious?'

'What happened at the party?'

'Fancy dress. A band. Ghosts and pumpkins.'

'Does she have a boyfriend?'

26

'Ask Lisa.'

'I'm asking you.'

He looked uncomfortable.

'It's best a teacher stays out of these things.'

Lund went outside, stopped the first girl she found, sat her down, talked to her until she got an answer.

Then she went back to the teacher.

'Oliver Schandorff. Is he here?'

'No.'

'Did you know Oliver was her boyfriend?'

'I told you. It's best we keep some distance.'

She waited.

'I'm their teacher. Not their guardian. Not a parent either.'

Lund looked at her watch. The interviews had run on for more than three hours and this was all they had. All anyone had. Meyer, out in the woods and fields near the airport with a search team, hadn't found a thing.

'Shit.'

'I'm sorry,' the teacher said.

'Not you.'

Me, she thought. She could surely have got this out of Pernille in a few minutes if she'd tried. Why was it the best questions only came when she had something – people, evidence, crimes – in front of her?

Two hundred and thirty-five three-storey terraced houses made up the place called Humleby, a tiny estate four streets from Birk Larsen's home. The colour of slate and gunmetal, they were built in the nineteenth century for workers at the nearby shipyard. Then the Carlsberg brewery expanded and the houses fell into the hands of men who made beer. They came onto the market slowly, sought after even if some needed much expensive restoration. Theis Birk Larsen had bought the cheapest he could find. Squatters had been in before, leaving behind their junk, mattresses and cheap furniture. It needed clearing, a lot of repair work. He'd do most of it himself, quietly, without telling Pernille, not until it was close to time to move in and escape the tiny apartment above the garage.

Vagn Skærbæk was helping. The two had known each other since they were teens, gone through a lot together, including a few appearances in court. To Birk Larsen he'd become almost a younger brother, uncle to the kids, steady employee in the transport company. Reliable, trustworthy, kind to Anton and Emil. A solitary man who seemed to have no life of his own once he took off the scarlet uniform.

'Pernille's looking for you,' Skærbæk said coming off the phone.

'Pernille's not going to know about this place. I told you. Not a word until I say.'

'She's phoning round, asking where you are.'

There was scaffolding on the outside, sheeting against the rotting windows. Birk Larsen was paying his own men to carry in new floorboards, guttering and piping, making them promise to keep quiet about the place when Pernille was around.

'The boys can have their own rooms,' he said, looking at the grey stone house. 'You see that top window?'

Skærbæk nodded.

'Nanna gets that whole floor, a staircase of her own and some privacy. Pernille a new kitchen. And me . . .' He laughed. 'Some peace and quiet.'

'This is going to cost a fortune, Theis.'

Birk Larsen stuffed his hands into the pockets of his red bib overall.

'I'll manage.'

'Maybe I can help.'

'Meaning?'

Skærbæk was a slight and fidgety man. He stood there shuffling from foot to foot even more than usual.

'I know where there's thirty B&O TVs going cheap. All we've got to—'

'You're in debt? That's it?'

'Listen. I've got buyers for half of them . . . We can share . . .'

Birk Larsen pulled a wad of notes out of his pocket, ripped off a few.

'All I need is to borrow a forklift . . .'

'Here you go.' He folded the money in Skærbæk's hand. 'Forget the TVs. We're not teenagers any more, Vagn. I've got a family. A business.' Skærbæk kept hold of the money. 'You're part of both. Always will be.'

Skærbæk stared at the cash. Birk Larsen wished he'd lose that stupid silver neck chain.

'How'd the boys feel if they had to visit their Uncle Vagn in jail?'

'You don't have to do this . . .' Skærbæk started.

Theis Birk Larsen wasn't listening. Pernille was riding towards him on the Christiania trike, so quickly the shiny scarlet box on the front bumped up and down over the cobblestones.

He forgot all about the secret house, about building work and where the money might come from.

She looked terrible.

Pernille got off, came straight up to him, took the collars of his black leather coat.

'Nanna's missing.' She was breathless, pale, scared. 'The police found your video rental card out near the airport. They found . . .'

Her hand went to her mouth. Tears started in her eyes.

'Found what?'

'Her top. The pink one with the flowers.'

'Lots of kids wear tops like that. Don't they?'

She gave him a sharp look.

'And the video card?'

'Did they talk to Lisa?'

Vagn Skærbæk was listening. She looked at him and said, 'Please, Vagn.'

'You want any help?'

Birk Larsen stared at him. He went away.

'What about that bastard kid?'

'She isn't seeing Oliver any more.'

There was a touch of red anger in his cheeks.

'Did they talk to him?'

A deep breath then she said, 'I don't know.'

He had his keys out, called to Skærbæk, 'Take Pernille home. And the trike.'

A thought.

'Why didn't you drive?'

'They wouldn't let me use the car. They said I couldn't move it.'

Theis Birk Larsen took his wife in his broad arms, held her, kissed her once, touched her cheek, looked her in the eye and said, 'Nanna's fine. I'll find her. Go home and wait for us.'

Then he climbed into the van and left.

'I'll drop you off at Gran's. You've got your key?'

The weather was closing in, the day ending in mist and drizzle.

Lund was driving out to Østerbro, her twelve-year-old son, Mark, in the passenger seat.

'You mean we're not going to Sweden after all?'

'I've got something to do first.'

'Me too.'

Lund looked at her son. But in truth all she was seeing in her head was the flat yellow grass, a teenager's bloodstained top. And the photograph of Nanna Birk Larsen, smiling like an older sister proud of her little brothers. Looking too grown-up with all that make-up.

She hadn't a clue what Mark was talking about.

'I told you, Mum. Magnus's birthday party.'

'Mark. Our flight's tonight. We decided this ages ago.'

He grunted and turned to stare out of the rain-streaked window.

'You look like a moose with the mumps,' she said.

Lund laughed. He didn't.

'You'll love it in Sweden. It's a great school. I'll have more time for you. We can—'

'He's not my father.'

Lund's phone started ringing. She looked at the number and began fumbling the headset into her ear.

'Of course he's not. He's found you a hockey club.'

'I've got one.'

'You must be sick of being the youngest at FCK.'

Silence.

'Aren't you?'

'It's called KSF.'

'Yes,' she said to the phone.

'KSF,' Mark repeated.

'I'm on my way.'

Mark began to speak very slowly.

'K . . . S . . . F . . .'

'Yes.'

'You get it wrong every time.'

'Yes.'

It wasn't far now which pleased her on two counts. She wanted to see Meyer. And Mark was . . . in the way.

'Not long now and then we go to the airport,' she said. 'You do have your key, don't you?'

*

30

Beneath a sullen monochrome sky a single line of twenty blue-clad officers moved slowly across the yellow grass, prodding the mud and clumps of vegetation with red and white sticks, search dogs snuffling at the damp earth.

Lund watched them for a moment then went into the wood. There a second team was working through the lichened trees, examining the ground, putting down markers, following another set of dogs.

Meyer was in a police jacket, soaked to the skin.

'How clear's the trail?' she asked.

'Clear enough. The dogs followed her from where we found the top.' He looked at his notes and gestured to a thicket ten metres away. 'We also got some blonde hair caught on a bush.'

'Where does it lead?'

'Here,' Meyer said, gesturing with the map in his hand. 'Where we're standing.' Another look at his notes. 'She was running. Zigzagging through the woods. This was where she stopped.'

Lund came and peered over his shoulder.

'What do we have close by?'

'A logging road. Maybe she was picked up there.'

'What about her mobile phone?'

'Switched off since Friday night.' He didn't like these obvious questions. 'Listen, Lund. We've gone over her route with a fine-tooth comb. Twice. She isn't here. We're wasting time.'

She turned and walked away, looked back to the marshland and yellow grass.

'Hello?' Meyer said with that dry sarcasm she was starting to recognize. 'Am I invisible?'

Lund came back and said, 'Spread out. Go over it all again.'

'Did you hear a word I said?'

The local intercom on one of the search team's jackets squawked her name.

'We've found something,' a voice said.

'Where?'

'In the trees.'

'What is it?'

A pause. It was getting dark. Then, 'It looks like a grave.'

The same sluggish twilight crept over the city, damp and dreary, wan and cold. In his campaign office, beneath the coral-coloured petals of the artichoke lamps, Hartmann listened to Morten Weber's answers. Poul Bremer wouldn't return to the school for another debate. Running the city was more important than begging for votes.

'Doesn't that suit him?' Hartmann said.

Rie Skovgaard placed a cup of coffee on his desk.

'Bremer's office announced the new allocation of funds while we were at the school. He was ready to come out with it whatever happened.'

'He knew about the twenty per cent. How's that possible, Morten?' Hartmann asked.

Weber seemed thrown by the question.

'Why ask me? Maybe he did his own survey. Makes sense. Promising money for education always wins you Brownie points.'

'And he got the same results? He knew.'

Weber shrugged.

'You shouldn't have cancelled,' Skovgaard said.

Hartmann's mobile rang.

'A young girl's missing. I had no choice.'

'It's Therese,' said the voice on the line.

Hartmann glanced at Rie Skovgaard.

'This isn't a good time. I'll ring you back.'

'Don't hang up, Troels. You're not too busy for this. We have to meet.'

'That wouldn't be a good idea.'

'Someone's trying to dig up dirt on you.'

Hartmann took a deep breath.

'Who?'

'A reporter rang me. I don't want to talk about this over the phone.'

'We've got a fundraiser here at five. Get here then. I can come out for a while.'

'Five it is.'

'Therese . . .'

'Take care, Troels.'

Weber and Skovgaard were watching him.

'Something we need to hear?' Skovgaard asked.

Theis Birk Larsen went to the student house in Nørrebro where Lisa Rasmussen lived with Oliver Schandorff and some other kids from

32

the school, pretending they were grown-ups, screwing around, drinking, smoking dope, acting the fool.

Lisa was outside wheeling away her bike. He took hold of the handlebars.

'Where's Nanna?'

The girl was dressed like a teenage tart, the way they all did, Nanna if he let her. She wouldn't look him in the eye.

'I told them. I don't know.'

His big fist didn't move.

'Where's that bastard Schandorff?'

Still staring at the wall.

'Not here. Not since Friday.'

He bent down and put his whiskery face in hers.

'Where is he?'

Finally she met his eyes. She looked as if she'd been crying.

'He said his parents were away for the weekend. He was staying there I think. After the Halloween party . . .'

Birk Larsen didn't wait to hear more.

On the way he called Pernille.

'I just talked to Lisa,' he said. 'I'm going to get her.'

He could hear the relief in her single brief sigh.

'It's that rich punk again. His parents went away. He's probably . . .'

He didn't want to say it, think it.

'You're sure she's there? Lisa said so?'

The evening traffic was heavy. The house was out on one of the new developments, south, near the airport.

'I'm sure. Don't worry.'

She was crying. He could see her tears. He wished he could touch them, brush them away with his fat, rough fingers. Pernille was beautiful and precious. Like Nanna, Emil and Anton. They all deserved better than he'd given them and soon they'd get it.

'Won't be long, sweetheart. I promise.'

When Lund was back among the bare dark trees Buchard called.

'The helicopter. Three forensic units. I hope you've found something?'

'A grave.'

'You left me out of the loop.'

'I tried. You were in a meeting.'

'I was at your leaving party. People don't say goodbye over breakfast . . .'

'Hang on a minute.'

Meyer was walking towards her through the wood. In his arms was a plastic forensic sheet. Something beneath. A body.

'Have you found something?' Buchard demanded.

Meyer put the sheet on the ground, opened it and showed her a dead fox. Stiff and dry, caked with earth. It had a cub scout kerchief around its neck along with the wire noose that had strangled it.

'We can put out a call for any kids nearby,' Meyer said, lifting the fox by its back legs. 'Animal cruelty's a shocking thing.'

'No,' Lund told Buchard. 'Not yet.'

'Pack up, come home and give me a full report. Maybe there's time for a beer before you catch your plane.'

Meyer was watching her, the stiff dead animal beneath his arm. Its eyes were black and glazed, its fur streaked with mud.

'Meet my new friend Foxy,' he said with a quick sharp grin. 'You'll like him.'

One more reception among so many. Part of the political calendar. A chance to meet, to negotiate, to forge alliances, confirm enmities.

The food came from an oil corporation, the drink from a transport magnate. A string quartet played Vivaldi. Morten Weber talked policy while Rie Skovgaard spoke spin.

Hartmann smiled and chatted, shook hands, made small talk. Then when his phone rang he excused himself and walked back to his office.

Therese Kruse was waiting for him. A couple of years younger than him. Married to a boring banker. A serious, well-connected, attractive woman, tougher than she looked.

'You're doing well in the polls. People in government are noticing.'

'So they should. We worked for this.'

'True.'

'Did you get the reporter's name?'

She handed him a piece of paper. *Erik Salin.*

'Never heard of him,' Hartmann said.

'I made some enquiries. He used to work as a private investigator. Now he's a freelance selling dirt for the highest fee. Newspapers. Magazines. Websites. Anyone who pays.'

He pocketed the note.

'And?'

'Salin wanted to know if you paid your hotel bills with your own credit card or the office's. If you buy lots of presents. Stuff like that. I didn't say anything, naturally . . .'

Hartmann took a sip of wine.

'He wanted to know about us,' she added.

'What did you say?'

'I laughed off the whole idea, of course. After all . . .' The smile was brief and bitter. 'It's not as if it was anything important. Was it?'

'We agreed it was best, Therese. I'm sorry. I couldn't . . .'

He stopped.

'Couldn't what, Troels? Take the risk?'

'What did he know?'

'About us? Nothing. He was guessing.' The caustic smile again. 'Perhaps he thinks if he asks enough women he's bound to strike gold. I think he's got something else though. I don't know how.'

Hartmann glanced at the door, made sure they were alone.

'Such as what?'

'He seems to have seen your diary. He was checking dates. He knew where you'd been and when.'

Hartmann looked at the name again, wondered if he'd heard it somewhere.

'No one sees my diary outside this office.'

She shrugged. Got up. The door opened. Rie Skovgaard looked at the pair of them.

With that stiff suspicious smile she said, 'Troels. I didn't know you had company. There are people in reception you need to meet.'

The two women stared at each other. Thinking. Judging. No need for words.

'I'm coming,' Troels Hartmann said.

Oliver Schandorff was a skinny kid of nineteen with a head of curly ginger hair and a sour unsmiling face. He was puffing on his third smoke of the day when Theis Birk Larsen burst through the front door.

Schandorff leapt out of his chair and retreated as the big and angry man marched towards him.

'Call her now,' Birk Larsen bellowed. 'She's leaving.'

'Hello!' Schandorff cried, skipping into the hall. 'There's a bell here. Private house.'

'Don't mess with me, sonny. I want Nanna.'

'Nanna isn't here.'

Birk Larsen began marching round the ground floor, opening doors, yelling her name.

Schandorff followed, at a safe distance.

'Mr Birk Larsen. I'm telling you. She isn't here.'

Birk Larsen went back to the hall. There were clothes on a chair by the sofa. A pink T-shirt. A bra. Jeans.

He swore at Schandorff and made for the stairs.

The kid lost it, raced in front, punched Birk Larsen's chest, yelled, 'Do you mind? Do you—'

The big man picked him up by his T-shirt, carried the kid back down to the hall, launched him against the front door, balled a massive fist in his face.

Oliver Schandorff went quiet.

Birk Larsen thought better of it. Strode up the open-plan stairs two at a time. The place was vast, the kind of mansion he could never dream of owning, however hard he worked, however many scarlet trucks he ran.

There was deafening rock music coming from a bedroom on the left. The place stank of stale dope and sex.

A double bed with crumpled sheets, crumpled duvet. Curly blonde hair poked out from beneath the pillows. Face down, naked feet out of the bottom. Stoned. Drunk. Both, or worse.

He glowered back at Schandorff who was following him, hands in pockets, smirking in a way that made Theis Birk Larsen want to punch him out on the spot.

Instead he walked to the bed, wondering how to play this, pulled back the duvet and said gently, 'Nanna. You need to come home. It doesn't matter what happened. We're going now . . .'

The naked woman stared up at him, her hard face a mix of fright and fury. Blonde too. Same shade. Twenty-five if she was a day.

'I did tell you,' Schandorff said. 'Nanna was never here. If I could help . . .'

Theis Birk Larsen walked outside wondering what to do. What to tell Pernille. Where to go next? He didn't like the police but maybe it was time to talk to them. He wanted to know something, find something. Or make it happen.

There was a sound overhead. A helicopter, the word POLITI underneath.

He hadn't thought much about the location when he came here. Nanna was in Oliver Schandorff's house. There was nothing more to know. Now he realized he wasn't far from the marshland east of the airport.

Pernille said that was the place where it all began.

Lund was back on the flat ground of the Kalvebod Fælled where they found the bloodstained top, looking at the map.

'Let's go home,' Meyer said, lighting one more cigarette.

Her phone rang.

'Are you coming to Sweden or what?' Bengt Rosling asked.

She had to think for a moment before saying, 'Shortly.'

'How about a house-warming party on Saturday? We could invite Lasse, Missan, Bosse and Janne.'

Lund was scanning the fading horizon, wishing she could slow time a little and hold back dusk.

'And my parents,' Bengt added. 'And your mother.'

Lund took one more look at the map, one more sweep of the marsh and the woods.

'Your mother's going to fix up the guest room,' Bengt said.

Three young kids walked past pushing bikes. They were carrying fishing rods.

Mark never went fishing. No one to take him.

'That would be nice,' she said, gesturing at Meyer to get his attention.

'I don't want her sleeping on the sofa,' Bengt said.

Lund wasn't listening by then. The phone hung in her fingers by the side of her blue cagoule.

'What's over there?' she asked Meyer.

'More woods,' he said. 'And a canal.'

'You did look in the water?'

He grimaced. Meyer was the kind of man who could look angry in his sleep.

37

'The girl ran the other way!'

Lund went back to the phone.

'We're going to miss the flight.'

'What?'

'You catch it. I'll come tomorrow with Mark.'

Meyer stood there, arms crossed, pushing crisps into his mouth between puffs on his cigarette.

'Do we have trained divers among the forensic teams? And gear?' Lund asked.

'We've got enough men here to start a small war. How about Sweden? Let's face it. That's the only way you'll get there.'

The two of them drove over to the canal. Walked up and down. There were tyre marks by a low metal bridge. Going off the edge of the muddy bank towards nothing but black water.

The bleak terrain mirrored Theis Birk Larsen's state of mind: a maze of baffling dead ends and pointless turnings. A labyrinth without an exit.

He drove and drove, into the dying grey sunset, away from it, finding nothing. Even the drone of the helicopter had disappeared. Pernille was with him every aching second, her shrill scared voice chanting through the phone clamped to his left ear.

'Where is she?'

How many times had she asked that? How many times had he?

'I'm looking.'

'Where?'

The Kalvebod Fælled he wanted to say. The place Anton came on a school nature trip once, and talked about bugs and eels for the best part of a day before forgetting the whole damned thing.

There were lights ahead. One of them was blue.

'Everywhere.'

The narrow lane stood above the slender canal, built from the earth that created it. Lund stared at the tracks, the lifting truck, the chain. The car emerging from the sullen water.

Look, think, imagine.

Someone parked on the lane, front wheels turned towards the water at the top of the slope. Then got out, pushed it. Gravity did the rest.

38

Meyer was next to her, watching as the car rose against the sky. Water poured from all four doors. The paint was black, the colour of the canal, but very shiny as if it was cleaned yesterday.

Ford hatchback. Brand new.

'Look up the registration,' Lund said the moment the number plate was clear.

The truck was parked on the bank, long crane arm extending over the canal. It turned the vehicle away from the water, dangled it over the grassy lane. Then three officers guided the Ford slowly down to the ground until it sat there, unremarkable except for the torrents of foul-smelling liquid gushing from beneath each door.

Meyer was off the phone. The two of them walked over and looked through the windows. Empty.

The divider was down on the boot hiding anything inside.

He walked to the back and tried the rear door. Locked.

'I'll get a crowbar,' Meyer said.

There were lights behind. Lund turned and looked. Not car lights. A van, she thought. It looked red in the beams of the police vehicles.

Birk Larsen was still on the phone when he reached the line of Don't Cross tape. So close he couldn't count the blue lights beyond it. They'd set up high portable floodlights, the kind they used at sports events.

His head didn't feel right. His heart was beating so hard it banged against his ribs.

'Hang on a second,' he said and didn't hear her reply.

Got out. Walked on.

'Where are you?' Pernille asked.

'On the marshes in Vestamager.'

A pause then she asked, 'Are the police still out there?'

Two cops came up and tried to stop him. Birk Larsen brushed them aside with a sweep of his huge arm, kept walking towards a low metal bridge across the narrow canal.

'I'll sort this out. I told you.'

'Theis.'

More cops now. They swarmed on him like angry bees as he kept walking forwards, batting away their clutching hands, phone locked to his head.

He could still hear her voice above the commotion.

'What's there, Theis? *What's there?'*

A sound ahead.

Water rushing.

Water rushing. It cascaded out of the rear compartment after Meyer levered it open. Gallons and gallons pouring onto the muddy ground.

The smell was worse.

Lund popped another Nicotinell in her mouth and waited.

After the water a pair of naked legs fell onto the shiny rear bumper. She shone her torch there. Naked ankles bound tightly with plastic fasteners.

Then movement. A snaking dark shape wound its way round and round the dead pale limbs, clinging to the skin, slithering down to the feet, over the bumper onto the ground.

One of the uniform cops started to puke into the yellow grass.

'What's the noise?' Lund asked, taking a step towards the car.

Meyer nodded at the retching man.

'Not him,' she said.

It was a loud coarse voice and it was furious.

Lund watched the last of the water drain from the rear, two more eels sliding their way to freedom, then walked forward and put her head inside. The blonde hair didn't look the way it had in the photos any more.

But the face . . .

The angry voice was bawling a name.

'Oh Christ,' Meyer said. 'The father's here.'

Theis Birk Larsen was a big strong man. It was a long time since he'd fought with cops. Some things you always remembered. Two swift punches, a roar and he was moving forward again, towards the black bridge.

Beyond that point he could see a car on the road next to a recovery truck. Busy shapes swarming there.

The phone was back to his ear.

'Theis!' Pernille cried.

'I'll talk to them.'

The cops he'd shaken off were at his back again. More this time. Too many.

A woman had left the car on the road and was walking steadily towards him. Beneath the harsh floodlights he saw she had a serious face, long brown hair, and shining, sad and interested eyes.

'For God's sake Theis . . .' Pernille whined.

They had him now, six cops, maybe seven. Had everything but his free arm with the phone.

Birk Larsen stopped struggling. Said again, as calmly as he could, 'I'm Nanna's father. I want to know what's going on.'

The woman stepped over one more line of red and white police tape.

She didn't say a thing, kept walking steadily towards him, staring into his face, chewing gum.

A voice, detached, not his at all, said meekly, 'Is that my daughter?'

'You can't stay here.'

Pernille was in his ear, his head, all in a single question, 'Theis?'

The woman stood in front of him.

'Is it Nanna down there?' Birk Larsen asked once more.

She was silent.

'Is it?'

The woman just nodded.

The roar was born deep in his belly, rose through him, burst into the damp night air. So loud and full of uncomprehending grief and fury it might have carried all the way to Copenhagen on its own.

But the phone was there. No need. As he struggled, screamed to see her, Pernille was with him shrieking, crying too.

Mother and father. Lost dead child.

Then all the fury, all the power, died. Theis Birk Larsen was a weeping, fractured man, feeble and distraught, held upright by the arms that seconds before had fought his boundless strength.

'I want to see my daughter,' he begged.

'You can't,' she said. 'I'm sorry.'

A tinny howling sound came from the man's right hand. Lund stepped forward, opened his fingers. Those of a labourer. Strong and scarred, the skin leathery and old.

He didn't protest as she took the phone from him, looked at the name on the screen.

'Pernille. This is Lund. Someone will be with you soon.'

Then she pocketed the phone, nodded to the officers to take Birk

Larsen away, went back to the drowned Ford, shiny and black, by the lifting truck.

Forensics were swarming there already. All the set procedures were in place. Officers in protective clothing. She didn't need to see any more.

Black car. Bright and shiny. Meyer was right. It was so very new and clean.

Lund found him smoking by the crane truck, shaking his head.

'We've got an owner,' he said. 'You won't believe this.'

Lund stood beside him, waited.

'The car belongs to Troels Hartmann's campaign office,' Jan Meyer said.

'Hartmann the politician?'

With a single finger Meyer flicked his cigarette out towards the canal.

'The Mayor of Education. Poster boy. Yeah. Him.'

Three

Tuesday, 4th November

Buchard arrived just after midnight. Then came the duty pathologist and his team. A huddle of forensic officers measuring tyre tracks, taking endless photographs, cordoning off the soaking muddy ground.

They trudged through the soaking rain leaving till last the bloodied, bruised corpse of a young girl still in her ragged slip, wrists and ankles tied with black plastic fasteners, dumped in the back of a shiny black Ford.

Lund talked to them all. She was officer in charge. No thoughts for Mark or Bengt or Sweden.

More camera flashes around the perimeter of the car. Then finally the team moved towards the open boot, starting to record details of the small, still body and its wounds, the dead face, the staring blank light-blue eyes.

Buchard asked, as he always did, about time of death. She told him what the pathologist said: no idea. Nothing had been reported over the weekend. It would take some time to establish.

The old man scowled.

'What a godforsaken place . . .'

'We don't know she died here. He didn't want her found. A day or two more, rain like this . . .' She glanced at the activity around the car. They'd move her soon. Someone needed to think about the family. 'The tyre tracks would have gone.'

Buchard waited.

'He knew this place,' Lund said. 'He knew what he was doing.'

'Cause of death?'

'They don't know yet. She was assaulted. Violent blows to the head. Signs of rape.'

'And this car? It belongs to Hartmann's team?'

'It's the best lead we have.'

Bengt Rosling rang. Lund walked away to take the call.

'What happened?' he asked.

'We found a girl. I'll tell you later. I'm sorry I didn't make it.'

Bengt was a criminal psychologist. That was how they met. Through a drug murder in Christiania. The victim was one of his patients.

'What about Mark?' he asked.

'He's with my mother.'

'I mean tomorrow. He's supposed to be starting Swedish lessons at school. In Sigtuna.'

'Oh. Right.'

'I'll tell them he'll be there on Wednesday.'

'We'll book another flight. I'll let you know the time.'

Buchard came over and asked, 'Is the girl connected to Hartmann?'

'I'll check.'

'If a candidate's involved report back to me.'

'I can't do this, Buchard.'

A horn was sounding. It was Meyer, cigarette in mouth, calling her.

'Use him,' she said.

The chief came close.

'This shouldn't be Meyer's first case. Don't ask. I'll call the Stockholm police and clear it.'

'No,' she insisted. 'It's not possible.'

Lund walked away, back towards Meyer and the car.

'You found this kid.' Buchard hurried behind her, talking to the back of her shiny wet blue cagoule. 'Would Meyer have done that? All he dug up was a dead fox in the woods.'

She stopped, turned, glared at him.

He looked like an old grizzled pug dog, had the same importunate eyes sometimes.

'Just one more day, Sarah.'

Silence.

'Do you want Meyer to talk to the parents?'

'I hate you. You know that?'

Buchard laughed and clapped his fat little hands.

'I'll work through the night,' Lund said. 'In the morning it's down to you.'

The morgue was deserted. One echoing antiseptic corridor after another.

Still in the black leather jacket and woollen hat, the scarlet cotton overalls, Theis Birk Larsen clumped across the clean tiles towards the single door at the end.

An anteroom.

Pernille there in her fawn gaberdine coat, turning to look at him, wide-eyed, face full of questions. He stopped two paces from her, no idea what to say or do. Felt shapeless words rise to his mouth then stay there, unfinished and uncertain, afraid to breach the cold dry air.

A big man, powerful, forbidding sometimes, silent, his gleaming eyes now pools of tears.

Ashamed when that broke her, made Pernille come to him, place her gentle arms around his shoulders.

She held him, damp face against his bristled cheek. Together they stood, together they clung to one another in close silence. Together they walked into the white room of brilliant tiles and medical cabinets, of taps and sinks and shining concave silver tables, of surgical implements, all the tools that codified death.

The cops led the way, the woman with the staring eyes, the surly, big-eared man. Walking towards a clean white sheet then stopping, half-looking at them in expectation, waiting. From the corner came a man in a surgeon's suit, blue mob cap, blue bib, blue gloves. There'd been doctors like this when Nanna was born. Theis Birk Larsen saw this picture clear in his head. The same colours, the same harsh chemical smells.

Without a word, without a glance, the man was beside them, lifting the white cotton.

Pernille edged forward, eyes widening.

All the while the woman cop watched, every gesture, every breath and move.

Birk Larsen removed his black hat, embarrassed that he still wore it. Looked at the bloodless, bruised face on the table, the dirty stained hair, the lifeless grey eyes.

Images filled his memory. Pictures, sounds, a touch, a word. A baby's cry, a much-rued argument. A hot afternoon by the beach. A freezing morning in winter, out on a sledge. Nanna tiny in the red Christiania trike Vagn fixed and painted, stencilling the logo *Birk Larsen* on the side.

Nanna older, climbing into it when she was sixteen, seventeen, laughing at how small it seemed.

Distant moments never to be recovered, unspoken promises never to be made. All the small pieces that once seemed so humdrum now shrieked . . .

See! You never noticed. And now I'm gone.

Now I'm gone.

Pernille turned, walked back to the anteroom, the gait of an old woman, broken and in pain.

'Is this Nanna?' the woman asked.

He glared at her. A stupid question and she didn't seem a stupid woman.

No, Birk Larsen wanted to say. *It was.*

Instead he nodded, nothing more.

Four of them face to face across a plastic table.

Plain facts.

Birk Larsen, his wife and their two young sons left for the seaside on Friday, returned Sunday evening. Nanna was supposed to be staying with friends.

'What sort of mood was she in?' Lund asked.

'Happy,' Birk Larsen said. 'She dressed up.'

'As what?'

'A witch.'

The mother sat there, mouth open, lost somewhere. Then she stared at Lund and asked, 'What happened?'

Lund didn't answer. Nor Meyer.

'Will someone talk to me! What happened?'

In the cold empty room her shrill voice bounced off the bare white walls.

Meyer lit a cigarette.

'The car was driven into the water,' he said.

'Was she interested in politics?' Lund asked.

Birk Larsen shook his head.

'Did she talk to anyone who was?'

'No.'

'At the Rådhus maybe?' Meyer wondered.

He scowled at the lack of an answer, got up and walked to the back of the room, making a call.

'Boyfriends . . . ?'

'Not lately.'

'How did she die?' Pernille asked.

'We don't know yet.'

'Did she suffer?'

Lund hesitated and said, 'We're not sure what happened. We're trying to understand. So you haven't talked to her since Friday? No calls? No contact? Nothing out of the ordinary?'

Narrow eyes, a bitter scowl, a note of sarcasm as he snarled, 'The ordinary?'

'Things you'd expect. It could be anything unusual. A little thing.'

'I got cross with her,' Pernille said. 'Is that ordinary? She was being too noisy. I shouted at her for running around with her brothers.'

She watched Lund.

'I was doing the accounts. I was busy . . .'

Birk Larsen wound his big arm round her.

'She just wanted to play with them. Just . . .'

More tears, Pernille shook beneath his grip.

'Just what?'

'Just wanted to play.'

'I'll have someone take you home now,' Lund said. 'We need to seal off Nanna's room. It's important no one goes in there.'

Lund and Meyer walked them to the door where the uniformed men with the car were waiting.

'If you think of anything . . .' Lund said and handed Birk Larsen a card.

The stocky father looked at it.

'How much do you know?'

'It's too early to say.'

'But you'll find him?'

'We'll do everything we can.'

Birk Larsen didn't move. There was a grim, hard set on his face when he asked again, more slowly, 'But you will find him?'

'Yes,' Meyer snapped. 'We will.'

The father stared hard at him then left for the car.

Lund watched them go.

'They just lost their daughter. And you're yelling at them?'

'I didn't yell.'

'It sounded like—'

'This is yelling!' Meyer bawled.

His voice was so loud the pathologist put his head round the corner.

Then, more quietly, Meyer said, 'I didn't yell.'

His bleak and watchful eyes caught her.

'He hates us, Lund. You saw that.'

'We're police. Lots of people hate us.'

'Picked his moment, didn't he?'

Half past two in the morning. Hartmann was there when they got to the Rådhus. Rie Skovgaard, the slick attractive woman they'd seen at the school, sat on his left. Hartmann's awkward fidgety middle-aged campaign manager, Morten Weber, was on the other side.

'Thanks for coming in,' Lund said.

'We didn't,' Hartmann answered. 'We just stayed. There's an election coming. We work late. Did you find the girl?'

'Yes.' Meyer stared at the politician in the blue shirt, blue trousers. 'She was in your rental car.'

Lund wrote out the number, placed it on the table.

'Who was the last person to drive it?'

Hartmann sat rigid in his leather seat.

'Our car?'

Meyer pushed the note closer to him.

'That's what we said. Can we have a little action now?'

'I'll check,' Morten Weber said. 'It'll take a while.'

'Why?' Meyer wanted to know.

'We've lots of cars,' Weber said. 'Thirty drivers. It's the middle of the night. We still have people working. Let me make some calls.'

He left the table and went off into a corner with his phone.

'What do they do, these cars?' Lund asked.

48

'Deliver campaign material,' Skovgaard said. 'Put up posters. That kind of thing.'

'When did you send a car to the school in Frederiksholm?'

'Probably Friday I guess . . .'

Meyer snapped, put his hands palm down on the table, leaned over and said, 'Guessing isn't much good. The girl's dead. We need to know—'

'We've nothing to hide,' Hartmann broke in. 'We want to help. It's past two in the morning. We can't pull answers out of a hat.'

'Was Nanna Birk Larsen connected to your political work?'

'No,' said Skovgaard straight away. 'She's not on any of our lists.'

'That was quick,' Meyer said.

'I thought you wanted quick.'

Weber returned.

'The campaign secretary's in Oslo right now.'

'Screw Oslo!' Meyer cried. 'This is a murder case. Get some answers.'

Weber sat down, raised an eyebrow at him, looked at Lund.

Checking the hierarchy, Lund thought. Smart man.

'So I asked the security desk. The keys were collected by Rikke Nielsen on Friday.'

'Who's she?' Lund asked.

'Rikke's in charge of our team of volunteers.' Weber shrugged. 'Anyone can volunteer. We use temps when there aren't enough.'

He glanced at Meyer who was now pacing the room, hands in pockets, like a cockerel pushing for a fight.

'You've phoned her?' Meyer demanded.

'Her phone's off. She's probably organizing the posters.'

Meyer nodded sarcastically.

'Probably?'

'Yes. Like I said. Thirty drivers to coordinate. It's a lot of work.'

'Stop!' Meyer was back at the table again. 'There's a dead girl and you're sitting here as if it's beneath you.'

'Meyer,' Lund said.

'I want answers,' he barked.

'Meyer!'

Loud enough. He stopped.

'Call headquarters,' she ordered. 'Give Buchard an update. Tell him we're going to interview the volunteers.'

He didn't move.

'It's past Buchard's bedtime . . .'

She locked eyes with him.

'Just do it.'

He went off to the window.

'Do you have any idea where this woman is now?' Lund asked.

Weber looked at a piece of paper. He highlighted something with a green marker.

'My best bet.'

Skovgaard took it, checked the names, then handed it on.

'The press,' she said. 'There's no need for them to know.'

Lund shook her head, puzzled.

'A young girl's been murdered. We can't keep this secret.'

'No,' Hartmann said. 'If it was our car we need to issue a statement. It's important no one can accuse us of hiding anything.'

'I don't want you making details public,' Lund insisted. 'You talk to no one but me.'

Skovgaard stood up, arms waving.

'There's an election going on. We can't afford to wait.'

Lund turned to Hartmann.

'The information we just gave you was confidential. If you choose to make it public and jeopardize a murder inquiry that's your choice. You can live with the consequences. And there will be consequences, Hartmann. That I promise.'

Weber coughed. Skovgaard went quiet. Meyer looked pleased.

'Rie,' Hartmann said. 'I think we can wait a while. Provided . . .'

The briefest, pleading smile.

'Provided what?' Meyer asked.

'Provided you tell us when you decide to go public. So we can work together. Make sure everything's right.'

He folded his arms. The shirt was the blue of the campaign poster above his head. Everything here was coordinated. Planned.

Lund took out her personal card, crossed out her name, wrote Meyer's there instead.

'Tomorrow morning ring Jan Meyer on this number,' she said. 'He'll update you.'

'You're not on the case?' Hartmann asked.

'No,' Lund said. 'He is.'

*

Weber left with the cops. Skovgaard stayed with him, still smarting.

'What the hell is this, Troels?'

'Search me.'

'If we agree to hide things the press could crucify us. They love the words cover-up. It gives them a hard-on.'

'We're not covering up. We're doing what the police asked us.'

'They won't care.'

Hartmann put on his jacket, thinking, looked at her.

'She didn't leave us much choice. They'd crucify us for screwing up a murder inquiry too. Lund knew that. It's nothing to do with us. Forget about it.'

Sharp eyes wide open, mouth agape.

'A girl's found dead in one of our cars? It's nothing to do with us?'

'Nothing. If you want something to worry about, take a look round this place.'

He pointed to the main office beyond the door. Eight, ten full-time staff working there during the day.

'Meaning what?'

'Meaning are we secure? The computers? Emails? Our reports?'

A caustic look.

'You're not getting paranoid about Bremer, are you?'

'How did he come up with that trick about the school funding? How did he know about the twenty per cent?'

Hartmann thought about the conversation with Bremer, what the mayor said about his late father.

'That cunning old bastard's up to something.'

She came to him with his coat, helped him on with it, zipped it up against the cold night.

'Such as?'

Hartmann told her a little about why Therese Kruse came to see him. About the reporter asking questions. He left out the personal details.

'Some of that had to come from in here. Had to.'

She wasn't happy.

'Why didn't you tell me?'

'I'm telling you now.'

He walked into the big office. Desks and computers. Filing cabinets, voicemail. All the private details of the campaign lived inside this room, deep in the heart of the Rådhus, locked securely every night.

'Go home,' she said. 'I'll take a look around.'

Hartmann came over, took her shoulders, kissed her tenderly.

'I could help.'

'Go home,' she repeated. 'You've got to cut the deal with Kirsten Eller first thing. I want you wide awake for that.'

He looked out of the window into the square.

'They said she was nineteen. Just a kid.'

'It's not our fault, is it?'

Troels Hartmann stared at the blue hotel sign and the yellow lights in the square.

'No,' he said. 'It isn't.'

'Why did you say we'd find him?' Lund asked.

They were in her unmarked car, Meyer at the wheel.

'You won't pull a trick like that on me again,' he said. 'In front of those clowns. Of all the people . . .'

His anger was so open and puerile it was almost amusing.

'I won't need to. I'll be gone. Why did you say that? To the father.'

'Because we will.' A pause. 'I will.'

'You don't make promises,' she threw at him. 'Read the book. Page one.'

'I've got my own book.'

'So I noticed.'

Meyer turned on the radio. A deafening, all-night rock station. Lund leaned forward, switched it off.

She checked the address.

'Turn here.'

A statue of a figure on horseback, sword raised. A grand illuminated building. A multi-storey parking garage. The place Hartmann's campaign team assembled before going out to plaster the city with his posters, leaflets, badges, hats and T-shirts.

The cars were on the second level. Identical black Fords, just like the one they'd pulled from the canal. Lund and Meyer walked round, looking at the same photo of Troels Hartmann plastered to the windows. One back door was open. Three hours earlier, in a vehicle identical to this, she'd seen the scarred half-naked corpse of Nanna Birk Larsen frozen in death in a torn, stained slip. Here there were

52

boxes and boxes of leaflets, and the same photo of Hartmann. That uncertain boyish smile, some pain behind his open, honest eyes.

A blonde woman walked round from the back, looked at her uncertainly. Lund showed her ID, asked, 'Rikke Nielsen?'

She seemed exhausted. Nervous too when Meyer came from the other side of the car, folded his arms, sat in the open boot and watched her.

'I need the name of a driver from the weekend,' Lund said.

'Why?'

'The number plate is . . .' Lund fumbled for her notebook.

'XU 24 919,' Meyer said unprompted. He got up, came close to the Nielsen woman. 'Black Ford like this one. We'd like to know who drove it last.'

Then he smiled, in a way he probably thought pleasant.

There were men carrying placards of Hartmann's beaming face to cars down the line.

'This is quite an organization you've got. You must keep a logbook.'

'Of course.'

'Can we see it? Please.'

She nodded, walked off. Meyer winked at Lund. The Nielsen woman came back. 'That was XU . . . ?'

'XU 24 919.'

Lund left him, watched the men with the placards and posters. It was cold in the parking garage. But not so cold.

One of the volunteers was a lanky figure in a worn and dirty anorak. He had the hood pulled up around his face. Put the posters in the back of the car. Turned. Grey sweatshirt. Face in shadow. Trying to hide.

Meyer's strained nice-guy act was wearing thin.

'I'm staying very calm here,' she heard him say behind her. 'So you stay calm too. I don't want to hear any more "ifs" or "buts" or "let me ask Mr Weber". Just give me the name of the damned driver.'

He was getting loud. The men stuffing the cars with Hartmann posters could hear. They were glancing at Rikke Nielsen. But not the one in the hood.

Lund turned to tell Meyer to cut the volume. When she looked again the figure in the grey sweatshirt and anorak wasn't there.

A black Ford in the line burst into life, roared out of the parking spot, back door open, scattering the smiling face of Troels Hartmann everywhere.

'Meyer!'

The driver had to get past her to reach the ramp.

Lund walked into the centre of the lane, stood there, stared through the oncoming windscreen.

Man in his late thirties, forties maybe. Stubbled, angry face, afraid, determined.

'For Christ's sake,' Meyer screamed and flew at her, caught her shoulder with one hand, dragged Lund out of the way.

Still accelerating the Ford raced past them, no more than a metre away.

Lund watched it, barely conscious she was in Meyer's arms and he was peering at her, breathless. Furious probably. She had that effect sometimes. The car turned the corner, headed up towards the roof. Meyer let go, set off for the ramp, arms pumping, handgun out, yelling. Lund went the other way, racing for the stairs, taking the concrete steps three at a time, up, up.

One floor, two. Three and there were no more. The roof was black and gleaming in the night rain. Ahead lay the grand baroque dome of the Marble Church softly lit against the city skyline. The car was parked by the far wall, headlamps blazing.

No gun. Still she walked towards it, trying to see.

'Police!' she called.

'Lund!'

Meyer emerged from the ramp exit, panting, coughing, barely able to speak.

There was a sound from the far side. A door opening and closing on a floor below. Lund dashed over to look, Meyer followed. A second set of stairs ran down the building. He'd come here to lose them. Managed it too.

They watched a figure reach the ground floor then flee into the night and the vast dark city.

Meyer in his fury leapt up like an animal, swearing, shrieking so loud she covered her ears.

They slept in their clothes, wrapped in each other, his grief in hers, hers in his.

Waking. Theis Birk Larsen unwound his arms without disturbing her, sat by the bed, quietly got up.

Washed his face, ate some bread, sipped coffee as the boys and Pernille slept. Then went down to face the men.

Twelve on that shift. Vagn Skærbæk, pale-faced, damp-eyed, among them. Vagn. Part of the family. The first person he'd called at two that morning, holding a conversation Birk Larsen could scarcely recall so punctuated was it by tears and cries and fury.

Vagn was a good man for hard times. Times Birk Larsen thought would never come again. He had a family. A rock to lean on, as he was a rock to them.

Sometimes the rock shifted on unseen sand.

He went into the office, took his black coat off the hook, put it on carefully, as he'd done for years. Then went out and stood before them, the boss as always, laying down the orders for the day.

Most of these men had worked for him for years. They knew his family, watched the kids grow. Brought them birthday presents. Read their homework. Wiped their tears sometimes when he or Pernille weren't there.

A couple were close to crying. Only Skærbæk could look him in the face.

Birk Larsen tried to speak but stood there saying nothing.

Work.

There was a clipboard. A list of jobs that defined the way the hours would pass. He took it, walked into the office. Went looking for something to do.

A long moment's silence. Vagn Skærbæk called to the men by the vans, 'Let's get a move on, huh? I'm not your babysitter.'

Then he came and sat opposite Birk Larsen. A small, insignificant man. Stronger than his puny frame suggested. Face not much changed from when they were in their teens. Dark hair, blank eyes, cheap silver chain round his neck.

'You do what you need to, Theis. I'll deal with the rest.'

Birk Larsen lit a cigarette, looked at the office walls. Photos everywhere. Pernille. Nanna. The boys.

'Some reporters called. I hung up on them. If they call back you give those bastards to me.'

Slowly the depot came to life. Cardboard cases moved beyond the window. Pallets got shifted. Vans went out into the street.

'Theis, I don't know what to say.' Same woollen hat, same red bib overall. Big brother, little brother. 'I want to help. Tell me . . .'

Birk Larsen looked at him, said nothing.

'Do they have a clue who did it?'

Birk Larsen shook his head, drew on his cigarette, tried to think about the schedule, nothing else.

'Let me know if there's anything . . .' Skærbæk began.

'The delivery on Sturlasgade,' Birk Larsen said, the first words he uttered that morning.

The man with him waited.

'I promised them a cherry-picker.'

'It's done,' Vagn Skærbæk told him.

Meyer waved a mugshot at the plain-clothes team in the briefing room. It was of an unremarkable man in a black T-shirt holding up a prison number. Balding, bruised, stubbly face, droopy grey hippie moustache. The long slash of what looked like an old knife wound scarring his right cheek. Staring at the camera, looking bored.

'His name is John Lynge from Nørrebro. He's not at home. He's a known criminal and we . . .' He pinned the photo to the notice-board. '. . . are going to put this bastard in jail. Talk to neighbours. People he worked with. Bars. Pawnshops. Dope dealers. Anyone who knows him. He's forty-three. Sad, solitary bastard . . .'

Lund listened from the adjoining office, sipping at a coffee in between talking to her son. She'd caught three hours' sleep in a spare room. Didn't feel too bad.

'He's got no plan,' Meyer announced as if this were a given. 'No bolt-hole. Sometime he's going to come up for air. And then . . .'

Meyer clapped his hands together so loudly the noise sounded like a gunshot.

Lund stifled a laugh.

'You're not getting out of Swedish lessons,' she told Mark down the phone. 'How can you? We're going to live there. Bengt can explain to the teacher why you're late. You won't be in trouble.'

Meyer held up a new photo of Nanna. Still pretty. No make-up, no forced sexy smile. Not trying too hard.

'We need to know everything about her. Text messages, voice-mails, emails. Anything that connects her to Lynge.'

Mark was getting sulky.

'We'll fly out tonight,' Lund said. 'I'll let you know when I've booked the plane.'

'Let's move,' Meyer cried and did the handclap again.

Then, when the team had left, he came through and said, 'Buchard wants a word before you go.'

The old man had Lynge's mugshot in front of him on the desk that was once hers. Meyer was going through what he'd learned from the files.

'Thirteen years ago he was caught flashing children in a playground. One year later he raped a girl. Fourteen.'

The chief listened. Lund stood in the door with her cold cup of coffee. She didn't like the look on Buchard's face.

'Six years after that he was put in a psychiatric prison. Released eighteen months ago.'

All this Meyer recited from memory, from a single look at the case records. Impressive, she thought. In a way.

'So why's he out?' Buchard asked.

Meyer shrugged.

'Because he was deemed no longer dangerous?' Lund suggested.

'They always say that.'

'Not always, Meyer,' Buchard said. 'Sarah?'

'We have to talk to him.'

Meyer threw up his hands in mock glee.

'That's the understatement of the year.'

He was playing with the toy police car. Running it to make the blue light flash and the siren wail. Just like a kid.

Buchard said, 'Cut that out. I'd like to talk to her alone.'

Meyer put the car back on the desk with exaggerated care.

'If it's about the case . . .'

Something in Buchard's face stopped him. Meyer raised his palms and walked out.

The moment the door was closed Lund picked up her bag and said, 'We've been through this. You know the answer.'

'Things change.'

'Chief! We don't have anywhere to live. Bengt's waiting for me in Sweden. Mark starts school tomorrow.'

She went for the door.

Buchard said, 'I came from the lab. The girl was still alive when she went into the canal. It takes twenty minutes for a car like that to fill up. Add to that the time it takes to drown.'

He was pulling out a file of photos.

'It's not my case,' Lund said, messing with her bag, rearranging the things she'd rearranged once before.

'She was raped repeatedly. In the vagina. In the anus. He wore a condom and took his time.'

Lund watched him read this from the file and said, 'Mark's so excited about moving. No!'

'She was abused like this for hours. All weekend probably. The bruises indicate she was held somewhere else before the woods.'

Lund got her coat.

'And then there's this,' Buchard said, holding up a small plastic evidence bag.

Lund looked, couldn't help it.

'Meyer showed it to the mother. She says she's never seen it before.'

Buchard cleared his throat.

'The girl was clutching it in her right hand when she died. My guess is he made her wear it. She ripped it from her throat when she was drowning. I can't think of any other explanation.'

Lund stood by the window, looking out at the bleak courtyard in front of the prison cells.

'This isn't the usual, Sarah. You know that. Rape a kid then kill her to shut her up.' She couldn't avoid those beady bright eyes. 'Do you think we'd even know she was dead if we'd left it all to . . .' He nodded at the door. 'Our new friend Meyer?'

'I'm not—'

'I talked to Stockholm. They've agreed you can report there when the case is closed.'

Then he walked away, left the photos, the files, the small clear evidence bag on the table. Walked out and left Lund on her own.

She thought about Mark and Bengt. About Sweden and a new civilian job in Stockholm. But mostly about Nanna Birk Larsen, a broken body in the back of a black Ford car dumped in a dank canal.

Lund picked up the bag, held it to the light.

It was a pendant on a gold chain. Cheap glass. Tacky. Different.

A black heart.

Meyer came back in from the corridor. He looked red-faced. Buchard must have told him.

'This is outrageous.'

'Couldn't agree more. We do things my way until the end of the week. If the case is still alive then you can have it.'

'Fine.'

It didn't look fine.

'We go by my rules. We treat people with respect, whether we like them or not. In the car you won't smoke, you won't drive at more than thirty miles an hour . . .'

'May I fart?'

'No. And I don't want cheese crisps or hot dogs everywhere either.'

'Any particular kind of underwear you prefer?'

She thought for a moment.

'How about clean?'

A school was a world in miniature, riven with gossip and rumour. When the teacher called Rama arrived that grey morning he felt the news flitting through the corridors like a mischievous ghost.

Then Rektor Koch told him, 'I can do it if you wish.'

'My pupil,' he said. 'My class.'

Five minutes later he walked into the room, no books in his hand, no smile on his face. Looked at them, all of them, not children, not adults. Oliver Schandorff with his wild ginger hair, his dope eyes, his sour face. Lisa Rasmussen, Nanna's best friend, though never so pretty or smart.

What did you say except the obvious? What did you offer but the banal?

His dark face morose, Rama said, 'It's just been announced . . .' He stopped, closed his eyes, heard the words' harshness even before he spoke them. 'The police say Nanna's dead.'

A quick communal intake of breath. Tears and moans and whispers.

'There'll be no more lessons today. You're free to go home. Or stay. The teachers will be here all day. We'll have counsellors available.'

A hand went up at the back. Someone asked the inevitable.

What happened?

The man they knew as Rama thought of his own family's journey, the difficult, perilous land they'd left behind. He was only a child then. But still he could sense from them how safe this city seemed by comparison.

'I don't know.'

Another hand.

'Was she murdered?'

Lisa Rasmussen's fingers flew to her face, a cry of grief and pain escaped them.

'You've all got questions I know. Me too. There are no . . .' A teacher was never lost for words. A teacher was always honest. 'Sometimes there are no quick answers. We have to wait for them.'

He thought of what Koch had told him. Went straight to Lisa, put an arm round her bent back, tried to meet her eyes.

'They need your help,' he said. 'Lisa?'

No answer.

'The police want to see you.'

She buried her face in her arms.

'You and Oliver.'

Rama looked up. He was there a minute ago. But now the seat was empty.

Lund showed Lisa Rasmussen a photo of the black Ford estate.

'You've seen this car?'

Lisa nodded.

'Maybe. One like it.'

'When?'

She thought and said, 'Friday. Before the party. I think they were dropping off some stuff.'

Lund held up the mugshot of John Lynge.

'And him?'

The girl stared at the bald man with the staring eyes, the grey moustache and scarred cheek, the police number in front of him.

'Did he do it?'

'Just tell me if you've seen him.'

Lisa peered at the photo and said, 'I don't think so. What did he do to Nanna?'

'Maybe he's been in the school. Or somewhere you and Nanna went together.'

A long moment, then she shook her head.

'No. I haven't seen him before.'

Lund put the photo away.

'Do you have any idea why Nanna said she was staying with you?'

'No.' The tears were back. She looked fifteen again. 'I thought maybe she'd gone off with someone.'

'Who?'

'I don't know.'

'Lisa—'

'I don't know!'

Another tack. They talked about the party.

'How was she?' Lund asked.

'Happy.'

'In a good mood?'

'Happy.'

'And . . . ?'

'And she left. I thought it was a bit early. But—'

'Why did she leave early?'

'She didn't say.'

'Did she leave with someone?'

'I didn't . . .'

Her voice trailed off into silence.

Lund bent down and tried to catch her eyes.

'I didn't see! Why do you keep asking me questions? What am I supposed to know?'

Lund let the outburst die down, bit into a piece of Nicotinell.

'Nanna was your best friend, wasn't she? I thought you'd want to help.'

'I don't know anything.'

The pile of photos was sorted carefully. Nothing physical. Nothing disturbing. Lund took out the last shot and showed it to her.

'Do you recognize this necklace?'

Black heart on a gold chain.

Lisa shook her head.

'Looks old,' she said.

'You never saw Nanna wear it?'

'No.'

'Are you sure . . .'

'I'm sure, I'm sure, I'm sure, I'm sure!' the girl screamed. 'I saw her at the party. I hugged her. I didn't know it was the last time . . .'

Lisa Rasmussen stared at the table, not at the photographs, never at Lund.

'I didn't know,' she said again.

'I checked,' Rie Skovgaard said. 'Lynge isn't a party member. He was a temp from an agency we used a couple of times. Could have been working for anyone.'

They were outside the campaign office, in the corridor, speaking in whispers. Hartmann looked as if he'd hardly slept.

'That's good,' he said.

'Only if people know. If we don't say something and the press get hold of this . . .'

'What?'

'They'll say we hired a killer and covered for him. If Kirsten Eller hears we can kiss goodbye to your alliance. We've got to issue a statement. Make the position clear immediately.'

Hartmann hesitated.

'I'm supposed to be your adviser, Troels. I'm telling you. We're standing on the precipice here. You don't wait until you're falling . . .'

'Fine, fine. Do it. But let the police know first.'

'Eller and the party?'

'Leave them to me.'

By midday the school was empty. Lund and Meyer were comparing notes in a deserted corridor, next to the lockers. On one side was a set of government health warnings about drugs and drink and sex. On the other a line of posters for movies and rock music.

Meyer had been busy. He had three witnesses who saw Lynge delivering campaign material to the school just after midday.

'And in the evening?'

'The car was here then too. Maybe he heard about the party and returned.'

'Are we certain this was the car?'

Meyer slapped some photos in her hand and grinned.

'They took pictures for the school website. Party time. Look in the background in the exterior shots. It was the car.'

His phone rang. While he talked she ran through the pictures. Behind kids in ghoulish costumes, masks and wigs, hideous monster outfits, was the black outline of the Ford.

Meyer was getting mad.

'I told you before that's out of the question,' he barked into the phone.

An angry Jan Meyer. That was something new. She looked at more photos. They didn't have Halloween like this when Lund was nineteen. Even if they had . . .

She wondered what her mother would have said.

'I'm not telling you again,' Meyer shouted. 'The answer's no.'

He stared at the phone. Swore.

'I don't believe it. She hung up on me.'

'What's going on?'

'Hartmann's issuing a press statement. Trying to get his scrawny arse off the . . .'

Lund slapped the photos in his arms.

'We're going to the Rådhus. You drive.'

Birk Larsen went out to the job in a daze, got there only to be appalled by his own lack of consideration, came straight home, sat with Pernille in the kitchen, not talking just waiting, for what neither knew.

Then Lotte arrived, her sister. Eleven years younger, as close to Nanna as she was to Pernille. Birk Larsen sat mute and lethargic in the corner, watched them hug and cry, envying their open emotions.

'What about the boys?' Lotte asked.

'We haven't told them yet,' Pernille said. 'Theis?'

'What?'

It was the first word he'd spoken in an hour.

Lotte sat at the table and sobbed. Pernille checked the school timetable, on the cork-board with the family photos.

'We'll pick up the boys after art. It ends at two.'

'Yes.'

Lotte was in pieces.

'What was she doing there? Nanna'd never get into a stranger's car.'

More black coffee. It stopped him wanting to scream.

Pernille moved photos around the cork-board for no good reason.

'We need to . . .' She sniffed, took two long breaths. 'We need to think about the boys.'

She was crying again but didn't want to show it.

Birk Larsen longed to do something. To be out of this place so badly. Knew that unspoken thought was a kind of betrayal too.

'We've got to tell them,' he said.

Lund walked into the Liberal Party office. It smelled of sweat and polished wood and old leather. Skovgaard, Hartmann's too-elegant too-confident political adviser, was on the phone talking about the press release.

'I want to see him,' Lund said when Skovgaard came off the phone.

'He's in a meeting.'

Lund said, 'Oh.'

Watched her go back to the computer, typing standing up, the way busy people did.

'Your statement's going out?' she asked.

Still typing.

'Can't wait any longer.'

'It has to.'

Skovgaard glanced at the door behind her, said very slowly, as if talking to an idiot, 'We can't.'

Lund walked over, pushed Skovgaard away when she flew at her, screaming, opened the door.

Troels Hartmann looked bemused. So did the woman next to him.

Kirsten Eller. The plump woman from the election posters.

She wasn't smiling. She didn't like to be disturbed.

'Sorry,' Lund said to the man in the pressed blue shirt. 'But we have to talk.'

One minute later by the window, Kirsten Eller out of earshot on the sofa.

Hartmann said, 'If the media think I'm lying . . .'

'This is a murder case. The details are confidential. You can't jeopardize our chances . . .'

'What about my chances?'

He was an unusual man. Blessed with a politician's charisma. An aura of blithe candour. He managed to say that without any obvious shame.

Her phone rang, she snatched it out of her bag, sighed when she saw the number, answered anyway.

'Bengt. Can I call you back?'

The sound of hammering. Distant.

'I'm at the house. The carpenters are here. What kind of wood do we want for the sauna?'

Lund closed her eyes. Hartmann wasn't walking away. That was something.

'What kind usually goes in saunas?'

'Pine.'

'Pine is fine. That sounds good.'

'But it depends on . . .'

'Not now. I'll phone you later.'

End of call.

Hartmann was walking back to the woman waiting patiently on his sofa.

Lund took his arm, looked into his eyes. There was something there . . .

'We're very close to catching him. Don't get in our way.'

'How close? Today?'

'I hope so.'

Hartmann hesitated.

'OK,' he said. 'I'll wait for that. So long as it is today.'

'Thanks,' she said.

'Polar pine.'

Lund stopped.

'Polar pine. It's better for saunas than ordinary. Has less resin.'

'Oh.'

Meyer was at the door, back from hunting round the corridors. Time to go.

Kirsten Eller was smiling when Hartmann came back.

'Bad news, Troels?'

'Not at all. It's no bother.'

She watched him.

'Really? You looked worried.'

'I said it's nothing.'

'If I'm to divorce Bremer this must be a marriage. Not a fickle affair.'

'Of course,' he said, nodding vigorously.

'Requiring frankness in all things.'

Hartmann smiled at her.

'There's no bad news, Kirsten. Can we get down to business?'

Just after two Pernille and Theis Birk Larsen waited on the grey pavement by the fountain, watched the kids come running from the playground, wrapped in warm coats, hats and gloves, backpacks on, brightly coloured kites waving in their hands.

Tuesday. They always made something.

Emil, seven, with his short fair hair, Anton six, ginger as his father once was. The boys came stumbling, trying to make their kites catch on the chill winter breeze.

Emil's was red, Anton's yellow.

'Why's Dad with you?' Emil asked straight out.

Into the grey street, watching the traffic. Cross the road carefully. Small hands in theirs.

Anton wanted to know if they could go and fly the kites in the park. Sulked when his mother said no.

The sky loomed dark and heavy. They packed the boys' things in the boot.

A call. Vagn Stærbæk anxious in Birk Larsen's ear.

'Don't come home yet,' he said.

'Why not?'

'The police are searching her room. Some photographers have arrived.'

Birk Larsen blinked, watched Pernille fasten the boys into their safety seats, buckles checked, a kiss on the forehead.

Not anger, he thought. Not now.

'How long will they be?'

'No idea. Should I get rid of them?'

Birk Larsen couldn't think of a thing to say.

'The boys, Theis. You don't want them to see this.'

'No. Call me when they're gone.'

So they got in the car and he said, 'Let's fly those kites. Let's do that.'

Two small cheers, fists punching the air in the back. Pernille looked at him.

No words needed. She knew.

Meyer was driving the way he usually did.

'Did Poster Boy get your vote then?'

'Meaning?'

'You smiled at him, Lund.'

'I smile at lots of people.'

'He kept looking at your jumper.'

She still wore the black and white sweater from the Faroes. It was warm and comfy. Bought it on the holiday just after the divorce, with Mark, trying to ease him through the shock. She liked them so much she got some more. Different colours. Different patterns. There was a mail order place . . .

'Last time I saw my granny she was wearing one like that,' Meyer said.

'That's nice.'

'Not really. She was in a box. I hate funerals. They seem so . . .' He slammed the horn as a cyclist got in the way. 'Final.'

'You made that up,' she said and he didn't answer.

The Faroe Islands were green and peaceful. A quiet, sleepy world away from the grimy urban landscape of Copenhagen.

'I'm sure he couldn't be stealing a glance at your tits. I mean . . .'

She didn't listen, let him ramble on. Get it out of his system.

In the green world of the Faroes nothing much happened. People got by. Seasons came and went. Cows farted. Just like Sigtuna.

'Where are we going, Meyer?'

'Lynge hasn't been in his apartment since last night. He's got a sister. She runs a hair salon in Christianshavn. He went to see her this morning. Turned ugly.'

Meyer grinned at her.

'Some men are like that.'

Lynge's sister was a good-looking woman with long straight hair and a mournful face.

'Where is he?' Meyer asked.

'Haven't a clue. He's my brother. I didn't pick him.'

Lynge was waiting down a side street when she opened up that morning. Forced his way in. Bad timing. All she had was five thousand kroner in the till. He took it, trashed the place a little. The sister was mopping up shampoo and conditioner from the floor as she spoke.

Lund walked round, leaving the questions to Meyer.

'Where do you think he's gone?'

'I don't know him any more. He's sick.'

'We know that.'

'No.' She tapped the side of her head. 'Not just there. He's sick. Ill. He needs to be in hospital.' She stopped mopping. 'I've never seen him that bad. It was just money. Don't put him back in jail. Not again. He'd get even crazier.'

'Does he have anywhere to go? A girlfriend?'

'No one wants to know him. Not after what he did.' She hesitated. 'There was a woman.'

'What woman?' Lund asked.

'A prison visitor. A volunteer.' The sister frowned. 'You know the kind. Christian. Never gives up. She contacted me a few weeks back. Begged me to get back in touch with him. Said it would help.'

They waited.

'It wouldn't help. I know him. Besides . . .' She looked around the little salon. 'I've got a life. A right to that. Haven't I?'

Meyer picked up a hairbrush, played with it.

'You've got a name for this woman?'

'Sorry. She came from one of the prison charities I think.'

The sister looked at Lund.

'He killed that girl on the TV, didn't he? I knew it was going to happen. They shouldn't have let him out. He was so scared.'

'When I get hold of him he will be,' Meyer murmured.

The woman didn't say anything.

'What?' Lund asked.

'This morning. He looked really scared. I mean . . . I don't know.'

'We need to find him. We need to talk.'

She started mopping again.

'Good luck,' the sister said.

Outside. Steady rain.

'Take my car. Get someone onto the prison visitor,' she told Meyer. 'Then call me.'

'Where are you going?'

Lund hailed a cab and was gone.

Mathilde Villadsen was seventy-six, half-blind, living in an old apartment block with her cat Samson and her second-best friend the radio. It was playing music from the Fifties, the decade she thought of as hers.

Then the swing band got interrupted by the news.

'The police have imposed a news blackout . . .' the reader began.

'Samson?'

It was time to feed him. The tin was open. The food was in the dish.

'. . . over the case of Nanna Birk Larsen who was found dead on Monday.'

She walked to the kitchen sink, turned off the radio. It was cold in the draughty flat. She wore what she did for most of the winter: a long blue woollen cardigan, a thick scarf round her wrinkled neck. The price of heating was terrible. She was a Fifties girl. A little hardship was a cross she could bear.

'Samson?'

The cat was mewing outside the flap into the corridor. In her old, loose slippers she shuffled to the front door, undid the chain.

It was dark in the stairwell. The kids were always knocking out the lights. Mathilde Villadsen sighed, got down on her painful knees, wished the cat wouldn't play these games.

In the gloom, feeling the cold stone through her stockings, she scrambled across the hall calling, 'Samson, Samson. Naughty cat, *naughty* cat . . .'

Then she bumped into something. Struggling to see, she felt with her fingers. Dirty leather, denim trousers above it.

Glanced up. A bald head, a scarred face in the flickering flame of a cigarette lighter, close to the cat's whiskers as it sat in the arms of a man above her.

He looked unhappy. Frightened.

'My cat . . .' she started to say.

The lighter got closer to Samson's face. Samson mewed and tried to scramble free from his strong arms.

In a low hard voice he said, 'Don't squawk. Get inside.'

There was a wedding dress on the mannequin, white satin covered in embroidered cotton flowers. Lund's mother, Vibeke, made them for a local shop. Not so much for money, more for something to do. Widowhood didn't suit her. Not a lot did.

'What does Bengt say about all this?'

She was a stiff-backed woman, always smart, always serious, with a brisk, sometimes caustic manner and a judgemental eye.

'I'm going to call him.'

Vibeke stood back and considered the dress. Put a stitch in the breast, another in the arm. Lund thought she liked the idea of women getting married. It narrowed their options. Tied them down the way God meant.

'So you haven't even told him you're not coming?'

'No time.'

Her mother uttered that short brief sigh Lund had known since childhood. Even so she remained amazed how much distaste and disapproval could be compressed into a single breath.

'I hope you don't chase this one away too.'

'I just said I would call!'

'Carsten . . .'

'Carsten hit me!'

The look, long and cold.

'Once. That's all. He was your husband. The father of your child.'

'He—'

'The way you behave. This obsession with your work. A man needs to know he's wanted. Loved. If you don't give them that . . .'

'He hit me.'

With great care Vibeke placed the needle in the shiny satin fabric at the neckline.

'Do you ever wonder if you asked for it?'

'I didn't ask for it. No one ever does.'

Lund's mobile rang. It was Meyer: 'I talked to the prison.'

'And?'

'He had three visitors in all. One's dead. One's moved. One's not answering her phone.'

'Come and get me,' Lund said and gave him the address in Østerbro. 'Twenty minutes.'

'Blue light taxi's on the way. I hope you tip well.'

The police people had left their marks and trails all over the apartment. Numbers and arrows. Puffs of dust where they'd looked for prints.

Anton, always the most inquisitive, stood outside her room and asked, 'What's that on Nanna's door?'

'Get away from there!' Theis Birk Larsen barked at him. 'Come to the table.'

The table.

Pernille and Nanna made it one empty distant summer three years before when there was nothing else to do but watch the rain. Cheap timber from the DIY store. Photos and school reports glued then lacquered onto the top. The Birk Larsen family frozen in time. Nanna turned sixteen, growing quickly. Anton and Emil so tiny. Faces captured in the place that was the heart of their small home. Smiling mostly.

Now the boys were six and seven, bright-eyed wondering. Curious, perhaps a little afraid.

Pernille sat down, looked at them, touched their knees, their hands, their cheeks and said, 'There's something we have to tell you.'

Birk Larsen stood behind. Until she turned to him. Then, slowly, he came and sat by her side.

'Something's happened to us,' Pernille told them.

The boys shuffled, glanced at one another.

'What?' Emil, the elder, though in a way the slower, asked.

Beyond the window the traffic rumbled. There were voices in the street. It was always like this. For Theis Birk Larsen it always would be.

Together. A family. Complete.

His great chest heaved. Strong, scarred fingers ran through greying ginger hair. He felt old, impotent, stupid.

'Boys,' he said finally. 'Nanna's dead.'

Pernille waited.

'She's not coming back,' he added.

Six and seven, bright eyes glittering beneath the lamp where they all ate supper. Static faces staring at them from the tabletop.

Emil said, 'Why's that, Dad?'

Thinking.

Struggling.

'There was a time we saw a big tree out in Deer Park. Remember?'

Anton looked at Emil. Then both nodded.

'Lightning struck it. Tore off a big . . .'

Was this real, he asked himself? Or imagined? Or a lie to let children sleep when the darkness came?

'Tore off a big branch. Well . . .'

It didn't matter, Birk Larsen thought. Lies could work too, as well as the truth. Better sometimes. Beautiful lies might let you sleep. Ugly truths never.

'You could say lightning's struck us now. It took Nanna away.'

They listened in silence.

'But just like the tree in Deer Park keeps growing we do too.'

A good lie. It heartened him a little.

He squeezed Pernille's hand beneath the table and said, 'We have to.'

'Where's Nanna?' asked Anton, younger, quicker.

'Someone's taking care of her,' Pernille said. 'In a few days everyone will go to church. Then we say goodbye.'

The boy's smooth brow furrowed.

'She won't *ever* come back?'

Mother and father, their eyes briefly locked. These were children. Precious, still trapped in their own world, no need to escape it.

'No,' said Pernille. 'An angel came and took her to heaven.'

Another good lie.

Six and seven, bright eyes glittering. Not a part of this nightmare. Not . . .

'How did she die?'

Anton. Had to be.

The words fled them. Pernille walked to the cork-board, stared at photos, the timetables, the plans they'd all made.

'How did she die, Dad?'

'I don't know.'

'Dad.'

'It just . . . happens sometimes.'

The boys fell quiet. He held their hands. Wondered: have they ever seen me cry before? How long before they see it again?

'It just happens.'

Lund and Meyer walked up the stairs, rang the bell, waited. The hallway was dark. Broken bulbs. It stank of cat piss.

'So you've moved in with your mother instead of that Norwegian?'

'Bengt's Swedish.'

'You can tell the difference?'

There was no answer from the address they had. Junk mail was piled up at the foot of the door.

Lund walked to the next apartment along. There was a light behind the frosted glass. The nameplate said Villadsen.

Meyer's radio squawked. It was too loud. She glared at him and banged on the door.

Nothing.

Lund knocked again. Meyer stood to one side, fists on hips, silent. She almost laughed. Like most of the men in homicide he wore his 9-millimetre Glock handgun on his waistband in a holster. It made him look like a cartoon cowboy.

'What's wrong?'

'Nothing.' She tried not to smile. 'Nothing at all.'

'At least I've got a gun. Where's . . . ?'

There was a rattle. The door opened just a couple of inches on the chain. An elderly woman's face, not clear in the darkness.

'I'm Vicekriminalkommissær Sarah Lund from the police,' Lund said, showing her ID. 'We need to speak to your neighbour, Geertsen.'

'She's away.'

Old people and strangers. Fear and suspicion.

'Do you know where?'

'Abroad.'

The woman moved as if to close the door. Lund put a hand out to stop her.

'Did you see anything unusual around the block today?'

'No.'

There was a sound from behind her in the apartment. The woman's eyes wouldn't leave Lund's.

'Do you have a visitor?' Meyer asked.

'It's just my cat,' she said then quickly slammed the door.

One minute later, back in her squad car, Lund on the radio, Meyer by her side. He was getting twitchy.

'I need back-up. The suspect may be at this location.'

'We'll send a car,' control replied.

They could see the apartment window from the street.

Meyer said, 'The lights are out. He knows we're here.'

'They're on their way.'

He took out the Glock and checked it.

'We can't wait. A man like that. An old woman. We're going in.'

Lund shook her head.

'To do what?'

'Whatever we can. You heard the sister. He's a lunatic. I'm not waiting till the old bird's dead.'

Lund leaned over the seat, looked him in the eye, said, 'We're staying here.'

'No.'

'Meyer! There's two of us. We can't cover the exits . . .'

'Where's your gun?'

She was getting sick of this.

'I don't have one.'

It was the look she saw the day before when they talked about Sweden. Utter amazement.

'What?' Meyer asked.

'We're going nowhere. We'll wait.'

A long moment. Meyer nodding.

'You can wait if you want,' he said then leapt out of the car.

Across the city, in a campaign car speeding through the night, Troels Hartmann took the last call he wanted. A news agency. Official this time. A journalist with a name he recalled.

The reporter said, 'We know about the car, Hartmann. Nanna Birk Larsen was found in one of yours. You kept it quiet. Why is that exactly?'

In the apartment above the depot, while Pernille quietly wept, Theis Birk Larsen sat with Anton and Emil, one on each huge knee, telling more stories about angels and forests, watching their faces, hating his lies.

Sarah Lund bit on another piece of Nicotinell, thought about Jan Meyer, thought about the dead girl who came out of the water.

Then she pulled open the glove compartment by the wheel, sorted through the packs of gum, the dead lighter, the tissues, the tampons and took out her gun.

Halfway up the dark dank staircase she heard the sound of breaking glass.

Lund ran the rest of the way, took hold of Meyer's arm as he smashed at the panel in the door with the grip of his gun.

'What do you think you're doing?'

'What does it look like?'

'I told you to wait.'

He broke more glass, opened up the hole with his elbow, put a hand through, looked at her and winked.

'You go left,' Meyer said. 'I go right.'

Hand through, searching. There was the sound of an old key turning an old lock. Then the door moved. Inside was as black as the night they'd just left. Meyer scuttled through and was gone in a stride. She went to the wall, edged forward, the Glock an unfamiliar shape in her right hand.

The place stank of mothballs and liniment, cat and washing.

Three steps and she bumped into a sideboard, nudged something with her arm, just managed to catch it before the thing fell to the floor. Lund could just see what she'd touched: a porcelain figurine, a country milkmaid grinning beneath her burden of buckets. Placed it back without a sound. Moved forward, stepped on something, heard a tinny mechanical voice break the silence.

'Your weight is fifty-seven point two kilograms.'

She got off the scales wondering what Meyer was saying to himself.

'Fifty-seven point two kilograms,' the thing said again.

There was a pained sigh from somewhere ahead. Then footsteps. A silhouette. Meyer, trudging in front of her, gun out.

No other sound. Three more steps. A door on the right, ajar. Laboured, arrhythmic breathing. She pocketed the weapon, walked through, fumbled her fingers against the wall, found a light switch. Turned it on.

In the dim yellow bulb of a single wall-light the old woman struggled, trussed like a farmyard bird, wrists and ankles, a cloth rag round her mouth.

Lund got down, put a hand to her shoulder, pulled off the gag.

A long high wail of terror and pain burst from the old woman's lips.

Meyer was close by, cursing.

'Where is he?' Lund asked. 'Mrs Villadsen?'

'What did she say?' Meyer snapped.

The woman was panting, gasping for breath. Terrified.

'What did she say?'

Lund looked at him. Listened. He got the message. Went back out in the dark apartment, feet tapping on the tiles.

She waited.

You take the left. I'll take the right.

Did that still apply? Yes, she guessed. Meyer was a little like her in some ways. There was one plan and one plan only. You stuck with it until something changed. He didn't like working with someone else either.

She undid the woman's ankles and wrists, told her to stay there, stay still.

A pair of scrawny hands clawed at her.

'Don't leave me.'

'I'll be right back. We're here. You're safe.'

'Don't leave me.'

'It's fine. Don't worry.'

Still the wrinkled fingers clutched at her.

'I need my cane.'

'Where is it?'

She gasped, thought, said, 'In the hallway.'

'OK.' Voice calm, steady. Which was how Lund felt. 'Stay here.'

She got to the door, bore left.

Kitchen smells. Drains, food. The cat. Another old lamp, frilly shade, faded yellow. A chair, a small desk. Striped curtains running to the floor. Gently moving as if the window behind was open.

In November.

Lund folded her arms, thought, moved forward, gently pushed the fabric aside.

The pain bit at her arm like a wasp sting, rapid and savage.

There was a figure coming from behind the stripes, silhouetted against the faint lights behind the window. His right arm was flailing, right and left, up and down.

Another flash of agony.

Lund yelled, 'Get back! Police! Get back.'

Fumbling like a fool for her gun.

The wall stopped her. He lunged forward. And now the light caught him. In his hand she saw a box cutter, short blade, sharp. Threatening.

He swore, slashed at her, so close she could feel the air move past her cheek.

A furious, insane face, mouth opening, yellow teeth grinning. He roared. One more cutting, sweeping slash . . .

Her fingers tightened on the gun butt. She raised it, pointed the barrel dead in his face.

John Lynge's eyes narrowed. He was sweating. Looked sick. Looked mad.

'Calm down, John. I won't hurt you.' No sound from Meyer. She knew what he'd be doing.

Lynge retreated a step. Her eyes were getting used to this light. She saw his shoulders, his arms.

Kept the gun straight on him.

'I didn't do anything!'

Frightened, she thought. That was good.

'I didn't say you did, John.'

Keep using the name. Keep turning down the heat.

He started rocking backwards, forwards, sobbing, hands to his face.

The blade was still there. Did he know that?

'You don't believe me,' Lynge grunted.

'I'm listening. Put down the knife.'

He flashed the box cutter at her. Didn't flinch at the gun.

'You're not putting me back in jail!'

Crazy voice. A man in agony.

'We're just talking, John. Let's do that. OK? The school . . .'

Stiff and furious, shaking, close to the edge, Lynge bellowed, 'I felt sick. I went to the hospital. I got back. The car was gone. Maybe, maybe . . .'

'Maybe what?'

'Maybe I dropped the keys when I was throwing up. I don't know.'

'What keys?'

'The car keys! You're not listening.'

He was getting madder all the time.

'You were sick. I hear you, John.'

He moved a step to the left. She could see him in the orange light from the street.

'You felt ill and you left the car. Put down the knife. Let's talk.'

'I'm not going back to that place. They'll know—'

'You won't—'

'John!'

A hard male voice from the hallway. Lund took a deep breath. Looked. Meyer was there. Gun up. Pointed straight at John Lynge's head. Ready.

'Drop the knife,' he said in a slow threatening tone.

'I have this, Meyer,' she said. 'It's under control . . .'

Lynge was running already. Meyer after him. Two dark shapes crossing the floor.

A scream and shattering glass. A tumult of bitter curses. Then a hideous crash outside. The sickening sound of flesh and bone on pavement.

'Meyer?' she said.

There was a figure at the window.

Lund walked to it.

'Meyer?' she said again.

John Lynge was unconscious, strapped to a trolley, tubes and apparatus everywhere, getting rushed down a hospital corridor. It was ten in the evening. Lund asked, for the third time, 'When can I speak to him?'

The surgeon didn't break his pace, just stared at her then said, 'Are you serious?'

'Is he going to live?' she asked when they got to the operating theatre doors.

Lund stopped, repeated the question at twice the volume.

No answer. Then John Lynge was gone.

'We've got prints,' Meyer told her. 'Forensics have got his boots.'

'And nothing to match them with. He says he went to the hospital!'

'Puh!'

'Have you ever heard someone say that, Meyer? Not I was screwing my girlfriend. I was in a bar. But I went to hospital?'

Nothing.

'He told me he left the keys at the school. When he came back the car was gone.'

'He was lying!'

Meyer looked at her and shook his head.

'He cut you, Lund. He'd have cut you again.' He came close. 'Cut your face to ribbons. Doesn't that bother you?'

'It doesn't mean he killed Nanna Birk Larsen. Check the hospital records.'

'Oh come on. Do you really think—'

'If he's got an alibi I want to know. Find out.'

She shouted that last order. Which wasn't like her. This man had got under her skin.

Lund took off her jacket, checked the sleeve of her black and white jumper. The thing was ruined. Lynge's blade had slashed a cut through the wool, opened up a flesh wound across the top of her arm just below the shoulder.

'You should get that seen—'

'Yes! I should. What about the old lady?'

'I called while you were yelling at the doctors. She's going to stay with some relatives.'

Lund nodded. Calm now. The cut hurt, not that she was going to show it.

'Go and get some sleep,' she told him. 'Tell them to let me know if his condition changes.'

He folded his arms, didn't move.

'What?' Lund asked.

'I'm not going anywhere until I see you talk to a nurse.'

The TV debate was over. A draw at best, Hartmann thought.

Outside, in the huddle waiting for their cars, he took Rie Skovgaard to one side, asked, 'Have you heard from Lund?'

'No.'

'Did you call her?'

'I can't get through.'

It was raining. There was no sign of their driver.

'We can't afford to wait any longer. Put a statement together.'

'Finally . . .'

'Give it to the reporter who phoned. He's legit. Tell him it's an exclusive. Win us some breathing space . . .'

Bremer strode up, jacket over shoulder, glanced at the rain, stepped back beneath the shelter of the roof.

'Crisis meeting?'

The two of them went quiet.

'I thought you were a little rusty tonight,' Poul Bremer said. 'If you don't mind my saying so.'

'Really?'

No points scored on either side. No balls dropped. But the way Bremer smiled throughout gave Hartmann pause. Every issue, every question he forced round to the question of character. Hartmann's lack of experience, of proven trust.

The old bastard knew something. He was waiting for the right moment to say it.

'Rusty,' Bremer repeated. 'You'll need to do better than that.'

'Still three weeks to the election,' Skovgaard said. 'Lots of time—'

'Pacing yourself. A wise move from what I hear. Goodnight!'

Hartmann watched him go.

'One day I will tear that old dinosaur apart,' he muttered.

'You really have to work on your temper,' Skovgaard said.

He turned his icy gaze on her.

'Do I?'

'Yes. It's good to come across as passionate. Energetic. Committed. But not bad-tempered, Troels. People don't like it.'

'Thank you. I'll try to remember that.'

'Bremer's looking for weak points. Don't hand him one on a plate. Your temper leaves you vulnerable. He's not the only one who's noticed.'

She didn't quite meet his eye.

'I need you to work on this.'

Skovgaard held up her phone.

'Ritzau news agency have heard about the car too. The story's out there.'

The black saloon came and parked in front of them. The Rådhus driver got out and opened the doors.

'I told you we needed to get this out early,' she said. 'Now we're racing round trying to clean up something we should have killed at birth.'

'Bremer's behind this.'

'Someone in the police more likely. How would he know?'

'Twelve years on that burnished throne. Maybe the Politigården works for him too.'

A long limousine ran past. Bremer wound down the window, grinned at them, waved like a king hailing his subjects.

'He's got someone,' Hartmann muttered. 'We need to know who it is.'

Ten minutes later the car pulled into the Rådhus. A crowd of reporters and cameramen flocked around them.

'Say what we agreed,' Skovgaard said. 'Be calm, be authoritative. Don't get mad. Don't go off script.'

'Whose script?' he said, and then they were in the middle of the mob, hands clawing at the doors to get them open.

The rain was heavy and constant. Hartmann pushed through the crowd to the steps of the building. Listening to the questions. Thinking about them.

'Hartmann? What's your connection to Nanna Birk Larsen?'

'Where were you on Friday?'

'What do you have to hide?'

A sea of hostile voices. When he got to the doors he stopped, watched the voice recorders come up ready to capture every word.

What he said would be on the radio in minutes. Captured for ever, repeated in newspapers, replayed on the web.

He waited till they listened then said, in as calm and statesman-like a manner as he could manage, 'A young woman was found dead in a car that my office rented. That's all I can tell you. The police specifically asked us not to comment. But let me say something—'

'When did you hear?' a woman shouted.

81

'Let me say . . . No one in the party or the organization is involved in this case. That's as much as I can—'

'Do you deny withholding information for the sake of the election?'

Hartmann looked. He was a stocky bald man of about thirty-five, cigarette in smirking mouth.

'What?'

The hack pushed his way nearer.

'This isn't a tough one, Hartmann,' the reporter bawled through the forest of voice recorders. 'Do you deny you deliberately deceived the public to win some votes. Is this what we can expect of the Liberal Party?'

He didn't stop to think about it. Was through the crowd so quickly Skovgaard couldn't stop him, had the man by the collar.

The smirk never left the bald hack's face.

'Yes,' Hartmann said close up. 'I deny that.' A pause. He let go, brushed the man's collar as if this were a joke. 'It's nothing to do with politics. This girl . . .'

He was off script. He was drowning.

'Troels?' Skovgaard said.

'The girl . . .'

Cameras flashed. A spiky crown of voice recorders bristled around him.

The hack he'd so nearly punched pulled out a card and thrust it into Hartmann's fingers. Not thinking he took it.

'Troels?'

Drowning.

She had his arm, quietly pulled him away, through the door, into the vestibule, through the inner courtyard and the gleaming silence of the Rådhus until they found safety behind its fortress walls.

Hartmann felt the paper in his hand. Looked.

It was a business card.

Just a mobile number. And a name.

Erik Salin.

All evening she'd sat in the dark front room watching TV, switching from news channel to news channel.

Now it was the main bulletin.

'Troels Hartmann is cooperating with the police in solving the murder,' the story said. 'He denies any connection to the girl or the crime.'

She'd seen his posters everywhere. Striking, handsome, more like an actor than a politician. He always looked sad too, she thought.

A noise from behind. She didn't turn.

He came and slumped by her side on the carpet.

'The car belonged to that politician,' Pernille said. 'They're looking for a driver.'

He had his head in his hands. Said nothing.

'Why don't they tell us what's going on, Theis? It's as if we don't matter.'

'They'll tell us when they've got something to say.'

His lethargy infuriated her.

'They know more than we do. Don't you care?'

'Stop this!'

'Don't you care?'

The TV was the brightest thing in the room.

'How could Nanna know this driver? Someone in politics? How—?'

'I don't know!'

There was a gulf between them. A chasm that was new. His big and clumsy hand went out to touch her. Pernille shrank back.

'Listen,' he said. 'I think it's best we go away for a few days. Maybe rent the cottage from last weekend.'

In the semi-darkness, their faces lit by the news about their daughter, Pernille looked at him, astonished.

'The police are here all the time,' he said. 'The boys keep seeing Nanna in the papers. On that damned thing. The kids talk to them at school.'

She started crying. His hand went to her damp face. This time she didn't shrink from him.

'And you,' he said. 'Watching it. Reliving it. Every minute of the day—'

'You want me to run away from Vesterbro when my daughter needs a funeral?'

They hadn't even used that word yet. Hadn't faced the thought.

Birk Larsen ground his big hands together. Squeezed his narrow eyes tight shut.

'Tomorrow we'll talk to the minister,' she said. 'We'll arrange everything. That's what we'll do.'

Silence in the wan kitchen light. The big man head in hands.

Pernille Birk Larsen picked up the remote, found another channel. Watched it.

Carefully, trying not to make it hurt more, Lund took off the sweater from the Faroes. Looked at the bloody gash. Wondered if the jumper could be mended. Not by her. But . . .

The wedding dress was still on the mannequin, needles and thread in the sleeves and collars.

They were the only things her mother ever made. It was like a one-woman campaign to marry off the female population of the world.

She left the jumper by the sewing box anyway. Her mother came yawning, grumbling out of her room.

'Do you know what time it is?'

'Yes.'

Vibeke glowered at the table.

'Please don't throw your clothes everywhere. No wonder Mark's such a messy boy.'

She saw the cut, naturally. Came, bent down, looked.

'What happened?'

'Nothing.'

'There's a cut on your arm.'

Meat stew and potatoes on the cooker. The gravy had congealed. The potato was dry. Lund spooned some of each onto a plate and shoved it in the microwave.

'A cat scratched me.'

'Don't tell me a cat did that.'

'It was a stray cat.'

They looked at each other. A kind of truce was called. On this anyway.

'Why do you insist on going to work?' Vibeke asked. 'Now you can have a proper life?'

The microwave beeped. The food was lukewarm. Enough. She was hungry. Lund sat down, picked up a fork, began to eat.

'I told you this morning. It's just till Friday. If it's a problem we can stay in a hotel.'

Her mother came to the table, a glass of water in her hand.

'Why should it be a problem? Why . . .?'

Her mouth full, Lund said, 'I'm sorry. I'm tired. Let's not argue.'

'We never argue. You always walk away.'

Lund smiled, picked up another forkful of meat and potato. She'd been eating this since she was a child. Nothing special. Sustenance. It never changed.

'It's delicious,' she said. 'I mean it.'

Her mother watched her.

'Bengt asked if you'd come to the house-warming party on Saturday. We're fixing up the spare room.'

She was watching the food, following how much got eaten, what got left.

'Bengt called here,' Vibeke said. 'This afternoon. He was wondering where you were.'

Lund's head fell. She swore.

'You didn't say I was here till Friday, did you?'

'Of course I did! Am I supposed to lie?'

Lund pushed away the food, got a beer from the fridge, went into her bedroom and called.

Bengt Rosling didn't get angry. Ever. It was beyond him. Or beneath. She never quite knew.

They spoke about parties and polar pine, made small talk, acted as if nothing had happened. Nothing was wrong.

He didn't know she was watching the news on her computer as they talked. She kept the sound low. It was all about Hartmann.

Come Friday she'd be in Sweden. With Mark, with her mother too for a little while. The new life would start. The past would slip away. Copenhagen and Carsten. The Vicekriminalkommissær's badge.

She felt better for speaking to him, put down the phone happy. Remembered straight away what she'd forgotten to say.

Before she could call back it rang.

Bengt, she knew. So she picked it up and, with a deliberate effort, found herself saying, 'I love you.'

'Wow! That just made my day.'

Meyer. The sound of him driving. She could picture the car going too fast through the black rain. Cheese crisps on the passenger seat. Chewing gum and tobacco.

'What do you want?'

'You told me to call about the hospital!' He was playing hurt. 'Lynge went in on Friday.'

'For how long?'

'He was there till seven the next morning. The idiot's a heroin addict. He screwed up his methadone or something.'

Troels Hartmann was on TV. Almost swinging a punch at a mouthy reporter.

He'd lost it over a simple question: Do you deny withholding information for the sake of the election?

She'd thought Hartmann a calm and reasonable man.

'Could Lynge have sneaked out?'

A noisy, chomping pause.

'Not a chance. They had him in a public ward. Medicated. Was there all night.'

'Will you leave those crisps alone? If they're all over the car . . .'

'I haven't had anything to eat all day.'

'Did you find Nanna's bike?'

'No.'

'What about her mobile phone?'

That was in Hartmann's car too. Which seemed odd.

'The lab got it working,' Meyer said. 'Her last call was on Friday. Maybe made from school. They're not sure.'

'OK. We go back there in the morning.'

'No, Lund. You're not coming.'

He was still eating crisps. She could hear him crunching them in that frantic way he had, as if there'd never be another packet in the world.

'Why not?'

'I ran into Buchard. Hartmann wants a meeting. It's about you.'

She thought about that.

'Get some sleep. Write your report.'

'Thank you. Sleep tight too, sweetheart.'

'Ha, ha.'

'Lund? Think about it. Hartmann didn't call you asking for that meeting. He called Buchard. Or maybe someone above Buchard. Or maybe . . .' The crunching could drive her crazy. 'Someone above him. We've got politicians on our backs now. My bet is every last one of them's calling upstairs trying to dump shit on our heads. Sleep on that.'

In the tiny bedroom, listening to her mother trawl around the kitchen tidying things, sweeping things, Sarah Lund followed the news on her computer. Watched Troels Hartmann carefully, second by second.

Four

Wednesday, 5th November

Hartmann arrived at headquarters just after nine, came straight to Lund's office. Sat in the bright winter sun streaming through the narrow window opposite her and Buchard. The sharp, severe Rie Skovgaard was next to him, following every word.

'I could have avoided all this shit last night,' he said. 'If I'd done the right thing and put out a statement straight away. Before you people leaked.'

This was politics, a world Lund had managed to avoid before the Birk Larsen case. She felt out of her depth. But interested.

The chief bent forward, caught Hartmann's eye, said, 'There was no leak from here. I guarantee it.'

'Has the driver confessed?' Hartmann asked.

Lund shook her head.

'No, and he won't. He's innocent.'

The face from the poster, handsome, thoughtful, benevolent, was gone. Now Troels Hartmann was getting mad.

'Wait a minute. Yesterday you said—'

'Yesterday I said he was a suspect. He was. He isn't now. That's the way it works. That's why we asked you to keep quiet.'

'But you're still saying someone used our car?'

'They did.'

'Maybe it was stolen,' Buchard added.

'Stolen?' He didn't seem happy with that idea. 'When are you making this public?'

'Not yet,' Lund said. 'We need to wait.'

'Wait for what?' Skovgaard wanted to know.

Lund shrugged.

'The driver was injured. We'll talk to him today. See what he has to say—'

'If our car was stolen,' Skovgaard said, 'the press must be told. The damage this is doing . . .'

Lund folded her arms, looked straight at Hartmann, not the woman.

'It could help us if the man we're looking for thinks we suspect someone else.'

'We can't keep playing this game,' Hartmann said. 'Rie can draft a release.' He turned to Buchard. 'You'll see a copy. It's going out. As soon as . . .'

Lund pulled her chair across the office, sat straight in front of him.

'I would really appreciate it if you waited.'

'I can't help that.'

'The damage this could do us . . .'

Hartmann's eyes lit up.

'What about the damage to me? It's done already. It's getting worse. Buchard . . .'

The chief nodded.

'You'll see a copy,' Hartmann promised. 'If you find an error tell us. I don't want to hear about anything else.'

'I appreciate that.'

'That's it.' Hartmann got to his feet. 'We're done here. Goodbye.'

Lund wasn't done at all. She got up and went into the corridor. Caught up with Hartmann and the Skovgaard woman as they walked towards the spiral stairs.

'Hartmann! Hartmann!'

He stopped. No smile.

'If you'll just listen to me—'

'The press are behaving as if I'm a suspect.' Hartmann stabbed his chest with a finger. 'As if I killed that kid.'

'On TV you said you'd cooperate.'

'We have cooperated,' Skovgaard said. 'Look where it got us.'

Lund stood in front of Hartmann, bright eyes shining, insistent.

'I need your help.'

Skovgaard said, 'We have to go.'

'Lund?'

Svendsen, one of the homicide team, came out of the incident room, beckoned to her.

'Your visitors are here.'

She touched Troels Hartmann's arm.

'Just a minute, please. We haven't finished. One minute. Spare me that.'

Two figures at the end of the long corridor. A giant of a man, grizzled features, long sideburns, black leather jacket. A woman in a fawn gaberdine raincoat, chestnut hair, an attractive face that looked lost and afraid. He held a black hat in his fidgeting hands. Waiting, in anticipation of something they didn't want to see. She stared at the shining black marble walls and clung on to his arm.

Lund strode towards them, businesslike, animated. Spoke briefly then they walked down the corridor, past Hartmann and Rie Skov-gaard who stood to one side.

No words spoken. No words needed.

Briefly the woman turned and stared then walked on.

'We're late,' Skovgaard told him. 'Troels. We have to go.'

Lund watched. Hartmann was trapped by the sight of them.

'Troels?'

Hartmann said, 'Was that . . . ?'

Lund nodded, looked at him, waited.

'Will it make a difference?'

'Yes.'

'You know that?' Skovgaard snarled.

'I know that if you put out a statement we've lost an opportunity. An advantage maybe.'

Lund sighed, shrugged.

'We've got so few. I'll fight to keep any I can.'

'OK.' He didn't look at Skovgaard glaring at him stony-eyed. 'Only till tomorrow. Then . . . Lund . . .'

She listened.

'Tomorrow,' Hartmann said, 'we make our position clear. What-ever you say.'

In Lund's room, coffee sitting on the desk, untouched, Theis and Pernille Birk Larsen listening.

'We've got a preliminary medical examiner's report,' Lund said. 'But he's not quite finished. A funeral—'

'We need to get away,' Birk Larsen broke in. 'We're going to the seaside this afternoon. All these damned reporters. The boys.' He looked into her face. 'You people coming round the apartment all the time. You can do what you like when we're not there.'

'If that's what you want.'

'What are they doing to her?' Pernille asked.

'Some more tests. I don't know exactly.' A lie, one she always used. 'We'll let you know when her body can be released.'

The mother was somewhere else, Lund thought. Lost in her memories. Or imagination.

The father again.

'Where will Nanna go?'

'Normally to a funeral director. It's your choice.'

Pernille woke.

'What happened to her?' She sniffed. 'What did he do?'

Lund opened her hands.

'I have to wait for the full report. I understand you want to know. It's . . .'

Theis Birk Larsen looked ready to put his big hands over his ears.

There was a knock at the door. An officer from the team. Said sorry, started asking for documents from her desk.

So many, and they said so little. Lund helped him. Got involved. Got lost for a moment. Never noticed the door was open.

But Pernille Birk Larsen did, and saw a chink, a brief shocking glimpse of the room beyond. The case office.

Photos on the wall. A pair of ankles bound with black plastic. Bruised legs on a silver table. A dead face, Nanna's, covered in wounds, eyes closed, lips purple and swollen. A bloodied eye. A broken nail. The slip with a stab mark. A top ripped and torn.

Arrows pointed to details, to bloodstains and slashes. Circles marked stains, notes described lesions.

Her body, side on, hands tied, legs bound. Lying on a table still as could be.

Pernille rises.

Breath pumping, heart racing, Theis beside her, walking to the door.

One noise: a pencil falling as she passes.

The spell broke. Lund looked, fury rising, dragged the officer with her, pushed him through, cried, 'Shut the door!'

She turned back to them.

'I'm sorry,' she said.

They stood in silence. The big man and his wife. Beyond tears, she thought. Beyond feeling.

'I'm sorry,' Lund said again and wanted to scream.

He was clutching the desk with one hand, his wife's fingers with the other.

'I think we should go now,' Theis Birk Larsen said.

They walked down the corridor like two ghosts lost in limbo, hand in hand, not noticing where they were going.

'Phone me any time,' Lund called after them, wishing there was something else to say.

Rektor Koch was too busy for the police.

'I need this school back to normal,' she said. 'We have a memorial service coming. I'll make a speech.'

'This isn't about what you need,' Lund told her.

They were in the corridor outside Nanna's class. Kids coming and going. Oliver Schandorff, Lund saw, hanging round, trying to eavesdrop.

'You can't possibly think the school's involved.'

Meyer came to the argument like a nail to a magnet.

'You know what? If you let us do our job maybe we can answer that.'

He gave her his best filthy look. When she left he said, 'Lynge arrived at noon and was told to leave his posters in the basement. Someone saw him hanging round the gym too.'

'Why?'

'No idea. Maybe he was feeling lazy. Or sick. Or liked seeing girls playing netball.'

'Maybe he lost the car keys there.'

Meyer shrugged.

'Who had PE afterwards?' Lund asked.

'No one. The next class was on Monday. No one reported any keys found. Surprise, surprise.'

They walked down the corridor towards the entrance hall.

'What do we have on the girl?'

Meyer went through his notes.

'Top pupil. Good marks. Popular. Good-looking. The teachers rated her. The boys wanted to sleep with her.'

'Did she let them?'

'Only Oliver Schandorff and she broke up with him six months ago.'

'Drugs?'

'Nothing. Didn't drink usually either. I got a photo from the party. No one saw her after nine thirty.'

Lund looked at the print in Meyer's fingers. Nanna in a shiny blue wig and a black witch's hat, Lisa Rasmussen next to her. Both smiling, Lisa like a teenager, Nanna more . . .

'She looks a very . . . grown-up kid,' Meyer noted.

'Meaning?'

'Meaning . . . she looks a very grown-up kid. Specially next to her friend.'

He turned up another photo. Nanna and Lisa again, maybe a moment before or after. Lisa with her arm round Nanna who was grinning, mouth open this time.

Lund looked at the wig and the hat.

'She went to all this trouble for a costume and left early?'

'Yes. Funny, huh?'

Lund looked down the corridor, looked at the lockers and the posters on the walls.

Meyer rattled his notebook at her.

'Got some answers?' she asked him.

'Got questions, Lund. That's a start.'

They took Lisa Rasmussen into an empty classroom.

Lund's first question.

'You never told us Oliver and Nanna fought on the dance floor. Why not?'

The teenage pout, then, 'It wasn't important.'

Meyer squinted at her.

'Your best friend got raped and murdered and that wasn't important?'

She wasn't going to cry. Today was hostile-to-cops day.

'We were dancing. Oliver came over. It wasn't a big drama.'

Lund smiled at her.

93

'Oliver threw a chair.'

Nothing.

'Was Nanna drunk?'

In a rising, nasal petulant voice she said, 'Nooooo.'

'You were,' Meyer said.

A roll of the shoulders.

'A bit. So what?'

'Why'd they break up?' he asked.

'I dunno.'

He leaned across the table, said very slowly, 'Why ... did ... they ...'

'She told me he was immature! Just a kid.'

'But you still thought she was with him?'

'I couldn't find her.'

Lund took over.

'What was the argument about?'

'Oliver wanted to talk to her. She didn't want to talk to him.'

'And then she left. Where was Oliver then?'

'Behind the bar. It was his turn.'

'You're sure?'

'I saw him.'

Meyer pushed a piece of paper over the table, looking at Lisa Rasmussen all the time.

'This is the bar schedule,' Lund said. 'His name's not on it. No one else remembered him working that night.'

She didn't look at the schedule. Just bit her lip like a little kid.

'What was she wearing?' Meyer asked.

A moment to think about it.

'A witch's hat with a buckle. A blue wig. She had a broom. Made out of twigs. Kind of this tatty party dress ...'

'It's cold out there, Lisa,' Meyer broke in. 'Didn't you think it was odd she had so little on?'

'She had a jacket in the classroom, I guess.'

'Then she'd have gone upstairs,' said Lund.

'But no.' Meyer came in like a shot. 'She went downstairs. Lisa told us earlier.' He looked at her. 'Downstairs right?'

'Downstairs,' the girl muttered.

'Then how'd she get her jacket?' Lund demanded.

'Yeah.' Meyer was on her now. 'How?'

'I don't know she had a jacket. There were people. Lots of . . .'

Lisa Rasmussen stopped, face red, looking guilty.

Meyer peered at her.

'I thought you weren't going to cry today, Lisa. Why's it so hard suddenly?'

'You don't know when she left or whether Oliver followed her,' Lund said.

'We know you're lying to us!' Meyer yelled. 'Did Oliver find the car keys? Did he screw her in the car to prove what a man he was? Did you watch for fun?'

Lund intervened, put an arm round the girl. Floods of tears now.

'It's important you tell us what you know,' she said.

In the squeaky frightened voice of a child Lisa Rasmussen whimpered, 'I don't know anything. Leave me alone.'

Meyer's phone rang.

'You need to tell us . . .' Lund began.

'No she doesn't,' Meyer said and got his jacket.

There was a warren of rooms making up the school's basement floor. They'd had Svendsen going through each in turn, grumbling about being on his own.

He found the broom of twigs with some plastic bags in an area set aside for storing pushbikes.

Lund looked.

Metal doors in rows. Cell-like chambers beyond them.

The blue wig was in one of the plastic bags.

'What about her bike?'

'I'm on my own,' Svendsen said for the fourth time that morning.

'Seal off the area. Get a full forensic team down here,' Lund ordered.

Weber was at his computer. Seemed to live there more with each passing day.

'Seen the new polls?' he asked.

'It's tomorrow's polls that matter,' Hartmann said. 'When they see there's an alliance . . .'

Morten Weber scowled.

'Until Kirsten Eller's name's on a piece of paper let's not count chickens.'

'I talked to them last night. It's done, Morten. Stop worrying.'

Skovgaard came off the phone. She didn't look happy either.

'You two seem close for a change,' Hartmann said. 'What have I done wrong now?'

'Eller's people think you're being evasive,' Skovgaard said. 'So do some of our own.'

'Tell them . . . tell them the car was stolen.'

Weber's phone rang.

'Why not tell them the truth?' he said before answering it. 'We're assisting the police.'

'The police have got their own agenda,' Skovgaard said. 'They don't give a damn about us.'

Hartmann bristled. The Lund woman intrigued him. He was willing to give her a chance.

'I'm not going to milk this, Rie. I'm not that kind of politician.'

Skovgaard said, 'You make me want to scream sometimes. Carry on like this and you won't be a politician at all.'

'That was Kirsten Eller.' Weber put down the phone. 'She wants to see you. Straight away.' Weber looked at Hartmann over his glasses. 'I thought you had this fixed, Troels?'

'What does she want?'

'Wouldn't tell a minion like me, would she? Pretty obvious, isn't it?'

Hartmann didn't speak.

'She wants some wriggle room,' Skovgaard said.

Both of them looked at him as if he should have known this.

'Who wouldn't?' Weber asked.

Hartmann got up.

'I'll deal with Kirsten Eller.'

Fifteen minutes later, Hartmann was alone in a meeting room in the Centre Party offices. Eller didn't smile.

'I underestimated the feelings in the group,' she said.

'How?'

'This mess with the police. It makes people talk about you. Bremer's backers smell your blood.'

'The car was stolen. The driver's innocent.'

'Why does no one know this, Troels?'

96

'Because the police asked us to wait. It was the right thing to do. What difference does it make?'

'A big difference. You could have warned me.'

'No. I couldn't. The police asked me to keep quiet.'

'Bremer phoned me this morning. He's offering to build ten thousand flats, social housing, minimal rents.'

'You know him. It'll come to nothing.'

'I'm sorry, Troels. There won't be an alliance. I can't. In the circumstances . . .'

Hartmann floundered for a reply, found his temper rising.

'Bremer's stringing you along. He just wants you to dither until it's too late for us to cut the deal. Then he'll drop you like a stone. You won't get the flats. You'll be lucky to get a mayor's seat.'

'It's the group's decision. There's nothing I can do.'

He was tempted to shout. To yell at her for being so stupid but he didn't.

'Unless, of course, you've got a better offer,' Eller said.

Bremer was in his media studio getting ready for a TV slot. Lights and cameras. A make-up woman. Hangers on.

Fighting to restrain his fury, Troels Hartmann barged in, walked over, looked down at the laughing figure in the white shirt, powder on his cheeks, said, 'You ruthless bastard.'

Bremer smiled and shook his grey head.

'I'm sorry.'

'You heard.'

The make-up woman stopped padding at him with a brush. Stayed. Listened.

'Bad timing for me, Troels,' Bremer said with a genial sigh. 'You too, I think. Later . . .'

'I want an explanation.'

They went to the window, a semblance of privacy. Hartmann couldn't help himself, was started before he got there.

'First you steal our plan. Then you double it and propose an unrealistic number of flats you know you'll never build.'

'Ah,' Bremer said, with a wave of his hand. 'You spoke to Kirsten. A terrible blabbermouth. I did warn you.'

'Then you exploit the death of a young girl and time it to

aggravate the situation ... precisely when we're trying to help the police and the parents.'

Bremer's face fell. He barged into Hartmann, wagged a finger in his face.

'Who do you think you're talking to? Am I supposed to time my proposals according to whatever mess you've got yourself into? Grow up, boy. You had nothing to do with the car yet still you chose not to announce it. I thought Rie Skovgaard had more sense than that.'

'What I do is my business.'

The Lord Mayor laughed.

'You're an infant, Troels. I'd no idea it was this bad. A clumsy alliance with Kirsten's clowns ... what were you thinking?'

'Don't go lower than you are, Bremer. It's hard I know ...'

'Oh dear. This is like dealing with your father all over again. The desperation. The paranoia. How very sad.'

'I'm telling you—'

'No!'

Poul Bremer's voice boomed round the studio, loud enough to silence everyone, Hartmann too.

'No,' he repeated, more quietly. 'You tell me nothing, Troels. Go find me a real man to fight. Not a tailor's dummy in a flash suit.'

The church was plain and cold, the priest much the same. They sat as he listed the options. For prayers, for music, for flowers. For everything except the thing they needed most: understanding.

It was like a shopping list.

'Can we have "A Spotless Rose is Growing"?' Pernille asked as she and Theis held the hymn book between them.

The minister wore a brown jacket and grey polo sweater. He peered over the page and said, 'That's number hundred and seventeen. A lovely hymn. One of my favourites.'

'I want it to be beautiful in here with plenty of flowers,' she added.

'That's up to you. I can give you the name of some florists.'

'She loves flowers.'

Next to her on the hard bench Theis Birk Larsen stared at the stone floor.

'Blue irises. And roses.'

'Is there anything else?' Birk Larsen asked.

The minister checked his notes.

'Nothing. Just the eulogy, but I suggest you write down some things. Do it at home. When you have the time.'

He checked his watch.

'You mustn't mention what happened to her,' Pernille told him.

'Only Nanna as you remember her. Of course.'

A long silence. Then she said, 'Nanna was always happy. Always.'

He scribbled a note.

'That's a good thing for me to say.'

Birk Larsen got up. The priest did too. Shook his hand.

Pernille looked around the cold dark building. Tried to imagine a coffin there, saw the stiff, cold body inside.

'If you need to talk to someone,' the minister said, like a doctor offering an appointment. There was a look of studied, practised sympathy in his eyes. 'Remember that all is well with her. Nanna's with God now.'

The man nodded as if these were the wisest, most fitting words he could find.

'With God,' he repeated.

They walked to the door in silence.

She stopped after two steps, turned, looked at the priest in the brown jacket and dark trousers.

'What good does that do me?'

He was taking back a chair. The notepad was in his pocket, like a carpenter's measuring book. Probably working out the bill in his head.

'What good?' she cried.

'Sweetheart,' Birk Larsen said, trying to take her fingers.

She shook him free.

'I want to know!' Pernille roared at the man on the steps, frozen on the way to the altar, trapped by her fury. 'What good does that do me? You with your sanctimonious words . . .'

He didn't recoil. He found a kind of courage. Came back, faced her.

'Sometimes life's meaningless. Without pity. It's a terrible thing to lose one's daughter. Faith helps to give you hope. Strength.'

Her breath was short, her heart pounding.

'To know that life isn't without meaning—'

'Don't give me this shit!' Pernille Birk Larsen screeched. 'I don't give a damn if she's with God. Do you understand?'

Her hands clutched at her breast. Her voice began to break. The man stayed where he was in front of the altar. Theis Birk Larsen froze, buried his face in his hands.

'Do you understand?' Pernille wailed. 'She's supposed to be with . . .' In the dark cold church a bird flapped somewhere, dry wings rustling in the eaves. '. . . with me.'

Lund was chewing Nicotinell. She looked at the ginger-haired kid, Oliver Schandorff. Screwed-up face, twitching fingers, seated in an empty classroom, nervous as hell.

'You left school early yesterday, Oliver. You weren't in class on Monday.'

'I felt ill.'

'Idleness isn't a disease,' Meyer said.

Schandorff scowled, looked ten years old.

'You've got an absence rate of seventeen per cent,' Lund added, looking at the records.

'Class lout,' Meyer chipped in with a wicked grin. 'Rich kid. Dumb, forgiving parents. I know you.'

'Look,' Schandorff cried. 'I had an argument with Nanna. That's all.'

Lund and Meyer exchanged glances.

'Lisa told you?' Meyer said. 'What else did she say?'

'I didn't do anything. I'd never hurt Nanna.'

'Why did she dump you?' Lund asked.

He shrugged.

'One of those things. Like I care.'

Meyer leaned forward, sniffed Schandorff's expensive sky-blue sweater.

'Guess she didn't like you doing dope either.'

Schandorff ran his hand across his mouth.

'Arrested for speed four months ago. Again two months later.' Meyer sniffed again. 'I'd say you're into some kind of I dunno . . .'

He looked at the kid, puzzled, as if seeing something. Leaned forward, a couple of inches from his face, Schandorff recoiling, scared.

'Wait,' Meyer said urgently, peering into his eyes. 'What's that?'

'What?'

'There's something. A tiny speck . . . I dunno. At the back of your eyes.'

Meyer reached out with a probing finger. Schandorff was at the back of his seat, couldn't go any further.

'Oh,' Meyer said, with a sigh of relief. Retreated. 'It's nothing. Just your brain . . .'

'Fuck you,' Oliver Schandorff muttered.

'Did you hand some of that shit to Nanna?' Meyer roared. 'Did you say . . . hey, let's turn on . . . oh and it's better with your pants down by the way.'

The ginger head went forward.

'Nanna didn't like it much.'

'Which?' Lund asked. 'The dope or the . . . ?'

'Either.'

'So you got punchy with her?' Meyer had his chin on his hands. A pose that said: going nowhere. 'On the dance floor. Threw a chair around. Yelled at her.'

'I was drunk!'

'Oh.' Meyer brightened. 'That's OK then. So after nine thirty what did you do?'

'I worked behind the bar.'

Lund pushed the sheet across the table.

'You're not on the schedule.'

'I worked behind the bar.'

Meyer again.

'Who saw you?'

'Lots of people.'

'Lisa?'

'She saw me.'

'No, she didn't,' Lund said.

'I was walking round. Collecting glasses . . .'

'Listen, brainiac.' Meyer was loud again, in a different way. Cold and threatening. 'Nobody saw you after nine thirty.'

Got up, pulled a chair next to Schandorff, sat so close they touched. Put an arm round his shoulder. Squeezed.

Lund took a deep breath.

'What did you do, Oliver? Tell your uncle Jan. Before he gets cross. We both know you won't like it if that happens.'

'Nothing . . .'

'Did you follow her outside?' Another squeeze. 'Hang around the basement?'

Schandorff wriggled out of his grip.

Meyer winked at him.

'Nanna had someone else, didn't she? You knew that. You were jealous as hell. I mean really.' Meyer nodded. 'Think about it. School rich kid. She was yours. How could some pretty chick from a dump like Vesterbro screw you around?'

Schandorff was up shouting, running his hands through his wild ginger hair.

'I told you what happened.'

His voice was a couple of tones higher. Young again in an instant.

'The car keys . . .' Meyer began.

'What . . . ?'

'You knew the car was there.'

'What are you talking about?'

'Nanna didn't want you. So you raped her. Dumped her out in the canal. On your way home—'

'Shut up!'

Meyer waited. Lund watched.

'I loved her.'

'Oliver!' Meyer was beaming. 'You just said you didn't give a shit. You loved her but she thought you were a jerk. So you did the thing any no-good little dope-smoking shit would. You raped her. You tied her up. Stuck her in the boot of that black car . . .'

Back on the seat, ginger head shaking side to side.

'Stuck her in there so no one could hear her scream then pushed her into the canal.'

Meyer slammed his fist so hard on the table the pens, the note-books jumped. Oliver Schandorff was a crumpled heap on the chair, silent, shaking.

Lund waited. After a while she said very calmly, 'Oliver. If you've got something to tell us it would be best to say it now.'

'Let's take him down the station,' Meyer cut in, reaching for his phone. 'Oliver and me need a quiet chat alone in a cell.'

The classroom door opened and two people walked in. A middle-aged man in an expensive-looking suit. A woman behind him looking worried.

'I'm Oliver's father,' the man said. 'I want a word with my son.'

'We're police officers,' Lund said. 'You're interrupting our interview. Get out.'

The man didn't move. The woman was watching him, expecting something.

'Have you charged him with anything?'

Meyer waved a hand in his face and said, 'Hello? Did you hear . . . ?'

A wallet. A business card waved in their faces. Erik Schandorff. Big-shot lawyer from a big-shot firm.

'Don't talk to me like that,' Erik Schandorff said.

'Oliver's helping—' Lund began.

'Dad?'

The cry of a frightened kid. No one could mistake that.

'I want to talk to him,' the father said.

Outside in the corridor, Meyer hissing and cursing beneath his breath, Lund watched through the window.

Father and son, Oliver head down, moving side to side.

Lifted it and then the father struck him full force across the face with the back of his hand.

'Happy families,' Meyer murmured, lighting a cigarette. 'Now if I'd done that . . .'

One minute later, rich lawyer, rich kid, quiet wife walking out. Not a word.

'See you soon, Oliver!' Meyer called as they left.

Lund leaned back against the wall, folded her arms, closed her eyes.

He was watching her when she opened them.

'I know what you're thinking, Lund. That it's vaguely possible I was a bit hard on him. But if that idiot hadn't walked in . . .'

'Fine.'

'No really. I knew what I was doing. I was in control. All the time. Honest . . .'

'Meyer,' she said, coming up to him, peering up into his wide-open, staring eyes. 'I said it was fine. Check downstairs again. Contact forensics. If Oliver drove the car they should know. Time the journey from here to the woods.'

She pulled the car keys out of her bag.

'Anything else?'

'You'll think of something.'

'And you, Lund?'

'Me?'

'Going to catch a movie or what?'

She nodded, left him, smiling when he couldn't see.

There were flowers on the sideboard, on the small iron mantel above the fire. Flowers by the sink still wrapped in their paper, bouquets on the floor.

Some were blue irises. Some roses.

Pernille stood washing dishes, staring out of the window.

A woman from the forensic department sat with the boys at the table Pernille and Nanna made, smiling at them. Cotton sticks in her hand.

She looked no more than twenty-two or so. No older than Nanna when she went out for the night.

'Is this really necessary?' Theis Birk Larsen asked.

'We need DNA,' said the woman in the blue uniform. 'For comparisons.'

Downstairs the car was packed. Suitcases with clothes. Boxes with kids' things. Vagn Skærbæk helped as he always did.

He had new toys. Cars. Cheap and tinny but Vagn was bad with money and Pernille lacked the heart to scold him. The men in the depot were like everyone else. Like Theis. Like her. Desperate to do something, lost for what that might be.

'OK?' the woman asked and didn't wait for an answer. Leaned over the table, got Anton first, then asked Emil to open his mouth.

Pernille watched from the sink, dishes in her hand.

They were back in Nanna's bedroom. Two men in blue walking round, putting up more stickers, making notes.

Lotte her sister, younger, prettier, still single, did most of the packing. Now she came and hugged each of them in turn.

'Take some flowers if you want,' Theis said.

Lotte looked at him and shook her head.

'Boys,' Theis said. 'Let's go see Uncle Vagn. Help him finish up downstairs.'

Pernille promised she'd be there soon and watched them go.

Soon.

She left the sink when he was gone. Looked around the untidy room.

In this small warm place an unexpected miracle had emerged between them. The magic that was family. Shared lives. Shared love.

Now men in blue tramped through Nanna's little bedroom, opening drawers they opened yesterday, talking in low tones, going quiet when they thought she could hear.

The boys rushed back up, snatched kites, snatched more toys. Showed her the tinny cars Vagn bought.

'Watch those sharp edges,' she said. 'Watch . . .'

They were gone, not listening, one of the men from the bedroom following, taking some of Nanna's books to the car in his blue gloved hands.

The cop who was left was old with a beard and a sad face. He looked uncomfortable. Couldn't meet her eyes. Grey head down looking at Nanna's bookcase once more.

She picked up her bag, ready to go.

The apartment was so full of the scent of flowers it made her head hurt.

Here we lived. Here we sat around the table, thinking this small, private bliss would never end.

And now we flee, we scuttle away in ignorance and fear as if the fault were our own.

Home. Covered in forensic stickers and their boot marks. Finger-print dust on walls that still bore Nanna's pretty face.

The bag went back on the old worn carpet. Pernille walked into her room, watched the man working. Sifting through the pieces of her daughter's brief lost life.

She sat on the bed, waited until he had the courage to look at her.

'I won't be long. I'm sorry . . .'

'What happened out in the woods?' she asked and thought: *I will not move, I will not leave until he speaks.*

A father. She could see it in his face. He understood. He knew.

'I'm not the one to talk to. Sorry.' He fiddled with the drawer of Nanna's desk. 'I'm working. You have to leave.'

Pernille stayed on the sheets of Nanna's tidy, made-up bed.

'I need . . .' His eyes were closed. She saw his pain, knew he saw hers too. 'I need to know what happened. I'm her mother . . .'

The desk again. He was doing nothing and both knew it.

'What happened to my daughter?'

'I'm not allowed—'

'There were photos. In your office. I saw . . .' Words, she thought. The right ones now. 'I see them in my head at night and I know . . . it can't be worse than anything I imagine. Not worse.'

He stopped, head bowed.

'It can't be worse. But . . .' She tapped her chestnut hair, her skull. Her voice was weak and faint, she made it so. 'In my head I see . . .'

The cop bent stiffly over the desk, didn't move.

'I'm her mother. Do I have to beg?'

No answer.

'Every day she dies in my head. Over and over and each time worse. We need to bury . . .'

He was shaking.

'I need to know,' she said again.

Then watched as he sighed.

Then, finally, listened.

Theis Birk Larsen looked round the depot. Helped Vagn Skærbæk move a cabinet to a truck. Watched as the boys played with their little tin cars. Checked their things in the back of the car: a family reduced to a set of luggage, ready to go.

'Any news, Theis?'

Birk Larsen lit a cigarette, shook his head.

Anton and Emil ran up, clinging to Skærbæk's red cotton legs. Begging for ice-cream money. Making him laugh.

'Do I look like a piggybank?' he said, taking out some coins. They scattered on the floor.

The old joke he always used with them: *no beer now, boys.*

'Who was this driver they caught?' Skærbæk asked. 'The paper didn't even print a name—'

'I don't know. They tell us nothing. Why would they?'

Birk Larsen stared around the depot trying to think the way he used to: of jobs and inventories, bills to be paid, invoices to be collected. Nothing worked. It was as if Nanna's death had locked them in a never-ending present, a frozen point in time with no escape. No prospect of release.

'We're just little people,' he murmured.

'No you're not.'

Vagn Skærbæk stood by him, ignoring the boys tugging at his overalls again.

'Thanks for running things,' Birk Larsen said. 'I don't know what . . .'

Too many words. He patted Skærbæk on the arm.

'You saved my skin, Theis.' Skærbæk's face was hard with anger. The silver chain glittered round his neck. 'I don't forget. That bastard's going to get what's coming to him. You just tell me if you want something done.'

'Like what?'

'When he gets a piddling sentence. And they let him out on parole. You tell me Theis . . . I want to . . .'

'Help?' Birk Larsen shook his head.

'If that's what you want . . .'

'She's dead.'

Poor Vagn. Dumb Vagn. Loyal as a guard dog. No brighter either.

'Dead.' One cruel, short word. 'Don't you understand?'

Still the flame was lit and with it a sudden burst of rage. Theis Birk Larsen hammered his massive fist on a cabinet, set it shaking on its feet.

'Where the hell's Pernille?'

Upstairs in the kitchen, surrounded by the flowers, choking in their scent.

The cop was on the phone. And worried.

'Pernille?'

He'd come up the stairs to look for her.

'We're not going.'

He rocked on his big feet the way he always did before an argument. Not that they had many, and those few he always won.

'I told the boys. The place is booked—'

'We're not going.'

'It's arranged!'

It wasn't that she lost. More that she never fought. That was over now. Lots of other things too. Things she hadn't recognized yet. But would.

'Nanna wasn't dead when the car hit the water.'

Her voice was flat and calm, her face too.

'What?'

'She wasn't dead. She was in the boot of the car. Trapped there. Drowning.'

Pernille walked into Nanna's bedroom.

Clothes. Belongings. Scattered round, pleading to be tidied. A mother's job . . .

She began to move the books, the clothes from one place to another, bright eyes shining, tears beginning to form.

Then she stopped, folded her arms.

'We're leaving now,' Theis Birk Larsen said, standing in the doorway. 'That's that.'

He was next to the fish tank Nanna wanted. Pernille found herself captivated by the swimming golden shapes trapped inside it. Peering out, unable to comprehend anything beyond the glass.

'No,' she said. 'We're staying here. I want to watch them find him. I want to see his face.'

Round and round they swam, puzzled by their own reflections, thinking nothing, going nowhere.

'They have to find him, Theis. They will.'

A moment pivoted between them. One that had never come before.

He fiddled with his woollen hat.

'We're staying here,' Pernille Birk Larsen repeated. 'I'll get the boys. You bring the cases.'

Lynge was awake. A bandage round his head, drips in his arm. Fresh cuts and grazes covered the old scar on his cheek. Traces of blood still caked his grey moustache.

'John?' Lund said.

Movement. Breathing. Eyes half open. She'd no idea if he could hear this. Any more than the impatient doctor she'd bullied to let her in there.

'I'm sorry this happened. Do you understand?'

The man's eyebrows flickered.

'I know you didn't harm the girl.'

He was connected to a machine with flashing numbers and graphs.

'I really need your help, John. I need to know what happened at the school. Who you met. Where you lost your keys.'

His eyes moved. Turned towards her.

'You parked your car. You took the posters inside. You went to the gym. Is that when you felt sick?'

Lynge coughed, choked on something.

A noise, a word.

'What? John?'

Another sound. An eye flicked wide open. A look there. Fear and pain.

'Basement.'

'You went there to deliver the posters. Is that where you lost the keys?'

'The kid got angry. Said I wasn't supposed to go near there.'

'John.' She got up, got close to his mouth, had to hear this. 'Who got angry? What kid?'

That wheezing sound again. She could smell him.

'Were there bikes there? Bikes?'

'The next one.'

Lund tried to picture that dank warren.

'The next room?'

'The boiler.'

A sound. The door opened. The doctor was back and he didn't look pleased.

'Who did you meet in the boiler room? John?'

Lund took out the photos from her bag. School portraits. Pointed to Oliver Schandorff, said, 'Did you see him? This one. Please. Look.'

The wheeze again. Then, 'No.'

'Are you sure? Take a good look.'

The doctor was with them, arms waving, saying, 'OK. That's it. You've got to stop. Leave now—'

'One minute,' Lund said, not budging. 'Just . . .'

She pushed him back, held the school photo over the sick man in the bed.

'I'm pointing my finger, John. One by one. Nod when I get to him. OK?'

One by one, kid by kid.

When she stopped on a tall dark-haired student, pleasant-looking, ordinary, John Lynge nodded.

'You saw him in the boiler room . . . ?'

'That's enough,' the doctor told her, grabbing her arm.

'John?'

The eye opened, caught her. His head moved, the slightest of nods.

Lund rose, threw the doctor's hand off her.

Said, 'Yes, it is.'

Meyer was smoking in the school playground when he answered her call.

'I need you to go back to the basement again,' Lund said.

A pause.

'Please tell me that was a joke.' He looked at the forensic men. He was hungry. So were they. And Svendsen was starting to get on his nerves.

'Go back down there.'

'Forensics are packing up. We've looked everywhere. How's Lynge?'

'He'll be out in a week. Is there a boiler room?'

'They keep it locked. No one can get in there except the janitor.'

'I'm on my way.'

He could hear the sound of traffic. The black rain-soaked streets were empty. She'd be with him in a matter of minutes.

Meyer started walking back down the grimy concrete stairs.

'It's bad to talk and drive, you know.'

'Are you in there yet?'

'We've got the janitor here.'

'I need to know what's inside.'

'All right, all right.'

He told the janitor to open the door.

'Are you in?'

'Yes! Just keep your pants on, will you?'

'What can you see?'

A pause. Then Meyer said, 'I can see the boiler. That's a surprise.'

Then, 'Just a bunch of old junk. Tables, chairs and books.' He cleared his throat. 'OK, Lund. So the kids could maybe get in here. But there's nothing to see.'

'Are you sure?'

'Hang on.'

'Did you hear me?'

Meyer made a disgusting noise down the phone.

'You're breaking up on me, Lund.'

Then muttered, 'For God's sake . . .'

Slammed the phone into his pocket, walked ahead, shining the beam of the torch one side, the other side. Up, down.

He'd thought about this earlier. The janitor said the boiler took an oil feed from a tank outside. No one had to go in there except for maintenance once a week. Every Friday afternoon.

There was a second door at the end. No handle. Looked as if it hadn't been used in years.

Meyer took out a handkerchief, edged the metal open. Peeked in, moved the torch around.

Kids had been here. At his feet the remains of a couple of joints were stamped into the ground. Beer cans. And . . .

Meyer whistled. The sleeve of a condom packet, foil torn, empty.

Noises behind. Something happening out in the main basement. Didn't care.

Pulled out his phone, dialled her number. Didn't wait before he said, 'I think you'd better get here. Lund . . . ?'

Deep in the concrete bowels of the school, there was no signal.

'Really . . .' Meyer whispered.

'Really?'

The sound made him jump. A torch beam in his face. Then on the ground.

'You must have been speeding. Admit it, Lund. You're as bad as me.'

She didn't answer. Just looked at the same thing that he did. A grubby mattress on the floor.

Bloodstains in the corner.

Bloodstains on the peeling grey wall.

Prints were appearing on the peeling plaster of the room in the school basement. Officers in white bunny suits tagging, drawing, taking photos. Lund on the phone to her mother's, telling Mark to do his homework, practise his Swedish.

'I could be here all night. Gran will help you.'

She'd gone back to the school hall to go through the flowers and photos on a small shrine set up for Nanna by the lockers.

'That's good,' Lund said. 'Bye.'

A picture there. Two girls dressed as angels. Nanna, maybe thirteen. Lisa Rasmussen.

A pair of red candles in front of it. A single flame flickering in the cold breeze running down the corridor.

'Who lit the candle?' Lund asked.

Meyer had been here five minutes before her. He looked young and guilty for a moment.

'I don't know. Does it matter?'

'You shouldn't interfere with things, Meyer.'

'Who said . . . ?'

She waved at him.

'Forget it.'

'Shouldn't we go and look in the basement?'

Lund straightened a photo of Nanna. Looked at the dead girl.

She held up a hand. Meyer shook his head, baffled.

'Your lighter. I'm giving up. Remember?'

'Oh.'

He threw her the silver Zippo. It looked expensive. She looked at the photos and the flowers, wished there was more she could offer than this. Knew that had to come. Then she lit the other candle and watched the tiny yellow flame flutter.

A small offering. Pathetic.

'We should look at the basement,' she said and followed him down.

Jansen, a ginger-haired officer from forensics, stood by the portable floodlights. Listed what they had so far. Blood on the mattress, the table, the floor. Some spots that could turn out to be semen. Hair.

A witch's hat. Nanna's it looked like.

And fingerprints. Lots of fingerprints.

'Access?' Meyer asked.

'There's the door from the basement,' Jansen said. 'And one from the school. Just needs a key for either.'

'A . . .'

'A different key,' he said.

Everything was visible under the bright floodlights. On the low table stood empty bottles of Coke and vodka, a Chianti flask. Plates of food. And pills. Red, green, orange. All the colour of children's sweets.

'Joints,' Meyer said. 'Amphetamine. Coke.'

Thirty minutes later Rektor Koch arrived at the school. They kept her out of the location. Too many people in bunny suits. Too much to see.

In a classroom upstairs Lund asked, 'What did you use that room for?'

'Storing tables and chairs.' Koch had brought her dog. A small brown terrier. Cuddled it for comfort. 'Books and the like. Nothing . . .'

'Nothing what?'

'Nothing special. I didn't know the pupils had access. They weren't supposed to have.'

Meyer walked in and said, 'Well they did. They had their own private party there. Right under your nose.'

'What did you find?'

Lund didn't answer. She said, 'The party was planned by the student council. Is that right?'

'It should have been locked,' Koch insisted. She held the dog more tightly. 'Is that where Nanna was?'

Lund took out her stack of school photos, pointed to the kid John Lynge had identified. Jeppe Hald. Nice-looking. Clean tidy black hair. Scholarly glasses.

'Tell me about him.'

Koch smiled.

'Jeppe's wonderful. President of the student council. Star pupil. We're proud of him. Fine parents . . .'

'Where does wonderboy live?' Meyer asked.

'He shares a flat with Oliver.'

Meyer said, 'Is Oliver a good pupil too?'

The smile again, less warm.

'They come from good families. The law. Both of them. I'm sure they'll follow their fathers into the same profession. Be a credit—'

'Better than being the offspring of some sweaty removals man from Vesterbro?' Meyer snapped.

The smile never cracked.

'I didn't say that. We're not prejudiced here. Against anyone.'

'So long as they pay the fees.'

Rector Koch glared at him.

'Oops,' Meyer said. 'I think I just got detention.'

'Thank you,' Lund told her and got him out of the room.

Jeppe Hald strode up and down the window of the office, watching the blue lights flash outside, listening to the occasional wail of sirens.

Lund and Meyer walked briskly in, threw their folders on the table.

Tall and skinny. Thick glasses. Harry Potter's taller geeky brother. Or that was the act.

'Why am I here?'

'Just routine,' Lund said pleasantly. 'Please sit down.'

'But I've got a physics essay to do.'

The two cops looked at each other. Meyer buried his head in his hands and pretended to weep.

While Hald was taking a chair Lund said, 'You met a man in the basement on Friday night. He was delivering election campaign material.'

Hald looked around at the empty chairs.

Meyer leaned forward, grinned cheerily.

'We tried to call your daddy but he was out getting fitted for a wig. The man in the basement?'

'I met him.'

'Why didn't you say so?'

Silence.

Lund said, 'You knew we were looking for a driver.'

'How was I to know he was a driver?'

Meyer raised his hands to his mouth, kissed his fingertips like a chef tasting the perfect dish.

'Superb. You do Shakespeare too?'

'Shakespeare?'

'First,' Meyer roared, 'we kill all the fucking lawyers.'

Jeppe Hald went white.

Lund scowled at Meyer.

'Shakespeare never said fucking. Don't teach the boy wrong. Jeppe. Jeppe!'

'What?'

114

'The driver lost his car keys. Did you happen to see them?'

'I'm here because of some missing keys?'

'What were you doing in the basement?' Lund asked.

'Fetching . . . fetching things for the bar.'

Meyer started picking at his nails. Hand closed to a fist.

'We found a room,' he said. 'Someone had a party. Do you know anything about that?'

Hald hesitated. Almost said no. Instead, 'I think the organizers had a room where they kept beer and soft drinks. Is that the one?'

'The one with beer and soft drinks, blood and drugs and condoms?' Meyer replied, still looking at his nails. 'That's the one.'

'I wouldn't know.'

Lund said nothing for a long while. Nor Meyer. They looked at their papers. Jeppe Hald sat at the table, barely moving, barely breathing.

Then she showed him a photo.

'Nanna's hat. We found it there. Did she go in that room?'

Shake of head. A shrug. No idea.

Meyer breathed a sigh so long it seemed to last a minute.

'I came down for the last beer about nine o'clock. I didn't see anyone.'

Slowly Meyer's head fell to his arms, and he lay there staring at the kid in the chair through half-closed eyes.

'You're sure you didn't go back later?' Lund asked.

A moment, a pause to be convincing. Then, 'I'm very sure.'

'No one saw you after nine thirty. What did you do?'

'Er . . .'

'Think, Jeppe,' Meyer said stifling a yawn. 'Think before you answer.'

Hald bristled. Looked more confident.

'The disco ball blew the fuses. I'd used the last one. So I went to buy more. I had to cycle a long way to get them.'

'We'll check,' Meyer muttered not looking up from his arms.

'When I got back Oliver was asleep in a classroom. He'd had too much to drink. I walked him home.' Folded his arms, looked the model pupil. 'We were there just before midnight. I put him to bed. Had to.'

'That's early!' Lund said brightly.

'I was going hunting the next morning.'

'Hunting!' Lund said, impressed.

Meyer grumbled something obscene into his sleeves.

'On the Sonderris estate. Our hunting club was holding a big event. I spent the night there.'

'I'm going to take up hunting in a minute,' Meyer muttered.

Lund scribbled on her pad.

'I'd really like to help,' Hald pleaded.

In a high-pitched squeal Meyer whined, 'I'd really like to help.'

'But that's all I know.'

Lund smiled at him. Said, 'Fine.' Wrote some more on her pad. 'Well . . .'

She closed her pad, shrugged. Jeppe Hald smiled back at her.

'That's it,' Lund said. 'Unless . . .'

She prodded the near-comatose Meyer.

'You want to ask something?'

Head straight up, face in the kid's.

'You won't object if I take a blood sample?' Meyer said very loudly. 'And fingerprints?'

He touched Hald's hand. The kid recoiled.

'I'll be as gentle as I can.'

Meyer waggled his big right ear at Jeppe Hald, listening, hearing nothing.

'Otherwise,' Lund added, 'I'm going to arrest you and we'll take them anyway.'

Jeppe Hald, the smart kid, star pupil, head boy, said in a young and petulant trembling voice, 'I'm not saying any more. I want to see my lawyer.'

Lund nodded.

'A lawyer. That's fine. Meyer?'

'Sure.' He took hold of Hald's arm. 'First you get your phone call, wonderboy. Then let me introduce you to the concept of a cell.'

Thirty minutes later. Meyer had people working the phones.

'I checked up on Oliver,' he told Lund. 'On Saturday he worked in a cafe. Met some woman. Went out and got drunk and took her to his parents' house. The two of them hung out there till Monday.'

One of the cadets came back with a package. Meyer groaned with delight.

'You're an angel.'

He stripped the thing from its wrapping. Lund watched. Big hot dog in a roll. Crispy fried onions. Remoulade sauce. Sliced cucumber pickles on the top.

Lund said, 'You sent a boy out to the *pølsevogn* and you didn't tell me?'

'I thought you only ate Swedish sausage.'

She stood there with her hands on her hips, big eyes boring into him. He took another quick bite of his food. Grimaced.

'Bastard,' Lund said. 'Where's the motive?'

'I was hungry.'

Silence.

'Oh. Right. Jeppe and Oliver. They're lying. Find the lie first. The motive won't be far away. Meyer Handbook of Detection. Page thirty-two.'

Lund still looked angry about the food and the sausage crack. The first mostly.

'I'll talk to Ginger and give you a call,' Meyer said.

'He'll just scream for a lawyer like Jeppe.'

'No,' Meyer insisted. 'Can't demand that unless we arrest him. If I just talk to him as a witness . . . I know the law. Mostly I abide by it. Also . . .'

'No.'

'You're a very negative woman sometimes. Just because I didn't get you a hot dog . . .'

'I want mouth swabs. I want blood samples.' A quick decision. 'Let's arrest them now.'

Meyer looked torn.

'Much as I adore that idea the lawyers won't be here for hours. We'll be sitting around on our hands until they turn up.'

'No. We search the flat. Check their emails. Phone records. Find the woman Schandorff says he spent the weekend with.'

He was eating and cursing between mouthfuls.

'Anything else?'

That tone of voice again. He had others. She'd heard them. Not often. But they were there.

'Why are you so angry, Meyer?'

The rest of the sausage disappeared while he thought about this.

'Because,' he said, 'I have feelings.'

Silence.

'Anything else?' he asked again.

'No.'

She thought about it.

'Yes.' Lund came and stabbed a finger in his chest. 'Next time you send a cadet out to the *pølsevogn*, get one for me.'

Lund decided to check with Buchard first. The chief was flicking through the morgue photos of the girl. Bloody eye, crouched, foetal corpse, lesions and wounds. Bruising. A violent, prolonged assault.

'What do you have on the boys?' he asked. 'Physical evidence from the room?'

'Nothing until the results come in. The DNA people are giving us priority.'

Buchard flicked through more photos.

'You do realize who the parents are?'

Lund frowned.

'Why should we care about that?'

He was in a foul mood for some reason.

'We've caused enough trouble as it is. We need to tread carefully.'

Meyer stuck his head through the door and announced, 'Hartmann wants a meeting.'

'About what?' she wanted to know.

'He wouldn't say. It sounded important.'

'Hartmann can wait,' Lund said. 'We're going to the flat.'

When she made for the door Buchard took her arm.

'What were we just saying? Troels Hartmann might be the next Lord Mayor of Copenhagen. We don't piss off people in the Rådhus without a reason.'

'We've got a suspect's flat to search . . .'

'I can do that,' Meyer cut in. 'Don't worry. I'll keep you posted.'

Buchard nodded.

'Good. That's settled.'

The chief walked out.

'Give Hartmann a ring,' Meyer said, following him down the winding corridor. 'It was you he asked for.'

*

118

Lund waited at the counter feeling awkward and uncomfortable. She didn't go out much, even with Bengt. After the last few days this touristy restaurant in Nyhavn seemed too ordinary. Too warm and human.

Hartmann was five minutes late, making excuses. While they waited for a table he asked, 'How are the girl's parents?'

Was that the politician, she wondered? Or the man?

'Is that why you asked me here? To talk about the parents?'

'You really don't do small talk, do you?'

'Not in the middle of a case. One like this.'

'I've got a press conference tomorrow. I want to say the right things.'

'Right for who?'

'For you. For me. Mostly for them.'

Men like this did sincerity so well. It was hard to see any cracks.

'Say what you like,' she told him.

'There've been so many surprises. Will there be any more?'

Without a blink.

'Not that I know of.'

'Can I say you know there's no connection between the crime and us?'

She nodded.

'I suppose so.' She watched him. 'If you think that's true.'

The waitress called. He'd booked a table.

'Is that all?'

Lund got ready to go.

He put his hand to her arm, very gently.

'I'm sorry. I know I made things difficult. There's an election going on. Some odd things have been happening.' Hartmann looked angry for a second. 'I never expected any of this.' He looked at her. 'Are you hungry?'

A plate of food went past. Meatballs and pasta. It looked a lot better than the hot dog Meyer never got her.

'I'll have some of that,' Lund said. Then, 'Just a minute.'

She went to the lobby, called her mother's. Got the loudest, friendliest greeting in months, then found out why. Bengt had arrived from Sweden, would be in Copenhagen for one night only.

'You must talk,' Vibeke crooned then handed the call over.

Don't need this now, Lund thought, listening to him talk about Mark's progress with his Swedish, the Sigtuna hockey shirt he'd found, the perfect wood for the perfect sauna.

She nodded all the while, seeing little in her head but a small and grubby room in the basement of a school, a mattress stained with blood, a table of drink and dope, a discarded witch's hat and a shiny blue wig.

'When will you be home?' Bengt asked.

Back to the awkward present.

'Soon,' she promised. 'Soon.'

A pause.

'When?'

He never pressed her. Never sounded upset or angry or cold. His pleasant, pacific nature was one of the things she loved. Or maybe it just made life easier.

'When I'm done. I'm sorry this came up. Truly. Let's talk later. I've got to go.'

Back at the table she got stuck into the food. They talked again about press releases. About cooperation. Close up Hartmann interested her. There was a frail naivety to him that was absent from the face on the posters. He was a widower. She'd checked that in the press cuttings library already, at the same time she had checked on Jan Meyer. Hartmann's wife died from cancer two years before. The loss had affected him. At one point it threatened to bring his political career – the only job he'd ever had – to a premature end.

She found he was staring at her, uncharacteristically shorn of the right words.

'What is it?'

'You've got . . .' His hand waved in her direction. 'You've got food on your face.'

Lund grabbed a napkin, wiped her mouth. Ate some more just as greedily.

It was a pleasant cafe. The kind of place couples went. Or men with their mistresses. If someone had walked in at that moment, seen her with this man . . .

'We're agreed then?' he concluded.

'You tell your story. We'll tell ours. Such as it is.'

'What about your life?' He smiled. 'I'm sorry. I don't know why I asked that. It's none of my business.'

'It's good. I'm going to Sweden with my son. My boyfriend lives outside Stockholm. I've got a job there. Civilian with the police.'

She took a quick gulp of wine, wished there was more food.

'Everything will be fine,' Lund insisted.

'How old's your son?'

'Twelve. And you?'

'I'm a bit older than that.'

'I meant . . .'

'I know, I know. We didn't get that far. My wife died. Mostly . . .' He shrugged, looked a little ashamed. 'I spend my time working. I've met someone though. Hopefully it's not too late.'

'The woman from your office,' she said and it wasn't a question. 'Rie Skovgaard.'

Hartmann cocked his head and looked at her.

'Can you see into my pockets too?'

He'd barely touched his food or drink. Hartmann looked as if he could stay there all night. Talking, talking.

'My boyfriend's over from Sweden,' Lund said. 'I have to go. Here . . .'

She took out some money for the bill.

'No, no, no.' He waved it away quickly. 'You were my guest.'

'So long as you pay. Not the taxpayer.'

'I'll pay, Sarah,' Hartmann said, waving a credit card.

'Thank you, Troels. Goodnight.'

Bengt went straight to sleep the way he always did. Lund got out of bed, pulled on a sweatshirt, went to the window, sat in the cane chair, called Meyer.

'What did you find out?' she whispered.

'Not much.'

Meyer was talking in a hushed tone too. It sounded odd.

'There's got to be something.'

'Forensics have taken a computer and samples.'

The dinner with Hartmann still intrigued her.

'Was there anything in Nanna's room that suggests she was going out to meet someone?'

'Can't this wait until tomorrow? I'm beat.'

'She must have had a date.'

'Yes, Lund. With Oliver. But you won't let me talk to him.' Noises

121

behind his quiet voice. Movement. A baby crying. 'There. Look. You've woken the whole house.'

She went out into the dining room, turned on a light, sat at the table.

'Do the parents remember anything new?'

'I'll ask them tomorrow. OK?' A grunt. 'Some idiot on the team told the mother the girl had drowned in the boot. She's going mad.'

Lund swore.

'You don't need to do that. I'll talk to them.'

'Can I go now?'

'Yes,' Lund said. 'Of course.'

She walked past Mark's room. He was still fast asleep. Bengt was awake but didn't want to show it. Everyone here was fine, Lund thought. They didn't need her at all.

Thursday, 6th November

The morning was dull and damp with drizzle. They ate breakfast together then Lund drove Bengt to the station. Talked about the weekend. Who they'd see in Sweden. What they'd do.

He listened in silence. Then she said, 'The house-warming party . . .'

'Forget about the party. I've cancelled it.'

She wondered: was that a stray note of displeasure in his voice? It was hard to tell. Anger was so foreign to him.

'Let's wait until your case is over, Sarah. Then . . .'

'I don't need to wait. I told you. We're coming Saturday, whatever.'

He gazed out of the window at the traffic and the morning travellers.

'I'm not inviting lots of people for you to call again and say you're not coming.'

That was sharp. Unmistakable.

'Of course I'll turn up! I'm looking forward to seeing your parents. And . . .' His little refrain of Swedish names from the other day came back to her. 'Ole and Missan and Janne and Panne and Hasse and Basse and Lasse . . .'

He was laughing. She could still get that out of him.

'It's Bosse, not Basse.'

'Sorry. Still learning.'

'Well. If you're sure . . .'

'I'm sure! It's a promise.'

She dropped him at Central Station then drove on to Vesterbro.

Lund sat on Nanna's bed trying to remember what it was like to be a teenager. The room was small and bright, messy and chaotic. Bags from inexpensive clothing companies, scribbled notes from class, books and magazines, make-up and jewellery . . .

A reflection of Nanna Birk Larsen's personality, her life.

She went through the diary, found nothing. Nothing in the school notebooks, the photos on the cork-board above her small desk.

Lund thought of herself at this age, an awkward, morose child. Her room was more untidy than this. But different somehow. It existed for her, an inward expression of her solitary, introverted nature. Here, she thought, Nanna had created a place for preparation. A private dressing room from which she would emerge to enchant the world outside, entrance it with her beauty, her clothes, her sparkling and obvious intelligence.

All the things the teenage Sarah Lund lacked this girl possessed in abundance. A loving mother too.

And now she was dead.

There was a path from this room to Nanna's shocking end in the canal at the Kalvebod Fælled. There were reasons, and reasons left traces.

She looked in the wardrobe, sifted through the clothes. A few had scissored labels, bought from a budget store perhaps. A few didn't. And . . .

Lund fought again to recall herself at this age. What did she wear? Much the same as now. Jeans, shirts, jumpers. Practical clothes for a practical life, not the attention of others. It was natural for an attractive teenager to dress to be seen. Lund herself was the exception. Yet the clothes she found sifting through Nanna's coat hangers seemed too good, too adult, too . . . knowing.

Then she brushed the hangers to one side, looked at the back where a small mountain of shoes stood, pair upon discarded pair.

Behind them something glittered. Lund reached in, felt Nanna's clothes fluttering against her cheeks like the wings of gigantic moths, retrieved what was there.

A pair of shiny brown cowboy boots decorated with coloured motifs, glitter, studs, tiny mirrors.

They shouted money.

No. They screamed it.

'My wife's here,' said a brusque male voice behind her.

Lund jumped, banged her head on the hanger rail.

It was Theis Birk Larsen.

He watched her rub her hair.

'Be careful what you tell her.'

Seated round the table, frozen faces captured in the surface.

'I'm sorry you were told,' Lund said.

The day had brightened. The flowers were fading. But still the place smelled of their sweet scent.

'The officer shouldn't have done that. He's been transferred so you won't see him again.'

Theis Birk Larsen, head down, eyes dead, muttered, 'Well, that's something.'

'It's nothing,' Pernille said. 'I want to know the truth. I want to know what happened. I'm her mother.'

Lund checked her notes.

'No one saw Nanna after the party. She was probably driven away in the stolen car. The one we found her in.'

Lund looked out of the window, looked back at her.

'She was raped.'

Pernille waited.

'She was beaten.'

Pernille waited.

'We think she fought back. That may be why he hit her.'

Nothing more.

'In the woods?' Pernille asked.

'In the woods. We think so.' Lund hesitated. 'But maybe she was held captive somewhere else first. We just don't know.'

The big man went to the sink, placed his fists knuckles down on the draining board, gazed out at the wan grey sky.

'She told us she'd be at Lisa's,' Pernille said. 'Nanna didn't lie to me.'

'Maybe she didn't.' A pause. 'Do you have no idea?' A glance at the shape at the window, the hunched back clad in black leather. 'Did you remember anything else?'

124

'If something was wrong Nanna would have told me,' Pernille insisted. 'She'd have told me. We're . . . We were . . .'

Words proved a struggle.

'Close.'

'When did she stop seeing Oliver Schandorff?'

'Is he involved?'

A long, broad shadow fell across the table. Theis Birk Larsen turning to listen.

'I'm just gathering information.'

'Six months ago or so,' Pernille said. 'Oliver was a kind of boy-friend.'

'Was she upset when it ended?'

'No. He was.'

Lund watched her.

'She wouldn't talk to Oliver on the phone. Nanna . . .' She leant forward, tried to hold Lund's wide and ranging eyes. 'If something was wrong she always told me. Didn't she, Theis?'

The silent man stood at the window, a giant figure in his scarlet bib overalls and leather jacket.

Lund's phone rang.

Meyer had something.

'OK. I'll come straight away.'

They stared at her, expectant.

'I have to go now.'

'What was that?' he asked in a low, brutal voice.

'Just a call. I saw a pair of boots in Nanna's room. They look expensive. Did you give them to her?'

'Expensive boots?' he grunted.

'Yes.'

Pernille said, 'Why do you ask?'

A shrug.

'I ask lots of questions. Maybe too many. I put my nose in where it's not wanted.' A pause. 'That's what I do.'

'We didn't buy her expensive boots,' Pernille said.

Interview room. The lawyer was brisk and bald and built like a hockey player. When Lund walked in he was yelling at a bored-looking Meyer who sat on the table edge, chin on fist, smiling childishly.

'You've ignored all my client's rights. You questioned him without a lawyer present . . .'

'Not my fault you wanted a lie-in. What's the big deal? I took him on a tour. Bought him breakfast. I'll change his stinking nappy if you want . . .'

'Come with me, Meyer . . .'

'There will be consequences,' the lawyer bellowed as Lund took him into the next room.

Meyer sat down, looked at her.

'They put Oliver Schandorff in the last free cell we had. So I drove Jeppe round a bit and dropped him off here at five.'

Wondering how bad this might turn out, Lund asked, 'Did you question him?'

'Have you seen his emails? Plenty. And he rang Nanna fifty-six times in one week. If you ask . . .'

'Did you question him without a lawyer present?'

'The lawyer said he would be here at seven. He didn't turn up till nine.' Meyer tried to look the picture of reasonableness. 'Like I said, I couldn't throw the little jerk into a cell. We just had breakfast together.' A small boy's gesture of guilt. 'It would have been rude if I hadn't talked to him, Lund.'

Buchard came through the door. Blue shirt. Grey face.

'We didn't have anywhere to hold the suspect last night,' Lund said straight off. 'The lawyer was two hours late. Meyer bought him breakfast.'

'He wasn't very hungry,' Meyer broke in, 'but it seemed the polite thing to do.'

'Maybe the kid thought he was being interrogated but . . .'

Lund left it at that. Buchard was unimpressed.

'Perhaps Meyer could explain this to me himself.'

'What Lund said,' Meyer told him.

'Write that in a report. Bring it to my office. I'll put it in your file with all the others.' A studied pause. 'After the hearing.'

When the chief left Lund got to her desk, started on the photos and the messages.

Meyer brightened.

'I thought that went pretty well. Didn't you?'

*

The press conference was packed. Cameras. Microphones everywhere. Troels Hartmann wore a tie this time, black. That morning he went to the barber that Rie Skovgaard chose, sat in the chair as she ordered the cut she wanted: short and severe, mournful.

Then the script.

'It's been a turbulent time. But I've been working closely with the police. The car was stolen. No staff were ever implicated. Our thoughts and sympathies go out to the girl's parents. Our priority all along was to help the police. Nothing more.'

'Is the driver a suspect?' a woman asked.

'The driver came from an agency. He's been cleared.'

A sea of voices, the loudest shouting, 'Is this the position of the police?'

Hartmann looked and saw the bald head and beaming smirk of Erik Salin.

'I don't speak for the Politigården. But I've discussed this with them. They're happy I make it clear our involvement was an unfortunate coincidence. We've nothing to do with this case. Speak to them if you want any more.'

Still the questions rained down on him.

A politician picked the ones he answered. Carefully. Hartmann listened to the clamour, thought of Bremer, waited in silence until the right question came along.

'Will you form an alliance with the Centre Party?'

A puzzled expression, bemused but knowing.

'You know,' he said, 'the world of local politics is rarely as dramatic as you people would have your readers believe. Thank you.'

He rose to leave.

The woman reporter was on her feet.

'You're forming an alliance?'

Nothing.

The political editor from one of the dailies pounced.

'Is Bremer wooing her too?'

There was the flash of a camera in his face. Stick to the script, Rie Skovgaard said.

'He is.' The room went silent, every eye upon him. 'Personally though, I think he's a bit old for her. Now . . .'

Sudden, raucous laughter.

A delicate balance, one that fell in his favour. The hacks hated Bremer as much as he did. At least that's what they said in their cups.

Troels Hartmann retreated to his office next door.

There Rie Skovgaard fussed over him. Adjusted his tie, his jacket. Looked girlish and pleased.

One short ticking-off for the departure from the script at the end. But that worked. So she was happy.

'I'm fine,' Hartmann said, retreating from her hands. 'Fine.'

'Troels. You've got a bunch of meetings ahead. Then a school visit. The cameras will be there. They'll want you.'

He stepped back to the window like a sullen child.

She played the same game. A pout. A practised one. She'd had her hair done before him. Black and sleek. Fitted dress hugging her slender body.

Weber rushed in brandishing papers. The draft of the alliance speech. He wanted it cleared with Eller.

'We'll read it in the car . . .'

'Take Morten with you,' Skovgaard said. 'Then the two of you can talk. Go over the points . . .'

Weber shook his head.

'There's nothing new. You don't need me. I've work here—'

'I'll hold the fort while you're gone,' she insisted. 'Go.' She waved at them. 'Go.' A smile. 'And talk.'

Sometimes they played chess together. He usually won. Because she let him? Hartmann wondered that sometimes.

'Go, boys!' Rie Skovgaard shouted like a scolding mother, waving her thin hands, flashing her rings.

'On Saturday night,' Meyer said, 'Jeppe Hald called Schandorff several times.'

'What about the woman Oliver was with?'

'Divorcee out for some fun. She said he was miserable and worried about something.'

Lund scowled at him.

'That's it?'

'No.'

That petulant ring to his voice was back. The smoking ban she'd imposed in the office was getting to him.

'What about the prints from the boiler room?'

'Half the school was down there.'

'What about DNA?'

'Still waiting. Ready?'

She looked through the glass door at the interview room across the passage. Oliver Schandorff, head down at the table.

'I want to be in there,' Meyer said. 'We're supposed to be working on this together.'

This was true.

'OK. You can come in. But leave the questions to me.'

He jumped to his feet. A short salute and click of the heels.

The moment they were through the door Schandorff, scruffy in a green polo shirt, pointed at Meyer.

'I'm not talking to him.'

'No,' Lund announced. 'You're talking to me.' Pause. 'Good morning, Oliver. How are you?'

'I feel like shit.'

She held out her hand. The kid took it. Then the bald lawyer they'd seen earlier did the same. Lund sat next to them. Meyer perched at the end of the room, on a stool in the light from the window.

'All we want to do,' Lund said, 'is ask you a few questions. Then you can go home.' No response. 'Nanna told her parents she would be at Lisa's. Was she meeting you?'

'No. I told you.'

'Do you know who she met?'

'No.'

From her folder Lund pulled a couple of photos of the fancy leather boots from Nanna's wardrobe.

'Did you give her these?'

He looked as if he'd never seen them.

'No.'

Meyer leaned back in his chair at the window, let loose a long yawn.

Lund ignored him.

'Why were you so angry that you threw a chair?'

The bald lawyer beamed and said, 'My client reserves the right not to answer.'

Lund ignored the man.

'I'm trying to help you, Oliver. Tell us the truth and you're gone from here. Hide behind this man and I promise—'

'She said she'd found someone else!'

'That's enough,' the lawyer said. 'We're going.'

Lund's eyes never left the ginger-haired kid.

'Did she say who?'

The lawyer was on his feet.

'My client's had a rough night—'

'Did she say anything else?'

'I said,' the lawyer cut in. 'No more questions.'

Schandorff shook his head.

'All I did was ask her if she'd come to the basement and talk to me. But she wouldn't—'

'Oliver!' the lawyer barked.

'Kid,' Meyer cut in. Schandorff glanced at him. 'He's not your dad. He won't hit you. I won't let him.'

'She wouldn't come with me.'

Lund nodded.

'So what did you do?'

'I called her a bunch of names. That was the last I saw of her.'

She picked up her papers.

'Thanks. That's all.'

Outside the room. Thinking.

'Nanna had a date. She had expensive boots no one knew about.'

'Oliver could have bought them,' Meyer said. 'He's lying. Maybe she was going on a date with him.'

'It feels wrong.'

'It feels wrong,' he muttered, reaching for a cigarette.

'Don't smoke in here,' she ordered. 'I told you that already.'

'I'll tell you what's wrong, Lund. You. You've been here so long you're part of the furniture. You think no one can ever replace you. That's what's wrong. You.'

Then he lit the cigarette anyway. Blew smoke in the air. Coughed. Said, 'My office. Mine.'

Svendsen stuck his head through the door.

'Forensics called. The samples from the boiler room were contaminated. There won't be any DNA profiles today.'

Lund said nothing. Looked at the photos on her desk. The boots.

'OK,' Meyer told him. 'We'll go back to the boys' flat.'

Svendsen sighed.

'We were there all night.'

'We didn't look hard enough.'

They left. Lund kept staring at the boots. The phone rang. It was the medical examiner. Wanting to see her.

Pernille waited on her own in the apartment with the flowers, the police tags and Nanna's clothes.

By midday she was ready to go crazy. So she drove to the school, saw an embarrassed Rektor Koch, then the charming, quiet, sad-eyed teacher Rama.

Learnt one thing only: the police held Oliver Schandorff and Jeppe Hald overnight.

Then she waited in an empty office, listening to the young voices outside in the corridor, dreaming she could hear Nanna's bright tones among them. Waited until Lisa Rasmussen came crying, running, throwing herself into the wide open arms of Pernille's gaberdine raincoat, shaking with emotion, sobbing like a little child.

Her hair was blonde like Nanna's. Pernille kissed it and knew she shouldn't. These two were friends. Sisters almost sometimes. These two were . . .

Pernille let go, smiled, stopped trying to rationalize something that was beyond comprehension. A child was a brief and blissful interlude of responsibility, not a thing to be owned. She'd no idea what Nanna did outside the little apartment above the garage. Didn't ask. Struggled not to think about it.

But Lisa knew. This short, slightly tubby girl trying so hard to be as pretty and clever as Nanna, and never quite succeeding.

Lisa dried her eyes, stood in front of her. Looking awkward. As if she'd like to go.

'There are things . . .' Pernille said. 'I don't understand.'

Silence. The little blonde girl shifted on her feet.

'Was Nanna upset by something?'

Lisa shook her head.

'What about Oliver? Was he involved?'

'No.'

A petulant teenage note in the denial.

'So why do the police keep asking about him, Lisa? Why?'

Her hands fidgeted behind her back, she leaned against the desk, said with a pout, 'I don't know.'

Pernille thought of the policewoman, Lund. Her quiet persistent manner. Her large and shining eyes that never seemed to stop looking.

'But you went to the party together. Did she say anything? Did she seem . . .' Words. Simple ones. Simple questions. Lund's way. 'Did she seem different?'

'No. She didn't say anything. She was just . . . Nanna.'

Don't get angry, Pernille thought. Don't say what you think . . . You're a lying little cow and it's written all over your plain fat face.

'Why did she say she was staying with you?'

The girl shook her head, like a bad actress in a bad play.

'I don't know.'

'But you're friends,' Pernille said, wondering . . . is this too much? Do I look hard? Do I look crazy?

Said anyway, 'You're friends. She would have told you her plans.' Voice getting louder, chestnut hair waving. 'She would have told you if there was something.'

'Pernille. She didn't. Honestly.'

Shake the child. Scream at it. Yell until she says . . . What?

'Was she angry?' Pernille asked. 'With me?'

'I don't know.'

'You have to tell me!' she cried, voice beginning to shatter. 'It's important.'

Lisa didn't move, grew calmer and more sullen with every angry rising note she heard.

'She . . . didn't . . . say . . . anything.'

Hands on the girl's shoulders, staring into those defiant stupid eyes.

'Tell me!'

'There's nothing to tell,' Lisa said in a voice flat and devoid of emotion. 'She wasn't angry with you. She really wasn't.'

'Then what happened?' Pernille snarled.

Shake the child. Slap her cheek.

'What happened?'

Lisa stood defiant. A look in her eyes that said: do it then. Hit me now. It won't make a difference. Nanna's still gone.

Pernille sniffed, wiped her nose, walked out into the corridor. Stopped at the flowers and photos by the lockers. Nanna's shrine.

Sat down among them. The third day. Petals falling. Notes slipped from their fastenings. Everything fading into a lost grey distance beyond her vision.

She picked up the nearest piece of paper. A childish scrawl.

It read, 'We will never forget you.'

But you will, she thought. You all will. Even Lund after a while. Even Theis if he can manage it, placing his boundless, shapeless love in the boys, in Anton and Emil. Hoping their young faces will obliterate Nanna's memory, supplant it with enough devotion to hide the pain.

Figures flitted quickly past lugging satchels, carrying papers, chatting in low tones.

She watched and listened. In these plain grey corridors her daughter once walked. Still did in a way, in Pernille's imagination, which made the hurt more keen. Grief should be an absence, a void, not the physical thing she now felt. Nanna was lost to her. Stolen. Till the thief and the deed became clear her death would mark them all, like the tumour of some cruel disease.

They were locked in the present, no way out. She got to her feet, walked up the steps, stumbled, fell.

A hand reached out. She saw a face, dark and kind.

'Are you all right?'

The teacher, Rama, again.

She took his arm, grabbed the handrail, got to her feet.

They all said that and never wanted the answer.

'No,' she murmured. 'I'm not.'

She wondered what Nanna thought of this handsome, intelligent man. Whether she liked him. What they talked about.

'Did Lisa say anything?' Rama asked.

'A little.'

'If I can—'

'Help?'

They all said that too. Reached for the same words. Perhaps he meant it. Perhaps it was one more trite sentiment, spoken automatically like a prayer.

Pernille Birk Larsen walked out of the school wondering if Theis was right. She was being stupid. The police were looking. Lund ought to know her job.

*

The woman from the estate agency gazed up at the scaffolding, the sheeted windows, the piles of material stacked by the door.

'It's got to be sold quickly. I want it gone.'

Theis Birk Larsen was in his black jacket, his hat, his rigger boots and red overalls. Work outfit, though work, the thing that seemed so important, now escaped him. The business was in Vagn Skærbæk's hands. Vagn could do the job. There was no choice.

'Of course,' she agreed.

'I'll take what I paid. I just want rid of it.'

'I understand.'

He kicked the scaffolding.

'The materials are included.'

Children played in the street. Kicked footballs. Laughs and shouts. He watched them, envious.

'It's a lovely house,' the woman said. 'Why not wait a few months?'

'No. It has to be now. Is that a problem?'

She hesitated.

'Not really. You saw the survey?'

She pulled out a sheaf of documents. Birk Larsen hated paper. That was Pernille's job.

'The survey shows dry rot.'

He blinked, felt sick and powerless.

'The insurance must cover that.'

She didn't look at him, shook her head.

'No. It doesn't. Sorry.'

A breeze struck up. The sheets flapped in the wind. Two kids on bikes rode by trailing kites from their hands.

'But . . .'

She pointed a manicured fingernail at the contract.

'It says there. No cover for dry rot. I'm sorry.' A deep and awkward breath. 'If you sell now you'll lose a lot of money. In this condition . . .'

He stared at the place, thought of all the lost dreams. The boys in their rooms. Nanna peering out of the top window now covered in black sheeting.

'Sell the damned thing,' Theis Birk Larsen said.

Troels Hartmann was on his hands and knees, painting with the toddlers in the kindergarten.

Morten Weber came to crouch beside him.

'Troels,' he said. 'I hate to interrupt your fun but the photographers have left. You've other places to go.'

Hartmann drew a childish yellow chicken on the paper, got squeals of delight from the kids around him.

Smiled.

'Are they fun too, Morten?'

'They're necessary.'

Hartmann pointed a finger at the young faces on the floor.

'These are the voters of tomorrow.'

'Well, let's come back tomorrow then. I'm more interested in anyone who's got a vote today.'

'They made us a cake.'

Weber frowned.

'A cake?'

Two minutes later they sat alone at a table away from the teachers and the kids.

'Try the cake, Morten.'

'Sorry. Can't.'

'The diabetes is a front. You wouldn't touch it anyway. You're so self-righteous.'

They were close enough for a crack like that, he thought.

'What about this reporter?' Hartmann asked.

'You mean Erik Salin?'

'He's on my tail, Morten. Why? Who is he? How did he know about the car?'

'He's a sleazeball looking to make a bit of money. Take it as a compliment. He wouldn't waste the time if you weren't in with a chance.'

'How did he know about the car?'

Weber squirmed.

'You think someone in the office leaked it, don't you?' Weber asked.

'Do you?'

'It had crossed my mind. But I can't imagine who.'

Hartmann pushed away the cake and his plastic cup of orange juice, listened to the kids giggling over their paintings.

'I've every confidence in our team,' Weber said a touch pompously. 'All of them. Haven't you?'

Hartmann was about to answer when his phone rang.

He listened, looked at Weber.

'We've got to go.'

Striding through the long echoing halls, around the central court-yard, Hartmann was livid.

'Where the hell is she?'

'She's going to call in a minute.'

Rie Skovgaard met him at the front door, was struggling to keep up as he marched towards their office, Weber following on behind, silent, listening.

'Eller says Poul Bremer made her a better offer. She's not taken it yet. She wants to know our reaction.'

'Our reaction is she can choke on it.'

Skovgaard sighed.

'This is politics.'

'No it's not. It's a beauty contest. And we're not playing.'

'Listen to her. Hear what she has to say. We could compromise on a few things . . .'

She stopped Hartmann outside the office door.

'Troels. You have to calm down.'

He cast his eyes around the inside of the Rådhus. Sometimes it looked like a jail. A very comfortable prison.

Skovgaard's phone rang.

'Hi, Kirsten. Just a second. We'll be with you soon.'

Call ended, she looked at Hartmann and said, 'Be polite. Keep cool.'

He was walking already. She lost it. Slapped him on the shoulder, yelled, 'Hey!'

Her voice was hard and shrill.

'Shut up and listen to me for once, will you? If we have Eller on our side we win. If we don't we're one more tiny minority begging for crumbs at Poul Bremer's table. Troels . . .'

Leaving again. Her hand gripped his blue lapels, dragged him back into the shadows.

'Do you understand what I'm saying? You can't get a majority on your own. You don't have the support.' She calmed down a little. 'Nothing can change that now. It's a fact.'

Hartmann held out his hand for the phone.

'Be calm,' she said and gave it him.

Hartmann called Eller. Small talk, then, 'I heard about you and Bremer. Well, that's the way it goes. There's no point in getting upset about it.'

He closed his eyes and listened. Talk of doors remaining open, offers that weren't quite final. The insistent, expectant tone never changed.

'I guess there won't be an alliance, after all,' Hartmann said. 'We should have coffee sometime. Take care. Bye.'

Skovgaard was white with fury. Weber was gone.

'There. How calm was that?'

The medical examiner was a long-winded man with a tanned face and a white beard. All the way to the morgue he talked about making cider.

'They've got good apples in Sweden. I'll give you the recipe.'

'That's lovely.'

They walked in, both pulled on gloves, and went to the table.

'This is an unusual case,' he said, lifting the white sheet.

She looked at Nanna Birk Larsen's body. Cleaned up now and showing the post-mortem marks.

'The blood in her hair clotted long before she hit the water. There's bruising on the arms and legs and down her right side.'

Lund looked. Thought she'd seen enough.

'Come here,' he ordered, pointing to the right thigh.

'We've been through this.'

The leg was covered in cuts.

'Abrasions?'

'No. Feel her skin.'

Lund did. It felt like skin.

'There's redness around the wounds,' he pointed out. 'When a body's been in the water that disappears. But it comes back after a few days.'

Lund shook her head.

'They're sores,' he said. 'She was kept on a rough surface. Maybe a concrete floor.'

'The school basement has a concrete floor.'

She touched the lesions. Thought about the hidden room with the bloody mattress and the drugs.

'How long was she like this?'

'Fifteen to twenty hours.'

Lund struggled with this information, tried to picture what it meant.

'Are you sure?'

'I'm sure. There was a series of rapes with several hours between them. But no DNA we can find so far. He must have used a condom. There's nothing under her nails or anywhere else.'

'Because of the water?'

He nodded.

'That's what I thought. But she was in the boot of the car. Look at her hands.'

He lifted up each one.

'Someone cut her nails.'

He let the hands fall back onto the white sheet. Lund picked up each in turn, took a close look.

'There are traces of ether in her liver and lungs,' he said, reading from a report. 'So she was drugged. Perhaps several times. This was all planned. He knew what he was doing. I wouldn't . . .'

He paused, as if unsure of himself.

'This isn't my field but I wouldn't be surprised if you found he'd done this before. There's a . . . method to it.'

Lund took the report from him.

'Does that help?'

She shrugged.

'Well,' he said. 'I'll send you anything else that comes along. Oh . . .' He smiled. 'And that recipe for cider.'

Lund went back to her office. Buchard was arguing with the bald lawyer outside the door. Struggling to keep hold of Oliver Schandorff and Jeppe Hald. The lawyer would be going in front of a judge to get them freed soon. From the look on Buchard's face the chief didn't have much hope of winning that particular argument.

Eller closed the door behind her. Sat down, placed her broad hands on her broad hips and said, 'That was some trick you played I must say.'

'No trick, Kirsten.'

'I hope not.'

He waited.

'I said no to Bremer. Don't think that was an easy decision. It's not a word he likes to hear.'

'I can imagine.'

'It wasn't much of a choice really. We're natural partners. He's just . . .' She smiled. 'The bastard who pulls all the strings.'

Still he said nothing.

'I hope you can live up to our expectations,' Eller added. 'My neck's on the line.'

'Your group . . . ?'

'. . . will do as I say. Now . . . shall we get down to business?'

Five minutes later, around the table in a meeting next to the campaign office, the negotiations began. Policies and appointments. Funding and media strategies. Rie Skovgaard took notes and made suggestions.

Hartmann and Eller cut the deal.

Meyer was back from searching the student flat again.

'Did you release those kids?' he asked.

'Yes.'

'We'll have to bring them back in.'

Lund scanned through some of the photos on the desk. Nanna's wounds. The boots.

'I don't think they did it,' she said.

'I'm sure they did.'

He had a memory card reader with him. Meyer placed it on her desk and plugged the cable into the PC.

'Take a look at this.'

The computer recognized what it was being given, fired up a window.

Shaky video came on the screen. The Halloween party. Kids in costume. Drinking beer. Screaming. Acting the way kids did when they knew no one was watching.

Lund watched. There was Jeppe Hald, bright, quiet Jeppe, star pupil, head boy. Screaming at the lens, drunk or doped or both.

Lisa Rasmussen in a short tight dress, sashaying, much the same.

'Where'd you get this?'

'Jeppe Hald's room. He recorded it on his mobile phone then saved it on a memory card.' Meyer looked at her. 'So he could watch it on his computer.'

Lund nodded.

'I don't think he's as bright as that school says,' Meyer added.

'Stop!'

Meyer froze the frame.

Nanna in her black witch's hat. Nanna alive and breathing. Beautiful, so beautiful. So . . . *old*.

She didn't look drunk. She wasn't screaming. She looked . . . bemused. Like an adult suddenly surrounded by a bunch of infants.

'Play,' Lund said.

Meyer set it running slowly. The picture panned from Nanna to Oliver Schandorff, wild hair, wild eyes. Schandorff staring hungrily at Nanna as he swigged at a can of beer.

'We didn't have parties like that at my school,' Meyer said. 'Yours?'

'They wouldn't have invited me.'

'I bet. Here we go.' Meyer let out a long sad sigh and sat down next to her. 'Show time.'

The picture changed. Somewhere else. Somewhere darker. A few lights. Drinks on the table. The place in the basement. Had to be.

Something moving in the background, getting bigger as the lens approached.

Lund leaned forward, looked at this carefully, felt her heart begin to race.

There was a sound. Panting, gasping. Oliver Schandorff naked, ginger head swaying as he writhed over the figure beneath him, naked too, legs splayed and not moving.

The contrast between him and the girl was striking. Schandorff all manic energy and desperation. She . . .

Drunk? Unconscious?

Couldn't tell. But not right.

Closer.

Schandorff's hands came and grabbed her legs, made her grip him. Her fingers rose as if to beat him off. He was like a madman, pushed them down, grunted, screaming.

Lund watched.

The lens shifted behind them, to Schandorff's back. Her legs had locked round him. Sex the teenage way. As if a clock somewhere was

140

running, saying, 'Do it now and do it quickly, or you'll never get the chance again.'

More grunts, more savage thrusts.

Closer. The black witch's hat they saw earlier, down over the eyes, over the face. Blonde hair. The hat moves . . .

'Shit,' Lund said.

Something had happened. The camera was off the couple. They heard him, sneaking up on them. Curses and swift movements. The girl just visible, scuttling to cover herself. Blonde hair, witch's hat, bare breasts. Not much more.

'I think I'll bring them in again,' Meyer said.

On the steps of the City Hall Troels Hartmann and Kirsten Eller stood next to one another, blinking in the bright lights of the cameras, smiling, shaking hands.

Waiting for Meyer, Lund watched it all on the news channel on her computer. Then went back to the video. The school.

One segment she'd skipped through earlier.

Nanna in her party dress. Hat on. Beaming into Jeppe Hald's phone. Raising a glass of what looked like Coke. Smiling. Sober. So elegant and natural. Not a kid at all. Not like the others.

And a few minutes later . . .

Naked in the basement, Oliver Schandorff thrusting at her like an animal.

'Be right, Meyer,' she whispered.

The caretaker was letting Lund into the school when Meyer called.

'I've got them both.'

'Don't question them yet.'

A pause.

'The last time I checked we had the same stripes.'

'I need to see something first.'

A long sigh.

'Don't worry, Lund. You'll get the credit.'

Her footsteps echoed down dark and empty corridors.

'Wait twenty minutes,' she said and cut the call.

The flowers on Nanna's shrine beside the lockers looked dead, the candles burned to stumps. Lund walked down the cold stairs to the basement, shining her torch, fumbling for light switches she couldn't find.

Past the Don't Cross tape. Into the hidden room. Lines and markers everywhere. Empty bottles circled, dusty with print powder.

She looked at the bloodstained mattress. There was one single large stain at the foot, then a line of red on the piping at the edge. Not so much blood. And it wasn't smeared.

Meyer didn't wait, didn't see why he should. He had Oliver Schandorff in Lund's office, seated in front of the computer, forced to watch the video. The pumpkin head. The drunken kids. The dope. The booze.

On his own now, free to act as he pleased, Meyer was more relaxed. He sat next to the kid, watched him as he stared at the PC, ginger hair everywhere, face screwed up with fear and pain.

'You've got two choices, Oliver,' he said in a flat, calm voice. 'Either you confess now . . .'

Nanna. In her witch's hat. Smiling. Happy. Beautiful.

'Or we watch the rest. And wait for your lawyer to come in the morning. If he can be bothered to get out of bed.'

The phone was moving, from the hall down the stairs. Into the basement. Towards the hidden room.

Two figures naked in the distance, beneath a single bulb, wrestling.

Schandorff couldn't take his eyes off the screen.

'I've got all night,' Meyer told him. 'But I know you two did it and so do you. So let's get this over with, shall we?'

Silence.

Meyer felt the faint stirrings of anger, tried to quell it.

'Oliver? *Oliver?*'

Lund took out the photos she'd brought. Close-ups of Nanna's body. Details of the sores, the lesions on her back.

The power was off for some reason so she checked them in the light of her torch. Held them up as she looked at the mattress, the spots of blood on the floor.

Took out a photo of Nanna's hands. Clipped fingernails.

Ran her torch around the room.

Checked the inventory.

No sign of scissors.

Took out her phone, looked at the screen. No signal in this underground tomb.

Oliver Schandorff sat rigid in front of the screen. Two bodies coupling. His own ginger hair bobbing up and down. He grabs her legs, makes her grip him. He pushes away her hands as they reach to claw at him.

The lens is up close behind. His back, his body pumping at her in a crazy, frenetic rhythm. Then confusion. Picture moving everywhere as he pulls himself away, confronts the intruder sneaking up on them.

Lips downturned like a naughty child, face full of shame and anger, Schandorff sat in the homicide office refusing to speak.

'Maybe Jeppe will talk first,' Meyer said.

There was Hald on the screen. Drunk. Out of control.

'You know he might be next door.' Meyer tapped Schandorff on the arm. 'Could be saying it was all you. Just you. Wouldn't be nice, would it?'

Meyer's hand went to his shoulder.

'He's not your friend, Oliver. Think about it. I know I yelled at you, son. I'm sorry. It's just . . .'

Schandorff sat there like a rock.

'Those pictures of Nanna after we got her out of the water.' Meyer watched him. 'I can't get them out of my head. Don't make me show them to you. Best for both of us if I don't do that.'

Lund wasn't ready to go outside and find a signal. More to do here. She pulled out a pair of forensic gloves and picked up a broken beer glass sitting in a ring of chalk.

Shone the torch on it.

Lipstick along the edge. Bright orange. Gaudy.

Got the photo of Nanna from the school set, shot at the party.

Nanna in her witch's hat, the only thing about her that seemed young.

Reached into the ashtray. Sifted through the cigarette ends and joint butts. Pulled out a rolled-up wad of tin foil. Pulled it open with her gloved fingers. Not dope. An earring.

In the light she saw three fake diamonds on a silver setting.

Back to the photos. Nanna and the other kids. Lisa Rasmussen.

It was four days now since they pulled Nanna Birk Larsen's body out of the chill canal by the airport. In all that time they'd scarcely worked without a lead. Chasing shadows running from them. A puzzle promising answers. Yet . . .

This case was like none she'd ever worked. It had layers and texture. Mysteries. Riddles. Investigations were never black and white. But never had she met one quite so grey and insubstantial.

Lund stared at the photo, Nanna and Lisa, smiling, happy.

Then there was a sound above her. Footsteps in the dark.

'Maybe it wasn't your idea,' Meyer said. 'Jeppe thought of it and you came along for the ride.'

He leaned over, tried to get Schandorff's attention.

'Oliver?'

Nothing. Just a miserable face locked on the computer.

'That would make a difference. If you told us. So what's it to be?'

Meyer leaned back in his chair, put his arms behind his head.

'Do we sit here all night and go through some more pictures? Or get it over with?'

Nothing.

'Fine.' There was an edge in Meyer's voice and he regretted that. 'I'm feeling hungry. Don't have money for two—'

'It's not her, you moron,' Schandorff snarled.

Meyer blinked.

That petulant, tortured teenage voice again. But finally Oliver Schandorff looked at him.

'The girl in the boiler room. It's not Nanna.'

Upstairs in the corridor, in front of Nanna's shrine. A stump of candle flickered in the dark.

Lund checked her phone. There was a signal.

Heard something, footsteps close to the door. Didn't think of hiding. Turned her torch towards the source.

'Lisa?'

The girl stood frozen in the bright white light, a glass vase with some roses in her hand.

'How did you get in?' Lund asked.

Lisa placed the flowers on the shrine.

'They were getting old. People forget.'

'How did you get in?'

'The gym door's open. The lock doesn't work. Everyone knows that.'

She brushed back her long blonde hair, looked at the photos and the flowers.

'When did you get to know Nanna?'

'At primary school. In our last year. Nanna picked Frederiksholm so I did too.' She moved the roses around. 'I didn't think I'd get in. Nanna's clever. Her dad had to find the money. My dad's got the money. But me . . . I'm stupid.'

'When did you fall out?'

Lisa didn't look at her.

'We didn't fall out.'

'We've got Nanna's phone. You never called her, texted her lately.'

Nothing.

'Nanna called you.'

'It wasn't an argument. Not really.'

'About Oliver?'

Straight away, 'I don't remember.'

'I think it was about Oliver. Nanna didn't care for him. You're in love with him, right?'

Lisa laughed.

'You ask some weird questions.'

'So you went to the boiler room.'

'Can I go now?'

Lund pulled out the earring.

'You forgot something.'

The girl stared at the evidence bag, swore, turned to go.

'We could waste a lot of time looking for the dress,' Lund said to her back. 'Or you could just tell me.'

Lisa Rasmussen stopped, hugged herself in her skimpy red coat.

'This is important,' Lund said. 'Was Nanna in the room? Or were you and the boys alone?'

Caught between being a kid and an adult.

'I was angry with her! OK?'

Lund folded her arms, waited.

'Nanna made all the decisions. She treated me like I was a child.

I was drunk. Then that creep Jeppe came in and started filming us. Oliver got mad. I tried to stop Jeppe. I tripped over some bottles.'

She rolled up her sleeve. Plasters and scratch marks. Long wounds, maybe stitches.

'Cut myself.'

'What happened?'

'Oliver took me to the hospital. We were there all night.'

She sat on a windowsill, plain young face lit by the street lamps.

'He was still mad about Nanna. I thought maybe I could . . .'

She rolled down her sleeve, hugged herself again.

'Stupid. Nanna was right.'

'Where was Nanna?'

'I don't know.'

'Lisa . . .'

'I don't know!' she yelled. 'Maybe half past nine . . . she came to the hall, put her hat on me. Gave me a hug. And said goodbye.'

She looked Lund in the face.

'That was it. She left.'

Lund nodded.

'Does my dad have to know? He'll kill me.'

Hartmann and Rie Skovgaard listened to the radio on the way to the reception. The news was calling the election already. The alliance had altered the game. A change to the long-established political system wasn't far off.

The Birk Larsen case seemed behind them. Ahead lay the hard work of the campaign. Meetings and press conferences. Shaking hands, winning votes.

And private conclaves of the inner circle of Danish politics, in the glittering rooms where right and left and centre gathered to spar gently with smiles and deft promises, trade polite insults, deliver discreet warnings disguised as advice.

Late that evening, exhausted, wishing for nothing more than to take Rie Skovgaard home to bed, Hartmann found himself faced with her father. A long-standing parliamentarian for the Liberal Party. Kim Skovgaard was a burly, genial man with clout. Not unlike Poul Bremer, who chatted amiably with his foes across the room.

The Lord Mayor's raucous laughter boomed over the gathering.

'I didn't realize Bremer was on your party list,' Hartmann said.

'Keep your friends close and your enemies closer,' Kim Skovgaard answered with a knowing grin. 'In the end we're all fighting for the same thing. A better life. We just disagree about the means.'

Hartmann smiled.

'Are you still implicated in the case?' Skovgaard asked.

'You mean the girl's murder?'

'Are there others?'

'We were never implicated. It was a coincidence. You'll hear no more of that.'

Skovgaard raised his glass.

'Good. It would have been hard to back you with those kind of headlines.'

'Dad . . .' his daughter intervened. 'Not now.'

He carried on.

'The Prime Minister . . . and a few others are wondering if you're on top of everything.'

'The campaign's under control. We'll win.' A smile. Lost amidst a sea of others. 'Excuse me . . .'

He walked through to the next room, took Poul Bremer's arm, asked for a word. The two of them strode to an empty space near the fireplace.

'So you won Madam Eller in the end, Troels,' Bremer said. 'Congratulations. I hope the price wasn't too high.'

'I know what you're up to.'

Bremer blinked behind his owlish glasses, shook his head.

'If I catch you playing any more games . . .' Hartmann came close, spoke in a gruff, determined whisper. 'I will take you to court. Do you understand?'

'Not a bit of it,' Bremer replied. 'I don't know what the hell you're talking about.'

'Fine,' Hartmann said, made to go. 'You heard.'

'Troels! Come back here.'

Bremer strolled to his side, peering into his face.

'I've always liked you. Ever since you were a novice here, struggling to make your first speech. Today . . .'

Hartmann tried to judge him, to sift sincerity from the histrionics, and failed.

'Today you defeated me. That doesn't happen often. When it does . . . I don't like it. Nor do I like it when in a fit of paranoia you accuse me of things of which I'm ignorant.'

Hartmann stood there, trying not to feel like a scolded schoolboy.

Bremer's big hand came up, thumb and forefinger rubbing together.

'If I'd wanted to crush you, don't you think I would have done it long ago?'

He patted Hartmann's shoulder.

'Think about that.' His smile turned to a scowl. 'You've ruined my mood, Troels. I'm going now. I hope you feel guilty. '

Bremer looked at him.

'Guilty. Yes. That's the word.'

They released Schandorff and Hald. Lund got Lisa Rasmussen to sign a statement, made sure she'd be taken safely home in a car.

On the way out she asked her again, 'You really don't know who she was going to meet?'

The girl looked exhausted. Relieved too. This secret had weighed upon her.

'Nanna was happy. I saw that. As if she was looking forward to something. Something special.'

When she was gone Meyer marched in brandishing papers.

'I'm charging them with perjury. Wasting police time.'

'Is that worth it?'

'Why didn't you call and tell me, Lund? Why haven't you said a word to me? I feel like a fool.'

She held up her phone.

'Basement. No signal. I tried.'

'No you didn't.'

He sounded like one of the petulant kids.

'You're in your own little world. Lundland. Nothing else in it.'

'OK. I'm sorry about that.'

'And I mustn't smoke. Or eat or yell at suspects.'

'Don't worry. I'll be gone soon.'

The pack of cigarettes came out. He brandished one, lit it, blew the smoke at her.

She sighed.

'We don't have a damned thing,' Meyer grumbled.

'Not true.'

'Are you serious?'

She found her voice rising. Must have been the cigarette. She wanted one so badly.

'We have plenty. If only you'd listen.'

He folded his arms, said, 'I'm listening now.'

Five minutes later with Buchard, pug-faced and serious.

She went through the papers, the photos she'd assembled, patiently, one by one.

'We know things about whoever did this. We know he drugged her with ether. He held her captive somewhere and abused her for fifteen to twenty hours. Afterwards . . .'

More shots of the body. Arms, hands, feet, thighs.

'He bathed her. Cut her fingernails. Then drove her to the woods where he knew they wouldn't be disturbed.'

Pictures of the track through the Pentecost Forest. Hair on the dead trees.

'There he played a game. He toyed with her. He let her run away and then caught her. Maybe . . .' She'd been thinking about this for a while. 'Maybe more than once.'

'Hide and seek,' Meyer said, and drew on his cigarette.

'We found designer boots in Nanna's closet,' Lund went on. 'Her parents didn't know about them.'

She passed round the photograph: brown leather and glittering metal.

'Nanna couldn't have bought them. Too expensive. The necklace . . .'

The black heart on a cheap gilt chain.

'We still don't know who this came from. Maybe a gift from whoever gave her the boots. Except it's cheap. And old.'

Lund placed in front of them the photo of Nanna and Lisa at the Halloween party, Lisa looking drunk, a teenager. Nanna elegant and smiling, wearing the black witch's hat as if it was an unwanted joke.

'This is the most important thing. Nanna had a secret rendezvous. She changed out of her clothes and left her costume at school. She was going to meet someone. Even her best friend had no idea who.'

Buchard groaned.

'You're not going to tell me it was a teacher, are you?'

Lund looked at him, said nothing.

'Right,' Meyer said. 'Tomorrow we start all over again.'

'Listen to me!' Buchard ordered. 'The schools fall under the remit of Troels Hartmann. He has to know what we're doing.'

'Fine.' Lund nodded. 'I'll call him tomorrow.'

'And I need you to stay on a little longer,' Buchard added.

Meyer closed his eyes, blew some smoke at the ceiling.

'I'm here till Saturday. Mark starts school on Monday. I've done all I—'

'With all respect,' Meyer cut in. 'I don't think she should stay. I know the ropes. And . . .' He frowned. 'Let's be honest. There hasn't exactly been much teamwork between the two of us. I think Lund should stick to her plan.'

Then he got up and left.

She was looking at the photos. Nanna in the witch's hat. Apart from the kids around her.

Buchard peered at her.

'Meyer's had nothing to eat,' she said. 'It makes him tetchy. No . . .' She waved a finger, corrected herself. 'Tetchier.'

'The school . . .'

'We have to look. We have to look very hard.'

Five

Lund was pulling on her black and white sweater, juggling a piece of toast when her mother said, 'I thought we were leaving tonight?'

'No. We'll go tomorrow afternoon.'

'Tomorrow afternoon? That's when the guests are arriving.'

'It'll be fine.'

'I can't stay in Sweden long. There are things to do.' She looked at the dress. 'There's a wedding on the way.'

'There's always a wedding on the way. We were hoping you'd be with us for a week. Meet Bengt's family.'

A grim laugh.

'You mean take your son to school while you go to work?'

'Never mind.' Lund gulped at her mug, pulled a face. 'It was just an idea. Do we have any hot coffee?'

She went to the percolator. No.

'Is this the kind of mother I've brought you up to be?' Vibeke asked, shaking her head. 'You haven't even talked to Mark while you've been here. Do you have any idea—?'

'It's been a busy week. I thought you might have noticed.'

Quickly, without a mirror, thinking about Nanna and the school all the time, she took an elastic band from her jeans and tied her long brown hair into a rough ponytail.

'He's twelve years old—'

'I know how old he is.'

'You know nothing about him! Or his life.'

'I have to go.'

151

'Do you even know he's got a girlfriend?'

Lund stopped. Struggled for a moment.

'Mark's like me,' she said. 'Very independent. We're not in each other's faces all the time. And yes . . . I do know about his girlfriend. Thank you.'

'I'm off,' said a voice behind that made her jump.

Mark, in a blue jacket, ready for school.

She followed him down the stairs.

A dull dry day. He had his scooter with him, started pushing it away the moment they were in the street.

'Mark! You haven't had breakfast.'

He slowed down, got off the thing.

'Not hungry.'

'I'm sorry about this week. I'll make it up to you. I promise.'

He got back on the scooter. She struggled to keep up.

'Gran said you had a girlfriend.'

Mark stopped, didn't look her in the eye.

Lund smiled.

'That's nice.'

She tried not to let the earring get to her. He'd got his ear pierced without even asking, by some stupid kid at school.

'What's her name?'

'It's not important.'

'You can invite her to Sweden.'

'I'm going to be late for school.'

'Mark? I'm interested in what goes on in your life.'

'She just broke up with me.'

Twelve years old and such pain on his young face.

'And you don't give a shit. You're only interested in dead people.'

Lund stood on the pavement. Seeing the boy he was at four or five. At eight. Ten. Struggling to separate that child from the surly, sad kid who stared at her now looking . . .

What?

Disappointed.

That was the word.

Mark turned his back on her, pushed himself down the street.

*

152

Hartmann came in at nine. Lund took him into her room.

'You told me we were off the hook?'

'I didn't say that . . .'

'You never mentioned a teacher.'

'It's one line of inquiry.'

'Into what exactly?'

Meyer stuck his head through the door, said, 'Are we going?'

Hartmann didn't move.

'What have you come up with now?'

Lund shook her head.

'I can't say.'

'These are my schools and my teachers. You will tell me.'

'When I can—'

'No. No!'

He was getting mad. She'd seen this temper before. On TV when he flew at the reporter. Now she had it in her face.

'I need to know who it is! Christ! I have to take precautions.'

'It's not possible—'

'You've made a fool of me once, Lund. It's not happening again.'

'I'm sorry. I can't put your election above a murder inquiry. It wouldn't be right . . .'

He looked livid.

'Don't you understand the damage you'll do? To teachers? To the pupils? To the parents? You spread suspicion like a farmer spreads shit. And you don't give a damn—'

'Don't you dare say that!' she yelled back at him.

Hartmann fell quiet, surprised by the sudden volume.

'Don't ever say that,' Lund repeated more quietly. 'I'm not a politician, Hartmann. I'm a police officer. I don't have time to think about all the consequences. I just have to . . . to . . .'

'What?' he demanded when she never finished the sentence.

'Keep looking.' She dragged her bag onto her shoulder. 'We'll be discreet. We won't start any rumours. We've no interest or desire to damage any innocent party. We just want to find out who killed that girl. OK?'

His sudden rage had fled. These outbursts, she thought, were sharp and unexpected, as much unwanted by Troels Hartmann as they were to those who heard them.

'Fine,' he said, nodding. He looked at her. 'Will you let me help?'

She said nothing.

'I want to, Lund. I'll ask the office to get copies of the personnel files. For the teachers. All the staff.'

'Send them to my office. I'll have someone look through them.'

'I want to help. Believe me.'

His phone went. The mask of the politician, unemotional, distanced, impassive, came upon him again in an instant. Lund left him to his call.

There was a smiling woman in the winding corridor of black marble, fair-haired, carrying a supermarket bag.

She asked Lund, 'Is Jan Meyer here?'

'In a moment.'

Lund went back to checking through the messages on her phone.

'I'm Hanne Meyer,' the woman said. 'I've got something for him.'

A wife. Lund remembered the call the other night. *Now you've woken the whole house.* A baby crying. Meyer had a life beyond the police station. The idea astonished her.

'Sarah Lund,' she said, and shook her hand. 'I work with him.'

'So this is what you look like!'

She was very pretty, with a scarf round her neck and a peasant dress beneath her brown wool coat.

'I've heard a lot about you.'

'I can imagine.'

'Ah.' She gave Lund a knowing look. 'He means well. It doesn't always comes across.' A pause. 'And he thinks you're . . . amazing.'

Lund blinked.

'Amazing?'

'He's to take two of these every hour,' Hanne Meyer said, giving her a bottle of pills. 'If that doesn't help you have to try the bananas.'

She pulled a couple out of her bag, passed them to the wide-eyed Lund.

'Whatever he tells you, Jan must *not* have coffee, cheese or crisps.' She tut-tutted. 'They upset his stomach.'

The woman clapped her hands: all done.

'New jobs are always difficult. Let's hope it works out this time.'

Meyer came round the corner. Old green anorak, sailor's jumper, embarrassed expression on his face.

'What the . . . ?'

'Hi, darling!' Hanne Meyer called cheerily.

Beaming, oblivious to all else, Meyer walked up, kissed her on the lips.

'What the hell are you doing here?'

She indicated the bananas and the pills in Lund's hands.

'You left them in the car.'

'Ah . . .'

Meyer shrugged.

She stroked his stubble, said, 'Take care. Have a good day, you two.'

He watched her every inch of the way, smiling, entranced.

When she was out of his sight his face dropped, turned dead serious.

Meyer took the fruit and the pills from Lund and tucked a banana in each pocket like a gun. Retrieved one, aimed it down the corridor, went, 'Kapow.'

'Amazing,' Lund said.

'What?'

'Nothing. Let's go.'

The campaign team was in place for the morning briefing. Eight workers, Rie Skovgaard running things. Hartmann left the Birk Larsen case till last.

'The press might get hold of something,' he finished. 'But it'll only be guesswork. We're sending the personnel files to Lund. Let's not get distracted. We've got more important work to do.'

'Wait, wait, wait.' Skovgaard waved at them to stay seated. 'You're saying they think it's a teacher.'

Hartmann packed his papers into his briefcase.

'That's one theory.'

'You know what that means, Troels? We're back in the story again. The press will involve you anyway.'

'It's a police matter . . .'

'You're Mayor of Education. If it's a teacher they'll hold you accountable.'

She never gave up. Never would.

He sat down again, looked at her and asked, 'What are you suggesting?'

'That we act first! Let's read those files before Lund gets them. Check we didn't screw up.'

'How could we have screwed up?'

'I don't know. I just don't want any surprises. Besides . . . Imagine if we passed on some information that helped them find the man. We'd pick up some credit instead of the blame.'

Hartmann gazed at her.

'Troels,' she added, 'if it's a choice between losing votes and winning them it's not much of a choice at all.'

'Fine. Do it.'

When the team left she gave Hartmann his schedule for the day, went through it line by line, minute by minute. The last event was a photo opportunity about social integration. Bringing foreign groups into the community. About role models, the immigrants Hartmann's team had picked to front the initiative.

'Shall we have dinner afterwards?' she asked.

'Sure,' Hartmann said without a thought.

'You can make time for me?'

'Sure.'

'Troels!'

'Oh.'

There was so little time for anything. Hartmann took her in his arms, liked the way her face brightened then. He was about to kiss her when there was a knock on the door. One of the City Hall employees. A young man. He looked embarrassed at walking in on them.

'You asked about some files? The schools?'

'I'll leave this to you,' Hartmann said and left.

Skovgaard sat the civil servant in front of her, listed the ones she wanted. Staff records for Frederiksholm High. Contracts. Assessments. Any complaints.

He listened, said nothing.

'Is this a problem?'

'The city records are for your use as an official? Not for . . . politics? I'm sorry. I have to ask.'

'No,' Skovgaard said. 'You don't.'

'But . . .'

'Hartmann wants this done. Hartmann's the Mayor of Education. So . . .'

He still didn't budge.

'What's your name?'

'Olav Christensen.'

'Is this a problem, Olav? If it is say so. You've seen the polls, haven't you? You know Troels Hartmann's the next Lord Mayor?'

A thin, sarcastic smile.

'It's not my job to dabble in politics.'

'No. It's your job to do what you're asked. So get on with it before I find someone else.'

In a small storeroom off the library, surrounded by books about English, about physics, about art, Lund and Meyer began talking to teachers one by one. About Nanna, about Lisa Rasmussen, Oliver Schandorff and Jeppe Hald. But mostly about themselves. What they did the previous weekend, a question Meyer asked while Lund watched, thinking, listening. Hunting for a flaw.

He ate a banana. Drank two bottles of water, smoked constantly. Consumed two packs of cheese crisps, against her orders. Looked at her between the endless procession of teachers. Said little. Didn't need to.

There was nothing in these ordinary, decent, dedicated people. They were teachers. Nothing more. Or so it seemed.

Pernille Birk Larsen sat in the chilly kitchen, hands on the table they both made. Stared at Nanna's bedroom door, the marks there, the arrows.

Knew now this had to be done.

Heard him downstairs, talking to the men. Low gruff voice. The boss.

Walked into her room. So much gone. Nanna's books and diaries. The photos and notes had disappeared from the cork-board on the wall. The place stank from their chemicals, so strongly it overcame the waning fragrance of flowers. Their pens and brushes and markers stained the walls.

She fought to remember *before*.

Her daughter here, so full of life and energy.

Pernille sat on the bed, thinking.

This had to be done. *This had to be done.*

She went to the small wardrobe, looked in.

The smell of Nanna lingered. A perfume, gentle and exotic. More sophisticated than Pernille recalled.

That lingering thought afflicted her again . . . *You never really knew her.*

'But I did,' she said out loud. 'I do.'

That morning the medical examiner's office called. The body was to be released. A service was needed. A funeral. The last scene in the bleak extended ceremony of a violent and premature death.

In the bedroom, deep in the fragrances of the wardrobe, Pernille fought to remember the last time she chose Nanna's clothes. Even as a child at primary school, seven or eight, she made that decision for herself. So bright, so pretty, so self-confident . . .

Later she'd walk round the house choosing her own. Take things from Pernille's drawers. From Lotte's when she stayed there.

Nothing constrained Nanna. She was her own person. Had been from the moment she could speak.

And now a mother had to choose the last thing her child would wear. A robe for a coffin. A gown for fire and ashes.

Her fingers reached out and fluttered through the flimsy fabrics. Through flowery prints and shirts, through shifts and jeans. They fell upon a long white dress, seersucker, Indian, brown buttons down the front. Cheap in a late summer sale since no one would want it for the cold winter.

No one except Nanna, who would wear these bright things rain or shine. Who never felt the cold. Never cried much. Never complained.

Nanna . . .

Pernille clutched the soft material to her face.

Looked at the floral smock next to it. Wished she could face anything in the world but this.

Theis Birk Larsen sat in the office with the estate agent, looking at numbers and plans. The name Humleby sounded like a curse to him now. A black and vicious joke that life had waited to play.

'You stand to lose a lot,' the woman said. 'The rot. The condition . . .'

'How much?'

'I don't know exactly.'

Pernille was walking towards them, wide-eyed, chestnut hair

unkempt, face blank and pale and miserable. In her hands were two dresses: one white, one flowery.

'Maybe as much as half a million,' the estate agent said. 'Or you could go ahead and renovate it. Takes time but then you might . . .'

He was looking out through the glass door. Not listening.

The woman stopped. Saw. Got to her feet, embarrassed. Made the noises they both knew now. Hurried words, stuttering condolences. Then fled from the office.

Pernille watched her go, watched her husband snatch a cigarette from the pack on the desk, light it anxiously.

'Is there a problem, Theis?'

'No. It was about selling the house. It's in hand.'

He rifled through the papers.

She held up the dresses.

'I need to know.'

She lifted the white one then the flowered one, as if this were the prelude to an evening. One of the social occasions they never went to. A dinner. A dance.

'Which one?'

He looked for a second, no more.

'The white is nice.'

Sucked on his cigarette, stared at the desk.

'The white?'

'The white,' he said again.

Rama, the teacher they saw earlier in the week, was halfway through the list. Same questions. Same uninformative answers. The man was thirty-five. Had worked at the school for seven years.

They asked everyone: what did you make of Nanna?

'Outgoing, happy, clever . . .' Rama said.

Meyer rolled one of his pills onto the table, stared at it.

'You two had a good relationship?' Lund asked.

'Definitely. She was a very clever girl. Hard-working. Mature.'

'Did you see her outside school?'

'No. I don't socialize with pupils. I'm too busy.'

Meyer glugged down his tablet, lobbed the empty water bottle into a waste bin.

'My wife's pregnant,' Rama added. 'Almost due. She works here too. Part-time now. Finishing up.'

'That's nice,' Lund said.

Meyer broke in, asked, 'Did you see Nanna at the party?'

'No. I did the first shift. I left at eight.'

Lund said, 'That's all, thanks. Can you send in the next person?'

She laughed.

'I sound like a teacher.'

Meyer stared at the empty yellow skins on the table.

'Did you eat my bananas?' he demanded.

'One.'

He got up, went to the window cursing, lit a cigarette.

The teacher still sat there.

'There's one thing a while back. A few months ago Nanna wrote an essay. For a mock exam.'

Lund waited.

'She wrote a short story.'

'Why's this important?' Lund asked.

'Maybe it isn't.' Rama looked at her. 'It was about a secret affair. Between a married man and a young girl. It was very . . .'

The teacher was searching for the right word.

'It was very explicit. She wrote it as a piece of fiction. It bothered me.'

Meyer came back to the table, looked at him, asked, 'Why?'

'I read a lot of essays. It sounded to me as if she was talking about herself. Talking about something she'd done.'

'Explicit?' Lund asked.

'They had meetings. They had sex.'

'Why didn't you mention this before?'

He squirmed.

'I don't know if it's important or not.'

'We need to read it,' Meyer said.

'It should be in the storeroom with the others. It was a mock exam. We keep them.'

They waited.

'I can help you look if you like,' Rama said.

The officer from the education department returned with a pile of blue folders underneath his arm. Skovgaard thanked him. Smiled.

'What do they say?'

'Model school. Private. Not cheap.' He flicked through some

folders. 'The teachers seem well qualified and enthusiastic. The grades are good.'

She stared at the pile of documents.

'No complaints?'

'Nothing I can see. But I don't know what you're looking for.' He waited for a response. 'If I did—'

'It's just routine. We want to know everything's in order.'

Olav Christensen seemed pliable, willing to help, even though she'd leaned on him earlier.

'Everything to do with Troels is usually in order,' he said. 'I wish . . .' he nodded back towards Poul Bremer's office, 'it was the same everywhere. Maybe soon.'

She wondered why he'd suddenly turned helpful. Held up a folder. Said thanks.

Ninety minutes Lund and Meyer spent going through the filing cabinets. The teacher had to leave them to take a class. Then Rektor Koch walked in, scowled at Meyer's cigarette, said, 'Have you found it yet?'

'It's not here,' he said.

'It has to be here,' Koch insisted.

'It's . . . not . . . here. We've been through everything.'

Lund brought over a file box.

'This was open when we came to it.'

Koch checked the names on the label, people who'd used it and when.

'One of our teachers is a linguist. He's writing a paper on trends in language. Word usage. I gave him permission to go through anything he needed.'

'Name?' Meyer demanded.

There was a pause, an uneasy look on the woman's face.

'Henning Kofoed. I find it hard to believe he wouldn't put it back. He's usually very meticulous. A highly intelligent . . .'

'Why haven't we spoken to him?' Lund broke in.

'He wasn't one of Nanna's teachers. He only works in the mornings. He's . . .'

Lund picked up her phone, her notepad and her bag.

'We need his address,' she said.

*

161

Hard wood and wicker seats. Candles. Gold crosses. Dim lights. A crucifix.

Pernille and Theis Birk Larsen sat next to each other in silence. She clutched the white dress. Freshly washed, freshly pressed, it smelled of flowers and summer.

On the leaded windows above them the winter rain hammered in a constant rattle.

After a while a man emerged. Black suit, white beard, a kindly face, a fixed professional smile. He took the dress, complimented them on the choice. Said, 'Ten minutes.' Then left.

It seemed much longer. They moved from seat to seat, stared at the walls. He took out his black woollen hat, turned it in his fingers. She saw, and tried not to watch.

Then the undertaker returned. The door was half open. A pale gentle light beyond. He beckoned them through.

Afterwards, in the red van driving slowly on the shining city road, Pernille said, 'She looked beautiful.'

Theis Birk Larsen stared through the windscreen, out into the grey rain.

Her hand strayed out, touched the bristle of his sideburn, the rough familiar warmth of his cheek.

He smiled.

'We've got to pick up the Thermos flasks,' she said. 'We can borrow two from Lotte.'

He tapped at a light on the dashboard.

'I need some screen wash.'

A small filling station. Cars and vans. Men and women. The ordinary life, the mundane passage, the daily routine. All this swam around them as if nothing had happened. Nothing changed or broken or lost.

He didn't reach for the pump. Didn't do anything except march into the shop, race to the toilet.

There, in this anonymous place, door locked, in his black coat and woollen cap, Theis Birk Larsen crouched over the basin, sobbing, shaking, bawling like a child.

Twenty minutes she waited. No one approached. No one spoke. Then he came out pink-eyed, red-cheeked. Scraps of paper towel clung to his stubble where he'd wiped his face. Tears still lurked, grief still lingered.

In his hands was a small plastic bottle. Blue.

'Here,' he said and placed the screen wash in her lap.

Henning Kofoed's home was a one-room flat behind the station. As squalid a bachelor place as Lund had ever seen. Books were thrown everywhere, food rotted on unwashed plates in the kitchen. Kofoed was a shifty-looking forty-year-old with a straggly brown beard and unkempt hair. He sucked on a foul-smelling pipe and regarded them with suspicion the moment they arrived.

'Why should I have this paper?'

'Because you took it,' Meyer said. 'For your ... What is it? Linguistic study. That's about how people talk, right?'

'In a very crude fashion ...'

'In a very crude fashion let me say this ... Find the fucking paper, Henning.'

'I probably misplaced it. I'm sorry.'

There was a computer in the bedroom. Meyer went through and started nosing around. Kofoed followed getting edgier by the minute.

'Did you read what Nanna wrote?' Meyer asked.

'I ... I ... read lots of things.'

'Simple question. You don't need a degree in linguistics to comprehend it. Did you read Nanna's story?'

Silence.

'I specialize in language. I look at words. Not the sentence so much. Did you know the word ciabatta never existed ... ?'

Meyer clutched his fists together and swore.

'Forget about ciabatta, will you? Find us the damned essay.'

'OK, OK, OK.'

He meandered into the adjoining room, started sifting through a jumble of files and papers scattered everywhere. The place looked like a record office that had been hit by a bomb.

Meyer glanced at Lund, smiled, pointed to the floor.

'Did you throw it away?'

'I'd never do that.'

He bent down over a set of collapsed drawers. Retrieved a plastic document folder.

'Ah! I knew I had it.'

He handed it over.

'Sorry. I'll show you out.'

Kofoed walked to the door, opened it. Lund stood where she was.

'I think we need to talk,' she said.

'About what?'

Meyer held up one of the magazines he found on the floor beneath the computer.

Hot Teenagers.

'About young girls.'

The teacher sat on the computer chair in the bedroom watching Meyer sift through the magazines, flick open the photos.

He was sweating a lot and Lund had taken away his pipe.

'Where were you on Friday?' she asked.

'At a conference in the city. About the language of youth.'

'When did it end?'

'Ten p.m.'

'And then?'

'I came home.'

Meyer leaned on the door frame, alternately scowling at the magazines and then Kofoed.

'Are there any witnesses?'

'No. I live alone. I work mostly.'

'When you're not playing with yourself,' Meyer grunted. 'Or looking at your girls.'

The teacher bristled.

'I don't like your tone.'

Meyer shook his head.

'You don't like my tone? I could arrest you for this.'

'Those magazines aren't illegal. I bought them here. Anyone can.'

'You don't mind if we take your computer then. You've got a portable hard drive down there too. What fun and games will we find on there?'

Kofoed went quiet. Went back to sweating.

'Oh, Henning.' Meyer came and sat in front of him. 'Do you have any idea how guys like you get treated in prison?'

'I haven't done anything. I wasn't the one they pointed the finger at . . .'

'I'm pointing the finger!'

'Meyer!' Lund looked at the shaking teacher. 'What do you mean, Henning? Who got the finger pointed at him?'

Silence.

'We're trying to help,' she said. 'If someone was under suspicion we need to know.'

'It wasn't me—'

'So you keep telling us. Who was it?'

Scared man. But he didn't want to say it.

'I can't remember—'

'I'm taking the computer,' Meyer said. 'You're going to jail. No job. No teaching. No chance to get close to the girls in the corridor—'

'It's not like that! It wasn't me. The girl retracted everything . . .' He was close to weeping. 'He was cleared. He's a nice guy.'

Meyer picked up a magazine, waved it in his face.

'Who?'

'Rama,' Kofoed said.

He looked ashamed of himself. More ashamed than when Meyer pulled out the porn.

'The girl made it up. He's a nice man. Kind to everyone.'

'Just like you,' Meyer said and threw the mag in his face.

Pernille sat at the table trying to smile for the teacher, Rama. The handsome, polite one from the school. He'd brought flowers, photos, messages from the shrine. Took the chair opposite looking serious and sorrowful.

'They're a bit wilted. I'm sorry.'

She took them, knowing they'd go in the bin the moment he left. And that Rama understood this too.

'Some of Nanna's class would like to come to the funeral. If that's OK.'

'That's fine.'

Rama smiled a brief, melancholy smile.

'You can come too. Please.'

He seemed surprised. Did they think she wouldn't want a foreigner?

'Thank you. We'll all be there. I won't keep you any longer—'

'Don't go.'

He wanted to, she thought. But Pernille was past worrying about what others wanted any more.

'Can you tell me something about her?'

'Like what?'

'Something she did.'

He thought about the question.

'Philosophy. Nanna always loved that. She was really into Aristotle.'

'Who?'

'He was Greek. She was in our drama group.'

'Acting?'

She never mentioned this. Not once.

'I told them what Aristotle said about acting. She was very interested in that. She thought our plays should last from dawn till dusk. Just like the ancient Greeks.'

'She was a schoolgirl,' Pernille said, cross suddenly. 'She had a life. Here. A real one. It wasn't a dream. She didn't need to make something up.'

A mistake. He looked embarrassed.

'I think it was a joke.' Checked his watch. 'I'm sorry. I have to go. I work at a youth club. There's an appointment. I can't miss it.'

Pernille looked into his calm, dark face. Liked this man. Looked at the table. Ran her fingers across the dimpled lacquered surface, stared at the photos and the faces.

'We made this together. Planed the timber. Glued it. Stuck the photos.'

The wood felt smooth now and worn. It wasn't always. There were splinters. Tears sometimes.

'You're alone,' the teacher said. 'Is that—?'

'Theis is downstairs. In the office. Doing . . .'

It was dark in there when she answered the bell. Not a single light.

Doing what?

Smoking. Hugging a bottle of beer. Weeping.

'Paperwork,' she said.

It wasn't paperwork.

Birk Larsen sat still and silent in the dark office. The door opened. Vagn Skærbæk walked in, turned on the dim light by the notice-board. Keys in his hand. Checked the line of hooks on the wall. Found the right place. Kept things in order.

Didn't see the man in the black jacket hunched over the desk, cigarette in hand, bottle in fist until Birk Larsen grunted something wordless.

'Shit! You scared me.'

The figure didn't move.

'Are you OK, Theis?'

Turned on the main light. Walked forward, looked.

'I'll go and get Pernille.'

A strong hand reached out and held him.

Birk Larsen's eyes were pink and watery.

Drunk.

He said, 'A week ago I had a daughter. She walked out of here. Went to a party.'

'Theis . . .'

'I saw her again today.' The eyes beneath the black hat closed, tears squeezed between the lids. 'It wasn't really her. It was like something . . . Something . . .'

'I'm going to get Pernille. You don't drink any more either.'

'No!'

His voice was loud and fierce. Vagn Skærbæk knew not to ignore it.

'Theis. I got this friend Jannik. He heard something.'

Skærbæk hesitated. Felt Birk Larsen's eyes on him.

'Heard what?'

'Maybe nothing.'

Birk Larsen waited.

'Jannik's wife works at the school. He said the police came back again.' Hands fidgeting with the silver chain. 'They started questioning the staff. All Nanna's teachers.'

Another cigarette. Another pull at the beer. He gazed at Vagn Skærbæk.

'Maybe she knows more than he told me.' Skærbæk licked his lips. 'The police are useless shits. If they weren't you and me—'

'Don't talk of that,' Birk Larsen snarled. 'Those days are gone.'

'So you don't want me to talk to Jannik's wife?'

Birk Larsen sat on the hard seat, staring into space.

'Theis . . .'

'You do that.'

*

Elections played on ideas. Themes. Icons. Brands. So Troels Hartmann found himself that night putting on tennis shoes then walking in his office suit, out to the sports hall, Rie Skovgaard by his side.

Basketball was a young sport. He was the young candidate. A photo opportunity. A chance to shake hands.

'Frederiksholm's a model school,' she said. 'There's nothing on any of the teachers. I've been through every file. Lund's got them. We're in the clear.'

The smell of sweat, the sound of a ball bouncing on wood.

'You've got a photo shoot. Then we meet some of the role models. We get youth, we get recreation, we get community. One strike, three hits.'

Hartmann took off his jacket, pulled his shirt out of his trousers, rolled up his sleeves.

'When do the civil servants go home?'

'Concentrate on why we're here. These people are important for us.'

They walked into the hall. Figures playing. Black and white. Moving quickly, noisily.

'Morten told me he noticed a couple of civil servants working late. Why would they do that?'

'I don't know!'

'He says we need to watch them.'

'Morten's paid to run your campaign. Not offer you advice like that.'

'What if Bremer's got someone inside? Causing mischief? Leaking emails. Getting hold of my diary.'

'Leave me to worry about that. You're the candidate. The public face. I can handle the rest.'

Hartmann didn't move.

'I went out of my way to fix this opportunity,' Rie Skovgaard added. 'We've got every media outlet that matters out there. Try to smile for them, will you?'

Onto the floor. Strong handshakes. Friendly greetings. One by one Hartmann talked to them, Iranian and Chinese, Syrian and Iraqi. Danish now, working for his integration programme. Unpaid role models for the communities around them.

Two teams. One with a gap for him.

Hartmann tied his laces, looked at the opposition, said: 'Ready to be thrashed?'

For ten precious minutes this was all there was. Racing around the polished floor, throwing the ball. Passing it. Physical exertion. No thoughts. No strategies. No plans. Even the flash of the cameras didn't bother him. The Rådhus. The Liberal Party. Poul Bremer. Kirsten Eller. Even Rie Skovgaard. All of them were gone.

A break in play. The throw came to him. Hartmann dashed, dummied, bounced, launched.

Watched the ball turn slowly through the air, descend to the net, fall through.

A roar. He punched the air. Pure emotion. No thought in his head.

The cameras burst like lightning. Smiling he turned, high-fived the nearest player.

Captured for ever: two men grinning happily at one another. Troels Hartmann in a blue shirt, victorious. The teacher called Rama, clasping his hand.

'She walks down the corridor and finds the right hotel room. She's about to knock. She wonders if this is wrong. Should she have come? It's so different being with him. So different from everything at home. The garage she played in as a little girl with its smell of petrol. Her room and all her things. Far too many things because she can't throw anything out. The kitchen where she spent hours with her mum, dad and two brothers, where they celebrated birthdays, Christmas and Easter. At home she will always be a little girl. But now . . . here in the hotel corridor . . . she's a woman. She knocks. He answers.'

Feet up on her desk in her office Lund was reading Nanna's story. Meyer walked in, arms full of food.

'For your sake there'd better be a hot dog for me.'

'No. Kebab.'

'What kind?'

A shrug.

'The meat kind. It's a kebab, Lund.'

He placed a white plastic box on her desk, then a couple of pots of sauce.

'No name,' she said. 'No description. Just a secret man she meets at various hotels.'

They flipped up the boxes and started to eat.

'All we have,' she went on, 'is a pair of boots, an old essay and some gossip among the teachers.'

'It's not just gossip.' He pulled out his notebook. 'I spoke to Rektor Koch. Rama . . . or rather Rahman Al Kemal was involved in something a few years ago. A third-year student said he groped her.'

'What happened?'

'She withdrew the complaint. Koch thinks the kid had a crush on him. Made it up when he didn't play.'

Lund emptied the entire pot of hot sauce on her kebab and took a bite. Meyer watched in horror.

'Go careful with that stuff.'

'Nothing wrong with my stomach. Why tell us about the essay if it was him?'

'We'd have found it anyway. Let's talk to him. He said he was at home with his wife. We can check that.'

Lund sifted through the personnel records.

'That incident should have been written up in his file.'

'Dead right,' he agreed.

She was rifling through the papers.

'Don't waste your time, Lund. We never got his file. Hartmann's people sent over all the rest. Not his.'

She was thinking.

'We did ask for them all, didn't we?' Meyer asked.

'Of course we did.'

Lund picked up the remains of her kebab and got her jacket.

'Well?'

Outside Rama's block in Østerbro she called home, got Mark. Spoke to him in the cobbled street, Meyer listening, not discreetly either.

There was a party. She issued instructions. Go straight home afterwards. Call if he needed her.

'We're leaving tomorrow,' Lund said. 'Saturday night. I'll book the tickets.'

She looked at the phone.

'Mark? Mark?'

Put it in her pocket.

Meyer said, 'How old's your boy?'

'Twelve.'

'Want some advice?'

'Not really.'

'You need to listen to him. A kid of that age has got a lot on his plate. What with girls and all the rest. His brain . . .' Meyer's voice took on a different tone, one she didn't recognize. 'It's at a certain stage of development. Just listen to him.'

Lund strode ahead of him, trying not to get angry.

'He says I'm only interested in dead people.'

Meyer stopped, stuttered some words she didn't hear.

'Must be his brain,' Lund said. 'Number four, isn't it?'

They found the place and rang the bell.

A blonde woman, very pregnant, very tired, answered the door and let them in without an argument.

Rama wasn't there. She said he had an appointment at the local youth club.

'You teach at the school too?' Meyer asked.

It was a nice, modern flat, only half-renovated. Stripped walls, naked doors. Barely habitable.

'Yes. Just part-time at the moment. The baby . . .'

While he talked Lund wandered round, looking. They'd fallen into this routine easily, without talking about it. The pattern seemed to work.

'Did you know Nanna Birk Larsen?' he asked.

The slightest hesitation.

'She wasn't a student of mine.'

Pots of paint, rolls of carpet waiting to be laid. No photos. Nothing personal at all.

'Were you at the party last Friday?'

'No. I get tired easily.'

Lund found nothing of interest, wandered back to the main room where Meyer stood with Rama's wife.

'So you were at home?' he said.

'Yes. Well, I wasn't actually at home.'

Nothing more.

171

Meyer took a deep breath and said, 'So you *weren't* at home?'

'We've got a little cottage on some allotments outside Dragør. We were there all weekend.'

Dragør. The other side of Kastrup. Not more than ten or fifteen minutes by car from where Nanna was found.

'This place is a mess,' she added. 'The floors were being sanded. We couldn't stay.'

'Ah.' Meyer nodded. His ears, Lund thought, looked bigger when he was curious. Which seemed impossible. 'So you were both there?'

'Rama picked me up at half past eight. We drove out there.'

'Let me get this straight . . .'

A lot bigger, Lund realized.

'You and your husband spent the weekend at your allotment?'

'Yes. Why do you ask?'

'No reason. I thought you might know something about the party at school.'

'Nothing, sorry.'

Lund walked towards the window. Felt her shoe stub against something. A roll of carpet. What looked like some blinds.

A black circle of plastic was curled on the floor. She bent down, picked it up. Thought of Nanna in the back of her car. Ankles tied. Wrists tied. By something like this.

Meyer said they used them in gardens. To secure building material too. For lots of things.

Lund took out an evidence bag, dropped in the tie.

'Do you want to talk to him again?' the woman asked.

'Not at the moment,' Meyer said, packing his notebook.

Lund came back and asked, 'Can I use the toilet?'

'Through there. I'll show you—'

'No need. I'll find it.'

'Your first child?' Meyer asked.

'Yes.'

Lund walked on. Still heard them.

'It's a girl.'

Meyer's voice brightened.

'A girl! Really! That's great. And you know too. Did you want to? Me, I like surprises . . .'

Plastic sheeting everywhere. A set of coat hooks. A painting.

'I could give you some good tips if you're interested.' Meyer's voice sounded cheery. 'The first few months . . . You need to make him work.'

Lund heard her laugh.

'You don't know my husband. He'll work. I won't need to ask.'

Very quietly Lund walked into the bedroom. Clothes. Photos. Rama younger, bare-chested, smiling in what looked like a swimming team. Army insignia behind. A military pool perhaps. Good-looking man. Fit and muscular. A calendar. A school timetable.

Lund looked in the en suite bathroom. New sink, new toilet. Bare walls. There was another room. The sign on the door said 'Nursery'.

It was dark. Just enough light from the street to see. Junk in the corner. Men's toys. A sports kite. A speedboat.

By the window a pair of men's hiking boots. She picked them up, looked at the sole, felt the mud there, rubbed it between her fingers.

Thought of the canal and the woods. And Dragør close by.

There was a bottle on an upturned box. White label, brown glass. Lund picked it up, made a note.

A cross voice behind said, 'You walked past the toilet.'

The bottle went back. The bag with the tie she slid into her pocket.

'Thanks,' Lund said and went straight back to the hall. Then took Meyer outside.

Rektor Koch was in Hartmann's office, Rie Skovgaard and Morten Weber listening.

'They suspect one of our teachers,' she said. 'You need to tell me what to do.'

'What do you mean?' Hartmann asked.

'They called me just now. Asking questions. They seem to know—'

'Know what? We've an agreement with the police. They'll talk to us first.'

'They seem to know something.' She squirmed on the seat. 'I don't want any damage. We've had enough bad publicity as it is. Should I suspend him?'

'Have they taken anyone in for questioning?'

'They're going to. A particular teacher. There was an old incident.'

'What incident?' Skovgaard cut in. 'I checked the files. There was nothing there.'

'It was . . . unproven,' Koch insisted. 'But it was on the files. I wrote it myself. Nonsense on the part of a stupid girl. The teacher was innocent I'm sure. The police only started to look at him because he was Nanna's form tutor.'

Hartmann asked, 'So that's why they're interested?'

'What other reason could there be?'

No answer.

Koch looked at the two of them.

'I've explained the situation to you. I've done my duty. It's your responsibility if the police or the newspapers come looking—'

'Don't worry about that,' Hartmann said with a wave of his hand. 'Give me his name. I'll talk to the police. I'm sure this is nothing.'

He got a pen.

'His name is Rama. We call him that. His full name is Rahman Al Kemal.'

She spelled it out. Hartmann started writing. Stopped.

'And he's a teacher at Frederiksholm?'

'I just told you.'

'And they're asking about him?'

An impatient sigh.

'Yes. That's why I'm here.'

He looked at Skovgaard. She frowned, shook her head.

'Is something wrong?' Koch asked.

'No. I just wanted to be sure. Will you . . . ?' He looked at her. 'Please step outside. Help yourself to a coffee. I'll be with you in a moment.'

He closed the door. Skovgaard got up.

'What's going on here?' Morten Weber asked.

'I just shook hands with a role model called Rama,' Hartmann said. 'At the youth club.'

'What?'

Weber glared at Skovgaard.

'He met a teacher from that school? And you didn't know?'

'I didn't see a teacher's name on the list. I went through every file myself. Troels wouldn't have been in the same room if I thought there was something wrong.'

'But there is something wrong!' Weber cried.

'Every single file, Morten!'

Hartmann watched them, torn, not wanting to take sides.

'Who gave you the files?' Weber asked.

Skovgaard swore under her breath.

'One of the civil servants in administration.'

Weber threw up his hands in exasperation.

'I told you!'

'They gave me the files. I looked at them. What else was I supposed to do? What . . . ?'

Weber was on his feet, red-faced, screaming.

'You could come to me, Rie. You could ask a question once in a while. Instead of marching off and doing whatever comes into your vapid little head—'

'Morten,' Hartmann intervened. 'Calm down.'

'Calm down? Calm down?' He pointed to the door. 'I've spent twenty years working these corridors. She comes from selling soap powder, spends ten minutes here and thinks she knows it all—'

'Morten!' Hartmann's voice silenced him. 'That's enough.'

'Yeah, Troels. It's enough.' Weber got hold of his bag. Stuffed in his papers with a shaking hand. 'Let's face it. If this election's going to be run from between your bedsheets there's not much room for me—'

Hartmann was on him, furious, fist in his face.

'I don't care how long I've known you. I won't take that. Get out of here. Go home.'

Weber did that. No more speeches. No more hurled insults. Picked up his bag and left.

Rie Skovgaard watched.

Then when Weber had left said thanks.

'I should have listened to him though,' Hartmann said. 'Shouldn't I?'

'I guess,' she agreed.

The car back from Østerbro.

'We need to check his past,' Lund said. 'He hasn't always been a teacher. Check his allotment and his alibi.'

She pulled out the plastic evidence bag.

'This goes to the lab. He's got a bottle of ether. I wrote down the brand name. Find out if it's the same kind that was found on the girl.'

Meyer wasn't happy. For a change.

'With all that evidence why didn't we wait until he got home? Now he can get rid of everything.'

Her phone was ringing. Hartmann was in the contacts list by now. She could see it was him.

Lund passed the mobile to Meyer.

'It's Poster Boy. You talk to him. He probably wants to complain.'

'Not the only one, Lund. What time's your plane tomorrow? Do you need a lift to Kastrup?'

Bedtime stories. Pernille reading. The boys in their pyjamas, chests against the soft duvets, elbows on the bed, waggling their feet.

'Is Nanna in the coffin?' Anton asked when she closed the book.

Pernille nodded, tried to smile.

'Is she going to be an angel?'

A long wait.

'Yes. She is.'

Bright baffled faces gazed at her.

'Tomorrow we say goodbye to Nanna. Then—'

'Some of the children at school are saying things.'

Anton's feet moved a little faster.

'What sort of things?'

'Someone killed her.'

Emil added, 'And there was a man who did something bad.'

'Who said that?'

'Some children in the class.'

She took their hands, gently squeezed their small fingers, looked into their sparkling eyes. Could think of nothing to say.

Five minutes later they were tucked up and quiet. She heard Theis moving, went downstairs. The garage was filled with furniture. Rented tables and chairs. He stacked and moved some, picked up more in one hand than most men could with two.

'The boys wanted to say goodnight.'

He heaved a table across the room.

'I had to get on with this.'

'They hear things at school.'

Nothing.

Pernille's hand went to her neck.

'I said it was the bogeyman.'

A trellis table. More chairs.

'Theis. I'm not sure it's a good idea to take them to the funeral. I mean . . .'

He didn't listen, didn't turn to look at her.

'They should say goodbye, I know. But there'll be so many people.'

A box of plastic plates and cutlery. He wiped his brow.

'I don't know how you and I will . . .'

The table he'd moved from right to left he now moved back where it came from.

'Would you please stop doing that?'

He put it down, looked at her in silence.

In the pocket of the blue checked shirt his phone trilled.

Birk Larsen listened.

'I'll find out more from Jannik tomorrow,' Vagn Skærbæk said. 'The woman hasn't heard anything new. I'll try.'

'OK.'

'So you need any help tonight?'

'No. See you tomorrow.'

When he came off the phone the garage was empty. He watched Pernille walk up the stairs. Then went back to moving tables, stacking chairs.

Mark seemed animated. As if he saw an opportunity.

'So if we're not going—'

'We are going,' Lund insisted. 'Bengt is having a house-warming party.'

Her mother was ironing. She was packing clothes, throwing them into an empty suitcase, squashing them down with her palms and elbows, ready to sit on the thing if need be.

'What if—?'

'Mark! There's no what if. We leave tomorrow. Gran's coming with us for a few days. That's it—'

Her phone rang. Bengt. Sounding anxious.

'Everything's fine,' Lund told him. 'Under control. We'll see you tomorrow night. We've almost finished packing . . .'

She covered the mouthpiece, mouthed at Mark, 'Pack!'

Then listened, heard a sound at the door. Vibeke answered. Lund looked. Troels Hartmann was standing there in a black winter coat looking every inch the politician.

Bengt said something she didn't quite hear.

'Of course I'm listening,' Lund said.

She took the call into the other room, watched as Vibeke got Hartmann folding a long tablecloth for the new house.

In Sweden.

The new life.

'Bengt,' Lund said. 'I've got to go.'

When she came back into the room Vibeke was asking him, 'So are you the coroner?'

'No,' Hartmann said, holding the long white piece of cotton.

'You've never folded a good tablecloth before,' Vibeke told him, shaking her head. 'I can see that. Look—'

'Mum. I don't think Troels Hartmann has time for that.'

Vibeke's mouth fell open.

'Hartmann?' She looked him up and down. 'You're different on the posters.'

In the kitchen, the two of them alone, he shook his head, like a man disappointed.

'You promised you'd keep me informed.'

'I didn't promise anything.'

She got a slice of bread, plastered on some butter and cheese, bit into it while he rambled angrily.

'You're looking at one of my teachers now. I had to hear about that from the school.'

Mouth half full, she asked him, 'Why did you tell your people not to give us Kemal's file? Where's the cooperation there?'

He shook his head, said nothing.

'We asked for all the files. On all the teachers, Hartmann. Why didn't we get his?'

'It's the first I knew about it. Believe me.'

'How come? You're the boss, aren't you?'

She finished the cheese, put the plate in the sink.

'Yes, OK, it doesn't look good. What do you want me to do?'

She raised an eyebrow, dried some dishes with a cloth.

'Cooperate.'

'I'm trying! I don't know why I didn't get his file.' Then, a tone lower, 'I don't know what's going on here. There's something, someone, in my office . . .'

Lund looked interested.

'Doing what?'

'I don't know,' Hartmann said. 'Snooping. Seeing things they shouldn't. It's an election. You expect dirt to fly. But not . . .'

He looked at her.

'If someone's broken into our system that's a crime, right?'

'If—'

'There's something going on. You could take a look—'

'I'm a homicide detective,' Lund cut in. 'Trying to find who raped and murdered a young girl. I don't do office work. And I want that file.'

'Fine.' He looked furious. Desperate too. 'I'll get it. There must be a duplicate. Somewhere.'

'Is there something special about Kemal?' she asked.

'He's one of our role models. He helps young immigrants who've got into trouble. I've got his party records for that. He's—'

'So if he did it you'll look bad? Is that it?'

Hartmann scowled at her.

'It damages your campaign.' She picked up an apple, thought about it, grabbed a bag of potato crisps instead. 'You lose votes.'

'You don't have a very high opinion of me, do you?'

Lund offered him a crisp.

'If this is your man that's all there is to it,' Hartmann said. 'No one in my office will stand in your way. I just want to know.'

'Is that all?'

He brightened a little.

'Yes. That's all. Your turn now.'

She laughed.

'What is this? A game? I've nothing to tell you. Kemal's one line of inquiry. There are questions we need answered. Where he was . . .'

'Fine. I'll have him suspended.'

'You can't do that. We don't have enough to arrest him.'

Lund got herself a bottle of milk from the fridge, sniffed it, poured herself a glass.

'You can't,' she repeated. 'I know you want a yes or no. I can't say yet.'

'When?'

Lund shrugged.

'I'm handing the case over to a colleague tomorrow.'

'Is he reliable?'

'Unlike me?'

'Unlike you.'

She toasted him.

'He's very reliable. You're going to love him.'

Eleven in the evening in Hartmann's private office. Under the blue light of the hotel sign he met Rie Skovgaard. She took one look at him and said, 'It's that bad?'

He threw his coat on the desk.

'I don't know exactly. Lund won't tell me anything she doesn't want to. They seem to think it's him. She just won't say it.'

Skovgaard checked her laptop.

'The pictures they took tonight are going out. I can't stop that. But no one knows he was a suspect, any more than you did when you shook his hand.'

'Who kept back that file?'

'I'm looking into it.'

She threw a set of dummy ads on the table. Foreign faces alongside white ones. Smiling. Together.

'The next run of the campaign was all about integration. We pushed the role model idea a lot. I'm going to pull them. We'll stop using the term. Focus on other issues till this blows over.'

'The debate tomorrow—'

'I'll get you out of it. This is a gift to Bremer. Let me make some calls.'

Skovgaard walked to her desk, picked up the phone.

'No.' Hartmann watched her. Still dialling. He walked over, put the phone back on the hook. 'I said no. The debate goes ahead.'

'Troels—'

'This is one man. A suspect. He hasn't been found guilty and even if he is that doesn't say anything about all the other role models. They've done plenty of good work. I won't let them be slandered through this.'

'Oh fine words!' she yelled at him. 'I hope they sound good when we lose.'

'This is what we're about. What I'm about. I have to stand by what I believe—'

'You have to win, Troels. If you don't it doesn't matter a shit.'

He was getting mad now. Wished he'd expended some of this on

Lund, watching him all the time with those glittering eyes while she munched on a sandwich and gulped at her milk.

'We owe these people something. Day in, day out, they work with these kids. Do things you wouldn't dream of. Me neither.'

He picked up a stash of papers, threw them at her.

'We've got the statistics. The proof it works.'

'The press . . .' she began.

'To hell with the press!'

'They'll crucify us if he did it!' She got up, came to him, put her arms on his shoulders. 'They'll crucify you. Like they did your father. This is politics, Troels. Save your fine words for speeches. If I've got to go into the gutter to get you into that chair I'll do it. That's what you pay me for.'

Hartmann turned away, looked out at the night beyond the window.

Her hand came to his hair.

'Come home with me, Troels. We can talk about it there.'

A moment of silence between them. An instant of indecision, of doubt.

Then Hartmann kissed her forehead.

'There's nothing to talk about. We're going ahead as planned. Everything. The posters. The debate. Nothing changes.'

Eyes closed, fingers at her pale temple.

'The civil servant who brought you the school files . . .' Hartmann said.

'What about him?'

'Make some room in my schedule. Tomorrow. I want to see him.'

Saturday, 8th November

Lund was pinning pictures of Kemal on the board, listening to Meyer read out what he'd found. Ten officers in the room, Buchard on his feet at the head of the table.

'Born in Syria. Damascus. Fled with his family when he was twelve. His father's an imam and frequents the Copenhagen mosque.'

Meyer looked around them.

'Apparently Kemal has severed ties with his family. They think he's too Western. Danish wife. No religion. After school and national service he became a professional soldier.'

Pictures of him smiling in a blue beret.

'Then he went to university and completed his Masters. Joined the school seven years ago. Two years ago he married a colleague. The school says he's popular. Well-respected—'

Buchard cut in, shaking his head.

'This doesn't sound like the kind of man—'

'He was accused of molesting a girl,' Lund said. 'No one wanted to believe it at the time.'

The chief still looked unconvinced.

'What does the girl say?'

'We can't reach her. She's backpacking in Asia.'

Meyer held up the evidence bag with the plastic tie.

'Lund found this in Kemal's apartment. It matches the one used on the girl.'

'And you've got ether too?' Buchard asked. He scratched his pug head. 'Lots of people use those ties. Ether . . . I don't know. This isn't enough.'

'We'll run through his alibi,' Lund said. She unsealed the first of a set of envelopes. Photos of Nanna. 'I want these pictures distributed around all the city hotels. She went somewhere.'

'Put a team on Kemal,' Buchard ordered. 'So we know what he's doing. Not too close. The funeral's today. We don't want to disturb the family.'

The chief cast his beady eyes around the table.

'It's bad enough as it is. Let's not make things worse.'

Twenty minutes later Lund and Meyer sat down to interview Stefan Petersen, a podgy, retired plumber who had one of the little houses on the allotments on the edge of Dragør.

'I've got number twelve. He's got number fourteen. In a year's time I'll have been there long enough to live in it all year round,' he said proudly. 'Can't choose your neighbours. But it's a nice place all the same.'

Meyer asked, 'On Friday? Did you see Kemal and his wife arrive?'

'Oh yes.' Petersen's attention was fully on him, not Lund. He liked talking to a man. 'About eight or nine I think. I saw something else later too.'

He looked pleased with himself.

'It's because I smoke cigarillos.' Petersen pulled out a packet of small cigars. 'Mind if I—?'

'Damned right I mind,' Meyer barked at him. 'Put those things away. What did you see?'

'Smoke if you want,' Lund said, taking a lighter out of his bag, flicking it for him.

The fat plumber grinned and lit up.

'Like I was saying . . . I'm a smoker. But the missus won't let me have a cigarillo indoors. So I sit on the patio. Rain or shine. There's a roof.'

Lund smiled at him.

'The Arab came out of his house. And drove away.'

'Kemal, you mean?'

He looked at Meyer as if she was being dim.

'What time was that?' Lund asked.

He thought about this, wreathed in a cloud of stinking fumes.

'I watched the weather forecast afterwards so it must have been about half past nine.'

'Did you see the car return?'

'I don't stay out all night. But it was there the next morning.'

She got up, shook his hand, said thanks.

When the plumber was gone Meyer marched up and down the office, as if claiming it for himself.

Lund leaned on the door, watching.

'Why would Kemal's wife lie about his whereabouts?' she asked.

'Let's find out.'

'We wait until after the funeral.'

'Why? Do you want me to call Hartmann and ask his permission?'

Buchard was at the door.

'Lund,' he said, jerking his thumb towards his office.

'What about me?' Meyer asked.

'What about you?'

She went to get away from the plumber's cigarillo smoke.

'The answer's no,' Lund said before Buchard got out a word.

'Listen to me—'

183

'I can help you by email. Or over the phone. Maybe pop over once in a while.'

'Let me speak,' the old man pleaded. 'That's not it. Did you check out the father?'

'Of course I checked out the father!'

'What did you find out?'

She frowned, trying to remember.

'Not much. Nothing interesting. Minor offences. Stolen goods. Bar brawls. It was twenty years ago. Why?'

Buchard helped himself to some water. He looked tired and sick.

'I got a call from a retired DCI. You know the kind. Nothing better to do than read the papers.'

He passed her a note.

'He says Birk Larsen was dangerous. Really dangerous.'

'Anything sexual?'

'Not that he'd heard. But he said we didn't know the half of it.'

'So what? We checked. He's got an alibi. It can't be him.'

'You're sure?'

Sure.

There was a word. Everyone wanted to be sure. No one was really. Because people lied. To others. To themselves sometimes. She even did it herself.

'I'm sure,' she said.

In the kitchen the boys ran around, Vagn's little cars in their hands. Theis Birk Larsen in black, ironed white shirt, funeral tie. Talking on the phone. Of Thermos flasks and tables, sandwiches and what to drink.

Anton stumbled, knocked a vase to the floor. The last of Nanna's flowers. Pink roses, more stalk than petal.

Stood with his brother, both heads down. Waiting for the storm to break.

'Go and wait in the garage,' Birk Larsen said. Not severely.

'I didn't mean . . .' the child started.

'Go and wait in the garage!' Their things were on the table. 'And don't forget your coats.'

When they left he heard the radio news. The first item: Nanna's funeral at St John's Church. As if she belonged to them all now. Not

184

the family that used to eat around the table, in the bright light of the window, thinking nothing would ever change.

'Many people have arrived to pay their respects,' the announcer went on. 'Outside there's—'

He turned it off. Tried to still his thoughts. Called, 'Sweetheart?'

An old word. One he'd used since she was a mouthy, pushy teenager looking for excitement. A glimpse of the rough world outside the middle classes where she belonged.

He remembered her clearly. Saw himself too. A thug, a thief. A villain. Getting tired of that life. Looking for a rock. Looking to be one himself.

'Sweetheart?'

It was her from the start. She saved him. In return . . .

A family. A home. A small removals firm built from nothing, their name on the side. It seemed so much. All he could hope to offer. All he had to give.

Still she didn't answer. He walked into the bedroom. Pernille sat naked and hunched on the bed. On her upper left arm, still vivid and blue as the day she got it, sat a tattooed rose. He remembered when she went down the hippie parlour in Christiania. They'd been smoking. He'd been dealing, not that she knew. It was Pernille's way of saying, 'I'm yours now. Part of that life you have. Part of you.'

He hated that rose and never said so. What he wanted of her were the very things she took for granted. Her decency, her honesty, her integrity. Her infinite capacity for blind, inexplicable love.

'Are you coming?'

The black dress lay on the bed with her underwear. A black bag. Black tights.

'I can't decide what to wear.'

Birk Larsen stared at the clothes on the duvet.

'I know . . .' she began.

Voice cracked, tears starting.

He heard himself shrieking inside.

'It doesn't matter, does it, Theis? Nothing does.'

Her hands went to her brushed chestnut hair.

'I can't do this. I can't go.'

He thought, as best he could.

'Maybe Lotte can help.'

She didn't hear. Pernille's eyes were fixed on the mirror: a naked woman in middle age, body getting flabby, breasts loose. Stomach stretched by children. Marked by motherhood. How it should be.

'The flowers should be right . . .' she murmured.

'They will be. We'll get through this.'

Birk Larsen bent down, picked up the black dress, held it out.

'We'll get through this,' he said. 'OK?'

Downstairs Vagn Skærbæk sat with the boys. Out of his red overalls. Black shirt, silver chain, black jeans.

'Anton. It was just a vase. Don't worry.'

Birk Larsen heard this as he walked through the round tables and chairs, looked at the white porcelain plates they'd rented, the glasses, the food under foil at the side.

'I broke a bottle once,' Skærbæk said. 'I did lots of stupid things. We all do.'

'We need to get in the car,' Birk Larsen ordered. 'We're leaving.'

The boys moved quickly, heads down, not a word.

Skærbæk looked at him.

'What about Pernille?'

'Her sister's going to take her.'

'Isn't Mum coming?' Anton asked, climbing into the car.

'Not with us.'

Skærbæk said, 'Theis, I was thinking . . . The woman at the school. It's best I don't talk to her.'

'Why not?'

Skærbæk shrugged.

'You've got a lot on your plate. Maybe she doesn't know a thing. Just gossip.'

'That's not what you said last night.'

'I know but . . .'

Birk Larsen bristled, stared at Skærbæk, a smaller man. A weaker man. This was always their relationship. One cemented by violence, by fists in the early days.

Finger in Skærbæk's face he said, 'I want to know.'

The civil servant called Olav Christensen was in Hartmann's office, looking at the campaign posters. About role models. Integration. The future.

Twenty-eight but he seemed younger. Fresh-faced. Biddable.

He was sweating.

'We have a small problem,' Hartmann said. 'The files you gave us on the teachers.'

A baffled smile.

'What about them?'

'One was missing.'

A pause.

'Missing?'

'It doesn't look good, does it, Olav? I mean we ask. You deliver.' Hartmann stared at him. 'That's the way it works, doesn't it?'

Christensen said nothing.

'I'm going to be boss of you and everyone who owns you soon. How about an answer?'

'Maybe it got lost when we moved the archives.'

'Maybe?'

'That's what I said.'

'This is the Rådhus. We've got documents going back a century. All kept in locked cabinets.'

Hartmann waited.

'They are,' Christensen agreed.

'There are no cabinets missing,' Skovgaard chipped in. 'Or reports of lost files. I asked your boss. He's sure of it.'

'Maybe there was an error made with the filing.'

The two of them waited.

'We have these trainees. Kids. I'm sorry. Mistakes happen.'

Hartmann got up, went to the window, looked out.

'Funny the one file they should lose is the one we wanted. The one that could embarrass us. The police needed that, Olav. They think I held it back. They think I've got something to hide.'

Christensen listened, nodded.

'I'll find out what happened and get back to you.'

'No,' Hartmann said. 'Don't trouble yourself.'

He came and stood very close to the man.

'Here's what happens,' Hartmann said. 'On Monday we order a formal inquiry. We get to the bottom of this. That's for sure.'

'An inquiry?'

Rabbit in the headlamps. Deer in the sights.

'But if the file turns up,' Hartmann added. 'It won't matter, will it?'

'I don't know anything about this.'

'Well. Then we're done.'

They watched him go.

'I remember him now,' Hartmann said. 'He applied for the job of director last year. Cocky little bastard. I didn't even put him on the short list. He's getting his own back.'

'You think he's doing favours for Bremer?'

'I don't know. He's got access to our network. Make everyone change their passwords. Let's take care.'

Hartmann looked out into the main office.

'Where the hell's Morten? I know I bit his head off but—'

'He called in sick. He's not a well man, Troels. He shouldn't be doing a job like this.'

'He's diabetic. It comes and goes. His moods are unpredictable sometimes. You learn to live with it.'

She came and sat on the edge of the sofa.

'I've been here five months. How long's Morten worked for you?'

He had to think.

'Off and on? For ever.'

'And how long have people regarded you as a serious contender to be Lord Mayor?'

Ambition. She was never short of it. Ambition was a good thing. Nothing happened without it.

Her hand fell on his cheek.

'We'll get by without Morten,' Rie Skovgaard said. 'Don't worry.'

It was bright and cold outside. A sharp winter sun. Weekend shoppers. Families out for the day.

Olav Christensen walked into the square and called.

'I want that file back,' he said.

Things were changing in City Hall. No one knew which way they'd go.

Silence on the line.

'Did you hear me?'

He was getting mad, which maybe wasn't such a good idea. But he couldn't help it. Hartmann was no fool. No naive good guy either. Christensen could see that in his eyes.

An inquiry . . .

Documents got tagged, counted in, counted out. It would take a day to discover that he'd retrieved the Kemal file along with all the others. Seen the trouble it might cause. Put it to one side just in case.

There was no way out. No excuse. No lie he could invent.

His head would be on the line in an instant. Career down the drain.

Still not a word.

'I did a big favour for you, man!' A kid walking past with a couple of red balloons stared at him for yelling. 'Don't screw me around. I want some help here. I told you before. I don't go down on my own.'

That was stupid. It sounded like a warning. Olav Christensen knew exactly who he was dealing with. Someone who issued threats, didn't take them.

'Look . . . What I'm trying to say is . . .'

He listened. Nothing there. Not even the slow rhythmic sound of his breathing.

'Hello?' he said. 'Hello?'

Brown brick spire against a pale blue sky. Bells in tumbling chimes. Cameras outside. Crowds in the street.

Lund thought of the case, of the investigations ahead.

Was he here too? The man who held Nanna hostage, raped her repeatedly, beat her, tormented the girl for hours on end? Forensics were getting somewhere. The soap on her skin was recent and unlike anything at home. There was blood beneath the mud in her nails, skin cut clumsily by scissors or clippers. How many explanations were there? Just one. He'd bathed her somewhere, washed clean her bruised, torn skin, clipped her fingernails as she fought him. Then set her running through the dark woods barefoot in her scanty slip. Until . . .

Hide and seek.

Meyer said that and Meyer was no fool.

This was a game. Not quite real. When he locked her alive in the boot of Troels Hartmann's campaign car and sent her screaming into that distant canal, he watched. The way another might enjoy a movie. Or a road accident.

Or a funeral.

A savage, unreal game.

What did he look like?

Ordinary. Criminals weren't a race apart, marked by scars or strange physical afflictions. Separate from their victims. They were one with them. A stranger on a bus. A man in a shop who says hello every morning.

Or a teacher who came to the same school day after day, impressed everyone with his honesty, remarkable only for his apparent decency in a world where few cared.

Lund looked around as she always did, lustrous eyes roaming. Looked and imagined.

Monstrous deeds had no need of monsters. They were the work of the everyday and the undistinguished. Cruel tears in the fabric of a society struggling to be whole. Wounds in the city's communal body, bleeding and painful.

She observed the sea of faces around her as she walked, found a space in the darkness by a pillar, sat down.

A place from which she could watch unseen.

The organ struck up wheezing. An old hymn. Lines from a Christmas carol she could barely remember.

Lund did not sing.

Lisa Rasmussen, across the aisle, did not sing.

Birk Larsen's right-hand man from the garage, Vagn Skærbæk, face streaming with tears, black hat clutched to his chest, did not sing.

The teacher known as Rama, seated in a pew with his pupils, did not sing.

At the front, seated by the white coffin, Pernille and Theis Birk Larsen did not sing, but sat with their boys looking lost, as if everything – the church, the people, the music, but most of all the shining white coffin that sat by their side – was unreal.

The priest. A thin man, with a craggy, miserable face. In black with a white ruff round his neck, he emerged from the gloom by the altar, glanced at the casket with its rose wreath, gazed slowly round the packed and silent rows ahead.

Said in a ringing, loud, theatrical voice, 'Today we bid farewell to a young woman. She was taken from us far too young.'

Hidden in the shadows Lund looked at the parents. Pernille dabbing at her eyes. Her husband, a lion of a man, a grizzled old beast. Head down, face rigid, staring at the stone floor.

'It's most unfair,' the priest said in a tone that reminded Lund of a letter to the bank. 'Beyond comprehension.'

She shook her head. No. This was untrue. It had to be.

'So we ask ourselves – what is the meaning?'

Kemal – Rama, she still thought of him this way – was three rows back in a black suit and white shirt. Dark hair clipped close.

'We question our faith, our trust in one another.'

Lund took a deep breath, closed her eyes.

'And we ask – how are we to move on?'

She stiffened at that dread, deceptive phrase. Loathed it with a vengeance. No one moved on. They swallowed their grief. They hoped to bury it. But it lived with them. Always would. A cross they had to bear. A constant, recurring nightmare.

'Christianity is about peace. Reconciliation and forgiveness. But it's not easy to forgive.'

Lund nodded. Thought: right there.

His voice took on a high, ethereal tone.

'Yet when we forgive, the past no longer controls us. And we can live in freedom.'

Lund looked at the man, in his black robe, white ruff. Wondered: what would he say if he was there by the canal that bleak cold night? Watching Theis Birk Larsen scream and rage. Watching Nanna's dead limbs tumble from the boot with the filthy rank water, seeing the black line of snaking eels writhe down her naked legs.

Would he forgive? Could he?

The organ struck up. She noted who sang and who did not. Then Sarah Lund walked outside.

They knew the teacher would be at the funeral. So Meyer went to the apartment to talk to his wife.

Midday and she was in a bulging white nightdress and black cardigan.

Didn't take long to get her talking about the accusation from the girl a few years back.

'It's a stupid old story,' she said. 'There's nothing to tell.'

'Rektor Koch wrote a report.'

'The kid made it up. She admitted it.'

'We spoke to a man from the allotments at Dragør. The plumber.'

Kemal's wife grimaced.

'He saw your husband go out about half past nine on Friday night.'

'He hates us. Doesn't mind borrowing our hedge trimmer. I always have to ask for it back.'

Meyer asked himself: what would Lund do?

'Did your husband go out?'

'Yes. He drove to the petrol station.'

'When did he get back?'

'About fifteen minutes later, I suppose. I went to bed while he was out. I was very tired.'

'I can imagine. When did you see him again?'

'About three. I woke up. He was lying next to me.'

Meyer thought about Lund's long pauses. That relentless, glittering stare.

He took off his anorak. The woman's eyes were fixed on the gun on his hip.

'So you didn't see him between half past nine and three the next morning?'

'No. But I'm sure he was there. He likes to read or watch TV.'

She smiled at him.

'Do you have a wife?'

'Yes.'

'Do you know when she's in the house? Can't you feel . . . ?'

Meyer didn't answer. Instead he said, 'Were you there all weekend? While the floors were being sanded?'

'That's right. The workmen were being difficult.'

He got up, started walking round the room, checking out the building material.

Looking.

'In what way?'

'They didn't turn up. Rama had to sand the floors himself. On Sunday he spent all day putting up new tiles in the bathroom.'

'So he was gone all day Saturday and Sunday? Did he leave first thing?'

She hugged herself inside the cardigan.

'I think you should go now.'

'Was he gone from six in the morning until eight in the evening?'

The woman got up, got angry.

'Why are you asking me these questions when you don't believe a word I tell you? Please. Leave.'

Meyer got his jacket. Said, 'OK.'

Forgive us our trespasses.

Pernille barely heard the Lord's prayer, the one she'd listened to, recited since she was a girl.

As we forgive those who trespass against us.

All she saw was the shiny white wood. The flowers, the notes. The coffin that hid the truth. Inside . . .

Lead us not into temptation but deliver us from evil.

Anton nudged her, asked in a clear, young voice, 'Why doesn't Dad have his hands together?'

Forever and ever.

'Shush,' she said, putting a finger to her lips.

'Why don't you?' asked Emil, staring at her hands.

The boys were in their best clothes, fingertips pressed together.

Her eyes filled with tears. Her mind with such memories.

Amen.

The sound came first. The low gentle fluting of the organ. Then shapes slowly rose around her, one by one. Flowers in hand. Faces blank and numb. Relatives. People she half knew. Strangers . . .

Roses placed on the casket by pale, trembling fingers.

'We've got something,' Anton said. 'Mum. We've got something too.'

He was the first of the family to stand. Theis the last, brought to his feet by Anton's gentle touch. Together the four walked towards her.

Towards it.

White wood and roses. A fragrance to hide a stench.

When they got there the two boys linked hands, placed a small map on the coffin. The city. Its rivers and streets.

'What's that nonsense?' Theis asked in a low furious voice. 'What is it?'

'It's for Nanna,' Emil said. 'So when she flies past she can see where we live.'

By the casket, four of them, both bound and separated by emotions they could not name.

Anton crying, asked, 'Are you cross, Dad?'

Are you cross?

Not an angry man. Not of late. Not since the children came along and made their lives whole.

She knew that. As did he.

And the boys, mostly.

'No,' Birk Larsen said, bending down to kiss both on their heads, taking their shoulders into his wide arms, holding them to him.

Pernille barely noticed. All she saw was the coffin. Her tears running down, salt stains on white wood.

His hand, rough callused fingers, reached out, entwined themselves in hers.

'Theis . . . ?' she whispered.

Pernille bent her head, puzzled how the single word her mind was forming could contain so much meaning, so much life and hurt and grief.

Looked into his coarse and grizzled face and said, 'Now?'

A squeeze of the fingers, a nod of the head.

They walked down the aisle, past the lines of mourners. Past pupils and teachers, past neighbours and friends. Past the inquisitive policewoman who watched them at the door with glittering sad eyes.

Out into the wan daylight, leaving Nanna behind.

Hartmann was listening to the hourly newscasts now. Couldn't stop himself. The police had put out another statement, as meaningless as most of the others. They had every available resource working on the case. Buchard, the pugnacious chief inspector, came on, sounding gruff and tetchy.

'We're following a lead but that's all we can say.'

And then the weather.

Rie Skovgaard came in, said edgily, 'My dad needs to see you.'

The debate with Bremer was an hour away. He pulled a tie out of the drawer, got up, tried it on in a mirror.

'Busy?' Kim Skovgaard asked taking a seat.

'Never too busy for you.'

'So you're going to the debate? You're going to talk about integration? Foreigners? Role models?'

'That's right.'

'Rie's worried about you, Troels.'

'Yes. I know.'

'She's a very smart woman. I'm not just saying that because she's my daughter.' He got up, came and put his hand on Hartmann's arm. 'You should listen to her more. But right now you should listen to me. Don't talk about role models. Not tonight.'

'Why?'

Skovgaard's voice changed, became stern and impatient.

'It's enough that one of your cars is involved in the Birk Larsen case. Anything the papers have about you and immigrants will be dug out of the archives and thrown in your face. Save your love for dark faces till later. When it wins some votes, not loses them.'

'And tonight?'

He straightened Hartmann's tie.

'Tonight you'll focus on housing. On the environment.'

'That's not going to happen.'

Skovgaard wasn't smiling any more, and that was rare.

'But it is. You don't seem to understand. I'm telling you to do this. Not asking. There are people watching you. In this place. In Parliament. You will do what I say.'

Hartmann stayed silent.

'It's in your best interests. Everyone's—'

'But . . .'

'I'm only trying to help my future son-in-law.'

He patted Hartmann's arm. It was a condescending gesture. Meant that way.

'You'll get your reward, Troels. And it won't be in heaven either.'

Hartmann and Rie Skovgaard were walking to the TV studio. What started as a discussion was boiling up into an argument.

'You knew he was coming,' he said. 'You fixed that.'

She stared at him as if he were crazy.

'No. Who do you think I am? Machiavelli? Dad was in the Rådhus. He turned up in front of my desk. What was I supposed to do?'

Hartmann wondered whether he believed her.

'But you agree with him?'

'Of course I do. It's obvious. To everyone except you. When you see an iceberg you steer away from it. You don't—'

'I'm not your little puppet,' Hartmann broke in. 'Or your father's.'

She stopped, threw up her hands in despair.

'Do you want to get elected or not? There are no prizes for losers. All your fine ideals mean nothing if Poul Bremer marches back into office.'

'That's not the only issue.'

'What is then?'

The producer was walking towards them.

Skovgaard beamed at him, turned soft and charming in an instant.

'Not now, Troels,' she hissed.

Lund found Meyer in the Memorial Yard, an open space on the ground floor of the Politigården. Quiet and solitary. A statue, the Snake Killer, good fighting evil. On one wall the names of a hundred and fifty-seven Danish police officers killed by the Nazis. On another a shorter list: those killed on duty more recently.

He was eyeing that wall, smoking anxiously.

'What was he like?' Lund asked.

Meyer jumped, surprised by her presence.

'Who?'

'Schultz.'

Hurt in his eyes. An accusation too.

'You've been checking up on me?'

'I looked through the press archive for Hartmann. I just thought . . .'

Four years before. She dimly remembered the case. An undercover narcotics cop in Aarhus was murdered by one of the gangs. Meyer was his partner. Sick on the day he was killed. His career had been shaky ever since.

'He was an idiot,' Meyer said. 'Went off on his own. If he'd waited a day I'd have been back on duty.'

She nodded at the wall.

'Then maybe there'd be two names there instead.'

'Maybe.' He shrugged. 'That's not the point.'

'What is?'

'We were a team. We did things together. Looked out for each other. That was part of the deal. He broke it.'

She said nothing.

'Like me forgetting to buy you a hot dog. For which I apologize.'

'Not quite the same.'

'Yes, it is.'

He pulled a half-eaten banana from his pocket, bit at it between pulls on the cigarette.

'Buchard wants to see us,' she said.

Back in their office. An empty packet of crisps sat on the desk. Along with a sceptical Buchard.

'Kemal leaves his wife to go and meet the girl. They have an argument in the flat,' Meyer said.

Lund was on the phone.

'He ties her up and drugs her. And drives home.'

Buchard propped his chin on his fist, stared at Meyer with his round, beady eyes. Said nothing.

'On Saturday morning he claims the workman has cancelled. But really Kemal has cancelled him.'

Buchard made to say something.

'The workman confirmed that,' Meyer said quickly. 'I tracked him down.'

Lund's voice rose from the other side of the office.

'There's time, Mum. Stop panicking. I said I'd be there. Why won't you believe me? OK?'

The call ended. She pulled a pack of Nicotinell out of her packet, eyed the cigarettes on the desk.

'So,' Meyer went on. 'He returns to the flat and the girl. He waits for it to get dark. Then he picks up the car at the school, drives back, carries the girl to the car and goes off to the woods.'

Lund came over, sat down, listened.

Meyer was warming to his idea.

'On Sunday he removes any traces, sands the floor and puts up tiles.'

'I'm going,' Lund said to Buchard. 'Talk to you soon.'

Meyer waved a hand in the air.

'Wait, wait,' he cried. 'What's wrong with it? Share the secret with dumb little Jan. Please.'

The two of them watched him.

'Please,' he repeated.

'How could he have driven Hartmann's car?' Lund asked.

Meyer struggled.

'He probably found the keys at the school on Friday night.'

Meyer watched Lund, waiting. So did Buchard.

'I don't think he's that stupid,' she said. 'In fact I think he's very clever.'

'Exactly,' Meyer agreed.

'If I were you,' she said, 'I wouldn't drag him in until you get some hard evidence.'

She smiled.

'But it's your case.' She held out her hand. 'Thanks for everything. It's been really . . .'

The word seemed to elude her.

'Really educational.'

He took her hand, shook it vigorously.

'You can say that again.'

'I've left my number. If . . .'

He stared at her.

'I'm sure you won't need it. But . . .'

Buchard sat on the desk looking miserable. Before he could say a word she shook his hand too, said goodbye.

Then walked out of the Copenhagen Police Headquarters. Career over. Job gone.

Case still open.

The cab had a dropdown TV. Mark one side, Vibeke the other, Lund watched the nightly news. A debate between Hartmann and Bremer. All the polls said the fight for City Hall was a battle between these two. One misstep might give the other the game.

'We haven't bought any beer or brandy,' Vibeke complained.

'There's plenty of time.'

'And chocolates to go with the coffee.'

'They sell chocolates in Sweden I believe.'

'Not *our* chocolates!'

Lund's phone rang. She looked at the number.

Skov. The detective she'd sent chasing information about Theis Birk Larsen after Buchard's tip-off from the retired cop.

Waited. Thought about leaving it. Answered anyway.

'What took you so long?' He sounded excited. 'I got the file from the retired DCI.'

'Oh.'

'Do you want to know what's in it?'

'Give it to Meyer.'

He hesitated.

'To Meyer?'

'That's what I said.'

The weather report. Lund picked up the remote, turned it off.

'What does it say?'

'It's a case from twenty years ago. Some kind of vendetta between dope dealers. It never went to court.'

Mark looked around the car, mumbled, 'I've forgotten my cap. Left it at Gran's . . .'

'It looks to me as if . . .'

'Mum?'

'I'll buy you a new one.'

The cop droned on, 'It's about a . . .'

'I don't want a Swedish cap.'

'We're not turning back now, Mark.'

Silence on the phone.

'I'm listening,' Lund insisted.

'Really?' Skov said. 'It involved a pusher from Christianshavn. Got beaten up. Almost killed. They never found who was responsible. Theis Birk Larsen was the main suspect. They questioned him.'

'Mark!'

He was rootling round the footwell, looking for something else.

'I forgot—'

'I don't care what you forgot,' she snapped. 'We're going.'

'Brandy and beer and cigarettes,' her mother murmured from the other side.

'Birk Larsen had a motive,' the cop said. 'The drug dealer had threatened to reveal something involving him. Was going to talk to us.'

'About what?'

'Don't know. He kept quiet after that. Real scared of Birk Larsen it seems. The man's got a reputation. Violence. Bad temper. Wait . . . I'm still reading this. There's a second file underneath.'

Then, so loud she took the phone from her ear, 'Christ!'

Mark was fidgeting, her mother still moaning.

'What is it?'

Silence.

'What is it?'

'They went back a month later to see if the pusher had changed his mind. Intelligence asked for it. They really wanted Birk Larsen.'

'And?'

'And nothing. They found him dead. I've got the pictures here. Jesus . . .'

'What?'

'This is worse than the first time. The guy looks like a piece of meat.'

'OK,' she cut in. 'You need to tell Meyer.'

'Meyer's busy.'

'Tell him to call me right away.'

'OK. Bye.'

The garage was full, the wake quiet. No speeches. No songs. Only tables covered with white cloths and flowers, portable chairs, simple food.

Theis Birk Larsen wandered among their guests, nodding, saying little. Watching the boys, Emil and Anton, grow puzzled and bored.

Pernille flitted from table to table. Listening, speaking rarely. Letting the gentle murmur of so many voices dull her pained, bruised mind.

This was a business. People still called. Customers. They had no idea.

By the door, on the extension, Vagn Skærbæk fielded them all, watching, sad-eyed in his black jumper, black jeans.

Coffee and water. Sandwiches and cake.

Birk Larsen walked like a ghost between tables, making sure cups were full, plates never empty. A waiter with nothing to say.

Then, in the office, by the hot silver urn, Skærbæk cornered him.

'Theis. I just had a call.'

'No business today, Vagn. I'm making coffee.'

'I just spoke to Jannik's wife. The woman at the school.'

Birk Larsen turned off the tap, put the half-filled cup on the table. Walked into the shadows, away from the people outside.

'Now's not the time—'

'No,' Skærbæk insisted. 'Now is the time.'

'I told you. It can wait.'

'I've got something.'

Birk Larsen looked at him. That plain thuggish face he'd known since childhood. More lined. The hair receding. Still a little scared. A little stupid.

'I told you, Vagn. I'm making coffee.'

Skærbæk stared at him. Defiant. Angry even.

'He's here,' he said.

Birk Larsen shook his head, stroked his chin, his cheek, wondered why he couldn't shave well on a day like this.

Asked, 'Who is?'

'The man they think did it.' Skærbæk's dark, tricky eyes were shining. 'He's here.'

A name. Said with that savage distaste Skærbæk saved for the foreigners.

Through the glass Birk Larsen stared.

The room began to empty. The wake was coming to an end. After a long time he walked out of the office, crossed the room with slow, ponderous steps, trying to think of the right words to say. The proper thing to do.

Pernille was thanking the teacher for the wreath.

Rama, smart and handsome in a dark suit, prepared and presentable in a way Birk Larsen knew he could never hope to emulate, said, 'It was from the school. From all of us. Students and staff.'

The man looked at Birk Larsen, expecting something.

Words.

'We need some coffee.'

Pernille stared at him, affronted by his rudeness.

'You want me to make some coffee?'

A nod.

She left.

Words.

'Thank you for welcoming us into your home,' the teacher said.

Birk Larsen looked at the table. The cups, the glasses, the plates with half-eaten food.

Lit a cigarette.

'It means a lot to her classmates.'

His voice was slick and sweet. Just a touch of the exotic there. Not like most of them, inarticulate. Strangers. Foreign.

'It means a lot to me,' Rama said and reached out to touch his arm.

Something in Birk Larsen's eyes stopped him.

Parks and recreation. Clean technology and environmental jobs. The interview was going well. Hartmann knew it. So did the studio. He could tell from the tone of the questions, the nodding heads behind the cameras in the dark.

From Poul Bremer's stiff responses too.

'You must be happy with all these ideas, Lord Mayor?'

The interviewer was a woman Hartmann had met before. Smart and attractive.

A nod of that grey magisterial head.

'Of course. But let's talk about something different. Immigration. Role models especially.'

He looked at the camera, then at Hartmann.

'Really, Troels. They're just a gimmick.'

Hartmann stiffened.

'Try saying that in your ghettoes.'

A genial laugh.

'We built good affordable housing for people who mostly arrived here uninvited. They seem grateful. We can't tell them where to live.'

Hartmann's temper stirred.

'You can try to address social inequality—'

'Let's go back to role models,' Bremer broke in. 'You seem so fascinated by them. Your personal invention. Why is this? Why are they so important?'

'Social inequality—'

'Why treat immigrants differently? I won't tolerate discrimination against minorities. But you wish to give the minorities rights that are denied to the rest of us. To people born here. Why not treat them like everyone else?'

Troels Hartmann took a deep breath, studied the man across the table. He'd heard these sly gambits so many times . . .

'That's not the point and you know it.'

'No I don't,' Bremer retorted. 'Enlighten me. What is the point?'

Hartmann fumbled for the words. Bremer sensed something.

'You don't seem very proud of your role models right now. Why is that?'

Poul Bremer knew something. It was written in that smirk.

Hartmann's hands performed contortions. His mouth opened. Said nothing.

In the darkness he heard a faint instruction.

'Stay on him. Camera one.'

A politician's career could disappear in an instant. With a single thoughtless action. A solitary careless word.

'I'm very proud of them.'

'Are you?' Bremer asked amiably.

'These people work unpaid to make Copenhagen a better place. We should thank them. Not dismiss them as third-class citizens—'

'This is wonderful.'

'Let me answer!'

'No. No. It's wonderful.'

A glance at the camera. Then Bremer's cold eyes fell on the man across the table.

'But isn't it true some of your role models are criminals themselves?'

'That's nonsense—'

'Be honest with us. One of them's involved in a murder case.'

The interviewer broke in.

'What murder case?'

'Ask Troels Hartmann,' Bremer said. 'He knows.'

'An actual case?' the woman asked.

'As I said. A murder. But . . .' Bremer frowned as if unwilling to elaborate for reasons of taste. The point was made. The bomb was dropped. 'Hartmann's the Mayor of Education. Ask him.'

'No.' The interviewer was cross now. 'This is unacceptable, Bremer. If you won't be specific you must drop this subject.'

'Unacceptable?' He raised his hands. 'What's unacceptable is—'

'Stop this!'

Hartmann's voice was so loud a technician near the table ripped off his headphones.

'Imagine you're right. Let's say this is true.'

'Yes,' the old man agreed. 'Let's say that.'

'Then what? If one immigrant makes a mistake does that implicate all immigrants? That's absurd and you know it. If that's so then what applies to one politician must apply to all of them.'

'You're avoiding the point—'

'No.' Hartmann no longer cared how this might look. 'These role models have achieved more for integration in four years than you've managed in all your time in office. Unpaid, without thanks. While you did nothing—'

'Not true—'

'It's true!'

Hartmann heard his own furious tones echo back at him from the dark belly of the studio.

Bremer relaxed in his seat, arms folded, smug and satisfied.

'I've got plans for Copenhagen,' Hartmann began.

'We'll hear more of this,' Bremer broke in. 'We'll hear more very soon I think.'

Kastrup. Fifteen minutes to departure. Their seats were halfway along the plane. Mark by the window. Vibeke in between. Lund in the aisle, phone in hand.

Meyer'd called.

'Did you hear about Birk Larsen?' she asked, cramming her bag into the overhead locker.

'No. But we've found the girl's bike. What did you want?'

'What bike?'

'A patrol car stopped a girl on a bike for riding without lights. Turned out to be Nanna's.'

A severe-looking flight attendant came up to Lund and ordered her to turn off the phone.

'The girl said she stole the bike from outside Kemal's place. We're picking him up. Where are you?'

'On the plane.'

'Have a nice flight.'

'Meyer. Keep an eye on Birk Larsen.'

She sat down. The flight attendant was at the front of the plane, haranguing someone else.

'Why?'

'Read the old case file like I told you. Don't let him near Kemal.'

She could hear him pulling on a cigarette.

'Now you tell me. The two of them just left the wake.'

'What?'

'I sent someone to pick up Kemal. He was there after the funeral. Birk Larsen had already offered him a lift. What's wrong?'

'Has Kemal arrived home?'

'Listen.' Meyer was getting cross. 'Birk Larsen knows nothing. If he did why would they have let Kemal into their place? Why—'

'Has he arrived home?' she repeated.

'As it happens, no. I don't have time for this. Go fly away.'

'Meyer!'

The line went dead.

The attendant came back, ordered her to put on her seat belt.

They were still at the gate, door open. Not for long.

Lund punched at her phone.

'I've already told you once,' the woman said. 'Turn off that phone and put on your seat belt. We're leaving.'

Lund stared at the dial. Hit the off button. Noticed Mark was looking at her. Her mother too. Probably had been for a while.

The pilot came on. Said the usual things.

Welcome on board your flight to Stockholm. Any minute now we'll push back from the stand. The weather is fine en route. We expect an on-time arrival . . .

Lund thought about Nanna and the teacher. Meyer and Theis Birk Larsen.

The flight attendant had her hand on the door. She was talking to the man outside on the gate. Getting ready to close it. Saying goodbye.

'Fetch the luggage,' Lund said, throwing off her seat belt.

'What?' her mother roared.

Mark punched the air, cried, 'Yes!'

Then Lund marched down the plane, waving her police ID in one hand, clutching her phone to her ear with the other.

Through the dark Theis Birk Larsen gunned the van. The teacher in the passenger seat talking.

About school. About Nanna. About families and children.

Words lost on the big man at the wheel.

From Vesterbro into the city. Past Parliament and Nyhavn.

The water. The empty ground around the Kastellet fortress.

Long dark roads becoming narrow and deserted.

The teacher went silent.

Then said, 'I think we passed the turning a while back.'

Birk Larsen drove and drove, into the black night, trying to think. Wishing he could find the words.

'So we did,' he said, and carried on.

In the cab from the airport Lund read over the details to the control room. Red van number plate UE 93 682. From Birk Larsen's removals company. A general call to stop and wait for orders.

Vibeke sat in the back scolding Mark.

'Of course you're going to Sweden. You don't think some silly trick of your mother's will stop that, do you?'

When Lund came off the phone Vibeke said in a long, low voice, 'Poor Bengt. Whatever must that nice man think?'

'Bengt doesn't just think of himself. He understands me better than you do.'

Her mother scowled at her.

'I hope so. For your sake.' A long, judgemental stare. 'So shouldn't you call him? Tell him there's no point in waiting at the airport any more?'

Lund nodded.

'I was about to. Thanks.'

Svendsen was outside the teacher's home by the time Meyer got there. Kemal still hadn't arrived. His wife had heard nothing. Theis Birk Larsen was missing. Not answering his phone.

'Where's Kemal's car?'

'Still in the garage.'

'OK. Go drive the route from Birk Larsen's house to here again.'

The detective bridled.

'We did that already.'

'You know that word I just used? Again?'

Svendsen didn't move.

'Shall I report Kemal missing?'

'What for?' Meyer asked.

'Lund talked to Skov before she left. Birk Larsen was dangerous.'

Meyer popped some gum into his mouth, came up to the man, looked around, started calling, 'Lund! Lund!'

Shrugged. Looked at the cop and asked, 'Do you see Lund here?'

The man looked at him, said nothing.

'From now on we do things my way. Understand? Lund's away with the fairies. Milking cows or something.'

The radio was squawking. A message about Birk Larsen's van.

Meyer called the control room and said, 'This is 80–15. I didn't put out a search for anything. What gives?'

'Vicekriminalkommissær Lund requested the search.'

Meyer tried to laugh.

'Lund's in Sweden. Cut the jokes.'

'Lund called five minutes ago and requested a search.' A pause. 'We don't do jokes.'

Then hung up.

'This is Theis Birk Larsen. Leave your name and number and I'll get back to you.'

Pernille held out the phone while the message played. Lund listened. The cab had gone on to take Vibeke and Mark home. She was alone with the Birk Larsen woman amidst the dirty plates, dirty cups, dirty glasses, uncleared tables of Nanna's wake.

'And you've no idea where he is?' Lund asked.

'He drove Rama home.'

Pernille looked pale, drained. And curious.

'What's so important?'

'Did anything happen before they left? Between the two of them?'

'I was talking to the teacher. Theis came over. He wanted some more coffee made.' She scanned the remains of the wake, the empty garage. 'So I went and made some. For the guests. What's this about?'

'Did your husband seem angry or upset. Or—?'

'Upset?'

Pernille Birk Larsen glowered at her. A strong woman, Lund thought. A match for her husband in some ways.

'How do you think Theis feels today? How do you think I feel? Take a look around. You've been everywhere anyway, haven't you?'

'Pernille.'

'Everywhere . . .'

There was a noise from the office. The man who seemed to be here all the time, one of the workers, was there.

She knew his name. They'd run some checks. Minor crimes. Just like Birk Larsen.

Vagn Skærbæk.

'Your husband may be about to do something stupid,' she said, watching the woman very carefully. 'It's important I find him.'

'Why? What would he do that's stupid?'

There was a young voice from the stairs. One of the boys, calling for her.

'My son needs me,' Pernille said then left.

Lund walked straight into the office, showed the man her card.

'You're a friend of his?'

He was dealing with some papers. Didn't look at her directly.

'Yeah.'

'Where did he go?'

Straight out, 'I don't know.'

More papers. She walked over, took them from his hands.

'Listen to me. This is important. If you're his friend you should help him. Where did they go?'

He had a silver necklace and a young man's face growing old. Lund had dealt with a generation of people like this. Not much money. Not many prospects. She knew what to expect.

'I've no idea.'

Sound at the door. Someone chewing, clearing his throat. She recognized his presence by now.

Lund was on the phone to control by the time she turned to face Meyer.

'I need you to trace two mobiles. Theis Birk Larsen's and Rahman Al Kemal's. Here are the numbers.'

She handed the phone over to Meyer and nodded: do it.

'God, you'll pay for this, Lund.'

'We don't have time. Vagn?'

He was back in the corner, hiding.

'Where are your warehouses?'

Meyer was on the phone, handling the numbers.

'Vagn?'

Out by the waterfront, north of the city, the deserted docks in Frihavnen. Rain like tears from an endless black sky.

The red van sauntered slowly to the end of the road. A line of concrete. A path by the water. No cars. No lights. Not a sign of life.

Theis Birk Larsen bumped the front tyres against the path, pulled on the brake.

They'd sat together like this for almost an hour driving through the city. Going north. Going nowhere. Scarcely exchanging a word.

Now he killed the engine. The headlights. There was just the dim bulb above the mirror between them.

The phone in Birk Larsen's suit pocket rang again. He took it out. Turned it off without answering. Put it back. Stared ahead.

'What's going on?' the teacher said. 'What . . . ?'

Birk Larsen reached down, opened his door, climbed out.

Pulled the jacket of his funeral suit round his big frame. Walked through the blustery wind and freezing rain out to the water's edge.

Turned, stared at the van. A dark face at the glass. Worried, grey in the single light.

Birk Larsen took out a packet of cigarettes, struggled to light one in the downpour. Shielded it with his powerful shoulder. Brought the flame to life.

Alone in his office Troels Hartmann was locked on to the news again. There was a time when he craved to be the lead item. Not now. Not like this.

'The battle for the mayoral post took a dramatic turn when Bremer accused one of Hartmann's role models of being involved in a murder case.'

Rie Skovgaard walked in, chanting the standard no comment at one more reporter looking for an interview. She came off the line, handed Hartmann a sheet of paper.

'The Centre Party want a meeting. I had to promise it.'

Hartmann turned off the TV. She was walking out.

'What did the police say?' he asked.

She stopped at the door.

'I can't get through to anyone. Troels?'

She didn't even look tired. She'd grown up in the brawling world of city politics from which his own father had been excluded. It was as if this all came naturally . . .

'You realize you've got to suspend Kemal and issue a statement. Otherwise—'

'Not until I've heard from the police. When I get a reason—'

'You have to do this! It's important we show you've got nothing to hide. This is about transparency.'

'No it's not. It's about giving in. Letting the pressure dictate what you do. Not what's right.'

He got up from the chair, found his jacket. Felt calm. Content this was the way forward.

'Bremer stirred this up for a reason . . .'

She leaned back against the door, shifted her head left to right. Dark hair moving. What was it Morten said? The Jackie Kennedy funeral look.

'You should have stuck to the script. No mention of role models. Just because Bremer went there you didn't have to follow.'

'I did what was right.'

'You fouled up.'

'Is that Daddy speaking?'

She broke, spat at him, 'No, it's me. I want you to win. Not throw away your chances for no good reason.'

'Whose chances, Rie? Mine? Yours? Your father's?'

She shook her head, narrowed those bright, piercing eyes.

'Is that how you see it?'

'I asked—'

'You know maybe I'm not the adviser for you. What's the point? If you ignore every damned thing I say.'

A turning point.

'Maybe not,' Hartmann said.

'Here's the truth, Troels. That teacher's guilty. It doesn't matter whether they convict him or not.'

'You think so?'

'If that's what the press say. And they do . . .'

He grabbed his coat from the stand.

'Talk to the police. If they say something . . . if they arrest this man. If they tell me he's guilty . . .'

'Too late.'

'Then I act.'

She watched him get ready to leave.

'Where are you going?' Skovgaard asked. 'Troels? Where?'

'Have they traced those phones yet?'

Meyer didn't answer. He was still on a call.

Lund was going through the documents on the wall, tracing the company premises, watched by a silent, surly Skærbæk.

She read them out to the control room. A warehouse at Sydhavnen. A depot in Valby. A warehouse at Frihavnen with no address.

'Where in Frihavnen?' she asked Skærbæk.

'I've never been to that one.'

There was a cupboard full of keys. She went through those.

'What about this workshop? Could he be there?'

'I told you. I don't know a bloody thing.'

Meyer came off the phone.

'We've got a trace off a mobile phone mast. Kemal's in Frihavnen.'

Port area. Not much used at night. Easy to hide, Lund thought.

'He's in Frihavnen,' she told control. 'Send out a car.'

No rain now. Just the Øresund's black water, Sweden somewhere in the distance. Waves reflected in the lights from across the channel. Birk Larsen stood at the edge, in the headlamps of the van. Back to the world.

A sound. He turned. The teacher was out now. Not running. Which he could. Younger and fitter. Could race all the way back to the city. Avoid Birk Larsen and the van.

Instead he walked to the water. Stared at the waves.

'I'm sorry . . .'

They never lost the accent completely. Never shrugged off who they were.

'My wife's waiting for me.'

Words. Where were the words?

'She's pregnant. I don't want her to worry. Maybe I should call and tell her . . .'

Another cigarette in Birk Larsen's fist. Barely touched. But now he raised it to his lips, dragged the harsh smoke into his lungs. Wished it would spread from there, fill his big body. Make him nothing. Invisible. Gone.

Words.

They should be about her. About no one else. Always.

'Nanna was a stargazer. Did you know that?'

The teacher shook his head.

'That's what they call it when you look up when you're born. See your mother's eyes. See something else. The sky.'

211

So many memories. A jumble of images and sounds. A child is a child. Its life flows like a river, never stopping, never fixed.

'We said she'd be an astronaut. Parents say . . .' He pulled on the cigarette again. 'We say such stupid things. Make stupid promises we're never going to keep.'

The teacher nodded. As if he knew.

Birk Larsen threw the cigarette into the water. Shrugged. Looked back at the van.

'She liked going to school, didn't she?'

'Very much so.'

Stamped his feet in the damp cold.

'I wasn't any good at school. Got into trouble. But Nanna was . . .'

Memories.

'Nanna was different. Better than me.'

There was a look on the teacher's dark face. The one they show parents.

'She was a very able student.'

'Able?'

'Hard working.'

'And she was fond of you, wasn't she?'

Memories. They burned like acid.

The man was silent.

'She told us about your lessons.'

Birk Larsen took a step towards him.

'People are talking about you, teacher.'

He was sweating. It wasn't rain.

'No matter what you've heard . . .' He shook his head. Didn't move. 'I can assure you. Nanna was my student. I would never . . .'

Birk Larsen waited.

'Never what, teacher?'

'I would never hurt her.'

Closer. His breath was sweet. Not mints. Something exotic.

'So why are people talking?'

Quickly, 'I don't know.'

Birk Larsen nodded.

Waited.

A long time. Then the teacher said, a touch angry, 'I didn't touch her. I never would. This is all a misunderstanding.'

'Misunder—'

'I'm going to be a father!'

Two men by the Øresund's cold expanse.

One walked to the van. Turned on the engine. Looked back at the tall hunched figure caught in the headlights by the water's edge.

Meyer hung on the phone, getting nowhere. Skærbæk was turning ugly in the corner. Pernille Birk Larsen had had enough.

'Do you get a kick out of this?' the woman stormed at them. 'You come to my daughter's funeral. I don't know what you think but . . .'

Keen, smart eyes turned on Lund.

'Theis hasn't done anything.'

Skærbæk leaned back against the office door, lit a cigarette.

'I believe he has,' Lund said.

Meyer came off the phone.

'There's no one at the harbour. They've looked everywhere.'

'Try the other warehouses.'

'Done what?' Pernille Birk Larsen demanded. 'You people—'

There was a sound. Lund looked, wondered about Meyer's weapon. He always had it.

The sliding door was moving upwards. Meyer was still on the phone.

Theis Birk Larsen walked in. Sharp black suit. Ironed white shirt. Black tie.

Looked at them. Cops first. Skærbæk. Then Pernille.

'Are the kids asleep?' he asked.

Lund couldn't stop staring.

'Where's Kemal?'

Birk Larsen's massive head lolled from side to side. There was something in his narrow, sly eyes she couldn't interpret, hard as she tried.

'I think he took a taxi.'

Lund glanced at Meyer. Pointed to his phone.

Birk Larsen walked for the stairs. His wife stopped him, asked, 'Where've you been, Theis? Two hours . . . ?'

'It's not so late.' He nodded at the apartment. 'I'd like to read them a story.'

'Wait. Wait!' Lund called.

He walked off, out of view.

Meyer got off the line.

'Kemal just called his wife. He's on his way home.'

Pernille Birk Larsen glared at them both, shook her head, swore, stomped off. There was just Skærbæk then. Silver chain at the neck. Giving them the fuck-you punk look of a teenager.

'Call off the search,' Meyer barked down the phone. 'Bring Kemal down to the station as soon as you can.'

He pocketed his mobile. Followed her outside.

'Well,' Meyer said. 'What the hell was that about?'

Lund called Sweden.

'This is Bengt Rosling. I can't take your call right now. Leave your name and number and I'll call you back.'

Best voice, trying not to sound apologetic because she wasn't. Not really.

'Hi, it's me. You must be busy welcoming the guests.'

All this she said while she was taking off her jacket, throwing it onto a chair in the corner of the office, scanning the documents on the desk.

Her desk?

Meyer's?

Didn't know. Didn't care. The documents mattered. Nothing else.

'I wish I could be there, Bengt.'

There hadn't been much new since the afternoon.

'The thing is . . . something came up in the case.'

Meyer walked in.

'I'm really, really sorry. Give everyone my best . . .'

She took a seat at the desk. It still felt hers. Rifled for her pens, her papers. Her place here.

'Tell them . . .'

He'd moved things. Her things. She felt a flicker of annoyance.

'It's a shame. But well . . .'

Meyer stood with his hands on the back of the opposite chair. Staring at her, open-mouthed.

'I'll talk to you later. Bye.'

Phone down, more sifting through the papers.

'Is he ready for questioning?' Lund asked.

'Look, look.' He seemed more amazed than angry. 'You can't do this. I don't know what you think—'

'I think you're right, Meyer.'

'I am?' he brightened. 'Oh great.'

'It isn't working. So I've decided to stay until the case is solved.'

'What?'

'Doesn't make sense going back and forth between here and Sweden. It's a mess. The Swedish police say—'

'Stop this, Lund.'

With his sticky-out ears and bright, hurt eyes Meyer suddenly looked very young.

'This is my case now. You're not staying here. End of story. We're done. The girl visited him on Friday night. Once he's admitted that I'm charging him.'

Lund took one last look at the files, picked up a couple, stood up.

'Let's hope he confesses then. Shall we go?'

'Oh no.'

Meyer stood in the way.

'I'm doing the questioning.'

'Don't make me talk to Buchard, Meyer.'

He bristled.

'I'm being nice here. You can sit in if you like.'

Kemal was at the table, black tie pulled down. Exhausted. Nervous.

Meyer sat on his left. Lund opposite.

'Want a coffee or a tea?' Meyer asked, throwing his files on the table.

He did all the policeman voices. Threatening. Sympathetic. Neutral now and calm.

The teacher poured himself a glass of water. Lund leaned over, shook his hand, said, 'Hi.'

'You're not under arrest,' Meyer recited from memory, 'but you have the same rights as someone who has been accused. You have the right to a lawyer.'

'I don't need a lawyer. I'll answer your questions.'

The teacher looked at Lund.

'There's something you should know.'

They watched him. Sweating. Trying to find the courage to say something. This didn't happen often, Lund thought.

'Last Friday I was supervising the Halloween party at school. My shift ended at eight thirty. I drove home to pick up my wife.'

She wondered what had happened in the van with Birk Larsen. What difference that might have made.

'We went to our house on the allotment. About nine thirty I realized we had forgotten to bring coffee. So I drove to the petrol station.'

Making it up, she thought. You are making this up.

'On the way back I remembered the workman was coming on Saturday. I drove back to the flat to clear things out of the way.'

Meyer shuffled forward on the table.

'Just after ten the doorbell rang. It was Nanna.'

They waited.

'She wanted to return some books I'd lent her. She was only there for two minutes.'

Meyer leaned back in his chair, put his hands behind his head.

'That's it,' Kemal said and finished the glass of water.

'She came round to return some books?' Meyer asked.

'School books?' Lund wondered.

'No, my own books. Karen Blixen. She seemed to want to give them back to me right then. I don't know why. I was surprised.' He shrugged. 'I just took them.'

'On a Friday night?' Meyer asked. 'At ten o'clock?'

'She was always looking for something to read.' He closed his eyes briefly. 'I know I should have told you this before.'

'Why didn't you?' Lund demanded.

He looked at his hands, not at them.

'There was an incident with another student. A few years ago. A false accusation. I was scared you'd think—'

'Think what?' Lund asked.

'Think I'd had some kind of relationship with Nanna.'

Dark eyes met hers.

'I didn't,' he said.

'That's it?' Lund asked.

'That's it. That's all I've got to say.'

Hartmann's car roamed the bars for a while, him in the back, phone off, radio off.

'It's got to be around here somewhere,' he told the driver.

A sign he remembered. A name.

'There! There!'

216

It was an old pub. Noisy. Busy. Full of men who'd taken on too much beer. Bottles on the table. Clouds of cigarette smoke in the air.

Hartmann strolled through the dark bar. Found Morten Weber finally, head back on his shoulders, curly hair grubby, all over the place.

There were six men around the table. Working steadily at their drinks. Saying nothing.

Hartmann stood in front of them, held up the plastic bag. Weber groaned, got up, came over.

The insulin was delivered to the campaign office. The place where Weber seemed to live.

'I saw you on TV,' he said, taking it.

The glass in his hand was whisky. Hartmann could smell it. The last in a long line he thought.

'You don't have time to play doctor, Troels.'

'Rie thinks you're sick. She doesn't know you so well. Yet.'

Bleary-eyed, Morten Weber tried to smile.

'I'm allowed one drunk day a month. It's in my contract, isn't it?'

'Why this one?'

'Because you yelled at me.'

'You asked for it.'

'Because I needed some time out of that marble prison. To think without you or her or some damned minion getting in my face. Besides . . .'

There was an expression he didn't recognize on Weber's sad, lined face. Bitterness, Hartmann realized.

'It doesn't matter, does it? You don't listen to me any more. Does she know you're here? Your new consort?'

He knocked back the drink. Went to sit at an empty table cuddling his glass. Hartmann took the bench opposite.

'You haven't even suspended the teacher yet, have you?' Weber said. 'From what I've heard you're right. But what does Kirsten Eller think?'

Hartmann said nothing.

'Has she dumped you yet, Troels? Or is she waiting till tomorrow? What's Rie's advice there? Go running to her? Go begging? Give her what she wants? That teacher's head on a plate?'

'I need you two to work together.'

'Oh do you? Just because you brought me some insulin it

doesn't . . .' His speech was slurred. His thoughts seemed clear. 'It doesn't make everything all right.'

Hartmann pulled his coat around him, ready to leave.

'I was trying to make amends. I'm sorry if I wasted your time.'

'Poor Troels. Always wants to do the right thing. But he listens to the wrong people. Poor . . .'

'I need you back in the office tomorrow. I need you to cut out these binges until this election's over. And get along with Rie.'

Weber nodded.

'Yes. I imagine you do. Now you're in the shit.'

A short, drunken laugh.

'You know it's only just started, don't you? All those hangers on who think they saw the spark of opportunity. They'll come for you, Troels. Once they think you've disappointed them. Watch out for the civil servants. Watch out for your own people. Bigum.'

Henrik Bigum, one of the senior party figures, a dour academic from the university.

'What about Bigum?'

'He loathes you and trouble's in his nature. He's the one who'll wield the dagger. But he'll get someone else to make the first move, naturally. You've no idea . . .'

He'd never seen such bleak fury in Morten Weber's face. Not directed at him anyway.

'When your wife died, Troels' – Weber banged his fist on the table – 'you were sitting here. And I was sitting there. Remember?'

Hartmann didn't move, didn't speak, didn't want to think about it.

Cheap, stupid pop music playing in the background. Loud voices. Men working through the prelude to a fight.

'You should listen to me, Troels. I deserve that. What else do I have?'

A last hateful look then Weber left the table and stumbled back to the bunch of drunks.

Hartmann had missed a call. Rie Skovgaard. He phoned her back.

'They found the girl's bike,' she said. 'It was at her teacher's flat the night she went missing.'

The music got louder. The fight was just a word, a push away.

'It's in the press already. Front page tomorrow. Pictures of you and Kemal. He's named as a suspect.'

Silence.

'Troels,' she said. 'I'm drafting the suspension papers now. I'm calling a press conference in an hour. I need you there.'

Buchard stormed into the office.

'How come our suspect's name's on television? Lund?'

'It's not a problem,' Meyer cut in. He nodded at the figure in the interview room beyond the glass. 'He's sitting right in there. We have him.'

'When the commissioner calls me it's a problem. Lund's gone from here for an hour or two and see what happens.'

'It's not Meyer's fault,' she said.

'What does the teacher say?' Buchard wanted to know.

Meyer sneered.

'Some crap about meeting the girl at his flat. She wanted to bring back some books.'

Buchard's lined face screwed up in bafflement.

'Books?'

Lund barely listened, kept running through the latest files on the PC.

'It's bullshit,' Meyer said. 'He sanded the floors. Removed everything.'

'They're renovating the flat,' Lund pointed out. 'That part's true.'

'Give me two hours with him, chief,' Meyer begged. 'I'll find out.'

Buchard looked unconvinced.

'The way you did with those boys?'

'I'll question him as a witness. I can—'

'He's lying,' Lund said and that stopped them.

Buchard folded his arms, looked at her.

'He's lying,' she said again.

'Search the flat,' Buchard ordered. 'Basement, the allotment in Dragør, everything. Locate the building waste. Tap his phone.'

Meyer didn't seem to be part of the conversation. Buchard was watching Lund scribble this down.

'Tell Hartmann what we're doing. And don't screw up with the press again.'

He was leaving. Meyer said, 'Talking about screwing up I need to talk to you in private.'

'Tomorrow,' Buchard snapped. 'Right now I want you working not whining.'

'So what do we do with him?' Meyer asked.

Buchard waited for Lund.

'We make him stay at his wife's house. Or a hotel,' she said. 'He's got to keep away from his flat and the place on the allotments. We 're searching them. We need his passport. We need him watched.'

Something nagged at her and Lund couldn't begin to guess what it was.

'He says he used his own car on Friday. We need to connect him to Hartmann's vehicle. He was a role model, wasn't he?'

The press conference was fifteen minutes away. Skovgaard was laying down the line.

'The suspension's effective immediately. I've got the paperwork. I've informed the administration.'

Hartmann looked at the documents she'd placed in front of him.

'You need to distance yourself from the whole thing. Say you regret your error of judgement. You support the police's efforts.'

He scanned through the statement, the apologetic, self-serving language.

'When they ask about role models, say you can't comment. If anyone . . .'

Hartmann got up from the desk and prowled the office, hands thrust deep in his pockets, blue shirt stained with sweat.

'If you're in the public eye and make a mistake it's important to apologize immediately. Put the whole thing to bed and move on. There are some fresh clothes in the wardrobe. You need them.'

He looked at the early edition of the newspaper on his desk. The teacher, Kemal, shaking his hand at the basketball match. Both of them smiling.

'I don't get this. He seemed a nice guy. No one has a bad word to say about him. I checked some of the records. There's a kid out there, straight and decent now. Would have been in jail if it wasn't for him.'

The first three pages were dedicated to the story.

'So I played basketball with him.'

Skovgaard was watching him with tired, worried eyes.

'And the weekend before he's supposed to have raped and murdered one of his own students.'

She looked deeply bored with this conversation.

'They're waiting for you, Troels. We need to sort out the lighting. The way you look.'

'Do you think he did it?'

'I don't know and I don't care. What I care about is saving you. I never realized it was going to be so hard.'

There was a knock on the door.

Lund stood there, waiting.

'What?' Skovgaard barked at her.

She walked in. Same old coat. Same black and white sweater. Same ponytail, long straight brown hair tied clumsily at the back.

This woman seemed to have attached herself to his life like a limpet.

'Hartmann said he wanted to be briefed,' Lund said, looking puzzled.

A shrug. Bright eyes boring into him.

'So here I am.'

'Aren't you supposed to be in Sweden?' Hartmann asked.

She smiled at that.

'Eventually. Kemal admits he met the girl at his flat. He says she left, but no one's seen her since. We're—'

'Give us the short version,' Skovgaard broke in. 'We've got a press conference.'

That smile again, a little different this time.

'The short version. He might have held her captive somewhere. We won't be charging him until we've searched his place. Maybe not then.'

'We read the papers,' Skovgaard said. 'We know all that.'

'I'll need mileage logs and documentation for any drivers using your cars over the last two years.'

'What for?'

'Kemal must have taken the car Nanna was found in. There has to be a connection . . .'

Hartmann stopped.

'He didn't drive that car.'

'It says in your records,' Lund insisted. 'The role models have access to them.'

'Not the campaign fleet. They're all brand new. Rented for a few weeks. Rie?'

She was watching him, arms folded, trying not to get drawn in.

221

'Rie!'

'The campaign cars are bright and shiny,' she said. 'We've got a point to make. The role models get the junk no one else wants to drive.'

'Wait a minute,' Hartmann said. 'You're going to charge him?'

'I said if we find more evidence—'

'But if Kemal never drove the car how could he even know it was one of ours?'

'Perhaps . . .' She was lost, and he'd never seen that before. 'Maybe . . . I don't know.'

Hartmann sensed something.

'We've only had those cars for two weeks or so. Maybe he's not guilty at all. We've got a press conference called about this in five minutes. What the hell are we supposed to say?'

'I don't run your press conferences, Hartmann.'

'If it wasn't for you we wouldn't need the damned things! You've been wrong before. Who's to say you're not wrong this time? You think I should suspend this man when you don't even have any evidence?'

'I just need some cooperation. You leave me to my job. I'll leave you to yours.'

She left with that. Skovgaard was watching him. He could hear the reporters assembling in the room next door.

Hartmann got the new suit, the clean shirt, started changing.

'Troels?' Skovgaard said. 'Don't even think of backing out. We've got the suspension papers. For your sake—'

'Kemal didn't do it.' He was grinning as he struggled into clean clothes. 'It's not him.'

Theis at the sink, broad back to her, pulling on a beer. Pernille at the table, watching him, pushing him to talk.

'They suspect the teacher,' she said. 'It's on the news.'

He sank some more beer and closed his eyes.

'Where did you go? What took you so long?'

'I don't know.'

Letters on the table. Bills. Late notices.

'I'll go to the house tomorrow. Do some work on it.'

She blinked.

'The house?'

'I've got to fix it up. Can't sell it till I do.'

He went to the drawer he always kept locked with a key she couldn't find. A habit from the past. Not the only place like that.

There were sheets inside. Architect's drawings.

'These were the plans. I'm sorry. I should have told you.'

'He was here,' she murmured.

Pencil projections. Dead dreams.

'We talked about Nanna.'

He folded out another sheet, smoothed it down with his elbow.

'I thanked him for the flowers in the church.'

He ran his finger over the drawings, said nothing.

'He touched her coffin.'

She looked at her fingers. The old wedding ring. The wrinkles. The marks of labour.

'I touched him.'

A rustle of papers. Nothing more.

In a calm, pleading tone she said, 'Why won't you talk to me?'

His eyes rose from the measurements and angles and drawings of beams.

'We don't know for sure.'

'You think he did it. Don't you?'

A long day. He never shaved well anyway. Now he looked like a miserable bear who'd strayed from the woods.

'Let's leave this to the police.'

Her hands flew across the table, swept away the papers of the home they'd never see.

'The police?'

Tears in her eyes. Fury in her face.

'Yes. The police.'

Bengt was still on voicemail. Vibeke was back at her sewing machine, running up another perfect dress for another perfect wedding.

An expression on her face that said: I knew it all along.

'Hi,' Lund said and threw her bag on the nearest chair.

Her mother turned off the machine, rolled back the white billowing fabric. Pushed the glasses down to the end of her long sharp nose.

'If you want a family, Sarah, you have to work for it.'

'I tried calling Bengt. He's not answering. I tried.'

Her mother said, 'Huh!'

'It's because of the party. He can't hear the phone.'

Vibeke came and sat next to her. An unexpected, almost apologetic expression on her face.

'I know you think I chased your father away before he died.'

'No.'

'I know you think that. I may not have been the best example for you . . .'

'We haven't broken up, Mum.'

'No. But you never let him close, do you? He's like the rest of us. Outside your life.'

'That's not true. You don't know us.'

Vibeke took the half-made dress off the stand, examined the seams.

'I just want you to be happy. I don't want you to be lonely in your old age.'

'You're not lonely, are you?'

Vibeke looked thrown by the question.

'I wasn't talking about myself.'

'I won't be lonely. I wasn't lonely before Bengt. Why should I . . . ?'

Now there was an expression she did recognize. Summed up in one word: *exactly*.

Lund turned on the TV and watched the news headlines. One story only. Troels Hartmann at his press conference, saying he wasn't suspending the teacher Kemal.

'Why in God's name not?' she whispered.

On the TV Hartmann answered.

'Rahman Al Kemal has been neither charged nor convicted. I won't take part in an act of character assassination. Bremer may be hell-bent on that. Let him square it with what passes as his conscience.'

His right hand rose, a gesture of politicians everywhere.

'Only if there's concrete evidence will there be a suspension.'

He leaned forward, an earnest face for the camera.

'It's the job of the police to convict criminals. Not politicians. We should stay out of their way except to offer every possible assistance we can. And that I will do. Thank you.'

A crowd of bodies rose, flinging questions. Lund watched, wished she'd got this on the recorder, could play back every word, catch every inflection, every expression on Hartmann's face.

'What if he murdered the girl?' yelled a reporter.

'As far as I know,' Hartmann replied, 'in this country a man is innocent until he's proven guilty. That's all . . .'

'That's all?' Lund murmured.

Then it was over. On to other news. The Middle East. The economy. She turned off the TV. Realized the room was dark and empty. Vibeke had gone off to bed without a word.

She was alone.

Sunday, 9th November

Dull morning. Lund walked into headquarters and was briefed by the leader of the overnight team. A security camera at the petrol station showed Kemal buying coffee at twenty to ten on the Friday night Nanna disappeared. He received a call from a launderette payphone around the same time. A place near his flat in the city. Twenty minutes before Nanna visited.

There was still nothing of use from the home. But if they could prove he'd arranged to meet her that broke his story. A lie.

The only other call he made was to the workman cancelling him.

Lund was thinking about this when she glanced into her office. Bengt was sitting there.

A quick smile. She closed the door, got some coffee from the flask.

'How'd you get here?' Lund asked.

'I drove last night.'

She handed him a cup, still wondering about the phone calls. Why would Nanna be in a launderette? Why wouldn't she use her own mobile?

'How did the house-warming party go?'

'Fine.' He looked tired and a little grubby from the drive. For once there was a touch of anger in his calm grey eyes. 'I sent people home at nine.'

She was wearing the black and white Faroese jumper from the day before. If she'd known Bengt was going to be there . . . She ran a hand through her untidy hair and thought: I'd still have worn it.

He came and put his hands on her shoulders. Professional face. Very serious. Fatherly.

'Listen, Sarah. It's not hard. Just walk out of that door, get in the car and we'll go home. You don't know those people. What about your family? What about Mark? He's supposed to be starting school.'

Lund walked to her desk, grabbed a folder.

'I want you to read the case. Here's the coroner's report. Here's what we found by the canal—'

'No!'

It was as close to a shout as she'd ever heard.

'I need your help,' she said calmly.

'You need? What about everyone else?'

She wasn't listening.

'He bathed her and clipped her nails. What kind of person does that? He removed every trace, carefully. Or there's some other reason I haven't guessed yet. Look . . .'

She got some of the morgue shots. Injuries. Bruises. Blood.

'The coroner thinks he's probably done this before. But I can't find anything similar.'

'I'm not interested in your case. I'm interested in you.'

He pointed to the door.

'The car's out there.'

There was a knock. Meyer came in. Sailor shirt, open-necked jerkin. Looking brighter and tidier than usual.

'I'm going to see Birk Larsen,' he said. 'But you don't need to—'

'I'll be right there.'

She grabbed her coat.

Bengt Rosling was a handsome man. That wasn't why she liked him. Loved him. He was placid, intelligent, patient.

'Please stay, Bengt.' She came and took his hand, smiled, looked into his eyes. 'It would mean a lot to me.'

He was wavering.

She picked up the folders, thrust them at him.

Then she quickly kissed him and went out to meet Meyer.

Rie Skovgaard had been through the vehicle files. The role models didn't use the cars.

'That's good news,' Hartmann said.

'We need a new campaign manager. If Morten isn't coming back.'

'He won't be.'

'I'll find someone. Knud Padde's here. He wants to talk to you. Alone. He's in your office.'

Padde held the assembly group chair, a mid-ranking party hack. Influential, important even at times. Tedious.

'Can't you—?'

'No. Go and talk to him.'

A trade union official, Padde was a bear-like shambling man with a bad suit, big spectacles and wild, uncombed hair.

'Have you seen the papers?' he complained the moment Hartmann walked in.

'Of course I've seen them.'

'The constituency's worried, Troels. The group wants a meeting. Today. One o'clock.'

'Knud. Not now. Kirsten Eller will be here in two minutes.'

'Why didn't you suspend the teacher? It looks as if you're covering for him.'

Hartmann looked him in the eye.

'According to the police the teacher's probably innocent.'

'That's not what the papers say.'

Padde was feeling unusually brave, Hartmann thought.

'I'm not sure we can take this pressure, Troels.'

Hartmann thought of his conversation the previous night with Weber.

'I'll deal with this. We don't need a meeting at one . . .'

'But there is a meeting. It's fixed,' Padde said. 'Best you be there.'

'You never told me he was a nut doctor,' Meyer said.

She was letting him drive again. It stopped him stuffing crisps and sweets and hot dogs into his mouth. Most of the time.

Lund didn't answer.

'Not that there's anything wrong in going out with your therapist.' She sighed.

'He's a criminal psychologist.'

Meyer raised an eyebrow as if to say: does that matter?

'He's the cleverest man I know.'

'Met him through work, eh?'

Silence.

'Am I right in thinking your ex-husband was a cop too?'

Silence.

'You're not the only one who can run background checks, Lund.'

Meyer shook his head. Stared at her as he took the corner.

'Watch the road,' she ordered.

'Do you know anyone outside the police?'

'Of course I do! Bengt—'

'Is a criminal psychologist.'

'I know lots of people.'

'Of course you do. I've asked Buchard for a meeting. About us.'

She looked at him. Big ears. Bulbous eyes. Stubble and that cocky haircut.

Meyer started to whistle. Then he turned the corner into Birk Larsen's street.

'Where's your husband?' Lund asked.

Pernille Birk Larsen was wiping down the kitchen table. The place looked too clean. As if the woman was trying to scrub away the memory of her lost child.

The tablecloth was unusual. Photographs and school reports were lacquered into the surface. Faces and words. A young Nanna, on her own, in the box of the red Christiania trike with a tiny Indian boy. The sons as toddlers.

A sweep of the tablecloth which was spotless already.

'He works weekends too.'

'We need information,' Lund said. 'We need to understand whether Nanna knew her murderer or not. Would you mind . . . ?'

The obsessive sweep of the hand, the cloth that removed nothing because there was nothing to remove.

'Would you mind doing that later please?' Lund said.

Pernille Birk Larsen didn't look at her. Just kept rubbing at the table.

Meyer rolled his eyes.

'It could be something she said,' Lund went on. 'Times she wasn't at home. Anything. Presents, books she borrowed . . .'

Pernille Birk Larsen stopped working with the cloth, leaned on both hands, glowered at both of them.

'You knew that teacher was a suspect. And you let him come to the funeral. Let me welcome him into my home.'

Meyer was shaking his head.

'He held my hand. And you said nothing!'

Lund shrugged, got up, looked around.

'And now you come asking questions!' Pernille shouted at them. 'It's too late.'

They didn't say a word.

'What are you doing about him?'

'We're searching his home,' Meyer broke in. 'As soon as we know something I'll call you.'

A look of bewilderment in the woman's intelligent, searching eyes. A connection she'd never made.

'Nanna was there?'

No answer.

'She was at his home that night?'

Lund shook her head, started to say, 'We can't go into details . . .'

'Yes,' Meyer broke in. 'She was there that night.'

Lund closed her eyes, furious.

'No one's seen her since,' he added.

Still livid, Lund said, 'This doesn't prove anything. We need information that links the two of them. We need . . .'

What? She wasn't sure either.

'We need a reason,' Lund said half to herself.

Pernille Birk Larsen picked up the cloth, wiped the clean table again.

'All I know is Nanna liked him as a teacher.' She waved at the girl's bedroom. 'Go round the place. Help yourself. There's nowhere you haven't poked your noses already.'

She glared at them.

'But keep me informed. You hear that?'

'Sure,' Meyer said.

Theis Birk Larsen and Vagn Skærbæk had picked up some fresh timber beams from the yard. They were in the garage stacking them in the van. There were jobs to be done. But the house in Humleby came first.

'I'll help you with the work, Theis,' Skærbæk promised. 'Just tell me what you want.'

Birk Larsen heaved some more timber into the truck, said nothing.

Skærbæk dodged a beam.

'Just as well you didn't touch him with all those police about.'
He picked up some more planks, threw them in the van. 'How can
an ape like that be a teacher? It's a sick world.'

Birk Larsen took off his black hat, looked at the wood. Fetched
some more.

'Know what?' Skærbæk checked around, made sure no one was
listening. 'He's finished. I promise you. Listen . . .'

He put a hand on Birk Larsen's black coat. Stopped him.

'We wait,' Skærbæk said. 'We've done this before. We know how.'

A sudden fury gripped Birk Larsen's stony face. He picked up the
smaller man by his overall, threw him towards the back of the van.
Grabbed him by the throat.

'Don't ever talk like that again. Ever.'

Skærbæk stood still, defiant, almost squared up to him.

'Theis. It's me. Remember?'

A shape at the edge of his vision. The lean, gruff cop came into
view, phone ringing. Birk Larsen let go.

'Meyer speaking,' the cop said.

The Lund woman was with him, walking round the place the way
she always did. Eyeing up everything as if she could record it with
those unblinking eyes.

Birk Larsen loaded the van and closed the door. Vagn had made
himself scarce without a sound. A talent he'd had since the two of
them were kids on the street.

Lund came up to Birk Larsen.

'If there's anything I can do . . .'.

'You know what you can do,' he said.

Kirsten Eller arrived, a look of mild outrage on her pasty face.

'This role model of yours is the prime suspect. In a murder case.'

'He may be innocent.'

'Not suspending him is madness.'

'That may be your opinion but it's not mine. Don't let this ruin
our agreement.'

'Our agreement?'

He waited. Rie Skovgaard studied her nails.

'Words on paper,' Eller said. 'That's all they are. Nothing more.'

There was coffee on the table and croissants. Barely touched.

'You mean you want out?'

'It's a question of credibility.'

'It's a question of principle.'

'Your principles. Not ours. I won't go down with you. I won't be held accountable. I won't—'

'What,' he cut in, 'are you saying?'

'If you don't make this go away I'll distance myself from you. We have to—'

A knock on the door. Morten Weber walked in. He looked as if he'd been shopping. Smart new jacket, red sweater, white shirt.

Hartmann and Skovgaard stared at him.

'Here's the document you asked me to find,' Weber said, coming over to Hartmann, a sheet of paper in his hand.

No one spoke.

Weber asked, 'More coffee?'

When there was no answer he smiled and left.

Hartmann looked at the colour printout. It was a page from Kirsten Eller's own website.

'What's it to be, Troels?'

He read the sheet carefully.

'OK,' she went on. 'I won't be seen with you. All joint arrangements are cancelled, including tonight's.'

Eller tidied her papers, dropped them into her briefcase with her pen. Got ready to go.

'What about your credibility?'

'What do you mean?'

Hartmann passed the paper across the table.

'You've been taking credit for my role models. It's here. On your home page.'

She snatched the page, read it.

'You liked our joint initiative so much you wrote about it.' Hartmann leaned back in his chair, put his hands behind his head. 'I'm happy to share the credit, Kirsten. But the trouble is . . . if there's blame to be apportioned you have to share that too.'

He leaned forward, smiled at her, added, 'That's what being accountable means.'

'This is blackmail.'

'No it's not. It's your website, not mine. Your responsibility. A matter of public record. Hang me out to dry and you'll find yourself swinging from the same line. But—'

'Thank you for the coffee,' Eller snarled.

'It was a pleasure. I'll see you tonight. As arranged.'

They watched her go then went back into the main office.

'She didn't like that,' Skovgaard said.

'I don't give a damn whether she liked it or not. I won't take lectures on accountability from some carpetbagging hack who'll climb into bed with anyone who'll have her.'

Morten Weber was at his desk. Hartmann walked over. Weber didn't take his eyes off his computer screen.

'I thought you'd deserted us.'

Weber scanned his inbox. Line after line of messages.

'I get bored on my own.'

Hartmann placed the page from Eller's website in front of him.

'How did you know?'

Weber stared at him as if it were obvious.

'I'd have grabbed the credit if I was running her campaign. You need to think like other people sometimes. It helps.'

'I'm glad you're back, Morten,' Skovgaard said.

He laughed, looked at her.

'Me too.'

Kemal's flat in Østerbro. The forensic team had pored over every inch of every room. All they had were two prints from Nanna Birk Larsen by the front door.

Meyer wanted more.

'Look,' the head forensic guy said. 'We've done everything. That's all there is.'

Lund read through the preliminary reports.

'What about the boots?' Meyer demanded.

'We analysed the mud. It's not from the crime scene.'

'What about the ether? Who the hell keeps ether in the house?'

'People with helicopters.'

One of the team pulled out a model helicopter.

'Boys' toys,' the forensic guy said. 'He likes them. This thing flies on a mixture of oil, paraffin and ether.'

'The neighbours?' Lund asked. 'What do they say?'

'There was a party on the third floor. A tenant saw him take out some rubbish at one thirty in the morning. That's all.'

Lund stared at him. The man wilted.

'Rubbish? At one thirty?'
'That's what he said.'

Twenty minutes later Kemal arrived for the reconstruction. He didn't look like a man expecting to be arrested. Smart jacket, grey scarf. Schoolteacher even on a Sunday.

'She never got much beyond the door?' Lund asked. 'That's what you're saying?'

'I buzzed her in. She rang the bell.'

'And then?'

'She felt guilty about some books I'd lent her.'

'You didn't go inside?'

'No. We talked here. At the door.'

'So why are her prints on a photo in the living room?'

'I was going to sand the floor. All the things were out here. It was the class photo. She looked at it before she left.'

'Why?'

'I don't know. She wanted to for some reason.'

'Then?'

'Then she left.'

'Did you see her out of the building?'

'No. I just closed the door. It's safe here. No reason . . .' He fell silent. 'I thought it was safe.'

'Why did you cancel the floor people?' Meyer asked.

'It was going to be too expensive. I thought I'd do it myself.'

'So you phoned him? At one thirty in the morning?'

'He had an answering machine. Why not?'

Lund checked the door, went in and out again.

'You took a call minutes before Nanna arrived.'

The man's dark eyes flickered between the two of them.

'It was a wrong number. That was when I was at the petrol station.'

Meyer said, 'What? You talk for ninety seconds on a wrong number?'

'Yes . . .' The two of them watched him struggling. 'He wanted to talk to the person who had the number before me.'

'The call came from a launderette just round the corner. Quite a coincidence, huh?'

'I don't know.'

Lund said, 'You threw out some rubbish.'

'On Saturday,' he agreed.

'On Saturday at one thirty in the morning. What was in the black bag?'

'An old rug.'

'A rug?'

'I took it to the bins on my way back to the allotment.'

Silence.

'If that's all . . .'

Silence.

'My wife's coming here soon. I'd like you gone by then.'

'Don't run away,' Meyer told him.

Back at headquarters Buchard listened to their briefing.

'So you don't have a bloody thing?'

'Kemal's lying,' Lund said.

'You found nothing at the flat.'

'He cleaned up. He took her somewhere else.'

The chief was stomping round the office like an angry dog.

'Where? You've checked everything. Flat, car, basement, allotment, youth club—'

'If you feel pressured by Troels Hartmann's campaign, chief,' Lund cut in. 'Do let us know. Only polite.'

Buchard looked ready to explode.

'I don't give a shit about politics. There's nothing here that makes the man a rapist and a murderer.'

'Kemal's lying,' Lund said again. 'He's got to have a place—'

'Then find it,' Buchard ordered.

Kemal's wife was walking round their apartment, looking at the walls covered in crimson fingerprint dust. There were markers everywhere.

He stood in the hall, not following her as she went round turning on the lights in each room, clutching at her big belly, face angry and confused.

'What were they looking for?'

No answer.

'What do they think you did to her?'

'They'll soon see they're wrong.'

'I don't understand why you didn't tell them before.'

He leaned against the wall, didn't meet her eyes.

'I didn't want you to worry.'

He wrapped his arms around her, persisted even when she tried to fight him off.

'I told you I'm sorry. I can't undo what's been done. We—'

She pulled away. Still furious. His phone rang.

'Rama speaking.'

He strode off, out into freshly sanded living room with its bare floorboards and the marks of the police forensic team everywhere.

She hated it when he spoke Arabic. A language she couldn't begin to understand.

Hated it when he got angry too. This was so rare. He was a placid, decent man. Yet as she listened to him, voice rising to a fury in that foreign tongue, she wondered how much she really knew him. How much there was still hidden in his life.

The tap on Kemal's phone caught the loud and angry exchange. Forty minutes later a woman in a cream chador was sitting in front of a computer listening to the phone tap.

Duty translator. She scribbled down the original, looked at it.

'What did he say?' Meyer asked.

' "Keep quiet. Don't go to the police or you'll regret it for the rest of your life." '

'Have you traced it?' Lund asked.

'Landline. Somewhere in the north-west.'

They listened to the tape again. There was a sound in the background. A long cry. He replayed it, slowed down but at the same fidelity. Full volume.

The translator listened, nodding.

'It's Isha,' she said. 'It's the evening prayer.'

Meyer was working on the computer.

'The phone belongs to Mustafa Akkad. No criminal records. Runs a small business renting lock-up garages near Nørreport Station.'

'Tell Svendsen to get Akkad in here,' Lund said as she went for her jacket.

*

The lock-ups were underneath a flyover. It was a grubby, desolate place. Metal doors covered in graffiti. Rubbish strewn in the lane. Bad drains.

Jansen was outside, blue plastic shoes on his big feet, ginger hair wet in the rain. A team of three technicians were working on the door.

'Only one of the garages isn't rented,' Jansen said. 'We thought we'd start there.'

They pulled on gloves and blue plastic shoe covers. Then the technicians got the padlocks off the door and slid it open.

Meyer was in first, Lund second, torches high in their hands.

In the wandering, searching beams the place looked like nothing but a junk store. Tables, half-dismantled engines, office storage racks, tents, fishing rods, furniture . . .

Lund walked through to the back. Lines of paintings in frames stood along both sides with some model ships and plaster statues.

At the rear of the garage, against the wall that ran parallel with the street, stood several large canvases. Cheap paintings, the kind a restaurant might use for decoration. They were stored oddly. Propped against each other, two frames high. Set at an angle of thirty degrees or so against the brickwork.

Lund looked and thought.

She went up close, removed all four frames. There was a door behind.

Her gloved hands fell on the handle. Unlocked, it opened easily. Lund stayed on the threshold for a moment, checking the interior carefully, looking for a figure trying to hide in the dark.

This place was smaller. More organized too. A couple of metal chairs stood together, nothing on the seats as if they'd been used recently. A lamp stand was next to them, the cable running to a socket in the corner.

Lund's torch checked the walls once more then she stepped inside, ran the beam down to the floor.

A worn, stained double mattress lay there, with a crumpled blue and orange sleeping bag on it next to an ashtray.

Closer. There was a child's teddy bear next to the makeshift bed. She got down, started looking more closely.

'Lund?'

Meyer had walked in and she'd barely noticed.

'Lund?'

She looked. He'd found a girl's yellow zipped top. There was a bloodstain on the front.

It was old and dark and big.

Yellow, she thought. The kind of thing a schoolgirl might wear. Childish even.

One o'clock. Hartmann watched the committee members assembling in the meeting room.

'The vultures are circling, Troels,' Weber said. 'Watch your back.'

'Anything from the police?' Hartmann asked.

'Not a thing.'

'Let's get this done with.'

When he entered they were scattered round the room, talking in fragmented groups.

Cabals and cliques. Every party had them.

Two women, the rest men, mainly middle-aged, in business suits. Long-term party workers.

'This meeting was called with insufficient notice,' Hartmann said, taking a chair at the head of the table. 'So let's keep it short.'

Knud Padde ruffled his curly hair nervously, glanced across the table, said, 'It's short notice, Troels. On the other hand. The situation with the press. The publicity . . .'

'Fine, Knud. Could we get to the point, please?'

'You're the point.'

Morten Weber's prediction was accurate as usual. It was Henrik Bigum who spoke. A lean, unsmiling economics lecturer at the university, bald with the severe, ascetic face of a judgemental priest. Bigum had put himself forward for election to the city council and the Parliament on several occasions. Never got past the short list. An intelligent, committed man, but caustic in private and addicted to scheming.

'Henrik. How nice to hear from you.'

The room was silent, tense.

Hartmann put down his pen, sat back in his chair.

'OK. Let's hear it.'

'We're all very fond of you,' Bigum went on, as if pronouncing a death sentence. 'Appreciative of the work you've done.'

'I hear a but, Henrik.'

'But lately your judgement and your honesty have been called into question.'

'Bullshit. By whom? You?'

'By events. The evidence suggests the teacher's guilty. By not suspending him you give the impression you're protecting the innocent when in fact you're protecting yourself.'

Morten Weber asked, 'Where's this on the agenda?'

'We're beyond agendas. Secondly, Kemal's file wasn't handed over to the police at the outset.'

Bigum looked round the table, addressing the meeting now, not Troels Hartmann.

'Why not? Does Troels have something to hide? Thirdly, confidential information has been leaked from this office. Very private information. Handed to people who can do us harm. We're losing votes. We're losing credibility. Our support in Parliament is fragmented and waning. Does it look as if you have the situation in hand, Troels? Not to me. Not to anyone.'

Hartmann stared at him across the gleaming table, laughed and asked, 'Is that it?'

'What do you mean?'

'I don't expect you to possess the assassin's skills of Poul Bremer, Henrik. But really . . . You abandoned your students for this?'

'Isn't it true? Everything, about the file, the police, the leaks from this place?'

'No. Everything you say has been taken out of context. These problems are dealt with. You don't need to worry—'

'If Troels doesn't withdraw his candidacy of his own accord,' Bigum interrupted, 'I propose a meeting be called for a vote of confidence.'

'Are you serious?' Hartmann.

'I am.'

'And who would stand in my place?' Hartmann gazed at him, waiting for an answer. 'Do you have any suggestions? I wonder—'

'That we deal with when the need arises. You're destroying what we've worked for—'

'This is not your decision, Henrik!' a lone female voice cried. 'It's not up to you.'

Elisabet Hedegaard, a nursery school teacher from Østebro.

Bigum took a moment to answer. This was an opportunistic stab in the back. Based on hope and the moment.

'It's in the constitution,' he said. 'Knud?'

'According to the regulations,' Padde said, pulling a copy out of his pocket, 'a majority of votes allows it.'

'What about the constituency?' Hedegaard asked. 'They chose Troels in the first place. They have a say.'

An old man Hartmann barely recognized snarled at her, 'We're looking for a solution to the problem, here. Some of us have been working for the party for decades. Not since yesterday . . .'

Hartmann sat back, stayed silent.

'The constituency has a voice,' the woman went on. 'What you suggest will only make matters worse.'

'They can be worse?' Bigum asked. 'We've got a candidate for Lord Mayor who's embroiled in a murder investigation. With leaks from his office. Numerous highly questionable decisions—'

'The constituency—' Hedegaard went on.

'The constituency decides whether Troels is fit to stand as a councillor,' Padde broke in. 'It's up to us to say who leads the campaign.'

'I propose . . .' Henrik Bigum began.

Theis and Pernille Birk Larsen turned up at headquarters just after two. Lund pulled out photos of some of the items from the lock-up. Meyer stood behind her, watching closely.

'I need you to tell me if you recognize any of these things,' she said.

A khaki rucksack.

Nothing.

A red notebook with a distinctive leaf pattern on the cover and a felt-tip pen.

'No,' the mother said.

The mattress with the teddy bear and the blue sleeping bag.

Theis Birk Larsen stared at the items.

Lund looked at him, looked at the photograph. Next to the mattress was a cup half full with orange juice. An uneaten biscuit on a plate. A bowl with the remains of what looked like curry. An ashtray with several stubbed-out cigarettes.

'Nanna didn't smoke,' he said. 'She always nagged me about it.'

Lund passed over a close-up of the teddy bear and a key ring. Two keys, and a plastic design of clover leaves and flowers.

'You've already got her keys, haven't you?' Pernille said.

'We thought there might be a second set.'

'I've never seen any of this.'

Then the yellow top with the bloodstain and a brand logo.

Pernille Birk Larsen's eyes opened wide, never left the photo.

'I think she's got one like that,' she said, still staring at the yellow fabric and the bloodstain on the left side, close to the zip at the waist.

'You're sure?' Lund asked quickly. 'You're absolutely sure?'

'Like it,' Pernille said, nodding.

'Thanks.'

Lund took the photos away.

'Where's he now?' Birk Larsen asked. 'The teacher?'

'He's in custody,' Lund said. 'He's under arrest until we've finished our investigation.'

He got up. Black jacket, red boiler suit.

'What do you know?' Pernille persisted.

'We can't go into details—' Meyer began.

'I'm her mother,' the woman cried. 'I have the right—'

'We can't go into—'

Lund interrupted.

'Apparently she went to his flat after the party. Maybe they had a relationship. We're not sure. She was taken somewhere. Perhaps this place. Then driven out to the woods.'

Meyer was grumbling wordlessly behind her.

'Thanks,' Birk Larsen said.

'Thanks,' the woman echoed.

There was nothing more. They left. Meyer sat in the corner of the office, smoking.

After a while he said, 'Lund?'

She was looking at the photos again. They had a potential ID of an item of clothing. It was the hardest piece of information they possessed.

'Lund?'

She met his gaze. Two days' stubble, big ears, glassy round eyes.

'That,' Meyer said, shaking his miserable head, 'was wrong.'

*

Buchard listened to Lund's report and shook his head.

'The mother identified the shirt,' Lund said.

'It's a kid's top,' Buchard complained. 'Millions like it. Forensics found nothing to suggest it was Nanna's.'

'The blood—'

'We haven't got the results yet.'

'There's enough evidence.'

Meyer watched in silence.

'Like what?' Buchard asked.

'Like a witness who saw Kemal carry something to his car.'

'No,' Buchard said. 'The only evidence you have is an inconclusive phone call.'

'And the fact that he lied!'

'If we charged everyone who lied to us half of Denmark would be in jail. Any judge with half a spine's going to tear us to pieces with this shit. Find Mustafa Akkad. Clear this up one way or the other. Or I'll get someone who can.'

Theis Birk Larsen went out to cost a job for the week ahead. Pernille hung round in the arcades outside police headquarters then, when he'd driven off, talked her way back inside.

She confronted Lund in her office.

'Why haven't you arrested him?'

'We don't have enough evidence.'

'How much do you need?' she yelled. 'You said she was at his flat. At the party. In the garage.'

'We're still looking.'

'And if you don't find more? After everything—'

'I told you,' Lund said. 'We're still working on the case. We're making progress. I understand—'

'Don't tell me you understand.' She stood there rigid, determined, right hand raised, finger wagging, like a teacher, like a mother. 'Don't do that. Do not tell me you understand.'

Back home. Back at the sink, manically washing dishes that didn't need washing, wiping surfaces that were already clean.

He'd returned, sat at the table, saying nothing. In their small quarter of Vesterbro he was a king of a kind. The man the neighbours asked for help when there were problems with tearaways. Even the immigrants would knock on the door sometimes and beg Theis Birk Larsen for advice. When Nanna was tiny, five or six or seven, she'd seized an Indian kid and made the bright-eyed little waif her first boyfriend.

Amir.

Pernille remembered the two of them together, hand in hand, giggling as she rode them down the street in the box of the Christiania trike. Remembered the way Theis dealt with a couple of local thugs who picked on Amir too. Not gently. It wasn't his way. But it worked.

Amir he defended. The boy was still in a picture on the table, in the scarlet box of the Christiania trike.

Nanna . . .

'They'll get him,' he said finally. 'In the end.'

'You know about these things?'

She glared at him as she stacked the plates.

'They never found enough evidence for you, did they? Not for everything . . .'

His face fell, became fierce.

Birk Larsen got up from the table, confronted her.

'Did I fail you? Am I a poor husband?' His eyes were sly again, but full of pain. 'A bad father?'

'I didn't say that. I said you of all people know the police don't find everything they ought to. Don't ask me to believe in them.'

He put his hands on her waist. She wriggled from him.

Birk Larsen cursed, got his leather jacket, put it on.

'I'm going over to the house.'

'Do that.'

She started washing the boys' dishes again.

'Go back to your stupid house and hide.'

'What?'

'It's what you do when things get difficult. Isn't it? Run away.'

She put down the dishes, pulled off her gloves, faced him, discovered a savage thrill in her own courage, found words she'd never dared speak before.

'That's what you did with Nanna.'

'What the hell does that mean?'

'When she wanted to talk. You never had time. Then you'd go. Down into the garage. Down to talk to Vagn. Isn't that right?'

'No.' He took a step towards her. 'It isn't.'

Pernille picked up the plates from the table, tidied them away. The boys were out with Lotte. She was glad of that.

'Why did she have so many secrets? Why didn't we know about her life?'

'Because she was nineteen years old! Did you want your parents knowing what you did then? Besides . . . You two stuck together like glue . . .'

'Because you weren't around.'

A roar like a lion, fury and pain.

'I was working. Paying for her school. Paying for all this. You were the one who let her do what she wanted. Go out at night, come back God knows when, never say who with or why.'

'Not me, not me.'

'Yes you. It didn't bother you at all.'

Tears in her eyes. Anger in her face.

'How can you say that? How *dare* you say that? I couldn't sleep until she was home.'

'That helped.'

'At least I didn't take it out on her.'

'And look where we are now.'

He waved a hand around the empty kitchen.

'Look at this,' Theis Birk Larsen said. 'This . . .'

But she was gone, back into their bedroom, slamming the door behind her.

He ate his sandwiches at his desk. Didn't want to leave the garage. Didn't want to work.

Vagn Skærbæk came in. Black cap, scarlet overalls, usual jaunty walk, silver chain round his neck.

'Rudi and I are going to the house. Are you coming?'

Birk Larsen huddled over the desk and the uneaten food, a cigarette in his fist. He shook his head. 'Is there something I can do, Theis?'

Birk Larsen stubbed out his cigarette in the bread. Skærbæk pulled up a chair, put his elbows on the table.

'You know how much she meant to me, don't you?' he said. 'You and Pernille. The boys. Nanna. You've been my family. I hate seeing all this.'

Birk Larsen watched him.

'It isn't fair, Theis.'

'I don't want to talk about it.'

Skærbæk said, 'OK.'

He didn't leave. Sat there. Waiting.

'What am I supposed to do?' Birk Larsen said eventually.

'I don't know.'

Birk Larsen stood up. A head taller than Skærbæk. A year older. Stronger by far. King of the quarter. Once anyway.

'It never lets you go,' Birk Larsen said.

'What?'

'What you've done. Who you are.'

Birk Larsen nodded at the van keys on the wall.

'Don't go to the house, Vagn,' he said. 'Send Rudi on his own.'

'OK.'

'I've got a better idea,' the big man said.

Svendsen's men found Mustafa Akkad when he walked back to the garages at Nørreport, straight into the arms of the team working there. By five that Sunday he was in an interview room with the woman interpreter. Lund was watching through the door, talking on the phone to Mark, telling him to get something to eat. Meyer came out and she ended the call.

'He won't say a word,' Meyer told her.

'We'll see about that,' she muttered and walked towards the room.

He didn't follow.

She stopped.

'What is it?' Lund asked.

'Are we sure he's involved?'

'Yes. Why?'

'He's got a clean record. He works. He's got four children. He prays five times a day.'

'So what?'

'So something doesn't fit.'

'Oh for Christ's sake. Where did you come from? Are they meant to wear badges or something?'

'There's something wrong! He could have removed all that stuff from the garage if he'd wanted.'

244

'But he didn't.'

'And he came back. To a murder scene. Please . . .'

'Watch me,' she said and marched into the room.

Akkad was a swarthy man of thirty-five. Leather bomber jacket. Scruffy gleaming black hair. Scared face that looked too young for his age.

Lund sat down, threw some papers on the table, said, 'Here's the thing. If you don't talk I throw you in a cell. With a couple of bikers we picked up pushing dope in Christiania. They're not into integration, Mustafa. Or didn't you know that?'

He suddenly looked worried.

'No language problems then.' She pointed to the door. 'So what is it? The cell? Or you talk? You tell me.'

The interpreter was still translating.

'He doesn't need this,' Lund said. 'Don't translate another word. He talks to me in Danish. Or he goes to meet his new biker friends. Listen.'

Akkad's eyes were on the table.

'Listen!' Lund shrieked in his face. 'The court doesn't care what you promised Kemal. Any more than I do. I can get you served with a deportation order in three days flat. You won't see daylight. We'll bundle you on a plane straight back to the place you came from.'

Finger in his face. That got some attention.

'Straight back, Mustafa. We'll make sure the police meet you at the airport.' She waited a moment. 'How are the police back home? Do they smile at you like we do? Are they nice?'

The translator was interpreting anyway. Lund let her chant on. It helped with the atmosphere.

'After that,' Lund said, speaking over the woman in the burka, 'I visit your wife and kids. Check their papers. See if I can send them after you.'

His face went down into his hands.

'Can you support them from a jail back home? Can they go to school? Go to hospital for free? Pick up benefits when they feel like it while everyone else goes out to work? Or maybe they'll be begging on the streets like everyone else—'

'I work!' he roared.

The armed uniformed cop at the door took a step towards the table.

'I work every hour I can.'

'You speak good Danish too,' Lund said, and folded her arms, sat back as if to listen. 'So why the silence?'

'It's not what you think.'

Meyer pulled up a chair.

'What is it then?' he asked.

Mustafa Akkad shook his head.

'Rama's a good man. You've got to believe me.' He stared at Lund. 'He wouldn't hurt anyone.'

He leaned back in his chair, closed his eyes.

'He just did something stupid.'

'What?' Lund asked.

'I went to his place that Friday night. He knew the girl would be coming by. I said I didn't want anything to do with it.' A shrug. 'But he needed somewhere. When I arrived the girl was hurt. She'd been beaten up. She could hardly walk. We carried her to the car and drove her to my garage. So she could hide from her family. Then I left . . .'

'Her family?' Lund asked. 'What are you talking about?'

'The girl. You keep asking me about the girl. I'm telling you . . . the girl Rama helped.'

'What girl?'

Mustafa Akkad said, very slowly, 'The girl from his father's congregation. The one you keep asking about. Abu Jamal's daughter. Leyla. They wanted her to marry some guy from home so he could come in here. So she tried to run away.'

'Shit,' Meyer muttered.

'If they found her I don't know what they'd do.' He glared at them. 'Not that you'd be much help. So Rama got her away from them. He hid her in my garage. Then somewhere else on Sunday. I don't know where.'

Meyer swore again then got up and walked out of the room. Lit a cigarette in the dim corridor. Looked down towards the end.

Kemal's wife was there. Big in an old khaki anorak. Phone in hand.

She said, 'Rama didn't come home. Where is he?'

'I don't know. I'm not his babysitter.'

'He went to pick up some shopping. He doesn't answer his phone.'

Lund came to the door, listened.

'I left lots of messages. He never got back to me.' She showed Meyer the phone. 'He always calls.'

Lund walked into Svendsen's office. He was there looking relaxed over a mug of coffee.

'Where's Theis Birk Larsen?' she asked.

'Last I heard he was at home.'

'I told you to keep him under surveillance.'

'Give me a million men and maybe I can do a quarter of what you ask.'

'Find out where he is,' she ordered.

He picked up the coffee mug, toasted her.

At quarter past six the scarlet van drew up by the front door of the deserted warehouse. Skærbæk got out first, looked around.

No one came to this part of the city much on a Sunday night.

Checked right, checked left. Remembered the old days when he and Theis worked the streets. A good team. Good partners too, most of the time.

'Clear,' he said and banged the driver's side. Then he took out the security card, opened the locks, rolled up the folding door, guided him in. Stood back and watched as Birk Larsen edged the vehicle into the half-empty interior.

A train went past. A shriek of a klaxon. Pigeons scattered round the inside of the building, flapped anxiously as they flew to the door.

Skærbæk popped on the lights then rolled the outside door back down.

The old days.

Birk Larsen had brought a sledgehammer with him. Skærbæk a pickaxe handle. Both men stood at the back of the van, swinging them idly, remembering.

'Theis—'

'Keep quiet.'

Skærbæk fell silent. Watched. Wondered.

It was Birk Larsen who walked up to the back, unlocked the doors, threw them open.

The teacher crouched by the racks still pretending to be white.

Smart black jacket. Preppy scarf. Shiny shoes.

Skærbæk had a torch. He shone it in the man's eyes.

Kemal got up, climbed out, opened his arms, looked at both of them.

Half angry, half terrified.

'Listen to me,' the teacher pleaded. 'I haven't done anything. I told you everything I know. I told the police—'

Birk Larsen upturned the sledgehammer, held it by the iron head, swung the shaft round, landed it in his gut.

Kemal went down, shrieking. Birk Larsen got a kick into his head, watched as he rolled round once on the floor, dragged him up by the leather jacket, threw him against the van.

Stood there, next to Skærbæk, waited.

'Your daughter was in my flat for a minute,' Kemal said, wiping the blood from his mouth. 'She brought some books back. Then she left.'

Birk Larsen upturned the sledgehammer, let the iron head hang down to the ground, swinging it like a pendulum.

'There was another girl there that night. Someone I was helping. I couldn't tell you. I couldn't tell the police.'

Skærbæk wiped his nose with his sleeve, banged his pickaxe handle against the van wall.

'I know I should have told you but I couldn't,' Kemal yelled. 'It's the truth.'

Birk Larsen nodded. Looked at Skærbæk.

'Gimme his phone,' he said.

'Theis . . .' Skærbæk began.

'Ring her,' Birk Larsen ordered, handing over the mobile.

The teacher stood by the back of the van, hunched over, rigid, hurting and scared.

'Go on,' Birk Larsen ordered. 'Ring the girl.'

Trembling fingers stabbed at the buttons. Rahman Al Kemal made the call.

As soon as she knew Lund left in her own car. Now she was out on the road, listening to the radio.

Control said, 'We have a possible kidnapping. We're looking for number plate PM 92 010. It's a red van from Birk Larsen's Removals. It left the garage around 6 p.m.'

Meyer was working up a team. She liked being on her own, trying to think.

'Theis Birk Larsen is six foot four tall. About forty-five years old. Exercise caution when approaching him. He may be violent. Apprehend immediately and . . .'

She put her phone headset on, called Meyer.

'What do you know?'

'Where the hell are you? You can't just walk out on me like that.'

'I did.'

'We've got the kidnap negotiators on standby.'

'It's not a kidnap, Meyer. He's going to kill him. What do you know?'

'We found Kemal's car near his house. Looks like there's been a struggle. Birk Larsen took a van.'

She was heading towards Vesterbro. This was Birk Larsen's territory. Surely . . .

'Places,' she demanded. 'Give me places.'

'Where the hell are you?'

'Places!'

He sighed.

'We've checked the garage and the warehouse next door. Trouble is Birk Larsen's got little cubbyholes all round the city.'

'Isn't there a warehouse at Teglholmen?'

There was a big industrial park south of Vesterbro. The closest deserted area in the city to Birk Larsen's home.

She heard the sound of papers being shuffled.

'Yeah but he hasn't used it in six months.'

'What does Pernille say?'

'I brought her in. She won't even speak to me.'

'Ask his best friend Skærbæk. If Theis is going to use anyone he'd pick him.'

'Yeah,' Meyer said. 'I notice things too. Skærbæk's not at home. Both of them have got their mobiles turned off.'

'Shit.'

'He used his credit card at a petrol station on Enghavevej about an hour and a half ago. That's in Vesterbro, three streets from where he lives.'

Lund pulled in to the side of the road. She was near the turning for Vesterbro, by the Fisketorvet shopping centre. Several roads converged here. She could head anywhere in the city.

'Wait,' he ordered. 'OK. We have a call from Kemal's mobile registered in P Knudsens Gade. Let me look at a map.'

She knew where that was.

'He's going south-east to Valby,' Meyer said.

'No,' she said. 'He isn't. I checked the Valby address.'

'For Christ's sake, Lund. Maybe he's taking the motorway. What about Avedore? They've got a depot there.'

She pulled out into the traffic.

'Would he use his own place?'

'My psychic powers fail me. You got any better ideas?'

'Birk Larsen isn't stupid. He knows we have a list of his depots.'

'Yeah!' Meyer yelled. 'They're all we have. Think of something, will you? Damned if I can.'

'Where did you say the call came from?'

'P Knudsens Gade.'

'I'll take a look. Tell the wife she'd better talk to you if she wants to see her husband again.'

'Yeah.'

The street was five minutes away, a broad, double carriageway lined with bare trees, running parallel with the motorway.

Houses and offices. Brightly lit.

Not the place for a killing.

Birk Larsen looked at his watch.

Kemal had tried the number repeatedly. Never got through. Now he sat on the ledge of the van door, pressing the buttons, getting nowhere.

'I couldn't give the girl away,' the teacher said, getting more desperate by the minute. 'It was an arranged marriage. You understand? You know what I mean?'

Vagn Skærbæk leaned against the wall, eyes closed, looking bored.

'I couldn't tell anyone. If her parents find her they'll hurt her again.' Kemal hesitated. 'Kill her maybe.'

'And?' Birk Larsen asked, swinging the sledgehammer from side to side like the pendulum on a clock slowing down to nothing.

'I was afraid they'd come after her. She'd run away from home.'

Skærbæk opened his eyes, looked at him, said, 'You sound like a man digging his own grave.'

'Why hasn't she rung back?' Birk Larsen asked.

'I don't know! How can I know? Nanna came round to return some books. That's the last I saw of her—'

'I said shut up,' Skærbæk yelled, then slapped him round the head.

'There is no girl,' Birk Larsen said. 'You're lying.'

'No! I left her a message. She'll ring back in a minute.'

'Long minute,' Skærbæk moaned.

Then the phone rang. Kemal glanced anxiously at the screen. A name: *Leyla*. A number.

He answered, stood up, showed it them.

Birk Larsen came over, took the phone off him. Answered.

A voice.

Gave the phone to Kemal. He tapped the speakerphone. The three of them listened.

'Leyla? This is Rama.'

'Rama?' She sounded sleepy. 'Is that you?'

'Don't be afraid,' he said. 'Everything will be OK.' He cleared his throat. 'I really need your help now, Leyla. I need you to say what happened on the Friday you came to see me.'

Silence.

'Hello?' he said.

'Where are you calling from?'

'Doesn't matter. Do you remember the girl you met? The girl from my school? Her father's with me. It's important you tell him what happened. Tell him she brought me some books—'

'Don't tell her what to say, you idiot!' Skærbæk shouted.

The girl began speaking in Arabic. Kemal answered in the same.

'Hey! Hey! Bin Laden!' Skærbæk screamed. 'This is Denmark. Speak Danish. Don't you understand?'

Birk Larsen snatched the phone, put it to his ear.

Said, 'Hello? Hello?'

Looked at the dead phone. Looked at Kemal, eyes bright in the gloom.

One moment.

One decision.

The teacher ran behind the door. Skærbæk screamed and went for him. Hand on the scarlet metal, Kemal rammed it back into his face, grabbed his pickaxe handle, punched it hard into Birk Larsen's chest as the big man came for him.

Ran for his life.

Panting.

Pigeons flapping frightened overhead.

Felt something take his legs from under him.

Down on the ground, chest heaving. Above him in the pale fluorescent light Birk Larsen raised the sledgehammer, swinging the head in a slow and certain arc.

She sat opposite Meyer in the low light of the office.

'Pernille,' he said. 'You have to help us. Kemal didn't kill your daughter. He had nothing to do with it. Theis has kidnapped him. Do you understand—?'

'No,' she cried. 'I don't! First it was that kid Scharndorff. Then the teacher. I don't!'

'If Theis hurts Kemal he'll go to prison. Do you understand that?'

She was quiet for a moment.

'Theis wouldn't hurt him.'

'Really?' Meyer asked.

He picked up the file photos on the desk. The bloodied corpse in Christiania.

'Twenty years ago a drug dealer was murdered.'

She looked at the grim pictures, didn't flinch.

'They thought Theis did it.' Meyer looked at her. 'I guess that was around the time the two of you got together. Did you not suspect—?'

'We're all different when we're young. Then we leave it behind.'

She stared at him.

'Didn't you?'

'Maybe. But this is now and he's making a big mistake.'

She picked up the photos, looked at them, turned them over.

'I told you. He'd never do that.'

'I always thought it was Vagn who came up with the alibis.'

'Screw you.'

'Vagn's with him too. They won't run from this.' He leaned forward in the dim light. 'Help me. Help Theis.'

Slowly, 'He wouldn't do it.'

Sirens outside. Cars setting off into the night.

'I know you lost your daughter. But Kemal's innocent. His wife's about to have a baby. He's a good man. Don't make it worse. You have to help me. I need to know where Theis is.'

Meyer watched her.

Silence.

'We can stay here all night,' he said. 'I've got all the time in the world. Have you?'

She glowered at him. They hated you even when you tried to help, he thought.

'Pern—'

'There's a place he uses sometimes. I don't know why. An abandoned warehouse.'

'What's the address?'

'I can't remember. It's out on Teglholmen. Somewhere.'

Lund drove up and down, looking, looking.

Finally, in the darkness close to the end of the road, she saw a red sign half-hidden behind a wire fence.

Birk Larsen Removals.

The phone rang.

'We're on our way to Teglholmen,' Meyer said. 'He's there somewhere. I've got an armed response unit on the way.'

'There already,' she said.

'What?'

'Birk Larsen's got a lock-up on the industrial estate. The lights are on.'

She gave him the number and a street cross reference.

'I've got Pernille with me,' Meyer said. 'We'll be there in two minutes. Wait for us. Lund? Lund?'

She put the phone in her pocket, got out of the car, shone her torch on the security gates.

Open.

Walked in.

Cold dark night. Thin clouds. Half moon. No wind. No sound or sign of life.

Except for the lights all round the building.

There was a side door covered in graffiti. Open. She went through, shining the torch ahead.

A short corridor. Lights at the end.

A man screamed, the cry loud and liquid, full of agony and fear. Lund began to run.

He didn't want to kill him. Yet. He wanted to hear. The sledge-hammer was gone. Now he had Skærbæk's pickaxe handle, kept swinging it into Kemal's guts and chest and limbs.

There was blood on the floor. One of the man's arms hung crazily broken at the elbow. Birk Larsen swung again, caught him in that dark and handsome face.

Another scream and not a word.

'Theis,' Skærbæk said.

He stood there shuffling from foot to foot, hadn't done a thing except watch and grumble.

Birk Larsen walked around the bloody heap on the floor, thinking of somewhere new to hurt. Kicked Kemal in the head.

'OK, Theis,' Skærbæk said.

Another thrashing blow with the wooden stick, another scream.

'Theis, for God's sake! He's had enough. Maybe . . .'

Birk Larsen glared at him, a fierce and frightening animal expression.

'Maybe what?'

'Maybe he's telling the truth.'

Birk Larsen cursed, swung the handle again, struck Kemal on the ribs.

Went for the sledgehammer.

'Theis!' Skærbæk pleaded.

A voice from the darkness.

'Theis Birk Larsen. This is Sarah Lund.'

Skærbæk found his spine, got between Birk Larsen and the man, said, 'Come on. We're done here.'

'You go running, Vagn,' the big man roared, and with one huge hand tossed him aside like a rag doll, sending him crashing against the van.

The sledgehammer came up, caressed Skærbæk's neck, drew back for a moment.

And then Vagn Skærbæk was gone.

A hand around a bloody neck, dragging Kemal from the ground.

'Sit up,' Birk Larsen ordered. 'Sit up! On your knees.'

The way they were on TV. In the videos of executions. Blindfolded men in faraway places. Waiting for death.

'Theis!' The voice was louder, nearer, higher. 'Stop. Stop now.'

But the heat was in him and the rage. They never abated easily.

He could hear her running across the concrete floor. Looked. In the harsh fluorescent light blue jeans and that black and white jumper.

'Kemal's innocent!' she yelled at him. 'Listen to me. He's nothing to do with it.'

The teacher was on all fours, bloody mouth dripping gore on the ground. Birk Larsen kicked him hard in the ribs, grabbed his hair.

'I said get up,' he barked, and looked into the bruised and bleeding face.

The head of the hammer stroked Kemal's neck. A single blow. To a kneeling man. Justice.

'Sit up!' he screamed.

In the van's headlights, shadows silhouetted against the wall. This was the right place, the right position. This was the point where the pain came to an end.

Another figure racing from the door.

'Theis! Put down the weapon. He didn't do it.'

The mouthy bug-eyed cop with the big ears.

The hammer. One long, strong swing.

He heard a gun cock, saw out of the corner of his eye the cop called Meyer had a weapon on him now, pointed, ready to go.

A shot. The sound echoed round the empty warehouse like a burst balloon. Birk Larsen blinked, hesitated. Was lost.

Then a third shape. A fawn raincoat. Long hair. A face, the precious face.

Pernille stood next to them, staring at him open-mouthed.

This is me, Birk Larsen thought. The me you knew existed even if you never dared ask.

This is me.

The hammer came back one more time.

'Theis!' Meyer yelled, gun out, barrel at him. 'Listen to me. Put the weapon down. I'll shoot you before you touch him. I swear to God.'

Pernille walked past them, straight towards Birk Larsen and the bloody heap on the grimy floor.

'Put it down!' the cop screamed. 'Don't do anything stupid.'

He hesitated and that was time enough. When he was ready again there were three more of them, black pistols pointed at his face.

As if that was enough . . .

But there was Pernille too, a stride away, her pale, pained face caught in the hard light of the bright strips. Pernille gazing at him as if to say: I knew but I never wanted to.

'Theis,' she said. 'Put it down.'

And so he did.

Rie Skovgaard and Morten Weber finished working the phones. Hartmann called a few more people himself. Spoke to police headquarters then, at eight exactly, walked into the meeting.

Knud Padde began.

'It's undesirable but necessary that we take a vote of no confidence against Troels Hartmann. May I—?'

'We're wasting time,' Henrik Bigum said wearily. He looked as if the result had already been declared. 'We all know where this is going.'

'Don't worry, Henrik,' Hartmann said. 'A vote won't be necessary.'

'I'm sorry, Troels. It will. We've decided to do this.'

'If you want I'll withdraw. You don't need to vote. Except for . . .' He smiled at Bigum. 'Whoever takes my place.'

'No, Troels!' Elisabet Hedegaard protested. 'Why? Why do this? Henrik speaks for himself, always . . .'

'Withdrawal's also an option,' Bigum agreed. 'If that's your choice.'

He took a pen out of his jacket. Offered it to Hartmann.

'You haven't checked your phone, Henrik? No private messages? No tips from Bremer's office? Not even the news?'

Bigum laughed, shook his head.

'I thought you might have done this with a little dignity. Resign and have done with it.'

'I just spoke to the police chief in charge of the Birk Larsen case,' Hartmann said. 'There's new evidence that proves beyond any doubt the teacher's innocent. He's going on TV in a few minutes. If you want to ditch me for defending an innocent man that's your prerogative. What it's going to do for the prospects of my successor—'

'Over to you, Knud,' Bigum bellowed.

Padde sat open-mouthed, unable to decide which way to turn.

'Maybe we should think about this,' he said eventually. 'Not vote now after all. If what Troels says is true we need to know the facts.'

'The facts!' Bigum was furious. 'The facts are Hartmann screwed this up from beginning to end. If you fall for a trick like this . . .'

Hartmann was nursing a cup of coffee. He looked at it. Made them wait.

'I think,' he said, 'we should all sleep on it and talk again in the morning. What's a few hours? Agreed?'

A long silence. Broken only when Henrik Bigum swore, got up, stormed out of the room. Then Elisabet Hedegaard squeezed Hartmann's hand, beamed at him, leaned over, whispered, 'Well done.'

Ten minutes later, alone in his office, in front of the TV.

'It's now evident that Hartmann's role model has been cleared of all suspicion,' the newscaster said.

A reporter was chasing Poul Bremer down a City Hall corridor, shoving a microphone in the mayor's face.

'I'm pleased the case has turned out this way for Hartmann's sake,' Bremer said with no conviction. 'But you saw the way he behaved. He was paralysed by indecision. Troels Hartmann isn't fit to be Lord Mayor. Not up to the job.'

Weber walked in, all smiles for once.

'Lots of people calling, Troels. The press would love to talk to you. Everyone's happy with the outcome.'

Skovgaard was behind him.

'Even in Parliament,' she added. 'People like a winner.'

Kirsten Eller came on the screen, smug outside her office.

'This is a happy moment,' she said. 'It proves Troels Hartmann is a trustworthy alternative to Bremer. That's why we placed our faith in him from the very beginning.'

Hartmann rolled back his head and laughed at the ceiling.

Then he turned off the TV.

'The press,' Skovgaard said.

'I don't want to talk to them till tomorrow. Put out a statement saying I'm glad justice has been done. Morten?'

Weber got out his notepad.

'Step up the poster campaign. Let's focus on our integration policy. Make a point of mentioning the role models. What a success they've been. Oh . . .'

He got his coat, put it on.

'I want another group meeting tomorrow. Don't call anyone till the morning. Tell them then. Say everyone who was here today needs to be there.'

'Short notice,' Weber said.

'Same as they gave me.'

Weber wandered off.

Troels Hartmann got Rie Skovgaard's coat, brought it to her. She looked happier than she had in days. Beautiful too, though exhausted. He worked everyone too hard.

'I'm hungry,' he said. 'And we need to talk.'

Theis Birk Larsen sat in a room with two uniformed officers going through the paperwork. Lund watched from outside with Pernille.

'What happens now?'

'We charge him,' Lund said.

'Where will he go?'

'A holding cell.'

The uniformed men nodded at the big man in the black jacket. He got up, walked out with them.

'When can he come home?'

Lund didn't answer.

'We've got two boys. When can he come home?'

'That depends on the charge.'

'Is he going to jail?'

Lund shrugged.

'This is all your fault, Lund. If it wasn't for you—'

'I'm sorry.'

'Sorry?'

'I'll have a car drive you home. Someone will be in touch after the hearing.'

'That's it?'

'Pernille . . .' She wondered if this was worth saying. Whether it might make a difference. 'We're not special. We're just like you. If people lie to us we think ill of it. We don't know whether their reasons are good or bad. All we know is . . . they're lying.'

Pernille Birk Larsen stood in the Politigården office, rigid with fury.

'You think I'm lying now?'

'I think there's a lot we still don't know.'

She waited.

'Fine,' Pernille said and walked off.

Meyer was at his desk, going through the latest papers.

'The Muslim girl's made a statement.' He looked like a tired schoolboy in his zip-up jerkin and striped T-shirt. 'She confirmed Kemal's alibi. She said it was her top we found. I've spoken to Kemal.'

She was listening, just. Mostly Lund was staring at the photographs on the wall. The car. The canal. The Pentecost Forest.

'The doctors say he'll recover,' Meyer added. 'He doesn't want to press charges.'

'It's not up to him.'

'Can you not do that again, Lund?'

'Do what?'

'Disappear on your own without telling me.'

'Birk Larsen is going to be charged with false imprisonment and grievous bodily harm. For starters.'

Meyer lit a cigarette, blew smoke at the ceiling.

'We did the right thing,' Lund insisted.

'We did nothing. The father's going to prison. Kemal's in hospital. Jesus . . .'

Knock on the door. Svendsen. He looked pleased with himself.

'Buchard wants a meeting with you two in the morning.'

'Thanks for keeping an eye on Birk Larsen,' Lund shot at him. 'Like I asked.'

Svendsen glared at her.

'If you ask for too much, Lund, you get it in alphabetical order. I talked to the chief about that already. He's straight on things.'

'A meeting about what?' Meyer asked.

Svendsen laughed.

'The commissioner's going to rip him apart tonight. I guess he wants to pass on some of the pain. Goodnight. Sleep tight.'

He closed the door behind him.

Meyer sat there looking shocked and worried, his big ears moving backwards and forwards as he chewed on some gum. Any other time it would have looked comical.

Lund kept peering at the photos on the wall.

'I'm not taking the fall for this,' Meyer said. He got up, got his jacket. 'I refuse.'

She was glad when he was gone. It was easier being alone.

Back to the photos. Nanna Birk Larsen. Nineteen years old though she could easily pass for twenty-two or -three. Curly blonde hair. Good with her make-up. Smiling at the camera easily, confidently. Not like a teenager at all.

They still didn't know this girl. Something was missing.

Lund went for her things, mumbled goodnight, walked off into the corridor.

Footsteps behind her. Meyer running, panting, wild-eyed.

'Lund,' he said. 'I'm sorry.'

'About what?'

'There's been an accident.'

Six

She slept in a chair by the bed in his hospital room. Bengt had a bandage round his head, a drip in his right arm, a cast on his left.

He didn't wake up. Not even when she came close to his face and whispered his name.

When the morning light began to filter through the dusty windows Lund looked around. They'd brought some of the things he'd had with him in the car when he crashed on the way to the bridge to Malmö.

A coat. A scarf and sweater.

A black leather briefcase. Some papers were sticking out of the top. They had the police stamp on them.

Lund checked him. Still sleeping. Then she began to look through the documents.

The file was thick, full of official reports. Autopsies and crime details. Photos and forensic material.

She sat down, spread them out on the floor in front of her, began to go through them one by one.

A voice broke her concentration.

'You're right,' Bengt said in a pained, croaky voice. 'He's done it before.'

Lund put the papers to one side, came and stood over him.

'How are you feeling?'

He didn't answer.

'They said you had concussion and a broken arm. The car's a write-off. You were lucky.'

'Lucky?'

'Yes. Lucky. You hadn't slept in a day . . .'

'I was so pissed off with you.'

She didn't say anything.

'I decided to drive home. I'd had enough. Jesus . . .'

Lund wondered if she was about to cry. Her eyes pricked. Her mind was wandering.

'I don't know why I'm like this,' she said softly. 'I'm sorry. I can't help myself. Sometimes . . .'

Bengt's hand came out and took hers. Fingers entwined. Warmth. Closeness.

'I read the file. It wasn't a crime of passion. It wasn't the usual.'

'We can talk about this later,' she said, and wondered if she meant it.

'Maybe he has a kind of method,' Bengt went on, eyes closed, thinking.

'We looked at that. We can't find any links to anything earlier.'

'That doesn't mean they're not there. He dumped Nanna in the water. You saw what it was like. Wild. Remote. There are probably more you don't know about.'

'Later, Bengt.'

'No.' His voice sounded cross, his eyes were open and flashing. 'Not later. You don't know what that word means. I'm telling you. It turns him on that only he and the girl know how and where it ends. To him that's intimacy. Like a love affair.'

'Later,' she said and turned on the TV.

They watched the news together. Buchard had put out a statement clearing Kemal. He'd been a suspect through a tragic coincidence, the chief said. Nothing about how the police had been misled.

That was the way of things. You were either right and a hero or wrong and a villain. There was no halfway house, no grey area. Not in the eyes of the media. Black and white. Nowhere else.

Same in politics, she thought, watching the rerun of Hartmann and Bremer bickering in a clip from their earlier debate on TV.

Nothing was different in their words, their gestures, their expressions. But before it was Bremer who seemed to have the upper hand, his sense of superiority obvious, the hint of victory in his eyes. Now that identical interview had a different, opposing tone. Bremer's statesmanship seemed smug and superficial. Hartmann's incautious and seemingly unwise defence of the teacher appeared brave and far-sighted.

It was the context that made the difference. But to understand the context one needed facts, waypoints, fixed positions from which to judge perspectives.

All of which the Birk Larsen case lacked.

'They said I can leave later today,' he said, switching off the news. 'I'll talk to my mother. We can move in with her.'

'You don't need to go to the trouble. I'm going home to Sweden.'

A flicker of something that might have been panic.

'Why?' Lund asked.

'You're busy. We've got workmen in the house. Your mother would find it odd.'

He closed his eyes for a moment. She looked at the bruising on his face. Wondered how long it would take to disappear.

'There's no shame in being wrong,' he said.

'Do you want some water?'

She got up. His hand reached out to stop her.

Bengt looked at her and said, 'Don't worry. You'll find him. Be patient.'

Lund sat on the edge of the bed.

'What if we don't?'

'You will.'

'We're at a dead end. I don't have any more ideas.'

'They're there. Keep going. What do you know for certain?'

'Nothing.'

'Stop this, Sarah. You know that's not true.'

'OK. On Friday the thirty-first of October Nanna Birk Larsen goes to a party at her high school. Earlier the same day a driver delivers campaign material for Troels Hartmann there.'

Lund got up, walked round the room, trying to think this through.

'The driver feels unwell. He loses the car keys and goes to hospital. About nine thirty Nanna leaves the party on her bicycle. Someone found the car keys and followed her.'

'Wait, wait,' Bengt interrupted. 'Stop there. This can't be spontaneous. He didn't just happen upon the keys and commit a crime.'

She shook her head.

'He must have.'

'He's not impulsive. He plans his actions and then he covers them up.'

'Bengt! The car was outside the school. That's what happened. No one could have known the driver was going to be taken ill.'

'It doesn't fit the profile I came up with.'

'What if your profile's wrong? I know you're trying to help but . . . what if everything's wrong? The way we're trying to see this. The idea there's a pattern. Some kind of logic.'

Lund got herself some water.

'A nineteen-year-old girl is snatched and held and raped repeatedly. Horribly. There's a kind of logic usually. But this . . .'

'Forget what you know. Forget everything I told you. Go back to the beginning. Then go back further. There's a method here, Sarah. A way of working he's established in his own mind.'

She waited.

'The scissors, the soap, the ritual . . .' He shook his head. 'I can't believe Nanna was the first. Go back further. Until you find something.'

'Further,' Lund whispered.

Out in the Kalvebod Fælled by the Pentecost Forest. A black shape emerging from the water. An eel slithering over a dead girl's naked limbs.

Events had shaped everything that came after. Events had stolen her head.

She kissed him carefully on the cheek, avoiding the bruises, then with a brief word of thanks she left.

The black Ford was stored in a garage used by the forensic department. It was in the basement of the headquarters, reached by a ramp that led to the yard by the prison where Theis Birk Larsen was now in custody.

The vehicle looked grubbier now it was dry. Mud-stained and covered in leaves. All the doors open and up on a ramp.

The forensic technician got her the current reports as Lund turned on the huge vertical fluorescent tubes that surrounded the car. Numbered markers were stuck everywhere, on the windows, on the doors, on the floorpan.

She looked at the paperwork. Nothing new.

Lund took off her jacket, walked round with the duty officer.

There was a sad chalk outline in the boot where Nanna was found. She felt she'd looked at it a million times. Lund pulled on some throwaway plastic gloves, sat in the driver's seat, the passenger's. Checked the mirrors, the glovebox, the door compartments. Sat in the back, did the same.

The man stayed on a bench outside watching her, bored.

She got him to raise the thing, checked underneath. Mud and sticks from the canal. Nothing else.

'Like I said,' he told her. 'There's not a thing on it. He got everything out from the inside. The water did the rest.'

He finished his coffee, threw the plastic mug into a bin.

'I've been here all night looking. You're wasting your time. There's nothing new.'

She went back to the paperwork.

'I promised my wife I'd remind her what I looked like,' the man said, pulling on his jacket. 'Is that OK?'

Lund had the tech report in front of her.

'It says here there were fifty-two litres of petrol in the tank when the car was found. Are you sure of that?'

He sighed.

'Yes. It was five or six litres short of a full tank.'

'You're sure?'

'I'm sure. Turn the lights off when you're done. Bye.'

'You're sure?' she shouted as he left.

'How many times—?'

'This is important. Could you have made a mistake? It was in the water—'

'No, no mistake. We checked that car over a thousand times. Five or six litres short of a full tank. Where's the problem? What did we do wrong?'

'I didn't say you did anything wrong.' She waved a document from City Hall at him. 'According to the logs the tank was last filled a week earlier. If that's the case it should be almost empty.'

He came over, looked at the log.

'Oh. I'm sorry. We should have . . .'

'So who filled it up?' Lund wondered.

*

265

It was sunny though grey clouds were gathering. Meyer was waiting for her in the yard outside forensics. He wore a shiny leather jacket she'd never seen before and fashionable shades.

Cool, she thought. He belonged in narcotics or robbery or the gang squad. Not murder. He took it personally. That was always a mistake.

'How's Bengt?' Meyer asked as he handed her a cup of coffee.

'What?'

'How . . . ?'

'Yes.'

'And you?'

'We need to check for young women who've disappeared in the last ten years.'

'Because?'

'In the city. All over the country. See if anything links to the Kalvebod Fælled. Or anywhere in Vestamager.'

Meyer took off his sunglasses and looked at her.

'How's Bengt? How are you?'

'I told you.'

'No you didn't.'

'He's fine. Can we get to work now?'

They had a room for lawyers' meetings in the main block of the Politigården, near the court. The woman was called Lis Gamborg. Birk Larsen looked at her smart business suit, her pearl necklace, her immaculate hair and wondered how he was going to pay for this.

He was in a prisoner's blue suit, unshaven, dirty, hungry.

'Take a seat,' she said.

A guard stood and watched, a handgun on his belt.

It looked bright outside the barred window.

'I'm your court-appointed lawyer. It's very busy today. We won't get a hearing for a few hours.'

He sat twiddling his thumbs, barely listening. Two decades ago, when he married Pernille, Birk Larsen had promised himself he'd never be in this situation again. Not that he mentioned this to Pernille. It was part of an unspoken pact between them. He would be a different man. No more tangles with the law. No more skipping dates for reasons he'd never reveal to her. He was young then. Angry and determined to mark his place in the world, with his strength, with his fists if need be.

Then along came family and he tried to forget what he once was. Buried young Theis. Tough Theis. Theis the thug who would never be needed again.

'Still,' she went on, 'that gives us time to talk about your case.'

'What's there to talk about?'

'The prosecution are going to charge you with attempted manslaughter, false imprisonment and grievous bodily harm.'

Birk Larsen closed his eyes.

He had to say something. Had to ask.

'How's the teacher?'

She kept looking at him as if he were a specimen. A zoo animal trapped in a cage.

'He'll recover. He says he won't press charges.'

Birk Larsen watched her.

'That's not enough. It won't get you acquitted. Not on charges like this.'

'The police told us it was him. The papers said it was him. No one did a damned thing.'

She took a deep breath.

'The judge may think there are some mitigating circumstances.'

'I'll plead guilty. Just tell me what to say.'

He didn't want to utter the words for fear of the answer that was coming.

'I just want to go home to my family.'

She said nothing.

'I need to go home.'

'I understand. In the circumstances we should hope for leniency.'

She put her slender hands together, leaned over the table, looked into his face.

'I'll try to convince the judge that you don't need to stay in custody. You've confessed. You came in willingly. You're not going to flee. You've got a family. A business to run—'

'I'd like to talk to my wife.'

The lawyer shook her head.

'You have to wait until after the hearing.'

His head went down.

'I'm sorry,' she added. 'Your friend? Vagn?'

'Vagn had nothing to do with this. He tried to stop me. Don't involve him.'

'He is involved. He's charged as an accessory.'

'That's not right!'

'It's a minor charge. He's free. I don't think . . .'

He waited.

'Don't think what?'

'He won't go to jail. I wish I could promise the same for you.'

Silence.

'Any questions?' she asked.

When he didn't answer she looked at the guard.

Part of the process. Part of a system that almost swallowed him once before. Theis Birk Larsen was back in the belly of a beast he hated, and that hated him. With no one to blame but himself.

Pernille was manning the phones. Lotte had arrived to help. Their usual luck. Every minute a customer was on the line demanding something straight away.

'I can't do that right now,' Pernille said to the latest. 'Let me get back to you. I will. I promise.'

Lotte waited until she put down the phone then asked, 'What's he going to be charged with?'

Another call.

'Birk Larsen's Removals. Please wait a moment.'

Hand over the mouthpiece.

'I don't know. Can you look after the boys for a while?'

'Sure. What did Theis do?'

Pernille went back to the phone and made excuses.

Lotte was still there, getting cross.

'He did something to that teacher, didn't he?'

'It's all my fault. I pushed him.'

Her hand ran through her straggly hair. She looked a mess and didn't care.

She looked at the appointments, wondered how all this was done.

One of the men came in asking for instructions. Pernille did her best. The phone went. Lotte answered.

'Do the job in Østerbro first,' she told him. 'Do it the way Theis would do it. Ask Vagn.'

He stared at her.

'Where's Vagn?' she asked.

'I dunno.'

'Just . . .' She waved a hand at him. 'Just do what you think. I'm sorry . . .'

'Pernille?'

Lotte had waited till he was gone.

'What?'

'The bank called when you were out. They said they need to talk to you.'

Buchard wore his best shirt, freshly pressed. Best suit. The uniform for a lecture from the commissioner.

He was straight from that and hurting.

Bent over that morning's papers, reading them in the grey light streaming through the window of Lund's office. Downturned mouth, shaking head.

Saying plenty without speaking a word.

Lund and Meyer sat next to one another, fidgeting like naughty children brought before the teacher.

Meyer broke the silence.

'We realize things haven't gone as well as they should.'

Buchard said nothing, just showed them another headline: 'Hartmann's Role Model Cleared'.

'If Kemal had told us the truth . . .' Lund started.

Buchard shut her up with a single caustic glance.

'I told you our working relationship wasn't the best,' Meyer added. 'Not that I'm kind of blaming anyone.'

'Kemal lied!' Lund said again. 'He had every opportunity to clear himself and didn't. If he'd—'

Buchard waved the paper at her again.

'All people see is this,' he snarled. 'Not your excuses.' A pause. 'The commissioner wants you off the case. We don't need this kind of coverage. Getting caught up in an election campaign . . . it's embarrassing. And now the father's charged with manslaughter.'

'Kemal doesn't want him prosecuted!' Meyer cried. 'Doesn't that mean anything?'

'It's up to the lawyers, not him. You screwed up, both of you.'

They stared at the carpet.

'Give me one good reason why I shouldn't kick you out of here right now?'

'Just the one?' Lund said straight off. 'I could give you . . .'

'Start then.'

'We know more about this than anyone. Bring in a new team and they'll take a week to go through the papers.'

'I'd rather wait a week and get it straight than have you two bringing the commissioner down on my head again.'

'We know more than we did yesterday.'

'I've got an appointment at the school,' Meyer added. 'I can clear things there. We'll bring this under control. Lund's right. Get someone else and they'll be starting from scratch.'

Buchard thought for a long moment.

'If this case is still going nowhere tomorrow you're off it. Both of you.'

He stood up, headed for the door.

'Stay well away from the Rådhus. And Troels Hartmann. I don't want any more shit from that direction. Understood?'

'Sure,' Meyer said.

Buchard left. Lund sat silent, thinking, arms tightly folded over her black and white sweater.

Meyer went out into the corridor, talked to the day team.

'We need to get this back on track,' he ordered. 'Go back to the school. Talk to everyone. Workmen, cleaners. Everyone.'

Lund got up and started going through the evidence bags, found the one she wanted.

'Get Nanna's picture out to all the taxi drivers,' Meyer said.

'We did that already,' Svendsen moaned.

Meyer turned on him.

'Every driver? Every last one in Copenhagen? No. I didn't think so. See who was working near Kemal's flat. Find out if she took a taxi from there. Anything!'

He came back into the office, grumbling.

'Jesus. How hard can it be?'

She had the City Hall vehicle logbook open.

'Send a photo of the car to all the petrol stations in the city,' Lund said. 'Ask if they saw it on the evening of October the thirty-first.'

'Why?'

'We missed something.'

She passed him the logbook.

'According to this there shouldn't have been much petrol left in the car. The tank's almost full. If he went to a petrol station—'

'He'll be on a surveillance tape. Yes. I know. I'm not stupid.'

'Good! Let's start with the petrol stations near Nanna's school.'

'Lund. If you were driving a stolen car with a kidnapped girl in the boot would you fill the car up yourself? The log might be inaccurate.'

She nodded.

'You could be right. Check it out with the security people at the Rådhus.'

Meyer laughed.

'Oh! Good joke! You heard what Buchard said. He'll have my balls if I go near that place.'

She stared at him. Hands on hips. Bright wide eyes. Expectant. Dogged.

'Don't look at me like that,' Meyer complained. 'I don't like it.'

She didn't move an inch.

'I'm not going to City Hall, Lund. That's that. You do what you want. I am *not* going.'

He went back towards the corridor.

'You told the father you'd find whoever did this, Meyer.'

He stopped, turned, scowled at her.

'Was that just something to say?'

'I also told my wife I'd hold down a job for more than three weeks. Which do you think matters most?'

She started saying something.

'No,' Meyer cut in. 'Not a word. I know the answer. Really. No need.'

Same people, same room. Yet everything now was different. The group meeting was beginning and the tension of the night before had vanished. Smiling, joking, acting as if nothing had happened at all they sat waiting, Knud Padde beaming more broadly than the rest.

He'd been on the phone to Rie Skovgaard already. Wondering what the available committee places were. Angling for promotion.

Troels Hartmann sat at the head of the table next to Elisabet

Hedegaard. The rest picked at croissants and pastries. He stuck to a single cup of coffee.

'Good morning,' Hartmann said and went through all the polite preliminaries. Thanks for their attendance. Apologies for the short notice.

Bigum sat at the far end of the table, slumped in his chair, trying to smile.

'There's no need for this to be long,' Hartmann began.

'Troels.'

It was Bigum. The smile looked ever more forced.

'Please. I would like to speak for a moment.'

Hartmann acted surprised.

'Of course, Henrik. If you wish.'

Bigum took a deep breath.

'I owe you all an apology. For the unfortunate course of events.'

No one spoke.

'It's been difficult for all of us.'

Padde had seated himself next to Elisabet Hedegaard who stared at Bigum, hand on her chin.

'I hope we all realize our disagreements only came about because of a mutual concern for the welfare of the party.' Henrik Bigum glanced at Hartmann. 'Nothing else, Troels. Nothing personal. So . . .'

An attempt at laughter. A deferential pass of the right hand.

'I'd like us all to bury the hatchet and move forward.'

'Thank you, Henrik,' Hartmann said with good grace.

'It's a pleas—'

'But you were right. This can't go on.'

Bigum squirmed on his seat.

'Troels. There's really no reason for you to withdraw now. The constituency and the group are behind you. Your stand on the role model—'

'Yes, yes, yes.' Hartmann waved him down. 'Don't worry. I'm not withdrawing.' He looked at each of them in turn, smile set to modest and self-effacing. 'Don't panic. Our common goal is to change the system here at City Hall. Right?'

They nodded, Bigum more vigorously than anyone else.

Hartmann rapped a finger on the table.

'We can't do this if we're fighting amongst ourselves.'

An approving murmur.

Hartmann played the crowd.

'I can't hear you!' He laughed. 'Am I right?'

Louder this time, and Henrik Bigum laughed too, said, 'You're right, Troels. You were right all along.'

Hartmann gazed at him the length of the shiny committee table.

'I know, Henrik. So I'm giving you the same choice you gave me yesterday.'

Bigum's smile froze.

'I'm sorry?'

Hartmann's face had changed again. Serious. The expression he used when facing Bremer.

'Either you step down . . .' He paused. 'Or we take a vote on it.'

Bigum shook his head.

'What?'

The room was silent. Hartmann had kept Weber out of this. He never liked conflict. Rie Skovgaard, standing close to the table, smiling, expectant, had worked the phones from six that morning. They knew precisely where he stood.

Bigum was getting angry.

'This is absurd. I've worked for this party for twenty years. As long as you, Troels. I was only acting in our best interest.'

'You went to Bremer, Henrik. You offered him a pact.'

The lecturer's bony, ascetic face flushed.

'I wanted to gauge opinion. Nothing more. We won't win outright. There are compromises to be made—'

'What's it to be, Henrik? Your resignation or a vote?'

Bigum looked at each of them. No one met his eyes. Not even Padde.

'I see.'

He got up, leaned across the table, glowered at Hartmann, said, 'Fuck you, Troels. You'll never be Lord Mayor. You haven't got the . . . the . . .'

'Stomach?' Hartmann asked.

Rie Skovgaard opened the door, smiling brightly.

'Fuck you all,' Bigum muttered and left.

Hartmann folded his arms and sat back in his chair.

Finally, Knud Padde said, 'Well. That's that. As chairman I will now give the floor to Troels.'

Hartmann got the coffee pot and poured himself another cup.

'That goes for you too, Knud. On your way.'

Padde laughed like a nervous child.

'Oh come on, Troels. I know I screwed up. But I worked hard for the party. I'm a loyal . . .'

Hartmann took a sip of his coffee.

'You're out,' he said, nothing more.

No one looked at him. No one uttered a word.

Skovgaard had the door open again, still smiling.

'That's why you dragged me here?' Padde said. 'To humiliate me?'

'Knud,' Skovgaard called, knocking on the door with her knuckles. 'We've a meeting to start. Please . . .'

He mumbled the first curse Hartmann had ever heard him utter then shambled out.

'Good,' Hartmann declared brightly. 'Let's get on with it.'

He beamed at the faces around the table. They were his now. No one else's.

'Elisabet. You'll take over from Knud as chair. Is that OK?'

She nodded, smiled.

'Now I'd like you to meet two new people.'

Skovgaard called out into the corridor.

'Sanjay? Deepika? Will you come this way?'

A young man and a young woman. Asian. Smartly dressed, professional. Straight from the role model programme.

'You may know Sanjay and Deepika from our youth organiz-ation,' Hartmann announced. 'Have a seat. Welcome. They're our two new group committee members.'

He waited. Then asked, 'Are there any questions?'

There were none.

Halfway through the meeting Hartmann came out to ask for some photocopies. Morten Weber and Rie Skovgaard were bickering over the machine.

'You never told me the knives were coming out,' Weber com-plained.

'You wouldn't have liked it.'

'This isn't a good time to start sacking people.'

'They asked for it, Morten,' Skovgaard said. 'How can we have a snake like Bigum sitting amongst us?'

'And Knud?' Weber asked. 'What did he do except behave the way he always did? Bending with the wind?'

'Knud's an example,' Hartmann answered.

Weber opened his mouth, in mock amazement.

'An example? Am I really hearing this from Saint Troels? Since when did you learn to wield daggers in the night?'

'Since I wanted to bring down Poul Bremer. They're gone. That's it.'

He slapped some papers on the machine.

'I want copies of these and some more coffee.'

'Get your own damned coffee! Bigum won't take this lying down. He'll cause shit for you in the party.'

'Listen, Morten,' Hartmann told him. 'We've been the nice guys too long. On the defensive. I had to act. I had to show I could be strong.'

'You did that. I hope you talked it over with Kirsten Eller. Bigum was close to her in case you didn't know.'

Nothing.

'Oh,' Weber snapped. 'You didn't. If you'd asked . . .'

Hartmann fought to keep his temper.

'I'll deal with Kirsten. You don't need to worry about that.'

'The problem,' said the bank manager, 'is you're paying for two places.'

He'd come to the depot to see her. Sat in the office, face a mix of shame and anger. She wanted to ask him: why now? Didn't he read the papers? Couldn't he see this wasn't the time?

But he was a bank manager. A man in a smart suit. Doubtless with a big house in one of the fancier suburbs. It was his job to chase small, struggling businesses in Vesterbro. Circumstances didn't matter. Only kroner in the bank.

'It won't go on for long.'

'It can't. You don't have the finances to sustain it. So . . .'

'So what?'

'When will you be able to sell the house?'

One of the men came through the door and said, 'The tail lift on the big truck's stuck.'

What would Theis do? What would Vagn say?

'Make two trips with the little one. We can't cancel.'

'If we do that the next job's late.'

She looked at him, said nothing. He left.

'I can put your loan on hold,' the bank manager said. 'That means you skip this month's payment. But . . .'

She was thinking about trucks and jobs and appointments. Work hard enough and the money came in. That was what Theis always said.

'Pernille? You've got a big overdraft. There's the cost of the funeral. We need some kind of—'

'Money?' she asked. 'Collateral?' She looked around at the office, the depot, the men outside. 'All this is yours anyway. What else can I offer?'

'You need a plan. Otherwise . . .'

'Theis will be home soon,' she said firmly. 'He'll find a solution. He always does.'

'Pernille . . .'

'You can wait till Theis comes, can't you? Or do you want to serve papers at the cemetery when I put Nanna's urn in the earth?'

He didn't like that. It was, she thought, a cruel thing to say.

'I'm trying to help.'

Her phone was ringing.

'You'll get your money. Excuse me. I have to take this.'

It was Theis, calling from the jail.

She went out into a quiet corner of the garage to talk.

'Hi.'

'Are you OK, Theis?'

'Yeah.'

She tried to picture him there. Had they put him in uniform? Did he get enough to eat? Would there be an argument? His temper . . .

'How are the boys?'

He sounded old and broken.

'They're fine. Waiting for you to come home.'

There was a long, asthmatic breath on the line, then he said, 'I won't be coming home today.'

'When will they let you out?'

'They want to keep me in custody.'

A couple of the workers were staring at one of the trucks. There was a problem there as well.

'For how long?'

'A week today I go back to court. Maybe then.'

She couldn't think of a thing to say.

'I'm sorry about . . .'

She'd never seen him cry. Not even when his mother died. Everything about Theis happened inside, hidden, trapped in silence. The emotions were there. She'd learned to feel them, to sense them. Never expected to see them made plain.

'I have to go now, love,' he said.

She was choking back the tears, for him, for her, for Nanna and the boys. For all the sad grey world.

Pernille had no words either and this seemed the worst thing, the greatest sin of all.

'Bye,' he said and then was gone.

Lund went to the brown-brick fortress that was the Rådhus, found the place in the basement that dealt with the cars. Stood there in her black coat, jeans and woollen sweater dealing with a tetchy old man in uniform who thought he had better things to do.

The parking garage was dealt with by a security office situated near the exit. There was a glass screen between the man and her, for reasons she couldn't begin to fathom. CCTV screens covered the building, the prison-like halls of the council quarters, the civil servants' offices, the basement, the garage.

'We're busy,' the security man said.

'This won't take long. I need to understand how your system works.'

He looked as if he'd worked here since the place was built a century or so ago. An unsmiling man of about sixty-five, half-moon spectacles he liked to fiddle with, bald with a fringe of silver hair. Self-important in his official blue jumper as if the city crest, three gold towers rising from the water, were a badge of office. More interested in his keys and cameras and pigeonholes than looking at the people around him.

'It's a garage,' he said. 'What do you expect? They hand in the keys once they've parked. They pick them up when they leave.'

There was a board behind him. Full of key rings. A driver came and asked for a car. The man got up, stretched out the half-moon glasses with his left hand so he could read the numbers. A long way. To the end of his sharp nose.

'You need to see an optician,' she said trying to be friendly.

He handed the driver a set, glared at her, sat down, said nothing.

'So the key to the stolen car should have been hanging there?'

'If it hadn't been stolen.'

'Who's responsible for filling up the cars?'

'Whoever's driving them, I guess. I don't deal with that side of things.'

'And is that always entered in the log?'

He didn't like that question.

'I can't speak for the electoral candidates. Talk to them.'

Lund hesitated, looked at him. Stood where she was.

'I'm talking to you.'

Then she walked into his office, placed the vehicle log in front of him.

'This is the log we took from here. Explain it to me. Does it mean no one filled the car?'

'You're supposed to stay outside the glass.'

'You're a city employee. You're supposed to help the police. Tell me about the log.'

'Doesn't mean a thing,' the man said. 'Drivers don't fill them in straight away. They wait till they've got time. Sometimes they don't fill them in at all.'

He peered at the entries.

'This driver never came back here. So he never filled in the log. Where's the surprise? Can I go back to my work now?'

He messed with his glasses again, peered at her.

'Unless you have some more questions?'

She walked out of the office, went to the door. Looked outside at the monochrome winter day.

No one helped the police much. They were an enemy of a kind. Even in the bowels of City Hall.

Lund went back and stood outside the glass as she was supposed to. He was still fidgeting with his spectacles, nervously it seemed to her.

'How do the drivers pay for petrol?'

He pressed the button for his mike.

'What?'

'How do the drivers pay for petrol?'

He thought about this.

'There's a charge card in the car. Look. This isn't anything to do with us—'

'We didn't find any charge card. What kind is it?'

'I don't know. We're security. We don't handle money. Now if you'll excuse—'

'I understand that. But you can look it up. See which petrol stations they usually use.'

'You want me to look it up?'

'Yes.' She smiled. 'And then I'll let you get back to work.'

He sat on his little seat, miserable pale face, fingers playing with his glasses.

'I promise,' she said.

The details were in a book in front of him. He scribbled on a piece of paper and passed them under the glass.

'Anything else?' he asked.

'Not right now, thanks.'

Meyer and his men were at the school wearing hard hats, looking at the building site that was to become the new wing.

'Talk to all the workers,' he ordered. 'Find out what time they arrived. When they left. Anything they saw. When you've done that talk to the cleaners. After that—'

His phone rang.

Lund.

'Are you coming to the school or what? We've got plenty to do here.'

'There was a charge card for the car. I don't have the card but I've got the number.'

A pause. The sound of traffic. He could see her juggling the phone, some papers, trying to drive, all at the same time.

'That Friday it was used at seven twenty-one in the evening. Petrol station on Nyropsgade.'

'Where?'

'Two minutes from City Hall.'

Meyer said nothing.

'We'll get hold of the surveillance tapes,' Lund said.

'We should do what Buchard tells us.'

She didn't answer.

'Can't you do this on your own?' he asked, and felt bad the moment he'd said it.

'Sure,' she replied in that lilting sing-song tone she could turn on and off at will. 'If you like.'

Then she was gone.

The men were looking at him.

Meyer threw the nearest his hard hat.

'You know what you need to do,' he said.

'Going somewhere?' the man asked.

'I'll be back at headquarters if you need me.'

The days were shortening. It was dark just after four.

Pernille Birk Larsen found herself alone in the office, fending off phone calls from irate customers, the media, strangers with odd offers of help.

The bank manager had been on the phone asking for financial information. So she'd been forced to find the key to Theis's private files to look for some missing bank statements. There was a picture in there: Theis and Nanna. Probably taken just a few weeks before, she guessed. He wore his black woollen hat and the guileless smile she loved. Nanna was beautiful, arm round her father's shoulders as if protecting him. Not the other way round. The way it was supposed to be.

She turned it over. A scribble on the back in Nanna's handwriting: *Love you!*

Pernille had never seen this photo. One more secret of Nanna's. And her father's. Nanna was always messing around in places she wasn't allowed. She took Pernille's clothes sometimes without asking. Hunted in other people's drawers for things she might want. It caused an argument from time to time. Never a serious one. They didn't have those. In some ways she wondered if they ever really connected with Nanna at all. Perhaps that was the inevitable distance brought about by her death. Perhaps . . .

Nanna was a curious kid, always looking for something new. Maybe she looked down here at Theis's private things too.

He wouldn't like that, Pernille thought. There was a side to him he wanted to keep to himself. She'd seen it the previous night. A huge, savage figure holding a sledgehammer over a bleeding figure on the floor of that distant warehouse. A man she loved, one she scarcely recognized at that moment.

A noise in the darkness of the garage made her jump. Vagn Skærbæk came out of the shadows. He looked guilty, furtive. There was a cut on his face and some bruising.

'Hi,' he said.

She put the photo away, looked up at him. Could think of nothing to say.

He stood hunched in his scarlet overalls, black woollen hat. The little brother. They'd known each other before she met Theis. Before she took the risk, felt the thrill of being with a man like him. The silver chain glittered at Skærbæk's neck.

'It was my idea,' Skærbæk said. 'Blame me. Not him.'

Pernille closed her eyes briefly, went back to the papers.

'Is he still inside?'

There was a pile of invoices. Some statements in red. She opened a drawer and brushed them inside with her hand.

'I can manage this, Pernille. Let me help you with the business. With the boys. I'll do whatever I can. I just . . .'

More papers. More bills. They seemed to be growing in front of her.

'I just want to help.'

Pernille strode up and slapped him on his cut, bruised face. As hard as she could.

He didn't flinch. Just put a hand up to his cheek. The wound had reopened with the blow. He wiped the blood away.

'How could you do that?' she asked. 'How could you?'

He swept away more blood with his hand, looked at her oddly.

'Theis thought he was doing it for you.'

'For me?'

'If it had been him, Pernille. If it was the teacher. What would he be now? Your hero? Or an idiot?'

She drew back her hand again. He didn't move.

'I shouldn't have told him,' Skærbæk said. 'I did my best to stop it. When I saw. Kemal would have been dead if I hadn't.'

'No. No more.'

He nodded. Went to the desk. Looked at the jobs for the following day.

She had to ask.

'Vagn. Back then. Twenty years ago. Before I knew him.'

'Yeah.'

'What was he like?'

He thought about this.

'Unfinished. Waiting. A kid. The way we all were.'

'The police showed me some pictures.'

'What pictures?'

'Someone murdered. A man. A drug dealer.'

'Oh.'

'What happened? Tell me the truth.'

'We all get stupid sometimes. Your parents thought that when you took up with Theis. Didn't they?'

'The police—'

'The police are trying to trick you.'

He came and peered at her. These two were close before she knew him. Thick as thieves.

'Theis didn't do anything, Pernille. Not a thing. OK?'

Kirsten Eller stuck out a flabby, sweaty hand.

'I'm so glad everything turned out well for you. All this unpleasantness was quite unwelcome.'

'Yes. Sit down.'

She planted her full frame on the sofa in his office.

'And you've sorted out your group. This is good.'

Hartmann took the chair opposite.

'I didn't have any choice, Kirsten. I had to do something.'

She had an image of a kind. Long coat to cover the weighty body. Permasmile. Owlish spectacles pushed back on a head of dyed brown hair as if she'd just come from a busy board meeting. Eller had been around City Hall for as long as he had. In a way she'd achieved more. By means he was beginning to appreciate.

'At least it's all over now,' she said. 'The polls are looking good. The media are starting to see which horse to back. So now we reap the benefits.'

'My thoughts exactly.'

She took a folder out of her briefcase and opened it.

'We have some suggestions for winning any floating voters out there. It's the undecided who'll put us in, Troels. Let's not forget it.'

He grinned at her, shook his head. Genuinely amused.

'What is it?' she asked.

'You're a wonderful actor. Quite a talent.'

The smile stayed. No response.

'Bigum would never have tried a trick like that without talking to you first. He went to Bremer. He came to you. And you gave him the nod.'

The smile went.

'Troels—'

'No. Please. Don't insult my intelligence by trying to deny it.'

'This is—'

'The truth,' he cut in. 'I know my people, Kirsten. I know Bigum. He's not big enough or brave enough to do this on his own. Maybe you went to him. I don't care.'

This was clear in his head now. He wondered why it had taken so long to see it.

'They were acting out of fear. Not strength. Not courage. Fear. I guess you could smell it.'

She held up her hands.

'Troels. Before you say another word . . . understand this.'

'I'm giving you two choices.'

Kirsten Eller fell quiet.

'Either I inform the press and they paint you for the untrustworthy, disloyal, conniving bitch you are.'

He waited, head to one side, listening.

'And the alternative?'

'You step down. Let your deputy take over.'

Kirsten Eller turned to look at Rie Skovgaard happily making notes.

'You need me, Troels. You all need me. Think of—'

'No, Kirsten. I don't need you at all.'

She waited. Not another word. Then Eller angrily gathered up her things, stormed to the door. There she turned and looked at him.

'This was about winning. Not you. Don't flatter yourself.'

283

'I won't,' he promised.

She bustled into Morten Weber on the way out. He watched her go.

'What happened there?' Weber asked. 'I thought we were having a meeting.'

Hartmann got to his feet.

'Rie!' Hartmann called. 'Line up some press interviews for me. Pick friends.'

'What the hell's going on?' Weber cried.

'I was going to tell you. There wasn't time. Kirsten's resigning.'

'Jesus, Troels! We've fought for this alliance—'

'She put Bigum up to it. She wanted me out all along.'

'You can't keep rocking the boat like this.'

'Morten.' Hartmann took him by his frail shoulders. 'Bremer's been one step ahead of us every inch of this campaign. It's time we set the agenda. It's time we moved more boldly than him.'

'By firing everyone in sight?'

Hartmann's temper broke.

'She went behind my back. She tried to cut deals with Bremer. Then with Bigum. You need to change your thinking. We can knock Bremer off his perch without those mealy-mouthed sons of bitches in the Centre Party.'

'No, Troels! We can't. On our own we don't have the votes.'

Hartmann shook his head. Rie Skovgaard stayed silent, smiling.

'How long have we played these games, Morten? Twenty years? Always the same rules. Theirs. From now on we play by mine. Call the minority leaders to a meeting tonight. Tell them I have an important proposition.'

'Half of them hate you,' Weber said.

'No more than they hate each other.'

'They're with Bremer!'

'Not if they've seen the polls. They're with whoever's going to win.'

He looked around the campaign office. There were posters everywhere, his own face. Modest smile. Blue eyes wide open. The new broom looking to sweep out the old.

Hartmann pointed to his portrait.

'That's me.'

*

'He filled the car the night Nanna died, ten days ago,' Meyer said.

They were in the office looking at the CCTV tapes. Black and white, split into four windows. Date and time in the corner of each grainy frame.

'The tapes run twenty-four hours a day. The chances of finding it after all this time are pretty slim, Lund.'

She was closest to the screen, looking. The numbers. The shadowy figures moving between the pumps.

Everything.

'Also,' Meyer added, 'all these people reuse the tapes. So if it's that old—'

'It's not this one,' Lund cut in, popping out the cassette.

'We've only got one left.'

'It's always the last.'

He took a deep breath.

'It's rarely the last, Lund.'

'Look at the screen. See something I can't. Please.'

He picked up a banana in one hand, a cigarette in the other. Lit the cigarette.

The video started. The date in the corner of the frames said 7th November.

'Shit,' Meyer muttered. 'It's from last Friday. Like I said. They reuse the tapes. That's why they're so scratchy.'

She took a sip of tepid coffee. Everyone else had gone home. A cleaner was sweeping along the corridor outside.

'Doesn't mean the rest of it's from the seventh, does it?' she said. 'When we had videotapes at home . . .'

Mark as a baby, back when she was married. They were all jumbled up together. Different months, different years. It was hard to keep track when you used the same cassettes over and over again.

'Fast forward,' she said.

Meyer worked the remote.

Black and white cars, hazy figures running around.

'Stop there,' Meyer said.

He clapped his hands and let out a whoop of joy. She looked at him. Big ears, big eyes. Big kid.

Meyer's face fell.

'I was trying to cheer you up.'

'It's the thirty-first,' Lund said.

'I know. That's what I was saying.'

Around eight p.m. He rewound, went too far, started moving forward more slowly.

They came to seven seventeen p.m. Four frames. Only one car.

It was a white Beetle.

'Shit,' Meyer muttered again.

'The clock's wrong. Why would you keep it accurate to the minute? Keep going forward.'

The Beetle left. No cars at all. Just empty concrete and the lights above the pumps.

Then at twenty minutes and thirty-seven seconds past seven a black car pulled onto the forecourt, to the pump in the right-hand upper frame, arriving with the jerky motion of a kid's stop-frame film.

Meyer squinted at the plate.

'That's the car,' he said.

It was raining. She hadn't seen that till now. Knew what it meant. Had to mean. It was that kind of case.

The door opened. The driver got out. He was dressed in a long dark winter anorak. The hood was pulled up over his head. He walked to the boot and the fuel cap.

His face didn't show for a moment.

'Sh . . .' Meyer began.

She put her hand on his.

'Patience.'

Round the boot to the pump. Face down every step.

'Come on, for Christ's sake,' Meyer whispered then took an anxious pull on the cigarette.

It was a pump with a card slot by the handle. They saw his hand go out, insert something, take it out.

No face.

He finished, went round the back to the fuel cap, then made for the door.

'Come on. Smile for the birdie. Just look at something, will you?'

Straight behind the wheel. Features hidden by the angle. The Ford drove off.

'Shit, shit, shit,' Meyer groaned.

'Wait a minute.'

She pressed the back button. Looked at the man working the pump.

286

Looked at his left hand. The way it stretched out and up to his head then took hold of something when he went to read the card numbers.

'I know who that is,' Lund said.

Meyer looked nervous.

'Don't tell me.'

'I'm going to City Hall. Want to come?'

Five minutes through the rain and the sparse night traffic. The security man was about to come off duty. He began squawking the moment Meyer waved the cuffs at him.

'I didn't do anything. I didn't do anything.'

'Good God,' Meyer said. 'I never heard that one before. You're coming with us, mate.'

'All I did was fill up the car.'

Lund followed as Meyer marched him to the door, thinking, listening.

'Before or after you snatched Nanna Birk Larsen?' Meyer asked.

The man in the blue city sweater looked at him aghast.

'I'm sixty-four years old. What the hell are you talking about? I didn't touch anyone.'

'Sit him on that bench over there,' Lund ordered.

'We need to take him in.'

Lund looked the old man up and down. Bent back. Lousy eyesight. He didn't seem to breathe too well.

'Tell us the truth,' Lund said. 'Tell us what really happened. Then maybe you'll keep your job.'

'My job? *My job?* It's because I was doing my job I've got you baboons in my face.'

Meyer shoved him onto the stone bench by the bike rack.

'They're never going to put you front of house are they, chum? Tell us what happened or you won't see daylight for sixteen years.'

The security man stared at him with a mixture of fear and outrage.

'Do I need to turn up your hearing aid, Grandad?' Meyer yelled.

'Where's the charge card?' Lund asked more gently.

He didn't say a thing.

'I'm trying to help,' she told him. 'If you don't talk now we're taking you in.'

'I took the card with me. I was going to put it back when I came in to work on the Monday. But then . . .'

'Then what?' Meyer asked.

'You people were here. Everywhere.'

'Why did you go to the school?'

'Why wouldn't I? My flat's round the corner. I walked home and saw the car there. One of our cars. Just left. I didn't understand. I knew the schedules. They were all supposed to be back.'

'And you had the keys?' Meyer said.

'No. They were still in the ignition. I guess the driver forgot them or something.'

He shook his head.

'I couldn't leave it there, could I? Keys in the ignition. Some thug would have had it before midnight.'

Lund was getting impatient.

'No. This isn't good enough. You could have called the campaign office. It was their car.'

'I tried,' he said very deliberately. 'They said the secretary was in Oslo. It's the city's car, you know. Not theirs. We own it. Our taxes—'

'You could drive me nuts,' Meyer spat at him. 'The girl—'

'I didn't know that girl. I didn't do anything. Except a favour.'

'What did you do with the car?' Lund asked.

'It belongs to Hartmann's pool. He's a flashy prick but that's not my business. Maybe he needed it. So I drove it to the petrol station, filled it up, and drove it back. Put the keys back.'

'Back? Back where?'

'Back here. Where else? There's a car park opposite. We keep the pool over there. So that's where I left it.'

She waited.

'I never gave it a second thought,' he said. 'Not until I read about the dead girl. And then . . .'

She sat down next to him.

'Then you kept quiet.'

He was fiddling with his glasses again. Licking his lips nervously.

Meyer sat down on his other side, gave him an evil smile, asked, 'Why?'

'A city official needs to stay out of politics. It's very important. We don't take sides. We don't get involved.'

'You're involved now,' Lund said. 'Very.'

'I thought I'd check the tapes to see who'd taken the keys. It was only right.'

'And?'

'It wasn't there.' He looked baffled. 'All I can think is whoever took the keys must have taken the tape too. How else—?'

'Oh for God's sake,' Meyer hissed.

'It's the truth. I'm telling you the truth. I'm sixty-four years old. Why would I lie? If they knew the tape was gone we'd all be in trouble. Those bastards upstairs can't wait to kick our arses. I've got one year left. Why should I carry the can for someone else? I brought that car back when I wasn't even on duty. And here you are treating me like I'm some criminal—'

'You are a criminal,' Meyer said. 'We've wasted a week chasing ghosts. There's a decent man in hospital and that kid's father in jail. If we'd known this from the beginning . . . Lund? Lund?'

She was on her feet, staring back into the Rådhus. The elegant tiled corridors. The shining wooden staircases. Crests and chandeliers. Plaques and memorials. All the trappings of power.

Someone had walked down here, taken the keys to the car in which Nanna Birk Larsen died. Taken the tape that would have shown who he was.

They'd been looking in the wrong place all the time.

'Show me. Show me where the car was.'

Meyer hesitated.

'The chief told us to call if—'

'Buchard can wait,' she said.

The council used a multi-storey garage across the road. Bare floors of grey concrete. The old security guy was getting scared.

'I parked the car here at half past seven that Friday.'

Third floor. Not a vehicle there any more.

'You're sure of the time?' Meyer wanted to know.

'Yes! Then I hung up the keys on the board behind our desk. Then I went home.'

Lund was looking at the ceilings, the walls, the layout of the place.

'Who's got access to your room?' Meyer said.

'Not many people. We're security, aren't we? But there was a party that night.'

'In City Hall?'

'Yes.' He scowled. 'One of their parties. Not what you'd call a party.'

He tried to smile at Meyer.

'Me neither. All piss and wind and cheap champagne. They always launch an election campaign with a party. A poster party they call it. Once the posters are ready they come and stand around and kid themselves they've won.'

'So what if there's a party?' Lund asked.

'You've got people coming and going. You can't keep track of everything. They leave their keys, they want their keys. You've got to show people where to find the room, take them for a piss.'

She waited.

'I wasn't there,' he said. 'If I was I'd try to keep control of things. But it's not easy. We don't man the place all the time. We can't.'

'So anyone could walk in and get the keys?'

'And the tape,' he added.

Meyer slapped his forehead and grunted, 'Wonderful.'

'Let's get hold of what's still there,' she said.

She turned to the security man.

'Whose party was it?'

He looked as if she ought to know.

'Hartmann. The one who keeps strutting round thinking he can boot old man Bremer out into the street. The ladies love him, I know. He makes a pretty picture. But honestly . . .'

A brief, grim laugh.

'Boys against men.'

Half past eight. Back at headquarters. Lund and Meyer in front of the PC, watching the security tapes. Buchard next to them, hands in pockets.

'We can't know who picked up the keys,' Lund said. 'Someone took that tape. But . . .'

She sat happy and comfortable in front of the screen, working the forward and back buttons, edging the video to the right place.

'At seven fifty-five this happened.'

Two cars left on the third floor of the garage. The black Ford on the far side of the image, a silver Volvo close to the camera.

At the right of the screen, two spaces along from the car in which Nanna died, a door opened from the staircase.

People started coming through. A family. Fresh from the party.

'Balloons,' Buchard said. 'You brought me here to see balloons?'

'Forget the balloons,' Lund said. 'Watch the background.'

A man. Two little kids with balloons. The Volvo was theirs. As they walked towards it a figure was just visible going through the shadows to the other vehicle. Little more than a shadow. A blur on the screen.

'How the hell do you see these things?' Meyer asked.

'I look. He's a man, about six foot two I'd say. At this point Nanna is still at the school party.'

The black Ford reversed just as Volvo man and his kids were getting into the car. Blocking the view.

'Later she stops by her teacher's. And then . . .'

The Ford headed for the exit, left of the screen, behind the car in front.

'Then I think she meets this man.' Lund watched the screen, caught by it, unaware she was smiling. 'Somewhere.'

She switched to another camera. The black Ford cruising along the garage. Then another on a corner. Turning towards the down ramp. The registration number was clear on the monochrome screen.

'That's him,' she said. 'XU 24 919. That's the car Nanna was found in.'

Cigarette in mouth, eyes shiny and tired, Meyer gave her a little salute.

'Thank you,' Lund said with a note of dry sarcasm.

'No, Lund. I mean it. Jesus . . .'

'We were wasting our time with the school. Nothing happened there. The car was back at the Rådhus garage all the time.'

'Someone's been taking the piss . . .' Meyer grumbled.

'We can rule out Hartmann and his staff,' she went on. 'We looked into them. The thing is . . .'

The two men waited.

'Nanna was going somewhere. The way she was acting at the party. Kemal said she picked up a school photo at his place for some reason. It's as if . . .'

'She was saying goodbye?' Meyer said.

'Maybe.' Lund shrugged, and tugged at the sleeves of her sweater. 'I think she was having an affair with someone. The parents suspect it too. They don't want to tell us. Perhaps they don't want to face it.'

'Birk Larsen's got history, chief. That teacher would have been dead.'

'Forget the parents,' Buchard ordered. 'They're stuck out in Vester-bro. What's going to get people like that into City Hall?'

Lund couldn't take her eyes off the screen.

'It's someone who cultivated her. Nanna was beautiful. Old for her years. Someone told her she was special. Gave her expensive gifts. Told her to keep quiet. To wait.'

She thought of the cramped bedroom above the garage in Vester-bro, full of books and souvenirs and mementoes. The clothes in the cupboard. The faint smell of a perfume that should have been beyond a teenager.

'Nanna had another life that no one knew about.'

'Doesn't work like that, Lund,' Meyer said. 'Someone had a clue.'

'Not Pernille. Or Theis maybe.'

'Someone,' Meyer insisted.

'Who've you told about this?' Buchard asked. 'The car being back in the City Hall garage?'

The question surprised her.

'No one except you. I'll get things started right now. Maybe there are some cameras in the street.'

Buchard strode out of the room.

'Maybe . . .' Lund said watching him.

The chief was in the corridor, visible through the glass. On his mobile.

'Is he calling his wife, do you think?' Meyer asked. 'Ordering a celebration pizza?'

Lund was back at the screen.

'What?'

'I was just wondering. You show him something like this. He doesn't say a word. Walks off. Calls someone.'

She waved away his smoke.

'I wish you'd stop that.'

'I worked in a little town down south before all this shit. No one ever complained about the smoke there.'

'Maybe you should go back.'

He looked a little down in the mouth.

'Can't,' Meyer said, nothing more.

Buchard marched back in.

'Check the guards' schedules and records. Pull in this old man who had the keys—'

'He didn't do it,' Meyer snapped.

'Bring me everything you can find on the staff.'

'It's not someone on the staff,' Lund said. 'They're not the kind of people to groom a pretty young kid like Nanna. Give her things she couldn't dream of. Pull tapes, fix keys, find places God knows where—'

'Look at the staff. Bring me what you find,' Buchard repeated.

She was thinking as she spoke. Couldn't stop even if she wanted.

'It has to be someone higher up. Someone who thinks they can get away with all this. Because we're beneath them. We're—'

'That's already been checked,' Buchard broke in.

'What?' Meyer asked.

Lund wanted to laugh.

'Checked? Who checked it? We're working this case. If we didn't check it—'

Buchard exploded.

'If I tell you it's been done it's been done. Now get going on the guards.'

Lund flew at him as he went for the door. Meyer wasn't far behind.

'No. This isn't good enough, Buchard. Who did you call?'

He was scuttling towards his office, back turned to them.

'Never mind who I call,' Buchard said and didn't even bother to turn.

'Wait, wait.' Meyer was mad too. 'This doesn't make sense.'

Buchard stopped, looked over his burly shoulder.

'Then I guess you must feel at home.'

'I want to know what's going on,' Lund demanded.

He turned. Big barrel chest pushed out. Face a picture of misery.

'Come with me,' Buchard said.

The two of them moved.

'Lund!' he barked at Meyer. 'Not you.'

She looked at the man next to her. Tried to smile.

Then followed Buchard, ignoring Meyer's bleats behind in the corridor.

The chief closed the door. She did smile then. She'd known this man all her working life. Had learned from him. Fought with him sometimes. Eaten dinner round his house. Even made up a foursome when she was married.

'You can tell me,' Lund said. 'It won't go any further. You know that.'

Buchard looked at her.

'You can tell that cretin too if you want. I don't mind.'

'Meyer's good,' Lund said. 'Better than he knows.'

The chief raised his hands. Took on that arrogant, scholarly pose he used when delivering a lecture.

'If I say they're not involved,' he told her, 'they're not involved.'

She cocked her head, looked at him in disbelief.

'Listen, Sarah. I want this solved just as much as you do.'

'So why are you tying my hands behind my back?'

He didn't like that.

'I'm your boss. I decide what you do. I've made myself clear.'

Then he left.

Meyer marched up, wanting to know what the chief said.

'Nothing,' Lund told him. 'When we checked Nanna's mobile how far did we go back with the calls?'

'I don't know. A week or so. There was no one from City Hall showing there. Just kids and home.'

'Can you check it again? Go back further?'

The phone was ringing back in the office. She marched off to get it. Meyer followed, whining all the way.

'What did Buchard say? Lund? Lund!'

The call was from a radio journalist asking for a comment on the case and Hartmann's campaign.

'We heard the focus is now back on City Hall,' the reporter said. 'Why is that? Is Hartmann a suspect?'

'Who told you that?' Lund asked.

'Sources.'

'Well, ask your sources what's going on,' she said.

She passed the phone to Meyer.

'What did Buchard say, Lund?'

Her phone beeped. A text message. She looked at it. Got her jacket and her bag. Didn't know what to think.

'I have to go.'

'Where?'

'Keep me informed,' Lund said and heard him bawling out the reporter as she left.

She left the car on the pavement outside the station, lights on, unlocked. Left her jacket in the driver's seat. Raced down the stairs in her black and white sweater and jeans.

Raining again. No moon. A few people fleeing the weather and a couple of drunks spoiling for a fight.

The train to Stockholm was close to leaving. That long journey over the water by the Øresund Bridge. One she could have made herself. Any time. If only . . .

Five hours later Stockholm. The new life. Bengt and Mark. A quieter job. A different world.

He stood by the platform, coffee cup in hand, left arm in a sling, face still bruised and swollen.

Lund stopped for a moment. Wondered what to say. What to do.

He hadn't seen her. Had turned towards the train. She could walk away now and she wondered whether that might be for the best.

Instead she strode up to him, said to his back, 'Bengt.'

Saw the pain, physical and inward, in his familiar, craggy face as he turned.

The first thing you did was make excuses. Always.

'Something came up again. I'm sorry. There was a . . .'

Her eyes were welling up. The words didn't come right.

'Things happening.'

She jerked a thumb over her shoulder.

'Can we talk about it in the car?'

Something different in his eyes. An expression she'd never seen before. A distance. A look that almost seemed like pity.

'Really,' Lund said. 'I understand why you don't want to stay at my mother's. I didn't think we'd be there long.'

A hope. A plan.

'Let's find a hotel,' she said. 'We can get a family room. It won't take long.'

He was shaking his head and she wanted to find the words that would stop him.

'We rushed into things, Sarah,' he said in a voice that seemed remote and impersonal. 'Maybe it's for the best. Moving to Sweden . . .'

That sharp stinging pain was back in her eyes.

'No! We didn't rush anything. What do you mean?' A single tear escaped and ran down her right cheek. 'I want to do this.'

Her sleeve went to her face, as if she were one more distraught kid at Nanna Birk Larsen's school.

'I want to be with you, Bengt. Please stay.'

'I can't watch this any more,' he said, then coffee cup in hand, embraced her once.

A short hug. The kind a friend gave. It didn't even feel like goodbye.

'Take care,' he said casually. Then climbed on the train.

Lund saw the station lights go blurry as she stood on the platform, watching the train pull out. Sobbing in a way she hadn't for years.

Words were never easy.

Not saying them anyway. What they signified, what the world meant in all its strange and impenetrable faces . . . these were matters that fascinated her in an obsessive, constant fashion.

She'd told Bengt she loved him. Not often. Not repeatedly. It seemed unnecessary. Importunate.

And it made no difference anyway. She was what she was and happy with it. The cost . . .

That rough wool sleeve fell across her face again, harsh against her eyes and skin.

For a moment the lights around her dimmed. She was back in the Pentecost Forest, amidst the dead trees with their shedding silver skin. Back chasing the man who chased Nanna Birk Larsen. Lost again, as Nanna must have been in those last few savage moments.

The dark wood . . .

Nanna fighting for her life amid the birch trunks. Her own struggle through the shadows of the girl's violent death, Meyer fighting to keep up by her side. They had all disappeared into the woods too. Faced with a choice of forks in the road. Left or right. Up or down. The straightforward pathway hidden from view.

Alone.

In a way she had been from the very beginning.

Perhaps that was what Bengt recognized. That when he was out of sight he was out of her thoughts. That nothing mattered except what she saw ahead of her with those gleaming, searching eyes.

And even that now seemed a lie, a joke, a phantom flitting, laughing through the shadows.

For her there was no pathway. No right direction, no correct course. Only the search for it. The chase not the conclusion.

The train pulled out towards the straight and certain track that led to the Øresund Bridge.

A turning not taken. A path that soon would be lost and overgrown.

They were all in the darkness, hunting the quarry within them and without. Meyer grappling to keep his job. The Birk Larsens fighting over how to bury their grief. Even Troels Hartmann, the poster boy of politics. A striking, intelligent man haunted by a demon beneath the surface. Of that she was sure.

So perhaps, Lund thought, she wasn't alone at all.

Meyer called when she was back in the car.

'Hello? Cat got your tongue?'

'What is it?'

'I went to forensics and made them take another look at her phone. There were fifty-three numbers on her contacts list.' He paused. 'We were only given fifty-two.'

She couldn't face talking to him.

'Can this wait till the morning?'

'I found a list of the calls she made going back a couple of months. I compared it to the data on the phone. Someone's screwing us around here, Lund. The list wasn't complete. She made calls we were never told about.'

'Where are you speaking from?'

'Outside. You think I'm stupid, don't you?'

'No. I don't. Do I have to keep saying this?'

'Here's the worst part. The first person to see those lists and take a look at the phone was Buchard.'

Lund kept driving.

'That can't be right.'

'It's right, Lund. I don't like this. If Buchard is covering for someone it's got to be Hartmann. Everything points there.'

'Not now,' she whispered.

'If we can't talk to Buchard who can we talk to? Huh? Who pulls his strings? Jesus . . .'

She took the phone from her ear.

'Lund? Lund!'

The headquarters building loomed ahead in the darkness, a pale grey palace, with so many curving corridors, offices and hidden corners, she could still lose herself there if she tried.

Sarah Lund kept going. Right past. On the way to what was, for now at least, home.

There were four minority parties on the Copenhagen City Council, right and left and somewhere in between, all bickering constantly, then pandering to Bremer to win a few prize committee chairs and paid appointments.

At a quarter to ten Hartmann had their leaders in his office.

He'd got a new shirt from the wardrobe, shaved, had Rie Skovgaard check him over. Combed his hair.

These people didn't get the smile. They were part of the game. They didn't need it.

'We represent five parties and five very different kinds of politics,' he said in a calm, practised tone. 'If we took the last election and added your votes to ours we would have had a clear majority.'

He paused.

'A clear majority. From what we've seen of the polls it's the same this time around. Maybe even better in our favour.'

Jens Holck, the leader of the Moderate Group, the biggest, the toughest nut to crack, sighed, took out a handkerchief and began to polish his glasses.

'Don't act bored, Jens,' Hartmann said. 'We're looking at the difference between victory and defeat. Bremer knows it. Why do you think he's playing these games with me on TV?'

'Because you keep inviting it, Troels.'

'No,' Hartmann insisted. 'I didn't. What happened to me could happen to any of us if he felt you threatened him. That's the state the Rådhus is in. That's why we need a broad alliance that gets Bremer out for good.'

Mai Juhl was a small, intense woman who'd created the Environment Party out of nothing. She carried plenty of respect and little goodwill. Politics was everything for her, which seemed odd to Hartmann since she'd achieved precious little in her time in office.

'That's all very well but what do we have in common?' she asked. 'How could we—?'

'We've plenty, Mai. Education, housing, integration. The environment too. You're not the only one to care, you know. We've more common ground among us than you think.'

'And the role models?' On most conventional issues Juhl swung to the right. 'You'd do anything to keep them.'

'Yes,' he agreed. 'I would.'

'We're a million miles apart there.'

Someone else agreed.

He looked at each of them, picking the subject carefully from the research Morten Weber had provided.

'Leif. Last time round Bremer promised you he'd reduce CO_2 levels? Never happened. What's he done for the elderly? Isn't that a key issue for you too? Bistrup? Did he create jobs like he promised? Jens? You used to say the city needed to attract families with children. What happened to all that?'

They didn't answer.

'Bremer took your well-meant commitments when he needed your support then threw them in the bin afterwards.'

He pushed their own election material across the table.

'If we were sitting round a TV studio now I'd tear you apart for this. You're asking for votes yet you never deliver on your promises. Because Bremer never delivers to you. It doesn't have to be that way. We can work together. We can compromise.'

He raised his shoulders in a gesture of indifference.

'We've all got issues we'll sacrifice. Me too.' Hartmann held up his own manifesto. 'This is a piece of paper, not the Bible. What matters is we win something. With Bremer you'll come away empty-handed and you know it.'

Hartmann got up, distributed Morten Weber's document around the table.

'I've drafted a collaboration between the five of us. Obviously it's only a beginning. Everything's up for discussion. You'll want changes. I welcome that.'

He went back to his seat, watched as they picked up the paper.

'I know it's a big step. But between us we have the talent and the energy and the ideas to make this city better. If we don't do something now he's back again. An administration stuck in the doldrums. No imagination. No fresh blood—'

'I think Bremer's done a good job,' Jens Holck broke in.

'So do I!' Hartmann said. 'Twelve years ago he was the right man. Now—'

'This is Copenhagen. Not paradise. I haven't seen anything from you that suggests you can be as good a Lord Mayor. Lately, more the opposite.'

'Fair enough. We should talk frankly. Let's see what the voters think.'

'And,' Holck added, 'you're on bad terms with Parliament. The Lord Mayor's there to negotiate the city's budget. If Parliament hates you they starve us. I really don't see this—'

'The way we deal with Parliament is through strength. If we have a broad alliance . . .' His hand swept the table. 'Then we can do better than Bremer. If they piss us off they piss off everyone. Don't you see?'

Jens Holck got to his feet.

'No. I don't. I'm sorry, Troels. I don't believe in you.'

'Won't you even look at the proposal?'

'I already did. Goodnight.'

Mai Juhl was leaving too.

'We couldn't do this without Jens,' she said.

The other three followed.

Alone in the office, in the blue light of the Palace Hotel's neon sign, Hartmann wondered whether he'd jumped the gun.

There'd never been a broad coalition like this before. Maybe it was madness. But madness had its place in politics sometimes. When the old order gave way a little chaos was only to be expected. That was when the bold would strike.

And he wasn't the only bold one around.

Morten Weber predicted Holck would reject the offer outright and the others follow. He rarely read the situation poorly. He also said they'd think about it offline. That before long someone would call.

Hartmann poured himself a brandy.

It took exactly seven minutes.

He looked at the name flashing on the phone and laughed.

Jens Holck was in the garden courtyard hidden in the heart of City Hall, smoking among the Russian vines and ivy next to the fountain.

'You're back in bad habits,' Hartmann said, looking at the cigarette. 'That's a shame.'

'Yes. It is.'

Holck was a couple of years short of Hartmann's age, about the same height and build, a one-time student leader, young-looking at first glance but worn down by underachievement. He had dark hair and black fashionable glasses, a bleak schoolmasterly face. He hadn't smiled much of late. Or shaved either. He looked a mess.

'Didn't I make myself clear?' Holck asked.

'Very. So why did you call?'

Holck's head went from side to side.

'In case I could make myself a little clearer.'

'Jens. We've got to do something. The city's drifting. Bremer's administration is disorganized. The finances are a mess. He only listens to himself.'

Holck took a draw on the cigarette, blew smoke over the fountain.

'He's like a dying king,' Hartmann added. 'We all know he's not long for this world. But no one wants to mention it. Or say a word in case the old man hears.'

'Then maybe we should wait for the funeral. And pick up the pieces from there.'

Hartmann looked around the courtyard. They were alone.

'Did you hear about his trip to Latvia?' he asked.

Holck's head bobbed up. He was on the audit committee. Rie Skovgaard had been fishing there too.

'What about it?'

'Officially it was a visit to a company. Inward investment. But the expense account—'

'Been snooping have we, Troels? I thought you were the good guy.'

'I don't mess with public money.'

'We see the expenses. There wasn't a thing wrong with them.'

'What you saw was tampered with. Thousands—'

'Oh for God's sake. Is this your new politics? I don't give a damn

301

if Bremer creams a little here and there. He's an old man and he's worked like a dog here. Always has. In spite of the miserable salaries and the godawful hours.'

'So we just carry on as we are?'

'Someone has to be Lord Mayor. Do you really think you're different?'

'Give me the chance.'

'And you *are* on terrible terms with Parliament. That's the heart of it. They don't like you, Troels. They don't like the way you preen yourself for the cameras. The women swooning. Your sanctimonious smugness. The way you think you're better than everyone else.'

Holck laughed, a short, harsh sound.

'Not me. I don't have that problem. I've known you long enough to see through the performance. Tell me. Are you running for the sake of Copenhagen? Or the benefit of Troels Hartmann? Which matters most?'

'You called to tell me this?'

'Pretty much,' Holck said, then threw the cigarette into the fountain and walked off.

Ten minutes later.

'You're wasting your time on Jens Holck,' Morten Weber said. 'He's Bremer's lapdog.'

'Then let's throw him the right bone. They were interested, Morten. They were wavering. If I'd got Holck on side they'd all fall in line behind him. In a heartbeat. Do we have any food?'

Weber bowed, said, 'At your service.'

Then went off to find something.

'So if we don't placate Jens Holck we're sunk?' Skovgaard said.

She sat on the desk, feet on his chair, chin propped on her hands. She didn't look unhappy with the idea.

'No,' Hartmann insisted. 'We know who we are. We're strong.'

Skovgaard held out her arm, flexed her bicep.

'I'm strong too. Feel.'

Hartmann laughed, came to her, tested her arm with his fingers.

'Not bad. One more thing.'

He bent down. Her arms went round his neck. They kissed. Fingers though hair. Grey business suit against black business dress.

She stayed in his embrace, said dreamily, 'It seems a long time since that happened.'

'When this is over I will take you somewhere with the biggest, softest, warmest bed . . .'

'When it's over?'

'Or sooner.'

'Is that a politician's promise?'

Hartmann pulled away from her, smiling.

'No. It's mine. Call your father and get him to talk to the Interior Minister. Tell me what I have to do. Just a word from Parliament. Holck will hear it.'

Morten Weber walked back in with a dinner plate full of sandwiches.

'The car park's crawling with policemen,' he said.

'Why?' Skovgaard asked.

Weber frowned.

'Search me.'

Lotte Holst was eleven years younger than her sister Pernille, pretty enough to hold down a job behind the bar of the Heartbreak Club for five long and eventful years. The place catered to businessmen, young executives, anyone with enough money to pay two hundred kroner for a weak cocktail. It was near Nyhavn, close to the hordes of tourists heading for the canal boats and the restaurants.

She had her hair up, glossy lipstick, a revealing halter dress open at the midriff, and a permanently bored smile as she served up bottles of Krug and vodka to the deafening music.

The money was good. The tips better. And sometimes there were surprises.

Around eleven one of the barmen came over and said she had a visitor.

Lotte walked to reception, saw Pernille there in her fawn raincoat, hair a mess. Put a hand to her own head, felt embarrassed, the way she always did as a kid.

Pernille was pretty. But she was the beautiful one. Everyone said that. No one knew why it was Pernille who got married, even to a rough and inarticulate man like Theis, not her.

Her sister was rocking to and fro. She looked terrible. There was a small storeroom next to the cloakroom. They went there, sat on beer crates. Lotte listened.

'I didn't want to bother you,' Pernille said.

'Then why . . . I mean. It doesn't matter. The boys are round with Mum. They're OK.'

'I know. I asked.'

'I have to work, Pernille.'

'I know that too.'

'Have you heard from Theis? When he's coming home?'

'No. The lawyer's doing her best.'

She hugged herself in the stained raincoat even though the little room was stifling.

'Did Nanna say anything to you about . . .'

The words died.

'About what?'

'I don't know. You were so close. Like sisters.' There was something accusing in her eyes. 'Closer than I got.'

'You were her mum.'

Pernille was starting to cry.

'She told you everything! She told me nothing.'

The door was open. One of the security men was watching them.

'She didn't . . .'

'Nanna had a life I didn't know about! I'm sure of it.'

'I don't know what you mean, Pernille.'

'What did she say? Were there problems at home? With me? With Theis?'

'No . . .'

'Sometimes we argued. She never stopped. Always coming and going. Taking things. Wearing my clothes.'

'She wore my clothes too,' Lotte said. 'Never asked.'

'Did she . . . ?' The tears again, closed eyes. An agony Lotte Holst didn't want to see. 'Did she hate us?'

Lotte put a hand on her sister's arm.

'Of course not. She loved you. Both of you. And the boys. She never said anything.'

'No?'

'No.'

'So it's just me?'

The security man was making signs. She wasn't supposed to take breaks from work. Not more than five minutes an hour.

'Something happened last summer,' Pernille said. 'Between her and Theis.'

She nodded, as if trying to recall a specific incident.

'When I look back I can see it. She was always Daddy's girl. She could wind Theis round her little finger. Then they suddenly stopped doing things together. She didn't tell me.'

'Theis thought it was too early for her to move out. She was a bit upset.' Lotte shrugged. 'That's all. She was nineteen. She wasn't a kid. It was nothing.'

'You're sure?'

'You have to stop thinking about it so much. Theis was a good father. He still is. Even if he did something stupid.'

The barman was at the door, beckoning her.

'I've got to go. I don't want to get fired. Listen.'

She squeezed her hands.

'I'll come round tomorrow and do what I can. Come on. You can get through this.'

She got Pernille to her feet, embraced her, took her to the exit.

Went back, made drinks for rich businessmen, smiled when they leered.

Then waited an hour till the break came again, walked into the toilet, took out the coke, snorted a long, expensive line, trying not to cry.

Tuesday, 11th November

Eight in the morning. Lund was watching the security tapes from the garage. Again. The family, the kids with the balloons getting into the silver Volvo. The black Ford pulling away.

Meyer came in with news. There was no sign of any connection between Nanna Birk Larsen and City Hall. She never worked there as staff or volunteer. Didn't even seem to have visited on a school trip.

'I've been through her things again,' he added. 'That key ring we found.'

He showed her an evidence bag.

'What about it?'

'They're not hers. Not for home.'

Lund had pushed those to the back of her mind.

She took the bag off him. They were Ruko keys. Used everywhere.

'They don't look like anything they use at City Hall,' he said. 'They have all these old fancy locks. I don't know . . .'

'Later,' she said. 'Can we enhance the picture? Zoom in on the driver and see what he looks like?'

'In theory.'

'Then let's do it.'

Meyer hesitated.

'Buchard says this has all been checked.'

She pointed at the reports.

'I can't see anything about it in here.'

'You heard him. I don't want any part in this.'

He came and sat down next to her. Looked almost humble.

'I really don't want to spell this out. But this . . .' He looked round the office. 'This is my last chance. Things didn't go too well in a couple of other places.'

'A couple?'

'I use that in a broad sense. I've got to keep this job. I have to.'

'Is that why he didn't kick us off the case?' she wondered. 'Because he's got us where he wants?'

Meyer stared at her with his big, sad eyes.

'If I was Buchard I would have fired us by now,' Lund added.

'The next time you're going to say something like that will you please warn me. So I can put my hands over my ears.'

'They're big ears. It won't work.'

'Thank you. If Buchard says it's been looked at—'

'No one's looked at this. You don't believe that either.'

He had his hands over his ears.

Quickly he took them away and said, 'He's coming.'

The chief marched in.

'You wanted to talk to me?'

Lund smiled.

'I wanted to say sorry about yesterday. We were both tired.'

Meyer nodded.

'Tired,' he agreed.

'No problem,' Buchard said. 'So long as we're making progress.'

'Progress.' She nodded. 'We are.'

'Good.'

He was ready to go.

'Who checked the contacts and the list of calls on Nanna's mobile?' Lund asked.

Buchard froze in the door.

'I don't know,' he said.

'Something might point to one of the guards. Maybe. I don't know.'

'Look into it.'

Another smile.

'I will,' she said.

They watched him go.

'What would you have been?' Lund asked. 'If you weren't a cop?'

'A DJ,' Meyer said. 'Did it when I was a student. I was very good. Except the face.'

He ran his hand over his bristle and cheeks.

'I don't know if I've got the looks.'

She laughed.

'And you?'

'Nothing,' Lund said. 'I'd have been nothing.'

'I did consider running a hot dog cart once,' Meyer added. 'You're your own boss there. Maybe one day soon. The way we're going. Lund?'

She was somewhere else.

'Nothing at all,' Lund said.

There was nothing to look at in the phone records. But twenty minutes later a detective stuck his head through the door with news. A taxi driver had appeared in the office after one more run by the night team pushing out pictures of Nanna. He said he thought he might have picked her up the night she died.

'I don't believe it,' Meyer said.

'Believe what?'

'This is the first time anyone's volunteered a damned thing about that poor kid. Didn't you notice, Lund? Everyone else expects us to be mind-readers.'

He rubbed his stubbly chin.

'They do want us to find this bastard, don't they?'

The taxi driver was called Leon Frevert, a tall, skinny man in his mid-forties. He had a long grey face that matched his cheap suit and smelled of cigarettes and sweat. Straight from a night driving a cab round the city.

'I'm not positive it's her,' Frevert said, looking at the photos they'd given her.

'Forget whether it was her or not,' Meyer ordered. 'Tell us what happened.'

He worked weekends driving a cab for one of the city firms.

'I picked her up on Friday. If it was her. We talked a bit. She wanted to go into town. I dropped her off on Grønningen, near the junction with Store Kongensgade.'

Long straight street at the edge of the city. Next to the Kastellet fortress. Nowhere near any of the addresses they'd looked at.

'You've got a receipt?'

'Sure. You're in trouble if you haven't.'

Frevert pulled a bunch of papers out of the pocket of his threadbare suit.

'I think it was this one. I picked her up near Ryparken. See.' He pointed to the receipt. 'The ride started at ten twenty-seven p.m. Finished at ten forty-five.'

Lund asked, 'What happened when you got to Grønningen?'

'She got out. I found a new customer straight away. Didn't even have to drive off. Plenty of work on Fridays.'

He scratched his thinning fair hair.

'The thing is we didn't go direct. We stopped. You don't get that so much with kids. They don't have the money.'

'Stopped where?'

'On Vester Voldgade. At the back of City Hall.'

Meyer closed his eyes and groaned.

'What happened there?' Lund asked.

'She got out and asked me to wait. I wouldn't do that normally. They just run off. But she seemed a nice girl. She wasn't drunk or anything.'

'What did she want at City Hall?'

'She didn't say. She went inside for a couple of minutes.'

'Did you see anyone with her?'

'No. She came out. And then we went to Grønningen. I don't want to waste your time. I can't promise it was her.' He glanced at the photos again. 'Maybe, but . . .'

'Thanks.'

She shook his hand, waved at Svendsen who was wandering down the corridor outside, asked him to take a statement.

Then the two of them sat in the office alone.

'There are lots of hotels around there,' Lund said.

'We've been round the hotels.'

'Then go round again. Ask them if they've seen a politician. If anyone from City Hall lives nearby. Are you working on the guards?'

He was getting tense and angry. Wouldn't look at her.

'Yes. I certainly am.'

'The taxi took her from Kemal's house to City Hall,' Lund went on.

'He said he wasn't sure if it was her.'

She didn't want an argument. Meyer was scared for his job. Torn, she guessed. Between what he thought was right and what he thought was smart. For himself.

'I've an appointment,' she said getting up, grabbing her jacket. 'Call me when you hear something.'

Rie Skovgaard had been putting out feelers to Parliament overnight. Hartmann's relations with the Interior Minister remained good.

'The problem's the Prime Minister. He thinks you're ambitious. You steal the limelight. He thinks you'll come for him if you unseat Bremer.'

Hartmann listened, shook his head.

'I'm not coming for him. Not for four years anyway.'

Morten Weber was reading the morning papers.

'At least the polls are staying with us. No one believed that nonsense about the girl.'

'If we've got the Interior Minister on board that's enough.'

'Only if the Prime Minister allows it,' Skovgaard said. 'He could still sink you.'

'This is ridiculous. We're in the same party. And they're backing Bremer?'

She was smiling at him.

'Out with it,' he said.

'There's one possibility. The Prime Minister's not doing well at the moment. He could use some of your limelight.'

Hartmann felt out of his depth for a moment. Skovgaard and Weber swam so easily in these muddy waters.

'What are you getting at?'

'He's never caught on to the integration issue properly. If we said his office helped put together our programme. Helped with role models. Some of the school projects . . .'

Hartmann laughed.

'Not a chance. We came up with that. They hated the idea.'

'Forget the past, Troels. If we give them credit—'

'For what?'

'For anything. So long as we get their backing.'

'It's a lie!'

Weber's head went from side to side.

'Lie's a very strong word. This is politics. What's true . . . what's untrue. After a while it doesn't matter so much.'

'Then what does matter?'

'What works,' Weber said, looking at him as if he were a simpleton.

'No. It's out of the question.'

'OK,' Skovgaard said and stared at the sheets in front of her.

'OK,' Weber agreed and read the paper.

A long minute's silence.

'I'm glad to see you're working well together,' Hartmann noted.

'We usually do,' Skovgaard replied.

'The answer's still no.'

Another long minute.

Then Hartmann took a long deep breath, looked around at the wooden walls, the leaded windows, the crests and gilt, up at the fancy artichoke lamp.

All the trappings of office. None of the power.

'What would we get in return?'

'We could invite him to your campaign meetings,' Skovgaard said.

'The most important thing is to get Holck into the deal,' Weber added. 'I hate this shit as much as you do.'

He shrugged.

'But if it can bring us the alliance . . .'

'Find out exactly what we can expect in return. I don't want any escape routes.'

'If we ask that question we've already said yes,' Weber told him. 'No going back.'

'No going back,' Skovgaard repeated.

'Cut the deal then make me an appointment. With the Prime Minister. If it gets us into office I don't give a shit who gets the credit.'

He got up from the table, walked out.

The two of them sat there, uneasy allies.

'Any news on why the police were in the car park?' Skovgaard asked.

'What?'

'You heard, Morten. You hear everything, even if you pretend you don't.'

'No news that I know of. I'll call Parliament.'

'I can do that. This is policy. You leave it to me.'

There was a new man round from the bank. Younger. Friendlier. Pernille had called the jail, tried to talk to Theis, failed. He was going to be kept in for another day at least. No phone calls but at least she might be able to see him later.

'Sorry,' she told the bank man. 'I can't talk to my husband.'

'No problem.' He spread out the papers in front of her. 'So let's assume the house will go on the market while you continue the renovations.'

'OK.'

'We'll extend your credit so you don't have to pay the instalments. Let's hope the house sells quickly so we can break even.'

'That's fine by me.'

'Then there's the account your daughter opened.'

She stared at him.

'In Anton and Emil's names. Where should that money go?'

Pernille brushed back her hair.

'What account?'

He pushed forward a statement.

'It's got eleven thousand kroner in it. She was a steady saver. It's a lot of money . . .'

'What kind of account?' she asked.

'It's a savings account for the boys.'

'Can I see?'

She snatched the statement before he could answer. Stared at the figures. Regular deposits. Hundreds of kroner a time. Never a with-drawal.

'Where did she get the money?'

'From a job?' the man suggested. He was blushing, embarrassed.

'She didn't have a job. She worked for us from time to time. But that was pocket money. Not this . . .'

He shrugged, said nothing.

The account was opened the previous January. Regular deposits every fortnight. They stopped in the summer.

'There's no rush,' he said. 'You don't have to make a decision right now. Well . . .'

A brief smile. He stood up.

'Unless there's something else.'

Pernille couldn't take her eyes off the bank statement. It sat on the table, above the family pictures captured in the surface. Taunting her. Laughing.

When he was gone she called the prison again. Found someone amiable.

'I'll come now,' she said.

The guard let Pernille into the tiny prison interview room then stood by the door. Theis sat hunched at a scratched wooden table in a bright-blue prison suit, eyes on the floor.

A moment of indecision. Then Pernille walked over, threw her arms round him, felt him clasp her, felt the tears rise in her face.

The two stayed locked together, rocking gently, his huge hand moving through her long chestnut hair as if looking for something that was lost.

Then they sat down opposite each other, Pernille's eyes swim-ming as she cried.

Finally he asked, 'How are the boys?'

'The boys are fine.'

He wouldn't look at her as he spoke.

'I talked to the lawyer. She's doing everything she can. When I get out I'll take care of the bank and the house.'

She turned away, wiped the tears. Felt a stiff hot flicker of anger and couldn't work out why.

'I'll fix everything,' he said. 'It'll be OK.'

Looking out of the window at the monochrome day beyond she asked, 'What happened between you and Nanna last summer?'

His head went up. His eyes – they were the part of him she liked the least – caught her. Unreadable. Aggressive sometimes.

'What?'

'You used to . . .'

The tears were coming again and she couldn't stop them, however hard she tried.

'Did you have an argument? Did you say something to her?'

Her voice was breaking and it was full of unintended blame.

'What do you mean?'

Two decades she'd been with this man. There were always secrets between people. Perhaps there had to be.

'Nanna opened a bank account in the boys' names,' Pernille said. 'She made regular deposits. She had a job. The account . . .' She said this very slowly. 'It had eleven thousand kroner in it.'

'You know she had a job! With us.'

'She didn't earn that kind of money with us.'

'Maybe I paid her extra. Or she saved it up.'

'Then why keep it a secret?'

'I don't know.'

She'd no idea whether she believed him or not.

'Nanna never said anything to you?'

'No.' He rubbed his bearded chin, closed his eyes. 'She was angry with me. I know that. I thought it was too early for her to move out.'

He reached over and took her hands across the table.

'I used to give her money to cheer her up sometimes. What she did with it . . .'

'Yes,' Pernille said.

'That's all I can think of.'

She watched him trying to smile. Trying to say what he always said.

I will fix this. Things will get better.

So she smiled back, squeezed his hands in return, came forward over the old wooden table and kissed him.

'Everything's going to be OK,' he said again.

*

313

Lund drove to the TV station to see a reporter who was making a documentary about the election campaign. The woman was following Hartmann and Bremer from beginning to end.

'I'm just interested in what happened on the night of the poster party,' Lund said.

They were seated in front of a screen, the woman flicking through unedited video.

'What do I get out of this?'

'Nothing.'

The TV woman blinked.

'It's only fair—'

'No it isn't. I could get a warrant in five minutes. If I do that you won't work again today. We'll take everything.' Lund smiled at her. 'If I think there's evidence here I can stop you using this.'

'So why should I show it you?'

'Because you don't have a choice.'

'I still want something.'

'If there's a story you'll get it first. If there's a story . . .'

Lund sat on the edge of the desk, not moving an inch.

'All I need is footage from seven p.m. to eight p.m.'

'The poster party was October the thirty-first?'

'That's right.'

'OK. I remember that. They were in Hartmann's office.'

Her fingers flashed across the keyboard. Then she scrolled through the footage. Poul Bremer came on the screen, laughing and joking, glass in hand.

'I love the way they pretend they respect each other. You should hear what they say in private.'

'Like what?'

'They smile and smile and hate each other's guts. And they'd climb into bed with anyone if it'd get a few votes.'

Lund was watching the screen, barely listening.

'Hartmann invited everyone into his office for a drink.'

Skovgaard, the leaders of the minority parties, Morten Weber, Bremer, all together, laughing and joking over glasses of wine.

'Does anything interesting happen?' Lund asked.

'Hartmann gives a short speech. Nothing special. No point in wasting effort on this bunch, is there? Either they're voting for him or they're not.'

Lund leaned forward, looked more closely. There was a figure in black at the back of the crowd. Talking to no one. Looking uncomfortable.

'Who's that?'

'Jens Holck. Leader of the Moderates. He's behind Bremer.'

'Was he there all evening?'

'Yep.'

Hartmann clinked a glass against a bottle. Poul Bremer came and stood next to him beaming, genial.

Lund wasn't watching them. Her eyes were on the figure at the back.

'So why's Holck putting on his coat?'

She didn't answer.

'Is there any more footage of him?'

'Why do you ask?'

'Curiosity.'

Lund nodded at the keyboard. The woman worked it, set the video to run more quickly.

The camera scanned the room. She went forwards, back, looking round the sea of bodies.

'I can't see him. I thought he was there. Sorry.'

'What's he like?' Lund asked.

'Holck? Been in politics for years. Serious. Bit of a loser. Nothing without Poul Bremer.'

She sat back in her chair, put her hands behind her head.

'Not exactly oozing charm if I'm honest with you. There was some gossip about him having an affair and getting found out. It never made the papers. His wife's divorced him though.'

'He had an affair? Is that true?'

The woman laughed at her.

'You don't know politics, do you?'

'Enlighten me.'

'They feed off gossip. Off one another. They live in this little world of their own and nothing else matters. I'll tell you something . . .'

Lund waited.

'Anybody who had an affair with Jens Holck must have been pretty desperate. Or they had a high boredom threshold.'

*

315

Lund called Meyer as she left the TV station.

'The car left at seven fifty-five. Jens Holck slunk out of the poster party fifteen minutes earlier and wasn't seen again.'

'Buchard's been asking for you,' Meyer said.

'Does Holck live near Grønningen? It might even be a hotel room.'

'I couldn't care less, Lund.'

'The talk in City Hall is that he's been having an affair.'

'We're not making inquiries at City Hall. Not with the politicians. Leave it. Didn't I mention Buchard was asking for you?'

'You did.'

'Were you listening by any chance?'

She looked at the phone. Tried to imagine Jan Meyer's face at that moment.

'Lund?' said a tinny, uncertain voice from the speaker. 'Lund?'

She found Troels Hartmann as he was leaving his office.

'I need two minutes of your time,' she said.

'Does your boss know you're here?'

'It'll only take a moment. I just wanted to apologize.'

'You need to leave,' Rie Skovgaard said. 'You've caused us no end of problems.'

'I know, I know. I'm sorry. This is a difficult case. Two minutes . . .'

Hartmann waved her into the office and closed the door.

'I need your help,' she said.

'I have a citizens' surgery on Mondays. You can make an appointment like anyone else.'

'What if I said your car wasn't at the school?'

'Then I'd say you'd screwed up again.'

'What if I said it was driven back here? To the City Hall car park?'

He was silent.

'That Friday night. When you held your poster party. All the group leaders. All your campaign workers.'

'What the hell is this about, Lund?'

'I need to know if anyone left the party early.'

'Wait, wait. I don't understand. You're saying the car was brought back here?'

'Did anyone leave early?'

316

Skovgaard walked in. She was on the phone. Saying, 'Can I speak to Buchard now?'

'Did Jens Holck leave early?' Lund asked.

'Holck?'

Skovgaard was through, whining to Buchard.

'Do you remember seeing him later in the evening?'

Hartmann shook his head.

'Your boss wants to talk to you,' Skovgaard cut in, offering the phone to Lund.

She stared at this woman. Attractive in a hard, unemotional way. It never seemed to touch these people that a young girl had died. No one except Hartmann, and that still interested her.

'Yes?' Lund said, taking the phone, not really listening.

When it was done she passed the handset back to Hartmann's smiling campaign manager.

'Get out of here,' Skovgaard said.

Lund looked around her. At the wooden walls, the panelling, the beautiful lamps, the expensive furniture.

'This place must feel like a castle,' she said.

'Go,' Skovgaard repeated.

Lund glanced at her, then, lingering more, at Hartmann.

'It's not a castle,' she said.

Back in her empty office Lund took a cigarette from Meyer's pack, rolled it in her fingers. Did all the bad things. Turned it round, tip to end, juggled it, smelled it. Lifted it to her lips, felt the dryness as she put it in her mouth, lit the thing and breathed in the choking smoke.

It didn't taste good. It didn't make anything better. It just was.

Outside Buchard was briefing the team, in a voice pitched loud enough for her to hear.

'Lund starts her new job in Sweden tomorrow,' the chief told them. 'Meyer takes over. Svendsen, you're Meyer's assistant.'

He'd taken her name off the door already. Now it simply said: Vicekriminalkommissær Jan Meyer.

Buchard came in to see her straight after. He looked at the cigarette.

'I've informed the Swedish police you're ready to start there. I refrained from telling them about your activities.'

'My gratitude knows no bounds.'

She took a suck on the cigarette and looked at him. Buchard wasn't good at shifty.

'I'm sorry things had to end this way,' he added.

'You're the only one in this place who rates Svendsen.'

A flicker of anger in his pug eyes.

'That's the last thing you have to say to me?'

'No. There's more.' The cigarette was starting to feel good now. 'But you've probably got calls to make.'

When he'd gone Meyer came in, stood by the sign with his name on it. He didn't seem happy.

'We couldn't find anything around Grønningen. Anything that links in Holck.'

Svendsen stuck his head around the door. He was smiling.

'There's a delivery from Sweden, Lund,' he said. 'You need to sign for it. Before you go.'

Emphasis on the last word then a big grin.

'I will,' Lund said. She pointed at the cigarette. 'When I'm done.'

Lund watched him wander off, turned to Meyer, pointed at the retreating Svendsen and said, 'He's theirs, Meyer. Not yours. Remember.'

Then she went to the window. A yellow removals van stood below, the driver waiting by the door.

'I've got some guy waiting in forensics,' Meyer said. 'So . . .'

She blew smoke out of the window, remembered how many times she'd scolded him for doing the same.

'You can keep the packet.'

One more pull, one more lungful out into the damp November air.

'Lund?'

'Thanks,' she said and didn't look at him.

When he was gone she went to the desk, went through the plastic evidence bags, found Nanna's keys, the Rukos on a red plastic ring, and pocketed them.

It was starting to rain. Bengt had sent back what things she had in Sweden. She opened up the first case. Clothes and bedding, nothing she could use.

So she signed for them, made a call to the company, ordered

storage, then watched the yellow van drive off with a part of her life still inside. Gone until she reached some point in the future she still couldn't begin to imagine.

The lawyer, Lis Gamborg, saw Birk Larsen in his cell.

'Vagn's been questioned. He confirmed he encouraged you to take revenge against the teacher.'

'He didn't do that. He tried to stop me.'

'That's what he says. It's to your advantage. Let's leave it there. Vagn will be charged as an accessory. He's not looking at jail.' She paused. 'You are.'

Birk Larsen took a deep breath, stared at the grey concrete floor, said nothing.

'I argued that you wouldn't try to abscond. That you'd suffered enough. You wouldn't interfere with witnesses, since you've already pleaded guilty.'

'And?'

She shrugged.

'And you're free to go.'

In his blue prison suit Birk Larsen felt like a child being gulled by a performer on stage. He didn't like tricks and maybe she realized that.

'Provided,' she added quickly, 'you don't leave Copenhagen. And under no circumstances must you interfere with the investigation again. I mean that, Theis. If you do anything else . . .'

'I won't do anything. I just want to go home.'

'Good. For your sake and your family's it's important you keep a low profile. Don't talk to the media. Don't get involved. Go back to the way you were.'

He stared at her.

'As much as you can. I'm sorry. That was thoughtless of me. You can get your things now. Theis . . .'

She hesitated over something.

'What?' he asked.

'People have got such sympathy for you. For Pernille. But sympathy's like a dripping tap. One little turn . . .'

The lawyer made a twisting gesture with her hand.

'Then it's off. What replaces it may not be so nice. Be invisible.

Be patient. I'll see you when we come back to court. If no one's heard a word of you in the meantime then maybe I can keep you out of jail.'

He nodded.

She smiled then left him alone, in his blue prison suit and black boots. Unshaven, unwashed. Thinking about the strange world beyond the door.

Pernille took the call, shrieked with a sudden burst of joy. Called Lotte round to look after the boys, shuffled on her coat before getting the car.

Her sister came straight away with a bagful of shopping, ready for the night. Sweets ready, and a book.

Families ran on these daily rituals, all taken for granted, all so painful when the reason for them was gone.

Lotte started running the bath, got the boys in. Pernille went for her keys.

One packet of sweets only, she thought, and looked in Lotte's shopping bag.

Plenty of crisps and snacks. Some shampoo. The kind of things a woman on her own bought in such small quantities it seemed ridiculous.

A pile of letters. Lotte must have picked them up on the way out, brought them round to read while she was babysitting.

The top one was square and formal, a card in an envelope.

It bore Nanna's name and Lotte's address.

Squeals from the bathroom, the noise of Lotte scolding them.

'I want the duck,' Emil cried.

'Not until you stop splashing,' Lotte said.

Without a thought Pernille reached in, took out the square envelope, ripped it open.

The card was silver with an ornate Christmas tree. An invitation to a staff Christmas party for a nightclub in the centre. Four weeks away.

She stared at it feeling cold and stupid and betrayed.

'Where's the duck?' Lotte asked by the bathroom door. 'Oh. Right.'

She'd found it. Then looked. Saw.

'Nanna worked with you all along,' Pernille said, the card in her hands. 'She gave them your address. That's why we never knew.'

Lotte came over, stared at the card, retreated, guilty.

'When did she start there?'

Little sister, little sister, Pernille thought. I never did trust you really.

'In January.'

Lotte had the evasive, shifty look of the naughty child she once was.

'She only started as a temp. She left last summer.'

Pernille held the card and waited.

Lotte licked her lips, tried to get hold of herself. Look convincing.

'She didn't plan it. She came to visit me and thought it seemed . . .' Lotte shrugged. 'Exciting.'

Pernille looked around their little apartment. The cramped rooms. The photos on the walls. The table they made. The books. The TV. The kids. The close and intimate thing called family.

'Exciting?'

'It just happened. I didn't see any harm in it.'

She didn't know whether to cry or scream. To fly at Lotte or run away.

Instead she asked, 'What happened last summer?'

Lotte folded her arms. Confident in herself now. Afforded an escape route.

'Maybe you should talk to Theis.'

'Charlotte. You're my sister. Tell me what happened.'

Sounds from the bathroom. The boys giggling, splashing.

'She liked the job. Then she started seeing someone. A man.'

'Who?'

'Someone she met there. I don't know who. She wouldn't tell me.'

'Did he give her money?'

Lotte looked sly again.

'Why do you ask?'

'Just tell me. Did he give her money?'

'I don't think so. It wasn't like that. She started to turn up late for her shifts. Then one day she didn't turn up at all. I was worried.'

Pernille knew what was coming, had to hear it.

'I called Theis,' Lotte said. 'I'm sorry. We found her in a hotel room. She was dead drunk. It was when you were away with the boys on the school trip. Nanna promised she'd stop seeing him. She promised Theis.'

Pernille laughed at the idea, laughed and held back her head, let the tears begin to flood her bright eyes.

'I'm sorry,' Lotte said again.

Pernille walked over, took the towels off her and the rubber duck.

'I want you to go now,' she said.

'Pernille—'

'I want you to go.'

The debate was in the Black Diamond, the angular glass building by the water that housed the Royal Danish Library.

Still the Nanna Birk Larsen case haunted Troels Hartmann. Rie Skovgaard and Morten Weber had bickered about little else in the car.

'Lund thinks the car was driven to City Hall,' Hartmann said as they walked into the library. 'Why? Why would anyone drive it back?'

'If any of this was important,' Skovgaard cut in, 'we would have heard of it. Lund's off the case. I told you.'

'So that's why the police were in the car park?' Weber asked.

'Doing what?' said Hartmann.

Weber shrugged.

'I don't know. Whatever police do.'

They got out, walked through the doors.

'This is a public event, Troels,' Skovgaard said. 'Time to smile.'

He wasn't in the mood.

'Why did she ask me about Holck?'

On the escalator, rising towards the busy crowds above.

'The only thing that matters about Holck is whether he's with us or not.'

'No,' Hartmann insisted. 'We need to know what's going on. I don't want all that shit again.'

'The shit came from Lund!' she barked at him. 'Lund's gone. Focus on the meeting. This is important.'

'I need to know!'

'Jesus, Troels . . .' Skovgaard muttered and wandered away.

Weber watched her, looked at Hartmann.

'For once I'm with her. Think about the meeting. We can deal with the rest later.'

Then they wandered off into the audience while Hartmann lugged his briefcase to the podium.

Bremer was there already. Immaculately dressed. Smiling as always. A little flushed under the lights.

'Welcome, Troels,' he said, shaking Hartmann's hand. 'You've been fishing in troubled waters, I hear. Did you catch anything?'

A laugh. A hard slap on Hartmann's shoulder. Then a wave to the crowd, some private gestures to people he maybe knew and maybe didn't.

All the politician's tricks and habits. Troels Hartmann had learned them, from Bremer mostly. Could summon them up too. But then . . .

A figure in a crumpled black suit entered from the right. Bremer leapt up, took Jens Holck by the hand, made a point of saying, 'Good evening, old friend. Sit by me, Jens . . . Sit.'

He pulled up a chair. Holck looked at it.

'No thanks.'

Walked on, looked at the empty seat next to Hartmann.

'Is this free? I've been thinking . . .'

'If you want it, Jens.'

'I believe I do,' Holck said and sat down.

Grønningen ran straight along the side of the Kastellet grounds for half a kilometre. There were buildings, apartment blocks, on one side only. Nanna's Ruko keys didn't work in any of the front doors.

After Lund wasted half an hour testing every lock there she checked the short road at the south, Esplanaden. Nothing.

She called Meyer.

'I need your help,' Lund said.

'You were wrong about Holck. He drove off in his own car that night.'

'Did you check if any party members owned flats around Grønningen?'

'We did. No one does. And there are no politicians living nearby. The Liberals own a flat on Store Kongensgade.'

'Whereabouts?'

'What are you up to?'

'Where?'

'Number hundred and thirty.'

Lund walked the short way into the street, checked the numbers. It was back to the north, closer to Grønningen. Store Kongensgade was a long and busy road that ran all the way from close to Østerport Station into the city itself. The taxi driver, Leon Frevert, said he dropped Nanna near to the junction between the two streets. She should have worked this out earlier.

On the left ran lines and lines of low, old ochre-coloured houses. The naval cottages of Nyboder, laid out in low rows in the dark like soldiers frozen to attention.

'It's on the fourth floor,' Meyer said. 'Where are you?'

A massive building. Red brick, white facings gleaming in the street lights. Grand communal entrance. Lots of bells. A Ruko lock.

'It's irrelevant,' he added. 'We've checked out Hartmann already. Lund?'

'What?'

'Where are you? What's going on?'

'Nothing,' she said, then put the phone in her pocket.

Two keys. One for the outside. One for the apartment.

Lund walked up to the double door, put the first key in the lock, turned.

Nothing.

Tried the second.

The door opened.

The lift was gleaming and ancient, double folding doors, room for no more than four inside.

She got in, pressed the button for the fourth floor. Listened to the mechanism whirr and hum.

The place seemed empty. She rose past offices and dentists' surgeries, past private apartments and places that bore no name.

Then the lift stopped. Lund got out and started to look around.

Meyer was back in forensics, going through the video from the car park again. The black car pulling away. The driver just out of sight.

'Stop it there,' he told the technician. 'What was that? It looked like a flash of light.'

'It's the fluorescent tube. On the way out. Flickering.'

'Go back, back. Take it step by step.'

Seven frames. Just visible in the driver's window, illuminated by a single brief flash of light, was the face of a man.

'Who the hell is that?' Meyer asked, trying to stifle his impatience. 'Can you enhance it?'

'I can try.'

His phone rang.

'It's Lund.'

'Good timing. We're about to find out who was in the car.'

'It was Troels Hartmann,' Lund said.

'What are you talking about?'

Silence.

'Lund? Lund? Where are you? What's going on? Talk to me. Please.'

'I'm in the Liberals' flat in Store Kongensgade. Nanna's keys open the door to the block and the door to the flat. Call forensics. Meet me here.'

'Hartmann?'

'That's what I said.'

The screen was rendering the enhanced image. A face was emerging out of the grey murk. Angular and handsome. Grim-set and familiar.

Meyer thought: Poster Boy. You're mine.

'We're on our way,' he said.

A full team were in place within the hour. Ten men in the blue uniforms of forensics, white bunny suits, white gloves at the ready. Floodlights. Cameras. Chemicals.

Lund had a second unit outside, in the courtyard behind the block, was walking among them, checking their work, offering advice and opinions, some of them well received, others plainly ignored.

Meyer brought her coffee. Buchard didn't say a word.

She took the two of them through the front door, into the noisy old lift.

'The taxi driver dropped her off on Grønningen at quarter to eleven. I imagine she didn't want anyone to know she was coming here. Nanna could have been in the flat four or five minutes later. It belongs to the Liberals. A donation from a supporter. They use it for work lunches, meetings, putting up guests.'

'Who lives in this place?' Meyer asked.

'Most of the units are offices or corporate accommodation. It was pretty much empty all weekend.'

They got to the fourth floor. Lund walked to the flat, showed them how Nanna's key worked.

'She had one for the front door too?' Buchard asked.

'Yes.'

Six technicians in bunny suits and blue plastic mob caps were working in the interior. The place was decorated like a luxury hotel suite. Red velvet wallpaper, old, stylish furniture.

'We've found her fingerprints already,' Lund said, handing them forensic gloves and shoe covers to wear.

When they were ready she led them in.

Posters of Troels Hartmann were scattered round the room. There was a broken glass table and splinters from what looked like a tumbler on the floor.

Lund walked to the table, showed them the marks on the carpet.

'The blood's Nanna's type. I've sent away for confirmation it's hers. There was some kind of fight.'

There was a heavy walnut desk by the window.

'We've got prints on the paperweight there. Nanna threw it at the mirror for some reason.'

Lund turned three hundred and sixty degrees on her heels, looking at the room. The broken glass. The disorder.

'She didn't just fight him. She got mad. Lost her temper I think. This wasn't random. Unexpected. She knew him. It was an argument. A lovers' tiff gone wrong.'

'We've got lots to send to forensics,' Meyer broke in. 'With a bit of luck we'll have a DNA result by tomorrow afternoon.'

Lund walked into the bedroom. The door was open, covered in forensic marks and stickers.

'Nanna ran in here and tried to block the door. He kicked it open.'

The bed sheets were ruffled as if someone had sat on them, nothing more.

'I don't think he raped her here. Or beat her up. That was to come. Somewhere else.'

Lund tried to imagine what had happened. An argument. A fight.

But Nanna didn't die for another two days. A big piece of the jigsaw was still missing.

She walked outside onto the terrace.

Meyer and Buchard followed.

Buchard stood still, Lund eyeing him.

'If you went down to forensics and checked the video you know perfectly well Hartmann was on the surveillance tape,' Meyer added. 'I got that in two minutes, Buchard. You're no fool.'

'I want to talk to Lund alone,' the chief said.

'Enough of that shit!' Meyer shouted. 'I'm sick of it.'

He slammed his hands on the iron railings.

'Buchard! Buchard! Look at me! I want to know what's going on. You owe us that. Both of us.'

The old man looked downcast, lost, defeated somehow.

'It's not what you two think.'

'What is it then?' Lund asked. 'You erased a name from her mobile. You deleted a call from the list.'

'No I didn't.' It was a weak, pathetic whine. 'It wasn't me.'

'Who was it then?'

He didn't answer.

'We're bringing in Hartmann for questioning,' Lund announced.

'And we want that information,' Meyer added.

He stood on the cold terrace, panting. Someone's servant. Not a happy one.

'Well?' Lund asked.

'I'll get it for you.'

'Good,' she said and then they left him there, pop-eyed and breathless in the dark.

The three of them were back in Hartmann's office feeling satisfied. The debate had gone well. Morten Weber said the minority leaders were meeting in the morning to discuss the alliance.

'If we've got Holck,' Skovgaard said, running to her computer, 'the rest of them will come too. What changed his mind?'

Hartmann was the only one who looked unhappy.

'I don't know. He didn't say. Why was Lund asking about him? What's all this about the car?'

Skovgaard waved him away.

'If Holck's involved I need to know.'

'I left Meyer a message.'

'That's not good enough.'

Weber was getting wine from the cupboard, putting out sand-wiches he'd brought.

'No surprises, Morten,' he said. 'That's what you want too.'

'No surprises.' Weber uncorked the wine, poured three glasses, toasted them both. 'Jens Holck's just following his nose, Troels. He knows you're going to win. Don't complicate things unnecessarily.'

Skovgaard's phone rang.

'Bremer looked worried as hell,' Weber added. 'He can feel the ground disappearing beneath him.'

Skovgaard spoke quietly into the phone, ended the call. Looked at Hartmann.

'That was the police,' she said.

'And?'

'They want to talk to you.'

'Oh for God's sake—'

'Troels. They want you to go to police headquarters. Now.'

'Is this about Holck and the car?'

'It didn't sound like it.'

'Then what could it be?'

'I don't know. They said straight away. Either that or they come here for you. I really don't want that.'

Hartmann's glass stopped halfway to his mouth. He slammed his hand on the table. Dark burgundy spilled over the walnut veneer.

Then he got his coat. So did Skovgaard. So, after she stared at him stuffing his face, did Morten Weber.

Ten minutes later they were crossing the open courtyard, heading for the spiral staircase that led to homicide.

Lund waited with Meyer and Svendsen outside the interview room.

'I only asked for you, Hartmann,' she said, looking at Skovgaard and Weber.

'I really don't have time for this.'

'We want to talk to you alone.'

'What's this about?'

Lund indicated the door.

'Just take a seat.'

Skovgaard was getting mad.

'If this is an interrogation say so. We've taken so much shit from you, Lund.'

Meyer smiled at her.

'It's just a few questions. A politician ought to help the police, surely.'

'If he wants a lawyer you can call one,' Lund added.

Hartmann glared at her.

'Why in God's name would I want a lawyer?'

They didn't answer.

Hartmann swore, walked into the room, indicated for Skovgaard and Weber to stay outside.

Lund and Meyer sat opposite him, showed him the video of the car leaving the parking garage.

'Looks like one of ours,' Hartmann said. 'But there are a lot of black cars out there.'

'Any idea who's driving?' Lund asked.

He shrugged.

'No. Why should I? If it's important I can ask one of our people to check.'

'You don't need to,' Meyer said. 'We're police remember.'

He hit some keys on the computer. Zoomed in. Face on the screen. Just to rub in the point he passed over a printout.

Hartmann stared at her.

'Right,' he said. 'It was after the poster party. I gave my driver the night off. So I borrowed a campaign car.'

Lund smiled. Svendsen came in with some coffee. Hartmann relaxed a little.

'You left the poster party early?' she said.

'I had a headache. And a speech to write.'

Lund poured him a cup.

'Where did you go?'

'We've got a flat on Store Kongensgade. I thought I'd go there to finish the speech. Why?'

'Who has a key to the flat?' Meyer asked.

'I do. There's a spare key in the office. Some other officers too, I think. I don't really know.'

'But you use the flat?'

'I told you. What is this?'

Lund shuffled some photos on the table, let him see them.

'The car you drove is the car Nanna was found in. It was driven back to City Hall that night. You drove it away.'

He shook his head, said nothing.

'What happened in the flat?' Meyer asked.

'It can't be the same car,' Hartmann said.

'What happened in the flat?' Meyer asked again.

'Nothing. I was there for a couple of hours.'

'So was Nanna Birk Larsen,' Lund said, fetching some new photos. 'She had a key. She was attacked there. Then driven away in the car you took.'

Lund pushed the photos from Store Kongensgade across the desk. Broken table, shattered mirror. Glass on the floor. Fingerprint markers.

'In our flat?' Hartmann asked finally.

'How long did you know her?' Meyer asked.

Hartmann couldn't take his eyes off the pictures. Slowly he flicked through them, mouth open, face frozen.

'I didn't know her. I never met the girl.'

Meyer snorted.

'The car. The flat. The fact you never mentioned any of this.'

'There was nothing to mention! I took the car. I went to the flat. I had a couple of beers. Then I decided to walk home.'

They said nothing.

'On Monday morning I came to pick up the car but it was gone. I assumed someone from the campaign office had gone in and found the keys. I left them on the table. Someone must have taken them.'

Meyer sighed.

'Why did you take the surveillance tape? So we couldn't see it was you in the car?'

'What? I didn't take any tape.'

'Your number was deleted from Nanna's mobile,' Lund added.

'That's not possible. I didn't even know the girl.'

'What did you do with the rest of the weekend?' Meyer asked.

Hartmann swore and got up.

Lund strode to the door, blocked it, looked at him. He was agitated and angry.

'Are you going to tell us or not, Hartmann?'

'Why the hell should I? My private life's my own business. None of yours.'

'This isn't about your private life . . .' Meyer began.

The door got pushed open. In walked Lennart Brix.

Brix.

Buchard's new number two. Fresh from one of the regional forces. A tall and striking man with an angular unsmiling face. He'd arrived two weeks before, kept himself scarce. Now he looked as if he owned the department.

'I'm the deputy chief here,' Brix said. 'Good evening.'

He walked straight over, shook Hartmann's hand. Stood next to him, turned to Lund and Meyer and Svendsen.

'I understand there's a problem,' Brix said.

Five minutes later. Lund lit her second cigarette of the month as she watched Hartmann leave with Skovgaard and Bremer by his side. Jan Meyer stood next to her chewing gum.

Brix saw the three of them out then came back to the office.

Black shirt. Black suit. Shiny black Italian shoes. He looked like a politician himself.

'Hartmann told me he took the car in good faith. He clearly left the flat before the girl arrived. He's willing to talk about the flat. You can question his employees as much as you need. You don't even have evidence she was raped there, Lund. She might have just had an argument with someone.'

'We don't want to talk to his employees,' Lund said.

Brix leaned against the door, watching her. A fixed, determined man.

'If you'd asked nicely you'd have discovered he had an alibi. You're looking for someone who had Nanna Birk Larsen all weekend. Hartmann left the flat around ten thirty and went to Rie Skovgaard's.'

'He said he went home.'

'His relationship with Skovgaard is a private matter. He wishes to keep it that way.'

'If these damned people told us the truth . . .' Meyer began.

'The next morning they went to a conference centre where they had meetings all day.'

'Can we check that?' Meyer asked.

'You don't need to.' He pointed at the pair of them. 'The next time you pull in someone like Hartmann I suggest you do your homework first.'

They watched him go. Lund passed the half-smoked cigarette to Meyer.

'Let's check the alibi. See if anyone else from City Hall uses the flat. Everyone in Hartmann's office comes in for questioning.'

She looked at Meyer.

'Are you OK with that?'

'Oh yes,' he said.

Svendsen came back in with a message. Pernille Birk Larsen was coming in. She wanted to see Lund urgently.

'We don't have time. If it's about her husband being in custody . . .'

'It can't be that. He got let out.' Svendsen shook his head, laughed. 'She didn't even come to meet him, Lund. You should feel flattered.'

Theis Birk Larsen walked home to Vesterbro. Twenty minutes in the rain through deserted streets.

Pernille wasn't there. Nor were the boys. In the kitchen, by the pot plants and the photographs, he phoned her, got nothing more than voicemail, waited five minutes, phoned again.

Just after eleven a door slammed downstairs. He ran down into the garage. Lights on. Vagn in his red overalls and black woollen hat, looking at the diary in the office.

Skærbæk looked surprised to see him.

'Have you seen Pernille, Vagn?'

'When did you get out?'

'Just now.'

'That's good. What happened with the teacher—'

'Have you seen her?'

Skærbæk looked baffled.

'Lotte came round to babysit. She wasn't here long and then they left.'

Birk Larsen stood by the office, hands in pockets, trying to make sense of this.

'Why?'

'I don't know.'

'Where to?'

'Christ, Theis! I don't know.'

Birk Larsen glared at him.

'You did talk to her?'

'I thought she went to pick you up.' Skærbæk hesitated. 'Didn't she?'

Birk Larsen went back upstairs. Called again. Got nowhere.

Pernille Birk Larsen brought her sister Lotte to headquarters. Dragged her there by the looks of it.

Lund listened then asked, 'Tell me about this club, Lotte. The Heartbreak.'

'It's for members. Private. Invitation only.'

Meyer sat silent, scribbling notes.

'What did Nanna do?'

'She waited on tables. I always kept an eye on her.'

'Nanna liked the place?'

'Sure. It was exciting. Different.'

'Different?' Meyer asked.

'Different from taking calls for a removals company.'

Pernille sat in the corridor beyond the glass. She'd refused to leave.

'How did you know she was seeing someone?'

'She missed some shifts and kept asking for time off. It seemed . . .'

She was a pretty woman, but with a sad and pasty face that spoke of late nights and maybe something else.

'It seemed innocent.'

'Then something happened?'

'One night she didn't turn up. I called Theis and told him about it. We drove around looking for her. I got a call from a hotel near the station. She gave them my number.'

Lund watched her, wondering.

'Why did she get a room?'

'She'd had too much to drink. She was upset. I think the guy had dumped her. He wasn't there. It was just Nanna.'

'Did she do drugs?' Meyer asked.

'I don't think so.'

'Did she talk about the man?'

'I think he was married or something. She was really secretive. She wouldn't tell me his name. Nanna . . .'

A long pause.

'It was kind of a time when a kid falls in love with someone different every week.'

'But she didn't,' Lund said. 'This went on for months.'

'That time. She always called him Faust.'

'Faust?' Lund checked, writing this down.

'It's not his real name.'

'It wouldn't be. Why did she call him that?'

'I don't know.'

Meyer chipped in.

'This was spring and summer. She didn't talk about him after that?'

'No.' Her eyes strayed to the figure in the corridor. 'Pernille thought this might be important.'

'She was right,' Meyer said and left it at that.

'Did she tell you where she and Faust used to meet?' Lund asked.

'Hotels, I think.'

'Do you know which ones?'

Lotte Holst was trying to remember something.

'It was hotels in the beginning. Later on I think they went to a flat.'

'A flat?'

'Yeah. I remember she said it was really cool. Old furniture. Very expensive.'

Lund waited. When there was nothing else she said, 'Whereabouts?'

'I don't know.' One more memory. 'All she said was it was near the old navy houses. The yellow ones they take you to on a school trip.'

'Nyboder?' Lund asked, staring at Meyer.

'I think so.'

'How about Store Kongensgade?'

Lotte blinked.

'Yes. That was it.' She looked at them both. 'How did you know?'

*

Lund got back to her mother's flat just after ten. Meyer called as she was walking up the stairs.

'There's no one called Faust on the Heartbreak Club's membership list. Hartmann's people have been on to say we can only talk to him through a lawyer from now on.'

'Is anyone from his office a member?'

'Not that I can see.'

The flat was dark and silent. And empty.

'It's an alias, Meyer. Remember Faust? The good man who was tempted by the Devil? Go to the club and ask around.'

'Can't you hear the music? Where the hell do you think I am?'

There was something in the background. Tinny disco and a million voices.

Lund kicked off her boots and turned on the kitchen light then opened the fridge.

Nothing.

There was a saucepan of stew on the hob.

'I can't see a politician prancing round this place,' Meyer said. 'People would know. But maybe he doesn't come here.'

She put the phone on speaker, placed it on a kitchen top and lit a low flame beneath the pan.

'What do you mean?'

'The club has a dating chat room on its website. People meet up online. Maybe that's it.'

The stew didn't look as if it would improve with cooking. Lund got it to tepid then picked up a spoon and took a taste from the pan.

'I'll have a specialist take a look,' Meyer said.

There was a Carlsberg in the fridge. She cracked the crown top and took a swig from the neck.

'OK,' she said, starting on her second spoonful. 'Let me know if something turns up.'

'Oh, lucky you,' Meyer moaned. 'Getting something to eat. I haven't had a bite since lunch.'

Lund looked at the pan.

'Yes. Lucky me.'

She went to the sofa with the stew, realized she was still in her coat, shrugged it off, threw it on the floor.

Then she turned on her laptop, sat there going from the pan to the beer to the computer.

Meyer was right. The Heartbreak had a dating section. Open to anyone, not just members of the nightclub.

She clicked for a new profile. Filled in the form as Janne Meyer. Female. Heterosexual. Password: bananas.

Her mother came back as she was waiting for the confirmation email.

'Where's Mark?' Lund asked.

'We went to see a film with Magnus. I bought them pizza afterwards. He wanted to spend the night at Magnus's. I said it was all right.'

Vibeke smiled sourly at her.

'You weren't around to ask.'

The confirmation message came through. Lund clicked on the acceptance link and found herself in the Heartbreak's dating forum.

'It's fine for him to stay there,' she said.

Her mother busied round the room doing nothing.

'How are you?' she asked.

'I've just eaten. It's been busy.'

'Are you getting anywhere?'

'Yes. I'm still doing things. Sorry.'

There was a search box at the bottom of the page. She typed in 'Faust'.

'Mark talked to his father today.'

The site was slow to load. Lund took another swig of beer.

'About what?'

'He's coming to Copenhagen. He'd like to see Mark. Mark didn't know if you'd be in Sweden or not.'

'This is dragging on. He can see Mark.'

'Yes. We noticed that.'

Vibeke came and stood at the door, staring at her with that mix of anger, sympathy and bafflement she'd made her own.

'The storage company called about the things Bengt sent back from Sweden. They wouldn't take your boxes into storage without an account. So I said they could leave them here. They're in the basement.'

Then she went to the bathroom without another word.

Lund was glad. She didn't know what to say.

Bengt.

That odd farewell on the station seemed an age away.

She looked at the laptop. There was one result called 'Faust'.

Lund clicked on it.

No photo. Just a silhouette. Next to it a quotation.

It read: 'Ruling the heart is the most difficult thing.'

Seven

Weber had everyone associated with the office assembled by eight in the morning. Hartmann stood to address them.

'This is unusual but the police need our help. They'll be here interviewing everyone today. You'll be summoned to headquarters one by one. I want you to talk to them frankly. Answer all their questions. We've nothing to hide.'

Olav Christensen was there.

'What's this about?' he asked.

'That's for the police to say. I can't go into details. I must stress that everything you hear is confidential. I'm counting on your full discretion.'

Hartmann looked round the office.

'Especially outside these walls. We're drowning in gossip as it is. We don't need any more.'

Then Weber ushered them out.

'Why was that creep Christensen here?' Hartmann asked when the door was closed.

'You said everyone with access to the office. He's here all the time.'

'He hangs around like a bad smell. Did you get Lund the material she wanted?'

'All the bookings for the flat. When it was used. Who by.'

'Troels?'

Skovgaard's voice had that silky, wheedling tone to it that grated sometimes.

'What?'

338

'The group leaders are on their way. You don't have to do this.'

'Send them in.'

'Troels!'

He walked into his office and waited.

Holck was first.

They got the best computer technician forensics could find, a young woman who looked no more than nineteen.

'Can you hack the site?' Meyer asked.

'Hacking's illegal. We're police. I can't believe you said that.'

'So how do we get in?'

'I ask nicely. If that doesn't work I say I'm coming round to check all the pictures on his PC.'

She was blonde with an amiable face and smile.

There was a piece of paper in her hand, a line of letters and numbers written on it.

'Voilà,' she said. 'See. Nicely didn't work, mind.'

Then she went into a part of the site Lund never saw on her laptop at home.

'These places have different levels. There's one for casual outsiders like you. There's something else for the privileged few. Something exclusive if you're prepared to pay for it.'

She typed more quickly and fluently than anyone Lund had ever seen. The light of the screen shone on her plain, confident face.

A list of names came up. Lund ran through them.

'Can you see any connections with Hartmann?' Meyer asked.

'Give me a chance.'

The forensics girl frowned.

'They're all fake names. This is a sleazy place, people. If it was just about, um . . .' She waved her hands in the air. '. . . matrimonial services they wouldn't need to hide like this.'

Another flourish at the keyboard.

'"Faust" is one of the more conventional names we have. Some are a bit more descriptive, shall we say?'

A line of entries came up in what looked like a spreadsheet.

'Not that our Faustian friend hasn't been busy.'

The entries kept flashing down the screen.

'He created this profile a year ago. He's been talking to a lot of women.'

She opened up some of the messages.

'Oh, what a charmer. He knows fancy hotels.' She winked at Meyer. 'Care for a suite in the Hilton?'

'Not right now. Where's the personal information?'

'Where do you think? In his wallet.'

The screen kept filling.

'Oh this is good. In April Faust contacts someone called NBL. Kids. I mean why not spell out your real name, Nanna?'

A few keystrokes and the messages narrowed down to that one identity.

'They meet. They're in contact regularly throughout the spring. They stop in the summer.' She scrolled to the end of the screen. 'He keeps trying to reach her but she doesn't reply.'

She scratched her cheek.

'Normally the other way round with me.'

'Can we see who Faust is?' Lund asked.

'Not directly. Places like this are too smart to store credit card details. I could try leaning on the site administrator.'

'Do it,' Meyer ordered.

'If you want my honest opinion it won't work. These people aren't fools. They don't want a service with trackbacks to their users. That just causes problems. They genuinely won't know who they are.'

'So we've no idea who he might be?' Lund asked.

'I didn't say that, did I?'

Another screen. Dates, times, long strings of numbers.

'These are the access log files. They show you the IP address of the networks he used when he went onto the site.'

Lund noticed her fingers fall still on the keys.

'What's wrong?'

'All these hits. He only ever uses two networks. Funny. Most people move around these days. Just two specific places is weird . . .'

She typed some numbers into a form.

'Most of the time he was using the internal Rådhus wifi network. The rest . . . Bear with me.'

More screens, more rapid typing. A page from a telecoms company. A baffling line of text and figures.

'The rest are from the router in the flat in Store Kongensgade.'

Meyer watched her.

'But you don't know who?'

She licked her finger, stuck it in the air, waited a moment, then said, 'Sorry. No.'

Lund's mind was turning.

'What about any other women he dated? Can you trace them?'

She took a swig from a can of Coke, thinking.

'I can try.'

Svendsen came through the door.

'Hartmann's alibi checks out. Rock solid. He was at the conference centre the whole weekend. Oh, and Lennart Brix is in your office.'

'Buchard can deal with him.'

Svendsen shook his head and leered.

'Buchard isn't here any more.'

Brix was playing with the toy police car on Meyer's desk. Spinning the wheels, laughing at the way they sparked up the red light on the top.

'Sit down,' he said. 'The people upstairs wanted me to have a word with you.'

'About what?' Lund asked.

She stayed on her feet. Meyer parked himself next to the window.

'About dereliction of duty in the Birk Larsen case.'

'Being lied to and messed about isn't dereliction of duty!' Meyer snapped.

'Some phone records slipped out of the system,' Brix said. 'You don't need to read too much into it.'

He pulled an envelope out of his black jacket.

'Here's a court order to requisition new records.'

Lund didn't take the paper.

'Buchard said he was going to do that.'

Brix thrust his hands into his trouser pockets.

'Buchard's gone. For now let's say he's on holiday.' He squinted at the rain beyond the glass. 'Bad time for it.'

He looked at them.

'Don't expect him back.' He put up a hand, beamed. It wasn't pretty. 'You've got me now. No worries. We'll manage.'

Then he headed for the door.

'I don't think Buchard was acting alone,' Lund said.

Brix stopped, looked at her, said, 'Come with me for a moment, will you?'

The two of them walked down the corridor.

'You've got a job with the Swedish police, Lund,' Brix said. 'I want you to finish your work here without any more fuss. And then . . .'

He made a shooing gesture with his long hands.

'Depart. Until then you report to me. No one else.'

When she got back to the office Meyer was staring miserably at the papers on the desk.

'I never thought I'd say this, Lund,' he grumbled. 'But I think I preferred the other one.'

Theis Birk Larsen sat opposite her at the table, beneath the chandelier. Pernille and the boys had spent the night at her parents. Anton and Emil were now at school. Just the two of them in the empty flat, Vagn Skærbæk barking orders in the garage below.

He stared at his hands. Struggled for the right words.

'I talked to Lotte,' he said, and she turned away from him, got up, paced the room. 'I should have said something. I know.'

Pernille stopped and looked at him from the bedroom door.

'Something was wrong and you never told me. You knew where she was working. You knew she was in trouble. You didn't say a thing.'

He kept wrestling with his hands, as if an answer lay there.

'Why?'

'Because she begged me not to. She didn't want to upset you.'

Pernille shook her head, eyes blazing.

'She didn't want to upset me?'

'That's right.'

'She could tell me anything.' Her hands flew out. Her voice cracked. 'Anything!'

Birk Larsen screwed his eyes shut.

'She promised it wouldn't happen again. She'd work for us. She promised she'd keep up with her schoolwork. Even though she was sick of it.'

Pernille went and stood by the bathroom door, back to him, back to everything.

342

'Nanna said she'd pull herself together. I had to trust her. What else could I do?'

She returned to the table, full of a calm, cold fury.

'What else haven't you told me?'

'That's it.'

He picked up his hat and keys.

'That's it!' she shrieked. 'And now you go to work? There must be more lies. More things I don't know.'

She glared at him.

'Come on, Theis. Spit it out.'

'There's nothing else,' he said gently. The stony look on her face hurt him more than all those lonely hours in a cell. 'Nanna knew she'd messed up. I didn't think she had to hear it from you too.'

There were tears in her eyes and he wished he could wipe them away.

'I wanted her to do well in school!'

'I know you did. But it wasn't just school. There was a reason why it was me she talked to. Don't you know?'

'Know what?'

'You never wanted to let her make the mistakes you made. That we made. You wanted her to be perfect because we weren't.'

'Don't talk to me about mistakes, Theis. I won't take that from you.'

She turned her back on him again. Walked towards the bathroom. Past the washing machine and the dryer. The clothes basket. The detergent.

There something happened. She shrieked and screamed, she clawed at the things around her. Clothes flew, glass shattered, washing powder broke and ran around her in a white, embracing cloud.

Birk Larsen went to her, tried to take her in his arms. She fought him off, crying, swearing, kicking, yelling.

Then she fell against the door, breathless and sobbing.

The moment gone, the fury abated. The reason for it still alive and painful between them.

Pernille walked into the bedroom, closed the door behind her. Slowly, with clumsy big fingers, he started to pick up the things from the floor. The sheets. The children's shirts and underwear. The small things that once made up the bond called family, a covenant that now lay shattered around them like the broken glass upon the floor.

Olav Christensen sat opposite Lund looking nervous in his grey civil servant's suit.

'You've never been in the flat?' she asked.

'No. Why should I? It's the party's. I work for City Hall.'

She was quiet.

'What's going on?' Christensen asked.

'You just had to say no.'

Lund scribbled down some notes.

'Did others use it after the poster party?'

'Why are you asking me this? I wouldn't know.'

'Why not?'

'I work for school services.'

'They say you're always in Hartmann's office.'

'He's the boss of education. I have to go there.'

'Do you like him?'

Christensen hesitated.

'It's not easy getting on his good side.' Then again, a little more anxiously, 'What's going on?'

'Does the name Faust mean anything to you?'

'Yes.'

She looked up from her notepad.

'He sold his soul to the Devil.'

Christensen looked briefly pleased with himself.

'Do you know anyone who uses that nickname?'

'No. But if the cap fits I'm sure there's plenty who'd wear it.'

Meyer rapped on the glass door. She went outside. The computer specialist had uncovered a message from a woman who'd written to Faust on the Heartbreak website. They had a name.

Lund took it, went back in to the interview.

'Am I done now?' Christensen asked.

'No. My colleague will continue. I have to go somewhere.'

She went out. Christensen sat at the table, sweating in his office suit.

Then Meyer walked in, looked him up and down. Took out a pack of cigarettes and a banana. One bite of the banana then a cigarette.

'I've got work to do,' Christensen said.

'You don't say?'

Meyer took another bite of the banana then rolled up his sleeves.

'I've been having a really shitty day so far,' he said, looking at the papers Lund had left. 'Let's see if you can make it better, shall we . . . Olav?'

Birk Larsen was alone in his scarlet truck, parked by the side of the road south through Valby. A pack of Tuborg on the passenger seat. Two cans gone, the third disappearing quickly.

He watched the cars and trucks. He smoked. He drank. And tried to think.

In the green fields, along the path, a man was walking his kids. Three of them and a dog.

The boys never had a dog. They wanted one so badly. No good in the flat. A house . . .

He thought of Humleby and the wreck there. All that money tied up in dry rot and crumbling brick.

Dreams didn't call to him. They were for fools. Birk Larsen thought himself a practical man, one who lived in the present, never thinking of the past, never fearing the future.

A man who worked and kept his family. A man who did his best and that was as good as goodness got.

And still it fell apart. One day bliss and hope. The next the quicksands shifting, cracks in walls that once seemed solid.

He hadn't spoken to Pernille since the row that morning. As far as he knew she was still in the bedroom, weeping through furious eyes. Vagn had taken over, gone through the schedules, allocated the jobs.

Vagn kept them on track. Kept him on track sometimes, not that Pernille knew.

Little Vagn with his stupid silver necklace. Pathetic Vagn who hung around them so much because he'd got nowhere else to go.

Three years ago, when he was in money trouble, Birk Larsen had let him sleep in the garage for a good six months. Vagn felt grateful and embarrassed. Turned up with pizzas they didn't want. Started spoiling the boys, buying presents for Nanna she didn't need.

Uncle Vagn. No blood there. But love?

When everyone else walked away Vagn Skærbæk would be there

till the last. He was a recluse of a kind, with no one but the Birk Larsens and his sick uncle to think about. A failure mostly. Nowhere else to go.

Birk Larsen snatched at the can, finished it, threw the thing out of the window.

He'd hated that last thought. It was part of the old him, the ungenerous, bullying thug that still lurked inside, grumbling to be let free.

That night in the warehouse with the teacher he'd had his moment. If it wasn't for Vagn Skærbæk he'd have taken it too. Kemal would be dead. And he would be locked up in a cell in a blue prison suit facing years inside.

The old Theis still slumbered, talking in his sleep.

He didn't know about generosity, about forgiveness, about grief. Only anger and violence and a fiery, urgent need to quench both.

The old Theis would stay buried. Had to. For Pernille's sake. For the sake of the boys.

For him too. Even in the bad days, when things happened he didn't care to remember, Theis Birk Larsen was aware of that nagging, awkward ghost in his head called conscience. Knew it picked at him, chipped at him, nagged him in the night.

Still did.

He looked at the three remaining beers, swore, threw them into the back of the van, wheeled round, then set off back into the city and the hospital.

The wing in Rigshospitalet was new and seemed to be made of glass. Its transparent walls amplified the anaemic November light until the day looked like summer. Bright, relentless, unforgiving.

Birk Larsen spoke to reception, waited as the woman made a call. Watched her face. Knew that she knew.

'He'll see you,' she said finally.

Then glared at him. She was a foreigner. Middle Eastern. Lebanese. Turk. He'd no idea.

'God knows why,' the woman added.

Kemal was in a wheelchair in a day room one floor below. His face was covered in bruises, wounds and plasters. His right leg was in plaster, horizontal. His left arm sat in a cast too.

346

'How are you?' Theis Birk Larsen asked when he could think of nothing else to say.

The teacher stared at him, face expressionless. He didn't look in pain.

'I get discharged tomorrow.'

A long silence.

'Can I get you something? A coffee? A sandwich?'

Kemal looked out of the glass window, looked back at him, said no.

'Any news on the case?' he asked.

Birk Larsen shook his head.

'I don't think so. They wouldn't tell me anyway. Not now.'

Teachers never impressed him. They were too full of themselves. As if they knew something that was kept secret from everyone else. But they didn't. They'd no idea about growing up in the Vesterbro of yesterday, walking to school among the hookers and the dope dealers and the leftover drunks. Trying to stay alive. Fighting to get to the top.

Fighting was Birk Larsen's first skill and he had the strength for it. Later he thought he'd learned to fight in different, more subtle ways. For Pernille's sake. For Nanna and the boys.

But there he was wrong. He was stupid.

Kemal watched him, didn't flinch.

'They said you won't press charges.'

The teacher said nothing.

'Why?'

'Because I lied to you. Nanna did come over that night. Briefly. But she was there. I should have said.'

He glanced at his phone.

'I'm waiting for the call. My wife's due any day.'

Birk Larsen looked at the bare white wall then the man in the wheelchair.

'I'm sorry.'

The teacher's head moved. A nod. Painful maybe.

'If there's anything I can do, Kemal, please let me know.'

The man in the wheelchair still said nothing.

'A baby changes you,' Birk Larsen murmured. 'Maybe you don't need changing. With me . . .'

Kemal leaned forward.

'There's nothing you need do,' he said.

They found the woman by the skating rink in Kongens Nytorv. Lots of middle-class homes, brown brick, four storeys. Lots of middle-class children in bright expensive clothes.

She was in the arms of a man who had to be her husband, laughing at a boy about Mark's age larking about on the ice.

Good-looking woman. Thirty-five or so. Long curly hair, bright happy face. Grey-haired husband. Older. Not so happy.

The kid came off and the husband took him to a stand to buy coffee and biscuits.

An only child, Lund thought. Like Mark. It was obvious.

The woman was on her own. Meyer marched over and asked, 'Nethe Stjernfeldt?'

They showed their IDs.

'Your office told us we could find you here.'

'What's it about?'

'We'd like to ask some questions about a contact of yours.' He looked round. The husband had got the coffee. 'From a dating site?'

She didn't say anything. The man strode over.

'I'm Nethe's husband. What is this?'

Lund said, as pleasantly as she could, 'We're police officers. We need to talk to your wife.'

He bristled. Possessive type. Superior.

'What's wrong?'

'Nothing's wrong,' Lund said. 'It's not serious. She might have seen something that's all.'

'If you could stay here,' Meyer added. 'We need a private word.'

They walked her to the edge of the rink. Nethe Stjernfeldt didn't look so happy.

'I don't know what you're talking about,' she said when Lund asked about the Heartbreak Club website.

'You've never used a dating service?'

Her face coloured.

'No. Why would I?'

'You've never been in touch with a man called Faust?' Meyer asked.

The boy was back on the ice. The woman looked at him, smiled, waved.

'Someone called Fanny Hill dated Faust,' Lund said. 'She had your email address.'

Nethe Stjernfeldt was glancing at her husband as he watched the kid on his skates.

'It's not a crime,' Meyer said. 'We just need to know if it's you.'

'It's not me. I've no idea what you're talking about.'

Meyer's mood was changing.

'On the fourteenth of December Fanny wrote to Faust to say she wanted to go out with him. Same time, same place. What do you know about that?'

'Nothing at all. This is my son's birthday!'

She started to walk away. Lund followed.

'Did you go to the flat on Store Kongensgade?'

Curly hair going from side to side as she shook her head.

'I don't know about any flat.'

Meyer got in front, put out a hand to stop her.

'We need to know who Faust is,' Lund said.

'Is this what the police do? Hunt through people's messages?'

'If they're not your messages, Nethe—' Meyer began.

'Leave me alone.'

She stormed off. The husband came over, glaring at them.

'If you want to talk to her call my office first. You can't just show up here and ruin a child's birthday party. What kind of people are you?'

'Busy people,' Meyer said. 'Busy getting lied to.'

He winked at the man.

'I guess you know how it feels.'

A flurry of curses and then he left.

'Have her followed,' Lund said. 'We need to talk to her when she's alone.'

It was just after six when Theis Birk Larsen got back home. The garage was empty. Upstairs he found Pernille helping the boys pack their things.

'Hi, Dad,' Anton said. 'You can't come.'

'Mum says you have to work,' Emil added.

Pernille was in her winter coat, suitcase by her side, watching them.

'Make sure you have everything for school,' she said.

Instead the boys ran to him. He picked them up in his arms. Small warm bodies in strong, old arms.

They smelled of soap and shampoo. Straight from the bath. Soon he ought to read them a story.

'Why do you have to work?' Anton asked.

'Because I do.'

He put them down, ruffled their hair.

'Can we talk, Pernille?'

'We have to be at my parents' for dinner.'

'It won't take long.'

Anton had a plastic sword, Emil a toy gun.

She took the things, pushed them into the bag.

'Go and play,' she said and off they ran.

In the kitchen, beneath the unlit chandelier, by the photographs, among the pot plants, next to the table Pernille and Nanna made.

'Ever since I first saw you,' Birk Larsen said slowly, hands in pockets, counting out every word in his head before he spoke. 'I . . .'

They wouldn't come. Not the way he hoped.

'No one knows me like you do.'

'Is that true, Theis? Do I know you?'

He sat down, began to knead his fists, not looking at her.

'I know I fouled up. I know . . .'

She didn't move, didn't speak.

'We have to try. We have to. We lost Nanna.' His narrow eyes closed in pain. 'I don't want to lose more than that. Without you . . . Without the boys.'

Something came clear.

'You make me . . . what I'm supposed to be. What I want to be. I'll do anything if you'll just stay.'

His eyes strayed nervously to hers.

'Don't leave me.'

His hand stretched out to hers, big and callused, rough and marked by years of labour.

'Don't leave me, Pernille,' Theis Birk Larsen said again.

*

350

Meyer was filling the office with smoke once more.

'We need to track down some other women who met Faust,' Lund said. 'Someone has to know who he is.'

A short figure went briskly down the corridor. Lund thought for a second then followed.

By the time she caught up he was beneath the colonnades of the circular courtyard, a box in his arms, fleeing for the exit.

'Buchard!' Lund called.

He kept walking towards the security office. She dashed across the central circle of marble slabs, grass poking between them. Stood in front and stopped him.

'The phone company's records are on your desk, Lund.'

He looked at her.

'You're in my way. Again.'

She stepped to one side, walked with him on the way out.

'It's a pre-paid phone card but the phone number's no longer in use.'

'And the name that was deleted?'

'I never saw it.'

The old chief glanced at her. All the stubbornness, the temper, the arrogance had left him.

'Believe that or not. It's true.'

'Why do you put up with this?'

'Are you serious?'

'Yes.'

They walked past the Memorial Yard, beneath the tall yellow lights and the iron stars on the walls.

'Either I get left holding the baby. Go count paper clips in some station in the sticks. Or I'm out. Forcibly retired. After thirty-six years they pin this shit on me.'

He turned to her.

'Good luck, Lund.'

She watched him go. Called, 'Who asked you to bury the information, Buchard?'

The old man didn't look back.

In her office Lund checked what he'd left. Pages of calls. Nothing to indicate whose number had been erased.

'What about the flat?'

'Hartmann's prints everywhere,' Meyer said.

'That fits with his story. Hartmann's got an alibi. What else?'

'We've got saliva, hair and fingerprints.'

'DNA?' she asked.

'Nothing that matches any database records.'

Meyer shook his head.

'There's hardly any blood to speak of. It could have been an accident.'

Meyer shrugged. She watched. He was thinking in a way he didn't when they first met. Not rushing to a conclusion. Now he was trying to see. To imagine.

'What is it?' she asked.

'You know that smug bastard Olav Christensen? The smart-arse from City Hall?'

'Yes?'

'One piece of incriminating testimony.'

He threw Christensen's file across the desk. She stared at the photo: young, thin face, staring eyes. Cocky.

'Some time ago Hartmann refused to promote him. One of the campaign team told me he took the teacher's file we asked for. He hates Hartmann. There's going to be an inquiry. Christensen could lose his job.'

Meyer had brought in a loaf of bread, some butter and some ham. She got a plastic knife, slapped all three roughly together, made something that approximated to a sandwich, bit into it.

'City Hall bitching,' Lund said, mouth full. 'It's not him.'

Meyer grabbed the food, the knife, made a sandwich of his own. Lund looked at it. His seemed so much better.

'Why not?'

'Why would anyone delete calls from some pipsqueak civil servant? Christensen doesn't have any class. Nanna met someone important through the Heartbreak Club. Not a pen-pusher.'

He sighed.

'Maybe. I don't know. When I talked to him he was squirming like a pig with piles. I was sure he was lying. If I'd had one thing to throw at him . . .'

'But you didn't.'

A rap on the door. One of the night team detectives.

'What?' she asked.

'We looked at some cold cases like you asked.'

'And?'

'I've got some names . . .'

A woman was walking down the corridor. Full head of curly hair. Pretty face. Not smiling any more.

'Let's do this later,' Lund said and walked out to meet her.

'I love my husband.'

Lund and Meyer sat side by side. He didn't smoke.

'He was away on business for two hundred days last year. Just me and my son. Week after week.'

Lund pushed a printout of the Heartbreak site across the table.

'You do have a profile, don't you?'

Nethe Stjernfeldt looked at the logo. A heart torn in two by an arrow.

'It was fun. That's all. Nothing serious.'

A glance at Meyer's notebook.

'Do you have to write this down?'

He put aside the pen.

'It was ridiculous. I put up this photograph.' She primped her hair. 'Half profile. You couldn't tell it was me. Could have been anybody. It was like . . . a million lonely men appeared. All of them rich and handsome. All of them single. Supposedly.'

'You checked?' he asked.

'No.'

There was a note of petulance in her voice. Lund kicked Meyer's leg underneath the table.

'Only one looked interesting. He was different.'

'In what way?' Lund asked.

'He took notice. He was interested in me. When I wrote something he read it. We were on the same wavelength. I could tell. You couldn't fake that.'

'Then you met?'

'I wasn't looking for an affair. I was just lonely.'

'You met him several times?'

She glared at them.

'You want the details? Where and when?'

'Not necessarily.'

'I thought I could control it. But . . .'

She smiled, remembering something.

'For a while I felt I was . . . crazy. I thought I could give up everything. My husband. My son. My job. Just run to him. Be with him. He made it that way. Then . . .'

A flash of ugly bitterness.

'I got too close. He didn't want a relationship. Just names on a website. A night in a hotel. So he stopped answering my messages. I woke up I guess.'

Lund asked, 'Have you seen him since?'

She was lost somewhere.

'This sounds stupid but I think he saved my marriage. I realized what's really important.'

'OK, OK,' Meyer snapped. 'We don't care if he ruins marriages or saves them. We just want to know who he is.'

'I can see that.' She watched them. 'Why? Why do you need to know?'

Meyer growled.

'This isn't a flea market, sugar. Just tell us.'

'I don't want to bad-mouth him. He dumped me. But he was a good man. He cared.'

'For God's sake just tell us his bloody name. Before the Pope makes him a saint or something.'

Lund looked at her.

'We need to know, Nethe. We will. One way or another.'

She looked at the door.

'I don't want to wait for your husband to turn up with a lawyer. But if I have to . . . Who's Faust?'

An hour and ten minutes later Hartmann was in an interview room listening to the lawyer Rie Skovgaard had found. A severe, middle-aged woman from one of the big city practices. A party supporter. She'd donated. He ought to remember her name.

'We've some time before they interview you,' she said, taking off her coat, bidding him to sit down. 'Let's make the most of it.'

'I've got to get out of here. This is ridiculous.'

'You're not going anywhere until they question you.'

'But—'

'They've got emails that can be traced back to you.'

'What business do they have going through my emails?'

She looked at her notes.

'A woman called Nethe Stjernfeldt has made a statement. She claims to have had sexual relations with you. She identified you as the man behind the profile Faust. The man who also met Nanna Birk Larsen.'

Hartmann got up, started walking up and down the room like a hungry cat.

'Are you going to say something, Troels?'

'I told them already. I've never met the Birk Larsen girl. I've got nothing to add. No statement to make.'

She waited. Disappointment on her lined and serious face.

'Shall we talk about controlling the damage?'

'What damage? I'm innocent.'

'Let's not get diverted by innocence, shall we? The police face a heavy burden of proof but . . .'

He shook his head, astonished.

'Burden of proof?'

'They've got the makings of a case. It's important they know your side of the story.'

'My side?' Hartmann laughed. 'Don't you see what's going on here? Every time one trumped-up effort fails they invent another. This is Bremer's doing.'

'Poul Bremer didn't invent the Stjernfeldt woman.'

He was silent.

'It sounds as if he didn't invent your messages either.'

'I never talked or met or communicated in any way with Nanna Birk Larsen. As they know.'

She scrawled something on her pad.

'I'll talk to Rie Skovgaard to see if we can take some civil action against them. I agree. The way they've acted is outrageous.'

'Quite.'

'Which is all the more reason to talk to them. You have to—'

'No.'

She folded her arms.

'You have to, Troels. If you don't what will they think? What would anyone think?'

Meyer stood outside in the corridor, yawning. Lund leaned against the wall.

'What's the big idea, Lund? Are we supposed to wait around all night?'

She looked at her watch.

'They've had enough time.'

A tall lean figure appeared. Lennart Brix striding down the corridor, on the phone, to the media by the sound of it.

Lund waited. Brix came and stood in front of her.

'It was the right thing to do,' she said. 'We had good cause.'

'Picking up a party leader? Without asking me?'

'Do we normally make appointments with murder suspects?' Meyer asked.

'It could have waited.'

'Hartmann's Faust,' Meyer said. 'He drove the car. He was in the flat. It has to be him.'

'Except,' Brix said, 'he has an alibi.'

'We're working on that,' Lund told him.

The door opened. The lawyer came out.

'He'll talk to you now,' she said.

Six of them in the room. Hartmann's lawyer and a clerk to take notes. Lund, Meyer and Brix.

And Troels Hartmann, pale, weary, angry and determined.

'My wife died two years ago. It was very sudden.' He sipped at a coffee. 'For a while I kept it to myself. I worked. I pretended there was nothing else.'

He stopped there.

'Go on, Troels,' the lawyer said.

'One day I got some leaflets through the door. A nightclub. I don't go to clubs but it advertised a dating chat room. You could talk to people. That's all it was. Talking.'

Meyer coughed into his fist.

'I created a profile. Under the name of Faust.'

'How many women did you meet?'

'That's got nothing to do with this.'

Meyer cocked his head to one side.

'More than ten, less than twenty,' Hartmann snapped. 'Something like that.'

No one spoke.

'I'm not proud of it.'

'You're in the public eye,' Lund said. 'Where could you go?'

'Just once in public. The first time. After that . . . if we got on . . . I had a cab pick them up.'

'And go where?'

'Mostly to the party flat on Store Kongensgade.'

'Then what happened?' Meyer asked.

Hartmann scowled at him.

'That's none of your business.'

'But it is,' Meyer insisted. 'Nanna Birk Larsen was there. Two days later she was found raped and murdered. I don't know whether you believe in coincidence in politics, Hartmann, but round here—'

'I never met her! I never even knew she existed.'

Meyer's head was still cocked.

'Let me refresh your memory.'

He went through the stack of papers on the table.

'We've got printouts of your emails. And Nanna's. Take a look.'

He passed over a stack of sheets. Hartmann started to read them.

'In April,' Lund said, 'you contacted her for the first time. She got back to you through the dating site. The messages continued until a few weeks before her murder.'

'No,' Hartmann said. 'I didn't write any of this. Look at the emails I do write. This isn't my style.'

'Your style?' Meyer said, laughing.

Hartmann pointed to the dates on the messages.

'These are months after I stopped using the site. I met someone. Rie. I didn't want to go on like that any more.'

He stacked the pages, passed them back.

'I put it behind me. I didn't write those messages.'

The lawyer said, 'Someone hacked into his email account.'

'In City Hall?' Lund asked.

'I told you before,' Hartmann said. 'I had concerns.'

'Anyone could have had access to the flat,' the lawyer added. 'The keys were kept in a desk. A visitor, someone else in City Hall could have copied them.'

'Oh please—' Meyer started.

'Listen to me! I admit I created that profile. I don't know who wrote those messages or how they got into the flat. They must have got my password. They pretended to be me.'

'My client has an alibi,' the lawyer added. 'He was with Rie

357

Skovgaard later that evening. They spent the weekend at a conference.'

Brix was staring at Lund, and letting Hartmann and the lawyer see it.

'Well?' the woman persisted. 'How is it possible in these circumstances that Troels Hartmann can be a suspect?'

'If I read one word of this crap in the press,' Hartmann threw at them, 'I will sue everyone in sight. This department. You all personally. I will not be libelled by Poul Bremer's puppets—'

'Enough,' Brix said. 'We need to talk about this.'

'What's the likelihood he's telling the truth?' Brix asked when they went outside. 'That someone could have been using his dating profile?'

'It's balls,' Meyer said. 'You'd need to have the password. And the computer that was used was in the party's flat.'

Lund was at the blinds, peering through them at Hartmann.

'What do you think?' Brix asked.

'We won't get any more out of him now. We need a court order to get his phone records. Why does he think Bremer's involved in this?'

'Because he's paranoid,' Brix said. 'Let him go. I don't want this in the media—'

'We don't do that,' Lund cut in. 'How many times—?'

'I don't want it leaked. Keep me posted. Don't do anything without clearing it with me first. I'm going to tell Hartmann he can go.'

When Brix had left Lund said, 'We need to talk to Rie Skovgaard. And the conference centre. Who confirmed the two of them were there?'

Meyer went to the desk and picked up the reports.

'Svendsen. According to reception they checked in at nine on Saturday. They rented a room and a large conference space. Then they checked out on Sunday afternoon.'

'Svendsen's a lazy bastard. How did they pay?'

A flick through the pages.

'Skovgaard's credit card.'

Meyer watched Hartmann walking down the corridor towards the spiral staircase. So did Lund.

'So Poster Boy's a serial philanderer,' he said. 'And I thought he was supposed to be a perfect gentleman.'

'Apart from Skovgaard who saw Hartmann? Let's find out.'

'I'll get someone to look. It will leak, you know. Someone's talking to the press. It's not you. It's not me.' He jerked a thumb towards Brix's office. 'But someone is.'

Her phone rang. Vibeke.

'Hi, Mum. I'll ring you back. And I'll be late. Don't talk to Mark about Bengt and Sweden. I'll do that myself.'

'Mark's father's here,' Vibeke said.

Lund struggled to separate her thoughts.

Hartmann.

Mark.

Theis Birk Larsen.

Carsten.

'If you want to see him,' her mother said, 'you'd better hurry.'

Theis Birk Larsen and Pernille sat next to each other around the table, beneath the Murano chandelier. The social worker they'd been sent was around forty, well-dressed, professional. She might have been a lawyer if they hadn't known.

'You've no previous experience of this?' she asked.

'No,' Birk Larsen said.

Pernille stared out of the window, barely listening.

'Neither of you has seen a therapist or been in counselling?'

He shook his head.

'Having a child together establishes a very strong connection. Losing that child has consequences for the relationship.'

She sounded as if she were reading from a textbook.

Pernille got up, leaned against the tiled kitchen wall, folded her arms.

'It's not our relationship I'm worried about right now,' she said.

'What worries you then?'

The woman had piercing blue eyes and hair that was too young for her.

'Do you have children?' Pernille asked.

'That's irrelevant. There's nothing you can do to solve the case. You have each other. You have your family.'

'I don't need your advice about my boys!' Pernille snapped.

The social worker reached into her bag and took out some leaflets.

'These pamphlets will give you an idea of what counselling can offer.'

She placed them on the table. Got up, pulled on her coat.

'I recommend our bereavement counselling groups. It can be helpful to talk to others.'

'We've got better things to do,' Pernille answered.

The blue eyes stared at her.

'It's not an offer. It's a condition of your husband's bail. If you don't attend he'll go back to jail. After the episode with the teacher he's lucky to be walking the streets at all.'

He saw her out, said thanks.

Back upstairs. Pernille leaning on the sink, staring out of the window.

'She said the bereavement counselling group have a meeting tomorrow.'

The call from the newspaper had come just before the woman from the council arrived. He'd taken it, kept it quiet. Knew he couldn't for much longer.

'The papers are going to write about the politician again,' he said.

'What are they going to say?'

'I don't know.'

She reached for the phone.

'The police won't tell you anything, Pernille. Don't you understand? It's not our business. Not for them.'

Lund was on voicemail.

She turned on the TV, hunted for the news. It was there. The murder team had taken in Hartmann for questioning. He'd been released after an interview.

Pernille turned up the volume, listened, rapt, eyes glistening.

A sleepy, high voice said, 'Mum? I can't sleep.'

Small shape at the door in pyjamas.

Theis Birk Larsen rose in an instant, scooped up Emil in his arms. Kissed him, whispered nonsense in his warm ear.

'Nanna was found dead in one of Hartmann's campaign cars,' the newsreader said. 'She'd been raped repeatedly, and reports say . . .'

He rushed the boy back into the bedroom, clutched him tightly, held the child's shaking frame to his.

*

Weber was watching the news when they got back to the Rådhus.

'Dare I ask how it went?'

Hartmann sat down.

'This is serious. We need to know who used the flat.'

Weber looked relaxed. No tie. Cup of coffee. Ready to sleep in the office again.

'I checked the records. It was mainly people we knew. People we trusted. The police have got all that.'

'No, no, no. That civil servant. Olav. He's been all over this office somehow. It has to be him.'

'Lund had him in along with the rest of us.'

Skovgaard listened looking gloomy. Hair swept back in a band now. Severe. Businesslike. Distant.

'What am I supposed to say to the press?' she asked.

'How the hell did they find out? The minute I was out of that room? Lund—'

'It's what the press do, Troels,' she said. 'Someone on the door could have tipped them off. Here or at the Politigården. There's no way you can bury a story like this—'

'Someone got my password. Someone used my profile to email that girl. And Nethe Stjernfeldt told the police about me. Jesus . . .'

In a sudden fit of anger he swept the papers off his desk, stood at the window in the light of the blue neon sign.

'What dating profile?' she asked in a cold and curious voice. 'Who's Nethe Stjernfeldt?'

Weber got up, mumbled something about taking a second look at the files, then left the office, closing the door behind him.

'Fine,' she said when Hartmann didn't speak. 'No answer. We'll start a civil action. Get a gagging order. We don't want more headlines. They get the papers tomorrow.'

'We're not bringing a civil action. Forget it. How can I hope to be Lord Mayor of Copenhagen if I'm in the middle of a legal battle with the police?'

'Is that the only reason?'

It had been almost six months now. Six happy months for the most part. She was good at her job, quick and sharp and imaginative. But the work pushed them together too closely. He needed distance. So did she.

'The police are looking for a man who contacted the Birk Larsen girl through a dating site,' he said, trying to keep the words as simple, as plain and boring as possible. 'It turns out it was through a profile I created. A long time ago. Before we ever . . .'

There was no expression on her face, no warmth or shock in her dark eyes.

'I don't know how this happened. After I stopped using it someone else got hold of the profile. Wrote to the girl. Sent her messages. Met her in the flat in Store Kongensgade.'

He came and stood in front of her.

'Don't look at me like that, Rie. You knew what I was like when you met me.'

He closed his eyes. The blue lights outside were so bright he could still see them.

'When did you stop?'

'When I met you.'

He came close, held out his arms. She walked to the desk for no reason.

'So now there are two things,' Skovgaard said. 'The flat and the dating profile. Make a list of the people who might know your password. Think about what you're going to say to the alliance tomorrow.'

She picked up the desk diary.

'I'll get Morten to update your appointments. I'll deal with the press. Go home, Troels. Keep out of the way. I don't want people to see you now, like this.'

'Like this?'

'Pathetic and sorry for yourself.'

He nodded, taking the blame. Put his arms down. Stuffed his hands in his pockets.

'Is that all you've got to say?'

'Is that all you've got to tell me? Is there more to come? More I don't know?'

'No,' he promised.

'I hope so.'

When Lund got back to her mother's flat she could hear Carsten, Mark's father, talking ice hockey. She took off her coat, went into the bedroom, got a new sweater, not black and white but white and black, put it on.

Then she went into the living room.

Carsten.

An athletic, engaging man. Too cerebral, too ambitious, too offended by the everyday to remain a police officer. He was talking Mark through some hockey rules, waving around a brand-new stick he'd bought.

Lund's son was watching. Caught. Engaged. As was Vibeke. Carsten still had that talent.

'Then it's easier to score?' Mark asked.

'Exactly. You can do it. We'll go and practise sometime.'

Lund stood in the shadows watching this exchange. Envying it. Fearing it.

Carsten turned. His hair was blonder than she remembered. Longer too. He had new fashionable plastic-framed glasses and a slick brown suit. No one would have dared to walk around head-quarters like that.

'Hi!' she said brightly, coming out of the dark to smile at him.

'Sarah!' Carsten cried, too loudly.

No embrace.

Mark was smiling too. For a moment she felt the brief and fragile bond of family between them.

Lund walked over, stroked Mark's hair, took no notice when he frowned and shrank away.

'So, Carsten. When did you get here?'

He held the hockey stick easily, like a pro. For Mark.

'This afternoon. It happened so suddenly.'

'They've rented a house in Klampenborg,' Vibeke said. 'Do you want some dinner?'

Lund nodded. Vibeke moved happily to the pans.

'The job came up last week,' Carsten carried on. 'The chance to come home . . . It was too good to say no. Brussels and two little girls . . . all we did was work.'

Mark got up, took the stick from him, practised a few strokes.

'And I missed this guy as well,' Carsten added, putting a hand round Mark's shoulder.

The two of them stood side by side, as if posing for a photograph.

Again Lund made herself smile.

'What about you and Sweden?' he asked.

'It's been postponed for a while,' she said immediately.

'I heard Bengt had an accident.'

Lund looked at her mother.

'It wasn't so bad.'

'He broke his arm!' Vibeke cried.

She handed Lund a plate of stew.

'The house-warming party was cancelled,' her mother went on. 'So was my trip to Løgumkloster.'

'I've been working on a case,' Lund said. 'It's not like Brussels. Nine to five.'

Carsten still had his arm round Mark. It looked possessive now, not an embrace.

'These things happen,' he said. 'But I suppose there's no rush.'

'Ha!' Vibeke again. 'How can there be? Bengt sent back their moving boxes. They're sitting downstairs in my basement. Untouched.'

Mark brightened again.

'Does that mean we're not moving?'

Carsten unwound his arm.

'I really have to go home and help. Thanks for the drink.'

He embraced Vibeke, kissed her. Got the warmest smile in return.

'It's always nice to see you, Carsten,' she said. 'Come any time.'

He hugged Mark. Rapped his knuckles on the hockey stick.

'I'll walk you outside,' Lund said.

The flat was on the third floor. She pressed the button for the lift.

'I don't want to pry. But I hope there aren't problems between you and Bengt.'

'We'll work it out.'

'Karen wants to know if you'd like to have dinner with us tomorrow. It would be nice. The girls can say hello to Mark.'

'I can't.'

The smile was gone. He never liked to hear the word no.

'Is it OK for Mark to come?'

The lift was slow. She pushed the button again.

'You want me to say yes so you can cancel again? The way you usually do?'

He folded his arms. Expensive raincoat. Expensive glasses. Floppy academic hair. Carsten had reinvented himself to be the man he wanted.

'You've lost weight,' he said. 'I don't see anything else that's changed.'

'I'm fine.'

Her phone went. The name Meyer flashed on the screen.

'I've left my phone number and address with Vibeke.'

'Good.'

She was walking back to the door listening. Carsten gave up on the lift and took the stairs.

'I talked to the conference centre,' Meyer said.

'And?'

'No one saw Hartmann until Sunday afternoon. He had the flu. It was Rie Skovgaard who held the meetings with sponsors.'

She heard the door go on the ground floor. Carsten leaving.

'Let's talk about this in the morning, Meyer. Goodnight.'

Thursday, 13th November

Just after eight, Lund and Meyer were watching the morning news in the office. Rie Skovgaard talking to a forest of microphones.

'The Mayor for Education spoke to the police last night,' she said. 'He cooperated fully and was able to provide them with information they hadn't previously gathered. I can't go into details but let me emphasize that Troels Hartmann has no – I repeat no – connection with the murder of Nanna Birk Larsen. He will help . . .'

'All the usual bullshit,' Meyer said.

He waved a typed sheet.

'I checked up on him. Forty-two. Born in Copenhagen. Son of a politician, Regner Hartmann. The father was Poul Bremer's bitter enemy. Lost every battle. Went to pieces. Died a while back.'

Skovgaard was fielding questions.

'Speculation made in bad taste by political opponents is deplorable,' she said.

Lund waved her coffee mug at the screen.

'So now the son's taking on his father's battles?'

'Been doing that all along,' Meyer agreed. 'Joined the Liberal youth branch at nineteen. Elected to the city assembly when he was twenty-four. Served on committees. Became group leader four years ago. Got to run the education department as a result.'

Lund was making the bread, butter and ham sandwiches again. She had one for him. Meyer bit into it.

'You do realize this man's never had a real job. He's spent his entire life playing round in that phoney world of theirs inside the Rådhus. No wonder he turns flaky the moment his little glass palace gets a crack in it.'

'The alliance will succeed,' Skovgaard emphasized to the cameras. 'Hello?'

He waved his sandwich in the air, scattering crumbs across the desk.

'Are we listening?'

'I'm listening.'

'He married his childhood sweetheart the year he became leader. She died two years ago. Cancer. She was six months pregnant.'

'That must have felt real enough,' Lund said. 'Any criminal record?'

'Not a thing. Whiter than white. Did you read the emails?'

'Yes. I don't buy the idea they were written by two different people. They sound the same. He always signs himself just as F.'

Meyer looked at the printouts.

'Can you see any differences?' she asked.

'No. So what? How many ways can you write . . . meet me in the Hilton at eight thirty, sweetheart? My turn with the condoms. Any preference, darling?'

Svendsen came in and threw some files on her desk.

'What's this?'

'Missing women from the last ten years. You asked for them.'

'Did you see anything?'

'No. Brix thought it was a waste of time.'

'Did you look?'

'Brix says you're barking up the wrong tree. If you want any more you're to do it in your own time. Not ours.'

'How many murdered women?'

Svendsen rapped his knuckles on the blue folder.

'I'm busy right now,' he said. 'Here you go.'

Coffee on the table and pastries, beneath the wan light of the pink artichoke lamps, the group meeting began. The four minority leaders and Hartmann.

Jens Holck looked a little better. He'd shaved. Put on a jacket.

'What's going on, Troels?' he asked. 'Was the girl in your flat? Yes or no?'

'Yes. At least that's what the police say.'

Holck sighed.

'This is wonderful. And you were there too?'

Skovgaard sat down next to Hartmann, started making notes.

'I was in the flat shortly before her.'

He looked at each of them.

'That caused a misunderstanding with the police. It's clear now.'

'And you drove the car?' Holck asked. 'What the hell is this? How can we even think—'

'Oh for God's sake, Jens!' Hartmann cried. 'Get off your high horse. I had nothing to do with that girl. I never met her. Never talked to her. I'm as shocked . . . as baffled by this as you are.'

'That doesn't help.'

'They're looking at City Hall. Isn't that obvious? Not me any more. But they're looking here. Someone had access to my computer. To my passwords.' He pointed at the door. 'Someone here. I'll help the police. What else can I do?'

'You could have told us all this before we read it in the papers,' Mai Juhl said.

'I didn't know! I was at a sponsor conference that weekend. If they thought I was guilty do you think I'd be here talking to you now?'

Holck was silent. So was Mai Juhl.

Morten Weber came to the door, tapping his watch.

'Let's stay calm,' Hartmann said. 'Are you happy with that? Are we still together or not?'

It was Mai Juhl who spoke first.

'You said this is the end of it?'

'It's the end of it.'

She glanced at Holck.

'Then I'm in.'

'What choice do we have?' Holck asked. 'If the alliance doesn't hold we're all finished.'

He got up, glowered at Hartmann.

'You got us into this corner, Troels. You can get us out of it. Step up, talk to the press. It's no good hiding behind Rie. This is your problem. Bury it or it'll bury all of us.'

Morten Weber watched them go.

'What happened? Are they still in?'

'Yes. Found anything?'

'The three of us are the only ones set up as users on the flat's PC. You, me and Rie. Who might have your password?'

'I don't know.'

'Maybe you forgot to log off.'

'It's not that. Someone's been snooping round here. Keep asking. Keep looking.'

'It's not easy. These are people we trust. Or we're supposed to.'

Hartmann looked at Weber. A man he'd known all his adult life. A solitary bachelor, carrying his insulin and needle around without a complaint. Doing the menial work, the drudgery. The dirty work when needed.

'I'm sorry, Morten.'

'About what?'

'About not listening to you.'

Weber laughed.

'That was yesterday! This is politics. Today and tomorrow. Nothing else exists.'

'Will you fix this?'

'If I can.'

Skovgaard came up. She was carrying her coat.

'Lund wants to talk to you again,' she said.

'No—'

'The lawyer says you have no choice. Leave by the side door. I've arranged a private car.'

She looked him in the eye.

'They're taking you to the flat in Store Kongensgade.' She passed Hartmann his gloves. 'Lund wants to put some questions to you there.'

Anton and Emil were in their winter jackets. Pernille was checking they had everything for school. At the office desk, red overalls, black hat, Theis Birk Larsen had been on the phone to the bank, talking calmly, trying to think things through.

The storm that had hung over them the night before had never broken. They slept in the same bed, not touching. Not sleeping really. Halfway through the night Emil had come in crying. Anton had wet the mattress for the first time in months.

The storm hadn't passed them by. It was simply waiting.

'They might give us an overdraft of a hundred thousand,' Birk Larsen said when she came in. 'With that we can pay the staff this month and sell the house.'

Just one month. He lit a cigarette and watched the smoke curl up to the grubby ceiling.

'Have you seen Emil's hat?' she asked.

He closed his eyes.

'Isn't it on the shelf? Where it usually is?'

'If it was there I wouldn't be asking, would I?'

He stubbed out his cigarette.

'OK. I'll find it.'

When he was gone she walked round the office, looked at the bank statements. Wondered what else she didn't know about. He'd bought a paper. The politician's face stared out from it. He wasn't arrested. Just questioned then released.

'Mum?' one of the boys called.

Anton ran in.

'Someone wants to talk to you.'

A tall man of about thirty stood silhouetted in the garage door. Dark designer ski jacket. Big smile.

'I'm here to talk to Theis Birk Larsen,' he said.

'If it's about a move my husband will be right down.'

'Pernille?'

He didn't wait for an answer.

'My name's Kim Hogsted.' He pulled out a business card. 'I'm a TV journalist. I rang a few times.'

He held out his card. She took it.

'I know you don't want to talk to the likes of me.'

'We don't.'

'It's the police.' He seemed earnest. 'I cover crime. I've never seen a foul-up like this. It must be awful for you. I can't imagine.'

'No,' she said. 'You can't.'

'Now there's a politician involved . . .'

He shrugged.

'What?' she asked.

'They'll try and keep everything under wraps. For you too.'

'What do you want?'

'We want to help. Give you the opportunity to tell your story. In your words. Not theirs. Not ours.'

She tried to imagine this.

'You want me to talk about Nanna?'

He didn't answer.

'What kind of people are you? It's best you leave. If my husband comes down—'

'Three years ago in Helsingborg a five-year-old boy went missing. The police hadn't a clue. We ran an interview. Offered a reward. They found him. Alive. You remember?'

'You really should go.'

'We can't get Nanna back for you. But we can put up a reward for information. I know you want to find out what happened. Think about it, please.'

'Leave!' she shrieked at him.

The reporter walked out into the daylight. She threw the card in the office bin.

Theis Birk Larsen was back with the hat.

'Shall I take them to school?'

'No! We already talked about this. Why do you keep asking twice?'

He stood stiff and awkward in the doorway.

'I'll meet you at counselling.'

'Emil!' Her voice was high and brittle. 'I told you not to bring that. Why don't you ever listen?'

Birk Larsen gently prised the toy from Emil's tight little fingers.

'Have a nice day, boys,' he said, and patted them on the head.

The Liberals' apartment was covered in forensic marks. Stickers and arrows. Numbers and outlines.

Troels Hartmann stood in the main room next to the grand piano. The party lawyer was with him.

'I parked outside and let myself in.'

'Did you see anyone on the way up?' Lund asked.

'Not that I know of. I wasn't looking much. It was just . . .'

'Just what?'

'Just another night.'

Lund waited. Wondered if he was going to say something else.

Hartmann looked at the shattered table. The broken mirror. The crumpled sheets on the double bed in the room beyond.

'What happened here?' he asked.

'Tell me what you did when you came in,' Lund said.

'I hung up my jacket. I remember having a headache. It was a busy week.'

He walked to the desk by the window. Meyer followed him.

'I sat here. I wrote some of the speech I was going to give.'

'What speech?' Meyer asked.

'It was for sponsors and businessmen. We were looking for support.'

Lund asked what he did with the car keys.

He looked at the shattered glass table.

'I left them on there. I didn't need them again.'

'I don't get it,' Meyer said. 'Why come here to write a speech? Why not just go home?'

Hartmann hesitated before answering.

'I think differently in different places. At home I get distracted. Here . . .' He looked round the room. The white piano. The chandelier. The velvet wallpaper and expensive furniture. The shattered glass. 'It was like a little island. I could think.'

'Why did you give your driver the weekend off?' Meyer asked.

'I didn't need him. Rie was going to drive. There was no point in having him waiting around.'

'So you dismissed him and took a campaign car from the City Hall? Then left it here?'

'Is that a crime? I wrote my speech. Then around ten thirty I walked round to Rie's. That's it. What else can I tell you?'

'This is enough,' the lawyer said. 'My client's assisted you as much as possible. If you're finished here . . .'

Lund walked to the window, looked out. Meyer was getting desperate.

'How did your speech go, Troels?' he asked.

'Quite well. Thanks for asking.'

'You're welcome. So you were with businessmen and sponsors all weekend?'

'That's right.'

He looked lost for a second. As if Meyer had tripped him.

'The truth is it was mostly Rie. I came down with flu. I was in bed until Sunday.'

Lund came back to him.

'How much did you drink here?'

'That's irrelevant,' the lawyer butted in.

'Forensics found an empty bottle of brandy and a glass with your prints on it.'

'Yes. I had a drink. To help with the flu.'

'A bottle of brandy?'

'It was nearly empty anyway.'

Lund sorted through her notes.

'The housekeeper had been shopping that day. She said she stocked up on everything.'

Hartmann glanced at the lawyer.

'She wouldn't throw out an unfinished bottle, would she? I had a drink. OK?'

Lund waited.

'It was our wedding anniversary. My wife and I—'

'So it was a special day?' Meyer said.

'None of your damned business.'

'You take sedatives,' Lund said. She picked up an evidence bag from the desk. 'We found your pills.'

'How low do you people intend to go? Does Bremer promote you afterwards?'

'Alcohol and drugs,' Meyer cut in. 'I'm shocked. You're a politician. You put up all these posters round the place. They're a dangerous cocktail, aren't they? So it says every time I take a piss.'

'I had a drink. I haven't taken any medication in months.'

'So you just had a really shit day?' Meyer's eyes were bulging. 'Is that what you're saying?'

Hartmann was walking up and down the room, looking at the marks on the walls.

'You drank a bottle of booze,' Meyer went on. 'You took some funny pills. One, maybe two.'

'This is getting tedious.'

'What's tedious is you telling us you came here, got shit-faced and still remember you left around ten thirty.'

'Yes! As it happens I do. I also remember which switches I touched. How many times I went to the toilet. Are you interested? Let me hold your hand and we can go and check the lift button together. How about it?'

Lund said, 'You took the lift?'

'Yes. Incredible, isn't it? I took the lift.'

Lund shook her head.

'According to the building manager the lift was out of service that Friday.'

He threw his arms open wide.

'Then I took the stairs. Does it matter?'

'Hartmann's told you what he did in the flat,' the lawyer insisted. 'Rie Skovgaard has confirmed he came to her afterwards and when.'

The lawyer went to the main door, ushered Hartmann towards it.

'My client's been more than helpful. We've no more business here.'

They watched him go.

'Why is that lying bastard lying to us?' Meyer asked.

Lund was looking in the bedroom at the crumpled sheets. No one had got underneath them. It was as if they simply sat on the bed. Talked even.

'Where did Nanna go?' she murmured.

Hartmann was passing the long ochre lines of the Nyboder cottages when Morten Weber called.

'How did it go?'

It seemed an odd question. There could only be one answer.

'It went well, Morten. What's happening?'

'Do you remember Dorte? The temp?'

'Not really.'

'The nice woman with back trouble? She went to my acupuncturist?'

'Yes, yes. I remember. What about her?'

Down the long drag of Store Kongensgade. Cafes and shops. On the left the grand dome of the Marble Church.

'She told me something interesting.'

Hartmann waited. When Weber kept quiet he said, 'What?'

'I don't like saying over the phone.'

'Jesus, Morten! Do you think they're tapping my calls now?'

A moment of silence then Weber said, 'Maybe they are. I don't know. We need to talk to Olav. You were right.'

The bereavement group met in a cold grey hall near the church. Ten people round a plastic table in a bare and cheerless room.

The Birk Larsens sat next to one another as the leader listened to their stories.

Cancer and traffic accidents. Heart attacks and suicide.

Tears from the living. Silence from the dead.

Pernille didn't listen. He nodded, said nothing.

Outside, on the bare branches of a tree, a ragged white scarf writhed and twisted in the wind like a lost prayer.

When it was their turn they barely spoke. No one pressed them. Only one, a skinny man whose head was erect and proud, even when he talked of his lost son, paid them any attention.

Perhaps it was embarrassment, Birk Larsen thought. He didn't care. The social worker said come or go back to jail. So he came and hoped it would help. Though looking at Pernille's frozen, emotionless face he doubted it.

Nothing helped except release. Knowledge. A waypoint passed. And that seemed further away than ever.

Outside he offered to put her bike in the back of the van and drive her home.

'I need some fresh air,' Pernille said.

'Are you sure?'

'I'll see you later.'

She pushed her cycle through the car park, out to the street and Vesterbro.

The thin man stopped her in the car park. His name was Peter Lassen.

'I didn't get the chance to say hello in there.'

She shook his hand.

'I hope it was some use to you.'

'It was fine,' she said.

He looked at her.

'I don't think you mean that.'

She wanted to walk on but didn't.

'I remember how awkward it felt the first time,' Lassen said. 'You can't relate to anyone. You think their pain's not like yours. And it isn't.'

'If I want your opinion I'll ask for it,' Pernille said with a sudden savagery.

Then pushed her bike away, eyes beginning to water.

By the road she stopped, ashamed. He'd been polite and pleasant. She'd been rude and caustic.

She went back, said sorry.

Lassen smiled a slow, soft smile.

'No need. Let me buy you a coffee.'

A moment's hesitation and then she said yes.

The cafe was tiny and empty. They sat in front of cappuccinos and biscotti.

'It'll be five years in January. I'd made lasagne. We sat at the table waiting for him to come home.'

There were kids outside the window, a long crocodile line of them heading off on a visit somewhere. Lassen smiled as they passed.

'We'd put new batteries on his bike lights. He knew the way. We used to cycle it together sometimes.'

He stirred the coffee he'd never touched.

'But he never came.'

One more round of the cup. She watched the froth subsiding.

'They said it was a red car. The police found paint on one of the pedals.'

He shook his head and, to her astonishment, laughed.

'I used to sit there by the turning in the road, looking for a scratched red car. Every evening around the time it happened.'

His delicate, pale hand waved at her.

'The car never came. So then I started sitting there during the day. It didn't come then.'

The brief amusement had left his face.

'In the end the only thing I could do was sit and wait. Day and night. Watching the cars. Thinking it will come. And when it does I'll drag that bastard out and . . .'

Lassen's eyes shut briefly and she saw on his face the mask of pain he still sought to hide.

'My wife tried to get me to stop. How could I? How? I lost my job. I lost my friends.'

He pushed away the coffee and the biscotto.

'Then one day I came home from the street and she was gone too.'

Outside a mother by the road, holding the hand of a child, waiting to cross. The everyday was special. For people like her, like

Lassen, there was nothing else, nor need of it. The everyday was holy, as precious as anything could be.

'There isn't a moment passes when I don't regret letting go of my loved ones. The red car didn't just take my son. It took everything I had. And still I never found him. Pernille?'

She turned away from the window, met his eyes.

'Do you understand what I'm saying?'

'But you still keep looking, don't you? How can you forget? What if you hadn't given up?'

Lassen shook his head. He seemed disappointed.

'You can't think of it like that.'

'But you do. You think . . . where is he? Where's the car? You don't stop thinking. You can fool yourself if you like. You can try to hide.'

'You have to let it go.'

He was starting to annoy her.

'Tell me you've forgotten then. Tell me you're OK with the fact that the bastard who killed your boy is still walking around out there.'

A glance outside the window.

'Maybe ready to do it all over again to someone else's son.'

Lassen said, 'What if they don't find him? What if you're locked in this hell for ever?'

'They'll find him. If they don't I will.'

He blinked. That hint of disappointment again.

'And then?' Lassen asked.

'You have to excuse me now. I've got to pick up my boys from school.'

She rose from the table.

'Thanks for the coffee.'

Hartmann's office. Weber had more sandwiches and coffee. There was a woman in the doorway and he fought for a moment to remember her name.

Nethe Stjernfeldt.

He got up quickly, walked to the door, saw Skovgaard's head go up.

She was as pretty as he remembered, slim and elegant. With that same anxious, needy look in her sparkling eyes.

'I'm sorry, Troels,' she said. 'I didn't want to come barging in.'

'It's not a good time.'

'I'm sorry if I said something wrong.'

'It's not your fault. I know what the police are like.'

'They came and threw all these questions at me. They had emails and . . . they seemed to know everything.'

'I talked to them,' Hartmann said. 'Don't worry. It won't go any further. Everything's fine.'

She was close. Her hand touched his lapel.

'Thanks for coming. But really I've got a lot of things to do.'

Her fingers brushed his jacket.

'I know. Ring me if there's any way I can help.' She smiled at him. 'Anything.'

Her hand flattened, touched his white ironed shirt, pressed. Hartmann retreated a step. She glared at him.

'I'll leave then,' she said.

'That would be best.'

He walked back into the office, stood next to Skovgaard as she read through the papers. Weber had made himself scarce.

'She . . . she wanted to apologize.'

Skovgaard's head never came up from the documents.

'Don't you trust me?' Hartmann asked.

Nothing.

He sat on the desk, made her look at him.

'Don't shut me out, Rie. That's all in the past. I told you.'

She folded her arms, stared at the ceiling, her eyes damp and unfocused.

'Rie!'

A knock on the door.

Olav Christensen walked in without waiting.

'I heard you want to talk to me,' he said.

'Morten!' Hartmann called.

They made the civil servant sit opposite them. Weber read through the material he'd assembled.

'You've taken a close interest in the flat, Olav,' he said.

'No. Not at all. I put up some guests there a few times.' He pointed at Hartmann. 'With the mayor's permission.'

'Hartmann just signed an approval slip. Your guests never turned up.'

His brittle show of arrogance was cracking.

'What am I? A hotel receptionist? I do what I'm told. Do I need a lawyer or something?'

Hartmann asked, 'Did you use the flat yourself?'

'I don't know what you mean.'

Weber placed a paper in front of him.

'Six months ago you asked Dorte if it was free at the weekend.'

Christensen took the document, read it.

'If I remember correctly that was for the Poles who were doing a report on the welfare system.'

'The Poles stayed in a hotel!' Weber snapped. 'I had dinner with them. Don't give me this shit.'

'Really? Then I don't remember.'

More paperwork.

'Several times a week you booked the flat for no-shows. Never went in the file. If it wasn't for Dorte—'

'Dorte isn't here. People changed their minds. Sometimes—'

'Do we look like idiots?' Hartmann pointed to Weber, to Skov-gaard sitting taping the conversation. 'Do we look as if we were born yesterday?'

'Don't blame me if you're in the shit. It's not my fault.'

'One more time. Did you book the flat for yourself?'

'You be careful what you accuse me of—'

'No, no, Olav! You're the one who needs to be careful.'

Hartmann waited a moment.

'Did you bring the girl there?'

'Of course not.'

'Did you make a copy of the key? Did you use my computer?'

He was laughing.

'So it's scapegoat time in the Liberal Party?'

Rie Skovgaard passed a document across the table.

'We had a security scan of the network this morning. They found key loggers on all our PCs. Someone was keeping track of everything. Passwords. What we typed. They could log in and pretend they were us.'

'What's this to do with me?'

'You've got a degree in computer engineering. You did this.'

'Me? A civil servant? No.' He smiled at the man across the

table. 'He's the one who needs to do the explaining. I read it in the papers.'

'I'm going to drive you down to police headquarters myself,' Troels Hartmann promised.

'He didn't kill the girl, Troels!' Skovgaard shrieked. 'He was at the poster party with us. It couldn't have been him in the flat.'

Olav Christensen smirked at them.

'You know what?' he said, getting up. 'I'm going to leave this in your hands. You people . . .' He shook his head and laughed. 'It's like Poul Bremer said. You're falling apart, aren't you?'

'If it wasn't you who was it?' Hartmann roared.

There were Christmas decorations in a box by the door. Christensen pulled out some tinsel, waved it at them.

'Santa Claus?' he asked.

Meyer was running through what they had.

'Hartmann saw plenty of women in that flat. He stopped for a few months. Then he started again.'

Blue lights from the headquarters yard flashed through the window.

'He tried to get hold of Nanna Birk Larsen. He was jealous. He went to see her. It all went wrong.'

'Someone must have seen something,' Lund said. 'A paper boy. A parking attendant.'

'No one's seen anything. Let's bring in Skovgaard again.'

'She won't say anything.'

'How the hell do you know? You talked to her last time.'

He felt the lapel of his wool zipper jacket.

'I have a way with women.'

Lund glanced at him, sighed, shook her head.

'He never called Nanna,' she said. 'His phone was turned off at ten twenty-nine that night.'

'A way with women,' he repeated very slowly.

She felt her head. A migraine was hovering.

'OK,' Lund said and threw the papers on the desk.

'That's that then,' Meyer announced.

He went off with his jaunty punk walk. Lund felt sure she'd arrested someone very like Jan Meyer once upon a time.

She picked up the phone records. Someone had called Hartmann at ten twenty-seven just before he turned off the phone. There was a list of names of callers somewhere. She found it. Looked. Thought of telling Meyer. Got her coat instead.

Back in Store Kongensgade she stood in the courtyard, looking at the circular iron fire-escape stairs running up the back.

Nethe Stjernfeldt came ten minutes after Lund called.

'What is this?' she asked. 'I told you everything—'

'You said you hadn't talked to Hartmann for a long time.'

'I haven't. I've got to pick up my son from youth club.'

'You rang him that Friday night. October the thirty-first. Ten twenty-seven p.m. I can prove it. I can prove you lied.'

The woman fiddled with her leather gloves.

'There's more, isn't there?' Lund said.

She looked around, saw they were alone.

'I promised my husband I'd never see him again.'

Lund waited.

'I missed him. I wanted to see him.'

'What did he say when you called?'

'He said it was over. I had to stop ringing him.'

'Then what did you do?'

She didn't answer. Just turned to leave.

'You got a parking ticket that evening. Here, on Store Kongensgade. You were too close to the corner.'

Lund caught up with her.

'Bad luck,' she said. 'I get that sometimes.'

'Does my husband have to know?'

'Just tell me what happened.'

Stjernfeldt looked up and down the long, empty street.

'I didn't like the way he cut me dead. I was home. On my own again. Going crazy.'

'So you came here to see him. What time, Nethe? This is important.'

'Doesn't the parking ticket say?'

'I want to hear it from you.'

'It was almost midnight. The lights were on. So I rang the bell.'

Lund looked at the shiny brass doorplate.

'Did he let you in?'

380

'No,' she said bitterly. 'He didn't even answer. I kept my finger on the buzzer until someone picked it up.'

'Then you talked to Hartmann?'

'I didn't talk to anyone. Whoever it was . . .' She shrugged. 'They didn't say a word.'

'You didn't hear anything?'

'I tried to get them to let me in. But then they hung up.'

Lund looked up at the big red-brick building.

'Did you drive home?'

'No. I was furious with him. I went into the courtyard and screamed his name.'

They walked back beneath the arch, stood in the open interior space.

'I saw a silhouette.'

She stopped and looked up at the fourth-floor windows.

'It wasn't him.'

'What do you mean?'

'It wasn't him! It didn't look like him.'

'How could you tell? It was dark.' Lund gestured at the building. 'It's high up. How can you be sure?'

'You really want to nail Troels, don't you?'

'I want the truth. How do you know?'

'He seemed shorter. Troels is tall. He holds himself well. The man I saw . . .'

She shrugged and looked at the street outside.

'It wasn't Troels Hartmann.'

Lund said nothing.

'He saw me,' Stjernfeldt said. 'He was looking directly at me. It made me feel uncomfortable. I didn't want to stay here. Troels wasn't in that flat any more. What was the point?'

Pernille drove the boys home listening to them bicker in the back. It never used to get to her.

Now . . .

'It's mine,' Anton said. 'Give it to me. You should've brought your own.'

'Mum, tell him to stop!'

The traffic was bad. The night wet. The noise of their voices filled her head but not so much it drowned out the dark thoughts.

'You're mean.'

'Tell him, Mum! I haven't played with it all day.'

'Can't you take turns?'

The stupid things parents said. Share what you have. Be quiet.
Be good and obedient. Tell us what you think, where you go, what
you do.

And who with.

'Mum! Tell him!'

'Shut up!' Anton wailed.

Or Emil.

When they screeched they both sounded the same.

'My toy! My toy! My toy!'

Like two little kettles coming to the boil.

There was a gap in the cars by the side of the road. She swung
the car violently knowing it would shake them in their safety seats.
Slammed her foot on the brakes. Listened to the tyres screaming.

Hit the pavement. People scattering and shouting around her.

They shut up then. They let her sit in the driver's seat, staring at
the figures milling round the car.

No damage done. Just a brief and insane turn off the steady
stream of traffic that was life.

'Mum?' asked a quiet, frightened voice from behind.

She looked at their faces in the mirror. Felt shocked she'd done
this. Put such fear into their unformed, fragile lives.

'Emil can have the toy,' Anton said. 'It's OK. We can take turns.'

She was crying again. Tears streaming down both cheeks, making
the night seem blurry. The wheel felt too heavy to drive. The car
stank of kids and petrol and Theis's cigarettes.

'Mum? Mum?'

Theis Birk Larsen was cooking supper when the boys came through
the door.

'You're late,' he said. 'What happened?'

'I picked up the boys. I told you.'

'I know, but the time. I was ringing round. I called Lotte . . .'

'I told you.'

He didn't push it.

'I made spaghetti bolognese.'

She didn't look right.

'I called the journalist who came this morning,' she said.

He stopped stirring the sauce.

'I set up a meeting. He'll be here soon.'

'Why the hell did you do that? Without talking to me? The police say I'm not supposed to go near the case.'

She laughed at him.

'The police? You're doing what they tell you now?'

'Pernille—'

'We need help. We need to get things moving. Someone must have seen something. They'll offer a reward.'

He had his eyes closed, his head up to the ceiling.

'If it's not Troels Hartmann then it's someone else.'

He went back to the stove, stirred the sauce.

'I don't like it.'

'Well that's the way it's going to be.'

'Pernille—'

'I've agreed and that's that!' she cried. 'Stay here and do the cooking if you like. I'll deal with it.'

Meyer kept running over the same points with Rie Skovgaard, again and again.

'So none of the sponsors saw Hartmann until Sunday?'

'As I've told you a million times, he was ill.'

Meyer shrugged.

'But he told me his speech went down well. I don't get it. Why are you covering for him? Your father's an MP. How's he going to feel when we drag you into court for aiding and abetting?'

She looked as if she'd changed for the interview. Smart pin-striped shirt. Glossy, well-brushed hair. A pretty woman. Beautiful even when she chose to smile.

'Is a man like Hartmann more important than your own career?'

'You don't know Troels Hartmann. And I'm not covering for him.'

'Do you know him, Rie? He didn't tell you he called himself Faust. He didn't tell you he was screwing around through that dating site.'

She smiled.

'Water under the bridge. Everyone does things they regret. Didn't you?'

'I always tell my wife. That's safest. That's the right thing to do.'

'Nothing's happened since we've been together.'

He got up, sat on the desk beside her. Read one of the emails.

'"I want you. I can't hold back. I need to touch you. To feel you."'

Another page.

'"I'm going to the flat now. Wait for me. Don't get dressed."'

He placed them in front of her.

'Every one signed F for Faust. How do you know he didn't write to Nanna Birk Larsen too?'

She sighed, kept smiling.

'How, Rie?' Meyer said. 'Please tell.'

No answer. He went back to the conference.

'What was wrong with Hartmann? Why did he have to stay in his room?'

He lit a cigarette.

'Flu. The same flu as before.'

'Man flu? It's not the real thing, is it? Real flu means you're stuck in bed, sweating like a pig, coughing, wheezing. Was that it?'

'Yes.'

'Lots of snot I guess.'

'Something like that.'

'Messy, huh?'

'Messy.'

'No, it wasn't.' He looked at his pad. 'I spoke to the maid who cleaned the room. She said it looked like there'd only been one person in there, not two. No snotty tissues. Nothing.'

'She must have the wrong room.'

'No. She didn't. You're covering for a murder suspect. That makes you an accomplice.'

He took a long drag.

'Will Daddy come and visit you in jail? Do you think he can get you privileges?'

Nothing.

'Is that how it works? One rule for you? Another for the dregs who pay your wages?'

'You're a man with a lot of hang-ups.'

Meyer waved a hand through the smoke.

'And where do they come from I wonder.'

'If that's all I'd like to leave now.'

One of the night team was at the door with a note.

'Wait a moment,' he said.

A message from his wife. Shopping list. Cucumber, milk, bread, sugar, olives, feta. And bananas.

She had her bag, her coat.

'So you were with Hartmann all weekend?'

'A million times . . .'

Meyer stared at her.

'Then why did you call his mobile phone on Saturday? When it was turned off?'

She stood there.

'You were with him, Rie? Wouldn't you know? Do people do phone sex when they're sharing the same bed?'

'I don't remember—'

'No, no. Don't think you can wriggle out of this.'

He waved the shopping list at her, keeping the writing to himself.

'I've got a call log from the phone company. You tried to phone him. Several times. Never got through.'

For the first time she looked vulnerable.

'It's as if you were worried about him. Which I don't think would be the case if you were in the same hotel room.' Meyer shook his head. 'I can't see that. Any way I look at it.'

He walked up to her.

'This is the last time I ask. You've lied and lied and I'm willing to let that go. But not for ever. Once more and you're an accomplice. Not a witness.'

He beckoned to the chair.

'Your choice either way.'

She didn't move.

'Did Hartmann come over to your place on Friday night? Think about it.'

She walked to the door.

'Last chance, Rie . . .'

Lund stood outside Hartmann's house. There were lights in the long windows on the first floor. A well-kept front garden. What looked like an extensive lawn at the back. The place was on an open well-lit street in Svanemøllevej, northern Østerbro, near the embassies. A detached villa. Ten million kroner at least.

There was money in politics.

She prowled around the gardens looking for signs of activity. Something buried. Something fresh. Walked across the long, dense grass, checked the back. There was a basement, the door old with peeling white paint. Leaves stacked up against it, a couple of feet high. Unused in ages. She looked at the single light inside the ground floor. This was a house for a family. A dynasty even. And all it had was the sad and handsome figure of Troels Hartmann.

She walked all the way round, saw nothing. Went through a side gate, found herself back at the foot of the stone stairs to the street.

No sound from inside. No TV. No music.

Lund rang the bell.

Rang again and knocked five times, loudly.

A woman answered. Foreign. Filipino maybe.

'Hi. Sarah Lund. Police. Is Troels Hartmann home?'

Without an argument she was in.

The kitchen was modern, immaculate. Expensive oven. Fancy central table. Spotless.

Cleaners, Lund thought.

A pizza was cooking in the see-through oven.

She stood in her raincoat and white and black sweater, rocking on her feet.

He could be anywhere in the house. So she waited, trying to be patient.

Hartmann came down the stairs, blue shirt, suit trousers, drying his hair.

Looked at her, open-mouthed.

He threw the towel on the table.

'I've answered your questions, Lund. I won't speak to you again without my lawyer present.'

'You said you didn't take any calls in the flat.'

He closed his eyes, shook his head.

'Do you ever listen to what people say to you?'

'All the time. You told me you didn't take any calls.'

He looked at the pizza. Slapped his forehead.

'OK. Nethe Stjernfeldt.'

'She told me.'

'We spoke for thirty seconds. No more. I made it absolutely clear I wasn't interested.'

He got some oven gloves, took out the pizza, slipped it onto a plate.

Lund watched. A man used to living on his own.

'She kept ringing me. Sending messages. It got tedious.'

'You're sure of that?'

'For the last time. I'm sure. I wrote the damned speech. I drank too much booze. Then I went to Rie's around ten thirty. I've told you that all along. I can't keep repeating it.'

He opened the back door.

'I have to eat now. Please.'

'Let's say someone else used your computer. Your car. Your flat. Who might know your password?'

'I've told you before. Someone got into our network.'

The housekeeper came back, picked up the rubbish, told Hartmann she'd see him the following week, then left, closing the door behind her.

'I want to help,' Lund said. His fair eyebrows rose. 'Honestly. I do.'

'Talk to Rie. She found something on the system. Anyone could have got the passwords. I use the same one for everything anyway. Rie's made a list for you. People we think you should look at. There's a civil servant—'

'I'd like that list.'

'There's a copy upstairs. I'll get it.'

On the staircase Hartmann stopped.

'Help yourself to pizza if you like. It's too much for me.'

'Just the list. But thanks.'

Lund watched him go.

It was an old house. She could hear the floorboards creak as he walked around, trying to find something.

Lund went into the adjoining room. A study overlooking the garden. She headed for the bookcase. Mostly they were political. Bill Clinton's autobiography. A couple of titles about JFK. There was a photo of the doomed president and Jackie. She was struck by the resemblance. Rie Skovgaard had the same cold beauty. Hartmann looked nothing like Jack. But he was handsome, gazed into the camera with a certain cocksure confidence.

Kennedy was, in Meyer's words, a serial philanderer too. A weakness he couldn't abandon. And Clinton . . .

She browsed the shelf. Pulled out the one piece of fiction she could find. A translation into Danish of Goethe's *Faust*.

Everything here was ordered and quiet and personal. So unlike the office in the Rådhus where he seemed to be under constant bombardment, from his own staff, from Bremer's machinations. And from her.

A diary sat on the desk by the garden window. She walked over, began to flick through the pages. There were a few curt, one-line entries. Nothing interesting. She was about to turn to that Friday when her phone rang.

Quickly she closed the pages.

'Lund.'

'It's Meyer.'

She could hear Hartmann walking down the stairs.

'I can't talk right now. I'll ring you back.'

'He doesn't have an alibi.'

She walked into the kitchen. He was there, carving up the pizza. Opening a bottle of wine.

Troels Hartmann smiled at her.

Politicians and women. They went together. He was a striking, interesting, intelligent man. She could see why. Could almost imagine . . .

'I got Rie Skovgaard to talk,' Meyer said proudly. 'She's no idea where he was the whole weekend. None whatsoever. She lied to the sponsors. She made up the story about him being ill.'

Hartmann was wrapping a napkin round the neck of the wine bottle. Then he poured himself a glass.

'What's going on, Lund? Where the hell are you?'

'That's fine,' she said brightly and ended the call.

'Anything wrong?' Hartmann asked.

'No. Did you bring me the list?'

'Here you go. Christensen. The one at the top. I'd start with him.'

'Thanks.'

Hartmann sat down, glanced at his watch, started on the pizza.

'Maybe I'll have a slice after all,' Lund said.

It didn't take long before Hartmann was in full flow, talking politics, talking tactics, talking about anything but himself.

Lund sipped her expensive red wine, wondered if this was a good idea. She stayed to entice him, to trap him. But he was doing the same to her. Had done this to many women, she thought. His personality, his looks, his energy and apparent sincerity . . . he had a magnetism she never encountered in the police.

Bengt Rosling was a good, kind, intelligent man. But Troels Hartmann, now she saw him alone, at his dining table, free of the police and the trappings of City Hall, was different. Charismatic and gripped by a visible passion, one most men she knew in Copenhagen would be reluctant to allow a stranger to see.

'Bremer . . . It's outrageous to have a man like that in power. For twelve years! He thinks he owns us.'

'Politics is about staying in power, isn't it? Not just getting there.'

Hartmann topped up her glass.

'You've got to get there first. Sure. But the reason we have power is to give it back.'

He looked at Lund.

'To you. We get everyone to work like fury and take a share of what we create together. Copenhagen doesn't belong to Poul Bremer. Or the political classes. It belongs to everyone. That's what politics means.'

He nodded, smiled. Aware, perhaps, that he'd made a speech, seemingly without wishing it.

'To me anyway. I'm sorry. I sound like I'm asking for your vote.'

'Aren't you?'

'Of course.' He raised his glass. 'I need every one I can get. Why are you looking at me like that?'

'Like what?'

'As if I'm . . . odd.'

Lund shrugged.

'Most people find politics boring. I get the impression you don't think about much else.'

'Nothing. We need to change. I want to lead that. I've always felt that way. It's me, I guess.'

'And your private life?'

'That comes second,' he said in a quiet, uncertain tone.

An awkward moment. Lund was smiling, out of embarrassment, out of a lack of anything to say.

'You think that's funny?' Hartmann asked. 'Why? I've dated half of Copenhagen, haven't I? Or so you seem to think.'

'Only half?'

He could have taken that badly. Instead Troels Hartmann broke into a broad smile and shook his head.

'You're a very unusual police officer.'

'No I'm not. How did you meet your wife?'

He thought about his answer.

'In high school. We were in the same class. We couldn't stand each other at first. Then we agreed we wouldn't live together. And under absolutely no circumstances . . .'

He held up his left hand, as if wishing to push something away.

'. . . would we marry.'

A short burst of laughter.

'But some things you can't control. Doesn't matter how hard you try.'

More wine. He looked as if he could drink the whole bottle.

'It must have been difficult.'

'It was. If I hadn't had this job . . . I don't know . . .'

Hartmann fell silent.

'Don't know what?'

'Sometimes life falls to pieces. You do something idiotic. Something that's not you. Never was. And still . . .' The wine was back in his hand. 'It's there.'

'Like calling yourself Faust on a dating site?'

'Quite.' His phone rang. 'If I'd been thinking straight I'd have called myself Donald Duck instead. Excuse me.'

'Troels? Where are you?'

It was Morten Weber.

'I'm at home.'

'They know your alibi's bogus.'

Hartmann smiled at Sarah Lund. Got up from the table, walked out into the hall.

'What do you mean?'

A long pause, then Weber said, 'Rie's on her way back from police headquarters. They really turned the screws on her.'

'Tell me, Morten.'

'They worked out she'd tried to call you when you were supposed to be together.'

'How long have they known?'

'A while. They took in Rie a couple of hours ago. Troels? It's important you don't talk to them. Come in here. Let's get the lawyer. We need to think this through.'

Lund was alone at the table. Same black and white sweater. She'd got make-up on for once, had done something to her hair. She looked good. Had prepared for this.

He felt a fool.

'Troels?'

Hartmann walked back into the kitchen.

'What are we going to do, Troels?'

He cut the call and put the phone in his jacket.

'Where were we?'

'You were telling me about yourself.'

'Right.'

'Don't you have to go?'

'Not yet. We can talk for a while.'

He gulped at the wine. It spilled down the front of his blue shirt. Lund passed him a napkin.

'I've got a press conference soon. Will anyone notice?'

She laughed.

'I think so.'

'I'd better . . . sorry.'

Then he went upstairs and left her alone.

Alone.

He'd gone up two floors from the sound of it.

Lund got to her feet. Strode back into the study. Found the diary she'd been looking through before. Skipped to the end of the previous month.

One entry.

Miss you. Lonely. Can't sleep.

More pages. Blank.

Then two, covered in an anxious scrawl. Nothing tangible, just disjointed thoughts and cries. Someone in torture shrieking at himself.

'Shall I turn the lights on?' Hartmann said just inches from her neck.

Lund jumped, mumbled something, turned.

Saw him in the shirt with the wine stain down the front.

He wasn't that clumsy and she should have realized.

She didn't speak.

'What was this?' Hartmann asked in a calm, cold voice. 'Were we supposed to drink all night until we became best friends? Then what? I confess? Is that it?'

His hard blue eyes wouldn't leave her.

'Is there really nothing you wouldn't do?'

He pointed upstairs.

'Do we go up to the bedroom and I tell you everything after?'

'You don't have an alibi. You lied to us. Rie Skovgaard . . .'

'So what? Does that give you the right to talk your way in here and read my diary behind my back?'

She watched, wondered what he'd do.

'Let me understand this,' Hartmann said. 'I take my own campaign car and drive to the party flat. Where I rape a nineteen-year-old girl, then kill her. Then drive the body out to the woods and ditch the car and the girl in the water. Is that right?'

'You lied to us. All that fine talk. About Poul Bremer. About politics—'

'What I do in public and what I do in private are two different things.'

'Not to me. Let's talk about this back at headquarters.'

'No. We talk about it here. So I do all this and I never think of covering my tracks. Why?'

'You did. You took the surveillance tape from reception.'

'I don't know a damned thing about that.'

'She went to your flat. The emails. Maybe . . .'

He came close, was getting mad.

'Maybe, maybe, maybe. I didn't do it. Can't you even consider that a possibility?'

'I'd be happy to. If you told me where you were that weekend.'

He was so close she could smell his cologne and the wine on his breath. Eyes blazing, Hartmann glared at her. Lund didn't move.

There was a rap at the door. A familiar voice crying, 'Police!'

'That's all you have to do,' Lund said.

'Troels Hartmann!' someone yelled.

Meyer's voice.

'This is the police. Open the door.'

*

392

Outside, Meyer and Svendsen were getting impatient. They could see the lights. They knew from Skovgaard he'd be here, got the arrest cleared by Brix after a fight.

'Dammit,' Meyer said. 'I'll take a look round the back. Call up for help. We'll break down the door if he doesn't come out in a minute.'

Sounds of footsteps. A light came on above them.

The door opened. Lund walked out, pulling her bag around her shoulder. She walked past him, down the steps, Hartmann following, stern-faced and silent.

'Let's go,' she said.

Meyer stood beneath the outside light, mouth open, staring, as did Svendsen.

Lund clapped her hands.

'Let's go,' she repeated.

The reporter came with a cameraman. They set up their equipment amidst the dust and chaos of the garage. Theis Birk Larsen stayed upstairs.

Pernille had written what she wanted to say on a single sheet of paper.

'That's fine,' he said when he read it.

'Will it do any good?'

'Sure it will. When we're done here we'll go up to the flat—'

'We're not going to the flat.'

The reporter looked ready for an argument. It was his job. Getting the story he wanted. She should have known that.

'We want to do the best we can, Pernille.'

'We're not going to the flat.'

A floodlight came on. It made the place look even grubbier.

'Very well.' He didn't look pleased. 'What about your husband?'

'What about him?'

'It looks better if you speak as a couple.'

'I decide how we do this. Not you. Not Theis.'

No answer.

'Take it or leave it,' she added.

Pernille waited.

'OK,' he said. 'Just you.'

*

Upstairs Theis Birk Larsen was finishing the boys' supper. Ice cream from the supermarket, on their special plates, beneath the Murano chandelier.

Nanna's face still stared at them from the table.

'Isn't Mum having pudding?' Anton asked.

'She has to talk to somebody.'

'We're going to the woods tomorrow,' Emil said.

'No, we're not,' Anton butted in.

'Yes, we are.'

'Shut up.'

The boys glared at each other.

'Why aren't you going to the woods?' Birk Larsen asked.

Anton toyed with his ice cream.

'Mum doesn't feel well.'

'Of course you're going to the woods. Mum thinks so too.'

Pernille came in from the stairs.

'They're offering a reward,' she said. 'The TV people. There was a neighbourhood collection too.'

Birk Larsen gave the boys more ice cream.

'Anton and Emil want to go to the woods tomorrow.'

'I know. I said I'd go with them.'

He couldn't stop looking at the photos pasted into the tabletop all those years ago. Nanna . . . what, sixteen? The boys as toddlers. A piece of their life, trapped in time.

It was a table. If she had her way it would stay with them for ever.

'When we went to counselling,' Birk Larsen said, 'they told us to think about what we have.'

She scowled at him.

'I know what I'm doing, thank you.'

His face was hard, his mood was black.

'So why aren't you here with us? Instead of talking to that guy downstairs?'

A long silence. Pernille smiled at Anton and Emil.

'Come on boys. Time for bed.'

They hadn't finished their ice cream but they didn't argue.

Birk Larsen threw his spoon on the plate as he watched her usher them out of the room.

Dirty cutlery and dishes. Bills and appointments. Burdens and cares.

All these things swept around him constantly, like a ceaseless tide of trouble.

He walked to the fridge, got a bottle of beer, sat in a chair and began to drink.

In the interview room at headquarters the lawyer looked as if nothing in the world had changed.

'My client admits his alibi was fabricated,' she said confidently. 'He wasn't with Rie Skovgaard.'

Hartmann sat next to her as she spoke. Lund and Meyer opposite. Lennart Brix listening at the end of the table.

'Any particular reason he lied to us?' Meyer wanted to know.

'Everyone has a right to privacy. Especially a politician during an election.'

'Irrelevant,' Meyer said. 'What were you doing that Friday, Hartmann?'

He stayed silent. The lawyer answered instead.

'As we've emphasized throughout, my client maintains his innocence. He never knew or had any dealings with Nanna Birk Larsen. He went elsewhere because he needed some peace. He asked Skovgaard to cover for him.'

'Not good enough—'

'He takes full responsibility for his fabricated alibi. It was necessary because he was in the public eye.'

Meyer was getting mad.

'Let me get this straight. You claim you were drinking yourself stupid all weekend because of your dead wife?'

'My client—'

'I'm not finished. Where were you, Hartmann?'

'My client doesn't want to comment. His private life is his own.'

'You'll go on TV and tell us how we're supposed to run this city. But you won't tell us one small thing to help out a murder inquiry?'

'Hartmann,' Lennart Brix broke in. 'Forty-eight hours ago you told me you had an alibi. Now you don't. If you won't make a statement there's only one thing I can do.'

He waited. Hartmann didn't say a word.

'Press charges and arrest you.'

'There are no grounds for that,' the lawyer cried. 'You don't have any evidence whatsoever to suggest Hartmann was involved with this girl. He's tried to cooperate as much as he feels able.'

Her voice got louder. She looked at Lund.

'At every turn he's been harassed by your officers while they stumble about their business. Harassed at home, where his house was searched without a warrant. In secret. Under the pretext of a personal conversation.'

She turned to Brix.

'Don't threaten us. Illegal entry. Illegal search. I could throw you all to the wolves now if I felt like it. Find the man who used Hartmann's email. The car, the flat . . .'

Meyer ran a finger along his notes.

'Olav Christensen has an alibi. A real one. We checked. If Hartmann would care to tell us the truth about his whereabouts we'll check his too.'

'Christensen's involved in this,' Hartmann said, breaking his silence. 'If you look at him . . .'

'Why won't you tell us where you were?' Lund asked, gazing at him across the table. The same way she had in the house when they were alone together, drinking wine, picking at the pizza.

Hartmann looked away.

'Christensen's in the clear,' Meyer insisted again. 'The administration backs it up.'

'Of course they back it up!' Hartmann bawled. 'They all belong to Bremer. They're the ones Olav must . . .'

He stopped, seemed to think of something.

'Must what?' Lund asked.

'I've got nothing more to say. If that's all I'd like to leave now.'

'No,' Brix said. 'You had your chance. You should have taken it.'

The three of them went to Lund's office. Brix wanted to draw up charges and put them in front of a prosecutor straight away.

Lund sat on the edge of her desk trying to think.

'The prosecutor's going to want blood, saliva and semen for that. We don't have it. I think we should wait. Let's see if we can find more. There's nothing to be gained from arresting him. It's not as if he's going to flee.'

'We can shove him in Vestre jail,' Brix said. 'That should get him talking.'

'No. This is wrong,' Lund insisted. 'When I talked to him he thought the girl had been killed in the flat.'

'So?'

'She wasn't. She was chased through the woods, two days later. She drowned in the car. Whoever did it must have heard her screaming. He tied her up. Put her in the boot.'

'That's just Hartmann being clever,' Meyer said.

'We need to think of the press,' Lund added.

Meyer picked up the phone and asked for the prosecutor.

'We can't make another mistake, Brix. Think of the teacher. You heard what the lawyer said. If we get this wrong she'll tear us apart.'

She paused, made sure this went in.

'It won't be just Buchard packing his bags.'

Back in the interview room.

'We're getting search warrants for your house,' Meyer said. 'If there's anything there we'll find it. We want access to your office and car. Your phone records. Your bank accounts. Your email.'

He grinned.

'You can't go back home. Maybe you should try sleeping on the street. Get closer to the voters, huh?'

'Very funny,' Hartmann muttered.

'There's a cellar and a summer house in the garden,' Meyer went on. 'I want the keys to those or we'll break down the doors. And I want your passport.'

'I take it from all this Troels is free to go,' the lawyer said.

'He can walk, can't he?'

Hartmann reached into his jacket, threw a key ring on the table.

'You'll have my passport in half an hour.'

Lund looked at the keys.

'It must be very important.'

'What?'

'Whatever it is that warrants all . . .' She picked up the keys and shook them. 'All this.'

'It's my life. Not yours. Not anyone else's. Mine.'

Then he left with the lawyer and Brix.

Lund pulled out the file for the party flat.

'I'm going back to Store Kongensgade. Do you have the caretaker's number?'

She was alone with Meyer for the first time that evening.

'What the hell happened at Hartmann's place?' he asked. 'Jesus, Lund. What did you think you were doing?'

She started going through the files, looking for the number herself.

'All you talk about is Hartmann. How screwed-up he is. Then after five minutes you let him off the hook.'

Lund found the number.

'What the hell are you up to? What aren't you telling me?'

She put the file in her bag and left.

'The press know you were questioned again,' Weber said.

'Holck and the alliance?' Hartmann asked.

'They're discussing it,' Skovgaard told him.

Hartmann took off his coat.

'Bremer wants to know if we should cancel the debate tomorrow. What do you want me to say?'

'We're not cancelling anything.'

He still wore the shirt with the wine stain.

'Rie?'

She didn't meet his eyes.

'Do I have a clean shirt? Can anyone get me a clean shirt?'

She didn't move.

'I'm sorry I couldn't keep quiet, Troels. They got my phone records somehow. I couldn't . . .'

He tried to read her face. Sorrow? Embarrassment? Anger that he'd asked her to cover in the first place?

'You don't have to apologize. It's my fault. I'll make sure they understand. This is my problem, not yours.'

Weber got a shirt from somewhere. Hartmann walked into his office to change. Skovgaard followed.

'Besides,' she said. 'It won't matter. Now the police know where you were they'll shut up. Maybe we should have—'

'They won't shut up. I didn't tell them. They're going to search the house.'

Weber came in to listen.

'They'll be all over me,' Hartmann added. 'All over this place too. We've got to check out Olav again. They don't want to.'

'I got as far as I could,' Weber said.

'What if Olav didn't use the flat himself? Maybe he lent the key to someone?'

'Who?'

'Who do you think? Who benefits? Who wins from all of this?'

Weber stared at him, astonished.

'Bremer? Poul Bremer's an old man. Him and a nineteen-year-old girl. I can't—'

'Bremer, Olav. Olav, Bremer.' Skovgaard looked furious. 'You're a murder suspect, Troels. And all you talk about is those two.'

'See who benefits—'

'You have to tell the police!' she cried.

'I don't owe those bastards a thing.'

'What does it matter that you went on a drinking binge? This is an election. We need to put this crap behind us.'

He was dragging on the clean shirt. There was a knock on the door.

Two men there, dark suits.

'Police,' the first said. 'We need you out of this office.'

Four more came behind carrying metal cases, two of them in blue overalls.

'All yours,' Hartmann said.

He went next door into the main office. Skovgaard followed.

'You told me you went drinking on your own. The date. Your wife—'

'Yes! That's right.'

'So why not tell them where you were!'

He closed his eyes, exasperated.

'Because it's none of their damned business.'

She put a hand to his chest to stop him leaving.

'It's mine, Troels. Where were you?'

'Don't worry,' he said. 'I've got this under control.'

Downstairs in the elegant arched basement that was the canteen Jens Holck was eating on his own. Reading the paper. Watching the TV news.

Hartmann found him.

'How's the food, Jens?'

'The usual.'

Hartmann pulled up a chair, sat opposite him, smiled, watching Holck's eyes, his face, his movements.

'So what's a man to think?' he asked. 'Did Troels Hartmann do it or not? They're saying now he doesn't even have an alibi. What's next?'

Holck cut into his meat.

'Good question. What is next?'

'What's next is finding the bastard who's responsible.'

Holck kept eating.

'Jens. Don't walk away now. When they clear me you'll regret it.'

He didn't look impressed.

'Will I, Troels? Does it matter? You promised this was the end of it. Now . . . it looks as if it'll never stop.'

'It's a misunderstanding.'

Holck shook his head.

'Jens. Trust me. Have I ever let you down?'

The news came on. Hartmann heard the girl's name. Everyone in the canteen stopped what they were doing, turned to the TV, saw Pernille Birk Larsen's interview. Blue checked shirt, notes in her hand, pale, taut face staring at the camera. Not frightened. Determined.

She began to read.

'I hope that someone saw something. Someone must know something. We need help. We need to hear. It's as if the police . . . I don't know what they're doing. Maybe they're not taking it seriously.'

The reporter asked, 'How do you feel about Troels Hartmann being a suspect?'

Eyes wide open, staring into the camera.

'I don't know about that. But if someone saw something I hope they'll come forward. Anything might be relevant. Please . . .'

'I won't distance the party from you yet,' Jens Holck said.

Hartmann nodded gratefully.

'But I can't be seen with you any more. I'm sorry, Troels.'

Holck picked up his tray and headed for the stairs.

*

Back in Store Kongensgade Lund waited in the living room of the Liberal Party flat. She looked at the broken glass again. The shattered table.

An argument? An accident? The smallest of fights?

Thought about the bedroom again.

Finally the caretaker arrived. He managed several buildings in the area and lived close by.

'You've seen Hartmann here before?' Lund asked.

'That's right.'

'With women?'

He grimaced.

'I'm a caretaker. You see lots of things.'

'Do you remember seeing this woman?'

She showed him the photo of Nanna.

He was looking round at the damage. Calculating.

'I've seen some ladies ringing the bell. I've seen him come in with them.'

'But not her?' she asked, showing him the photo again.

'No. I think she must have had her own key. She used to let herself into the flat and wait for him.'

Lund wanted this clear.

'She was with Hartmann?'

'That's what I said. A couple of months ago. I was changing a washer next door. I saw her outside. I heard him talking.'

'You didn't see him?'

'Who else could it have been?'

She put the photo back in her bag.

'When do I hear?' the caretaker asked.

'Hear what?'

'I saw it on the news. There's a reward. Fifty thousand kroner. When do I hear?'

She took a deep breath and sighed.

'It was him,' the man insisted. 'I swear it.'

Twenty-five minutes later she was at the door of the apartment, talking to Pernille Birk Larsen.

'I need you to waive the reward.'

The woman wouldn't let her in.

'We didn't offer it.'

'If you talk to the TV people they'll do as you say, Pernille. I know how hard it is—'

'No you don't. You've no idea.'

The husband was lurking in the background, listening.

'You're not surrounded by her things. You don't keep getting her post. People don't look at you in the street as if this was all somehow your fault—'

'All that will happen is lots of people who want that money will contact us with useless information. Because they've done that we'll have to take every one of them seriously.'

'Good.'

'We don't have the officers. Things that matter will suffer.'

'What things?'

'I can't tell you. I know you feel we should be more open with you. But we can't be.' She glanced at the man in the background. 'We've said too much already. I thought you'd appreciate that.'

Pernille walked back into the living room. Theis Birk Larsen stood where he was, staring balefully at Lund.

'You have to make Pernille understand this is wrong, Theis. Please.'

He walked to the door and closed it in her face.

Friday, 14th November

Meyer phoned when she was just out of the shower. Straight away he began complaining about the flood of calls coming in after the appeal and the reward.

'I talked to the parents,' Lund told him. 'They won't help. I'm sorry. We're going to have to deal with all of them.'

'Wonderful. Anything else?'

'I want more on Olav Christensen.'

'Get someone else to deal with that, Lund. Not me.'

Mark walked in looking for breakfast.

'You're up early,' she said.

He slunk off to the table in silence.

'I'm bringing in Morten Weber again,' Meyer told her. 'See you.'

Mark poured himself some cornflakes.

'How was dinner round at your father's?'

A long pause then, 'OK.'

'And his girls? Are they nice?'

Lund had broken out a new jumper from its wrapping from the stock she'd bought by mail order. Thick wool, dark brown, black and white lozenges.

Mark was staring at it.

'They've got a lot of different clothes,' he said.

The milk ran out when he tried to pour it. He held up the carton.

Lund sighed, came and sat down at the table, tried to take his hand until he snatched it away.

'Listen. I know everything's a mess. Bengt's coming back to Copenhagen soon. He has to teach. We'll talk. We'll work it out.'

He picked at the half-dry cornflakes.

'At least now you can go to the Christmas concert at school.'

Mark played with the earring for a second then gave up on the cereal.

'Do we have any more milk?'

She went to the fridge.

'No. Grandma has gone shopping. She'll be back soon.'

He sat in front of his food, head on hand, miserable.

Lund tied up her hair, got ready to go.

'Mum?'

'Yes?'

Mark looked awkward.

'It doesn't matter.'

'No. Tell me.'

'You don't need to wait for Grandma to get back. If you've got to go . . .'

She smiled at him, touched his arm.

'You're so sweet.'

He was looking at her in a way she didn't recognize.

'What is it?'

'Nothing. Go to work.'

Meyer had Morten Weber in the office.

'So you don't know what Hartmann was doing that weekend either? And you're his what?'

'Campaign manager. Not his nanny.'

Meyer didn't like this man. He seemed slippery.

'He looks to me like a guy who needs one.'

Weber groaned.

'How many times do I have to tell you this. You've searched our office. You've confiscated our computers. I told you already. We are having them checked.'

'Forget computers. Who visited Hartmann at his home on Sunday morning?'

No answer.

'Don't know? Someone who looks like you, Morten. You went into his house.'

'Yes. That's right.'

'Why?'

'I was worried. I hadn't heard from him. So I went over there.'

Meyer's wife had sent him off to work with two apples and a strict order to eat both. He started peeling the first with a knife, munching on the pieces.

'What did you do there?'

Weber folded his arms and said, 'I looked for Troels. I've got a spare key. Why not?'

'And after that you went to the dry cleaners.'

'So what?'

'The cleaner confirmed you brought his clothes in on Monday. The ones he wore on Friday. Why get them cleaned?'

'They were in the house. He wears them a lot in public—'

'Why did they need cleaning?'

'Because they were dirty?'

Meyer finished half of the apple.

'So you're not his nanny. You're his maid.'

'I went to his house because I was worried. That's all there is to it.' He got up from the table. 'I'm leaving now. We've got an election to fight.'

'Why didn't you phone him, Morten? If you were so bothered?'

'Hartmann had nothing to do with the girl. You're wasting your time. And ours.'

'Rie Skovgaard called Hartmann that weekend. Over and over again. I've got your phone records. You didn't try once.'

Weber shrugged.

'Maybe I had other things to do.'

'No you don't. You're a bachelor. You live for the party. Always have. Always will.'

Meyer grinned.

'I've got your number. You knew where Troels Hartmann was all along. You knew what he was doing. Just the two of you. It's your little secret. And when I find out . . .'

Morten Weber laughed in his face.

'Good luck,' he said. 'I'm leaving now.'

In the office in City Hall Skovgaard and Hartmann were going over the day ahead.

'There has to be a link between Bremer and Olav,' he said. 'A conference? Something . . .'

'We haven't found one. Cancel the debate.'

'Not a chance. People will think I'm in jail.'

'If you told the truth we wouldn't be in this situation.'

He didn't respond.

'You have to cancel the debate. Some of the assembly members are talking. They're saying you might not be fit for office. They can block your nomination.'

'They wouldn't dare.'

'It's Bremer's call. He can do it, Troels. If he wants rid of you . . .'

Hartmann's eyes lit up.

'If? What do you mean if?'

Weber came in, grumbling about the police.

'Olav?' Hartmann asked.

'People say Bremer doesn't know him.'

'What do you expect them to say?'

'I'll keep checking. But really it doesn't feel right.'

'Wonderful,' Hartmann moaned. 'I'm starving.'

He walked back into the main office to get a pastry.

Weber looked at Rie Skovgaard.

'The police still suspect him,' he said.

'Of course they do. He won't tell them where he was. Here . . .' She passed him a slip of paper. 'The computer people who found that thing on the network. It's a sniffer. Logs every keystroke on every account. I told them to keep it there. It didn't just trap our passwords. It got Olav's too. He changed it last night. That's the new one.'

'What the hell am I supposed to do with . . . ?'

Hartmann marched back in, dropping pieces of croissant everywhere.

'I've got a meeting with the committee clerks,' he said. 'Call if you hear anything.'

Downstairs in a corner of the echoing lobby Olav Christensen was sweating. He'd called six times that morning. Never got through.

'No, no. I need to talk to him personally. When's he going to be free?'

He listened. From the dark recess he could see the policewoman Lund walk into the building. Christensen fell further into the shadows.

'This is important,' he said. 'Tell him he has to call me as soon as possible. This is urgent. OK?'

She was walking towards him. Christensen started to head down the stairs towards the basement. The canteen. The security office. Out the back way to the car park, anywhere.

'Olav?' she called.

Too late.

He stopped. Tried to smile.

'Spare a minute?'

Lund got the civil servant to find them a spare desk in the library. He sat there in front of the morning paper, phone on the desk, massaging his temples.

A worried man.

She took the chair opposite and smiled.

'What's this about?' he said. 'I've talked to you.'

'Just a few more questions.'

'I'd really like to help. But it's supposed to be my day off.'

'Then why are you here?'

'I came in for a meeting. It starts in a few minutes.'

'What kind of meeting?'

'Just a meeting.'

'It's cancelled,' she said and took out her pad, looked at the notes, looked at him.

'You told us you didn't know about the key to the party's flat.'

He had his hand to his face, trying to look confident.

'That's right.'

'But you booked it for people. Lots of times. We've got the details from the book in Morten Weber's drawer.' Another brief smile. 'The same drawer where the key's kept. You did know about the flat. And the key.'

'I never touched the key.'

She looked around the library. Shelves and shelves of old books. Empty desks and chairs.

'Must be hard getting on in a place like this. Waiting to fill dead men's shoes. And Hartmann doesn't give you the job you want.'

'Is ambition a crime?'

'Do you make enough money?'

He grinned.

'Do you?'

'You are a smart puppy,' Lund said.

An ironic smile.

'Thanks.'

'No. I meant I ought to feel guilty when I kick you. I don't. But I ought to.'

She reached into her bag, pulled something out. He looked at it.

On the polished walnut table Lund spread out Olav Christensen's last payslip.

'You get an extra five thousand kroner every month on top of your basic for consulting services.' Lund watched him. 'What services?'

He sniffed, went quiet for a moment.

'I do some things for the environmental people. In my own time.'

'A busy puppy too. But you work for the Education Department, don't you?'

Christensen laughed, shook his head, muttered, 'I don't believe this.'

Lund pushed the payslip under his nose.

'What don't you believe? It's all here. Except who gives you this money.'

He picked up the piece of paper, said nothing.

'There must be some documentation for the amount and why you get it.'

'Ask payroll.'

'I did. They'd no idea.'

She took the slip from him and put it back in her bag.

'They're getting back to me today. They promised they'd find out. It seemed a puzzle to them too.'

She let that hang.

'Public money, Olav. One thing you can say about a place like this . . .' She looked at the rows and rows of books again. 'There's going to be a record somewhere.'

He nodded.

'So why not tell me now?'

'There's nothing to tell. I did some work. I got paid.'

'You can do better than that.'

'I'm busy right now.'

He got up, walked to the end of the room, out into the corridor.

Lund put her away her notebook, watched him from the door. Christensen was in the shadows of an arch along the way. On his phone already. And shaking.

Vagn Skærbæk was fielding calls again. Theis Birk Larsen wouldn't come to the phone.

'For the love of God,' Skærbæk grunted when the last one finished. 'The weirdos we get.'

'Pull out the lead,' Birk Larsen said.

'What if it's a customer?'

The big man walked over, yanked the wire from the wall.

'Two vans to Valby, and you'll drive one of them.'

Pernille came down. They'd barely spoken that morning.

'I can't go on the cub trip,' she said.

'Why not?' Birk Larsen asked.

'The funeral director called. I have to see the headstone. Make sure it's ready.'

Birk Larsen closed his eyes, said nothing.

'I don't know how long—' she began.

'The boys really want to go—'

'I can't do it!'

He glanced at Skærbæk.

'I can cover, Theis. No problem.'

'Yeah,' Birk Larsen said. 'I'll take the boys. Of course.'

He handed over the keys of the truck.

'Find someone, Vagn. Pay double if you have to. Pernille?'

He looked round the garage. She was already walking out of the door.

It was frosty in the playground where the cub trips met. No one on the tyre swings. No kids playing on the slides.

Just one woman he barely knew standing alone, smiling at the boys as they ran up in their blue uniforms, excited, ready to go.

They leapt onto the tyres and started to play.

Birk Larsen walked up to her, looked around.

'We're late. I'm sorry.'

'That's all right. I've been trying to call. There was no answer.'

Birk Larsen scanned the deserted playground.

'This is where we're supposed to meet, right?'

'Yes, but . . .'

He'd seen this look before. Was beginning to recognize it. At school. In the shops. It was a distanced, embarrassed kind of sympathy.

'You didn't get my message?'

She had something she didn't want to say. She wanted to run, to be anywhere but here, with him and the boys.

'No. I didn't.'

'The trip was cancelled this morning.'

'Cancelled?'

'I tried to go through with it.'

He stood there in his black hat and black jacket, feeling stupid and slow. The boys were shouting, starting to argue.

'Why was it cancelled?'

She struggled for an answer.

'Too many people pulled out.'

He waited.

'A lot of them saw the TV last night. They didn't think it was the best thing to do.'

Birk Larsen watched them on the tyre swings, barked at Anton to be more careful.

'Why?' he asked. 'What did we do?'

'I'm really sorry,' the woman said. 'Everyone feels for you. They just—'

'The boys have been looking forward to this trip.'

She looked guilty. He felt miserable for making her feel this way. At least she'd had the courage to come and tell him.

'I know. And we'll do it in the end. I promise.'

'When?'

'A couple of weeks. I don't know. When things—'

'Boys!' he shouted. 'Anton! Emil!'

They stopped what they were doing and looked at him from the tyres.

'We're going. Come on.'

'I'm really sorry,' she said.

'Yeah.'

Anton ran up, always the first to talk.

'When are the other kids coming, Dad?'

'The trip's cancelled,' Birk Larsen told him. 'Grandma and Grandpa want to see you. Let's go.'

He left them with Pernille's parents and went back home. Vagn Skærbæk had called in some help. The business was like that. There was always someone who'd come in to pick up a day's work when it was going. Birk Larsen didn't like using drifters. He preferred men he knew. Sometimes there was no choice.

Skærbæk was still in the depot loading cases.

Pernille wasn't back.

'What happened to the trip to the woods?'

'Got cancelled,' Birk Larsen said. 'The boys are at their grand-parents.'

He was thinking. Wondering how long Pernille would be gone.

'Can you give me a hand, Vagn?'

'Sure. With what?'

Birk Larsen got some of the flat-packed cardboard boxes they used for crating smaller things.

'Let's go upstairs.'

Nanna's bedroom. The police marks he ignored. All he saw was the mess. The books. The pens. The pot plants, the perfumed candles. The cosmetics and creams.

And the bed with its reindeer-skin cover, the coloured sheets, the patterned pillows.

These things seemed to have been here for ever. A part of him – a stupid part he knew – once believed they'd never disappear.

He went to her cork-board, cast his eyes over the photos there. A decade or more of a life cut short. With the boys, with her parents. With friends and teachers.

Nanna smiling, always. Nanna the kid. Nanna, lately, the teenager looking to shrug off childhood and march straight into an adult world she craved, not knowing what lurked there. What the cost might be.

'Everything goes. Everything.'

'Theis—'

'Everything. The clothes go in plastic bags. Just as usual.'

'Did you talk to Pernille about this?'

'Be careful not to break anything. OK?'

Skærbæk stepped into the bedroom, stopped by his side.

'If that's what you want.'

He popped open one of the cardboard cases.

Birk Larsen didn't move. Stood in his dead daughter's bedroom, staring at what remained.

'No.' He took the box. 'I'll do it myself.'

Morten Weber found an empty office in the education department. One man there tapping idly at a computer.

'I need some statistics for Hartmann,' he said. 'I can do it myself . . .'

'Take a seat. Everyone's gone to lunch and I'm joining them.'

Then he was on his own.

Weber chose the desk furthest away from the door. Typed in the username and password Rie Skovgaard gave him. One second and he was in.

Same email system the campaign office used, different linked network. Olav Christensen's email account stared at him. He scanned the messages.

Got partway through when Christensen walked in carrying a set of folders.

Weber tried to think.

'Can I help?' Christensen asked. 'We don't normally see political people in here. Just us.'

'No, no need.' He was floundering. 'Someone told me there was a virus.'

Weber got up quickly from the desk and realized straight off he hadn't logged out of Christensen's account.

The young civil servant was on him immediately.

'You're tech support now, Morten?'

He looked at the screen, swore, logged himself out.

Bunched up a fist, jabbed Weber hard in the chest, pushed him against the desks.

'They sent you to make me the scapegoat, did they?'

Christensen's phone rang. He took it out of his pocket, glanced at the screen.

'Did Hartmann put you up to this?'

'It's a virus,' Weber said and tried to push back.

Got another punch in the ribs, a kick in the shins. Christensen had him by the lapels, shoving him into the shadows by the wall.

Weber looked at the door.

No one.

'Don't give me that shit!' Christensen barked at him.

Footsteps down the corridor.

Weber fought free, stumbled for the door, got out into the light. Half-walked, half-ran.

Behind he heard the phone again and Olav Christensen's low, frightened voice as he answered it.

Morten Weber stopped. He'd taken a file into the office as a pretext. It was important. Confidential. He'd left it there.

And Christensen was an arrogant, pushy kid.

A playground bully. Someone else's puppet.

Slowly, quietly, Weber walked back to the education office and slipped through the door, listening.

Christensen had retreated into a corner, his back to the door. He sounded scared.

'We've got to talk. For Christ's sake! What am I supposed to say?'

Weber edged forward, hearing every word.

'They're checking my payslips. They want to know where the money comes from. You've got to do something.'

The folder was still on the desk. Weber realized he could get out without being seen.

'Fuck it!' Christensen screeched. 'I need some help. No, no. Either I talk to him in person or I'm spilling the beans. I'm not going down for this. I'm not going down for him.'

Morten Weber picked up the folder and stood where he was. Olav Christensen turned, saw him, fell silent.

Put the phone in his pocket.

Weber wondered if he'd ever seen anyone this scared in the grandiose surroundings of City Hall.

'Who were you talking to?'

Christensen looked dumbstruck.

'Olav. If you've done something wrong . . .'

Christensen picked up his briefcase. He was in a daze.

'We can help you,' Weber said. 'Come on . . .'

The civil servant was scouring the office, unlocking filing cabinets, taking documents.

As he headed for the door Weber stood in front of him.

'Talk to me and I can do something.'

'No,' Olav Christensen said. 'You can't.'

Lund was back at Hartmann's house watching Meyer, Svendsen and three other officers go through it room by room.

She'd got a call from headquarters about the payslip.

'Someone in City Hall has to know who ordered that money to be paid,' she told the officer handling the inquiry. 'Check Christensen's records. Check the audit trail. It's important. Who, when and how.'

When she was off the phone Svendsen stuck his head round from the kitchen and said with some sly amusement, 'The Swedish guy . . . your ex, has been trying to get you.'

She ignored him.

'The diary's interesting,' Meyer said.

It was the one Lund saw, but briefly.

Meyer flicked through the pages.

'He's been keeping it ever since his wife died. Then that Friday he stopped. Why?'

'What do you think?'

Meyer licked his fingers and turned more pages.

'Something happened and he's not proud of it. Or he did something he didn't want to write down. Listen to this.'

He read out from the page.

' "I'm beside myself. I have to let this go before it kills me." '

'This is a waste of time,' she said.

'Lund!'

It was Svendsen again, phone in hand.

'No,' Meyer cut in. 'She doesn't want to talk to her ex.'

'You need to call Morten Weber. He caught Olav Christensen talking to someone about his payslips. Then the guy took off from City Hall.'

'I want Olav Christensen taken into custody. I want those payslips explained.'

'Now we're wasting our time,' Meyer grumbled.

'Olav Christensen knows who was using the flat on the side. He's been doing someone a few favours.'

Meyer folded his arms and sighed.

'Says who?'

'Morten Weber by the sound of it. Put a trace on Christensen's phone.'

She picked up her bag and headed for the door.

'There's no point in looking here.'

'We haven't finished, Lund!'

It was cold outside and dry. Lund popped in a Nicotinell and drove back to the centre.

Theis Birk Larsen sat at the kitchen table, tapping the truck keys, waiting for her footsteps on the stairs.

He hadn't changed out of his work clothes. He didn't feel right. Feel settled. The flat, their home was changing, and they were changing with it.

'I'm sorry I'm late,' Pernille said when she came through the door. 'Did anyone call for me?'

'No.'

She had that animated expression that came from thinking about Nanna. The only time she looked alive. He was starting to hate it.

'I'm glad I went. They were using the wrong lettering. It wouldn't look right.' She listened. 'Where are the boys?'

'At your parents'.'

'Why?'

Birk Larsen glanced at the faces frozen into the table.

'We've got to talk about this. Pernille. We've got to . . .'

She wasn't listening. Eyes wide she was staring past him, at the open door to Nanna's room. She walked towards it, went in.

Bare walls, bare cupboards. No desk, no carpet. No photos. No clothes. Just the single bed stripped of everything but a mattress. Not a thing in the window. Not even a plant.

He stayed at the table, back to her.

'Where are her things?' she asked in a cold, bleak voice.

'Anton's pissed the bed three nights running. Emil says crazy things. If you listened to the boys you'd understand.'

She marched back to the table, said again, 'Where are her things?'

'In the van. I'm putting them in storage in Valby tonight. We'll keep everything. We just don't need it here.'

With a sudden violent movement she went for the truck keys on the table.

Birk Larsen's hand closed over them.

'Give me them.'

'No. We can't go on this way. Stuck like this. I'm not allowing it.'

There was a look on her face he didn't recognize for a moment. Then he put a word to it: hatred.

'You're not allowing it?'

She flew through the door, down to the garage. Was at the spare key rack in the office by the time he caught up with her.

'Listen to me, Pernille.'

She kept scrabbling through the nests of rings.

'Listen to me! The cubs cancelled the trip because of that shit on TV. Do you understand what's happening?'

She pushed past him without a word, went to the parked van, tried the doors.

'Take it out on me. Not the boys. They don't deserve it—'

'Just open it, will you?'

Birk Larsen hesitated.

'Don't talk to me like that. I don't deserve it.'

'Open it!'

He pulled out the keys, hit the remote. She scrabbled at the back of the van, dragged the door open.

All the photos and the furniture. Everything that was left of

Nanna's life stared back at her from the grubby rear of a scarlet removals truck.

'I'll take it to the warehouse. It won't be damaged. Nothing's going to get lost.'

She got on the step and climbed inside.

Birk Larsen rubbed his eyes with the back of his hands.

'Pernille . . .'

She got hold of the photos first. Then with her spare hand the bedside lamp. Climbed down from the back of the van and looked at him.

'I'm going to take this upstairs. Then I'm going to pick up the boys.'

'Pernille—'

'Am I just a face here?' she asked. 'Someone to sleep with? A servant to do your washing and look after your kids? Not to talk to. Not ask about . . . about . . .'

The words wouldn't come, for either of them this time. The social people had told them to put Nanna's death behind them. Clearing her room made sense to him. It was doing what he was told, and ever since he'd married, that, he thought, was what people wanted. The new, obedient Theis. Not the one from before.

'When I come back . . .' she said, face hard set and furious.

A long moment. One in which he felt his heart stop. They never argued outright like this. Never talked much sometimes. There wasn't the need. Now, trapped in this dread limbo, everything had changed. Thoughts that went unspoken now burst into the air alive and thrashing, demanding to be heard.

'When I come back I want you to be gone,' she said and that was that.

He stood there stiff and still as a pillar, struggling with his ravelled thoughts. Wondering if there could ever have been another way. A different set of actions. Another fork in the road.

Thought of only one thing to say.

'OK,' Birk Larsen murmured and watched her walk away.

Lund was at the wheel of her car, Lennart Brix in her ear.

'What in God's name are you doing now?'

'I tried Olav's home. He's not there. I've got an address for his sister.'

'Why are we looking for him?'

'Because he's involved. Have we traced his mobile yet?'

'No, Lund. I called off the search.'

She took her foot off the pedal. Let the car coast for a moment.

'Why did you do that?'

'We've got a witness who saw Hartmann with bloody clothes on Saturday morning.'

'Since that idiotic reward we've got fifty people claiming they saw everything.'

'I want you to concentrate on them.'

'If they knew something why didn't they come forward until there was money on the table? Christensen knows who was with Nanna.'

A long sigh down the phone.

'I really don't have time for this. You've got your orders.'

'Olav was taking bribes to give someone access to the flat. Every month he gets a fixed sum straight out of City Hall. Brix? Brix?'

She thought he'd gone. Then he said, 'Who ordered the payment?'

'That's what I'm trying to find out. I need his phone traced. He's in a panic. He's calling someone. Get me a name.'

Another silence.

'He made a call in Vester Voldgade about half an hour ago.'

The long street that ran past City Hall. Not far away.

'Thank you for that,' she said. 'Who to?'

'An airline.'

Skovgaard came off the phone.

'Bremer's moving on the selection. He's called the group chairs together. There's going to be a meeting tonight.'

'They'll get Olav before that. Call Lund and find out.'

Weber watched her go into the adjoining office.

'Troels. If they don't find him you're going to have to tell the truth. You know that, don't you?'

'We've already been through this.'

'Bremer's going to declare you unfit to be elected. There's no comeback from that. No grubby deals. No alliances. You're finished. For good. You'll have to quit the party. Forget about politics. It's over.'

'They'll find him!'

'And if they don't?' Morten Weber looked around the small office.

At the posters of Hartmann smiling. 'All this gets pissed away just because you don't have the guts to . . .'

Hartmann was on his feet, furious.

'They'll find him,' he bellowed.

Poul Bremer walked through the City Hall parking garage, briefcase in hand, aide by his side.

In the shadows Olav Christensen lurked, silent, thinking.

'The press have to be told something,' Bremer said. 'I haven't heard a word from Hartmann or the police. I've called an emergency meeting of the group chairs. We need to decide on Hartmann's eligibility. This scandal damages us all. The matter's a slur on the political class.'

The woman was nodding.

'I'm assuming we'll decide Hartmann is unfit,' Bremer added. 'It seems inevitable. But it's important we're all agreed on this. Unanimous. If there's dissent the problem will only fester.'

Christensen marched out of the darkness, straight up to Bremer.

'We need to talk,' he said.

'And who the hell are you? Press? Not now.'

Christensen's eyes flared with fury.

'You know who I am! I'm Olav. I've been trying to reach you.'

Bremer kept walking.

'Olav?'

'Yes. Christensen. In Hartmann's division.'

Bremer shook his grey head.

'I'm sorry. I don't know what this is about and I'm too busy. I don't know you.'

'Yes!'

Christensen's shriek echoed round the garage.

'I'm the one who helped you. Remember? Without me you're screwed, man.'

Bremer stopped and looked at him. He told the aide to walk on.

'Helped me do what?'

'You know perfectly well.'

'No. I've no idea what you're talking about.'

'You needed the flat.'

'The flat? What flat?'

'I fixed the keys for you. When you wanted them—'

'No, no, no. Calm down. I didn't ask for any keys.'

Christensen stood in the chilly garage, open-mouthed.

'Who asked you to do this?' Bremer repeated. 'Was it Hartmann?'

'You mean he didn't even mention me?'

Bremer closed his eyes for a moment.

'For the last time. I've no idea what you're talking about. If you know something we should call the police.'

He pulled out his phone.

'What did you say your name was again?'

Bremer fumbled with the buttons on the phone.

When he looked up he was on his own.

Two minutes from City Hall Lund got a call from Meyer.

'I've got someone here who wants to talk to you,' he said.

'I don't have time.'

'Tell him yourself.'

A voice she had to place said, 'It's Carsten.'

'I'm going to have to call you back.'

'It's about Mark.'

'He said you had a nice time.'

'Mark hasn't been to school all week. I talked to his teacher. They thought he'd already moved to Sweden.'

'I'll have a word with him,' Lund said.

'We're past that, Sarah. When you can find the time to discuss your family phone me. Don't take too long. I'm not having my son screwed up by you.'

Silence.

Then Meyer was back on.

'You still there, Lund?'

'Yeah.'

'We've found Olav.'

Mark and Carsten disappeared from her thoughts.

'Where?'

'If you're near City Hall you should be able to see him. Just look for the blue lights.'

Three ambulances, two squad cars. A gurney on the ground. Blood on the shiny black street.

The uniform officer she spoke to said Christensen was crossing

419

the street when he was hit by a fast car that drove off. No one saw the driver. No one got a registration number.

Lund walked towards the ambulances. Olav Christensen was in the office suit he always wore. Head a mess. Neck broken she guessed. Blood streaming from his mouth and nose.

Eyes still open. All the arrogance gone. Just fear now, sharp and real.

He was looking at her as she bent over him.

'Take nice slow breaths,' the ambulance man said.

'What is it, Olav?' Lund asked.

He was convulsing in tortured rhythmic throes. Gouts of gore came with each breath. No words.

'Olav. Tell me.'

Someone called for oxygen.

'Olav . . .'

In one moment his eyes glazed over then closed. The tension in his neck relaxed. The clinical mask went on. His head turned to one side.

'Olav?'

The medics pushed her away. She watched the familiar dance around a dying man. Walked to the side of the road. Begged a cigarette from one of the uniforms. Smoked it in the shadow of the Rådhus, beneath the golden statue of Absalon.

There were lights on inside. It always seemed that way. But no one walked out to see Olav Christensen die on the black wet cobblestones of Vester Voldgade. They were all too busy with themselves.

The car that killed Olav Christensen was a white estate. They knew no more than that. Lund put out a bulletin straight away. The savage injuries to Christensen indicated it had been travelling at speed when it hit him. There had to be damage.

The best witness she had, an off-duty parking attendant from the City Hall garage, was adamant the collision was deliberate. Christensen had been crossing the empty road when the car pulled out of the side and went straight for him.

Meyer was there with Svendsen and some night men.

'I want Christensen's computer taken into forensics,' she said. 'I want his office searched and everyone in his department questioned. See if anyone close to him drives a white estate car.'

Svendsen went off to City Hall.

'You're sure this was deliberate?' Meyer asked.

'Where are the skid marks? He was accelerating straight at Christensen. He wanted to kill him.'

Lund looked at the Rådhus.

'The parking attendant was finishing work. He said he saw Christensen before. He was in the garage. He spoke to Poul Bremer.'

Meyer stopped in the street.

'Bremer?'

'Bremer,' Lund said. 'Come on. Let's talk to the Lord Mayor.'

City Hall was abuzz with rumour. Skovgaard had confirmed what she could to the police. On the way to the meeting she briefed Hartmann.

'He died in the street.'

'They're sure it was him?'

'Absolutely. Lund was there. She tried to talk to him.'

She put a hand to his arm.

'You have to tell them where you were.'

They were at the top of the main staircase. Lund and Meyer were walking up.

Hartmann pounced.

'Not now,' Lund said. 'I don't have the time.'

'Is he dead?'

Lund kept walking.

'Yes.'

'Morten overheard a conversation. Olav was talking to someone about the money.'

'I know, I know.'

Down the long corridor, beneath the tiles and mosaics.

'Stop this!' Hartmann barked at her. 'You know I'm not involved. Why not say it?'

Lund and Meyer walked a touch more quickly.

'We don't have time,' Meyer said.

Skovgaard's temper was fighting its short rein.

'Troels could lose his seat because of this crap!'

421

Meyer stopped and stared at both of them.

'You lied to us, Hartmann. And you . . .' He stabbed a finger in Skovgaard's face. 'You gave him a fake alibi. Don't pretend we owe you a damned thing.'

'Am I above suspicion?' Hartman pressed him. 'You're investigating Olav. Not me. That's all I need to know.'

Lund started walking again. Meyer stayed for a moment.

'You know what? I've worked out what you guys do here. You talk and talk and talk. But never listen.'

Then he walked on.

The two cops were disappearing down the corridor, towards Bremer's department.

'I'll remember this,' Hartmann shouted after them.

Poul Bremer looked relaxed, confident. Baffled.

'You had a meeting with Olav Christensen before his accident?' Lund asked.

'I've never met the man as far as I know. He hung around the garage and just leapt out and started haranguing me.'

Meyer had his feet up on the polished coffee table, making notes.

'You say this was unplanned?'

Bremer's grey eyes fixed her.

'I'm the Lord Mayor of Copenhagen. I don't hold meetings in car parks. I told you. I've never spoken to him before.'

'What did he say?' Meyer asked.

'He started talking rubbish. He said he'd been helping me.'

'With what?'

'I didn't understand. He was talking about the key to a flat.'

'What flat?'

'I've no idea. I assumed he'd confused me with someone else.'

'You're the Lord Mayor of Copenhagen,' Lund said.

'I didn't know this man. I didn't understand what the hell he was talking about. Phillip . . .'

A tall, bearded figure had walked into the room. City Hall suit and tie.

'This is my private secretary, Phillip Bressau,' Bremer said. 'Since you seem to think this is important I'd like him to listen.'

Bremer shook his head.

'I don't understand. Why all these questions about a traffic accident?'

'It wasn't an accident,' Bressau said. 'You two are working on the Nanna case, right?'

'Is this true? He was killed?'

'We're looking into it,' Lund said.

'Dammit. I won't take that kind of evasive nonsense from my staff. I won't take it from you. What's going on here?'

'When Christensen spoke to you did he mention any names?'

'No! He realized he'd made a mistake. Then he walked off.'

Lund waited. Nothing more.

'Every month,' she said, 'five thousand kroner were paid into his wages. Above his salary.'

Bremer turned to Bressau, perplexed.

'No one can tell me what the money was for,' Lund went on.

'The mayor has nothing to do with this civil servant,' Bressau broke in. 'He worked for education—'

'Someone gave him the impression he was doing you favours, Bremer. To do with the flat in Store Kongensgade and the girl.'

'What?'

The old man sat on his comfy leather chair, rigid, astonished.

'Is this an accusation?' Bressau asked.

Meyer was swearing, his head in his hands.

'It's a question,' Lund said. 'I'm trying to find a connection here. We need your help . . .'

Poul Bremer was thinking.

'Did he mention a name?' Lund asked again.

'Is this about us or Troels Hartmann?'

Meyer leaned back in his chair and let out a long howl.

That shut them up.

'It's about murder,' Meyer cried. 'It's about a nineteen-year-old girl who was raped and then dumped inside a car and left to drown.'

Bremer and his civil servant stayed silent.

'It's about finding out what happened while all you fine and important people . . .' Meyer's hand waved around the grand office. '. . . do nothing but protect your backs.'

'Help us,' Lund pleaded.

Meyer pulled out a cigarette, lit it in the face of Bremer's furious complaints.

Then he blew smoke up towards the mosaics and gilt of the ceiling.

'Do what Lund says,' he added. 'Or I stay here all night.'

Poul Bremer wasn't like his election photos. He seemed older. Skin more florid. Eyes more tired.

'Tell Bressau what you want and he'll look into it,' he said. 'Keep me informed on a regular basis. I require that.'

They didn't move.

'Is that enough?' he asked.

Meyer took his feet off the table, stuck the cigarette between his lips, stood up.

'We'll see.'

On her own in the kitchen Pernille Birk Larsen listened to the radio news, keeping it quiet so that the boys in their bedroom couldn't hear.

'After the mother's appeal several witnesses have come forward in the Nanna case. The police have searched the Liberals' office and Troels Hartmann's home. Hartmann himself has been questioned.'

Lotte came through the door with some takeaway food from round the corner.

Pernille watched her start to open the boxes. She didn't want her sister in the house really. Not after the deceit over the club. But Theis was gone. She couldn't bear to ask another favour of her parents, who'd never liked him and would wear that told-you-so look for ever.

'Tomorrow we meet the cemetery manager at the grave,' she said in a whisper.

'OK.'

Lotte got some plates, forks and spoons.

'What about Mum and Dad?'

'It'll be just us.'

'Us?'

'You and me. And the boys.'

'What about Theis?'

She didn't answer.

'I know you're mad at him, Pernille. But you have to talk. You can't shut him out.'

Nothing.

'Maybe he shouldn't have packed her things without asking. But for God's sake—'

'This is none of your business.'

'He didn't do it to upset you! He did it because he wanted to help.'

'To help?'

'You've got to get past this. Don't you see? If you let it destroy more than it has already—'

'It . . .'

'I mean—'

'Someone killed Nanna!' Pernille said as loudly as she dared. 'It didn't happen yesterday. Last week. Last year.'

She stabbed her head with her finger.

'It happens now. Every day. You don't . . .'

She didn't feel hungry, didn't want any food.

Lotte said, 'I know they have to find him. But that's not more important than you and Theis and the boys.'

Pernille felt the fury rising inside her and realized she was growing to like it.

She glared at her sister. Lotte was still beautiful. Lotte never had kids, never had those kinds of cares. Never had a husband or anyone who stayed for long.

'Who are you to lecture me?' Pernille asked her. 'Who are you to tell me what to do?'

Lotte was starting to cry and it didn't matter.

'I'm your sister—'

'Nothing's more important. Not me. Not Theis. Not the boys. Not you—'

'Pernille.'

'If you'd told me what Nanna was up to I could have stopped her!'

Lotte sat at the table, hunched and tearful, silent, eyes downcast.

'I don't trust you any more than I trust him. How can I?'

Giggles from the bedroom. She wondered if Anton would finally have a dry night.

'Anton! Emil!' Pernille called. 'We've got dinner!'

The boys yelled gleefully.

425

'They shouldn't see you crying, Lotte,' she said. 'Either stop it or go.'

Lotte went to the bathroom, dried her eyes. Wondered about the coke in her handbag. Hated herself for even thinking of it.

Then she went back and picked at the food, listened to the boys laughing, watched Pernille glued to the TV.

At eight thirty she walked downstairs to the garage. Vagn Skærbæk was there, calling round anxiously.

He hadn't located Theis. Had no idea where he might be.

'Who did you phone?'

'As many as I trusted. I told them not to start any rumours. We don't want it all over Vesterbro.'

He and Theis were like brothers. Theis always dominant, but the two of them close. If anyone could find him . . .

'I'll take a drive round,' Skærbæk said. 'I can think of a few places—'

'What did he say when he came round your place?'

Skærbæk pulled on his jacket. Black, like Theis's, but cheaper.

'Nothing.'

'He must have said something—'

'He said nothing! I was at home watching TV and he rang the doorbell. He mumbled something about it all being his fault.'

'And you let him go?'

'What do you want me to do? Slap him round the head? Would you try that?'

'Vagn—'

'I didn't know she'd bitten his balls off. I went to get him a beer and he was gone.'

It was cold in the garage. Lotte was in the skimpy top she wore to the Heartbreak. She hugged herself and shivered.

'Does he know the urn's being buried tomorrow?'

'Yes. I guess. If Pernille told him.'

She was out of ideas.

Vagn Skærbæk took out his car keys.

'I'll drive around. I'll find him.'

Then a bleak aside, to himself more than her.

'I mean . . . it's not like it's the first time.'

*

Poul Bremer sat in front of the group leaders, the holders of the keys to City Hall, arguing for a formal investigation of Hartmann the following evening.

'I've always admired Troels as a hard-working and clever politician. But the evidence is against him and he seems unable to give a credible explanation. This is a sad occasion . . .'

Bremer looked at each of them, Jens Holck more than the others.

'We've no choice. We have to vote for his appearance before the Electoral Commission. He needs to explain himself.'

'Hartmann's not been charged,' Holck broke in. 'Why not leave this to the police?'

'We all know Troels. We all like him . . .'

'The whole council could have been sued if he'd pilloried the teacher the way you wanted,' Holck added. 'Should we risk doing the same to him?'

'I've known Troels longer than any of you. I understand how you feel.'

The statesman's smile.

'Especially since you were about to enter into an alliance with him.'

He came round and patted Holck on the back.

'Right, Jens? But parties aside, it's our duty to maintain the public's confidence in the political system. We have to ask ourselves how long our own credibility can withstand such a prominent member of our assembly being questioned daily as a suspect in a murder case. If we're to—'

The doors broke open. Hartmann stormed in.

'I'm sorry. Am I interrupting?'

'You weren't invited, Troels.'

'No,' Hartmann snarled. 'I wouldn't be. Have you told everyone the police are now investigating the case here? In the Rådhus? Did you tell them they're looking at the civil servants? That they interviewed you?'

Bremer stood his ground.

'This is a private meeting. You were the subject. That is why you weren't invited.'

Hartmann looked at the group around the table.

'If you've got questions ask them! Don't listen to this devious old bastard. Ask me!'

427

Bremer laughed.

'If that's what people wish. Have your say. While you can . . .'

Hartmann walked in front of them.

'I know you're worried about the damage. Reporting me to the Electoral Commission doesn't solve a thing. I've nothing to do with this case . . .'

'You'll find that out soon enough,' said Bremer.

Bremer's phone rang. He walked away to answer it, then went to the fax machine in the corner of the office.

'Someone bought Olav's services and his silence,' Hartmann went on. 'With the help of funds paid for by City Hall. Don't ask me how. The police are investigating.'

Bremer was coming back with a sheet of paper from the machine. He was reading it carefully.

Hartmann was in his stride.

'The Lord Mayor neglected to mention any of this information even though he knew of it. He wants to get rid of me to help his own campaign.'

'Oh, Troels,' Bremer said. 'You're so full of accusations for others, and silent when it comes to answering for yourself.'

'I will not—'

'We've traced the money Olav Christensen was receiving.'

He brandished the paper.

'Phillip Bressau came across it hidden in the accounts. He's given the records to the police. They're on their way. There. Are you happy with my recounting of the facts now?'

He passed the paper round the table.

'It's true the money came from the pay office,' he added. 'It was in connection with environmental reports, supposedly. Reports made for the schools service. Money for so-called consultation, paid for directly from the Mayor of Education's budget.'

Hartmann snatched the sheet as Jens Holck read it.

'Don't be ridiculous. I don't know every damned person who's on my payroll! Any more than you do. This is one more piece of nonsense.' Hartmann was floundering. 'It's a mistake. The police can clear it up.'

The people around the table were silent, wouldn't look at him.

'If I was using this man,' Hartmann yelled, 'would I put him on my own payroll? It's a fabrication . . .'

Bremer took his seat at the head of the table, watched Hartmann ranting.

'A fabrication,' Hartmann repeated more quietly. 'Like everything else. From the beginning. Jens . . .'

He took Holck's arm.

'You know I wouldn't do this.'

Holck didn't budge.

'Someone's changing the damned records. Someone in this place—'

The door opened. Meyer was there with his big ears and miserable unshaven face.

They all turned and looked and waited.

'For God's sake . . .' Hartmann began.

Meyer rapped on the shining wood.

'Time for walkies, Troels,' he said.

The melee was there already. Flashing cameras, shrieking reporters. Meyer told a cameraman to piss off. Svendsen got his hand on Hartmann's head as he thrust him into the back of the squad car parked on the cobbled courtyard beneath the golden statue of Absalon.

Rie Skovgaard and Morten Weber watched from the gates. The pack ran after the blue police car with 'Politi' painted on the side in white. Hartmann sat slumped in the back, heading back to headquarters again.

'This time, Hartmann,' Meyer said from the front seat, 'you tell us the truth or you will spend the night sweating in a cell.'

Back in the committee room Bremer walked over to Holck who was on his own, smoking by the window, watching the commotion outside.

'If you want a life in politics, Jens,' he whispered, 'you'll vote with me.'

Holck looked pale and worried. He chewed on the cigarette. Said nothing.

'And if you're smart you'll get the rest of Hartmann's lapdogs to do the same. Right now I could cut you all loose if I wanted and rule this place on my own.'

'Poul—'

'No, Jens. Don't talk.'

The old man looked cruel and vengeful. There was an opportunity here and he was determined to take it.

'He got out of there before,' Holck said anyway.

'Not this time. But you choose.'

His voice grew louder. The others looked at him the way they used to do. In meek obedience.

'All of you,' Bremer said, 'must choose. Do it wisely this time.'

From the corridor Lund watched as Svendsen dealt with Hartmann in the detention room.

Standard procedure. Happened every day. But not to a man in a fine business suit, a politician of Hartmann's stature.

Svendsen counted out his belongings. Seven hundred kroner and some change. Twenty euros. Two credit cards and a phone.

'Now remove your jacket and put it on the chair.'

A uniformed officer wrote down a tally of the items.

'Your tie,' Svendsen said.

They watched.

'Shoes on the table.'

Hartmann did it.

'Now lift your arms. I need to search you.'

The uniformed officer got up and twisted the venetian blinds. Lund saw no more.

Back to the office, Brix in a chair, looking at the paperwork.

'So we can prove Hartmann was behind the payments to the civil servant?' he asked.

'It's a bit complicated,' Meyer said. 'But from what the Bressau guy came up with it looks that way.'

'Has he said anything?'

'Not a word.'

Brix looked at Lund.

'We should focus on the hit-and-run driver,' she said. 'We know that couldn't be Hartmann.'

'I want you on the Nanna case. That's Hartmann. Not the civil servant.'

Lund picked up the paper from Bremer's press man.

'I talked to people in Hartmann's department. No one's even

heard of this arrangement. Yet Bressau can pull it out of the files in five minutes flat.'

'So he kept it quiet,' Meyer said.

'Hartmann tried to fire Olav! He gave us his name!'

Brix didn't budge.

'If he's innocent why won't he say so?'

'I don't know! But this doesn't add up.'

'Then we bring in the prosecutor,' Brix said. 'Maybe that'll loosen his tongue. One way or another that stuck-up bastard's going to talk.'

She played with Meyer's toy car, listened to the little siren.

'Are we here to find Nanna Birk Larsen's murderer? Or to make some kind of political point for the man who runs City Hall?'

Brix smiled. She hadn't seen that much before.

'Just this once I'll forget you said that, Lund. Perhaps, when it comes to Hartmann, you lack your customary objectivity.'

'What the hell does that mean?'

Brix turned to Meyer for support. Meyer stared at the desk.

'Thanks,' Lund threw at him. 'Great teamwork.'

Then she picked up her bag, walked out of the office, slamming the door behind her.

Brix watched her go.

'You can do it yourself, Meyer. Get on with it.' The smile again. 'Good work.'

'Maybe we should listen to her, chief.'

'Why?'

'When Lund gets an idea . . .'

Brix waited.

'There's usually something in it. Haven't you noticed?'

Lennart Brix looked at him with sorrowful eyes.

'Oh dear,' he said. 'You were doing so well too.'

'What?'

'Two steps forward. One step back. Don't stumble again. You can't afford it.'

On her way out Lund stopped to chase the night team.

'Call any accident repair shops. Tell them to look for a white estate. Damage to the front and left wing. Let me know.'

Morten Weber was waiting in the corridor.

'You've got to listen to me, Lund. This is out of control.'

'Talk to Jan Meyer. He's on duty. I'm not.'

'Hartmann didn't kill that girl. It's absurd.'

'So he should tell us where he was. It's not hard.'

Weber was struggling with something. This interested her.

'It is hard.'

'Why?'

'He's a proud man. He needs his dignity. Pathetic I know but there you are. It doesn't make him a murderer.'

She waited.

'Troels isn't as strong or as confident as he seems. You know that, Lund. You can read people.'

'This isn't about reading people.'

'He's a fool sometimes. I don't know why I put up with it.'

'You should tell this to the judge. I don't think it'll work. It doesn't for me.'

She walked towards the exit. Weber followed.

'Let me talk to him,' he pleaded.

'You must be joking.'

'Jesus, Lund. He's about to be excluded from the election! It's the only thing that matters to him.'

She stopped.

'Is this a joke to you people? A young girl dead. Raped. Murdered. And every time we ask you what's going on you lie and duck and dodge our questions?'

To his credit Weber looked embarrassed.

'Well?' she added. 'Is it a joke? A kid? Battered then dumped in a car to drown? Do you want to see the photos, Morten?'

She took his arm.

'Come on. Let's look at them and laugh.'

Lund was getting angry. It didn't happen often. She liked the release.

'We've got ones of the autopsy too if you'd like—'

'Stop this, Lund. It's beneath you.'

Bright eyes staring, hand on his jacket.

'Beneath me? Nothing's beneath me. Not if I can find out who killed Nanna Birk Larsen. If you know where Hartmann was tell me. Or else get out of here. Stop wasting my time.'

Weber did nothing for a moment, then shook his head.

'I can't. I'm sorry.'

'Sleep well,' she said and showed him to the door.

Lund picked up Mark from a party, drove him back to Vibeke's listening to the radio. Hartmann had been arrested on suspicion of Nanna's murder. He was going to be reported to the Electoral Commission and stripped of his right to stand for election.

'Does it have to be so loud?' Mark asked.

She turned it off.

'Was the party fun?'

The Birk Larsen case felt hardwired inside her head.

A long, long pause then he said, with a pained drawl, 'It was OK.'

'I know you haven't been at school all week.'

She looked at him for an answer, got none.

'I know it's difficult to go back after you've said goodbye. I'm sorry. But you can't skip school. Mark?'

He was gazing out of the window, watching the rainy night pass by.

'I won't accept it. Do you understand?'

He thought for a while.

'Is it OK if I go and stay at Dad's for a couple of days?'

She stared at the black wet road ahead.

'When did you talk to Carsten about this?'

'Is it OK?'

'No. It's not OK. When did you talk to him?'

'What does it matter? I spend all my time with Grandma anyway. Not with you.'

'You know what your father's like. He promises something and then . . . he forgets.'

He sighed and stared at the dashboard.

'You know how upset you get when that happens. I won't have it. They only just moved here. They've got things to do.'

'He said it was OK.'

'When did he talk to you about this? When?'

'I'm not one of your suspects, Mum.'

'Where were you all week anyway? What did you do?'

His face was back at the window.

'Everything's fine at Dad's house. They've got a room for me.'

'It's still not going to happen.'

He thrust his feet deep into the footwell, locked his arms together. Torn between child and teenager.

'I know it's been difficult, Mark. But don't worry. I'll deal with it. Nothing's changed. We're still the same.'

'It's not the same. You damn well know it.'

'Mark—'

'I don't want to talk about this.'

'Mark—'

'It's my life!' he yelled. 'You don't own me.'

Eight

Saturday, 15th November

Nine in the morning, outside Vibeke's flat. Mark with his things. Skis and hockey gear. Sports bags and a small suitcase.

Hands in pockets, looking older. Lund couldn't stop herself coming close to him, carefully running up his zip, straightening the collar of his jacket.

'It's all right, Mum.'

'No it's not. It's cold.'

Winter coming on. A bite in the wind. Another year passing. Mark growing older, growing further away from her.

He didn't shrink from her touch. She was grateful for that.

Eyes locked on the distance, impatient to go.

'Dad's coming.'

Shiny red Saab. Sports wheels. Darkened windows. Men's toys.

Mark looked at it and smiled.

'See you,' he said, then picked up his things, threw them on the back seat, climbed into the front.

Carsten wound down the window. He looked good. Dark business coat, different glasses. Hair too long for the police, but the police he'd left long behind. Along with her. Carsten was ambitious in a way she never quite understood. It was about money and position. Not achievement, not how Lund measured it.

The man she once married, once slept with and loved, smiled at her briefly, a touch of regret, of shame even in his placid, managerial face.

And once you hit me, Lund recalled. Just once. And no, I never asked for it.

The shiny red Saab rolled across the cobbles.

Lund waved and smiled at both of them. Stopped the moment they were round the corner.

'Hello?'

Meyer was behind her, his car a few feet away. She never noticed.

'Is he moving out?'

'Just for a few days,' she said a little sharply.

'First the Swede. Then junior. I hope your mother stays put.'

She stared at him. Cruelty wasn't part of Meyer's odd personality. He was both simple and complex at the same time. In a way she liked that.

'Any news about the car?'

'No.'

'We need to check the Rådhus garage again.'

'Maybe. Brix came up with something. I don't know where.'

She said nothing.

'He's the chief, Lund. You've got to stop fighting him. He's not taking orders.'

'Brix doesn't need to take orders. He knows what they want.'

The leather biker's jacket again. It was getting scruffy.

'What's that supposed to mean?'

'It's how it works. You don't think Poul Bremer calls Brix and tells him what to do. He doesn't have to. Brix knows.'

She knew too.

'Fix Hartmann. Any way he can.'

She'd thought this through, tallied the idea with every small occurrence in headquarters that had puzzled her.

'It's called power. And all of us . . .' Theis and Pernille Birk Larsen too. 'We don't really count.'

'Brix found some information on a property Hartmann owns. He's got a cottage he didn't tell us about.'

A sheet of paper came out of his jacket pocket. Lund looked at it. Pointed at the stamp of the City Hall property register department at the top.

'I wonder how we came to have that.'

'We have to look. Brix is there already. Do you want to come?'

The cottage was ten kilometres from the city near Dragør, not far from Kemal's more modest allotment. Six cars, two unmarked, stood around the drive. Red tape marked the garden boundary. A single-storey wooden bungalow, modest and run-down, almost engulfed by a ragged wood of conifers.

Svendsen was leading the team. Lund and Meyer walked in, listening to him.

'Hartmann inherited the place from his wife. Looks like they started to spend money on it then gave up when she died.'

The kitchen was a mess. Dirty plates over a modern stove. The only light came from the open door and some floodlights the forensic team had assembled.

Lund looked at the windows. Every one was blocked. By sheets. By a duvet. By tablecloths.

'The weekend Nanna disappeared two neighbours saw a black car in the driveway. This is where he was.'

In the living room two officers in white suits were tramping round marking items of interest, taking photos.

'The description fits the campaign car Nanna was found in.'

The windows here had mattresses piled up against the glass.

'Did anyone see him?' Meyer asked.

'No. But we've got fresh prints. They're his. And there's this.'

He picked up an evidence bag from the table. The evening newspaper from Friday, October the thirty-first.

'It was taped over the broken window.'

Lund looked at the shattered glass at the top of one of the long frames by the sunny side of the bungalow. There was blood on some of the shards that lay scattered round the polished wooden floorboards.

Brix marched in.

'Hartmann needed somewhere isolated,' he said. 'He got it. He didn't have a key with him so he broke the window to get in.'

Lund took a cushion off the sofa, sniffed it. The place had a lingering, residual smell. It was stronger on the soft cotton of the cushion.

'Then he covered the windows so no one could see what he was up to,' Brix added.

Svendsen pointed back to the kitchen.

'The utility room has a cement floor. That's where he kept her tied up. There's blood there.'

She walked through to the next room. A double bed. Crumpled sheets. Blood there too but not much of it.

'What did you find here?' she asked.

Svendsen glanced at Brix.

'We're still looking, Lund.'

Brix checked his watch.

'I'm going back. When you get some hard evidence let me know. I'll put it in front of the judge.'

He walked up to Lund, caught her eye as she scanned the room.

'Can I count on you?'

'Always,' she said.

Then he left with Svendsen, the two of them talking in low, inaudible voices.

Meyer stayed, studying the room much as she had, following her lead.

There was a purple towel wrapped up tightly and stuffed beneath the bottom of the bathroom door.

Lund nodded at an air vent in the wall. A balled-up newspaper had been shoved into the grille.

'Forensics didn't mention gas,' he said. 'This place stinks of it. If Nanna was here there'd be traces.'

Lund shook her head.

'Would you leave your car out in the drive where anyone could see it?'

'This isn't right,' Meyer said. 'I don't give a shit what Brix thinks. We'll check out the hit-and-run driver.'

She walked outside, took a deep breath. The woods reminded her of the Pentecost Forest not so far away.

'What do we tell Brix?' he asked.

'He's busy talking to the judge. Let's not disturb him.'

Pernille Birk Larsen sat in the kitchen, fawn raincoat on, mind wandering, letting the phone ring.

It was Lotte who finally answered it.

'The undertaker needs to talk to you, Pernille.'

She couldn't take her eyes off the things around her. The table, the photos, the things on the wall. And through the door Nanna's room, now back as it was. Empty yet preserved, like a shrine.

'Tell him I'm on my way,' she said, and went to the door.

Downstairs the men were working as always. Vagn Skærbæk supervising carts and slings, crates and boxes.

He followed her to the car.

'Have you heard from Theis?'

'No.'

'So you don't know what the hell . . . ?'

His voice died under the force of her gaze.

'There's an office job from Brøndby to Enigheden. Is it being dealt with?'

'I sent Franz and Rudi there.'

He held the door as she climbed into the car.

'Maybe you should call him, Pernille.'

She placed her hands on the wheel, didn't look at him.

'I'm grateful you're taking care of the business, Vagn. Stay out of this.'

That plaintive, pale face at the window. The silver chain. The too-young, eager worried look.

'Yeah. Well. I'll try to get hold of him. If the two of you . . .'

A car pulled in behind her. Pernille Birk Larsen's head fell against the wheel.

It was Lund.

'I was told your sister was here.'

'Why do you want to know?'

'I want to ask her some questions.'

She made for the garage and the apartment.

'How sure are you it's Hartmann?'

Lund didn't answer.

'The reward helped, didn't it?'

There was a note of desperation, of guilt in Pernille Birk Larsen's voice.

Lund looked at her and said, 'I can't talk about the case. Sorry.'

Then she walked inside.

Lotte Holst was doing the washing. She looked as mutinous and unhelpful as her sister.

'I've told you everything. What else is there to say?'

'You're the only one who knew about this affair. I still don't understand—'

'It was Hartmann, wasn't it?' Lotte asked as she ran through the boys' clothes, stuffing them into the machine.

'What happened over the summer?'

The sister kept sorting the washing in silence.

'I read the emails on the nightclub's dating site,' Lund said, taking the printouts from her bag.

'I don't work there any more.'

'The emails are odd. He still wants to see her but her answers become more and more infrequent. Did she tell you it was over?'

Lotte hesitated.

'No. But she was going cold on him. I could see that. Maybe there was someone else. I don't know.'

She threw in some powder, closed the door, turned on the machine.

'Nanna was a big romantic. The way teenagers are. Not that she thought she was a teenager. I think she maybe went from one big love to another. Probably in the space of a week.'

'Did Hartmann meet her at the nightclub?'

'I never saw him there.'

'What about the first weekend of August? Lotte. This is important.'

She walked back into the living room, said nothing.

'On the Friday,' Lund went on, 'he writes that he's leaving the next day. He's desperate to see her. He called her. But—'

'But what?'

'We can't trace any calls by Hartmann. He didn't go anywhere that weekend.'

Lotte got her bag, pulled out her diary, checked it.

'We had a VIP event that day. You get big tips.'

'What happened?'

'I do remember something. I had to ask her to put her phone onto silent. It was going all the time with the messages.'

'Who from?'

'I don't know. She wouldn't answer them.'

Lotte went quiet.

'What?' Lund asked.

'I remember she asked me to take her orders out for her. She had to talk to someone outside. I was pissed off. She was always asking me to cover. Sticking her nose into things. Taking my clothes.'

A sudden flash of anger.

'Nanna wasn't an angel. I know I'm not supposed to say that—'

'Did you see the man she met?'

440

'There was a car. I went and looked. I wanted to know what was so important I had to do Nanna's work for her.'

'What kind of car?'

'A car. I don't know.'

'Saloon? Estate? What colour?'

'I don't know.'

'Did you see the driver?'

'No.'

'The make? Anything distinctive. Any . . .'

Lund's voice was running away from her and she couldn't stop it. Lotte was shaking her head.

'Nothing at all,' Lund said. 'Are you sure?'

One thought.

'It was white, I think.'

Rie Skovgaard read the letter and said, 'That didn't take long.'

'What is it?'

She showed Morten Weber. A formal note from the Rådhus secretariat demanding they vacate their office premises by the following morning.

'They can't do this.' Weber waved the letter in the air. 'They can't do this! The Electoral Commission don't even meet until tonight.'

'Oh for Christ's sake. He's in jail facing a murder charge. What do you expect?'

'The lawyer's going to talk to him. We'll find a way out.'

She looked ragged, at the end of her tether. Hair a mess. No make-up. Tired, angry eyes.

'As long as Troels doesn't talk there is no way out.'

Two forensic officers in white suits knocked on the open door, walked in, began to look at the room. Skovgaard marched into Hartmann's adjoining office. Weber followed.

'Can't you have a word with your father, Rie? He's got connections.'

'Connections?'

'Yes.'

'Tell me what happened. What did Troels do that weekend?'

'I don't know—'

'Don't lie to me! I called you to say Troels was missing. I'd no idea where. You said he'd gone drinking.'

'Rie—'

'You weren't worried because you knew where he was.'

'It isn't—'

'He told you. He couldn't tell me. Do you know how that feels?'

He didn't have an answer.

'What was he doing?' Skovgaard asked again.

Weber sighed, sat down, looked old and tired.

'Troels is my oldest friend.'

'And what am I exactly?'

'I promised him I'd never say a word!' He looked at her. 'To anyone.'

'What's the big secret then? Another woman? Are we going through all this because he can't bring himself to tell me he's screwing around again?'

'No.' Weber shook his head. 'Of course not.'

'So it was his wife then? Something to do with her?'

He didn't meet her furious eyes.

'Answer me. I know it was their anniversary. What did he do?'

Weber was shaking, sweating. He needed a shot. Needed a drink.

'What,' Rie Skovgaard asked again, 'did he do?'

Lund waited for Hartmann in the same visiting room Theis Birk Larsen had recently used. He arrived in a blue prison suit, was made to remove his shoes, watched carefully throughout by the guard.

She sat, hands on her jeans, too hot in the woollen jumper. Black on white, a rolling pattern of snowflakes.

He hadn't shaved. Looked broken, a shadow of the bold and handsome politician of the Rådhus.

It took a while but finally Troels Hartmann pulled up a chair.

Eyes shining, desperate, Lund looked at him and said, 'I really need your help. The night in the flat . . . did you notice a white estate car?'

Hartmann stared at her, silent.

'Was it in the courtyard when you left? Or in the street?'

He looked out of the window at the thin winter sun. She didn't know whether Hartmann was listening or not.

'Does anyone at City Hall drive a white estate?'

'As far as I know, Lund, I've been arrested for driving a black car. Why are you taunting me with this nonsense?'

'It's important.'

'If you're looking for a white car why the hell am I in jail?'

'Because you put yourself here. We found your wife's cottage. I know what you did that night.'

Hartmann's blue-clad arms closed round his chest.

'Rolled-up towels under the door. Mattresses in front of the windows. Newspapers in all the cracks and an open gas oven.'

He sat mute and sullen.

'Maybe you were interrupted. Maybe you chickened out. I don't know.'

His face was back to the window.

'Is it so demeaning for a man to say he got drunk and tried to kill himself? Would that lose you votes? Or Rie Skovgaard? Or just your own self-esteem?'

The man in the blue prison suit was somewhere else.

'Was it worth the price?'

No answer.

'I don't really care, Hartmann. I want your help. Then you can get out of here and play your games in the Rådhus. While we try to work out who among you murdered Nanna Birk Larsen.'

'You don't know anything,' he muttered.

'Don't I? It was in your diary. When your wife got sick the doctors told her she needed treatment. She refused. She was pregnant. She knew it could harm the child. So . . .'

He was looking at her now and for the first time she thought she saw Troels Hartmann frightened.

'I think you feel guilty. I think it nags you every day. What if we'd said yes? She'd be alive. Maybe the child would be too. If not there's always the chance of another.'

His blue eyes shone with anger.

'I think you feel guilty,' she said again. 'And that night you realized that, however hard you worked at your precious hollow world inside the Rådhus, your life, the one you loved, was never coming back. So you gave up.'

Lund nodded.

'Strong, fearless, decent Troels Hartmann let his demons win.

And the memory of that frightens you so much you'd rather rot in jail than admit it. So . . .'

She sat back, smiled at him. Relieved that finally, in this long tangle of lost threads, one stray line had finally reached some semblance of completion.

'Are you going to help me?'

She waited. Nothing.

'You flatter yourself you've got so much to lose. You haven't, Troels. Honestly.'

Meyer had a list of white cars using the City Hall garage.

Lund took some headache pills and didn't look at it. She'd tried so hard with Hartmann. She'd joined the dots and let him know it. And still nothing changed. Still the route to Nanna's killer lay hidden in the shadows.

If he wasn't going to talk he could damn well rot in a cell.

'I checked the barrier,' Meyer went on. 'A car left the garage right after Olav talked to Bremer.'

She reached for the paper.

'Which one?'

'Second from the bottom.'

'Phillip Bressau. He's Bremer's private secretary. What do we know about him?'

'Wife and two kids. Bremer's right-hand man.'

'And the car?'

'Hasn't been back to the garage since. He came to work in his wife's yesterday.'

'Bressau.'

She got up, reached for her bag.

Five figures by a hole in the ground, brown earth shovelled over green grass. A cold and sunny winter's day. Pigeons flapping in the bare trees. Anton and Emil in their black warm clothes. Pernille pale and severe in the fawn raincoat. Lotte dressed too brightly.

The cemetery superintendent wore a green industrial suit and galoshes. He held out the turquoise urn.

So small, inside nothing but dust.

'Do you want to place it?' he asked.

Pernille took the vase, bent down, lowered it into the ground with trembling fingers.

Stood back. Looked. Felt as if she were in a dream.

'Is it Nanna?' Anton asked.

'Yes,' Lotte said. 'She's ashes now.'

'Why?'

Lotte hesitated.

'So it's easier to get to heaven.'

The boys looked at each other and frowned. They never liked Lotte's stories.

'Isn't that true, Pernille?'

'What?'

Lotte tried to smile at her.

'Yes,' Pernille said. 'It's true.'

'When's Dad coming?' Emil asked.

The cemetery man was carrying over a large wreath with a crown of roses.

'He'll be here later,' Lotte said.

'Why isn't he here now?'

Pernille was staring at the wreath.

'What's that? I didn't ask for it.'

He shrugged. Placed it by the hole for the urn.

'It arrived this morning.'

'Who sent it?'

'I didn't see a card.'

'It's lovely,' Lotte butted in.

Pernille was shaking her head.

'You have to know where it came from.'

Lotte had some single white roses. She handed one each to the boys and told them to place them by the urn. They obeyed. Small black figures in the sun. They might have been playing on a chilly beach by the Øresund.

'Well done,' she said when they had finished.

Pernille stared around her. The small square lake full of rotting wood and algae. The monuments with their mould and fungus. The place stank of decay. She began to feel sick.

Then she bent down, picked up the giant wreath, gave it to the cemetery man.

'Take it away. I don't want it here.'

Lotte was staring at the grass. The boys looked scared.

'I don't want this plot,' Pernille said. 'I don't like it. There must be another one.'

With the wreath in his arms the man in the green suit looked embarrassed.

'You chose this one.'

'I don't want to bury her here. Find another place.'

'Pernille,' Lotte said. 'It's lovely. We all agreed. It's perfect.'

Voice rising, Pernille Birk Larsen glared at them all.

'I don't want this wreath. I don't want this plot.'

'There's nothing I can do,' the man said. 'If you want somewhere else you have to talk to the office.'

'You talk to the office! I paid you, didn't I?'

She walked away and stared at the small lake.

The rotting wood. The algae.

A figure in scarlet striding along the path.

Vagn Skærbæk took one look at Pernille and marched straight up to Lotte.

'Have you heard from him?' he asked.

'No. Where is he?'

He glanced at the woman by the water.

'A wreath arrived without a name,' Lotte whispered. 'She's getting all sorts of ideas. I don't know . . .'

Skærbæk took the wreath, walked to the water's edge.

'Pernille. We bought it. Rudi and me had a collection at work. I'm sorry. We didn't know what to write so we just asked them to deliver it.'

She looked at him, expressionless.

He held out the laurel wreath with its crown of roses.

'It's from us.'

She shook her head and went back to looking at the dead water.

'When's Dad coming?' Emil bleated.

On the other side of Vesterbro, in one of the poorer, rougher, dirtier areas he used to frequent as a young ambitious thug, Theis Birk Larsen was drinking. Long glasses of strong lager from the Vesterbro Bryghus. A shot of akvavit.

The way it was. The way the long days passed before Pernille.

Chasing money on the street. Working with the dealers and the gangs. Snatching at whatever might be passing.

There was a time he could have walked into this bar and silenced them all with a stare. But that was long gone. None knew him now. The thug of old had mutated into the industrious, decent father with a small business seven blocks away, one that kept him away from these old haunts and these old habits.

His big hand gripped the cold glass. The beer went down to a rhythm. Blocking the pain not killing it. But that was enough.

Behind he heard the clatter of billiard balls, the foul-mouthed chatter of the young kids doing what he once had.

Maybe even worse.

These were bad times even though he tried to pretend otherwise. The hunt for money and opportunity. The desperate business of staying alive. Life had never been harder and no shell a man might build could keep him safe from that fact. Or protect his family.

Theis Birk Larsen smoked and drank and tried to still his thoughts, listening to the childish too-loud pop music on the radio and the clatter of billiard balls on the tables.

Somewhere an urn with what was left of Nanna was disappearing into the earth.

Nothing he could say or do would change that. He'd failed her. Failed them all.

He finished the beer, head starting to spin. Looked round. Once he'd been king of these places. His voice, his fists had ruled. Another Theis. A different, harder man.

Would he have saved her? Was that the lesson he was supposed to learn? That a man was what he was, however much he tried to change, to conform, to obey, to be that shapeless, untouchable thing called good.

The teacher, Kemal, had forgotten his roots too. And paid the price.

If only . . .

He lurched to his feet, staggered towards the exit, stumbling against a kid by the billiard table.

Birk Larsen pushed him roughly to one side the way he always did once upon a time. With a warning and a curse.

Stumbled on. Didn't see the outstretched foot of the kid to follow. Fell hard and grunting to the floor.

Memories.

So many fights and none he lost. Some that went so far . . .

He rolled through the muck and cigarette ends on the floor, listening to their laughter. Groaned as he got to his feet.

Snatched the cue from the kid who'd tripped him, held it like a sword, a weapon. Like the sledgehammer he'd wielded above the shrieking, bleeding foreigner in the depot, Vagn Skærbæk whimpering all the while.

The kid had a black jacket and a black woollen hat. An expression that was both scared and defiant.

Theis Birk Larsen knew this face. He'd lived with him all his life.

So he swore and threw the cue on the table, then staggered outside, wondering where to go.

These streets, once home, were foreign to him now. He got to a deserted archway, started to take a piss. Had barely finished when they pounced. Five of them, heads in hoods, fists flying. A billiard cue thrashing him round the head.

'Hold him,' someone screamed, and two weak arms tried to pin Birk Larsen to the wall he'd pissed against. A boot flew at his groin.

Kids.

He threw off two, got the third by the scruff of the neck, launched himself across the narrow street, pinioned the weak and skinny figure against the crumbling plaster of the wall.

Big fist pulled back, ready to strike. One hard, vicious punch and this was a day the kid would never forget, would leave enough damage to last the rest of his meagre life.

Birk Larsen held back the blow and stared.

The hood had fallen. The face that looked back at him, so full of hatred, was a girl's. No more than sixteen. Ring through the nose, tattoos over the eyes.

A girl.

In that moment they fell on him with such a fury he knew he was lost to them.

Boots and hands and knees. The cue and flailing fingers. They took his wallet, his keys. They swore at him, spat at him, pissed on him. Birk Larsen did what he'd never done before, rolled into a ball like a victim, cowered on the ground. A pose he'd seen so often, but never for himself.

One hard blow to the head and the day grew dark.

Then a voice, older, angrier, crying.

'What are you doing? What the . . . ?'

He lay in the gutter, drunk and hurting.

And they were gone.

A bleeding hand went to the wall. He staggered to his feet.

A woman. Middle-aged. Holding a bike.

'Are you all right?'

Head against the cold brickwork Theis Birk Larsen started to throw up. Blood and beer. Some of the blackness inside him.

'I'm calling the police,' the woman said.

He vomited some more. Put a hand to her shoulder. She shied away from him, wriggled out of his grasp.

'No police,' he muttered, coughing, then stumbled out towards the light.

She left him. Alone again he found he couldn't stand. Like a felled tree Theis Birk Larsen tumbled slowly onto the broken stones of Vesterbro, knelt there, knelt then keeled over, letting the darkness roll over him like the black swampy waters of the Kalvebod Fælled.

Back in the interview room, Hartmann faced his lawyer.

'The evidence is circumstantial, Troels. On this I wouldn't expect the judge to extend your custody. But if they find something in your cottage . . .'

He sat in his blue prison suit, silent and miserable.

'The more you tell me, the more I can help you.'

Nothing.

'Do you understand?'

Nothing.

She tidied her papers, uttered a small dyspeptic sigh of disapproval.

'Well then. I'll come back tomorrow. Perhaps you'll be of a mind to talk to me then.'

He watched her sort the documents into a pile and place them in her briefcase.

'What's going on at City Hall?'

She stopped and gazed at him.

'What do you think? The Electoral Commission has gone along with Bremer's wishes. They've made their final decision.'

'Final? You're sure about that?'

She had a hard-set face.

'I'm a criminal lawyer. Not a political one. As I understand it the decision is made. It simply needs to be approved by the council tonight.'

The lawyer stared at him.

'Then you're gone, Troels. Shame. I put money into your campaign. What on earth was I thinking?'

He was barely listening.

'What time's the meeting?'

The woman folded her arms.

'I'm glad you've decided to talk to me. Perhaps we could discuss your defence?'

'Can you get me a copy of the council constitution?'

A pause, then, 'Why?'

'I need to know something about the Electoral Commission. I need the detail—'

'Troels! You're facing a murder charge! Have you lost your mind?'

A grim smile, a second long, no more.

'No. I haven't. Get me Brix. Tell him I'm ready to talk. I'll let him know what I did that weekend.'

She reached into her bag and retrieved her notepad.

'Finally. Let's hear it.'

The smile again. Longer this time, and more confident.

'I'm sorry. I don't have time.'

He snatched the pad from her and started writing.

'I want you to contact the prosecutor. Ensure we have a meeting as soon as possible. It's important the police drop the charges before the end of the afternoon.'

'You can't get out of here for another day at least.'

He finished the note.

'Give this to Morten.'

'I can't.'

'All it says is that he should tell the truth. That's what they want, isn't it? That's what you want.'

She hesitated.

'I have to get out of here by tonight. Please help me.' He held the note across the table. 'And thanks for the contribution.'

*

Phillip Bressau was on the phone when Meyer and Lund walked into his office.

He put his hand over the receiver.

'The mayor's not here.'

'No problem,' Meyer said. 'We came for you.'

'Can't this wait until tomorrow?'

'Five minutes. Then you're done.'

They sat around a coffee table, Lund taking notes, meek and obedient like a secretary.

'Before the poster party that Friday,' Meyer said. 'There was a gathering in Hartmann's office. You went along?'

Bressau was neatly dressed for a Saturday. Well-pressed suit, blue shirt, tie.

'Yes. For a while.'

'Did you see Hartmann there?'

'No. I didn't stay. Work to do.What is this?'

'Just routine,' Lund said. 'When you met with Hartmann on the third of August . . .'

'What?'

'Hartmann says you met that weekend.'

'I didn't meet Hartmann.'

Meyer looked at Lund.

'Are you sure?' Lund asked.

'Absolutely. Is that what he said?'

'Yes.'

'It can't be right.'

Bressau pulled a diary out of his jacket.

'No. August the third I was in Latvia on an official visit with the mayor. We left on Saturday morning. Hartmann wasn't a member of the delegation.'

'Well, there you go,' Lund said and scribbled something.

'Is that it?'

Bressau got up from the table.

'Not quite,' Meyer said. 'Can I have your car keys?'

'What?'

'We'll sort out a loan.'

'It's not here.'

'Where is it?'

'Why do you need my car?'

'I'm nosy like that,' Meyer told him.

Footsteps at the door. Poul Bremer marched in, glared at them, said, 'What the hell's going on here?'

Bressau shrugged.

'They're questioning me now.'

Jan Meyer laughed.

'You people. You're so sensitive. We just have some problems with Hartmann's movements. That's all. Really—'

'Is that why you've been questioning the security staff about Bressau's car?'

Poul Bremer looked furious. The two cops fell silent.

'Nothing happens here without me knowing,' the old man said. 'Looks like I'm going to be talking to your boss again.'

Bremer nodded at the door.

'Close it behind you, please.'

On the way back to headquarters Lund put out a call for Bressau's car. A white estate, registration number YJ 23 585.

'I want the car taken in for forensic investigation.'

Meyer was driving. Not so fast any more. No cigarettes. No banana.

'If he called Nanna twenty-one times from Latvia someone must have noticed,' Lund said.

Meyer nodded.

'There were ten people on that little jamboree,' he said. 'Seven were businessmen.'

'Anyone who wasn't in Bremer's camp?'

'Just the one. Jens Holck from the Moderates.'

She remembered the figure in black, scuttling out of Hartmann's poster party in the TV reporter's video.

'Let's get his address,' Lund said.

When Theis Birk Larsen came to he was in a hard single bunk bed in a small whitewashed room that stank of stale booze, men and sweat. Bedrolls and backpacks littered the floor. There were others around him. Half-naked men under thin sheets, snoring and groaning.

His limbs ached. He was covered in cuts and bruises.

The door opened. Someone walked through and said, 'I see you're awake.'

A light came on. The man crouched by the side of the bunk. He had an ancient brown cardigan and long white hair. The lined and whiskery face of a fallen saint.

'How are you feeling?'

'Where are my things?'

'You got beaten up. They took most of your stuff.'

He half-sat up in the bed. The bunk above was so low he could go no further.

'Where am I?'

'The Holy Cross hostel. I'm the duty warden. You were lying in a doorway in Skydebanegade. You didn't want to go to the hospital. You didn't want to call home. So we brought you here. Nothing broken. We checked.'

He tried to struggle out of the bed but couldn't.

'You talked about your daughter.'

Back on the hard mattress, staring at the iron frame, thinking, hurting.

'You're Theis Birk Larsen,' the warden said. 'Some of the Vesterbro men know you. You had a reputation I gather.'

Birk Larsen wiped his hand across his face, looked at the blood.

'It's OK. Stay where you are. I'll get you some soup.'

One last effort. He took hold of the iron frame.

'No. I can't stay.'

On the edge of the bed. No boots. No coat. Nothing of his he could see. Just a damaged man of middle age, once king of the quarter, now an old and bloody fool.

'A night here would be for the best,' the man said.

Birk Larsen tried to move and couldn't. With a long, pained groan he fell back on the sheets.

'Maybe we can help, Theis.'

'No you can't,' he said straight off.

'Maybe . . .'

'I said you can't.'

Birk Larsen's powerful hand, cuts on the knuckles, bruises on the wrist, rose, pointed to a crucifix in the corner.

'You can't help and he can't either.'

A fleeting expression on the man's grey and bloodless face. It wasn't pleasant.

'I'll get you some soup then,' he said.

The arguments at the cemetery went on and on, and were never resolved. It was dark by the time they left. Lotte drove. The boys sat silent and scared in the back.

Pernille watched the city lights as they threaded through the Saturday traffic. She hadn't spoken since the blazing row in the cemetery office. Vagn had returned to the depot to work on some orders. Lotte felt left in charge.

'What do two hungry boys want for dinner?' she asked as brightly as she could.

They'd pass Tivoli on the way. The fairground would be lit. If she'd had the money she'd have taken them there out of desperation.

'I don't know,' Emil said in a slow, bored, lilting voice.

'Dad's big pancakes and jam!' Anton cried.

Emil hit him for that. Lotte heard it.

Pernille sat in the passenger seat still crazy from the argument.

'OK,' Lotte said. 'Pancakes it is.'

Traffic lights. Groups of men and women heading off to the bars. Saturday night in the city.

'In that case,' Lotte added, smiling at them in the mirror, 'we're going to need some milk and eggs.'

She turned to her sister.

'Pernille?'

That wild-eyed look Lotte hated.

'It's OK,' she added quickly. 'I can make them.'

'Lotte.'

Pernille's hand was on the door. It looked as if she was ready to step out into the moving traffic.

'Can you watch the boys tonight?'

'Sure. If you want. Why?'

Pernille didn't answer. She turned and said, 'You go to Auntie Lotte's house tonight and eat pancakes. OK?'

Not a word, then Anton asked, 'Aren't you coming?'

She was back looking through the traffic again, at the lights and the people on the street.

'No.'

A junction. Bars. Neon. People. Anonymity in the night.

'Let me out here.'

Lotte kept driving.

'Let's go home. I'm sure Vagn's found Theis by now.'

Pernille picked up her bag.

'Let me out here,' she said again.

The car kept on.

She was screaming now.

'I said let me out here! Let me, let me, let me . . .'

Eyes clouding over, heart beating, Lotte pulled in to the side of the road.

Her sister was gone in an instant without another word.

Hartmann was back in the interview room with his lawyer and a prison guard, facing Brix across the table.

Calm now. Something of his old self. Talking about that Friday, the party, the round of meetings, of get-togethers in the winding, labyrinthine corridors of the Rådhus.

'Do you believe in God?' he asked Brix.

'I came here for this?' the lean policeman grumbled.

'No. You came for your own enjoyment. To see me squirm.'

'Troels . . .' The woman lawyer was looking worried. 'Brix is doing you a favour.'

'A favour,' Hartmann murmured.

Brix sighed and looked at his watch.

'I don't believe in God,' Hartmann said. 'Never did. But sometimes I wonder if that's just a kind of . . . cowardice. Because the worst thing of all would be believing, putting everything you have in that simple faith. Then waking up one morning and discovering it was all one big, cruel joke.'

'Troels . . .' the woman said again.

'Don't you understand?'

The question was aimed at Brix, not her.

'That night in the Rådhus. It was our anniversary. I was surrounded by all these smiling, glittering people. I had my face on the posters. Everyone loved Troels Hartmann.'

A cold and incisive glance across the table.

'The man who would bring the Bremer years to an end.'

Hartmann laughed, at himself, at his own stupidity.

'And it didn't mean a damned thing. I knew it right then. All the champagne, all the food and congratulations. I just thought of her. Of how much I missed her. Of what I'd lost. For good . . .'

Eyes closed, remembering.

'They didn't see a thing. Just Troels Hartmann, going about his business. Laughing, joking, smiling. And all the while I was asking . . . why?'

Hartmann's fingers tapped at his chest.

'What did I do to deserve all this? All this . . . meaningless . . . shit.'

He shrugged.

'I was the priest who got a letter from God and it read . . . well more fool you. So I did what a good brave man does. I slunk off and got stinking drunk. There . . .' He nodded at Brix. 'A confession.'

'And then?'

'I couldn't face Rie. So I got a cab and went to the cottage.'

His eyes drifted to the window and the dark night outside.

'My wife always loved that place. It was hers.'

'The window?' Brix asked.

'When I got there I realized I didn't have a key. So I smashed it. Cut myself a little. Drunks do.'

'And you were alone?'

'With a lot of memories.'

'Hartmann . . .'

'Don't ask me how it happened. I can't explain. I've tried. Believe me. Maybe because I was drunk and stupid and pitiful. And weak.'

He tapped the table and said more loudly, 'Weak. The weak man said that if I was to put an end to this shit it was best it happened in our cottage.'

Dry, hollow laughter.

'Can you imagine how idiotic that is? She loved that place.' His eyes closed in pain. 'What she would have thought . . .'

Brix and the lawyer waited.

'So I stuffed mattresses over the windows, towels under the doors. Then I turned on the gas, got on the bed and waited.'

There was a knock at the door. Meyer walked in, looked at Brix, said, 'Got a minute?'

'Not now.'

456

'It's important.'

'Not now!'

Meyer grunted and left.

When he was gone, Hartmann continued.

'When I woke up the next morning the door had blown open. I never closed it properly I guess. Or maybe I was a clumsy drunk. Or perhaps . . . she'd come along and said, no more of this, Troels. No more. I can't explain it so don't ask. Then Morten came and found me and drove me home.'

'Morten Weber will corroborate this story,' the woman added quickly.

Brix was silent.

'That's it,' Hartmann concluded.

'And you didn't tell us any of this because of the election? You were worried about your reputation?'

Troels Hartmann met his gaze.

'There's nothing I've said to you in confidence that didn't make it into the papers the next day. That worried me, I admit. I was concerned for Rie as well. I wanted to keep her out of it.'

A long breath, a long look.

'But mostly I was ashamed. Afraid. I thought that by admitting it I might let that black thing back into my life. Which makes me a bigger fool than even I appreciated. Because really . . .'

Hartmann laughed.

'I just set it free.' He watched Brix's eyes. 'Can you understand that?'

'Yes,' the policeman said. 'I can.'

'Well, that's it.'

He hesitated.

'Are you going to plaster that all over the papers now?'

'I don't think so,' Brix said.

He nodded to the guard.

'Take him back to the cell.'

The man in uniform moved. Hartmann evaded his arms.

'I told you the truth! What is this?'

The lawyer was agitated.

'This is the truth,' she said. 'Morten Weber confirms his story.'

'I'm sure he does,' Brix said. 'Perhaps I'll charge him as an accomplice.'

457

He gestured to the guard.

Hartmann was on his feet, arms up, still resisting.

'I need to be in the Rådhus. Now!'

The guard grabbed him. Hartmann held up his hands.

'Call Morten! Is this Bremer again?'

'Out!' Brix ordered, and watched him dragged from the room.

Next door Meyer was going through more reports from forensics. Brix walked in, saw the stamp on the cover, said, 'I hope to God they've found some hard evidence Nanna Birk Larsen was in that cottage.'

Meyer shook his head.

'Not a thing. Not a single head of hair. No evidence of sexual activity. No sign of violence. Lund said—'

Brix snatched the report from him, tore through the pages.

'Forget Lund. There were traces of blood in the utility room.'

'Yes. Fish blood. Very old.' Meyer leaned back in his chair. 'Is fishicide a crime? I don't recall—'

Brix's phone rang. He listened. Barked, 'No, I damned well didn't. Let me deal with it.'

He glared at Meyer.

'Has Lund put out a call for Phillip Bressau's car?'

'You mean the white car he can't account for? The white car he's hiding from us? Yes. She has. Bressau's probably the hit-and-run driver.'

'Bressau's wife and children are at Soro police station. They were stopped by a patrol. The car doesn't have a scratch.'

'It's a white car from City Hall. I don't believe it, Brix. The car that killed Olav Christensen came from there.' Meyer was close to losing it. 'Every time we step inside the Rådhus those bastards go out of their way to lie to us. Why doesn't this bother you? Who did you just speak to?'

'You're a big disappointment to me sometimes. Where's Lund?'

Meyer ran his finger down the address list and the tally of white cars. Life had been too busy to get far with them. He hadn't even checked two thirds down the list. Until then.

'Oh shit,' he muttered then grabbed for the phone.

*

458

Lund didn't answer Meyer's call. She'd tracked down Jens Holck to a half-finished block of flats in Valby and was listening to him talk about the Latvia trip.

'You saw Phillip Bressau?'

'Only on the plane over and then back again. He doesn't say much. Bremer and Bressau went to some meetings in Riga. The rest of us stayed in Saldus.'

Holck looked tired, unshaven. He might have been drinking.

'Did Bressau make many calls?'

'I don't remember. I've got to go now.'

'Do you still have the itinerary for the trip? Hotels. That kind of thing. It would be a big help.'

He looked at his watch.

'I'll have a look,' Holck said. 'Wait here.'

She watched him go back into the building. A light went on upstairs. Lund walked over to the garage, wandered down the ramp.

The place was a converted warehouse. The basement seemed big, probably had some industrial use once.

She pulled out a torch. Shone it into the black maw ahead.

Nothing.

Walked further.

At the very end stood a shape draped in a black tarpaulin.

Lund looked at her phone. No signal.

She walked up to the tarpaulin, dragged it off from the front.

Stood back and looked.

A white estate car. Windscreen smashed and smeared with blood. Front a wreck. Blood there too. Driver-side mirror hanging against the door.

Enough.

She cut the torch, marched back into the cold, gloomy night, went back to the unmarked police car.

No keys.

Lund checked the dashboard, the floor. Kept looking.

Went into the glovebox. Snatched the Glock from beneath the packs of Nicotinell and tissues.

Held it low. Looked around.

'Holck?' Lund called. 'Holck?'

*

Meyer was driving like a lunatic, blue light flashing, alone. Fielding a stupid call from Brix in his ear.

'Did Lund call?' Meyer asked.

'Don't ever walk out on me,' Brix bellowed. 'Get back here.'

'I'm going to Holck's house. He had an affair with Nanna. He got the key to the flat from Olav.'

'The accounts show Hartmann approved the money.'

'Oh wake up, man! Holck doctored them. He's been fitting up Hartmann all along. Holck's got a white estate. No one's seen it since Olav got killed.'

'That doesn't prove anything.'

'I gave Lund Holck's address! She's there on her own. Send some patrol cars now.'

'What about Hartmann?'

'Hartmann's nothing to do with it! We need to get to Lund now! You know what she's like. She'll walk in blind on her own.'

A long pause. Meyer threw the car round the side of a sluggish delivery van, slammed on the horn, forced a couple of vehicles coming the other way onto the kerb.

'I'll send one car,' Brix said. 'Keep me posted.'

Lennart Brix called Hartmann back to the interview room and ordered him to take a seat.

'Have you heard from my lawyer?'

'I want to ask you about Jens Holck.'

'Oh for Christ's sake. I've told you everything I know. There's an important vote at—'

'Could Holck have doctored your books?'

'What are you talking about? What books?'

'The accounts that show you authorized the money for Olav.'

'So now you think Jens did it?'

'Just answer the question.'

'Maybe. I run the department. I don't do book-keeping.'

A glance at his notes then Brix asked, 'Has Holck been acting strangely?'

'What kind of a question is that?'

Brix's phone rang.

'She's not at the address I gave you,' Meyer said. 'The house was for sale.'

'Is she at City Hall?'

'No. I called. You've got to put out a call for her.'

'It's not the first time Lund's gone off on her own.'

'Listen to me, Brix! There's something really wrong here. She's on her own and I'm damned sure Holck's our man.'

'You've been sure in the past too.'

'Are you going to help me or not?'

Brix took the phone away from his ear, looked at Hartmann.

'Where's Jen Holck living at the moment?'

'What's going on?'

'Holck isn't at his house. Do you have another address for him?'

'I don't know. He got divorced a few months ago. I think he's been living with relatives.'

'What relatives?'

'I don't know. What's going on?'

Brix picked up the phone.

'Hartmann says he's staying with relatives. He doesn't know where.'

He cut the call. Hartmann was staring at the clock on the wall. Twenty past eight.

'If you think Holck did it why am I here?'

Brix waved to one of the guards.

'Take him back to his cell.'

'Oh, for pity's sake,' Hartmann whined. 'The meeting starts soon.'

He struggled as the guard grabbed his arm, fought a little, not much.

'You know I didn't do it. Do you think you can bury all this when I get free? Do you think that's going to happen, Brix?'

The tall cop stopped by the door.

'Here's the deal,' Hartmann said, leaning across the table. 'I walk from here. I do nothing about the persecution. The false arrest. The illegal search and entry. The trouble I could cause you . . . I forget everything.'

Brix was listening.

'In return you keep what I told you private. Truly private. No leaks to the press. No hints about a suicide attempt. Nothing. You say Hartmann was interviewed because of a misunderstanding. Found innocent, released. End of story.'

Brix took a deep breath, put a long finger to his cheek.

'I could be Lord Mayor within a week. It's best we have good relations. We should start that now.' He held out his hand. 'Don't you think?'

'Stay there,' Brix ordered.

Then he walked out into the corridor and called control.

'Put out a search for Lund.'

No sign of Holck anywhere. Lund walked down into the basement for a second look.

Torch in left hand, gun in her right, she moved ahead, searching, sweeping.

The place smelled of damp and dust and spilled oil. There were sets of tools in racks on the walls. A stack of wooden pallets. An engine in pieces. A half-built piece of furniture, a wardrobe maybe, bare wood with hammers, screwdrivers, nails and a saw by the side.

No sign of Holck.

She moved on, past bags of cement, past tiles and bricks.

The Glock trembled in her hand. She'd never fired it, not outside the practice range. The white beam of the torch shook with her movement. Caught nothing.

Stupid, she thought. Going in on her own. Not calling Meyer. Bringing in back-up, some help.

Why did she do this?

Lund had no idea. It was how she was. Who she was.

The woman who clawed her way to the rank of Vicekriminalkommissær in homicide. Kept her job through results, not politics or some concept of equality she privately despised.

She was a good cop. A good mother. Someone who cared.

But she was on her own, still. Maybe always would be. An outsider. An awkward fit, with her plain clothes, simple ponytail, her shining eyes that never ceased looking.

Lund went in alone because she felt like it. She wanted to be first. To see their faces when they came later, following.

Usually it worked.

One last flash of the beam into the corner. A row of ceramic shapes, baths and washbasins, toilets and bidets.

Lund swore, turned, was walking to the exit, determined to call Meyer, furious with herself for being so stupid, so impetuous.

A shape flitted through the dark, left to right.

The gun stayed where it was. Down. A weapon wasn't her first natural response and never would be.

She wanted to talk first. She wanted to know.

'Holck . . .'

The shape again. Something his hand. A wheel brace, four steel iron legs, like a weapon from the Middle Ages.

Closer.

Too close.

She could hear him. The sweep of his arm.

The gun moved but not much and not quickly.

He dodged to one side, was replaced by something flashing through the torch beam towards her.

The hard iron fell on Sarah Lund's skull, sent her crashing to the hard floor.

It was a business hotel in Bredgade just off the shopping street of Strøget. A hundred kroner for a Scotch. Not much less for a beer.

Pernille sat at the bar, bag by her side. Third stop of the night. Hard spirits in every one.

The way it used to be when she was young and nothing really mattered. When she could sneak out past her parents, go down to the rough areas, the forbidden places, see where the night took her.

By her side was a man she'd have laughed at back then. Portly, self-satisfied, tanned, in a suit that was a touch too small for him. But he was buying.

'I've got my own company,' he said, ordering some more drinks. 'I started it from scratch.'

It was a hotel bar. They were the only people there. The locals never came. Only visitors stranded in the city, lonely for the night.

'It took me five years.' He was Norwegian. 'I've got thirty employees, a branch in Denmark, and production in Vietnam.'

The television was on. It was talking about a fresh turn in the City Hall elections.

He moved his seat closer, saw she was watching the TV.

'A nasty case. It made the papers in Oslo.'

'The council will vote on excluding Hartmann,' the newsreader said. 'He's due to be charged, though we're now hearing from sources this may not . . .'

He touched her arm.

'Do you travel a lot?' The man laughed. 'They say life's nothing without travel. They don't do it for business. Twenty nights a month . . .'

He toasted her.

'But sometimes you get to talk to a nice lady, in a nice bar. It's not so bad.'

He was smiling and it was close to a leer.

She took a long swig of the drink. She didn't much like it.

Didn't much like anything any more. The boys. Lotte. Theis. Locked in this endless search, the hunt for an explanation, a reason, her life had entered a strange limbo. She couldn't sleep, couldn't feel, couldn't laugh, think straight.

Pernille thought of her old self, the pretty young girl, the one who flitted from bar to bar in dark and dirty Vesterbro, tempting the young blades till she found the right one.

Nothing mattered.

Then and now.

She looked at the man next to her. Wondered what he was like at that age. Cocky. Good-looking. Weak and obedient.

'Let's go to your room,' she said.

The Norwegian stared at her, dumbstruck.

Pernille got up, picked her bag off the floor.

With anxious fingers he grabbed his key.

'Put it on the tab,' he said to the barman then followed her to the door.

The room wasn't big. Double bed. Shiny table. Laptop on a desk. The kind of bad-taste furnishing no one bought but a hotel.

He was flustered, nervous, fumbling with the key, slapping the wall for the light switch.

There were clothes on the bed. A shirt. Underpants.

He grabbed them off the sheets, threw them into a cupboard.

'I didn't know I'd have company. Do you want a drink?'

It was the size of Nanna's room. Nothing personal here. Nothing she would remember.

'When I was a student I worked as a barman at the Grand Hotel in Oslo.'

He said this as if it was one of his great achievements. Like starting his own company and having a factory in Vietnam.

Two gins from the minibar. A single bottle of tonic. He bounced the bottles on the tiny tabletop, splashed the spirit into the glasses.

'Ha! See! I still have it.'

No, smaller than Nanna's she thought. A box for a faceless man. A place outside the life she knew.

'Gin and tonic. No ice. No lemon.'

He shrugged. He was drunker than she had realized. So, perhaps, was she, though there was a sense of clarity here. Of purpose even.

The drink was in her hand. She didn't touch it, didn't want it.

She thought of Theis. Rough, coarse Theis. No manners, no fine words.

No delicate thoughtful touches, only a direct and physical embrace.

Yet there was something sensitive, even tender in him. Had to be. Why else did she love him, marry him, bear him three children?

The Norwegian was different.

Drink in hand, drink on breath, he stood next to her, brushed aside her long chestnut hair, damp from the rain. Stroked her cheek with his pale fingers.

Tried to kiss her.

The glass fell from her fingers. Bounced booze on the plush hotel carpet.

'I'm sorry.' He sounded concerned more than disappointed. 'I'm not much good at this.'

It was a lie, she thought.

'I thought . . .' He shrugged. 'No matter.'

He picked up the glass, put it on the minibar. When he turned she was on the bed.

Puzzlement and hope in his face. A nice-looking man. No name.

Not at all like Theis, who could only dream of going to a place like Vietnam. Who struggled to pay ten workers let alone fifty.

'Another drink?' he asked.

She said words she'd not uttered in years, and then to one man only.

'Take my clothes off.'

He laughed, looked foolish.

'Are you sure? I mean . . . you seem a bit . . .'

She closed her eyes. She let her head roll back, mouth half open.

She smiled.

A kiss then. He was on her. Fumbling, feeling. Boozy lips against her neck. Panting too quickly, as if trying to convince himself.

Pernille lay back on the hard double bed, let his arms engulf her, as he writhed and tugged desperately at the dark blue dress.

These clothes she wore when she placed Nanna's urn in the brown earth. She didn't want them any more, or anything to do with them.

Theis Birk Larsen drank his soup, found what things he still had left, checked his cuts, begged plasters. Got dressed in his scarlet work suit, his black leather jacket.

The white-haired man from the hostel watched him.

'You're sure you don't want to stay? It's not the Radisson I know . . .'

'Thanks for your help. I have to go.'

Handshake. A firm, determined grip.

'You're welcome. Any time.'

He tidied away the bedclothes.

'I lost something that mattered once,' the man said. 'How and why doesn't matter. But that's what happened.'

It was nearly nine in the evening. He pulled on his black woollen hat.

'Life wasn't worth living. And all the guilt made me do awful things. I hated myself. What I'd become.'

He handed Birk Larsen a lighter and a pack of cigarettes.

'Keep them. I hated life itself. But today I see there's a plan behind everything.'

He said this as if it were the most natural thing in the world.

Birk Larsen lit a cigarette.

'What seemed like the end turned out to be a beginning.'

Smoke in the little room that smelled of booze and sweat and men.

'God gives us hardship for a reason. Not that we understand that when we're up to our necks in shit.'

'A plan?' Birk Larsen said and couldn't stop the sneer.

'Oh yes. There's a plan, Theis. For you. For me. For everyone. We're walking down the road that's given us whether we know it or not. What's waiting at the end . . .'

Birk Larsen took a deep pull on the cigarette. He didn't want to see this man again. Didn't like the way he looked at him, demanding answers.

'Say something, Theis.'

'Say what?' Birk Larsen snapped and felt ashamed at the sudden fierceness in his voice. 'Before I met my wife, before the kids I did a lot of bad things.'

He glared at the man.

'Not your kind. Beyond your league. I hurt people because I thought they earned it. I did . . .'

His narrow eyes closed in pain.

'Enough of this shit.'

There was a crucifix on every wall, a slender broken figure staring down at each shambling body that passed through the door.

'It was a long time ago.' He pointed at the figure of Christ in his agony. 'But I don't think that guy's quite forgotten. So all I got was parole. A little time with my family. And now that's done.'

Too many words. He was back to the cigarette, sly eyes stinging in the smoke, watching the man from the hostel.

'I'm sure there's something, Theis. Some help, some comfort that gives you and your family hope.'

'Yeah,' Birk Larsen said. 'There could be.'

He looked at the man.

'I just don't think you'd find it very Christian.'

Finally the white-haired man seemed out of words.

'Goodnight,' Birk Larsen mumbled then walked outside into the damp cold street.

A sudden start, a bright red pain at the back of her skull. Lund came to on the floor of the basement garage, tried to stand, could barely move. Her hands were tied, her ankles too. The place was lit now. She was by the white estate car. Not far from the half-made wardrobe and the tools.

Scrabbled on the floor, breathing in the dust, the oil fumes, the smell of sawdust.

And cigarette smoke.

She managed to work herself round until she saw the tiny red fire flickering in the corner.

Eyes adjusting.

Holck sat on what looked like an oil barrel, puffing on a cigarette. A man deciding what to do.

You talk, Lund thought. The gun was gone. Nothing left.

'Untie me, Holck. You know this can't work.'

He didn't answer.

'Come on.'

Silence.

'We can work something out.'

She sounded pathetic, wrong.

'How about it?'

He kept smoking, looking at her. Looking round the garage.

'Headquarters can trace me.'

Holck threw something through the shadows. It landed in front of her. Phone, smashed and cracked.

'I suppose you want to know,' he said.

'Untie me.'

He laughed.

'Which way's it supposed to be? If I tell you . . .'

She didn't speak.

'No, really.' He sounded coldly amused. 'I'm interested. If I tell you I kill you. If I don't . . .'

He tossed the cigarette towards her. It spun fizzling into a pool of oil.

'Oh. I still kill you. In that case . . .'

'Untie me, Holck.'

He cocked his head as if listening for something.

'So quiet out here. Don't you love it?'

'Holck . . .'

He got up, came to her.

'I told headquarters where I was going,' Lund said quickly. 'They're on their way.'

He had his wallet out, was looking at something.

'Do you have children?'

She was shaking. The cold. The fear.

He came close, crouched down, showed her his wallet.

'You got kids? These are mine.'

A girl and a boy, laughing with a woman who smiled at the camera.

Holck's fingers ran over each figure.

'My wife.' He shook his head. 'My ex-wife. She won't let them see me much.'

'Holck—'

'You wanted to know. You never stopped asking. Now look where you are.'

He tapped his own chest.

'And you're blaming me now? Me? I never wanted to kill anyone. Who does? Never. Not even that filthy little whore.'

'Jens—'

'That slimy bastard Christensen wouldn't let it go. He wanted money. A job. He wanted . . .'

A fierce, crazed anger contorted Holck's miserable grey features.

'This shit's cost me too much already.'

'I know,' she said, trying to bring down the temperature. 'That's why we need to talk. You've got to untie me. We can sort this out.'

'Yes.'

Hope.

'I'd really like to.'

'Let's do it then. Untie me.'

'But it's not that simple, is it?'

'Holck . . .'

He stood up, looked around.

'I knew you'd understand.'

Walked over, lifted the rear door of the white estate.

Lund struggled, got nowhere, tried to think.

Then he was back, hand on her jacket, dragging her across the filthy floor.

Shattered handset on the ground.

'That's my phone, Holck!' she cried.

They were at the back of the car. He was looking for something. A weapon. Beat her unconscious. In the boot. In the river. Just like Nanna.

'It's my phone. Not the police one.'

He stopped.

'I told you. They're on their way. The police phone's in the car.'

'Where?'

She didn't speak.

He went and got the wheel brace, held it over her, said again, more loudly, 'Where?'

'In my bag.'

'Don't go away,' Holck said and laughed.

One minute, maybe two. Lund shuffled back across the floor, towards the half-made wardrobe and the tools.

There was no second phone. No magic beacon that would bring the police to this lost, dark semi-industrial part of the city where Holck lived alone, in a half-finished warehouse block owned by relatives who'd decamped to Cape Town for the winter.

Only a handbag full of chewing gum and tissues, mints and rubbish.

He started sifting through it. Got angrier with each failed second. Ripped open the glovebox. Saw nothing there but Nicotinell packets and parking receipts.

He didn't know why he showed her the photo of his wife and kids. Didn't know why he didn't kill her straight off, shove her bleeding corpse into the back of the white car, drive out into the distant woods, find a river, a canal. Push Lund and the white estate into the dank waters where they'd stay for ever.

Lost. Unseen. Forgotten.

Holck took one last look.

He hadn't wanted to run down Olav Christensen. The creep had left him no choice. That was life. No choices anywhere. Just a long road that kept getting bleaker, narrower with every passing day.

'Bitch,' Holck spat as he slammed the car door shut then went back to the black hole that led to the garage and Lund.

Scrabbling on the floor, towards the sawdust and the tools, the crooked shape of the half-finished wardrobe.

A hammer. A chisel. Some nails and screws and dowels.

And a saw.

Hands tied, fingers trembling, she closed on the handle, got it to her legs, trapped the blade between her knees. Began to work at the plastic tie that bound her.

A noise. He was back. Scrabbling somewhere in the pool of darkness by the entrance.

Pictures in Lund's head.

A man who thinks ahead. Needs things. Plans things.

A sound, rustling plastic.

A black bag to hide a body in the boot.

Metal clattering, blade against blade.

Knives or scythes or something else that cuts, a weapon to pair with the wheel brace, tools for the task.

Footsteps.

When he came into the light Holck had the black bin liner beneath his right arm and was stretching out a line of industrial tape between his hands.

Nanna went into the river alive, but at least she had her mouth free and could scream.

Holck strode forward, to the space behind the car.

Looked round.

Shouted, 'Bitch!'

Looked round again, not believing he could be so stupid.

Got a torch from the car boot, flicked it on.

A bright monocular beam seeking her. Like a hunter after a wounded deer. Its white beam ranged, a single blazing ray of light.

Five minutes, ten.

In the basement garage there was no thing called time. Only a man and a weapon, and a woman he sought in the shadows.

Behind a concrete pillar Lund lurked, trying to still her breathing, to make no sound.

Trying to convince herself the threats she'd made were not as idle as they seemed. That someone was coming. Even though she drove here alone. Told nobody. Not even Meyer.

They'd find her somehow.

Maybe.

Maybe.

He was close to the piles of cement sacks, torch ranging across the floor. Then she saw it. The Glock lay where it fell when Holck clubbed her with the wheel brace. A grey shape dimly shining, not far from the white estate.

Wait and hope.

Or act and win.

She wondered why she asked the question. There really was no choice.

He was down the far side of the basement. The gun four strides away, no more. Maybe he hadn't seen it. Maybe he felt so powerful, so in control, he'd no need of any other weapon but his strength.

Lund ran.

Not four strides, five. She was leaping for the weapon when she saw him. Tall in the darkness, waiting all the time.

The gun was a lure for fools, she thought, as Holck snatched it from the floor with his left hand, punched her in the head with his right, sent her shrieking down to the stone floor.

Dust in the mouth. Bitterness and fear. She scrambled, crawled, half-kneeled before him.

Looked up, saw the Glock pointing straight in her face.

A second sound, another direction.

Another beam of light.

'Hold it, Holck!'

Another voice, one she recognized.

She tried to move. Holck's boot came out and kicked her in the gut.

Winded, aching.

Turning she saw him. Doing what he was taught for once.

Weaver Stance. Two hands, main elbow straight, support just bent. Gun steady, aim deliberate.

'Put down the gun,' Meyer ordered.

Holck stood unsteadily above her, the weapon at Lund's head.

'Drop it, Holck. For Christ's sake.'

Lund crouched, didn't look at the man. Thought about Mark. And Bengt. And Nanna Birk Larsen.

'Put the fucking gun down!' Meyer bellowed.

Holck wasn't moving. Wasn't going to. Death by cop. And sometimes they took one with them.

'Come on, Holck! Gun down. You. On the ground. Now.'

He was staring at her and she knew it somehow. So Lund looked at him.

The Glock slipped down to the side of Holck's legs. He was shaking. Eyes wide and terrified. Lost.

'Tell my kids . . .' he said and slowly, with an ambiguous intent, brought the weapon up to her scalp.

Three rapid explosions echoing round the empty, dusty garage.

She saw him jump with each, saw the pain and shock in his eyes.

The force took him backwards, sent him crumpling into a broken heap on the floor.

She hugged herself and waited.

Meyer was approaching. Regulations. Torch on the man, gun ready.

Lund looked at the still shape beyond her.

Watched for movement. Saw none.

Ten minutes later, medics putting clips in the wound in the back of Lund's head. A corpse in a body bag, blood seeping through the seams.

In a flood tide of blue flashing lights, amidst the cacophony of sirens, Jan Meyer leaned against his car, smoking furiously with a shaking hand.

Watching Lund. Thinking. Wondering how many different outcomes there might have been. Were there other words? Other stratagems? Or did the road lead one way only, straight to the inevitable end?

Lennart Brix walked over. Blue raincoat. Burberry scarf tied carefully at his neck. He might have come from the opera.

Looked around then said, 'How did you know where to go?'

Meyer watched her sitting in the ambulance, expressionless, letting the medics do their work.

'The same way Lund did. I called his ex-wife.'

Brix held out his right hand, palm open, upwards. His leather gloves would have suited the opera too.

Meyer finished the cigarette, dispatched it into the dark, stood up and took the gun out of his holster. Checked the magazine, removed it. Held the gun by the grip, barrel down and placed it in Brix's gloved hand. Then the magazine.

'There'll be an investigation. There has to be.'

'Yeah.'

'You'll be informed. The girl's parents need to be told.'

He patted Meyer on the back.

'Well done,' Brix said. 'Now get some sleep.'

They let Hartmann go at ten. Lund was across the corridor, getting looked at again, as he collected his things.

'Don't you owe me an explanation?' Hartmann asked Brix.

473

'I don't think so. Do you want to sign for your things or not?'

Hartmann picked up his tie and watch. Put a signature to the form.

'Do we have a deal?' he asked tentatively.

'About what?'

'About . . . what I told you.'

Not a flicker of emotion on Brix's grey immobile face.

'We only disclose statements to the public if a case comes to court,' he said. 'Since it won't . . .'

'Thanks.'

'Don't thank me.'

Hartmann was staring at the watch. The time.

'No need,' Brix added with a smile.

Another torch. This time that of a police doctor, shining it in her eyes.

'You've got minor concussion. Go home and relax.'

'I'm fine,' Lund said, carefully pulling the black and white sweater back over her head, noting the tears that wouldn't mend, realizing she needed to buy another.

The door opened. Bengt came in. Arm in sling. He looked more shocked than after the car crash.

'I'm not done yet,' the doctor said.

Bengt took no notice.

'If the stitches come undone you'll have to get new ones.'

He came and held her.

Still Lund looked out into the corridor, saw Hartmann putting on his grey coat, walking for the door.

The doctor coughed.

'I said I hadn't finished.'

Lund gently stepped back from Bengt. Looked at the corridor again.

'I said I'm fine.'

But Hartmann was gone.

Morten Weber had the car outside.

'It was Holck. He took Sarah Lund prisoner. She's lucky to be alive.'

Hartmann watched the city lights, thinking ahead.

'Who told you that?'

'Your lawyer. All charges have been dropped. She says you could sue the living daylights out of them.'

'I'm not suing anybody. Where's Rie?'

A pause.

'It was too late to help, Troels. They voted. You're excluded from the election. I'm sorry.'

'We'll see about that. Where is she?'

'Bremer's called a press conference.'

Hartmann looked out of the window. Winter night. Someone he knew, not liked but knew, was dead. Another man on the city council with a life that was withheld from those around him.

Troels Hartmann realized he wasn't alone. Wasn't afraid any more. Wasn't bound by the demons that once haunted him.

'No one's ever going to know about the cottage,' he said.

'You confessed to the police.'

'No one's ever going to know about that. We're back in business, Morten.'

'Troels!'

'I'm a wronged man!' Hartmann roared. 'Don't you understand?'

Weber was silent.

'I'm the victim here. As much as that Birk Larsen girl—'

'Not as much,' Morten Weber pointed out. 'If you're going to play the sympathy card, best play it carefully.'

'Good point.' Hartmann took out his phone, wondered who to call first. 'Let's work on it.'

The hotel room was wrecked. Smashed mirrors. Bad paintings on the floor. Vagn Skærbæk looked at Pernille, silent on the bed, half-dressed.

The drunk Norwegian was scared.

'I didn't know she'd go crazy! I got a number off her phone. It was me who called you.'

Skærbæk was still in his work clothes. Hands in pockets. Black hat. He bent down, looked into her face.

'Pernille.'

She stared at him and said nothing.

'Is it OK?' the Norwegian pleaded. 'I didn't do anything. Nothing happened. I thought she wanted it and . . .'

He looked at Skærbæk. It was supposed to be man-to-man.

'She went berserk. I mean . . . I didn't know she was married. I thought she wanted a little company—'

'Piss off out of here,' Skærbæk yelled then bundled him out of the door.

Went back to her. Knelt by the bed.

'Pernille. I think you should get dressed.'

He set a chair upright. Got her tights off the bed.

She wouldn't take them.

'Oh for God's sake.'

He struggled to get them on her feet. Gave up.

'Where are your shoes?'

No answer. He looked around. Found the black boots.

'I've been trying to get you. The police called.'

The boots weren't easier.

'Pernille! I can't dress you.'

She looked at him. Said nothing.

'They found who killed her.'

Wouldn't move. Wouldn't help him. The boots again.

'Do you get what I'm saying? They caught him. He's dead.'

Nothing on her blank face. Not a word.

'He's dead,' Skærbæk repeated.

She took the boots off him, slowly pulled them on. Vagn Skærbæk looked round the room. Did what he had to sometimes. Cleaned up a little. Straightened the flowers, the broken lamp.

Got her out of the hotel.

He'd brought a small works van. It smelled of fusty carpets.

'Lotte's with the boys at your parents'. Have you heard from Theis?'

Nothing but lights and traffic. Not a word.

'For God's sake, Pernille! Will you say something?'

Past the Rådhus, past the station, down the long straight drag of Vesterbrogade. Into Vesterbro, past cafes and bars, past the side streets with their drug dens, past the hookers and the partygoers, the people of the night.

'One day,' she said, 'we went to the beach and I wanted to teach Nanna to swim.'

Past the school where the boys went and the church where her white coffin rested.

'We stood out in the sea. I said . . . first you have to learn to float.'

Towards home.

'Nanna was scared. But I said I'd hold on to her. Always. No matter what. I'd hold her.'

Her hand went to her mouth. Tears. A sudden convulsion of grief.

'Never let go,' she sobbed. 'Never.'

Back in Vibeke's apartment Lund watched the evening news. Her head didn't hurt too much. The beer helped.

Brix stood outside the warehouse block, looking serious for the camera. He liked being on the TV.

'Jens Holck was shot in self-defence after threatening an officer with a firearm. He was killed by another officer on the scene. Evidence points to Holck being the man we were looking for in the Birk Larsen case.'

The reporter tackled him about Hartmann. Brix was unmoved.

Bengt came into the room and sat beside her.

'We had strong reasons to believe there was a link with the Rådhus. Unfortunately Holck appears to have doctored some records to make it appear Troels Hartmann was responsible. I'm happy to say Hartmann was an innocent victim in all of this and has gone out of his way to help the police throughout.'

'Sarah . . .'

'A minute,' she said.

He reached over, took the remote, turned off the TV.

'You should talk,' he said.

'About what?'

'About how you feel?'

'How do I feel?'

'Guilty.'

'No,' she said immediately.

'Frightened?'

She stared at the dead screen and shook her head. Then she took a swig of the beer.

'You will have a reaction,' he insisted.

Still watching the dead screen.

'Is that a professional diagnosis?'

'If you like.'

'That's not the problem.'

More beer.

'What is?'

She looked at him and said nothing.

Bengt sighed.

'OK. I know what I said about the profile. That there could be more victims.'

'Not likely if it was Holck. He couldn't lead the life he did if he had that behind him.'

'So there you have it. I was wrong. It happens.'

She looked at him again, was silent.

'I'm not as smart as you, Sarah.'

He squeezed her hand. She didn't respond.

'I don't see things. Imagine things. I can't.'

Not a word.

'I wish you couldn't sometimes too. Don't you?'

Lund finished the beer, thought about another.

'We don't get to choose who we are, do we?' she said.

'In some ways. Be glad that it's over.'

He reached out and gently stroked the hair from her forehead.

'Be glad you don't need it all in there any more.'

She was staring at the blank TV. Hand reaching for the remote.

'Come to bed, Sarah. For God's sake, let it go.'

Nine

The Electoral Commission met in emergency session at nine in the morning and revoked its decision of the previous night. Troels Hartmann was back in the race, exonerated, a victim of circumstances. No one knew of the suicide attempt. Not even, Hartmann hoped, Poul Bremer.

Two hours later, in the Liberals' office, Morten Weber was trying to instil some hope in the troops.

'We've got a job to do. We have to explain to the voters that Troels is innocent. We know that. So do the police. But the voters have to understand.'

Eight campaign people there and Hartmann.

'Many of our financial backers have pulled out,' Weber went on. 'Without money there's no campaign. So we need to get them back onside.'

'What about the alliance?' Elisabet Hedegaard asked.

'Forget the alliance,' Hartmann said. 'If we get the votes they'll come. Where else can they go?'

Hedegaard looked unconvinced.

'We go to the polls a week on Tuesday. We all know what that means. By next Saturday people have made up their minds. There isn't time.'

Morten Weber grimaced and looked down the table.

Hartmann stood up, looking the part. Meeting their eyes, making each of them feel special.

'What Elisabet says is true. Time's against us. The media too.

479

Maybe Bremer's got more tricks up his sleeve.' Hartmann shrugged. 'All I know is this. If we don't try we will lose. So why not give it our all? Why not fight? Why not dream?'

He laughed. Enjoyed this small stage, this tiny audience.

'I don't recommend a jail cell for political meditation. But it works, in a way. When I sat there . . .'

His eyes drifted off to the distance. All of them, Weber even, were caught by the moment.

'In my blue prison suit I thought of who we were.' He nodded at them. 'Of you. Of what we're fighting for. None of that's changed. Our ideas, our ambitions are the same. Do we want them any less today than we did yesterday?'

His fist thumped the table.

'No. I want them more, with a passion. I want a City Hall that can't play fast and loose with the police just because someone here feels like it.'

A murmur of approval. A lighter mood. One that swung his way.

'Do we make the best of it? Or do we give Poul Bremer what he and his henchmen have been angling for all along? Another four wasted years?'

Weber clapped. So did Elisabet Hedegaard. Then all of them.

Hartmann smiled, gazed at each in turn, remembered every name. Almost all had been ready to ditch him. Every one he would now thank personally, in fulsome tones, with a private phone call later, for the support they'd shown.

'Let's get moving. I'll see you out there.'

He watched them go.

'Have you talked to Rie?' Weber asked. 'There's a lot we have to do.'

'I know, I know. I've left a thousand messages. She doesn't call me back.'

Someone rapping at the door. Poul Bremer, winter coat, scarlet scarf and beaming smile, looking as if he was about to audition for the job of Santa Claus.

'Troels!' A loud and cheery voice. 'I'm so sorry to interrupt. I had to come by to say . . .'

He came in, took off the scarf. The smile fell.

Sincerity.

'To say welcome back.'

'That's very kind of you.'

Weber muttered something dark and wandered off to his desk. Bremer walked into Hartmann's private office, helped himself to some coffee then sat on the sofa, shaking his head.

'Holck, Holck. He was always a solitary soul. But this. I don't understand. Why? We went to Latvia together. He was a bit down in the mouth but . . .'

He took a biscuit and picked at it.

'A capable man if unimaginative. The Moderates will fare better without him in the end. Not this time round. As far as this election's concerned they're lost. As are Kirsten's troops and all the other fleas that hang on the backs of others wishing to feed off them.'

That broad grin again.

'One way or another you've left them all in ruins. It's you and me now. I'd congratulate you if I thought it was intentional.'

'Do you have something to say?'

Another sip of the coffee then his intense grey eyes turned on Hartmann.

'I do. I'm very sorry about what's happened. Believe me. Last night I thought we were doing the right thing in the circumstances. Mistaken circumstances but they were the only ones we knew.'

He waited. A political moment, one Hartmann recognized.

'And I'm sorry, Poul, if I accused you unfairly in the heat of the moment.'

Bremer shrugged.

'No need. Don't give it another thought. I won't. Now we must look forward. We've all been touched by this. Not just you.'

Hartmann took the chair opposite.

'And?'

'There's a common consensus. A rare consensus. I talked to the others after we reversed the decision to exclude you. An easy decision, I might add. We all agree this is a time to bury our differences and turn around the public sentiment. The cynicism. The shock. The perception of chaos. It's understandable but it's wrong, as you well know. Our most crucial task is to win back the confidence of the voters. That's the legacy Jens Holck has bequeathed us. We have to renew our contract with the people. Convince them of our worth. Are you with me?'

'You always make a good speech.'

'This isn't about me. Or you. It's about . . .' He waved a hand at the elegant room, the mosaics, the sculptures, the paintings. '. . . this place. Our castle. Our natural home. The Rådhus. Tonight we hold a press conference. I'll talk about a new desire on the part of all the parties to work together for the common good and clean up the mess Holck left us. Are you with me?'

'What are you saying?'

'We've agreed to a *borg fred*. A truce. We put a halt to these personal attacks. The frenetic nature of the debate. The hostile climate. A gentlemen's agreement. We behave ourselves.'

'A *borg fred* . . .'

'Peace in the castle. It's happened in extraordinary circumstances before. The election goes on. We simply mind our manners. Bring down the temperature.'

The grey eyes were on him.

'Talk about policies not individuals. I'm sure you can agree to that.'

Bremer got up from the sofa.

'That's how things stand. I suggest you throw your weight behind us. I'm being generous, Troels. You're in no fit state to fight anything. Not now.'

The smile, the outstretched hand.

'Can I count on you?'

Hartmann hesitated.

'Let me think about it.'

'What's there to think about? There's a consensus. Call them if you like. I'm giving you a chance to come back into the fold. You'll look a fool if you stay outside. But if that's what you want . . .'

'Whatever's best,' Hartmann answered.

Poul Bremer glared at him.

'I'll take that as a yes. The joint press conference is at eight. We'll expect to see you there.'

By late morning Svendsen's team had got hold of Holck's bank and credit card statements. They showed a string of purchases at expensive fashion stores and jewellery companies.

'We can trace her boots directly,' Meyer said.

Lennart Brix sat in the office looking at the photos, no expression, no emotion on his face.

'What about the necklace?' Lund asked. 'The one with the black heart?'

Meyer shoved the photo from the lab in front of Brix.

'She had this in her hand when she was found,' he said. 'We think he made her wear it. Nanna ripped it from her neck when she was drowning.'

Lund persisted.

'Did Holck buy her the necklace?'

'It probably wouldn't show on the records. If he did he must have paid cash down on one of the junk stalls in Christiania or somewhere.'

'What makes you say that?' she asked.

Meyer shuffled uncomfortably on his chair. He looked pale, exhausted. It was rare for anyone to die at the hands of a Danish police officer. The media were fascinated. An internal inquiry was inevitable.

'From what we can gather the necklace is old. Twenty years or more. It's hand-made. Cheap gilt chain. Glass . . .'

He was staring at her and she knew that look now. It said: why do you keep pressing? Why can't you just accept there are things we'll never know?

'What does a black heart mean, Meyer?'

'The hippies in Christiania . . . they had a fashion for them back then. It was kind of a badge for the drug gangs. Now they just get bought and sold on junk stalls.'

Brix spoke for the first time.

'We can't waste time going back two decades.'

Lund reached over and sifted through the evidence pile. The necklace was there in a plastic bag. She picked it up. Looked at the gilt chain. Unmarked. Not tarnished.

'This hasn't been worn for twenty years. If Holck bought it . . .'

Meyer carried on.

'Jens Holck transferred money personally to Olav's account. Not just the five thousand he was giving him through City Hall. Blackmail. We found his prints in Store Kongensgade too. We got these in his home.'

Meyer spread out some photos on the table. Lund shuffled her chair closer. Holck with Nanna somewhere in the country. Happy, loving. Holck was smiling. Barely recognizable.

'It's obvious they were having an affair. His wife confirmed it. She didn't know who he was seeing. Just that he was obsessed with her. And she was young.'

Meyer scratched his head.

'They always mention that, don't they? I guess he was proud.'

'And happy,' Lund added.

Brix looked bored.

'What do we know about his movements that Friday?'

'He was at the poster party. Nanna went to the Rådhus later. Probably to pick up the keys so she could let herself into the flat.'

Lund went back to Holck's photos. Another set. It was colder. Both of them in winter coats. Laughing. Nanna too old for her years. Holck a different man, holding her. In love. It was so obvious.

A memory from the night before.

That filthy little whore.

'Did anyone see Holck that weekend?' Brix asked.

'No. His ex-wife had the kids and was blocking access. She was giving him a hard time over everything. We don't have anyone who saw him at all.'

Brix nodded.

'And the car we found at Holck's?'

'No doubt about that,' Meyer said. 'It was the car that killed Olav.'

Lund kept flicking through the photos. Holck and Nanna, a couple. Twenty years apart. Happy as could be.

'What do you think, Lund?'

Brix's question took her by surprise. She threw the pictures on the table.

'Sounds like a good case,' she said without much conviction.

'Your enthusiasm overwhelms me.'

She said nothing.

'Well done,' Brix declared, got up, patted Meyer on the shoulder, left the room.

Not long after Lund was packing her things again. It was Meyer's office now.

He was watching her. He looked concerned.

'What are you going to do?'

She had a cardboard box, was putting things into it.

'I don't know. Bengt and I have to talk. Mark too. We'll work something out.'

Meyer started playing with his toy police car. Gave up on that and began pacing the office, cigarette in hand.

'What about you?' she asked.

'Me. There'll be an investigation of the shooting. Bound to take weeks.'

'You don't have to worry. You did the right thing—'

'Why the hell didn't that idiot just drop the gun? God knows I tried—'

'Meyer—'

'What the hell could I do?'

He looked shocked and scared and defenceless. And young, with his big ears and guileless face.

Lund stopped packing, came and stood in front of him.

'You couldn't do anything else. You didn't have any choice.'

Close up his eyes were glistening. She wondered if he'd been crying.

Meyer sucked on his cigarette, glanced nervously around the office.

She remembered finding him in the Memorial Yard, staring at the name of his dead colleague. Meyer was marked by that event. Couldn't shake it off.

'I'm glad you did it. How could I not be? You saved my life.'

He picked up the little car again, ran the wheels along the desk. Didn't laugh when the blue light fired.

'So now what?' he asked. 'The case is closed, right?'

An ashtray and a commendation plaque went into her cardboard box.

'What do you mean?'

'Oh please. I can see what you're thinking. I can read you by now.'

'What am I thinking?'

'You tell me.'

'I'm just tired. Like you. That's all.'

Brix came back. The legal department had ruled. There was sufficient evidence to prove Holck was Nanna Birk Larsen's murderer. Meyer agreed to tell the parents.

'What about Sweden, Lund?' he asked. 'Any news?'

She picked up the box.

'Not yet.'

Brix scratched his ear, seemed uncomfortable.

'I've got a bottle of a very good malt whisky in my room. If you're willing. We ought to celebrate, you and all the others. It's been a long and difficult road. For you two especially. Maybe . . .'

He coughed. Looked at them. Smiled without the slightest side or hint of sarcasm.

'Perhaps I didn't make it easy sometimes. Life's never going to be simple when politics comes into play . . .'

'I'll have a drink,' Meyer said and left the room.

'In a minute,' Lund told him.

Brix headed off down the corridor. She could hear laughter there. No voices she recognized.

Alone, Lund went to her files. Pulled out the folder of missing women. Ten years. A handful. Nothing promising. The man she'd set to work on this was an old cop, not well. Once a fit officer, good in the field. Now confined to hunting through old papers, looking for lost gold.

Ten years was not enough. So he'd gone back further. Twenty-three by the time Brix had dragged him off the job.

Thirteen missing women. Young. No link to City Hall or politics. Nothing to connect any of them with a man called Holck. Nothing to link them to a single, serial killer either. That didn't mean there wasn't one.

She turned to the last, the oldest. Twenty-one years before.

The colours in the photograph had faded. Mette Hauge. Student. Twenty-two. Long brown hair. Vacant, friendly smile. Big white earrings.

Lund looked at the cold case sheets and sat down.

The phone never stopped and there was only Vagn Skærbæk there to answer it. Lotte hung around him in a low, half-revealing top. He knew why.

'I don't give a shit about your deadline,' he yelled then slammed down the phone. 'Fucking reporters.'

He scowled at her.

'Don't you get cold going round like that?'

Then he went back to work on one of the engines.

'Have you heard from Theis?' she asked.

'He's on his way in. God knows where he's been.'

Lotte smiled at him, fluttered her eyelashes. As if he'd fall for that by now.

'Vagn. We don't have to tell Theis about yesterday. It wouldn't help. We could keep it between us.'

'You want me to lie now? Jesus. I'm working Sunday. Trying to keep the vans on the road. Is there anything I'm not supposed to do round here?'

Footsteps at the garage door. Theis Birk Larsen turned up. Black jacket, black hat. Cuts on his face. Unshaven.

Lotte found a nervous smile.

'Hi, Theis. Did you hear they found him? The police say they'll be here in an hour.'

He didn't look at either of them. Just walked to the office, started to look at the week's schedules.

'I heard. Where's Pernille?'

'Where the hell do you think?' Skærbæk shrieked.

Lotte looked at her feet. Birk Larsen turned his narrow, cold eyes on the small man in the red suit, twitching nervously a couple of strides away from him.

'What?'

Skærbæk's temper broke.

'Don't give me that shit.' He jabbed a finger at the stairs. 'She's where you should be. Here. What the hell's wrong with you?'

Birk Larsen turned to him, big head to one side, fixed him with a stare, said nothing.

'You didn't bother coming to the cemetery, did you? Too busy, huh, you pisshead? We ran round everywhere looking. We were there with Pernille and the boys. Where the fuck were you?'

Lotte stepped back, ready for the explosion.

Skærbæk took one stride forward, looked up at the huge man in the black jacket.

'You've lost it, you worthless piece of shit. Everything round here's fucked and I'm not holding it together for you. Not any more.'

He took off his work gloves, slapped them on the engine of the van.

'Fix this stinking mess yourself.'

Swept the tools and the cans from the workbench. Stormed out, kicking an oilcan on the way.

Birk Larsen watched, looked at Lotte.

'What's gone on?'

She was quiet. Scared.

His big hand fell on her shoulder.

'I want you to tell me what's happened, Lotte. I need to hear it now.'

In the kitchen, winter sun streaming through the windows. Pot plants. Pictures. School schedules on the wall. The door to Nanna's room was open. Everything back the way it was.

Pernille sat at the table, staring at the surface. Her back to him as he came through the door.

He walked to the stove and got himself a cup of coffee.

Didn't look at her as he said, 'I was in the house in Humleby last night. It doesn't look too bad. I'd got further than I thought.'

At the table. The morning paper. Nothing on the front page but a huge photo of Jens Holck and a smaller one of Nanna.

Pernille looked pale. Hungover. Ashamed maybe. He didn't want to think about it. Wouldn't.

He picked up the paper, his long, stubbly face held by the page.

Holck's photo was a politician's portrait. He looked decent, friendly, reliable. A pillar of Copenhagen society. A loving family man.

'They say he's dead,' Birk Larsen murmured.

Her eyes were as wide as he'd ever seen. Glistening with the coming tears.

'Theis. There's something I have to—'

'It doesn't matter.'

A single heavy teardrop ran down her right cheek.

With his big, rough hand Theis Birk Larsen reached out and brushed it away.

'It doesn't matter at all.'

More tears. He wondered why he couldn't join her. Why he owned the feelings but not the words.

'God I missed you,' he said. 'One day and it felt like for ever.'

She laughed then and two gleaming rivers appeared, so free and flowing he couldn't staunch them even if he wanted.

Her hand reached out, touched his chin, his brown beard going grey. Stroked his cheek, the wounds, the bruises. Then she leaned over and kissed him.

Her lips were warm and damp, and so was her skin. Over the table, with its mosaic of frozen faces he held her and she held him.

The way it was supposed to be.

Hartmann didn't break the news until the afternoon. It still left Weber furious.

'A *borg fred*? I can't believe you agreed to this, Troels. A truce benefits no one but Bremer. It's a way of silencing you. He's treating us all like naughty schoolchildren. If you go along to that meeting we're finished.'

Hartmann nursed his coffee, looked out of the office window, thought about a few days outside the small enclosed world of City Hall. With Rie somewhere. Alone.

'We don't have any choice.'

'Oh! So now it's fine Bremer stays in office.'

'No. It isn't. But he's backed us into a corner.'

Hartmann swore under his breath.

'God that man's got timing. If I do what he wants I can't criticize him. If I don't I look like the solitary troublemaker with a questionable past. We're screwed. Aren't we?'

No answer.

'Aren't we, Morten? Unless you've got some ideas?'

Weber took a deep breath. Was still out of words when the door opened and Rie Skovgaard came in with a face so pale and furious he beat a rapid retreat next door.

'I tried to phone you,' Hartmann said. 'You weren't home.'

'No.' She threw her bag on the desk, sat down. 'I was at a friend's house.'

'I'm sorry I never told you.'

'Why didn't you?'

'I was . . . I said I'm sorry.'

She came and stood in front him.

'Three days after your lost weekend you were asking me to move in with you.'

'I meant it.'

'So why didn't you tell me?'

'Because . . . I was drunk. It was stupid.'

'You could tell Morten. But you couldn't tell me. Is it going to make the papers?'

'No,' Hartmann insisted. 'Brix gave me his word.'

'That means a lot.'

'I think it does this time around. They won't look good if the truth comes out either. Forget the police, Rie. I didn't want to make things worse with you. Sometimes . . . I don't know what you want. I'm the one saying we should get a house somewhere. Have kids.'

'Now it's my fault?'

'I didn't mean that.'

'Then why say it? Oh screw it. I don't give a shit anyway.'

She got some papers out of her case, started to go through them.

'At least let me try to explain.'

'I don't want to hear it.'

She looked at him. No expression. It might have been a glance over the table at a committee meeting.

'Troels, it's over. We're still in the campaign. I've worked my heart out for that. I'm not quitting now. Tell me truthfully. Did you really agree to a truce with Bremer? You know what that means?'

'I told him I'd do what was best. He didn't leave me any options.'

'Well you've got them now. There won't be a truce.'

'That's my decision. Not yours.'

Rie Skovgaard reached over and took his diary off the desk.

'While you were pissing off everyone you could find and playing the martyr with the police I was working. You've got an extra appointment today. Tell me you still want to be Poul Bremer's poodle after that.'

Mette Hauge's father lived on a farm on the city outskirts near Køge. Lund drove out there alone. The place was mostly derelict from what she could see. The commercial greenhouse was empty with cracked windows and missing panels. There was no car, only a cheap motorbike parked by the back door.

It took a while for Jorgen Hauge to answer. He was a fit-looking grey-haired man in a blue boiler suit, not unlike the one Theis Birk Larsen had worn recently. Perhaps seventy.

He seemed puzzled when she showed him her police ID and asked about his daughter Mette.

'Why do you want to know? After all this time?'

'Just a few questions,' Lund said. 'It won't take long.'

Hauge lived on his own with a few chickens and an ancient sheepdog. The house was tidy and clean. He seemed a punctilious, careful man.

While he made coffee she walked round, looking. A photo of a young girl playing on the beach. Then a few years later posing on a couch. Prizes for cattle and pigs at shows.

'It was twenty-one years ago,' Hauge said when he came back. 'She disappeared on the seventh of November. A Wednesday.'

He looked at her.

'It was raining. I was worried about the drains.'

He brought more photos to the table.

'She'd just moved to Christianshavn. First place she had after leaving home. They said she was on her way back from handball. We called the police.'

News cuttings from the time. The same photo of Mette everywhere. Pretty.

'Two, three weeks later there were only a couple of officers on the case. They never found her.'

Another cutting. Wreaths. A headstone.

'So we buried a casket without a body.'

'Is it possible she committed suicide?'

He didn't seem to mind the question.

'Mette got depressed sometimes. She was a student. A bit naive. I think she hung around with some of the hippies for a while. Christiania and that. Not that she ever told us.'

'Was there any kind of note?'

'No. She didn't kill herself. I know . . .' He ran a finger across the cuttings. 'Your people told me a father always says that. But she didn't kill herself.'

'Did she have a boyfriend?'

'Not that we knew of. Like I said, she'd just moved to the city.' Hauge looked around the room. 'This place is a bit boring when you're young, I guess. It's a long time ago. I don't recall. She had a life . . .'

'Did anything puzzle you at the time?'

He bridled at that.

'Oh yes. One day you've got a daughter you love more than

491

anything in the world. The next she's gone for ever. That puzzled me.'

She got up, said, 'I'm sorry I bothered you.'

'Here's another thing. After all this time how come I get a visit from you people twice in one week?'

Lund stopped.

'What do you mean?'

'I had an officer here asking the same questions.'

'What was his name?'

'I wrote it down somewhere. He spoke funny. Didn't really hear all he said.'

Hauge sifted through some papers on an old desk by the window.

'Maybe I left it in the living room. I'll get it for you.'

She followed him, looking at the walls.

Photos and paintings everywhere. Family and landscapes.

Then one of Mette. It was black and white. Looked like student days. Hair dishevelled. Cheap T-shirt.

Necklace with a black heart.

She stood in front of the photo, unable to breathe for a moment.

Looked again.

Hand-made by hippies in Christiania, Meyer said. Not many of them around.

It was the same necklace. She knew that as certainly as she knew her own name.

Hauge came back.

'Where did she get that necklace?' Lund asked.

'I don't know. She was in the city by then. A gift maybe.'

'Who gave it to her?'

'Do you think she'd tell her father? Why?'

'Did you ever see it again? In her belongings after she died?'

'I don't think so.'

He gave her the name of the man he'd spoken to. She wondered why she was surprised.

'Do you mind if I take this photograph with me?' Lund asked. 'You'll get it back. I promise.'

Meyer went to talk to the family. Sat around their odd kitchen table. Told them what he knew. Holck met Nanna through the dating site.

He used Hartmann's identity to conceal what they were doing. The affair ended.

'Why did he do it?' Pernille Birk Larsen asked.

The two of them clasped hands together like teenagers.

'It looks like he was in love with her. Crazy. She broke it off. Holck persuaded Nanna to meet him one last time in the Liberals' flat. After that . . . we don't really know.'

Birk Larsen kept his eyes on Meyer and said, 'How exactly did he die?'

'He . . .'

Close to a stammer, Meyer struggled.

'He threatened the life of a colleague. So we had no alternative. He was shot.'

'Did he say anything?' she asked.

'No. He didn't.'

'And you're sure it's him?'

'We're sure.'

The couple's fingers worked together, entwined. A glance between them. A nod. A flicker of a smile.

'We'd like Nanna's things back now,' Pernille said.

'Of course. My colleague Sarah Lund's no longer on the case. If there's anything you need, call me from now on.'

Meyer placed his card on the table.

'Any time. About anything at all.'

He got up. So did Theis Birk Larsen.

The big man stuck his hand out. Meyer took it.

'Thank you,' Birk Larsen said.

A glance at his wife.

'From both of us. Thanks.'

Bengt Rosling was in the kitchen, cooking with his one good arm, Vibeke watching, smiling.

'When we get away from here things will be fine,' he said.

A bottle of Amarone. Pasta and sauce.

Vibeke toasted him.

'I need the place to myself again. Sarah . . .'

The door went. Her voice lowered.

'She needs someone to keep her in check.'

Lund walked in. Anorak damp from the drizzle outside. Hair a mess.

'Hi!' Bengt said, getting a third glass, pouring some wine.

'Can we talk?' she said.

'Now? We're making lunch. Your mother's helping me.'

Lund waited, said nothing.

'Here we go again,' Vibeke grumbled and walked into the living room, closing the door behind her.

Lund took the files out of her bag. Threw them on the table. Trying to control her temper, but not much.

'Well . . . ?' he asked.

'You talked to the father of one of the missing women.'

He sat down, gulped at the wine.

'You pretended you were a police officer. I could pull you in for that right now.'

'No, you can't.'

'Why not?'

'Because your boss Brix called me three days ago. He'd heard about my ideas. That maybe the man had killed before.'

He picked up the Mette Hauge folder, opened the first page.

Pretty girl. Dishevelled hair. It was a mugshot. Lund had checked. Mette had been cautioned over soft drugs.

'I told Brix what I thought. He brushed it to one side. He seemed determined to get Hartmann in the frame.'

'Really?'

'He was very arrogant in the way he dealt with me. I found that irritating.'

'I never realized your ego was so fragile.'

'That was uncalled for. I wanted to prove I was right. The Hauge file was old but it looked the most promising. They found her bike not far from where Nanna was dumped. So I went and called on the father.'

More wine.

'That's it,' he said.

'And what did you find out?'

He didn't say anything.

'What did you find out, Bengt?'

He held out the second glass. She didn't take it.

'Last night you told me you were wrong. There was no connection to any of the old cases. But you went out there. You know that wasn't true.'

'One case. Tentative.'

'Tentative?'

She pulled the black and white photo out of her bag.

'Look me in the face and say you never saw it. I want to know what it's like when you're lying. I never looked for that before.'

He glanced at the photo, frowned.

'It's probably just a coincidence. There might be thousands of those necklaces.'

'Now,' she said. 'Now I know what it's like.'

She went and stood over the sink, trying to think, trying to calm down.

'Sarah . . .'

He was behind her. Touched her shoulder briefly. Thought better of it.

'I love you. I'm worried about you. I didn't want this hanging around us for ever . . .'

She turned and faced him.

'What did you do afterwards?'

'I took some notes and gave them to Brix.'

She closed her eyes briefly.

'You gave them to Brix? Not me?'

'We weren't speaking. I was pissed off with you. How could I?'

Lund nodded.

'How could you?'

She picked up the folder and the photograph, stuffed them back in her bag.

'Sarah . . .'

Lund left him bleating in the kitchen, with his wine and his pasta and her mother.

Hartmann's unscheduled appointment proved to be with Gert Stokke, the head of Holck's council department. Skovgaard stayed to listen.

Stokke was a tall man approaching sixty. Civil servant's suit. Subtle, intelligent face. Bald as a coot and slippery.

He sat down, looked at Skovgaard first then Hartmann, and said, 'This had better be in confidence. I don't like coming in on Sundays. People talk.'

'Thanks for being here, Gert,' she said, and ushered him to the sofa.

'You realize the risk I'm taking?'

'Yes.' She glanced at Hartmann. 'We do. And we appreciate it.'

'Well . . .'

Stokke had worked in City Hall for more than twenty years. Three years before he was appointed to run the department Holck headed.

'Of course,' he said, 'I had access to all the accounts and budgets. This is public money. It's a very important job, and much under-appreciated if I might say so.'

Hartmann checked his watch and glared at Skovgaard.

'Am I keeping you?' Stokke asked.

'Tell us about Holck,' she said.

'Cold man. During the summer he changed. He was always so conscientious. Not likeable. But he was on top of his job.' A shrug. 'Then things started to slide.'

'How?' Hartmann asked.

'He took a day off and told me his child was sick. Then his wife called and asked me where he was. Men have affairs. It's none of my business.'

'Why am I listening to this, Rie?' Hartmann asked. 'None of it's new. Holck's dead. I've got a press conference.'

He got up from the chair.

'Gert,' she said. 'You knew Holck had an affair and that he used our flat?'

Hartmann stopped at the door.

'I knew about the affair,' Stokke agreed. 'I wasn't sure about the flat. Not entirely. I heard rumours about it. Once I wanted to send him some papers and he said that I should send them by taxi to Store Kongensgade.'

'Jesus,' Hartmann muttered.

'It could have been for a meeting with you.'

'You knew he used our flat?' Hartmann shook his head. 'Do you understand what you could have spared me? Why the hell didn't you say so? They threw me in jail—'

496

'I told Bremer,' Stokke said quickly. 'He knew all about it. He's Lord Mayor. If it's for anyone to speak out surely—'

'What?'

'Months ago. When I first knew about it. I asked for a meeting. Bremer said he was going to take care of it. He'd have a word with Holck.'

'When was all this?'

'May, June. He's Bremer! The Lord Mayor. If he says he's in control of something who am I to argue? Don't look at me like that, Hartmann. I'm here, aren't I?'

A sound at the door. Morten Weber bustled in.

'Troels. You're late for your castration. The press conference is assembling. Bremer wants to meet everyone beforehand.'

Weber caught the atmosphere.

'Gert?' he said. 'What the hell are you doing here?'

Jan Meyer was in the office with his wife. The kids. Three girls. Seven and five and two. They'd brought him two new toy police cars. Went *vroom vroom* with them on the desk top.

'Let's go out for a Sunday meal,' his wife said.

He had the eldest on his knee, arms around her waist.

'I'd really like to go home if that's OK.'

'Fine,' she said. 'Home.'

'We do have food at home, don't we?'

His voice grew big and bold, like a cartoon giant.

'I want big steaks and lots of ice cream. And candy and Coke. And then . . . more big steaks!'

'We can pick up some pizza . . .'

A shape beyond the glass. Lund stern-faced and anxious. She'd stopped at the door.

'Wait here,' Meyer said. 'I've got to talk to someone. It won't take a moment.'

Out in the corridor.

'What's up, Lund?'

'I don't know.'

She touched her head. He looked at her fingers.

'You're bleeding. The doctor said you'd need that restitched if they came out.'

'We've to go back to the canal. I think there's more out there.'

'Lund . . .'

The kids were waving at him from the office. They were making eating gestures. His wife didn't look happy.

'I'll tell you on the way.'

'No. Tell me now.'

'I'm not crazy, Meyer.'

He didn't speak.

'There's more,' she said. 'Shall we go?'

Lund drove, Meyer read her files. The radio news was on. Holck's death. A police officer held hostage. Brix saying the Nanna Birk Larsen case was closed. A truce rumoured at City Hall as the politicians drew in their horns and tried to ride out the blaze that had suddenly burst into life in their midst.

He was looking at the photo of the necklace. In Nanna's hand. Around the throat of Mette Hauge twenty-one years before.

'It's the same,' Lund said. 'Don't you think?'

'Looks like. Why does this girl stand out?'

'They found her bike. You can read it at the end of the report.'

Meyer got the page.

'Frieslandsvej?'

'Runs through the Kalvebod Fælled. By the main canal. Close to the Pentecost Forest. You cross the canal and you're in the woods. The bike was about seven hundred metres from where we found the car.'

There was a map of the area provided by the local nature foundation. Meyer pored over it.

'There's little canals criss-crossing this all the way to the coast. You could dump half of Copenhagen out there and we'd never find them.'

'Holck was studying in America when Mette Hauge went missing.'

She passed him a photocopy of a bachelor's degree certificate from the University of California in Santa Cruz.

'He never came back all year. It couldn't be him.'

'All you've got is the necklace.'

'And the bike. I know it's the same man. It has to be.'

'We've already searched the canal.'

'He wouldn't go back to the same place.'

Meyer waved the map at her.

'This could take years.'

They passed Vestamager Station, the last on the metro line. Then the road ran straight, south to the Øresund.

Low, flat land. Nothing but the outline of dead woodland on the right.

'We just need some help,' Lund said. 'Don't worry.'

There was a pumping station. Two night-duty officers from headquarters. They followed Lund and Meyer through a door, down some stairs, into a dark interior of clanking machines and pumps. The water company had sent an engineer. He was used to visitors. Liked to tell the history. When the Germans invaded Denmark they were looking for any excuse they could find to ship out the local men and put them to work in Nazi labour camps.

So the Copenhagen government invented phoney schemes to keep them at home. One was land reclamation. The project had no practical purpose. But it kept hundreds of Danes out of the hands of the Germans for a while.

'And now,' he said over the sound of the machinery, 'we keep pumping. Eighty per cent of the ground round here is below sea level. If we didn't the Øresund would want it back.'

He had a better map. Meyer looked at it and sighed. The drainage network was even more complex than it first looked, spanning the entire area like a watery nervous system on a haphazard path to the sea.

'Here's the bridge where we found Nanna,' she said, pointing to the spot on the map. 'Where does the canal go?'

'All of the canals take drainage water to the seawater reservoir. That's why they're there.'

Her finger traced back from the point of Nanna's death to the ditch where Mette Hauge's bike was left.

'This is impossible, Lund,' Meyer grumbled. 'Where the hell do we start?'

She stared at him, puzzled. It seemed an uncharacteristically oblique question.

'We start by thinking like he did.' She was showing the company man the map again. 'What's this?'

'A drain line that flowed onto the old road.'

'What road?'

'The old road,' he said as if she was supposed to know. 'We closed it down twenty years or so ago. We didn't need it. No one went there. Why would they?'

'This is where we look,' Lund said, tapping her finger on the map. 'Get divers out to all the canals and ditches that lead off it. We need to drag the lake.'

'Oh no,' the engineer said, laughing nervously. 'You can't do that. We'd have to close down everything if people know you're looking for a body.'

'Shutting it down's the best thing to do,' Lund said. 'Let's say forty-eight hours.'

She looked at the night men.

'Bring more people in.'

'You can't! There's a hundred and fifty thousand homes on the system. Hospitals. Old people's homes.'

'We'll be as quick as we can.'

There was a tall figure at the top of the steps. Long coat, long face.

Brix came clunking down the metal stairs.

Lund walked straight to him.

'They never found Mette Hauge's body,' she said quickly. 'Her bike was close to where Nanna was left. The black necklace was Mette's. We've got to search the canals. It's the same man.'

'OK,' Brix said. 'Send in the divers.'

She couldn't believe how easy this was.

'I'll get onto the air force for some F-16s,' he added. 'Alert NATO. Anything else? Can we get a submarine in here?'

'Listen. Holck wasn't in the country then.'

'So he didn't kill Mette Hauge. There's a surprise. But he did murder Nanna. That's what matters. I read your boyfriend's memo. It's just theory. The case is solved. Holck had an affair with Nanna. His prints were all over the flat.'

'They could be old. Where did Holck take her? We still don't know. It wasn't that warehouse he was staying in. There's nothing there—'

'Just go home, will you? Work things out with your boyfriend. Then catch a plane to Sweden. Please.'

He started walking off.

She was getting mad and wished she wasn't.

'That's what you want, is it? For me to shut up. Did Bremer ask for that too? Is that part of the deal?'

Brix turned and looked at her.

'I'm a patient man, you know. But everything runs out in the end. Didn't you notice?'

'I'm telling you, Brix.'

He held out his hand.

'I want your police ID.'

She tried to argue. He wouldn't listen. Lund handed it over.

'And the car keys.'

Meyer had seen something, was walking over.

'You need all the help you can get, Lund,' Brix said. 'Thank God you're off my budget so I don't have to pay for it.'

He threw the car keys. Meyer caught them.

'Cancel everything she asked for. She's someone else's problem now.'

Meyer drove her home, trying in his own way to offer some comfort.

'We could have pissed around there for the rest of our lives and never found a thing. Come on.'

Her head was bleeding again. She dabbed at it with a tissue. In the end left the bloody stump of paper stuck to the back of her scalp.

'And anyway the water guy said they checked the bacteria level daily. The bit you were talking about was near the water supply. They'd have picked up something.'

'It was twenty-one years ago. Forget the canal for now. Why did Nanna go to the flat? She was looking forward to something, remember? Those pictures of her at school. She was happy.'

'She liked Holck. That's why she was happy.'

Lund looked at him and blinked.

'OK. Maybe that doesn't work,' Meyer confessed. 'But you never know everything.'

'Why didn't they go to the flat together?'

'Because he's a politician. He can't be seen in public with a nineteen-year-old girl. And maybe—'

'Oh for pity's sake. Do you think I'm crazy too?'

'Of course I don't. I'm driving you home, aren't I?'

'You always make a joke of things when they turn awkward.'

'I don't think you're crazy, Lund. OK?'

'You need to check the Mette Hauge file. It was a big case back then. They conducted seventeen hundred interviews. There has to be someone who links into Nanna.'

Meyer groaned.

'I need to do it?'

'Yes. Brix has my ID. I can't get into the archives. Do it tonight. Look for recurring names. Locations.'

'No.'

'See if there are any—'

'No!' Meyer roared.

Silence.

'This has to stop,' he said finally. 'It's turned into an obsession.'

She looked out of the window and said, 'I understand you'll feel bad if it wasn't Holck.'

His hands came off the wheel. Clapped them, then went back to driving.

'In case you didn't notice, I shot Holck for your sake. Not Nanna's. She was already dead.'

Silence.

'Why is it you're so aware of everything around you? But not yourself?'

He hesitated.

'Not even your own family.'

'You did the right thing, Meyer.'

'I know I did the right thing. It's not about that. The case is closed. Done.'

She wouldn't look at him.

'You're the only one who can't understand that. You need to talk to a psychologist or something.'

'So I am crazy?'

'I didn't mean it that way.'

'There's another way?'

'Oh for the love of God . . .'

She undid her seat belt, grabbed her coat.

'Stop the car. Let me out here.'

'Don't be so childish.'

The folders went into her bag. She put a hand on the door, started to open it even as the car was moving.

'Calm down!' Meyer yelled.

'Stop this thing and let me out.'

'Do you even know where you are?'

Lund looked at the street lights. Somewhere near Vesterbro. The wrong side of town for her mother's place.

'Yes,' she said. 'I know.'

Hartmann walked into the press conference, Skovgaard by his side.

'Why are we even here?' she said in a cold, hard whisper. 'You heard what Stokke said. Bremer could have cleared you from the outset . . .'

Another wood-panelled room. Paintings, old and new on the walls. Reporters assembling. Cameramen adjusting their gear. The party leaders in a huddle by the podium.

Weber was with her for once.

'You can't ignore the facts,' he said. 'This is a travesty.'

Mai Juhl came and shook his hand.

'It's good of you to come, Troels. After all you've been through.'

'All he's been put through,' Weber muttered.

'No problem, Mai,' Hartmann said. 'Will you give me a minute?'

Poul Bremer had just walked in, was reading some documents. He saw Hartmann approaching.

'I'm glad you came. Let's get on with it.'

'We need to talk.'

The reporters were taking their seats.

'No, Troels. Not now.'

'You knew Holck transferred that money to Olav Christensen.'

Bremer thrust his fists into his trouser pockets, looked at him, mouth open, eyes narrow.

'Did I? Says who?'

Hartmann didn't answer.

'Ah. Let me guess. One of the civil servants?' Bremer smiled. 'Makes sense. They always watch their own backs first.'

'You knew,' Hartmann told him. 'Don't try to wriggle out of it.'

'Of course I didn't know!' He patted Hartmann's shoulder. 'Troels . . . you've been through a lot. It shows. You really must learn to control that temper of yours.'

Hartmann didn't rise to the bait.

'Listen,' Bremer went on. 'Holck's civil servants are squabbling among themselves. They know I'm going to conduct a closed hearing into this mess. They'll invent any nonsense they can to dodge the blame.'

The genial smile, the twinkling eyes.

'You've been through hell. I can see why you're suspicious. Holck and maybe some of his people deceived all of us. We need to clean up this mess together. We will. Agreed?'

No answer.

'Or would you rather believe them than me?' Poul Bremer asked. Another pat. Another smile. 'Good. Let's get started.'

More reporters through the door. Bremer beaming from the podium. A well-prepared speech about how Holck's exposure had come as a shock to all. How one city councillor above all others had unfairly borne the brunt of the fallout.

'We've all witnessed the unreasonable accusations Troels Hartmann has been subjected to,' Bremer said, putting a hand on Hartmann's shoulder. 'Never for one moment did I believe them. But politicians must respond to events and we did, in good faith but mistakenly. Now, in City Hall, we declare a *borg fred*, a truce. We bury our differences for the benefit of Copenhagen . . .'

Hartmann turned to him and said, his voice caught by the microphone, 'You're the head of the finance committee.'

The old man stopped, glared.

'What?'

'You're the head of the finance committee.'

No smile. No warmth now.

'We'll talk about this later,' Bremer said in a low, hard voice.

Hartmann wouldn't be silenced.

'How could the committee not know that Holck authorized the money, not me? How's that possible? You lied to me . . .'

Bremer was stuttering, caught between the audience and Hartmann.

'As . . . as we've already agreed—'

Hartmann took the microphone from him.

'The Liberal group will not be a part of this farce,' he said, watching the reporters start to scribble furiously. 'If we do what Poul Bremer wishes we'll never know the full truth of Holck's actions, and who was party to them.'

One of the TV political hacks cried out, 'What do you mean, Hartmann? Say it.'

'I mean that the Lord Mayor knows more about this case than he's told any of us. And the police.'

Bremer stared at Hartmann, at the other leaders, furious.

'I've no further comments for the moment,' Hartmann added. 'As far as the Liberals are concerned this election's like any other. We fight every seat and we fight to win.'

He left the podium. The press divided, half to him, half to Bremer demanding answers.

Back in his office Hartmann told them to speak to all the financial backers who'd dropped out. Brief them on the situation. Find new ones.

Skovgaard was on the phone. Weber was tugging at his unruly head of hair.

'We're going to have the media down our throats demanding an explanation, Troels. What am I supposed to say?'

'When I've clarified things with Stokke we'll put out a statement. Fix a meeting with him.'

'Stokke's a civil servant. He won't come forward. He's not going to put his career on the line for us.'

'It's his duty to tell the truth,' Hartmann insisted. 'I'll meet with him. We'll work this out. Oh for Christ's sake, Morten. Don't look so worried. You wanted out of the truce, didn't you?'

'I did. But you haven't learned yet, have you? Throw a stone at Bremer and you get a boulder back. I'll try . . .'

He wandered off into the main room.

Hartmann was alone with Skovgaard. Hands in pockets. Tongue-tied.

She'd come off the phone.

'Did I remember to thank you?' he said. 'For all the work?'

'It's what I'm paid for.'

Hair back. Attractive face tired and lined. But she thrived on pressure. Liked the tension. The race.

'I'm sorry I've been such a mess, Rie.'

'Me too.'

She didn't leave then and she might have.

The briefest of laughs.

'Still, that was quite a performance. Stealing the limelight from Bremer in front of everyone. I forgot you had that in you.'

'What else could I do? Bremer knew. It was written in his face. He knew and I don't think he even minded if I saw it.' A glance outside the window. The Copenhagen night. The blue hotel sign. 'He really thinks this all belongs to him.'

'Morten's got a point. He'll come back at us somehow.'

Hartmann took a step towards her.

'Do you think there's any chance . . . maybe we could go out for a meal tonight? I'm still trying to get the taste of that jail food out of my mouth.'

He wore a self-deprecating smile. Didn't mind begging.

'Not tonight. I'll start drafting a press release.'

'Maybe tomorrow—'

'You really need to think about what you're going to say to Stokke. If he won't play this game we're done for.'

Theis Birk Larsen made some calls. People he hadn't talked to for a long time. People he hoped never to have to deal with again.

But life changed.

He said what was needed then put down the phone.

Pernille was at the kitchen table, out of earshot he hoped, reading the paper.

He took the chair opposite. Pernille looked at the photo on the front page. Jens Holck.

'They say he was a family man,' she said. 'Our age.'

He pushed the paper to one side.

'I'm glad he's dead. I suppose it's wrong of me, Theis, but I am. We're supposed to forgive.'

She looked at him, as if seeking some answer.

'How can you forgive? How?' A pause. 'Why?'

He grimaced, stared out of the window for a moment.

'I've made some calls about the house. The estate agents say they're almost done with the paperwork. I'm going to see her tomorrow.'

He lit a cigarette and waited. She was still looking at the paper. Finally she put her hands on his arm, smiled, said, 'I'm sorry. What did you say?'

'The sooner we sell the house the better.'

'By Christmas maybe?'

'I've got to get a good price. Those bastards at the bank are at our throats . . .'

She ran her hand down his strong arm. Put her fingers to his stubbly cheek.

'It'll be fine,' he said. 'You never thought you were marrying a millionaire, did you?'

She laughed at that, the first time he'd seen her laugh since the blackness fell upon them out on the Kalvebod Fælled, that dark damp night a lifetime before.

'I was young. I never knew what I was marrying.' Fingers on his skin again. 'Just that I wanted him.'

The agency details for the house were on the table. She looked at the plans. Three floors. A garden.

'Humleby,' she said.

Theis Birk Larsen watched her, felt a warm rush of hope and love run though him.

A sound downstairs. The big door opening.

'I'll deal with it,' he said.

The garage seemed empty. Just the goods they fetched and carried. Valuable goods.

Birk Larsen called, got no answer.

Thought about burglars and how much he relied on the little man called Skærbæk. An old friend he treated so badly at times.

He picked up a wrench and walked round to the office, turned on the light.

A figure emerged from the dark. Slight and young.

An Indian man, with scholarly glasses and a fetching round face that looked ready to burst into tears.

'Hello,' he said, and came and shook Birk Larsen's hand. 'The door was open. You don't recognize me, do you?'

Birk Larsen shrugged.

'No. I don't. It's late. We're closed. Can I—'

'I'm Amir. Amir El' Namen.'

He pointed to the door.

'You remember my dad? With the restaurant?'

A flash of memory, a sudden pang of pain.

Two children, no more than six, riding to school hand in hand, tight in the scarlet box of the Christiania trike. Little Nanna and the Indian boy, Pernille at the pedals, happy and beautiful. Vagn Skærbæk never approved. Birk Larsen wasn't sure either. Pernille thought it was sweet, so sweet she'd invite Amir in for parties, make him Western clothes. Ride him and Nanna around and around giggling as it bounced and crashed across the cobbled streets.

That was one of the photos captured on the table.

They'd half-watched as Amir turned from a foreigner who spoke no Danish into one more local kid. Different skin but not different.

And besides, Birk Larsen remembered, Nanna loved him. Amir was her first boyfriend. For two years, maybe three. And then . . .

'You're Karim's youngest,' he said, and found the memories contained more smiles than pain, and one of them sprang to his face.

'I've been in London. Studying.'

'I remember. Karim told me. You're getting married, right?'

He had a bag over his shoulder, a fashionable khaki jacket. A student with money. He didn't find it easy to speak. He seemed – and this was ridiculous, surely – scared.

'Amir. What can I do for you?'

'Will you move some things for me? Tomorrow?'

'Move what?'

A pause.

'Things for the wedding. Some tables and chairs.'

'Tomorrow? No. It's the middle of Sunday night. You can't expect us to drop everything. I mean . . .'

Amir's face fell. He looked ashamed.

'I'm sorry. I didn't mean to offend you. I just . . . It's OK. I'll make some other arrangement.'

Birk Larsen breathed a deep sigh, walked to the desk, got the schedule.

'Look. I'll try to find someone for you.'

'Mr Birk Larsen . . .'

'What?'

He walked up, looked hopeful.

'I really need it to be you.'

'Me? What difference does it make?'

'I need it to be you. Please.'

Two little kids in the box of the Christiania trike. Nanna's first boyfriend. So sweet, so meek, so deferential. No different now.

'I'll pick you up at lunchtime,' Birk Larsen said. 'One o'clock in the restaurant. You'll have to help me.'

'Of course.'

He held out his hand.

'Thank you, sir,' Amir said.

Lund's mother was seething that Bengt had left.

'What in God's name did you say to him? To make him run out like that?'

Lund had taken over her work desk. Covered it with reports taken from headquarters. Removed the white, half-finished wedding dress from her mannequin and pinned photos of Nanna and Mette Hauge to the headless shape instead.

'I told him he had to stay in a hotel.'

The TV news was on. She heard Hartmann's name. Turned to see the story about the conflict with Bremer, and the promise of revelations about Holck.

Vibeke was in her blue dressing gown, skinny arms folded, staring at her like a judge from an ancient drama.

'Hartmann accused Bremer of failing to disclose his knowledge of Holck's actions,' the news said.

'You told me the case was over.'

Lund watched the TV closely, took in Hartmann's words.

'Mark's moved in with his father, Sarah. You've kicked out Bengt. You treat me as if I'm just here for your convenience.'

Lund turned up the volume on the TV.

'I want an explanation!' Vibeke cried. 'Why?'

'Because it's important, for Christ's sake! Important. You know what that word means?'

That unforgiving basilisk stare. Then Vibeke said, 'I talked to your Aunt Birgit. I'm going to stay with her for a few days.'

The news got less interesting.

'Are you taking the train? Because I'll need your car.'

Vibeke closed her eyes and turned her face to the ceiling.

The doorbell rang. Her mother wasn't moving so Lund left the TV and walked out briskly to answer it.

No one there. She walked out into the hall, looked up the stairs, down them. Heard the door slam far below.

Gone. And – this was her first thought – no CCTV in Vibeke's damned building.

She walked back to the apartment, caught something with her foot, looked down.

There was a padded envelope on the doormat. No name. She picked it up. Knew the shape straight away.

A video cassette.

Her mother went to bed. Lund cut the envelope carefully. She didn't have gloves so she used a remnant of Vibeke's satin to handle it.

An old tape, the label scratched off. The way some were in City Hall security.

She slotted it into the TV and watched.

Picked up her phone.

'Meyer?' she said.

Thirty minutes later he arrived, red-faced and cursing.

'Will you ever leave me alone?'

'You came didn't you? Sit down.'

'This is like a bad affair. All the danger and none of the sex.'

Lund got the remote.

'Not that I'm asking,' he added quickly.

'You've never had an affair, Meyer. You wouldn't know how.'

After that he sat down like an obedient little boy.

The video came on.

'So why am I here?'

'It's the missing tape. From the CCTV system at City Hall.'

The security office came on screen. People leaving for the evening.

Meyer pulled at his right ear.

'How the hell did you get this?'

'Someone left it on my doormat.'

She passed him the padded envelope. It was now in a freezer bag from the kitchen.

Then Nanna walked on the screen, still beautiful in black and white. Hair a little untidy. Not a teenager. That seemed impossible. She was smiling, nervously but affectionately too.

Looking up. Looking around. An expression on her face that seemed to say: farewell.

A man walked in from the left. Jens Holck. Took something from his pocket. A key ring it looked like. Nanna came to him, embraced him.

Lund pushed out another stub of Nicotinell and began to chew.

'Is Holck seen leaving the Rådhus?' Meyer asked.

'Half an hour later.'

'There's nothing there we didn't know already.'

'You've got to learn to look, Meyer. How many times do I have to say this?'

She started rolling back the tape.

'I did! We see him give her the keys. They make a date. And then she goes to the flat.'

'I know you can't help the fact you're a man. But really. They don't make a date. Look!'

Meyer's bug eyes fixed on the screen.

'Can't you see? Holck's face. He's not happy. If Nanna had come back to him why would he look so miserable?'

A final hug, a kiss that was friendship not passion. Holck looked like a man who'd lost everything. And Nanna as happy as the child she dreamed she no longer was.

Meyer nodded.

'OK. It still doesn't mean he didn't meet her at the flat.'

He got up and started nosing around. Looking at the reports on the work desk. The photos on the mannequin.

'Where's your mother?'

Lund froze the video.

'Meyer. You have to help me.'

Nothing.

'If you have the slightest doubt . . .' she started.

He waved the freezer bag and the envelope at her.

'I don't like this. Someone delivers a tape and we're back in all that shit at City Hall again.'

'It doesn't matter where it is.'

'You only get stuff like this if they've something to gain.'

'You're very cynical sometimes. Maybe they just want to help.'

Meyer looked mournfully at the frozen picture. A miserable Holck kissing a joyful Nanna.

'Oh crap,' he said.

Monday, 17th November

First thing that morning Hartmann had Gert Stokke in his office. The civil servant looked shifty.

'All I'm asking is you tell the truth. That you say you told Bremer about Holck using our flat.'

'You don't want much, do you?'

Stokke had a long grey bloodhound face and pink, watery eyes.

'I can't get involved with you and Bremer.'

'You already are,' Rie Skovgaard said.

Morten Weber leapt in.

'Do you think he'll reward you for keeping quiet, Gert? You know him. You're a civil servant. He can't dump this on Holck any more. So he'll pick on the department. You'll be the first to go.'

Stokke scowled at the three of them. A smart man, cornered.

'And you're on my side? My friends now, huh? Go stab one another. Leave me out of it.'

'If Bremer survives this you're gone,' Weber said.

The civil servant shook his head.

'Bremer's never going to admit we had that conversation.'

'There must be minutes,' Skovgaard said.

A moment's hesitation. Then he said, 'Bremer didn't want it minuted. He said he'd have a quiet word with Holck. Then it would be over with.'

Weber swore and slammed his papers on the table.

'I'm sorry. If I come forward I'm finished. I always thought you'd make a good Lord Mayor, Hartmann. Maybe next time round.'

'There won't be a next time,' Hartmann grumbled. 'We need you, Gert.'

'Who'd hire me if I spoke out? I'm fifty-eight. What about my pension?'

Skovgaard was livid.

'So Troels should pay the price instead? When he did nothing?'

'Leave it, leave it,' Hartmann cut in. 'Let's not pressure Gert any more. If he won't do it, he won't do it. It's up to him.'

He held out his hand. Stokke took it.

'Thanks for coming anyway,' Hartmann said, and watched the civil servant button his jacket and leave.

Weber had a copy of Stokke's minutes from the original meeting.

'Is it there?' Hartmann asked.

'No. Look for yourself.'

He passed over the sheets.

'We should have leaned on him more,' Skovgaard said.

Morten Weber shook his head.

'Pointless. He's terrified of Bremer. Won't work.'

Hartmann stopped on the second page.

'It says here there's an appendix. Where is it?'

'Probably technical documentation,' Weber suggested.

Hartmann wasn't convinced.

'Stokke's a good civil servant. I can't believe he wouldn't set down something. It's financial impropriety for God's sake. He'd want to cover his back.'

'He's terrified of Bremer. I told you.'

'Maybe. Are we friendly with anyone in Holck's department? That big woman—'

'You mean Rita?' Skovgaard asked.

'If that's what she's called.'

'Yes. I know Rita.'

'Well,' he said, throwing the minutes at her, 'you know what to do.'

Then she started bickering about a media strategy. Hartmann didn't listen. Weber was on the phone again. Getting heated.

'What is it?' Hartmann asked when he was done.

'You're going to have to talk to that lawyer of yours again, Troels.'

'Oh for God's sake. Not Lund.'

'Not Lund. Bremer wants to sue for libel.'

Vibeke's car was a ten-year-old green Beetle. Lund didn't feel minded to drive it very carefully.

The laundry was in Islands Brygge. She'd used it once before when the police couldn't find the right person.

A charity. Sponsored by the city. Most of the people working there were disabled in some way. A few deaf from birth.

The manager remembered her.

'Why does everybody think that because someone's deaf they can lip-read?' he moaned when she turned up. 'It's not true. Even if they can they probably only pick up a third of what they see.'

The place handled many of the big city hotels. She walked past industrial washing machines, piles of sheets and pillows. The air was hot and humid, and sickly with the smell of ironing and detergent.

'I'll take a third,' she said.

'You need to know the subject matter, the context.'

'I can do that.'

He stopped.

'I imagine you can. If anyone can help it's Ditte. She's a smart little thing. Deaf and dumb. Bright as they come.'

She looked about twenty, long fair hair, immobile face. Working a commercial ironing machine with a steady, practised ease.

Lund spoke, the manager signed. The girl watched Lund mostly.

Bright as they come.

Ditte's fingers flew.

'She wants to see your badge.'

Lund fumbled in her pockets. The girl's eyes never left her.

'I forgot it. It's supposed to be my day off. I must have left it at home.' She smiled at the manager. 'I've been here before. He knows me.'

Nothing.

'I can give you my card.'

Brix hadn't taken those.

Ditte read the card carefully and then they went and sat in a storeroom.

The video was on her laptop. Lund took her through it slowly, rewinding when necessary. That wasn't often.

The girl signed, the man talked.

'She came because he promised to give her some keys.'

Frozen on a frame. Nanna looking at Jens Holck. Begging.

'She wants to pick up something she forgot.'

Ditte's fingers twisted and turned.

'She doesn't want him to come with her.'

The girl stopped, eyes locked to the screen.

'What is it?' Lund asked.

The man's hands gestured. Ditte responded, slowly.

'She says this is very sad. The girl's saying she told him it was over.'

'Does she say what she forgot?'

'She came to get her . . .'

The hands stopped.

'Her what?'

Nothing.

'Do you want me to rewind it?'

Ditte made a soft, meaningless noise, not vowel, not consonant.

'No,' she says. 'Let it play.'

'They went away somewhere for the weekend.'

Ditte nodded. Happy with something. She turned and looked at Lund. Fingers very certain.

'She says she left her passport in a drawer in the flat afterwards.'

Lund took a deep breath.

'Her passport? Are you sure about that?'

Ditte was back, trapped by the screen.

'Her plane leaves tonight,' the manager said.

'Her plane? Where to?'

The laundry girl looked puzzled. Lund halted the video. Let her catch her breath.

'Take this slowly. There's no rush.'

'She wants you to play the video,' the man said.

So Lund did.

'The man asks her where she's going to. But she just asks for the keys. She says she's met someone else. Someone she loves very much. Someone she's going away with.'

Two faces on the screen, love and hate in the same moment. Both dead.

'He asks her where she's going again.'

Lund closed her eyes.

'And she says Paris. But Paris . . .'

Ditte stopped. She looked cross.

'What about Paris?'

The hands again.

'It isn't Paris. She's lying.'

'How do you know?'

She pointed to the video.

'When the girl speaks she won't look him in the eye.'

Lund nodded. The hands flew again.

'Just like you, when you said you'd forgotten your badge. And it was your day off.'

The laundry girl sat at the laptop smiling at Lund. Proud of herself.

'I won't get into trouble for this, will I?' the manager asked.

'No,' she said. 'I promise.'

*

Outside, in the hard seat of Vibeke's green Beetle, travelling back into the city, she called Meyer.

'Nanna's plane was leaving that night. She lied about the destination.'

She could hear the sound of papers getting slammed on the desk. Meyer had her on speakerphone. He was probably making rude gestures at the handset as she spoke.

'We never came across anything to suggest she was going on a trip.'

'She said goodbye to her parents. Goodbye to her friends at school. To Kemal. To Holck. You saw that too.'

'Did I? Who was she going away with?'

'Get all the passenger lists. Talk to the airlines.'

'No problem. I've got nothing else to do.'

'Did you check the old cases?'

'I'm looking at them now. I can't see any link. Except for Mette Hauge's bike and really—'

'Check the departures and find out who she was travelling with. The Hauge girl—'

The phone clicked.

'Meyer?' Lund said into the neck mike. 'Meyer?'

Nanna's room looked different again. Pernille had relented. Got some Birk Larsen boxes. Carefully started stashing her belongings.

Moving things. Changing things.

There was a globe on Nanna's desk. Marked with ink stars for all the cities she wanted to visit one day. London and Rome. New York and Beijing.

Pernille looked at it. A simple piece of plastic. Placed it in the cardboard box and walked back into the living room. Looked around.

All their life had been here, from Nanna to the boys. All the love and squabbles. All the pain and joy.

On the door in crayon were the height marks. Red for Nanna, green for Anton, blue for Emil. The junk the police had posted was gone. She could see the place again without being reminded of the world outside and what it contained.

Lives were never still. They shifted always. Or they weren't lives at all. She'd forgotten this in the dreadful limbo that had consumed them. Forgotten it before, perhaps, in the comfort of their cramped apartment above the grubby, busy depot. Bringing up kids. Feeding Theis. Enjoying his strong arms around her when they were alone.

Never still. You either moved with time or it flowed past heedless. Left you stranded in the bare, cold sand.

She walked downstairs. The woman from the agency had called. Theis was talking to her. Knuckles still raw from whatever happened two nights before. Face grim and dark.

Pernille knocked on the door, went in, sat down.

The woman said, 'I really think you should take the offer. I know it's not wonderful. But the market's not very good. With your finances the bank expect the money.'

'The bank,' he muttered.

She smiled, and said to Pernille, 'Now that it's all over a clean break might be nice.'

Pernille froze.

Quickly, the estate agent added, 'I don't mean over with, of course, but—'

'When would they move in?' he asked.

'Very soon. The money—'

Pernille said, 'We'd like to talk about this. Can you wait outside?'

She seemed shocked, but went.

'Stinking banks,' he muttered.

The plans were on the desk. Some drawings. The agency photos.

'I never had the time to look at it.'

'No . . .'

'What's it like? Is it nice? Is there a garden?'

'It's Humleby. Three floors . . .'

'Would the boys like it, Theis?'

'Their own rooms? They could have a train set. Of course they'd like it.'

'And the school's not far . . .'

'Pernille.' He eyed the woman beyond the glass. 'The dragon out there just told me she's found a buyer. The price is lousy but . . .'

She didn't speak.

'The bank would love it.'

Her fingers were running across the photos. Grey Humleby brickwork. A garden.

'But if you've changed your mind—'

'No, no. Take the offer.'

She looked at him.

'We need the money, don't we?'

'Money,' he said.

Lund found the taxi driver, Leon Frevert, polishing his Mercedes on a rank by the tourist ferry stop in Nyhavn.

He didn't want to talk.

After three monosyllabic answers Frevert said, 'I told you everything I knew. I picked up a fare. I took her somewhere. What else is there to say?'

'Did she have a bag?'

He started on the windscreen. She thought of Ditte. Frevert wouldn't look her in the eye.

'It's been almost three weeks. This is ridiculous.'

'Did she have a bag?'

He put down the cloth, glanced in her direction.

'Maybe she had her wallet in a bag. I don't know.'

'I meant a travel bag. A suitcase. A rucksack.'

'No. She didn't.'

'You're sure?'

'If she had I would have put it in the boot.'

The car ahead moved off. That left him second in line. She felt sure Frevert would have driven off given half the chance.

'Did she tell you where she was going afterwards?'

He looked thinner than she recalled. More careworn.

'What I said before. City Hall and Grønningen. That's all I know.'

The first car left. Frevert was next.

'She didn't mention the airport?'

'Definitely not. I would have driven her there. A good ride that.' He scratched his thinning hair. 'Now you mention it though—'

'What?'

'She asked me to wait.'

'To wait?'

'Yeah. I remember now. She said she had to go round the corner and then she'd be straight back. So could I wait?'

He laughed.

'On a Friday night? I was nice to the kid when we went to City

Hall. But there were plenty of customers. I couldn't hang around there.'

For a moment he looked bleak and ashamed.

'Jesus. What if I had?'

'Where did Nanna want to go next?'

Frevert was thinking.

'I think she said Central Station.'

The station was opposite Tivoli. Lund could think of only one reason why Nanna would want to go there.

She went straight to the left luggage department. There was an officious-looking youth in a blue uniform behind the counter. He said that after three days every box got emptied and any uncollected contents taken into store.

'If you give me a key I'll find it,' he added. 'There'll be a charge.'

'I don't have a key.'

'What's the number?'

'I don't have the number.'

'In that case,' he said very brightly, 'you don't get any luggage.'

'It's a travel bag. Handed in around October the thirty-first.'

He looked about eighteen. She could see the storage area behind the counter. Rows and rows of bags.

'Is this bag yours by any chance?'

'If you let me behind and tell me where to look I'll find it.'

He folded his arms.

'Anything else you'd like? A free ticket, first class, to Helsingør? A cheeseburger?'

She pulled out her police business card, gave it to him.

'Sarah Lund. You called us about a suspicious suitcase.'

He read it, put it in his pocket.

'Let's see some ID.'

She started climbing over the steel gate beside him.

'I can find the bag myself.'

Lund marched past him, ignoring his shouts, got to the back, dragged a bag off the shelf. The date was recent. Nanna's had to be somewhere else.

'You stop this now! I'm an official of the railroad.'

'I'm trying to help,' Lund said, running quickly down the lines of shelves.

'I'm getting mad now.'

He stood there, thin arms folded.

'You're getting mad?' she yelled at him. 'I came in on my day off as a favour to someone in transport. And I've got a spotty teenager on my case. Fuck off over the road and take a fairground ride, sonny. Grown-ups have got work to do.'

Face red, he started bleating, arms flapping.

'You . . . oh . . . You!'

'Mickey Mouse is waiting,' she said, pointing out to Tivoli.

'You stay here!' he shrieked. 'I'm fetching my boss.'

Lund moved quickly.

So many bags. Most of them black. The kind men bought.

Nanna was pretty and liked pretty things.

Voices at the end of the room. Someone getting loud.

Lund half-ran until she saw it. Pink and fashionable. A brand name. The kind Jens Holck might have bought on City Hall expenses.

She looked at the name tag. Frederiksholm High School on one side. Vesterbrogade 95, Lotte's address on the other.

Of course Nanna kept it there. She'd never want Pernille and Theis to know.

Lund picked up the bag and rushed out with it, ignoring the flapping, screeching teenager at the counter.

Meyer didn't put the phone down on her.

'Do you have the passenger lists?' she asked.

'No.'

He sounded reluctant to speak.

'You're driving somewhere, Meyer.'

'SAS are on strike. I'm going to the airport. OK?'

'Good. I've got her bag.'

She was back in the green Beetle, going through Nanna's belongings, the suitcase open on the passenger's seat.

'Any indication where she was going?' he asked.

A sketchpad. Trainers. Swimsuit. Warm clothes. Price tags on most of the things. She reeled them off to Meyer.

'Anything to suggest who she was going with?'

'No.'

Lund had a spare pair of forensic gloves from home. Bit the pack open with her teeth, snapped them on.

'I'm going to ask the Birk Larsens,' Lund said.

'For God's sake, don't do that. Yesterday I told them we'd closed the case. Those two need a break.'

'Yes, well . . . I'll work something out.'

'Lund!'

Birk Larsen turned up outside the Indian restaurant on the dot. Pernille called.

'The bank won't help us, Theis.'

'What are you talking about?'

'They won't help us with the house. Maybe we could take out a loan against the company?'

'The company's got enough loans. We're selling the house, aren't we?'

She sounded calm. Happy almost.

'I'm there now. In Humleby. You haven't put up any curtains.'

'Curtains! Why do women always think of curtains! There's plumbing and wiring and—'

'Even without the curtains it looks beautiful.'

Birk Larsen stopped in the street. Broke into a broad smile. Laughed at the gloomy winter sky.

'Women,' he said.

He heard her happy voice down the line. Could see her face in his head.

'Baby?'

He hadn't called her that in ages.

'Baby?' Pernille echoed. 'Do I answer to baby?'

'You used to. Why not? What I'm going to do, baby, is call the estate agency. Tell them the sale's cancelled. And they can shove their commission up their tight backside.'

Silence.

'If that's OK.'

Silence.

'If,' he said again, 'that's OK.'

'It's a house, Theis. We never had a house. What about the money?'

'I'll find a way to make it work.'

'Where do we get the money?'

'You never asked before. Why start now?'

'Can I bring the boys over this afternoon? Can you come? We can show them the place together.'

He saw Amir in the window of the restaurant. Gloomy and anxious, just like the previous night. He was with his father, who looked no happier.

'You bet,' Birk Larsen said.

Phone in pocket. He clapped his big hands. Beamed at strangers. Felt . . . whole.

There were places for the money. It wasn't the first time he'd steered through stormy waters to keep things afloat. The calls he'd been making would be all the more useful now.

Across the road Amir and his father were outside the restaurant, arguing. The old man pointing an accusing finger, shouting so loudly Birk Larsen could hear him. The babble of another tongue.

The father had his hand on Amir's arm. The young man broke free with a ferocious burst of Danish curses.

Two little kids in the box of a red Christiania trike. Off to school. Trapped for ever in a photograph on a table.

They all grew up. They all went somewhere, a few into an endless night.

Amir walked over the road, came to him.

'Is something wrong?' Birk Larsen asked.

'Let's just get out of here.'

Then he walked to the scarlet van.

Skovgaard was on the phone chasing the missing document from Stokke's minutes. Morten Weber had spent an hour with Bremer's people trying to clear the air. Mai Juhl waited in Hartmann's office, getting impatient on her own.

'What does the old man have to say?'

'Bremer's about to start the hearing into Holck's department. You're expected. Either you issue a correction and withdraw what you said or he'll sue you.'

Hartmann waved to Juhl. Got the faintest of smiles in return.

'So I'm supposed to retract it and look like a complete fool?'

Weber shook his head.

'There are ways around these things, Troels. We could say you'd been under a lot of pressure after the false arrest. Bremer will put out a sympathetic message if you give him what he wants.'

'Forget it.'

Mai Juhl had much the same idea. That probably came from Bremer too.

'Don't paint yourself into a corner, Troels.'

'Bremer knew I was innocent. He let me sit in a jail cell, face a charge of murder. When all along he could have picked up the phone and—'

'So you say. But can you prove it?'

'He thinks he owns us, Mai. Maybe he does.'

'Be practical. We're all sorry about what happened. But you need friends. Don't cut yourself off—'

'What exactly do you want me to do?'

Skovgaard walked in.

'Not now,' Hartmann said, barely looking at her.

'Yes, now.'

She was smiling. There were some printouts in her hand. Something in her eyes . . .

'Go on, Mai.'

'If you change your mind we can stop the libel suit. Word won't get out.'

Hartmann took the papers and started to read.

'There are six mayors and Bremer,' Juhl went on. 'He won't leave you education. He wants me for that. But you'll get one of them. Maybe . . . environment now.'

'The last man in that job prospered, didn't he?' Hartmann said, still going through the documents.

'I'm trying to help. There are people out there who don't think you're worth it. Prove me right. Prove them wrong. Let's do this the proper way. Draft the letter. OK?'

He barely moved. It wasn't a nod, not really.

But Mai Juhl snatched at it. Picked up her jacket, said cheerily, 'Thank God for that. See you shortly.'

Then left.

Hartmann stared at the world beyond the window. Thought about possibilities and directions. Choices to be made.

'Troels?'

523

Weber had walked in and he'd barely noticed.

'The hearing's soon. We need a plan.'

No answer.

'Hello?' Weber called. 'Anyone in?'

'I'm in,' Hartmann said. 'Here's a plan. Tell Bremer we'll work out a denial afterwards.'

Weber squinted at him.

'You're going to withdraw the accusation?'

'Afterwards.'

'Right . . .' Weber said.

She walked through the garage, ignored the hard stares of the men in their red uniforms, went up the stairs, rang the bell.

'Hi, Pernille.'

Lund smiled, tried to appear friendly.

'Is it a bad time?'

'We're moving. I'm going to see the house.'

'We need to number the evidence in the case. It's just a formality.'

'What?'

A gap. An opportunity. Lund walked in, stood in the kitchen. So many things. Little vases and plants, animal silhouettes in the window, dishes on the side. She could never create a home like this.

'I need to go through Nanna's belongings again. The last time, I promise.'

'Meyer said you were off the case.'

'Tomorrow. It's my last day. Didn't he mention it?'

She didn't know whether Pernille believed that or not.

'It's just a detail. Is this a bad time? You don't need to be here. If you have to go . . .'

'I do have to go. Most of her things are in boxes. Will you lock the door behind you?'

'Sure.'

Lund looked around the lovely kitchen.

'Your new place is bigger?'

'It's a house.'

'It's going to be beautiful.'

Pernille stared at her.

'Just remember to lock up,' she said and left.

Lund listened to her footsteps down the stairs.

When she was gone Lund took off her jacket and went to the first box. Emptied trinket boxes and books and homework diaries onto the threadbare carpet.

Went through everything. Six boxes in all.

An hour and a half later she sat desolate in Nanna's bedroom, belongings everywhere, as if an angry child had thrown a tantrum.

Nothing. No sign of a secret assignation. No mention of a trip.

Lund buried her head in her hands, wanted to scream.

Then she looked up, looked around with those big eyes again.

Think.

Think like Nanna.

Look.

Imagine.

There was a blue plastic globe in the corner. She'd seen it earlier. The cross marks on famous cities. Places Nanna surely wanted to visit.

It was a lamp too. An electric cable ran out of the back. Lund took the globe from the box, placed it on the desk, found a socket, turned it on.

The bulb lit up all the bright colours of the countries and continents. Slowly she moved it around on its base. America, Australia, Asia, Africa . . .

Between the tips of the two capes, in the South Atlantic at the base, something darkened the blue of the sea.

Paper. Letters. Documents.

A secret place for a kid who wanted to go somewhere.

Lund shook the globe.

Took out the plug, sought the way in. Nanna must have had one. She knew how to take this thing apart and put it back together without a sign.

But Nanna was nineteen, with nimbler fingers. Getting cross Lund gave up, picked it up, crashed the thing on the desk, shattered the base and the light fitting, smashed it with her fist.

The plastic gave. The world divided at the equator. Two equal halves, the southern hemisphere with a secret cache of documents.

Last pair of forensic gloves on. She turned the contents on the floor, sat down, legs splayed, went through everything piece by piece.

Letters and cards. A Valentine's heart. A flower. A photo. So old.

A blonde-haired girl, little more than four or five. Next to a dark-haired kid shyly holding her hand. A playground behind. Sand and a slide. The two of them together in the box of a Christiania trike.

Lund stared.

Didn't notice the footsteps behind. Didn't see Pernille Birk Larsen looking over her shoulder at first.

When she did she asked, 'Who's this in the picture?'

Lund got up, showed the photo to her.

'This is Nanna, isn't it?'

The mess, the upturned boxes. The chaos returned.

'Who's the boy, Pernille?'

'You said the case was closed?'

'Who is it?'

Pernille took the photo, gazed at it.

'Amir. A little Asian kid from round the corner. He was Nanna's sweetheart for a while. They were . . .'

The word eluded her.

'They were tiny.'

'Where's Amir now?' Lund asked.

Meyer called when she was back in the car.

'Nanna wasn't going from Kastrup, Lund. She was booked on one of the budget airlines from Malmö. Flight to Berlin. Friday at one fifty in the morning. There was another passenger. He didn't make the flight.'

'Amir,' she said.

A long pause.

'I do wish you'd stop doing this to me. He lives two streets from Nanna. But I guess you know that.'

'Amir El' Namen. He came to see Theis last night. He's moving and he's using the Birk Larsens. He asked for Theis to do the job himself.'

'Where are you?'

'Near the station. Meet me.'

Meyer looked at the long corridor, the dark marble walls, the lights. He couldn't get out without passing Brix's office. It looked empty . . .

'What's going on?'

Brix came up behind him, made Meyer jump.

'If it's about Lund, I haven't seen her. I swear.'

'The Birk Larsen woman just called. Where is she?'

'I've got an appointment right now. Let me call later and explain.'

Brix blocked his way.

'Explain now.'

'Nanna was headed for Berlin with someone—'

'I don't give a shit about Berlin. The station's reported some luggage stolen. By Lund. Cut out this misguided loyalty and tell me where she is.'

Meyer didn't like that.

'It's nothing to do with loyalty. It's to do with the facts. Holck didn't know Nanna would leave from Malmö. So he went to Kastrup. Here . . .'

He opened the folder he was taking to Lund.

'These are Kastrup security pictures from that night. Holck's in them. Perfect quality. Unmistakable.'

The gloomy politician slumped against an information desk in the departures area. Rubbing his eyes by the ticket desks. Looking old and dejected on a shiny bench seat by the escalators.

'Jens Holck stayed there till two in the morning. He doesn't meet a soul.'

Brix gazed at the photos.

'He didn't kill Nanna,' Meyer said. 'I'll call you later, shall I?'

No answer. So he left.

Amir asked Birk Larsen to go to an address on an industrial estate in Amager. He didn't want to talk. Just clutched his student bag and watched glumly as the low houses and industrial buildings ran past the window.

Birk Larsen liked conversation when he was in the cab. Was determined to have it.

'You were in London, right? I never went. One day—'

'I was at college. It was my father's idea.'

'And you just got back?'

He didn't understand why Amir had his stuff out here. It seemed an odd place to keep tables and chairs.

'No. I got back during the summer.'

'I never saw you.'

'No.'

'You should have come round, Amir. Nanna would have liked that. I remember the two of you playing together.'

He laughed.

'God she used to give you hell. She hated dolls, you know. I always thought that was because she had you instead.'

It seemed a good joke. One he could crack now. Didn't work on Amir.

'Did you talk to her when you got back?'

He was back at the window, staring at the dead land beyond. Birk Larsen looked at the address Amir had given him, looked at the road sign, the numbers.

'No, well. We're nearly there.'

A closed gate, a derelict industrial unit behind it.

Birk Larsen checked again.

'Number seventy-four. This is it?'

Amir was frozen in the seat, clutching his bag as if it were the most important thing in all the world.

'Amir? Is this the place? Is this where we pick up the things for your wedding? What . . .'

He was crying. Just like he did as a little kid when Nanna pushed him too far. Big tears rolling down from underneath his black student glasses.

'There isn't going to be a wedding. It's cancelled.'

Birk Larsen wondered what to do.

'Amir . . . I don't know why we're here.'

He took off the shoulder bag, opened it.

Mumbled, 'I wish . . .'

Nothing else.

'You wish what? What?'

'I was always scared of you,' Amir said. 'When we were little and Nanna took me to your home. I was scared of you when I came back this summer. Didn't dare come round, thinking about what you'd say, what you'd do when you . . . got to know.'

Birk Larsen squinted at him, said, 'Know what?'

'Me. Nanna. Us. She always said I didn't need to. That you'd come round. That you and her mum were just the same once. Stupid. In love. But . . .'

He rubbed his eyes with the sleeve of his jacket the way a child would.

'I was still scared and I thought . . . it's just going to make it worse, isn't it? When you know—'

'Know what?'

'It was me she loved. The immigrant kid from round the corner. We were running away. And then . . .'

He thrust the bag into Birk Larsen's hands. There was a white padded envelope inside. Something else.

'Then something . . . I don't know . . .'

He took off his seat belt. Climbed out. Went to stand by the padlocked gate, looking at the derelict factory that meant nothing, was nothing. Birk Larsen understood this somehow now.

The envelope was addressed to him and Pernille. Inside was a small digital video cassette. Birk Larsen looked in the bag. There was a camera. The cassette fitted.

He found the play button.

Hit it.

Felt his heart stop.

A cold day. Not long ago. Nanna in her heavy coat, hair a mess. Not looking nineteen at all.

'Is it recording?' she asks.

A voice from somewhere. Amir's. A little tetchy as he tries to work things out.

'Yes.'

She says good. Takes a long deep breath, smiles. A woman's smile.

Looks into the lens and Theis Birk Larsen's blood runs cold as he listens to a voice he knows he'll never hear again.

So bright, so sweet, so full of hope it makes him ache with a desperate sense of loss.

The voice says in a laughing, naughty tone, 'Hello, Mum. Hello, Dad.'

A wink.

'Hi, Anton and Emil, the world's best Teletubbies.'

A pause and her face is so serious and old Theis Birk Larsen feels the tears sting his narrow eyes in an instant.

'When you all watch this it'll be Monday. You'll think I'm in school. But I'm not.'

She turns her head to one side, the cheeky way she always does to win an argument.

'I know you'll be angry with me. But don't worry. I love you all so much. And I'm fine. With Amir. Little Amir.'

A shrug.

'Not now. My first boyfriend. He came back this summer. We met . . .'

Her eyes drift to the man behind the camera. She looks embarrassed. Laughs it away.

'Well. We hadn't seen each other for three years. But it was like yesterday. You always told me, Mum. When it happens you know. It doesn't matter what people think. Doesn't matter what the world thinks. When it happens, when you find the right person, nothing can stop you. And you mustn't let it.'

A low deep moan rises from Birk Larsen's lungs.

Her blue eyes fix on the camera, on them.

'We've always loved each other really. It just took a while to admit it. Mum, I think you always knew. Amir's got a friend we can stay with. I don't know for how long. Till things calm down.'

He holds the camera closer, as if in some irrational part of his mind he believes this is her. Nanna breathing. Nanna alive.

Nanna saying, 'I want you all to know I've never been happier. So please . . . I hope you can forgive me. I think you can. You ran away, didn't you? I remember the look in your eyes when you told me, Mum. So much love.'

Her hand reaches out, touches the unseen man behind the lens.

'If Amir and me can be as happy and as good as you . . .'

She is crying now and he always hated to see that.

'See you, Mum and Dad.'

She blows a kiss.

'Love you, Teletubbies. I'll call you soon. I'll love you always.'

Tears and laughter. The camera moves. A wall with graffiti. A line of bikes. Two streets from their home in Vesterbro. He recognizes the bricks.

Then Nanna and Amir. She's bright and sparked by hope. He's quiet and bashful and can look at nothing but her.

With shaking fingers Birk Larsen placed the camera on the passenger seat then buried his head in his hands and wept.

*

530

Poul Bremer ran the hearing. Jacket off. Blue shirt. No tie. A man at work.

'Next we'll hear from the head of Holck's administration. Gert Stokke. Gert?'

The grey man in the grey suit came into the room, took a seat.

'You know the form,' Bremer said. 'We're investigating Holck's department. We need you to shed some light on this case.'

Stokke nodded, looked at each of the leaders round the table.

'As you can see from the documents I had a conversation with Holck. I tried to get him to understand that something was wrong. But he didn't want to know. I was unable to convince him.'

'And then?' Bremer asked.

Stokke puffed out his cheeks, said eventually, 'I brought it up at a later date. He was no more cooperative. With hindsight I see I should have informed someone. I apologize for this. We have systems in place now . . .'

'And Holck himself . . .' Bremer prompted. 'He had a bullying nature which was not known to most of us, I believe.'

'He was forthright,' Stokke agreed. 'And convincing. He told me he'd deal with the matter directly. I assumed he was telling the truth. What else could I do?'

Bremer put his hands together, like a priest taking confession.

'I think we've all learned lessons from this sad episode. As far as I can see you did what you could. No further questions are needed. So thank you—'

Hartmann put up his left hand.

'I have a question if you don't mind.'

Bremer waited for a moment then said, 'Go ahead, Troels.'

'Just so we're absolutely clear, did you tell anyone about Holck's actions?'

'No one.'

Hartmann picked up the folder in front of him.

'I'd like to hand out some documents.'

He walked round, placing the sheets in front of each, Stokke first.

'These are minutes from a meeting between Gert Stokke and Bremer. They discussed planting trees. There are references to an appendix which wasn't included with the file copy. It was mislaid, I imagine. Is that right, Gert?'

'I'd have to check the records—'

'No need.' Hartmann picked up another pile of documents. 'I've managed to recover the appendix anyway.'

Stokke blinked.

'It was in a safe place, hidden there by the head of administration of Holck's department.'

A wave to Stokke.

'You, Gert.'

The civil servant's eyes locked on the document in front of him.

'Let me refresh your memory,' Hartmann went on. 'This is your note of a report you gave to the Lord Mayor about what you call the worrying conditions in Holck's administration. It cites, for example, the payment of five thousand kroner a month to a civil servant named Olav Christensen, who worked in my department, not that any of my payroll team or my administration were aware of this relationship. Or that there's any clear indication why Christensen was paid in the first place.'

Bremer sat flushed, speechless.

Hartmann turned to the council members.

'This appendix was never part of the official minutes. It was Gert Stokke's secret insurance policy. A way of making sure that if the sky fell he could at least say we were warned.'

Hartmann pointed to the document.

'And here it is. Proof that the Lord Mayor knew about Holck's wilful and illegal misconduct in office long before the rest of us. Proof that the Lord Mayor withheld from the police information that could have revealed the real murderer of Nanna Birk Larsen long before they did.'

He looked across at Bremer.

'Would the Lord Mayor care to comment?'

Nothing.

'No?'

'Well,' Hartmann said, getting up from the table, leaving them with the papers, 'thanks for listening.'

Lund and Meyer were out looking for Amir. He'd come back to the city after seeing Theis Birk Larsen. Picked up his car. Hadn't been seen since.

They'd tried the father's restaurant. The cemetery.

Nothing.

As Meyer cruised through Vesterbro his phone rang.

'His mobile is registered on a tower near Tårnby. Not far from the airport. Maybe he's trying to get out . . .'

He wheeled the car round, headed for the road out to Kastrup.

Lund thought. Remembered the picture. Two little kids and a red Christiania trike.

'He's not going to the airport.'

'The mobile—'

'I know where he is.'

The traffic was light. It took twenty-five minutes to get there.

Meyer grew more sullen and morose as he realized where they were headed.

Down the narrow lanes, along the ditches and the canals. Past the dark wood where the dead trees gave no shelter.

Their headlights caught the low metal bridge. A shape midway along.

Meyer checked his gun, realized Brix still had it. Lund scowled at him, got out, walked straight towards the figure by the canal.

There was a bouquet of flowers at his back. Amir sat on the edge, looking at the black water, arms through the railings, dangling his legs in the air.

Like a kid.

A second squad car pulled up on the other side, blue lights flashing. Two men raced out. Lund waved them back.

She walked up.

'Amir El' Namen?'

She gestured for Meyer to take out his ID then bent down to talk to him.

'We're police, Amir. It's OK. You're not a suspect.'

He kept looking at the water.

'Witnesses saw you at the airport in Malmö.'

She went to the edge, leaned on the ironwork, wanting to see the eyes behind his thick black-rimmed spectacles.

'There's something I need to know,' Lund said. 'Who knew? Who did Nanna tell?'

Finally he looked at her.

'Who knew, Amir?'

'No one knew. We weren't stupid.'

'Someone must have known. Someone who kept an eye on Nanna . . . Or saw you together. An ex-boyfriend, maybe. Think.'

He did.

'Someone saw us. But he couldn't have known. It's not possible.'

Lund got closer.

'Who saw you?'

'It was when I picked her up to take her luggage to the station. He got out of a car. I didn't really see him. I don't know who he was.'

Meyer sighed.

'So what did you see then?' he asked wearily.

Amir glared at him.

'A red uniform. But he couldn't have known.'

Meyer shook his head.

'What do you mean a red uniform?'

'I mean a red uniform. Like they wear.'

'Who?' Meyer asked.

'His people. Their people. The overalls. Birk Larsen's.'

Thirty minutes later Brix arrived, gave Lund her ID card without a word.

'The river search team you wanted is on their way. I expect you to find something.'

'What about the water supply?' Meyer asked.

'They'll close it for twenty-four hours. No more. What did the Indian boy say?'

'We're looking for one of the removals men. Someone who works for Birk Larsen. That's the link.'

Brix was scanning the arriving cars.

'The link to what?'

'To Mette Hauge. She'd moved from her dad's place to the city not long before she disappeared.'

She waited, wanting to get this clear in her own head.

'When you move home,' Lund said, 'you let strangers into your life. Mette did. Nanna . . .'

Vagn Skærbæk looked at the orders, the schedules, the money owed. They were doing some night work off the books to make ends meet.

It wasn't easy.

Theis Birk Larsen was back from a cash run out to the docks, looking beat but happier than he had of late.

'You know I'm calling in extra people,' Skærbæk said. 'What with the work, the calls. We don't have enough.'

'So long as the jobs cover it.'

Skærbæk nodded.

'They will. Don't worry. I can add up.'

'Good.'

There was a ring at the door.

'Go upstairs, Theis. You look beat.'

Skærbæk watched him leave.

The man was lean, around their age. Bloodless face. Sick-looking.

'You could have come earlier.'

'I couldn't. I was busy. The guy who owns the taxis is giving me a hard time. He wants me to do more shifts.'

'Yeah well. Theis needs you more. And you owe him. So don't screw us around again. Get your overall on. We've got work to do.'

'Cash?'

'Yeah. Cash.'

'Nothing . . . you know—'

'Nothing what?'

'I don't want trouble, Vagn.'

Skærbæk shooed him into the room with the lockers.

'Just do the job. There's still a uniform with your name on it. Even if you do mess us around. This is a family firm, remember?'

'Family. I know.'

The scarlet overalls were where the new man left them two weeks before, the last time he'd worked. He picked up the red cotton, checked the name on the tag anyway.

It said: *Leon Frevert*.

Lund looked up and down the canals, wondered what secrets they hid. Scuba divers had been working for two hours, dropping into the water from inflatable boats. Other officers were scouring the weed banks and bulrushes at the edge. Floodlights everywhere.

Even Jansen, the ginger-haired forensic officer who never seemed to question Lund's orders, was starting to have doubts.

Around eight, during a break to move the scuba team to a

different patch he came up, said, 'We've searched two of the smaller canals. God knows how many there are left.'

'Try the old drain line. Twenty years ago most of this area was off limits. He'd know that, he'd have made use of it.'

'All of this was off limits twenty years ago. The army used it as a firing range. No one came here. To dump a car . . .'

She was barely listening. Lund was trying to imagine what might have happened.

'Don't assume she's in a car.' She thought of Bengt, going behind her back, tracking down Mette Hauge, convinced he was right. 'Don't assume anything.'

Meyer had spoken to Mette's father again. She'd used a removals firm to take her from her home into a new apartment in the city. He'd no idea which one. But the police report said her belongings went to a warehouse registered to a company called Merkur. It had long since gone out of business.

'The last person it was registered to was someone called Edel Lonstrup,' Meyer added. 'I've got an address. Maybe tomorrow . . .'

It was almost ten.

'Let's go now,' Lund said.

'Isn't it a bit late?' Meyer asked.

'Yes. Twenty years.'

Lonstrup was in Søborg, on the edge of an industrial zone. It looked more like an abandoned warehouse than a home. The metal gates were unlocked. So were the doors to the run-down metal shack that greeted them at the end of the drive. Meyer pushed in. Boxes everywhere and dusty junk. The name Merkur was stencilled on a few. At the back was a long window with a light on. They could see a kitchen. A few pot plants.

Someone lived here as well.

A bloodless face came to the glass, put a leathery hand to her cheeks, peered out.

In her grey dressing grown, with her lank unwashed hair, she didn't look as if she got many visitors.

They sat in the kitchen, watching her eat. The place seemed to be made out of the junk she'd collected: unmatched crockery, a rickety stove, an ancient radio. Merkur closed down ten years ago after her husband died. She said she didn't have a list of staff, any paperwork at all.

'What happened to it?' Meyer asked.

'I threw it all out. Why keep it? If this is about taxes or something go down to the cemetery and talk to him.'

'Did one of your employees switch to Birk Larsen's company?'

'Employees? It's the moving business. They're all gypsies. They worked for us one minute. The competition the next. God knows what else they got up to on the side.'

Her face hardened. A memory.

'That's why he hung around with them, not his family. For the drink and the women and whatever else was going on.'

'Birk Larsen?'

'Who's Birk Larsen?'

The woman had no TV as far as she could see. No papers on the table. Nothing that linked this place to the world outside.

'Does the name Mette Hauge mean anything?' Lund asked.

'Who?'

'Mette Hauge. She had some things in storage.'

'Aage sold everything he could before he went bust. Other people's belongings too. If he hadn't died he'd be in prison. All to get drunk and hang around with scum.'

'So you didn't keep anything?'

'Take a look. What you see is ours. No one else's.'

A voice emerged from the dark behind them, younger, more frail. It said, 'We've still got some things in the garage.'

The woman behind them looked forty but was dressed like a teenager from another time. Long woollen cardigan, a colourful, tatty T-shirt beneath. Jeans. Her hair was in pigtails, turning from brown to grey. She had the face of a child, scared and mutinous at the same moment.

'Go to your room,' Edel Lonstrup ordered.

'What things?' Lund asked.

'Dad's things. Lots of them.'

'They're just old boxes!' the mother bawled. 'Go back to your room!'

'We need to take a look,' Meyer said. 'Show us.'

Boxes of papers, no order, no logic in the dusty garage full of junk and cobwebs. A few crates had the company logo. The word Merkur in blocked blue type with a wing flying out from the left.

Lund sorted through ancient computer printouts. Meyer emptied box upon box onto the floor.

'What exactly are we supposed to be looking for?'

'A man.'

He kicked a crate. More papers flew around the room, more dust.

'Nope,' Meyer said. 'Not there.'

The daughter stayed and watched from the shadows.

'How old were you twenty-one years ago?' Lund asked her.

'Seventeen.'

'What were they like? The men your father employed.'

'Rough. Frightening. Big. Strong.'

She clutched her grubby cardigan as she spoke.

'My mother said to stay away. They weren't like us. They were . . .'

The daughter stopped.

'They were what?' Meyer asked.

'They were moving men. All like that.'

'All?'

Lund left the boxes and walked up to her.

'The man we're looking for might have been different. Not much older than you. Twenty, twenty-five. Perhaps he worked here part-time.'

'They came and went . . .'

Lund was trying to imagine. If Bengt was right this man was organized, clever, persistent. He didn't snatch women in the night. He hunted them, wound them in. Charmed them even.

'He was probably different to the others. Better maybe. Smarter.'

She didn't speak.

'He'd like talking to girls. I think he'd talk with more respect than the others. More sympathy.'

A picture was starting to form in Lund's head.

'He'd be nice. Not rough. Not nasty. Next to them he'd seem charming, maybe. Was there anyone like that?'

Silence.

Lund took out a photo of the necklace with the black heart.

'Have you seen this before?'

The woman came out of the darkness, into the light for the first time. She was, Lund thought, extraordinarily pretty, but damaged by something. The isolation. The loneliness.

Nothing.

'Let's go, Lund,' Meyer said. 'Is there somewhere I can wash this shit off my hands?'

The daughter pointed to the door. Waited till he was gone. Watched Lund.

When he was out of earshot she said, 'There might be someone.' Nervous, she turned her head, made sure Meyer wasn't listening. 'It won't come from me, will it? My mother won't—'

'No one needs to know.'

'They only want one thing. Men.'

'Was he like that?'

She was remembering.

'No. The others didn't like him that much. They'd be messing round. Drinking. Smoking. Not doing a damned thing. He worked. He made sure they kept to the schedule if he could. They didn't like that.'

'What did he look like?' Lund asked.

She shrugged.

'Just ordinary. There was a picture of him with my father. But Mum threw it out. He was supposed to become the manager but I don't know . . . something happened.'

'What?'

'I said. I don't know. One day he was here. Then he never came back.'

Lund watched her face.

'Did you miss him?'

Almost forty, dressed like a teenager, long hair turning grey. A life gone to waste.

Nothing.

'If that was me,' Lund added, 'I wouldn't have let anyone throw out that picture. I'd have gone back and got it. Kept it somewhere my mother didn't know. That's what pictures are for, aren't they? Memories.'

Lund came closer. The daughter had the same fusty smell as the garage and the living quarters stuck onto the side. Damp and dust and cobwebs.

'We need that picture . . .'

The long thin arms in the threadbare cardigan came out and gripped her tightly.

'You mustn't tell . . .'

The daughter glanced at the windows into the kitchen. There was no one there. Then she went to the back of the garage, carefully began to move sets of old shelves to one side.

Found something at the bottom. Began to sort through it.

Meyer had returned. He started towards the woman. Lund's arm went out to stop him. Her thumb jerked at the door and she mouthed, 'Out.'

She found the photo so quickly Lund wondered whether she looked at it every day. It was spotless, no dust. A good clear picture.

'That's my father. This is the man I was talking about.'

Lund examined the faces.

'It was twenty years ago,' the daughter said. 'Why are you looking for him? What's he done?'

Lund said nothing.

'It can't be anything bad,' the woman with the greying pigtails added. 'He wasn't like that.'

Pernille sat at the kitchen table watching the video on Amir's camera, trying to blink back the tears.

Theis was next to her, his hand on hers.

'Was Amir involved?' she asked after she watched Nanna blow them a farewell kiss.

'No. The police said he waited for her at the airport in Malmö.'

She brushed her eyes, her cheeks with the sleeves of her shirt.

'Why didn't she tell us? Why keep it a secret?'

He kept staring at the last image of Amir and Nanna, frozen in time, all smiles. Couldn't speak.

'The Lund woman came and went through all her things again.'

She shook her head. Felt bleak and defeated again, just as she had before.

'Something's not right, Theis.'

His fingers left her hand.

'Don't start this again. They said the case was closed.'

'So why did Lund come over?'

No answer.

'They haven't found him,' she whispered. 'You know that. They haven't found him.'

A knock on the door. Leon Frevert stood at the threshold in his red overalls and black cap.

'What?' Birk Larsen asked.

'Sorry but . . . Vagn wants you to come downstairs.'

'Not now.'

The tall thin man looked scared, but he wasn't moving.

'I think you need to come, Theis. Please.'

Birk Larsen grunted and said, 'OK.'

The men were all there, full-timers, part-timers, some he barely recognized. In their red uniforms, lined up in the office. Talking among themselves, not smiling, not looking at him as he came through the door.

Vagn Skærbæk stood at the front of the group, arms folded, talking and nodding.

The leader, always.

They had rows sometimes. People walked out. Didn't always come back.

That, Birk Larsen thought, was the business.

His business.

So he walked straight in, said, 'What the hell is this? Either work or go home, will you?'

Skærbæk turned and faced him. Shifty-looking, glancing at the floor.

'Theis—'

'Not now.'

'Now, Theis. We have a problem.'

Skærbæk met his eyes finally. Silver necklace glittering. Face serious, resigned.

'What's that?'

'This house of yours in Humleby. Don't get us wrong. We're glad it's working out. We really do but . . .'

He frowned.

'It's getting in the way. We come here to work for customers. Instead we keep stopping to move bricks and wood and all that shit to Humleby. This can't go on . . .'

Birk Larsen closed his eyes, tried to find the words.

'Truth is, Theis, you won't have that place fixed up by Christmas the way things are going. So we've decided. Sorry. But this is final . . .'

That nod of his little head.

'We're going to fix it for you.'

A warm roar of laughter, someone slapped his back. Birk Larsen looked at their beaming faces.

'A couple of us are going to work each evening and a couple more at weekends.'

'You bastards . . .' Birk Larsen muttered, shaking his head, wiping his eyes.

'The basement's first. Then the kitchen and the bathroom.'

He pulled out a list of materials.

'Rudi's cousin's a plumber so we get that stuff at cost and a little on the side. He needs moving soon so we can do a deal. The rest will cost you beer.'

He nudged Birk Larsen's elbow.

'Best start saving, Theis. These guys drink. And . . .'

Skærbæk fell silent. They all followed the direction of his puzzled gaze.

Lund and Meyer walked into the garage, were doing what they always did, looking around.

Birk Larsen swore then marched out to meet them.

'We've got new information,' Meyer said. 'It changes things.'

Birk Larsen stood in front of his men outside the office.

'Last time you told us this was done with.'

'I know. I was wrong. We have to reopen the case.'

'I want you to leave.'

'We can't do that.'

'If you want to talk to me again, do it through the lawyer.'

'It's not you we want to talk to,' Lund cut in. 'It's one of your men. Vagn Skærbæk.'

'Oh for fuck's sake,' Birk Larsen bellowed. 'What?'

Lund walked past him, went to the office, noticed one lean figure scuttling to the back of the room, jerking his baseball cap over his face. Thought of what the daughter had said: they're all footloose. Gypsies.

It wasn't Skærbæk. He'd stayed where he was, glaring at her.

'You should leave Theis alone,' he said. 'Hasn't he been through enough?'

'Can we have a word, Vagn?'

Wide eyes, silver neck chain glittering, he came out, stood next to Birk Larsen.

'What is it, Theis?'

'They want to speak to you.'

'About what?'

Meyer said, 'You're coming with us.'

'Why?'

'Get in the car or we arrest you. What's it going to be?'

Skærbæk looked at Birk Larsen, head to one side, bemused.

'Is this a joke?'

'No joke,' Meyer said. He looked at his watch. 'It's ten thirty-seven. You're under arrest.'

He reached into his back pocket, took out the handcuffs, waved them at Skærbæk.

'Is that what you want?'

'Take it easy, for Christ's sake.'

Pernille was there now.

'What's going on?' she asked.

'Search me.' Vagn Skærbæk saw the cuffs waved again and said, 'I'm coming. I'm coming.'

The tall figure at the back of the office was still hiding in the shadows, pulling his baseball cap down over his eyes. Lund wanted to look but Meyer was getting impatient.

'If there's news,' she told Pernille Birk Larsen, 'we'll call.'

Hartmann was in front of the press conference. Black suit, black shirt and tie.

'The charge against the Lord Mayor could hardly be more serious. He knew about Jens Holck's criminal activities. Gert Stokke wrote the minutes of the meeting.'

He held up the papers Skovgaard had found.

'This is the proof. We'll distribute copies. Because Bremer never came forward with this knowledge I was discredited. More importantly the city of Copenhagen was deceived by the man elected to lead it. Bremer deliberately misled the police and their inquiries. He wasted their time and our money to cover for a killer. All out of nothing more than his own political gain.'

Hartmann looked round the room.

'We deserve better than this. We must get better. I've reported Poul Bremer to the police.'

'What did the police say?' one of the reporters called out.

'They'll investigate. I regret the focus of this election has shifted once again.'

'Will he be charged?'

'That's up to the police.'

Erik Salin was in the front row. Bald head. Beaming smirk.

'Five days left to the election, Hartmann. Aren't you getting a bit desperate?'

They all waited.

'I'll let the people decide that,' Hartmann said. 'Thank you.'

Thirty minutes later he was back in his office watching Bremer respond live on the news.

He might have predicted the reaction.

'This is all a lie,' the Lord Mayor said. 'I never had that conversation with Stokke. These so-called minutes are forged. Fabricated for the occasion.'

'By Troels Hartmann?' the interviewer asked.

'I doubt it. I see this as a civil servant's attempts to wash his hands of a problem of his own making. I'm the victim. Hartmann has chosen, knowingly or not, to be his mouthpiece. I would have hoped for better—'

Weber hit the off button.

'Bremer's dumping it in Stokke's lap. What else do you expect him to do?'

'Stokke's a big boy,' Skovgaard said. 'You should be too.'

'Is that so?'

'Yes. This is going to bring Bremer down.'

Weber dragged on his coat.

'I thought we were here to beat him with better ideas. Not by playing his own shitty game more grubbily than he does. Oh to hell with this. I'm sick of the rotten taste of it in my mouth.'

'What was that?' Hartmann barked at him.

'You heard, Troels! I spent years making you what you are.'

'Did you?'

Weber looked him up and down.

'Damned right. The new guard. Clean and honest. Frank and fearless. And here you are trying to scrape the barrel like the worst of them. Jesus . . . You think you're up to it?'

He pointed a finger at Skovgaard.

'Do you think she is? The Jack and Jackie show's falling apart and the two of you can't even see it.'

'That's enough, Morten.'

Weber scowled.

'I haven't even started. You're not supposed to wander onto the dark side, Troels. That's my job. Leave it to the professionals.'

He was gone before Hartmann could answer. Rie Skovgaard sat fuming in her chair.

Hartmann perched on the desk.

'I'm sorry. Morten turns brittle under pressure.'

'That was brittle?'

'I think so. I've known him a long time. That's how it shows.'

Skovgaard seized her papers. Hair up now, severe. Dark eyes restless. Looking everywhere but him.

'I was wondering if you'd like a drink.'

Head to one side, eyes examining him, she said nothing.

'OK,' Hartmann said with a shrug. 'Just an idea . . .'

Weber marched back in. He was holding a gigantic bouquet of lilies.

'Here.' He thrust them into her arms. 'These arrived for you. Maybe you're supposed to turn them into a wreath or something.'

Then marched out.

'Flowers,' Hartmann said.

'You're very observant sometimes, Troels.'

'Someone must appreciate you a lot.'

A smile, finally.

'Can you call the police now?' he asked.

There was a constituency meeting next. Weber relented and shared the car with Hartmann. They listened to Bremer's statement on the radio. Halfway through Weber asked the driver to turn it off.

545

'What did you mean, Morten? About the Jack and Jackie show?'

'Oh come on. You see yourself that way. So does Rie. Don't you know that was an act too?'

'I'm not acting.'

'You're a politician. Don't be so stupid.'

Hartmann shook his head.

'Why do I take this constant abuse from you?'

'Because we make a good match. Better than you and Rie. More honest anyway.'

Weber patted his knee.

'Don't be offended. I want the best for you. Both of you. She'll make a good sidekick once she learns her limitations.'

'Same for me, I imagine.'

'You're getting there.'

'Why am I wrong about Bremer? Does it matter? If the end's right, who cares about the means?'

'Doesn't work that way.'

'I need to know I can rely on you, Morten. I need to know you won't walk out. Throw a fit about Rie . . .'

No answer.

'I know what I'm doing,' Hartmann said.

'I believe you think you do.'

Hartmann held out his hand.

'Come on, you grumpy old bastard. We're in this together.'

Weber took his hand, shook it.

'We always have been, Troels. And I'm not grumpy by the way. The thing is—'

Hartmann's phone rang. Skovgaard. He put it on speakerphone so that Weber could hear.

'I talked to the police,' she said. 'They'll look into the allegations against Bremer.'

'When?'

'When they get round to it. They're reopening the Birk Larsen case.'

Hartmann stretched back into the seat, wanted to scream.

'What?'

'They're looking for someone else. They don't think Jens Holck killed her after all. Lund and Meyer are back on the investigation. They're out in Vestamager. They've shut down the waterworks and started searching all the canals.'

'Find out more. We've a right to know.'

'It's a murder case, Troels. We don't have the right to know anything.'

'If Holck's innocent it's just a matter of time before they start banging on my door again. Find out what you can.'

A long pause.

'They ruled you out, didn't they?'

'Since when did that mean a damned thing?'

He finished the call, told Weber what was happening.

'They can't come for you, Troels. How could they?'

Hartmann watched the city run past beyond the window.

'Five days. One more punch. One more low blow. That's all Bremer needs. By the time we get clear he's back on the throne. You're the strategist. If you were advising him, what would you do?'

'If I was his strategist?'

'Yes.'

Morten Weber laughed.

'Then you'd be dead already.'

Vagn Skærbæk sat in their office chewing nervously on a plastic cup of coffee. Lund kicked off the questioning.

'You worked for Merkur twenty years ago?'

'I worked for lots of people over the years. You go where the money is. So what?'

She showed him the photo Aage Lonstrup's daughter had found for them.

'God, I was beautiful back then.' Skærbæk stroked his chin. 'I still am, don't you think?'

'How long did you work there?'

'Three or four months. He was a nice guy but some of the others were idiots. A lot of boozing went on. I'm not much of a drinker.'

'Did you know Mette Hauge?' Meyer asked.

'Who?'

'A young woman called Mette Hauge. Merkur moved her into the city. Dark-haired girl. Early twenties.'

'Are you kidding? We'd move someone every day. Two sometimes. I don't remember. How'd you expect—?'

'How well did you know Nanna?' Lund cut in.

He stared at her.

547

'I first held her when she was a week old. Does that answer your question?'

'Not really. Did you know about her boyfriends?'

'Not the politician. There was that rich kid from school who used to come round drooling. She had the sense to get rid of him.'

Lund watched him closely.

'Did you know she was planning to travel that weekend?'

'Travel? Where to?'

'Talk to us about that Friday, Vagn,' Meyer said. 'You spent the evening at a nursing home with your uncle. That's right?'

'I told you that already.'

'You're a single man. You spend Friday night with your uncle?'

'Yes. Every Friday.'

'What about the rest of the weekend? Choir practice? Feeding the ducks? Knitting?'

Skærbæk rolled back his head, looked at the ceiling and said, 'Ha, ha.'

'You beat up the teacher.'

He glared at them.

'You should never have told Pernille he did it. Wouldn't have happened without you idiots.'

'Where were you?'

'At work! Like I told you! Theis and Pernille took the boys away for a break. I offered to cover. I've known Theis since for ever. They're like family. I'd do anything for them.'

'Have you seen this before?'

Lund passed him a photo of the necklace.

'No. Can I go now? It's been a long day.'

'What about the other Merkur movers? Still know them?'

'Twenty years ago? You're kidding. Old man Lonstrup died. The rest were clowns, like I said. You know if you can't work out who killed Nanna maybe it's time your bosses found someone who can.'

He closed his eyes for a moment, looked as if he was in pain.

'You've got to stop putting Theis and Pernille through all this. Do you people have no feelings? Christ . . .'

Lund looked at Meyer.

'Stay there,' she told Skærbæk.

*

548

They updated Brix in the adjoining office, watching Vagn Skærbæk through the glass.

'He knew Nanna,' Meyer said. 'It's possible he helped Mette Hauge move. He's agreed to prints and a DNA swab. We're checking them now.'

Brix got up and took a closer look at the man beyond the glass. Skærbæk was chewing on his empty plastic cup, spitting out the pieces. He looked bored and exhausted.

'Any news from the woods?'

'No. But they'll work through the night.'

'Check Skærbæk's alibi again. Take a look at his family, his friends.'

'We need to see if any other missing women had contact with a removals company,' Lund suggested. 'Think about it. You invite these people into your life. They see your home. Your routine. You trust them . . .'

'You could say that about a priest. A doctor. A postman . . .'

'I'm saying it about Vagn Skærbæk. Merkur—'

'Wait,' he broke in. 'We're working on the murder of Nanna Birk Larsen. Maybe there's a connection to a girl who disappeared twenty years ago. I don't know. All you have is a necklace. I'm not letting you dig up every cold case on the files—'

'Brix—'

'Take a look at him!'

Skærbæk had bitten through half the cup, done nothing else all the time they'd left him.

'That guy can't even change a light bulb. The idea he's been running rings round us for twenty years . . . I don't believe he's been doing it for twenty days.'

Lund glanced at Meyer, stayed silent.

'You've got seventeen hours left in the woods. Then the water supply goes back on. If there's nothing but a necklace to link Nanna to the Hauge girl you drop that line altogether. Understood?'

Meyer gave him a little salute.

'I want this case under wraps. No leaks. Not even to Hartmann.'

'When do I get my gun back?' Meyer asked.

'When forensics are done with it.'

'There are other guns, I believe. Sir—'

'You just shot a man dead, Meyer. Three bullets. No mistake. Maybe it's best you stay away from firearms for a while. We were wrong about Holck. I don't want any more screw-ups.'

No answer. Brix left.

'At least he said we,' Meyer noted.

Lund was watching Vagn Skærbæk through the glass.

'He's not stupid,' she said.

When they let Skærbæk go he went straight back to the garage in Vesterbro, talked to the Birk Larsens in their kitchen over coffee.

'They haven't a clue. You want to know what I think? They're so desperate they're going to go through everyone. Every guy who works here, Theis. Same thing. What did you do all weekend? Let's have your fingerprints. Lick this. Sit there. Jesus—'

'What did they ask about?'

'Just that. What did you do all weekend? Why don't you have a girlfriend? Stupid things.'

'What sort of things?' Pernille asked.

'Like what I knew about Nanna's boyfriends. Did I know she'd been seeing the politician. All kinds of stuff. It's a joke.'

Birk Larsen's narrow eyes turned on him.

'Did you know about Nanna and Amir?'

Skærbæk squinted, shook his head.

'The Indian kid? The one she used to hang about with when she was little?'

'Yeah.'

'Know what?'

'They were going out together again.'

Skærbæk thought for a moment.

'You mean like . . . now?'

'Now,' Birk Larsen snapped.

'I don't know jack shit about anything. I haven't seen that Indian kid in years. What is this? I spent the weekend looking after the business.'

Pernille said to no one in particular, 'Why do they think it's one of the men?'

Birk Larsen shook his head.

'They don't tell anyone a damned thing,' Skærbæk said, getting louder. 'I told them to stop messing you around. They don't care. They don't give a fuck about anyone's feelings. Jesus . . . Nanna.'

His eyes were getting glassy.

'They said . . . how long did I know her? Nanna? Only since she was a baby. It's disgusting—'

Birk Larsen put a hand on his shoulder,

'Calm down, Vagn. It's like you said. They're just trying it with anyone. I'm getting a lawyer for this. We need some peace and quiet. I'm not having these bastards marching through the door any time they feel like. Pestering . . .'

'I appreciate that,' Skærbæk said.

Lund picked up her voicemail as she arrived back at the empty flat in Østerbro. There was only one message. Bengt.

'Hi, it's me. I know it was stupid, but I'd like to explain. I'm still in Copenhagen. Your mother wasn't at home. I hope everything's all right.'

She walked up the stairs, thought she heard a noise on her landing. Looked round. Saw nothing.

'Call me,' Bengt said.

Then a voice came out of the shadows, and a tall shape.

Lund fell back against the wall, eyes darting, trying to make sense of what was happening.

'Your neighbour let me in,' Troels Hartmann said.

'You surprised me.'

'Sorry.'

'Why are you here?'

He came out into the light.

'You know why I'm here.'

'If it's about the report you filed with us on Bremer you'll have to wait. Someone will get back to you.'

He watched her work her key into the lock.

'They haven't yet.'

'We're busy right now. I can't help you. I'm not on that case.'

She opened the door. He walked forward and put an arm out to stop her.

'What are you doing in the woods?'

Lund dodged under his arm, went inside.

'It's just an exercise. Nothing. Goodnight.'

Then she slammed the door.

'Fine!' Hartmann yelled from the other side. 'So you won't mind me telling the media what's going on in the woods is nothing to do with me? Or Nanna Birk Larsen?'

He was halfway down the stairs when she came to the door and said, 'Get in here.'

Lund changed her jumper while he watched. Black and white for white and black.

'I'm on my way out. Make this quick.'

'Quick as you like. I just want a straight answer.'

Looked in the fridge. Still time for a beer.

'I've only got one, Hartmann. Do you want some?'

He stared at the Carlsberg.

'That red wine I gave you was five hundred kroner.'

Lund shrugged, cracked open the bottle, swigged from the neck.

'Tonight I said Bremer was covering for a killer.'

'I wouldn't repeat that if I were you.'

He didn't like that answer.

'There was Christensen—'

'Could go down as a road traffic accident. Hard to prove intent in a dead man. Not sure Brix will think it's worth trying.'

'How certain are you Holck didn't kill Nanna?'

The beer tasted good.

'Pretty certain. Well, as much as anything.'

Lund had bought the last box of sushi in the local store. She didn't like sushi much but there was nothing else left that was quick and simple.

'If it wasn't Holck who was it?'

'If I knew that would I be sitting here drinking beer from the bottle and eating cold rice and fish?'

He took a chair on the other side of the table.

'How long before you come back to me? What the hell will people think?'

'They'll think the case is closed. Do you want some sushi?'

'You don't like it, do you?'

Lund pushed the box away.

'We're making progress, Hartmann. Stop worrying.'

552

'What kind of progress? How close are you to an arrest? Hours? Days? Weeks?'

'I'm a police officer. Not a clairvoyant.'

More beer. She looked at him.

'I haven't finished the bottle,' Lund said, waving the Carlsberg at him. 'You can still have some if you want.'

Hartmann looked briefly disgusted by the idea.

'They'll take your report seriously. If Bremer was aware of Holck's misconduct in office something will happen. In time.'

'Great.'

He got up to leave.

'I was wondering, Hartmann.'

'Wondering what?'

'The missing tape from City Hall security.'

'What about it?'

'We were looking for that all along. We thought we could nail you with it. In fact it clears you. There's Holck on it, with Nanna.'

Hartmann looked bewildered.

'Who sent it?' he asked.

'I thought you might be able to tell me.'

'I've no idea.'

'Well . . .' She pulled back the box of sushi, ate some more anyway. 'I guess we can assume someone at City Hall is still interested in you and Nanna anyway.'

'What's that supposed to mean?'

'They didn't give us the tape till now. When you're in the clear. Why is that?'

'Tell me,' Hartmann said.

'If they took it to protect you they can't have watched it, can they? Otherwise they could have saved you from jail.'

He was struggling with that idea.

'You need to make connections, Hartmann.'

'Like what?'

'Someone steals a videotape to protect you. They make sure we don't get our hands on it. But they never watch it. Then, when you're cleared, we get it. Why?'

Nothing.

Lund finished the beer.

'Here's what I'd guess. They gave it to us now because they think there's more shit coming your way.'

'And why didn't they watch it?'

She looked at him.

'Maybe because they couldn't bear to. Because they thought they'd see you there with Nanna. Guilty as hell.'

His handsome politician's face was so immobile it might have been chiselled from stone.

'Just a guess. That's all.'

Ten

Lund got caught in the morning rush-hour traffic on the way to Vesterbro. Meyer sat in the passenger seat giving her an update on Vagn Skærbæk.

'Only child. Parents are gone. Mother died when he was born. That might indicate an odd relationship with women.'

'Don't throw psychology at me. I've had enough of that crap for a while.'

'Fine. At fifteen his father disappeared. Probably went off chasing drugs and hookers in Amsterdam. So little Vagn moved in with his uncle. No education to speak of. I thought he might have done some time but there's nothing much.'

He flipped the pages he had.

'The only reason we get to talk to him is when we're trying to nail Theis.'

'What do you mean?'

'If Theis needs an alibi Vagn's his man. Three cases where Vagn's evidence got him off the hook. I spoke to that retired guy who called in. He thought they were part of a team.'

'What about kids? A wife? Ex-wife?'

'Nope. Lives on his own in a cheap studio half a kilometre from the Birk Larsens. We went through it. Nothing that puts him in Vestamager or anywhere else of interest.'

'There has to be something.'

'He's godfather to the Birk Larsen boys. Seems very close to the

555

family. Sometimes he's lived with them for a while. Maybe he was abusing Nanna behind their back.'

Lund just looked at him.

'OK. I withdraw that remark. Theis or Pernille would surely have known and he'd be the one feeding the eels. Also . . .'

He stopped.

'Also what?'

'Nanna looked happy. Didn't she? I did a couple of abuse cases. Those kids . . . you can see it in their eyes. Years after. That Lonstrup woman with the pigtails and the grey hair—'

'No one abused Nanna,' Lund said as she came off the motorway and looked for the care home. 'She wrapped Jens Holck round her little finger and kept it secret. Nanna was Theis and Pernille all in one.'

It was a modern place, two storeys, red-brick.

'There's a scary thought,' Meyer said.

The manager of the care home was a jolly, plump woman with dyed blonde hair and a perpetual smile. She loved Vagn Skærbæk.

'I wish we had more like him. Vagn visits his uncle every Friday.'

'You're sure about the thirty-first?' Lund asked as they walked down the long white corridor, past elderly men and women playing cards.

'Yes. I'm sure. The nurse on duty always enters visitors in the guest book.'

She had it with her and showed Meyer the page.

'Vagn checked in at eight fifteen.'

'It doesn't say when he left.'

'He didn't. He fell asleep in a chair. His uncle wasn't feeling well. Vagn came in to say goodbye when he left the next morning. Eight o'clock or so.'

Lund asked, 'So he told you he was here all night? No one saw him?'

The woman didn't like that.

'Vagn's stayed before. He was here.'

'But no one saw him?'

'He put his uncle to bed. He does that for us. Why are you asking these questions? Vagn's a diamond. I wish we—'

'Had more like him,' Meyer said. 'Got that message. Where's his uncle?'

A small room with a small, old man in it. He walked with a stick and looked frail.

They sat and had coffee, listened to his stories. Looked at the pencil drawings of windmills and fields that Vagn drew when he was a child. His uncle seemed to carry part of Skærbæk's childhood with him. One last link to the life that went before.

'Did Vagn ever talk about girlfriends?' Lund asked.

'No.' The old man laughed. 'Vagn's a shy boy. He keeps things to himself. They used to bully him when he was a kid in Vesterbro. If it wasn't for a few nice friends they'd have picked on him all the time. You see . . .'

They waited.

'See what?' Meyer prompted.

'Vagn's a gentle soul. It's a hard world out there. I don't think it's been easy for him.'

His kindly face turned miserable for a moment.

'I did what I could. But I couldn't be there all the time.'

'Does the name Mette Hauge mean anything?'

His face brightened.

'There's a lovely girl here called Mette. Is it her?'

'What about Nanna Birk Larsen?'

The smile was gone.

'Vagn took that poor girl's death very hard.'

Lund looked at the photos on the walls. A black and white portrait of a woman she took to be his late wife. Vagn when he was younger.

'How's that?' she asked.

'They're the family he never had. I was just me. My wife died young. It was selfishness that made me take him in. I was lonely, you see. I never regretted it.' He looked round the little room. 'All those years later, and still he comes to see me. There's miserable old bastards here who don't get a minute from their own son once a year. I see Vagn every week. *Every* week.'

'He was here the night you felt poorly?' Meyer said. 'Two weeks ago? How did he seem?'

'We watched TV. We always do.'

The programme guide was on the table. Meyer picked it up. Lund got out of her chair and started to walk round the room, looking at the photos, the uncle's belongings.

'That night,' Meyer said, '*Columbo* was on. And a gardening show. And then *Star Search*. What did you watch?'

'I remember the detective with the raincoat. But I didn't feel well.' He scowled. 'I'm getting old. Try to avoid it if you can. But Vagn got me my pills and I was better after that.'

Lund glanced at Meyer.

'What kind of pills?' he asked.

'I don't know. Ask the nurses. I take what they give me.'

She came back with a wedding photo. A couple from years ago, stiff and unsmiling in a black and white portrait.

'Who are these people?'

'Vagn's parents. That's my brother.' A pause. 'The layabout.'

'What did they do?'

'I think she was pregnant already. Not that you talked about things like that back then.'

He was laughing at his own joke.

'What did they do?'

'They worked in a hospital. Not good people, I have to say.'

The old man took a deep breath.

'He had such a rotten start in life. These kids . . .' His voice was rising. 'They need discipline. They need an example. They need to be shown the way to behave. And when they step outside then . . .'

He stopped, as if surprised by his own sudden outburst.

'Then what?' Meyer said.

'Then they need to know there'll be consequences. I never had to do that. Not with Vagn. But some of the youngsters you see . . .'

They checked the nursing notes on the way out. Skærbæk had given his uncle phenobarbital, a strong sedative.

Lund was driving again.

'How many?'

'Just one. It's enough to knock out a horse. He'd still have to pass the nurse's office to get out. You saw the security . . .'

Lund shook her head.

'I looked upstairs when you were talking to the nurses. There are other exits. He could have got out if he wanted.'

'Then he's smarter than he looks.'

'I told you. He is.'

Meyer went quiet.

'What is it?' she asked.

'You heard that old man. You heard the manager. They all love Vagn.'

'Doesn't mean a thing, Meyer.'

'What?'

'It doesn't mean a thing!'

'He goes and sits with his old uncle most Friday nights? When the average Copenhagen working-class male can't wait to hit the beer? That—'

'It . . doesn't . . . mean . . . a . . . thing.'

'If it wasn't for Skærbæk Theis Birk Larsen wouldn't have a business from what I've seen.'

Lund was thinking.

'Weak kid, bullied at school. Parents gone. Brought up by an uncle.'

The rain came on suddenly. The windscreen turned opaque. Meyer reached over and turned on the wipers.

'I wish you'd let me drive.'

'We'll do a line-up. See if Amir can identify him.'

'You're clutching at straws. Any news in the woods?'

She turned the wipers up to double speed. Watched the sheets of rain envelop the car.

'If we don't find anything on Vagn then Brix will shut down the Hauge case,' Meyer said. 'We need more than a few pills and an old photo.'

'I know that, thanks.'

Theis and Pernille Birk Larsen talked to the lawyer, Lis Gamborg, in the kitchen, around the decorated table. Complained about the police, about the constant visits, the ceaseless questioning.

The woman listened then said, 'I sympathize but there's really nothing you can do. It's a criminal investigation. A murder case.'

'But they're not doing anything,' Pernille said. 'Nothing useful. They keep saying it's solved. Closed. And then the next day they come back and it starts all over again.'

'The police usually have good reasons, Pernille. Even as Nanna's parents you've no right to know.'

'No right?'

'In law, no. I can talk to headquarters. Ask that they don't turn up without warning.'

'That's not good enough,' Birk Larsen broke in. 'We won't have anything to do with them. We're finished. We won't hand over the videotape either.'

'They can get a warrant.'

'I don't want them here. I don't want them in my home . . .'

'I'll talk to them. See what I can do.'

'One more thing. They're harassing one of our drivers. A close friend.'

Pernille stared at him.

'This is about us, Theis.'

'I won't let them pick on Vagn. He always stood up for me. I do the same for him.'

'Theis—'

'The bastards took him in for questioning. If it happens again I'd like you to help.'

The lawyer made some notes.

'I can do that, of course. But the police wouldn't question him without a reason.'

He tapped the table.

'I want you to help him.'

'Of course.'

Lis Gamborg took out a business card, passed it over.

'Give him my number. Tell him to call any time.'

Vagn Skærbæk had been complaining to anyone who'd listen. Most of them had now gone out on jobs. He was left with Leon Frevert, the two of them shifting a pile of household belongings into one of the smaller scarlet vans.

'Being questioned like a criminal sucks. It's like I did something wrong. Like somebody grassed on you.'

Frevert had ditched the black wool hat for a baseball cap. The peak was turned round to the back now. He looked ridiculous.

'And there you are, these idiots throwing the same things at you hour after hour.'

He watched Frevert lug out some carpet to the van.

Anton and Emil were kicking a football around the yard.

Frevert returned and picked up a box of crockery.

Skærbæk came up close, looked him in the face.

'Someone put them up to this. Was it you?'

Frevert was taller but skinny, older.

'What do you mean, Vagn? What would I have to tell them?'

'Some bastard did . . .'

Frevert laughed.

'You're getting paranoid. They're just hitting on anyone they can.'

A young voice crying, 'Vagn, Vagn.'

'Are you playing with my football?' Skærbæk cried. 'I told you that was my football. How dare . . . ?'

He made a gorilla shape, face furious, wandered outside on comic legs.

The boys squealed, ran around. Skærbæk caught them both, got Anton under his right arm, Emil under his left.

Was lugging them around like that, listening to them scream happily, when Birk Larsen came down with Pernille and a woman in a business suit.

Skærbæk let the boys go.

'My ball,' he said. 'Remember that.'

Then they were off, giggling, kicking it round the yard again.

The woman went to her car. Birk Larsen gave Skærbæk a business card, said to call the number if the police were round again.

Skærbæk said thanks, put it in his pocket.

'We're going to get some guttering, Theis. Leon can come. I'll fix it.'

'Yeah. I'm going to let a squirt like you put up guttering. Leon can stay here. I'll show you how it's done.'

The boys were on Vagn again, tugging at his red overalls.

'These kids need a trip to the toy store, Pernille. I'll come back later and pick them up. OK?'

She stood and watched him.

It took a long while but eventually she said, 'OK.'

In the mahogany office, from the shadows by the window, Hartmann told them about the meeting with Lund.

'Wonderful,' Weber said. 'If it wasn't Holck, who did it?'

'Damned if I know.'

'Does this mean we're back in the frame?' Skovgaard asked. 'They'll be looking at the flat? At us?'

Hartmann shrugged.

Weber leaned back in his chair, closed his eyes, and said, 'You were supposed to have the police on Bremer by now. What happened to the report you filed?'

'He's guilty. They'll get round to it.'

'When, Troels? A month or two after we lose the election? I warned you not to play that old bastard's game.'

'The police will question Stokke. He can't lie to them. Bremer's running out of time.'

'So are we,' Skovgaard said. 'Bremer's still in for the debate tonight.'

'Why shouldn't he be?'

She looked at him as if the question were idiotic.

'If we were in that position I wouldn't let you out in public. What's the point? I don't get it . . .'

'Amateurs,' Morten Weber scoffed. 'Why do I work with amateurs?'

Hartmann waited.

'Gert Stokke's gone missing,' Weber said. 'I got a call a couple of minutes ago. The police came for him but he wasn't there. Stokke lives on his own. No one's seen him since yesterday's hearing.'

He let it sink in.

'Your key witness just went walkabout, Troels. Now what do we do?'

'Find him,' said Hartmann.

Skovgaard walked out of the office, went to her desk, started making some calls.

'Not easy finding a man who doesn't want to be found,' Weber said.

'The surveillance tape.'

'What about it?'

'Find out who gave it to the police.'

He got his jacket, came over, tapped Morten Weber in the chest.

'You do that. No one else.'

*

562

Lund and Meyer went to Humleby. Skærbæk was out at a roofing suppliers. They looked at the house. New window frames, new doors. Scaffolding and fresh paint. Timber and glass waiting to be fitted.

'Is Birk Larsen inside?' Lund asked one of the men in red overalls in the street.

She left Meyer checking on the progress of the ID line-up, walked through the open, half-finished door, over the tarpaulins, carefully picking a path among the plasterboard and the buckets, the tools and drill cases.

He was in what would one day be the living room. Big windows. It would be full of light once the plastic was replaced with glass.

Birk Larsen was by a stepladder, working on the ceiling.

'The doorbell doesn't work,' Lund said, chewing on Nicotinell.

She took a look around.

'I've got some questions about Vagn.'

He took a deep breath, picked up a bucket, walked to the other side of the room.

Lund followed.

'What exactly did he do that weekend, Theis? When he was minding the business?'

Birk Larsen moved some chipboard to the wall, took out a retractable knife, popped up the blade.

'You left Friday night, right after Nanna went to the school party. Did you plan all that in advance?'

'No. Why do you keep asking the same questions?'

'Because people keep giving us the same answers. When did you know you were going away?'

'The night before. Pernille's mother called to offer us the cottage.'

'Did you talk to Vagn during the weekend?'

'I didn't want any calls on Saturday. It was a holiday. There was a problem with a hydraulic lift on Sunday. We talked.'

'How many times?'

He didn't answer, just shifted some more chipboard.

'Did his relationship with Nanna ever strike you as odd?'

That struck home.

He came over, stood in front of her.

'I've known Vagn for more than twenty years. His father abandoned him. His mother drank herself to death. He's always been

563

our friend. It doesn't matter what ridiculous stories you come up with. I don't give a shit. Is that clear?'

He marched to the door, held it open.

Lund followed, stopped at the threshold.

'One of your people saw Nanna and Amir together that day. He's the only one who knew she was running away. I need to know if it was Vagn.'

'Get out,' he said, jerking a thumb at the dull day outside. 'I've got nothing more to say.'

She walked to the front steps.

Turned. Looked at his stony, stubbled face.

'Vagn's mother didn't drink herself to death. She died giving birth. To him.'

'Get lost—'

'Theis!'

The half-finished door slammed in her face.

Lund went to the hole for the letterbox, yelled through it, 'He lied to you. Think about it.'

Down the curving corridor on the eastern wing. The line-up room had floor-length one-way glass. A platform on the suspects' side. Chairs and tables on the other. The lawyer Birk Larsen had hired stood with Lund and Meyer watching as Amir went up and down the line of six men, all in identical khaki uniforms, each with a number round the neck.

'Do you recognize anyone?' Lund asked.

'I don't know. I only saw him for a second.'

'Take your time. Take a good look. Think about what you saw. Try to remember a face.'

Amir adjusted his heavy spectacles, went closer to the glass.

'No one can see you,' Meyer said. 'You don't need to worry.'

Amir shook his head.

'Did you see him face on or in profile? Think about it.'

He looked.

'It might be him. Number three.'

'Number three?' Lund repeated.

Skærbæk.

'Maybe.'

'Is it him or not?' Meyer wanted to know.

'Or maybe number five.'

The lawyer let loose a long, pained sigh.

'I don't know.'

Lund put a hand on his shoulder.

'Amir?' the lawyer said. 'How far's your flat from the Birk Larsen garage?'

'Two streets.'

'You've walked past the place most of your life. You used to go there as a kid, to play with Nanna?'

He said nothing.

'So,' the woman added, 'you could just be recognizing a face you know.'

Lund nodded to one of the uniform men to take him back to the office.

The lawyer looked at both of them.

'I can't believe you did this. Number five's one of your detectives, isn't he? Even if he'd picked Vagn . . . Of course he's seen him. In the garage.'

She looked at her watch.

'We're going now.'

'No,' Lund said. 'You're not.'

Back in the office, Skærbæk in his scarlet overalls, hat on, scowling, bored.

'No one saw you in the nursing home from ten at night until eight in the morning,' Meyer said.

'Why would they? I was asleep in a chair. In my uncle's room.'

'Right. And the rest of the weekend you were in the depot.'

'Correct.'

'But no one saw you there either, Vagn.'

'I was on my own. The hydraulic lift wasn't working. I stayed in the garage. I like working on things. Why should Theis pay for a mechanic if I can fix it?'

'Your phone was turned off.'

'I was fixing the lift. People could leave messages if they wanted.'

'But no one can confirm you were there.'

'Theis and Pernille can.'

Lund stood at the door, watching him answer, thinking about the way he spoke.

'You're forty-one years old, Vagn. Why don't you have a wife and kids?'

'I never met the right girl.'

'Maybe women don't like you,' Meyer said.

'And you still spend time with Anton and Emil,' Lund added.

'Sure. I'm their godfather. There's nothing wrong with spending time with your family.'

Lund shook her head.

'But they're not your family.'

He met her eyes.

'You don't understand. I feel sorry for you.'

'You and Pernille,' Meyer cut in. 'Did you maybe have a little fling when Theis was inside one time? Is there some history . . . ?'

Skærbæk turned to the lawyer.

'Do I have to answer that crap?'

'Go ahead,' she said.

'No.'

Meyer lit a cigarette.

'So what the hell's in it for you? I don't get it. All the time. All the investment. What do you get out of it?'

'Mutual respect.'

'Mutual respect? For what? You're a sad old loner hanging round the family.' Meyer pointed across the table. 'With that stupid silver necklace? I mean . . . what kind of forty-one-year-old weirdo—?'

'Were you envious of Theis?' Lund asked.

'You haven't seen Pernille when she gets mad.'

She came and sat next to him.

'You and Theis were friends as kids. He grew up and got everything. A business. A family. The good life.'

'And you just go to work each day and hang grinning off their coat-tails,' Meyer said. 'You spend your day dealing with shit. Then watch Theis go home to his wife and kids.'

'Is this your life you're talking about?' Skærbæk asked with a stupid, childish grin.

'You're a loser,' Meyer snarled. 'No future. No family. A dead-end job. And then the boss's beautiful daughter starts hanging out with a raghead . . .'

'You've got a filthy mouth for a policeman.'

The lawyer put her notebook on the table.

'My client's happy to answer relevant questions. If you have any. If not . . .'

'Do you know what phenobarbital is?' Lund asked.

'I haven't done anything wrong.'

'Why do you hang around them?' Meyer wouldn't let this go. 'You're always there. When Theis goes out to beat up the teacher you've got to tag along. Why?'

'Because I owe him! OK?'

They'd touched something and Lund had no idea what.

'Why do you owe him, Vagn?'

'Go look it up. You're idiots. You know that? You drag me here . . . throw names at me. Do you think I don't know what that's like?'

Vagn Skærbæk got to his feet.

'Idiots. I want to go now.'

'Stay here,' Lund said.

Svendsen was lurking outside.

'They've found something out in Vestamager,' he said.

'What?'

'They're not sure. They're working on it now. It's not easy.'

'Let's go,' Lund said.

Svendsen nodded at the figure in the scarlet suit in the interview room.

'What about him?'

'Get his passport if he has one,' Lund ordered. 'Tell him he can't leave Copenhagen.'

A thought.

'Go back to the records. We're missing something here.'

Svendsen hated being asked to do things twice.

'What am I supposed to be looking for this time?'

'Something to do with Vagn and Theis Birk Larsen. Something . . .'

Skærbæk was slumped at the desk, picking pieces off his plastic cup again. Playing the fool.

'Something that connects,' she said.

Three full days of campaigning left before the weekend. The dead lull of the following Monday. Then the election. The meetings went on and on, this time at the Black Diamond, the Royal Library by the water. A room full of supporters, a handful of media. Wan winter light through the massive windows.

Hartmann smiled and nodded as the audience made for the exit.

He strode to the door, dealing with the faithful.

Smiles and handshakes. Shoulders patted. Thanks exchanged.

Outside the black glass shone in the rain. Hartmann stared at the bleak grey water. Waited for Skovgaard and the car.

Alone for once he felt strangely free. He knew the long battle to topple Bremer would be exhausting. But not this much. He felt drained. Surrounded on all sides by inimical and invisible enemies. Lacking the weapons to fight them.

Rie Skovgaard was the first to him from the car.

'Stokke . . .' Hartmann began.

'We can't find him. You're going to have to think about withdrawing your allegations.'

'If I do that I may as well pull out of the election. What are the police doing?'

Her hair was always up now. Not free around her shoulders, the way he preferred.

'I've no idea. I'll get us some food. God knows when we'll get the chance to eat again.'

He watched her walk off. Stood on the steps, battered by the wind and drizzle. Not caring much.

Alone.

A man emerged from the shadows. He wore a black coat and sunglasses in spite of the dismal day.

Closer, then he stopped by one of the campaign posters against the glass. Troels Hartmann smiling for the world, confident, modest, youthful. Energetic and fresh.

Ten strides and Hartmann was with him.

'You run a good campaign,' Gert Stokke said.

In the half-light Hartmann turned, checked the pavement around them. Empty.

'The old king's dying. The new king waits by his bed. Long live Troels Hartmann.'

Stokke saluted.

'They're looking for you, Gert.'

Mouth downturned, balding head greasy from the rain, Stokke said, 'Why the hell did I get mixed up in all this? I should have stuck to filing minutes. Letting Holck and Bremer get away with it.'

'But you didn't.'

'I do my job and I try to do it responsibly.'

'I know that.'

He laughed.

'Do you really? Is that why you threw my name into the ring? Without even warning me?'

Hartmann leaned against the black glass, stared at his own reflection.

'Sometimes events have a life of their own. There's nothing we can do to control them. I know that better than most by now.'

That dry laugh again.

'You've got a fine turn of speech. But civil servants don't trade in rhetoric. It's wasted. Sorry.'

'You lied to me. You said there were no minutes.'

'What else could I do?'

'You've got to go to the police.'

'How can I? You know that's impossible.'

Hartmann waited, then said, 'What about your career?'

'What career? I'll be lucky to get out of this with a pension. I'm sorry. This was a mistake. I don't why I came . . .'

He started to walk off. Hartmann caught up with him.

'You've got a career if I win.'

The car was waiting.

Stokke stopped, took off the sunglasses, looked at him warily.

'A civil servant learns before anyone else never to trust a politician's promises.'

'You can believe mine. After the election we need good, honest loyal people. I don't doubt you fit that bill. You wouldn't have noted that minute otherwise.'

'Ah, the words. They come so easily.'

'If we win, Gert, I'll find a good position for you. Better than the job you have now. Better-paid too.'

He held out his hand.

'If I win.'

Stokke was laughing again, more freely this time.

'What's so funny?' Hartmann asked.

'I got a message from Bremer's people. They said the same.'

Hartmann walked to the car, opened the back door, looked at him.

Stokke rubbed his chin with his hand. Thinking.

'You've got to ask yourself, Gert. Who do you trust the most?'

'No.'

Hartmann struggled for something else, some other lure.

Then Stokke walked to join him at the car.

'What I have to ask myself,' the civil servant said, 'is who I mistrust the least.'

He climbed in the back. Rie Skovgaard came round the corner with some sandwiches.

'We're giving Gert a lift,' Hartmann told her. 'So he doesn't get lost again.'

Pernille stayed in the garage to talk to Leon Frevert.

'That weekend when . . .'

He heaved some cardboard boxes onto a stack, looked embarrassed by her questions.

'Were you around, Leon?'

'No. Vagn called and said he didn't need me after all.'

He went back to the boxes. A hard worker. Strong in spite of his slight build.

'But you were supposed to work?'

'Yeah. Saturday and Sunday. It didn't matter. I've always got the taxis.'

He went outside and got more cases. She followed.

'Vagn said there was no point in coming in. We only had one customer and they'd cancelled. So I went back to the cab. No problem. It was fine.'

She looked around the garage, thinking. Wondering about Lund. The questions the odd and persistent policewoman asked. The repetitive way she went about them.

'So a job had been cancelled?' Pernille asked.

Frevert took off his baseball cap and scratched his balding scalp.

'It was funny really.'

Pernille's breath turned shallow and rapid. She couldn't stop looking at this pallid, thin man who wouldn't meet her eyes.

'What was funny?'

'We were supposed to move for an office supply store. Couple of days later I ran into the owner. He was ranting and raving at me for cancelling on them. I thought Vagn said they cancelled on us. But he said Vagn had phoned to say we couldn't do it.'

Frevert picked up another crate.

'I'm sure he had a good reason.'

He lugged the load to the van, closed the doors.

'That's the lot then?'

She couldn't move. Could barely stand at that moment.

'Vagn wants the van in the morning, Pernille. I'll drop the keys off at his place tonight when I'm done.'

He looked round the garage.

'I'm taking a holiday soon. You won't see me for a while. Is that OK?'

She went back upstairs, sat at the table for a long time doing nothing. Then she listened to the messages on the answering machine.

It had to be him first.

Cocky as ever.

'Hi, it's me. I'm on my way back. I think the police get it finally. They'll keep their distance from now on.'

Pernille had her chestnut hair tied back in a ponytail. Like Lund. She wore a thin sweater over a white shirt. Summer clothes for some reason.

'I'd still like to take the boys to the toy store. I saw the coolest water pistols. They'll love them.'

As if nothing had happened, she thought.

'They've got some new ones. Three different kinds. See you soon. Bye.'

Theis Birk Larsen came up the stairs. She looked at him, saw his face, knew at that moment.

Almost said it.

Back in the nightmare. Trapped in limbo.

'Are the boys ready to go out?' Birk Larsen asked.

'If we want them to.'

Anton and Emil's young voices drifted through from their room. They were playing well together for once.

Birk Larsen looked at their coats on the table. Put them on the hooks.

571

'Maybe we should eat together tonight. We can watch TV with them.'

He was staring at her, wanting her approval.

'Good idea,' Pernille said and it was almost a whisper.

Not long after they heard the sliding garage door. A bright voice that seemed to be a part of the place calling, 'Hello? Hello?'

Birk Larsen walked down the stairs first. Pernille followed.

Red suit, silver chain. Cheeky grin.

'Hi, Theis. Did you get my message?'

Birk Larsen stayed at the foot of the stairs, said nothing.

'What about the boys? Are they ready?'

Pernille joined her husband. The two of them stood together.

'They can't go today,' Birk Larsen said. 'Anton's got a cold.'

Skærbæk's face turned suspicious.

'What do you mean he's got a cold? He was fine this morning.'

'Yeah, well . . .'

Pernille was silent.

Skærbæk stood there.

'You always got me to lie for you, Theis. You're so bad at it yourself.'

'Vagn,' Birk Larsen groaned. 'Not now.'

'This is ridiculous. I love the boys. I was really looking forward to picking them up.'

He looked ready to cry. Or lose his temper.

'Yes,' Birk Larsen said.

'Can't you see what they're trying to do? They're trying to break us up. They can't find the bastard who did it so they turn on us.'

'Did you lie to us, Vagn?'

A long pause.

'What did they say? Tell me.'

Together they stood there in silence.

'Jesus . . .'

He turned to go.

'Vagn,' Birk Larsen said.

Skærbæk turned, pointed an accusing finger.

'I always stood up for you, Theis. And you, Pernille. You know that.'

'Vagn!'

The door went up.

'Always!' Vagn Skærbæk shrieked, then walked off into the rain.

The TV studio was in Islands Brygge, brand new, low blue lights everywhere. Bremer turned up just before they were due to go on air, apologizing, looking flustered.

They sat at the interview desk, Hartmann making notes, Bremer fidgeting nervously. The cameras were dead and silent. The circus had yet to begin.

'I have to tell you, Troels,' Bremer said in a low, spiteful voice, 'I find your conduct appalling.'

Hartmann glanced at him then went back to writing.

'Instead of jumping to conclusions you could have come to me and checked these ridiculous accusations.'

'Shall we begin the debate with that?'

A make-up woman came over and started to put powder on Bremer's sweating forehead. Someone called four minutes to go. The lights went down.

'Or with you fleeing to the police to file stupid reports?' Bremer retorted.

'You lead, I'll follow.'

Bremer laughed. Caught him with a sly look.

'You can no longer accuse me of covering for a murderer. The police know Holck didn't do it. I've told his wife.'

'Have you spoken to Olav Christensen's mother? Asked her opinion?'

'You don't know a thing. To think I once believed you worthy—'

'Save your breath. Save it for the police.'

Bremer grasped at the glass of water in front of him, gulped some down.

'There won't be any charges. Unless they go for Gert Stokke.' He brightened. 'Oh, look. Here comes Rie Skovgaard. She'll probably bring you the same news.'

Hartmann got up to speak to her.

'I talked to the police,' she whispered. 'Bremer has witnesses who'll say he never spoke about Holck at the meeting with Stokke.'

'There were no witnesses. The minutes make that clear.'

'There are now. It's going to be Stokke's word against the Lord Mayor's. Troels?'

Hartmann walked back to the table. Sat down in the interviewer's seat, close to Bremer.

'Stokke's going to be fired,' Bremer said, eyeing the camera. 'That'll be the end of it. And the end of you.'

Hartmann leaned over, whispered, 'Can you feel the world crumbling beneath you, old man?' Looked into his hooded grey eyes. 'You're like a decrepit actor who doesn't know it's time to leave the stage. The only one who doesn't see it. Tragic in a way.'

A pause.

'And when it's over, Poul, people will try to forget about you. What you were. What you stood for. You'll just be one grubby little detail in the history of this city. No plaques. No streets named after you. No monuments. No flowers on your grave. Just a dirty sense of shame.'

Bremer stared at him, mouth gaping, shocked, speechless.

'Do you think you can save yourself by conjuring up witnesses?' Hartmann asked with a smile. 'It's pathetic.'

Someone called one minute. The lights went up.

'Your house is built on lies and it's starting to burn all round you. Before long you won't see the world for flames. And then you're just ash and cinders. You're gone.'

He got up, went back to his own seat.

Bremer gazed at him with such bitterness and hatred.

'And what about you? Are you any better?'

'Yes,' Hartmann said. 'Yes, I am.'

'So tell me how you think the surveillance tape disappeared. How could the party's flat be connected to this poor child's murder and no one notices, not one of you?'

Hartmann stared at the notepad, scribbled doodles on it.

'Who stole that tape, Troels, and kept it secret even though it seems to exonerate you? How come Skovgaard suddenly gets a tip about Gert Stokke?'

No answer.

'You're no better than me,' Bremer snarled. 'You just don't know it.'

The interviewer strode past them, took her seat, said, 'We're nearly on.'

More lights. The cameras closed in, lenses hunting.

Poul Bremer smiled.

So did Troels Hartmann.

Two scuba divers in the dank and muddy waters of the canal on the Kalvebod Fælled, dark shiny shapes in the floodlights. Lund and Meyer watched as a portable gurney was lowered down to them on ropes.

The men above pulled something to the surface. It looked like a chrysalis the size of a man. Blue plastic. Shiny and held with tape.

Four forensic officers got it to the bank. The duty pathologist waited in a white bunny suit, medical case by his side.

Gloves on, he took a scalpel, ran it down the plastic. Opened up a flap, got ready to wind it back.

'All sensitive souls retire now,' the man said and no one moved.

It stank of rotten flesh and rotten water.

Torches ran over it, caught yellow bone. Ribs and a skull.

Brix waited on the upper bank. Lund stayed as close as the pathologist allowed.

'There,' she said, spotting something. 'What's that? Try scraping it.'

'It's not the body.'

'I can see it's not the body.'

With the back of his scalpel he wiped the grime and mud from the tape that bound her.

A word emerged. Blocked blue letters. MERKUR, with a flying wing to the left.

Lund started walking to the car.

Driving through the dark night Meyer got a call from headquarters.

'Well?' she asked.

'I think they found what Vagn was talking about. Twenty-one years ago there was an incident in Christiania. Probably down to selling dope or something. Vagn got badly beaten up. Might have been killed.'

'Theis stopped them,' Lund said.

'I sometimes wonder why you ask questions.'

It wasn't far to Vesterbro. Skærbæk lived in a public housing project near the meat-packing district.

'There had to be something tying them together.'

'So why would Vagn kill his daughter?'

'Let's ask him,' she said.

It was an ugly white block, three storeys with a supermarket in the basement. At the end of the road the hookers were out for the night. Jaded girls trying to look pretty, showing their legs to the cars streaming towards them over the Dybbølsbro bridge.

They were some of the cheapest flats around. Long lines of small units joined by an exterior walkway with an iron grille fence at the front. Skærbæk lived on the first floor. Svendsen was outside the door already. The apartment was empty. No one had been home all day. He'd left the Birk Larsens. He wasn't at the nursing home.

Svendsen started for the stairs. Lund and Meyer paced the walkway.

'Let's add this up,' she said. 'Vagn gave his uncle the medication at ten. Nanna arrived at the flat in Store Kongensgade one hour later.'

'The timing works for me.'

'But how did Vagn know where she was?'

There was someone up ahead walking past the pale grey doors.

Tall figure, skinny. Baseball cap. He pulled the peak over his face as soon as he saw them.

'Maybe he kept an eye on her,' Meyer suggested. 'He knew where to go.'

'How? She just happened to go to the flat to get her passport. It's not a routine.'

The man in the baseball cap had gone back to the lift. Pressed the button.

Lund and Meyer got there behind him. He turned away from them, took a phone out of his pocket, looked ready to make a call.

'We questioned him twice!' Meyer said. 'We should have arrested him.'

Whoever he was calling hadn't answered.

'Let's take the stairs, Lund. We could wait for ever.'

She followed back the way they came.

Then stopped, looked back.

The man in the baseball cap never made the call. But he couldn't stop himself turning. And then she saw.

'Hey,' Lund cried. 'Hey!'

He was starting to run, dashing down the narrow corridor towards a distant stairwell.

'Meyer!'

Lund turned to follow, found herself in darkness, struggling to get her bearings.

Fast footsteps on metal. Iron railing, iron steps below. She'd got halfway down when she saw it.

White Mercedes. Taxi sign on the top.

Leon Frevert. The last man to see Nanna alive.

Meyer was running for it too, trying to leap on the bonnet.

He didn't have a gun, she thought. Thanks to Brix.

'Meyer!'

Didn't matter anyway. The Mercedes wheeled out of the parking area, tyres squealing and smoking.

Lund got to their car first. Passenger seat. Blue light out of the glovebox, popped flashing onto the roof.

'This time, Meyer, you drive.'

'Who the hell was that?' he asked, falling into the seat.

She didn't answer. Just called headquarters.

'I want a search for Leon Frevert. White Mercedes. Taxi sign. Registration HZ 98050. Approach with caution. Frevert's a suspect in the Birk Larsen case.'

Meyer took the car out so quickly she had to catch her breath.

Maybe he turned right into Vesterbro. Or over the Dybbølsbro bridge, back to the city, or out to Amager, to the bridge to Malmö.

He slammed on the brakes, sending the flock of mini-skirted hookers scattering onto the pavement.

'Which way?' Meyer asked. 'Which way, Lund?'

To the woods, she thought. To the dead trees of the Pentecost Forest. In the end it always goes there.

'Lund! Which way?'

The wet shining roads led everywhere.

'I don't know.'

Leon Frevert had a brother. Svendsen brought the man to Frevert's dismal studio apartment off Vesterbrogade.

He was called Martin. An accountant with his own company in Østerbro. Dark suit and tie. Younger than his brother, not so skinny or so grey. More money, Lund thought. More brains.

Meyer looked round the place.

'Doesn't your brother believe in furniture?'

Martin Frevert sat on the single chair. There was a sofa, a single bed. Nothing else.

'Last time I was here the place was fully furnished. Three weeks ago,' he added before either of them could ask.

Lund asked, 'What's missing?'

Frevert looked around the place.

'The table. All his CDs. His stuff.'

'So you didn't know he'd given notice?'

'He never told me. Leon always said he liked this place. His choice.'

They'd found a ticket to Ho Chi Minh City via Frankfurt. Due to leave the following Monday. Bought two days before.

Meyer said, 'He didn't tell you he was going to Vietnam?'

'No. He went there on holiday a year or so ago.'

Martin Frevert scowled, looked guilty.

'He used to go to Thailand too. It was the girls, I think—'

'Oh come on,' Meyer said. 'He'd got tickets. Got money. He'd packed his bags. Sold everything. And he didn't tell his baby brother?'

Frevert looked incensed.

'He didn't tell me! What do you want me to say? Why would I lie to you?'

'What about girlfriends?' Lund asked.

'Not recently. He used to be married.'

'Kids?' said Meyer.

'No. It didn't end well.'

'Friends then?'

Martin Frevert glanced at his watch.

'Leon doesn't have many friends. We'd have him round for dinner now and then. But really . . .' He shrugged. 'What was there to talk about? He drove a taxi. He humped cardboard boxes around the place.'

Lund ordered Svendsen to take Frevert to headquarters to make a formal statement. Then she walked to the plain wall at the end of the room.

It was covered with newspaper front pages from the very beginning of the Nanna case. Photos of Hartmann. Of Jens Holck and Kemal. But most of all pictures of Nanna, smiling.

'The brother didn't know,' Meyer said. 'This creep kept it all to himself.'

'We had him.' Lund stared at the front pages, the felt-tip pen marks around Nanna's photo on every one. 'We had him and we let him go.'

She walked out, went down the stairs to the car park. Blue lights flashing. Cars everywhere marked and unmarked. Forensics turning up.

Svendsen was smoking by the metal steps.

'He dumped the cab near Birk Larsen's place then picked up his own car,' Svendsen said. 'We've got an alert out for it. His phone's off. We'll get a trace the moment it comes back on.'

'Why didn't we know Frevert worked for Birk Larsen? You interviewed him.'

Svendsen looked at her, said, 'What?'

'You interviewed him. Why didn't we know?'

'He came in as a witness. Not a suspect. You never asked us to check him out.'

'Lund . . .' Meyer began.

'Are you an intern or something, Svendsen?' she barked. 'Do I need to tell you your job?'

'He was a witness!' the burly cop yelled at her.

Meyer retreated.

She stabbed a finger towards Svendsen's face.

'If we'd known he worked for Birk Larsen we wouldn't be standing here looking like idiots. We'd have Leon Frevert in a cell.'

'Don't blame me for your fuck-ups.'

'You,' she said, waving a finger in his bull face, 'are a lazy man. And there's nothing I hate more than laziness.'

She walked back towards her car. Meyer was making conciliatory noises behind her.

'We've been working round the clock!' Svendsen shouted. 'I'm not having that bitch call me lazy. You hear that!'

She got behind the wheel.

'They're doing their best,' Meyer said through the window. 'Give them a break.'

'Find Leon Frevert and I might even buy them a beer. Get his description out to the media. Bring in Vagn Skærbæk for questioning again.'

'Lund . . .'

She started the car and edged out into the road.

'Lund?' Meyer said, running at the window. 'What the hell do we want Vagn for again?'

'Company,' she answered and drove off.

Morten Weber was listening to the radio news, grim-faced, weary. A couple of reporters and photographers had ambushed Hartmann on the way into the Rådhus, following him up the stairs until Skovgaard turned on them.

Weber turned up the volume as Hartmann took off his coat.

'Sources in police headquarters indicate the killer of Nanna Birk Larsen has still to be found. There is new speculation about the coming elections. The case continues to haunt Troels Hartmann since the Liberal Party flat is known to be connected to the crime. The basis for the police report filed by Hartmann against the Lord Mayor appears to be crumbling. New witnesses have stated that Bremer was not privy to the conversation . . .'

'Turn it off,' Hartmann ordered.

The office was strewn with papers. Committee minutes and constitutional documents.

'Let's go back to the police and get an update. Rie?'

She nodded, looking glum.

'Send out a press release stating that we maintain our position on Bremer. Emphasize that I've been cleared of all suspicion.'

'I hope the public believe that,' Weber grumbled.

Skovgaard asked, 'What did Bremer say to you, Troels?'

'He accused me of covering up details in the case.'

'What details?'

'The surveillance tape. The party flat. He seems to think we got the information on Gert Stokke deceitfully somehow.'

Skovgaard said nothing.

Weber checked his phone.

'I hate to make a bad day worse,' he said, 'but that slimy bastard Erik Salin's waiting outside for you. He says he has to talk to you. It's important.'

'To him or me?'

'I'd guess him. Ignore it . . .'

Hartmann went into the main office. Erik Salin was on the sofa, helping himself to a glass of wine. He'd started working on special projects for one of the dailies, or so he said.

'What does that mean?' Hartmann asked.

'Right now that means you.'

Hartmann sat back on the leather sofa and waited.

'Thing is,' Salin said, taking out his notebook, 'I don't get some of this story. The surveillance tape, say.'

'Been talking to Bremer?'

'I talk to lots of people. It's my job. I just want to get this straight. Wasn't it really convenient for you that the tape disappeared? It's got you on there taking the car keys.'

'It's also got Holck with the girl. So it suited him more than me, don't you think?'

'I guess. But Holck was dead by the time the tape showed up.' A thin, sarcastic smile. 'Didn't help him much then, did it?'

'Erik . . .'

'So the party flat was left untouched for more than a week? Is that right?'

'Seems to be. I'm running an election campaign. Not an accommodation agency.'

Salin looked surprised.

'You're running the Liberal group, aren't you? There were lots of meetings during that time. And you never used the flat. Don't you find that strange?'

'Not really. We hold meetings here. In the campaign office.'

'I guess.' Salin smiled at him. 'I'm sorry to pester you with all this. New editor. You get all the pressure.'

'You are aware, Erik, that the police have cleared me of all suspicion?'

'I do know that. I have to ask. What with stuff flying around. Like all these rumours about Rie Skovgaard.'

Hartmann said nothing.

'You must have heard them, Troels? It's everywhere. Supposedly she got the tip on Stokke by spreading her legs for Bremer's press guy Bressau.'

He picked up one of the papers, found a photo of Bressau with Bremer. Put it in front of Hartmann.

'Can't blame the guy. Skovgaard's hot in a kind of . . .' He scratched his bald head. 'A cold kind of way.'

Salin was grinning.

'Word is she took him to a hotel the night they let you out of jail. Worked a little pillow talk on him. Got favours in return. If it's true Bressau's finished, of course. I guess we'll have to see. People always say I'm in a shitty business. But it's not much different to yours, is it?'

Hartmann waited, thinking.

Then he said, 'I know you people think you own my private life. But if you're going to stoop to playing Peeping Tom with my staff you've crossed the line.'

He got to his feet.

'I don't want to see you here again.'

Salin scooped up his notebook and his pen.

'You put yourself in the public eye, Troels. You've got to expect some scrutiny.' That snide grin again. 'People have the right to know who they're voting for. The real person. Not the pretty face on the posters. Not the bullshit they're fed from your publicity machine.'

'Goodnight.'

'Still, I guess if she's willing to go that far for her man you have to wonder.' Erik Salin came close, looked into Hartmann's eyes. 'What else would she do? And here you are accusing Bremer of impeding the investigation. It's a bit rich, don't you think?'

'Isn't there an opening on a gossip column somewhere, Erik? Sounds more up your street.'

'Ouch! That hurt.' He nudged Hartmann gently in the ribs. 'Just kidding. I will need to get back to you, Troels. With some more questions. Don't freeze me out.'

'Erik—'

'You won't kill this by not talking to me. That's a promise.'

Vagn Skærbæk was in Lund's office demanding his lawyer.

'No one's charging you,' Meyer said. 'We just want to know what Leon Frevert was doing round your place.'

Red overalls, black hat. He looked as if he never climbed out of them.

'So that means I'm not a suspect any more?'

'Where's Frevert likely to hang out?'

'That's an apology? Jesus. You people . . .'

Lund looked at him.

'You want us to find out what happened, don't you, Vagn? You're one of the family.'

'Leon was bringing back the keys for the van. He did a job. He's not working tomorrow. I'm closer to him than the garage. He was going to drop them through my door.'

Lund wrote that down.

Meyer got up from the desk, started looking at the one photo they had of Frevert. Not a good one.

'How well do you know him?'

Skærbæk frowned.

'Leon's been hanging round the removals business for years.' He took off his black cap. 'If he'd been a bit more reliable we might have given him a job. But I don't know. You never got friends with the guy. There was always something . . .'

He stopped.

'Something what?' Lund prompted.

'He was married for a while. When that went tits up he turned a bit weird. You think I'm a loner? I'm not. Leon . . .' He frowned. 'Definitely.'

'Where do you think he might go?'

'God knows.'

'Was he working for Birk Larsen when Nanna went missing?' she asked.

Skærbæk took off his hat, played with it, said nothing.

'Well?' Meyer asked.

'I don't think he's been around for a few weeks. I don't carry a job list in my head. He worked a lot during the summer, off and on.'

'How did he get the job there?'

'Through me. There's an agency we use for casual work when we need people. He was looking for some cash on the side.'

'When did you first get to know him?'

Skærbæk's dark and beady eyes were on her.

'Through Aage Lonstrup. He was a casual when I worked there.'

Lund sat back, thought about it.

'You're saying twenty years ago Leon Frevert worked for Merkur?'

Skærbæk's face was still unreadable.

'Did he do it?'

She didn't answer.

583

'People in your business see a lot of empty buildings and ware-houses.'

Lund passed him a notepad and a pen, placed it next to Meyer's toy police car.

'I want a list of all the places Frevert would know from the business.'

He laughed.

'All of them? You're kidding. I mean . . . there's a million places.'

'Get started,' Meyer said. 'When you're finished you can go.'

Skærbæk nodded.

'So . . .' His voice was cracking. 'I brought this bastard into their home.'

He closed his eyes, let out a low moan.

'Vagn . . .' Meyer began.

An accusing arm, thrust at both of them.

'Thanks to you Theis and Pernille think I killed Nanna. Now I've got to go back and tell them . . . maybe . . . maybe . . .' The volume and the anger fell, turned inwards. 'Maybe I did in a way.'

Lund watched him.

'Just write the list,' she said.

She listened as Meyer talked to the night team in the briefing room. Next to the map of the city on the wall were some fresh photos of Frevert, pictures of Nanna and Mette Hauge, some of the other women from the missing persons files.

All the standard procedures. Background to Frevert's activities over the previous two decades. Tracking down girlfriends, the former wife, workmates, neighbours. Staff from the closed Merkur. Something that might link him to Mette Hauge.

'I want to know where his cab went after he let Nanna out,' Meyer said. 'Let's get his phone records. Every call he made that weekend. OK?'

Lund watched them go. Svendsen came into the room, didn't look at her.

He had an evidence bag and some old file records.

'What's that?' Lund asked, making him look at her.

'I tracked down some storage space Merkur used to rent. The tax people impounded everything over unpaid bills. Pile of crap so they've never got round to selling what they took. From what I can gather some of Mette's stuff may be still there. The tax people have given me an entry card and some keys. Whether anything's still there . . .'

'Good,' Lund said.

Svendsen looked at her.

'Good,' she repeated.

Meyer watched him leave.

'You never did the teamwork course, did you, Lund?'

'Depends on the team. The body we found is Mette Hauge. How many more are out there?'

'We've got enough on our hands already. No time to look for more. Did he tie her up too?'

'Mette was long dead when she was bound. Fractured skull. Fractured clavicle, forearm, femur and shoulder.'

He looked at the photos in front of her.

'He wasn't kidding, was he?'

'What are we missing, Meyer? Nanna was kept for the weekend. Raped repeatedly. Thrown alive into the boot of a car. Drowned. Mette was beaten to death, wrapped up in plastic sheeting, bound with Merkur tape, dumped in the water.'

There was more information about Mette Hauge on the desk. She was wrapped in the sheeting wearing a torn cotton dress. No bra. No underwear.

'It says she was taking self-defence classes. Judo. She was a fit, muscular girl.'

'She'd fight,' Lund said. 'If someone came at her. She'd fight for her life, fight well I guess. How can these be the same but different?'

'You mean it's not our guy?'

'I don't know what I mean. Maybe he had some sort of relationship with Mette. It went wrong. That made him mad. Nanna was different.'

She picked up the evidence bag with the entry card and the key to the warehouse.

'If there was a relationship we could pick up something from her things.'

'Tomorrow,' Meyer said.

'No. Now.'

Meyer got his jacket.

'Look, Lund. Maybe you don't have a life but I do. My youngest's got an ear infection. I promised I'd be home.'

'Fine. I'll tell you about it in the morning.'

'Oh for pity's sake. You're not going on your own.'

She read through the file record.

'OK,' Meyer said. 'That's it. Time for a little frank speaking.'

His hand slammed on the papers she was shuffling.

'Lund. I've been watching you for two weeks. You're falling apart.'

She looked at him.

Meyer folded his arms.

'I'm saying this as your friend. You need sleep. You need to get this case out of your head for a while. I'm driving you home now. No arguments. No . . .'

She smiled, patted him on the chest, got her jacket, walked down the corridor.

Footsteps behind her. Lund didn't look back.

'This better not take long,' Meyer yelled.

She drove. The warehouse was in a deserted part of the docks. Two fluorescent tubes outside.

Meyer got a call from home. Apologies. Baby talk to a child.

'Poor darling. Does it hurt?'

'If it's an ear infection . . .' Lund said lightly.

She got out of the car, looked at the place, left the door open. Meyer didn't move.

'I'll stop at the chemist on the way home. I won't be late, I promise. Hang on a minute . . .'

Lund was at the door. It was a security card system.

'Hey!' Meyer cried. 'The chances of that thing working are about equal to me making the next Pope. Just wait will you?'

She popped in the card, heard the lock clank. Opened the door. Turned, waved the card at him and walked in.

Meyer was screaming at her.

'Lund! Goddammit! Lund!'

Just heard him say, in a voice more sympathetic than angry, 'I'm sorry, love. It's just that she's really crazy right now. I've got to keep an eye out—'

The red metal door was on a massive spring. It slammed shut behind her, its iron voice booming through the darkness ahead.

Theis Birk Larsen refused to talk to the two detectives who came round demanding access to their records. Pernille was less reticent. She stood in the office with the two of them, fielding their questions. Asking some of her own.

They were asking about staff and when they worked.

'Of course we make a note of who goes on each job,' she said.

The two of them were hunting through calendars, worksheets, ledgers. Didn't ask permission for anything.

'What's this about? What are you looking for?'

One of them found a financial ledger, started flicking through the pages.

'We want to know when Leon Frevert worked here.'

'Why?'

He didn't answer.

'Those are our accounts. They're private. Nothing to do with you—'

'We've got a warrant. We'll take what we like.'

'They're the accounts!'

He grinned at her.

'Everything goes through the books, does it? We work with the tax people too, Pernille. I can pass this on—'

'What do you want?'

'I want to see the paperwork that lists who's worked here and when. Every day for the last year.'

She marched to the filing cabinets. Got what they wanted. Threw it on the desk.

'You're welcome,' she said and went upstairs.

Theis was washing up at the sink. The basil plant and the parsley were dying on the windowsill. She hadn't watered them. Never thought of it.

Pernille stood next to him, trying to catch his eyes.

'They're looking for Leon Frevert. They're asking where he's been. How long he's worked for us. They want to—'

'There's no point in getting involved,' he cut in angrily.

'Yes but—'

'There's no point! Every day they point the finger at someone new. This morning it's Vagn. Now it's Leon. Tomorrow it's probably me—'

'Theis—'

'I can't believe we did that to Vagn. We were stupid enough to think there was something in it.'

'Theis—'

'If it wasn't for Vagn we wouldn't have this place. If it wasn't for Vagn . . .'

His voice drifted into silence.

'Maybe you should call him,' she said.

'I tried. He didn't answer.'

A small, scared voice from the shadows.

'Did something happen to Uncle Vagn?'

Anton walked out in his blue pyjamas, sat on the step, looked wide awake.

'Were the police here again, Dad?'

'Yes . . . I lost something. They came to return it.'

Folded arms, bright face. Always the one with questions.

'What did you lose?'

Theis Birk Larsen looked at Pernille.

'Well, it was supposed to be a surprise. But . . .'

He pulled a set of keys out of his pocket.

'It's these. We're moving. We've got a house.'

Pernille smiled, at Theis, at Anton.

'You get your own room,' she said. 'We can sit outside in the summer. You can have a slide in the garden.'

The boy got up, frowned.

'I like it here.'

'You'll like it there better.'

'I like it here.'

'You'll like it there better.'

The hard tone in Theis Birk Larsen's voice silenced the boy.

'Go to bed, Anton,' he ordered and the child went straight away.

Lund was on the sixth floor, poking round the storage spaces, when Meyer called.

'What the hell are you doing in there?'

'I found the floor where Merkur's stuff's kept.'

The building was still used regularly. The lights worked. The concrete was swept. Each floor was allotted to a company. Everything was stored behind chipboard doors.

'You said this wouldn't take long.'

The key Svendsen found had the number 555 scrawled on the label in pencil. Lund looked at the nearest door. Five hundred and thirty.

'You do realize you locked the door behind you? I can't get in.'

He sounded anxious. Almost frantic.

'I'll be back down in a minute. What are you doing?'

'Right now? Taking a leak. You did ask.'

Meyer finished peeing into the water by the dock. Called home again. Got ticked off again.

'I told you. She's not right in the head. I can't leave her on her own.' He listened to the list of complaints. 'I can't leave her! You know why.'

Women, he thought after the desultory, angry goodbyes.

He looked at the building. It wasn't the wreck he was expecting. Graffiti all over the front. From the smell some people weren't as particular about peeing in the water instead of peeing against the walls. But there were low security lights on every floor, good strong doors. No exterior CCTV. Apart from that . . .

He pulled the torch out of his anorak pocket, shone it the length of the grey cement facing.

On the right something glittered. He walked over, found his feet scrunching through broken glass.

Looked down.

Fresh.

Shone the light on the window above.

Broken.

A commercial waste bin was pushed up close to the wall. With that someone could climb inside.

He pushed back, shone the torch on the floors above.

Said, 'Shit.'

She walked along until she reached door 555. Same chipboard slab. Same basic lock mechanism. Sliding bolt with a padlock.

It was half open.

Lund didn't have any gloves with her. So she pulled her sleeve down until the wool covered her fingers then slowly prised the door back.

The space beyond was half empty. What lay there was stored at the rear.

Cardboard boxes, like the ones in Birk Larsen's garage. But these had white tape with blue lettering. The name Merkur with the flying wing to the left. The same tape that bound Mette Hauge.

It looked mostly junk.

The phone rang.

She looked at the ID.

'I said a minute, Meyer. One of my minutes. OK?'

'There's a broken window at the front. Someone's been here.'

'Makes sense. The door was forced when I got to the Hauge unit.'

'What floor are you on?'

'The sixth. The top one.'

Silence. Then Meyer said, 'OK. I can see your torch now. You're at the window.'

Lund tucked her hands in her pockets, tried to think.

'What window? I'm not using a torch.'

The silence again.

'Stay where you are, Lund. You're not alone. I'm coming in.'

She walked to the corner of the cold, dry room. Stood in the darkness. Turned her phone to vibrate, not ring.

Someone was out there. She could hear their footsteps. Up and down. Searching.

Something silver glittered in a nearby box. Lund looked. A heavy metal candlestick. She picked it up and walked back into the corridor, looking right, looking left in the waxy low security lights, walked on, seeing nothing but concrete and chipboard and dust.

Jan Meyer ran back to Lund's car, cursing Brix for taking his weapon. Hunted through the Nicotinell packets and the tissues in the glovebox until he found the Glock.

Full magazine. Chewing gum on the grip.

He put it on the roof of the car, plugged in his headset, called her again.

'Lund, are you there?'

'Yes,' she said in a whisper.

'Good. I'm on my way.'

He climbed through the broken window, lowered himself gently onto the floor inside. Yellow chipboard doors. Concrete floor. Nothing.

Hit the call button.

'Lund? Can you hear me? Hello?'

No answer.

'Lund!'

A noise. A reluctant mechanical growl. Cables moving, wheels turning.

A voice in his ear.

'Shit!'

'Lund!'

'Meyer. He's got the lift and he's coming down. I'm on the stairs. The lift!'

It sounded like a rusty metal animal stirring from a long sleep. Meyer walked the concrete corridor. Found the place. Buttons on the wall. Folding metal door. Cables falling and rising beyond.

Got out the Glock. Fell against the wall.

'I'm by the lift,' he said.

He could hear footsteps on the stairs, rapid and anxious. Drowned out by the approaching squeals of the tin cage falling from above.

A light. A clank. The lift stopped beside him.

Gun out. Waiting for the folding doors to slide. To move.

Nothing.

Waited.

Nothing.

Barrel pointing, turned the corner, aimed it straight ahead.

Nothing but an empty cage, a single bare bulb bright in the ceiling.

Meyer looked around him, saw blank space.

Confused.

'The lift's empty,' he said.

Footsteps racing down the stairs. Getting closer.

'I'm coming up for you.'

'I don't think he's here.'

Her voice sounded shrill and scared in his head.

'He's gone down. He's with you—'

'I'm coming . . .'

Walked for the stairs. Saw the chipboard door come flying out to meet him.

Wood slammed into his face, hard metal bolt and padlock smashed against his waist.

A shout. A cry. His?

Meyer was on the floor, stunned and hurting.

Angry, swearing too.

Fingers reaching for the gun.

The gun.

The lost gun.

He rolled, he groaned. Looked up. Saw the black Glock.

Eyes widening.

A roar as big as the world. A flash of flame.

Jan Meyer bucked back against the impact, felt a bright sharp spear of pain grip his body.

Frozen on the cold floor, limbs wouldn't move. Saw the gun over him again.

Said . . .

Nothing.

What words were there?

He thought of his daughter, crying at home. Thought of his wife and their last few angry words.

The second roar was bigger and behind it was nothing but blood and pain.

One word in it. His, spoken in a voice that died the moment it was uttered.

'Sarah . . .' Meyer said, and then was gone.

Lund flew down the stairs, stumbling, shrieking, thinking but not thinking, flailing at the dead space ahead with her arms.

The floors lost their numbers. When she got to the last she kept running, round and round, as if there were more. As if the cold, dry staircase led somewhere for ever.

But it didn't. She was there. And just a few steps away was Meyer. A still shape on the ground. Noises. Someone running.

Lund knelt by him.

Breathing, gasping. Blood from his throat. Blood on his chest.

'Jan. Jan. Look at me.'

Hand to his face. Warm red gore.

Chest, she thought.

Ripped at the vest. Saw flesh. Saw the gaping wound.

Got the phone with her bloody fingers.

Called.

Outside an engine gunning.

Waited.

Waited.

Waited.

An ambulance. Lights, sirens, noise.

Inside now. Medics in green uniform working, screaming, hands flying, pushing her out of the way.

A mask over his face.

Cries.

'More fluid.'

Machines beep. Tyres squeal. The world turns.

'Oxygen saturation low. Pulse high.'

A line in his arm. Big eyes wide and scared.

Lund sat on the bench, watching, beyond tears.

'He's going,' someone said. 'Paddles!'

'Keep ventilating. More fluid.'

Meyer rocking and twitching, wires through the blood.

'OK. Charging.'

A machine on the wall.

'Clear!'

Meyer leapt.

'Again.'

Meyer leapt.

Hands on chest. Massaging.

Words in her head.

'Will he? Will he?'

No one hears.

One hour later. She sat on a bench in the corridor, close to the theatre. Still sticky from his blood. Still lost in what happened.

Forks in the road. Choices made.

If she'd let him go home to his sick kid with earache.

If they'd gone in together, as every rulebook said.

If . . .

Brix marched towards her. Evening suit. White bow tie, fancy dress shirt.

'I came as soon as I could,' he said.

Down the corridor men in green smocks talked in low voices behind masks.

'Any news?' Brix asked.

A nurse ran into the theatre carrying a plastic sac of fluid.

'They're operating.'

She watched the people come and go through the swinging doors. Wondered what they were thinking.

'What were you doing in the warehouse?'

'What?'

He repeated the question.

'We thought there might be some evidence in Mette Hauge's belongings. Someone had the same idea.'

Brix said, 'Leave this to me. And this time you really will do what I say.'

Meyer's wife Hanne was coming towards them. Face immobile, bloodless. Blonde hair tied back. Walking in a daze.

'Where is he?' she asked.

'In the theatre,' Lund said. 'I'll come with you to the office.'

'No.'

Brix glared at her.

A tall man, dignified in his evening dress.

This was what they did. Times like these belonged to them.

He put an arm round Hanne Meyer's shoulder, walked her down the corridor to the place next to the theatre.

Lund stood there alone and watched them.

Stood there and didn't, couldn't move.

Eleven

Wednesday, 19th November

Seven thirty. A misty morning. Traffic gridlocked on the wet city streets. Hartmann and Bremer locked in an ill-tempered live debate in a radio studio not far from the Christianborg Palace.

Environmental policy and industrial regeneration. Hartmann pushing his green credentials.

'We need to make the city attractive to eco-friendly companies—'

'You can't pander to industry for the sake of the environment,' Bremer broke in.

He looked tired and crotchety. Hartmann was following Rie Skovgaard's advice. Playing up the charm. The new young face of Copenhagen politics. Mild, listening, reasonable, caring.

'No one's talking about pandering—'

'But what about some common ground?' the interviewer cut in. 'One way or another the two of you will have to work with each other after the election. Can you do that now?'

'I can work with anyone,' Bremer declared. 'The issue is Hartmann's credibility.'

'The needle's stuck, Poul. We're here to talk about the environment.'

'No, no, no. Everything hangs around the murder case. The unanswered questions . . .'

Hartmann smiled at the woman chairing the interview.

'We've been through this a million times. I've been cleared. My office has been cleared. The police themselves have said this—'

'Credibility. It goes to the heart of the matter,' Bremer insisted.

'How can we work with a man about whom we all have so many doubts?'

Hartmann shrugged, eyes on the interviewer.

'I'm saddened you're using this tragic case for your own political capital gain. Now we have a good police officer critically ill in hospital. This is surely not the time—'

'You brought that poor man into it. Not me. From what I hear he wasn't your biggest fan . . .'

The clock on the wall. Second hand moving. Hartmann timed his interjection.

'We will work with anyone who shows good faith and commitment to a common cause. That rules out the Lord Mayor and his party. I take no pleasure saying this but I'm sure listeners who've heard this strange outburst will understand.'

'No . . .!'

'Thank you,' the interviewer said. 'That's all we have time for. And now . . .'

The news came on. Poul Bremer was up, an artificial smile, handshakes all round. Then he left.

Rie Skovgaard looked happy.

Hartmann listened to the news. Meyer was still unconscious in intensive care after surgery.

Someone was rapping on the glass window of the studio. Erik Salin.

He blocked the route to the exit. Poul Bremer must have passed him. There was no other way out.

Hartmann went out, kept walking.

'Got a minute, Troels?' Salin said, catching up.

'You had more than that yesterday.'

He headed for the exit, another meeting, another interview.

'I've been asking about the envelope your security tape was in. It's the same type that your office uses.'

Hartmann stopped, raised an eyebrow.

'I took one when I was there yesterday.'

'Really, Erik? Will an envelope get you the Pulitzer Prize?'

Salin beamed.

'You're good at this. I've got to hand it to you.'

Hartmann walked off to the toilet.

'Hey,' Salin said. 'Don't mind if I come, do you? Anything for a story, huh?'

'Stop wasting your time.'

He followed Hartmann, watched him at the wall.

'I talked to the people in your campaign office. They've been so busy they had to rent rooms for meetings.'

Hartmann took a leak, stared at the white tiles.

'This is so interesting.'

'Well, I think it is actually. Why waste money renting rooms when you have an empty flat? In these straitened times?'

Hartmann went to the sinks, washed his hands, looked at his face in the mirror.

'Your obsession with small details is deeply impressive.'

'The devil's in the details, they say. And what a devil. Takes your tape. Keeps it for a while even though it . . .'

He paused, waited for Hartmann to turn and briefly look at him.

'Even though it *appears* to put you in the clear. Then they stuff it into one of your envelopes and give it to the police. And for more than a week someone makes sure no one – not a soul – goes in the flat where Nanna was just before she died. Would have been even longer probably if the police hadn't got there first.'

Salin grinned at Hartmann's reflection in the mirror.

'You're a smart man, Troels. You can see something here stinks. It's on your shoes. Not Poul Bremer's.'

Hartmann walked back up the stairs. Rie Skovgaard was waiting.

'So even if you didn't do it,' Salin said, keeping up with him. 'Someone close to you thought you did. Believed it so much they wanted to cover for you. If your own people don't trust you, if they think you're capable of murder, why the hell should . . . ?'

Hartmann broke, had him by the collar of his blue winter coat, hard up against the glass wall of the radio station, Skovgaard bleating at his back.

'Print one word of that you little worm and I'll make your life a misery.'

He was bigger than Salin. Hadn't punched out anyone since he was a student. But it felt right now.

'Troels!' Skovgaard yapped behind him, tugging at his arm.

'Come on,' Salin said, staring at the balled fist, grinning into

Hartmann's face. 'Do it. You've got your political adviser balling the opposition to get you secret papers. You've got someone close to you who thinks you raped and murdered a teenager. How's Mr Clean feeling today? Starting to realize it's a long way to fall?'

She got Hartmann's arm before he could strike. Held on to it with all her frail weight.

Hands up, beaming as if he'd won the game, Erik Salin said, 'They're just questions, Troels. That's all. You're a politician. You're supposed to deal with them.'

Hartmann threw some more abuse at him and stormed off towards the door.

Skovgaard stayed. Confronted the reporter, mad as hell.

'Who the hell put you up to this? As if I can't guess.'

'The public's got a right to know.'

'They've got the right to know the truth. Don't let one word of this drivel get into the paper, Erik. Or you'll be back to taking pictures through bedroom curtains.'

Salin tut-tutted.

'Ooh. That hurt.'

'I know where you came from, you bloodsucking creep.'

'Same here.' The smirk. 'Your media relations suck, Rie. Surprising really. Phillip Bressau's a slick guy. I thought he might have . . . you know, drilled things into you a bit better.'

Lost for words, glad Hartmann was gone, Skovgaard stood her ground in front of Erik Salin, shaking with fury.

'Or did I get that wrong too?' he asked.

Lund slept in the hospital. At eight the following morning she got some food then took a tray back to the ward. Hanne Meyer sat where she had the night before. She looked ten years older.

'I got something to eat,' Lund said. 'Can I sit down?'

'They played with magic markers last night.'

Lund looked at Hanne's hands. They were covered with childish drawing in blue and red ink.

Red hands. Bloody fingers. The images wouldn't go away.

'They drew some pictures to cheer up their sister. She's got an ear infection.'

Her voice was high and cracked. One step from a sob.

'Jan told me. How old is Marie?'

'Neel's the youngest. Marie's the middle one.'

'So . . .'

Lund tried to remember the names. She'd heard them often enough.

'Ellie's the oldest?'

'Ella. She's ten.'

Lund wondered about Mark. What he was doing. What he thought of her.

'Tell me what happened?'

'He waited in the car while I went in. And then . . .'

She wasn't so sure herself. The night, the blood . . . the guilt. Her head wasn't right.

'He realized there was someone inside.'

Hanne Meyer started to dab at her eyes with a screwed-up tissue. Lund thought about putting an arm round her shoulders. But didn't.

A surgeon came through the door. Green cotton, mob cap, mask down.

Meyer's wife was up in an instant.

The doctor was giving orders to a nurse.

He had an X-ray. Put it on a light screen by the door.

They came and looked.

'The operation went well but he lost a lot of blood. Look here . . .'

Bones and tissue, tears and dark lines.

'The first bullet went right through him. The second was going for his heart. But he's got this cigarette lighter . . . ?'

Metal. Shiny. Lund hated that Zippo.

'The bullet hit that. Changed direction. Penetrated his left lung. There's other damage . . .'

The wife pointed at the film. Bones and flesh and tears.

'Is he going to live?'

He looked at the X-ray. Lund closed her eyes.

'He should live. He's not regained consciousness yet. We'll have to look at what else has gone on there. It's not over . . .'

Hanne Meyer was hugging him, tears streaming down her cheeks. Lund watched, felt awkward. Like an intruder.

The surgeon pulled something out of his pocket. The silver lighter. Dented. Mangled.

'This is for you. Tell him if he starts smoking after all the trouble we've been to he'll have me to deal with next time.'

Crying, laughing at the same time, she took it.

'You can see him now.'

Hanne Meyer half-ran into the room.

Lund followed the surgeon down the corridor.

'Did he say anything?'

'I told you. He's been unconscious ever since he came in.'

'When can I talk to him?'

'When he wakes up.'

She folded her arms.

There was a look in his face she recognized, but rarely saw in hospitals.

Evasion.

'What's wrong?' Lund asked.

'He's suffered some serious injuries. We still don't know how bad. I want to hope. We all do.'

'When?'

'Come back tonight. Then we'll see.'

The car felt odd without him. The office too.

Brix was briefing a meeting next door. She sat alone for a minute then walked in and listened.

'We're lucky Meyer's still alive,' Brix said. 'I want Leon Frevert. Assume he's armed and dangerous. We don't let this one go. We've got our own reasons now. Any questions?'

None.

'Good. Let's get to it.'

He watched them leave.

'Whoever was in that building knew about Mette's things,' Lund said when they were alone. 'He read about us dragging the canals.'

Dark, open-necked shirt. She couldn't quite picture him in evening dress any more. Brix was sending out a message. In charge, wanting results.

'I've put a new team leader on the case.'

'Why?'

'Go home. Stay there. We'll need to interview you.'

'Brix. I know more—'

'You can't possibly lead this investigation now.'

'Why not?'

He shook his head.

'Are you serious? You went in that building on your own. Meyer was shot with your weapon.'

'I didn't have the gun with me, for God's sake. Meyer must have taken it out of the car.'

He winced.

'Do I have to hear this? You can tell that to the investigations board.'

'We have to find Leon Frevert!'

Silence. That hard, merciless stare again.

'We'll leave that to the Germans now. Frevert's car was found near the ferry port. We think he sailed to Hamburg last night.'

'Why?' she asked straight off.

Brix walked out of the room. Lund followed.

'He didn't go to Germany. He doesn't have his passport. We found it in his flat. He doesn't have any money. Frevert had changed just about everything he had into Vietnamese currency. If he was going to flee anywhere—'

'Well that's what he's done.'

'Whoever shot Meyer isn't stupid!'

'He got the money before he saw the newspaper. Isn't it obvious?'

He made for his office. She stood in the door, blocking the way.

'No. It's not.'

Brix folded his arms.

'Give me two hours,' she begged. 'I just want to make some calls. If I've got nothing I'll do whatever you tell me.'

'That would be a first.'

Svendsen was marching down the corridor. He had a sheet of paper in his hand.

'Leon Frevert was seen at Høje Taastrup Station two hours ago. We've got CCTV. It's him. A uniform guy went after him but he ran off.'

A suburb on the western edge of the city. Easy access to motorways. Frevert could get anywhere from there.

'Do we have any patrol cars in the area?' Lund asked.

'I'll check.'

'Lund—' Brix began.

'He's on foot,' she said to Svendsen. 'He'll need a vehicle. Contact the banks. He doesn't have any money. Watch the brother.'

'Lund!' Brix shouted.

She looked at him. Svendsen looked at him.

'Keep me posted,' he said.

Vagn Skærbæk arrived at the garage just after eight. His red overalls were in a bag. The black fisherman's hat he kept.

Got out of the removals van, gave Theis Birk Larsen the key to it.

'The keys to the garage, the gate and the flat are in the bag.'

He looked miserable and weary.

Birk Larsen nodded. Old jeans. Black sweatshirt. Silver chain. Black windcheater.

'Right,' he said.

Skærbæk went back to the van, took out another bag. Bright yellow. The name of the toy store on the side.

'This is for the boys,' he said, handing it over. 'Do whatever you want with it.'

'Vagn,' Birk Larsen said as he walked off towards the gate. 'Vagn!'

Skærbæk stopped, hands in pockets. Stopped and looked.

'Let's go upstairs and sort this out, can we?'

'What's there to sort?'

'Lots.' He took Skærbæk's arm. 'Come on.'

In the kitchen, light streaming through the plants at the window. They'd picked up since Pernille watered them. The place looked almost normal.

She sat next to Birk Larsen, served coffee and bread and cheese.

Skærbæk smoked, didn't eat.

'Leon told us some things about you,' Pernille said. 'They sounded strange.'

He sucked on the cigarette.

'We should have talked to you first, I know. But . . .'

Her eyes were glistening again.

'We've all been crazy.'

'You can say that again.'

She looked at him.

'But they still sound strange. To me . . .'

No answer.

Birk Larsen said, 'Leon told us you cancelled a big customer that Saturday.'

Skærbæk laughed.

'Oh yeah. That guy. He wanted to pay cash. I only do that when you ask for it, Theis. Not on my own . . .'

They watched him.

'So I said we could either put it through the books or he does it himself. Maybe I was wrong . . .'

'The police said you lied about your mother,' Pernille told him.

'Yeah. They said that to me too. My uncle always told me she drank herself to death. Then last year he told me the truth. God knows why he made that one up. But what . . .'

The cigarette got stubbed out in the saucer.

'What's this got to do with anybody?'

Amidst the smoke, the anxiety, the embarrassment, she said, 'Nothing.'

'Those bastards have had us jumping through hoops from the beginning.' Birk Larsen shook his grizzled head. 'You just bore the brunt of it this time round.'

He looked across the table.

'We're really sorry, Vagn.'

'We are,' Pernille added softly.

Skærbæk sat unsmiling, playing with the packet of cigarettes.

'What did you tell the boys?'

'Nothing,' Birk Larsen said.

'Jesus.' He took off the black woollen hat, began kneading it in his fingers. 'What a fuck-up this is. I'm the one who should apologize. I brought that bastard Leon in here. The agency . . .'

Birk Larsen coughed, looked at his hands.

'Did they tell you where he is?' Skærbæk asked.

'No. I don't want to think about it. We're going to finish the house. Get out of this flat. Right?'

Pernille said, 'We're going over there today with the boys. Anton doesn't like the idea of moving. So we want to make it as easy as possible.'

The phone rang. She went to answer it. The bag with Skærbæk's red overalls sat in the middle of the table.

He put a hand on it.

'Aren't we supposed to be on a job in fifteen minutes?' Vagn Skærbæk asked.

'Yeah,' Birk Larsen said with the slightest of smiles.

Pernille came back.

'It's the lawyer. The police want to come round and check the flat. They want to see if Leon's been in here.'

'Oh for God's sake.' Birk Larsen's huge fist thumped the table, the photos, the faces there. 'I'm sick of having these people on our backs. Don't let them in. Vagn!'

Skærbæk gulped at his coffee, picked up the bag. Followed him down the stairs.

Frevert was on the move, tracking back into the city. They had a report of him trying to use a cash machine in Toftegaards Plads in Valby.

'We were there two minutes later,' Svendsen told the team in the briefing room. 'Gone . . .'

'Keep an eye on the parks,' Lund ordered. 'Look out for hostels. Look out for—'

The phone on the desk rang. She picked it up. Switchboard with someone asking for her by name.

'Is that Lund?'

'Speaking.'

'This is Leon Frevert.'

Lund stopped, looked round at the officers in the room, silently gestured with her hand, mouthed the word, 'Trace.'

'Where are you?'

'Never mind that. I just heard all this bullshit on the radio.'

Svendsen ran to the closest laptop, started hammering at the keys, grabbing for a headset.

'I didn't kill that girl. Are you serious?'

'We need to talk to you, Leon.'

'You're talking to me now. I didn't kill her. Understand?'

'OK. Let's meet somewhere.'

'I didn't shoot anyone either.'

'I'm listening.'

'First time for everything they say.' He was mad. 'I told you I let her out of the cab that night. I told you about the station.'

'You didn't tell us you knew her, Leon.'

Svendsen was getting somewhere. Signalling with his hands.

'You haven't a clue, have you?'

'No. So tell me. Where are you? I'll come and get you. Just me. We can talk. All we want's the truth.'

Silence. Then a click.

'Leon? Hello?'

Svendsen hit the keys again, tore off the headset.

'He's on Roskildevej. Couple of kilometres out of the city. Don't ask for any more. He just turned off the phone.'

Lund sat down.

'Why did he talk for so long?' she asked.

'He doesn't know we were tracking him,' Svendsen said.

'Then why did he turn off his phone?'

Svendsen scowled at her.

'What is it now?'

'Roskildevej . . .' Svendsen began.

'Roskildevej's three kilometres long, we don't have a clue where he is or what kind of car he's driving. Get me the brother.'

'OK! OK!'

Svendsen stormed out of the room, shaking his head.

Lund stayed at the desk. Looked at the photos on the walls. Nanna and Mette Hauge.

Leon Frevert. A thin grey solitary man.

The scarlet van was full of the boys' things. Model aeroplanes, plastic dinosaurs. Mobiles and posters for the walls. The job before ran late. The road was blocked by a broken-down car into Humleby. Vagn Skærbæk was yelling at the driver in front to clear the road when Birk Larsen's phone went.

Looked at the number. Pernille.

'Where's that dinosaur shop?' he said straight away. 'We haven't got enough stuff for Anton's room. We wanted to put a few surprises in there.'

'You can't take the boys to the house, Theis.'

'Why not?'

'The police are searching it.'

'What?'

'They're looking everywhere Leon's been working.'

'I've had enough of this shit,' Birk Larsen said. 'That's our house.'

'Theis—'

He cut the call.

'Problems?' Skærbæk asked.

The car ahead was moving.

'Nothing I can't deal with.'

It took another ten minutes to get there. Three plain-clothes detectives he'd never seen before were in the downstairs living room, going through the bags of belongings, emptying black plastic sacks of building material onto the floor.

Birk Larsen marched in, stood, hands in pockets, face like thunder.

The cops looked at him.

'You can't be in here.' A flash of the ID. 'We're working.'

'This is my house.'

'Your wife gave us the key.'

Birk Larsen jerked a thumb at the door, looked at all three of them, said, 'Out.'

'We have to search the place,' one cop said.

'Get out!' Skærbæk yelled.

The cop pulled a piece of paper out of his pocket. He was young and slight. They all were.

'We've got a warrant.'

'I don't give a fuck about your warrant.'

Two steps forward. The three of them retreated.

'You have to leave,' a cop said gingerly.

'You found Leon yet?' Skærbæk shouted. 'You found anything? It's a house, you bastards! You have no respect. No decency . . .'

Another cop rushed up from the basement.

'There's no one here.'

'Fine,' the young cop said. 'We'll come back later.'

Birk Larsen bunched his fist at the man's face.

'Don't come near us again until you've talked to the lawyer. Understood?'

They watched the cops go. Then Skærbæk ran downstairs, into the basement. Looked around. Came back up.

'They didn't make too much mess, Theis.'

Birk Larsen had barely moved. Frozen with fury, with a sense of his own helplessness.

'We can get the boys' room ready for them,' Skærbæk added. 'I took out a lot of the crap from the place myself anyway. All that shit in the basement.'

'What shit?'

'The blinds. The broken bathroom stuff.' Skærbæk stuck his hands in his pockets, looked at him. 'That stinking old mattress. You don't need the kids to see all that crap.'

Another TV studio. Another round with Poul Bremer.

Hartmann was getting ready in his office, Morten Weber helping him pick the right clothes.

Not young this time. Sober grey suit, immaculate white shirt. Dark tie.

Hartmann looked at himself in the full-length mirror in the office wardrobe. Looked at Weber's world-weary face.

'Can we still win on Tuesday, Morten?'

'Miracles happen. Rumour has it anyway.'

'How?'

Weber scowled at the tie, told him to wear something brighter.

'What does Rie think?'

'I'm asking you.'

'If Bremer stumbles the votes come to you. Sometimes elections aren't so much won. They're lost. This is a two-horse race now. The minority parties are squabbling among themselves as usual. No one's going to turn to them. It's going to go to the wire, that's for sure. So . . .'

Nothing more.

'So what?'

'So keep your head, play everything straight, and let's pray the iceberg hits him this time, not us.' Weber waited. 'I thought you might at least look a little impressed by my uncharacteristically upbeat assessment of our chances.'

Hartmann laughed.

'I am. Truly, Morten. That bastard Salin's still on my back about the damned surveillance tape.'

Weber smiled. Awkwardly.

'Someone took it from security,' Hartmann said. 'Someone sent it. Someone kept people out of Store Kongensgade. Or at least tried to. Ask Lund.'

Weber watched him put on the new tie. Nodded.

'Why don't we just let some things ride?'

'Because we daren't. What's wrong?'

'Nothing's wrong. I looked at the logs. The only package that went out of here that day was sent by Rie. It doesn't say where. I'm sure it was just routine.'

The shirt was brand new. The label was still on a button. Weber got a pair of nail scissors, cut the cotton thread and took it away.

Looked at Hartmann's hands. Gave him the scissors.

'You could use those, Troels. People look at everything these days.'

'Rie sent a package? And she handled the bookings for the flat.'

'Oh forget it, will you? There were no bookings.'

'We used other places instead. That was Rie too, wasn't it?'

'I don't know and I don't care. We've better things to think about.' Morten Weber brightened. 'Still . . . I do have good news.'

'What?'

'Bremer just fired Phillip Bressau.' Weber shrugged. 'I've no idea why. He's one of the best men on his team. I wouldn't want to lose someone like that six days before an election.'

Hartmann couldn't think straight.

'You look good, Troels,' Weber said. 'Smile at the camera, keep your temper. Go wipe the floor with that old bastard.'

Outside in the long corridor, by the brown-tiled steps. The phone rang.

'Troels! You asked me to call.'

It was Salin.

'I talked to the lawyers, Erik. We'll sue you personally if you print any of those lies. And the paper.'

Laughter down the line.

'I'm actually trying to help. Don't you get that?'

'It seems to have escaped me somehow.'

'You're no idiot. You know someone's been working to cover things up. Maybe they did it without your knowledge. I don't know. But they did it.'

'Enough. No more calls. No more questions. No more communication. Understood?'

He stopped at the head of the broad staircase, beneath the iron lamps, by the paintings of a naval battle covering most of the long, high wall.

Rie Skovgaard was at the foot of the steps in her coat, ready to leave. So was Phillip Bressau. The two of them stood on the blue carpet with the emblem of Copenhagen, three towers set above waves.

They were arguing. Furiously. As he watched Bressau's hand came out and grabbed her collar, then her red scarf. She stepped back, yelling abuse into his face.

Angrier than Hartmann had ever seen her.

'Hartmann?' Salin said in his ear. 'Are you still there?'

Skovgaard stormed off. Bressau stayed there, hurling insults as she headed for the security office exit. Then he picked up his brief-case. Looked around.

Looked up the long staircase, saw Hartmann.

Scowled, walked off in the opposite direction, towards the main doors.

'You heard,' Hartmann said and cut the call.

Martin Frevert was in Lund's office, wilting under her questions.

'We've got all the details. You rented a car on the Internet. It was picked up at a petrol station near Valby.'

'So what? It was for my company.'

'Where's your brother?'

'I told you already. I don't know.'

Papers on the desk. She pushed them over.

'You withdrew thirty-two thousand kroner from the bank. Was that for your company as well? I don't have time for this. I can walk you straight to a cell as an accessory to murder if you like. Save us all some time.'

Silence.

'OK,' she said. 'Enough. I'm taking you in.'

'I didn't give him the money!'

He took an envelope out of his jacket. Threw it in front of her.

'Good. Where are you meeting him?'

'Listen. Leon's a bit weird. But he didn't kill that girl. He couldn't hurt anyone.'

'You've no idea how often I hear that. Where are you meeting him?'

Silence.

'My partner was shot last night,' Lund said. 'If you want to help your brother you should make sure I find him before . . .' Her finger went to the window. '. . . anyone out there.'

'It's not you he's scared of.'

'Who is it then?'

'I don't know. Leon's mixed up in something. He's not the brightest guy. If he sees an opportunity—'

'What's he mixed up in?'

'I think there was some smuggling going on. When I talked to him I thought he was scared about that.'

'Not about us?'

'No.' He said that emphatically. 'Leon said he tried to help you. But you kept doing a shit job.'

'Where are you meeting him? And when?'

'He's my brother. I don't want him hurt.'

'Me neither. Where is he?'

Martin Frevert stared at the envelope on the table.

Lund looked at her watch.

The house in Humleby was in darkness. It looked too big, too cold, too dusty and bare for a seven-year-old with an active imagination.

Anton walked through the door, stepped carefully over the sheets.

Listening.

They were talking about all the things that weren't there. Toys and furniture. Beds and cookers, toilets and fridges.

Grown-up things.

It was a grey cold place and he hated it.

'This house sucks,' Anton said.

His father's face went red and angry, the way it often did.

'Is that so?'

'I don't want to live here.'

'Well, you're going to.'

The boy walked to the stairs, found a light switch, looked down.

A basement.

That was new.

A voice from behind.

'Leave him alone, Theis.'

He went down the steps. Looked around.

His mother cried, 'Emil! Come and look at your bedroom. It's nice.'

Footsteps on the wooden boards above.

Three floors and a cellar. One and a garage was enough in his real home.

Dim light from a street lamp fell through a couple of small blue-tinted windows. Enough to see the place was full of junk and dust. Rats too probably. Other things that lurked in the shadows.

A barbecue. He ran his finger along the lid. Looked at the mark it left in the dust. A football, white with black spots, tucked inside a box.

Anton took it out, booted it. Watched it bounce off the bare grey walls.

Aimed it at the tools, kicked it again from side to side.

A loud metallic clatter.

His eyes went up to the ceiling. He could see the look on his father's angry face already.

Don't touch. Don't mess. Don't fiddle. Don't interfere.

Don't do anything because it's bound to be wrong.

He went to get the ball, stepping softly so no one could hear.

The sound had come from a piece of rusty tin that had fallen off the wall. The blue light from the little window fell straight on it. Pipes and stopcocks and the bottom of a piece of equipment. A boiler maybe.

Something else. Small, made out of card. Maroon with a gold crest.

He picked it up, opened the pages.

Nanna smiling.

Shook a little when he saw the blood, dried, like a red puddle in the corner.

Thought of his father just above him. What he'd say. What, in his fury, he might do.

Stared at the photo.

Nanna smiling.

'Anton!'

The deep voice was loud. On the edge of angry.

'We're going for pizza. Are you hungry or not?'

Don't mess. Don't look. Don't do anything.

It was Nanna's passport. He knew what they looked like because once, not long ago, she'd shown him the thing that now sat grubby and bloodstained in his trembling fingers. Made him swear it was a secret, would tell no one, not even blabbermouth Emil.

'Anton!'

On the very edge of angry.

He placed the passport beneath the old pipes, carefully picked up the tin door and pushed it back where it was, all without making a sound.

Then he walked upstairs, looked at his father stamping his feet, getting mad.

'This house sucks,' Anton said again.

Martin Frevert arranged to meet his brother on a Russian coaster moored by one of the distant piers in the sprawling commercial port area to the north of the city.

Lund had Svendsen drive her there, issuing orders all the way. Don't approach until she's arrived. Have boats in the water close by.

The pier was in darkness and deserted. One vessel at the end of the jetty. Old, red, decrepit. The name *Alexa* on the bows.

Three unmarked cars there when she arrived. No lights. Nothing to draw attention.

The SWAT team leader, in black with a sub-machine gun tucked beneath his arm, met her.

'We've got the rental car,' he said. 'It's behind one of the containers. Nothing in it. We've seen a light on board. He must still be there.'

Lund looked round.

'Good,' she said. 'I don't want this to turn into a shooting match. I need to talk to this man.'

With all the gear the man looked ready for war.

'I mean that,' Lund said.

'I'm sure you do.'

'I'm going in alone to try and speak to him.'

'What?'

'You heard. If he tries to run take him into custody. He can't get far from here.'

She looked around. Dark and silent. The SWAT guy sounded sensible. They had this under control.

Lund stepped out, started walking towards the metal staircase to the coaster.

Lights behind. A car coming straight towards her.

Closer.

Closer still.

She spun on her heels. The car kept coming. Lund leapt in front, listened in fury to the squeal of brakes. Banged on the bonnet, yelling, 'Hey! Hey!'

The SWAT man was with her, some of his men too.

Lund walked round to the driver's door.

'Police,' she started to say.

A tall man in a long raincoat got out of the back, waving ID.

He thrust the card in her face.

'We're from the prosecutor's office.'

'I don't give a damn. This is a live operation. Turn off those headlights now.'

'Lund?'

'That's me.'

'We're launching an investigation—'

'I'm so impressed. We're taking in a murder suspect so get in your car and get going. I'll see you in my office tomorrow morning.'

Another one joined him. Shorter, heavier, bearded, full of his own importance.

She vaguely recognized this one. Bülow. Once a cop. Now with the prosecutor's people.

'No you won't, Lund,' he said, holding the door open. 'You'll come with us now.'

'You've got my report.'

'In the car—'

'Speak to Meyer,' she said without thinking.

Bülow came and stood in front of her. Cold eyes, rimless glasses.

'That would be difficult.'

'I talked to the surgeon. He should be coming round by now. Listen . . .' She pointed back to the coaster. 'We've got the prime suspect for the Nanna Birk Larsen murder cornered in there. Will you kindly fuck off out of here?'

'Assign command to someone else. You—'

'Call Brix!' she bellowed.

'Talk to him yourself.'

The first one handed over his phone.

'Brix?'

A long silence.

'What's going on?' Lund demanded.

'Meyer went back into surgery forty-five minutes ago. It wasn't as simple as they thought.'

'What do you mean?'

'He's in a coma. On life support. His family's here. There are . . .'

She looked at the coaster, the black night.

'Decisions to be made.'

Lund remembered now. They used Bülow to prosecute police officers.

She wondered what they'd do. Take her arms. Push her head into the back like anyone else.

'You've got to go with them.'

'Meyer—'

'Meyer's no use to you now. I'm sorry. It's . . .' She thought she heard his voice breaking. 'It's not good. None of this.'

Her fingers went loose. The phone tumbled from her hand, clattered on the damp cobblestones of the pier.

'Get in the car, Lund,' someone said.

Bülow marched round the room asking the questions. The other one made notes.

'Let's hear this again. You were in the warehouse on the phone. You heard a shot and then another.'

They were in her office. Meyer's office. The toy patrol car sat on the desk. The basketball net was still on the wall.

'You find Meyer wounded on the ground floor.'

Lund was crying very slowly, wiping her eyes with the rough sleeve of the black and white woollen jumper. Thinking of Meyer, the sad wife Hanne. Forks in the road.

'How is he?'

Cold eyes. Rimless glasses. They never left her.

'The surgeon doesn't expect him to regain consciousness. Which means all we have is you. Your side of the story, Lund. Nothing else.'

The tall man said, 'We just want some answers. Then you're free to go.'

The heavy one scowled at him, sat down, scowled at her.

'It was your idea to go out there? Did you tell Brix?'

'No. He was off duty. There was no reason.'

She looked at them.

'The doctor seemed confident.'

Or she thought he did. Maybe . . .

Bülow ignored the question, began again.

'You left your gun in the glove compartment? Why wasn't it locked?'

'Meyer was in the car.'

'How did he know it was there?'

'Because we worked together.'

'So he took your pistol. And someone you didn't see took it from him. Shot him.'

Lund couldn't lose the memory of him, bleeding, eyes wide open and terrified, leaping with the shocks in the ambulance.

'You didn't see him?'

She wiped her nose with the back of her hand.

'I heard footsteps. When I got to the ground floor there was a car driving off outside.'

'Did Meyer see him?'

'I don't know. How would I? Maybe.'

'But you're sure it was Frevert?'

She closed her eyes, squeezed the lids tight shut. Tried to stop the tears.

'I didn't see him, Bülow. Who else could it be?'

'Don't get smart. If you didn't see anyone you don't know whether Meyer took your gun. Or the man who shot him.'

Lund looked at him. None of this touched Bülow. He was distant from her, from Meyer. How it was supposed to be. How she was meant to feel about Nanna Birk Larsen but couldn't.

'Why don't you ask Leon Frevert? I'd like to leave now.'

Brix was outside the glass, on the phone, gesturing to the pair from the prosecutor's office.

Bülow went out and talked to him.

The tall one glanced at the door, took the opportunity.

'I know it's hard to talk about this. But we've got a job to do. You appreciate that.'

'I'm done here. You know where to get me.'

She stood up, got her bag, found herself crying again. Bülow was coming through the door.

'So you're sticking to your statement, Lund?'

'Oh for God's sake! Of course I'm sticking to it. I told you the truth.'

'Right. Get your coat. We're leaving.'

They drove back to the pier. Dismal sheets of black gusting rain. Twice as many police vehicles as before. Floodlights. Don't Cross tapes. Forensic officers.

Up the gangway. The coaster looked so old it barely seemed seaworthy. Over the wooden deck. The ship smelled of spilled fuel and recent paint.

'The coastguard have had this vessel under surveillance for eighteen months,' Bülow said as they walked inside. 'People smuggling. Drugs. The crew cut loose somewhere. We're looking for them.'

'What about their contacts here?'

'All in good time.'

He opened a heavy metal door, smiled at her. She couldn't work out why he'd suddenly turned friendly.

'It looks like you were right about Leon Frevert.'

There were officers in what looked like a map room, poring over charts.

'They were going to sail for St Petersburg tomorrow. The crew were on shore getting shit-faced for the occasion. These people . . .'

'So . . . ?'

They walked through another door, down stairs. Open this time. An old computer. A fire extinguisher from the ark. Radios. Signs in Russian.

The bright sparks of camera flashes.

They were two floors below the deck, next to a hatch that opened to black sky. From the opening something dangled.

Feet down. Body swaying gently with the movement of the ship.

Lund walked round, thinking, looking.

Grey suit, grey face. Leon Frevert wasn't much changed in death, even with a noose round his skinny neck.

The rope ran from the floor above. Bright blue. Nautical. Two officers were struggling to pull the body into the side for recovery.

'Maybe he thought the crew weren't coming,' Bülow said. 'Too many things here he didn't want to face.'

He had a piece of paper in a plastic evidence bag.

'This is the closest we'll get to a confession.'

She took it. One word in a childish scrawl, all capital letters. UNDSKYLD.

'Sorry,' Lund said.

She stared at Bülow.

'Sorry? Is that it?'

'What do you want? Chapter and verse?'

'More than this . . .'

'He had a receipt in his pocket.'

Another plastic bag.

'Leon Frevert filled up his car about thirty kilometres from the warehouse where Meyer was shot. Twelve minutes before you called for an ambulance.'

She peered at the piece of paper.

'No one drives that fast, Lund.'

'The receipt could be wrong.'

'We've got him on video there. With the car.'

Too many ideas, too many possibilities crowding her head.

'This can't be right.'

She looked at the body swinging above them. They'd got hold of it. Gripped Frevert by his jacket, started pulling him in.

'I'm asking you for the last time,' Bülow said. 'Do you want to revise your statement?'

Pernille was making bread, happy working in the kitchen while Birk Larsen stomped around the room, making plans.

'If everything goes OK we could move in next weekend. I need to work on the heating . . .'

She rolled the soft dough.

'Anton's really upset.'

'That's new,' Birk Larsen grumbled. 'He'll come round.'

'Getting a dog's a good idea.'

'I thought that was for Emil?'

'It's a dog, Theis. They'll both love him. Anton can have it as a birthday present.'

He winked.

'Well in that case, maybe you'd better lower your voice.'

'They're down in the garage, playing. They can't hear.'

He came and stood in front of her. Picked a chunk of raw dough from her fingers. Put it in his mouth.

She peered into his narrow eyes. Looked into his badly shaven face. Theis was still a boy in some ways. Rough and unfinished. In need of something. Her usually.

Pernille came and hugged him, kissed his bristly cheek, whispered, 'We'll never be the way we were. Will we? Not again?'

He touched her chestnut hair with his right hand, stealing some more of the dough with his left.

'We'll be who we were. I promise.'

She held him tightly, face against his broad chest, listening to the rhythm of his breathing, feeling the life in him, the strength.

Downstairs Vagn Skærbæk was playing with the latest toy. A black battery car, radio-controlled. It ran around the garage between packing cases and trucks.

Anton had the control. Skærbæk was the target.

Backwards and forwards it leapt across the concrete. He jumped and squealed trying to get out of the way.

Finally it bounced against his white trainers.

'Got me!' Skærbæk cried. 'Dead!'

Stood there, eyes wide open, tongue lolling from his mouth.

Anton didn't laugh.

'It's cool, huh?' Skærbæk said. 'You can race it round the yard at the new house.'

'Can I take it upstairs, Uncle Vagn?'

Skærbæk picked the thing off the floor and held it out for him.

'It's yours. You can do with it what you like.'

Anton snatched for it. The man above him in the red suit jerked it from his fingers.

'When you get to the new house.' He crouched down, looked the boy in the eyes. 'Everyone gets nervous about something new.'

'Do you?'

'Yeah. If you don't know what's going to happen. But it's fun to change. You should . . .'

'There's something in the basement.'

Silence.

'What do you mean?'

'Nanna's passport's there. With blood on it.' Anton looked scared. 'Don't tell Dad. I'll get into trouble.'

Skærbæk laughed, shook his head.

'What makes you say things like that?'

The boy snatched for the car again. Skærbæk kept it from him.

'Anton . . . it's because you're afraid of moving. You don't need to be afraid. You should always tell the truth. Not lies.'

The boy folded his arms.

'I'm not lying. I saw it in the basement.'

He reached and took the car. Skærbæk didn't try to stop him. Then Anton walked upstairs.

The boys were in bed. The three of them sat round the kitchen table, in front of the dirty plates and cutlery.

Birk Larsen was smoking. Face like a basilisk.

'What else did Anton say?' Pernille asked.

'Nothing,' Skærbæk told her. 'Just that he saw Nanna's passport there.'

'Bloody kids,' Birk Larsen grumbled. 'I've been there hundreds of times and I haven't seen it. Have you?'

'He's just jumpy, Theis. It's all got to him. God knows . . . it got to all of us, didn't it?'

'Where?' Pernille asked.

'He said it was in the basement. There was nothing there to begin with. Just some rubbish I cleared out the other day.'

'Why would her passport be in the basement?' Birk Larsen asked. 'Nanna didn't even know about Humleby.'

'I can go and take a look if you like.'

'There's nothing there, Vagn.'

Pernille's fingers worked at her temples. The smell of bread was gone from the kitchen. Now it was just cigarette smoke and sweat.

'Then why,' she asked, trying not to get mad, 'did he say there was?'

'It's Anton! He can say what he wants. I'm not having him making up shit like this. I'll talk to him in the morning.'

She wasn't going to stop.

'The police never found her passport. They asked us time and time again.'

He stared at her. The other Theis. The cold one saying: don't ask, don't come near.

'I'd really appreciate it if you didn't talk to Anton about it,' Skærbæk said. 'I promised . . .'

Pernille was on him in an instant.

'Of course we're going to talk to the boy. We'll go over there tomorrow and take a look. I want to know—'

'It's not there!' Birk Larsen roared.

She closed her eyes for a moment, fought the anger.

'It's not there,' he said more quietly. 'And tomorrow's his birthday.'

'Theis . . .'

His big hands cut the air above the table.

'That,' Birk Larsen said, 'is it.'

Out in the main TV studios in Amager, minutes to go before the last broadcast debate of the election, Poul Bremer was arguing minutiae with the production team.

'I'm the biggest party. I go last,' Bremer said.

The producer didn't look ready for a fight.

'The agreement was,' Rie Skovgaard said, 'we draw lots.'

'I didn't sign up for that. We do things the way we've always done them. The leading party has the final say. That's what's going to—'

His phone rang. Bremer walked away to take it.

'Maybe we should drop the idea about drawing lots,' the producer said. 'If it's going to cause trouble.'

'We had an agreement.'

Bremer was listening intently to the call, looking directly at Skovgaard.

'We're on air in ten minutes,' the producer said.

Poul Bremer walked over, all smiles, all pleasantness.

'Let's draw lots after all. I'm feeling lucky.'

Grey eyes on Skovgaard.

'When we're done here there'll be nothing left to play for anyway.'

*

Hartmann was still in the dressing room, on the line to Morten Weber in City Hall.

'Why was Bressau fired, Morten? I want the truth.'

'He messed up big time, I guess. Aren't you supposed to be on TV soon?'

'Why was he fired?'

Weber hesitated.

'This place is always swimming with rumours. If you believe every one of them—'

'Tell me the truth, dammit! I just got another call from that bastard Salin. Crowing that he's nailed me. He won't say what. Bremer's got it and planning to hand it over after the debate. I need to know. What is it?'

'He's just trying to get to you. Succeeding by the sound of it.'

'Where did Rie send that package? To Lund?'

'I don't know and frankly I'm not going looking. I've got better things to do.'

'Could Rie have kept people out of the flat?'

'Of course she could. Anyone in the office could.'

'Did you check what she did that Friday night?'

'I'm not here to spy on people.'

'I asked—'

'No, Troels. I'm not playing this game. That's final.'

The line went dead. When he turned Rie Skovgaard was in the door.

'Is everything OK?' she said. 'It's time now.'

He didn't answer.

'This is the last TV debate of the campaign.' She was back to being professional, looking him in the eye. 'Whatever impression the people get today they'll take with them into the voting booth.'

One more product to be sold. A puppet for her father to manipulate from Parliament.

'All the polls say this is between you and Bremer. The minorities convince no one. It's the two of you.'

He nodded.

'If they mention the murder case stick to what we agreed. You'll do whatever you can to help the investigation. You're the new broom. You stand for candour and clarity. Bremer's the one with skeletons in the cupboard. Don't go anywhere else . . . dammit, Troels, are you even listening?'

His eyes were on the studio outside. Bremer there. Confident. Beaming.

'Troels. This is important.'

She went quiet, looked nervous. A studio assistant came to the door and asked him to take his seat.

Hartmann stepped out towards the bright lights, turned and looked at her in the shadows.

'I know what you did.'

'What . . . ?'

'I know all about it. Bremer knows too.'

No answer.

'About Bressau. About the surveillance tape.'

She stood rigid, face emotionless, eyes fixed on him. Saying nothing.

'About how you tried to keep people out of the flat.'

'No, no. This isn't what you think.'

The studio man was back.

'We're on the air now, Hartmann. If you want to be part of this you'd better get in here.'

'Troels!'

He walked towards the bright lights and took his seat.

Ten minutes into the live debate, they were throwing around the case for higher taxes. Hartmann couldn't take his eyes off the old man two seats away. He looked as if he'd won already. Couldn't wait to walk into the council chamber, smiling, triumphant. Four more years on his shining throne.

Then it came.

'Taxes are important,' Bremer said with that calm, magisterial air he'd mastered over three decades of working Copenhagen's political circles. 'But just as important is the character of those we choose to represent us.'

He looked directly into the camera.

'The murder of Nanna Birk Larsen—'

'Wait,' the interviewer cut in. 'We're here to talk politics—'

'Politics is about ethics and morals, first and foremost,' Bremer said, glancing at Hartmann across from him before returning to the lens. 'The voters have a right to know . . .'

622

Hartmann sat back, listened.

Bremer's face now wore a look of resigned indignation.

'I've been accused of withholding information. I've even been reported to the police. All at the instigation of Troels Hartmann. The very man who deliberately withheld information himself, impeded the progress of a criminal investigation . . .'

Hartmann raised a finger, lacked the energy to interrupt. Found himself looking back at Rie Skovgaard by the studio door.

'How can it be that his party flat was left untouched until the homicide team found it?' Bremer demanded. 'How could a surveillance tape suddenly disappear and then just as suddenly turn up? How?'

Finally, Hartmann found his voice.

'The police have given me their word that Bremer's accusations are unfounded. These are the desperate efforts of a man who'll do anything to cling to power.'

'Power?' Bremer's voice had risen above its natural register. His face was flushed. He was loosening his tie. 'Then they've been misinformed. When they see the proof I have . . .'

The interviewer was getting flustered.

'Briefly—'

'This goes to the very heart of the matter!' Bremer shrieked.

Hartmann wondered at his temperament. His state of mind.

'If you're so convinced of your own fantasies, Poul, go to the police. I've nothing to fear from the truth. Unlike you—'

'You sanctimonious little shit,' Bremer spat at him.

Silence.

Then Hartmann said, 'Copenhagen deserves policies, not personal abuse. If the police want to talk to me they know where to find me.'

'When I'm done you'll be back in a cell again, Hartmann. Where you belong—'

'Excuse me! Excuse me! I've been cleared.'

A shouting match now. The interviewer had lost control.

'Before I came on air—' Bremer began.

'This is what twelve years in power does to you,' Hartmann barked at him.

Bremer's eyes were down on the studio floor. His face was red. His breathing agitated.

'I have information—'

'No, no,' Hartmann shouted over him. 'All you can do is come here and try to sling mud. Not talk politics. This is unworthy of the Lord Mayor of Copenhagen. You're unfit to hold the office.'

'Unfit?' Bremer's voice was close to falsetto. 'I have information—'

'The system's in a rut,' Hartmann interrupted. 'We live under a despotism ruled by one wretched old man who instead of engaging in debate treats political colleagues as pawns then vents his arrogance on the voters.'

Hand at his neck, jerking at his shirt, gasping for breath. Bremer said, 'I have proof that—'

Hartmann was on him.

'You've nothing. You're just trying to sidetrack the debate from your own failings. This is what you always do. Try to turn the spotlight on others to hide your own corruption and lack of vision.'

Bremer stared at him, lost for words. Lost for breath.

'Corruption, Poul,' Hartmann added, in a clear, confident voice. 'There I said it. The worm of corruption eats you as we watch—'

'I have proof—' Bremer bleated.

'You've nothing.'

He looked at the old man in the grey striped suit. Bremer was clutching his right arm. His mouth was open and working.

'I . . .'

Poul Bremer let out a low, frightened moan and rolled off the studio chair, onto the floor.

Eyes glassy behind the statesman's spectacles. Face immobile. Sweat on his brow.

Hartmann was by his side in a moment. Loosening his tie.

'Bremer?' he said. 'Bremer?'

Lund was back in Bülow's office. On the second floor of head-quarters, the opposite side to homicide. Down a long black marble corridor, through places she'd never before seen.

'Why didn't Meyer go with you?'

'He didn't think it was worth going there.'

'Did you give him an order?'

'No. I just wanted a quick look. He called and told me he'd seen a broken window. And that there was a light from a torch on the floor near me. It was Frevert's, not mine.'

Bülow sat down, looked at her.

'Frevert's?'

'OK. I'm sorry. I'm tired. It was . . . someone's torch.'

He looked pleased.

'So we do agree Frevert wasn't there, right?'

She'd been thinking about this.

'He had more to tell us. He just didn't want anyone to know. Frevert was scared of someone. Maybe he saw something he wasn't supposed to.'

'So even though he wrote that note he didn't murder Mette and Nanna?' Bülow asked.

'You don't know he wrote that note. You don't know he killed himself.'

'Your career seems based on wild guesses.'

'No,' Lund said. 'It isn't. Someone got inside the warehouse. He knew we'd be looking for something there. The storage unit for Mette's belongings was broken into. He must have taken what we were looking for.'

'You were supposed to go to Sweden, Lund. Did Meyer want the case for himself?'

'What do you mean? He wanted it to begin with. Then Buchard asked me to take it on—'

'You argued—'

'Of course we argued. A case like this. It was nothing.'

'Did Meyer complain to his superior about nothing? He told his wife you weren't yourself that evening. You were crazy. He said there was no reason for you to be at the warehouse.'

'Meyer wouldn't have come if there was no reason—'

'He's not the only one to notice the state you're in,' Bülow said. 'Obsessed. Detached from reality.'

'Who said that? Brix? Svendsen?'

'Never mind who said it. Is it correct?'

'No. And I've saved Brix's arse twice already.'

She leaned over the table, looked at Bülow and the assistant.

'I need to know what he removed from Mette Hauge's belongings. If we find that—'

'If someone was there,' Bülow cut in. 'Apart from you and Jan Meyer.'

'What?'

'Follow me,' he ordered.

Three rooms along. A forensic officer she half-recognized. A computer with speakers.

Bülow stood behind him. Lund sat when he told her to.

He held up an evidence bag with Meyer's phone in it.

'When you were inside the warehouse Meyer pressed a shortcut he used for taping interrogations with suspects. Listen.'

The technician hit the keyboard. Meyer's voice came out of the speakers.

'Lund? Can you hear me? Hello?'

'Lund!'

'Shit!'

'Lund!'

'Meyer. He's got the lift and he's coming down. I'm on the stairs. The lift!'

'I'm by the lift.'

A long pause. A mechanical sound.

'The lift's empty. I'm coming up for you.'

'I don't think he's here.'

'He's gone down. He's with you—'

'I'm coming . . .'

Her head jerked back in shock with the first explosion. Her mind went blank with the second. She could hear Meyer's shrieks and groans.

Bülow's face had changed. She thought he was trying to look sympathetic.

'You haven't slept for three days. It's dark. You hear a sound and you think it's the man you want, somewhere in the building. You draw your gun. The gun you brought with you into the building. You run down the stairs.'

'Oh please—' Lund whispered.

'You throw open the door and shoot. What else could you do? What else would anyone have done in the circumstances? Someone's there. He reaches for your gun. You fire. He grabs again. You fire again.'

Lund's clear, acute eyes turned on him.

'Then you realize you shot Meyer. You're distraught. You call an ambulance. In the sixteen minutes before it arrives you fake the break-in. Then you place your pistol at Meyer's side and wait.'

He paused.

'What do you think, Lund?'

'I think that's the most stupid thing I've ever heard.'

'There's no trace of anyone but you and Meyer in the building.'

'You're a failed cop looking for somewhere new to fail again.'

'We didn't find anything!'

Still her eyes didn't leave him.

'That's because you don't know how to look.'

The other one came in.

'We questioned Meyer's wife, Lund. He came to just before they took him back into surgery.'

He passed over a statement.

'The one thing he said to her was your name. Sarah. He said it over and over again.'

'He thought it was important,' Bülow added. 'I guess it could be a declaration of love. But that doesn't seem likely from what I gather about your relationship.'

He passed over a charge sheet.

'There'll be a preliminary hearing tomorrow. You know the procedure. You've the right to one phone call.'

Bülow gave her back her mobile then the two of them left the room.

Lund followed.

'This doesn't make sense.'

They kept walking. A uniformed man on the door stopped her, pushed her back inside.

Lund looked at the phone on the table. Called.

'It's me,' Lund said. 'I need your help.'

Bülow walked round the circling corridors, found Brix in his office in homicide.

'I want her flat searched,' he said. 'Take her clothes and shoes to forensics. I need her records. You've got twenty minutes.'

Brix laughed at him.

'You'll get it. In good time.'

'Twenty minutes, Brix. It's not just her I'm looking at.'

'According to the record Lund's never fired her gun. She never wore it on duty. Never took it with her. They all know that.'

'You took her badge from her a few days ago then gave it back. Why was that?'

'Because she was right and I was wrong. She saw things . . .' He shrugged. 'Things I didn't get. No one else did either. She's not the easiest of people but—'

'You knew she was unbalanced. Why else would you have done it?'

'I did it because she pissed me off. She's good at that and she doesn't care. But she cares about the case. More about that than anything else, I think. Her family. Herself. I don't know why—'

'Yeah, yeah,' the short man moaned. 'Bore me with all that another time. Twenty minutes . . .'

There were four cells for women. The other three were full of screaming drunks. Lund sat on the solitary chair and looked around. It seemed different on the inside. Smaller. A single mattress. Sheets and a pillow. A sink and a Bible.

She wore a blue prison tracksuit. There was a bowl beneath the bed.

Lund looked at the officer on duty.

Tried to remember his name.

He gave her some soap and a towel. Walked out. Closed the door. Looked through the hatch.

'Any chance of some food?'

'It's not food time,' he said and closed the shutter.

Hartmann and Skovgaard were back at the Rådhus, alone in his office. Outside the city was starting to sleep. Bremer was in hospital, in a stable condition. There'd been talk of the effect on the election. Nothing about Nanna Birk Larsen on the news. Just the king of Copenhagen looking mortal for the first time in his long life.

'You lied to me, Troels,' she said, sitting in front of his desk like a junior come to an interview. 'To me. You and Morten . . .'

'What?'

'How can you share a secret with him? But not me?'

'We've been there,' he said and thought to himself: this ended days ago. It died and no one noticed.

'I was mad at you!'

He waited.

'That night when everyone thought you were finished I ran into Phillip Bressau. We went to a hotel and sat in the bar. He said you were a lost cause. I should switch sides. There was a job going.'

And if I do fall, Hartmann thought, she'd be there. Alongside Bremer in an instant.

'I knew something was going on. His phone kept ringing.'

She looked him in the face.

'He asked me if I wanted a nightcap. In his room.'

Hartmann nodded.

'Very generous of him.'

'I could hear he was talking about Stokke. About our apartment. Bressau had had a couple of drinks. He wasn't . . .' She frowned. 'He wasn't so discreet. That's how I knew Stokke was involved.'

'What happened?'

'You mean did I go to bed with him?'

Hartmann didn't answer.

'Does it matter? At least I know Bressau. I didn't go on dating sites. I didn't screw strangers.'

Nothing.

'What's it to you anyway?' she said. 'I listened. I had a drink. Then I went home.'

He got up, walked around the room.

'That Friday night. You went looking for me?'

'Did I?'

'You went to the flat. You knew something happened there.'

'No. I didn't. The next morning I went to the conference centre without you. And lied for you there. What is this? What do you want? Some kind of pure virginal honesty when you feel like it? Then we turn as nasty and as crooked as everyone else if it's needed—'

'I never asked for that.'

She laughed.

'You don't have to, do you? You just need it to happen but never want to know. Bremer's the same. Maybe it goes with the job.'

'I expect certain—'

'I can't help what you expect. I didn't go near the flat. I didn't touch the stupid surveillance tape. I'd do a lot for you. But I wouldn't cover up for murder.'

She got up, turned on the smile. Came to him, touched his shoulder, his shirt.

'Come on. You know that. People have been screwing round with this office for weeks. Olav got into the system . . .'

He removed her hand from his jacket.

'Olav's dead. Would you have taken the job? With Bremer?'

'I've got a job, haven't I? I gave up a partnership in the ad agency to come here. Took half the pay—'

'I thought it was commitment.'

'It *is* commitment.'

'Would you have taken the job?'

She closed her eyes. Looked near to breaking. He liked that.

'I haven't given it any thought. We've got work to do here.'

'I can do that myself, thanks.'

'Troels—'

'I want you to go home. I want you to stay there.'

'This is ridiculous.'

He looked at her. She met his eyes. She always could.

'I'm not a piece of meat you can buy and sell. Tell your father, will you?'

'I never thought you were!'

'Just go,' he said.

Twelve

Thursday, 20th November

Lund's lawyer and Bengt Rosling began the meeting in Brix's office at nine fifteen. She was still in her cell, still in the prison suit.

'My client moves for her release,' the lawyer said. 'She's willing to cooperate within reason. You have no proof against her. She denies the charges. Since the question of guilt's undecided she shouldn't be here.'

'Tell that to the judge,' Bülow said.

'All the people you can interview have been interviewed,' the lawyer retorted. 'Lund is the last person to commit new crimes. She has a son—'

'The son lives with her ex-husband.'

'She's been under great mental stress lately. She was a hostage and has been in two shooting incidents. Her record in the police is impeccable.'

Bülow laughed.

'If you think you can get her out on the grounds that she's crazy, forget it. She shot her partner. She's going to court.'

He got up.

'Release her,' the lawyer added quickly, 'and she's willing to let you see her psychiatric file.'

Bengt Rosling, still in a sling from the accident, placed a folder on the desk.

'What file?' Brix asked. 'She wasn't getting any treatment from us.'

'It wasn't a police psychiatrist,' Rosling replied. 'There's reason to believe she's suffering from paranoia and anxiety attacks. She may be suicidal.'

Bülow grabbed the papers, read them, laughed.

'Did you write this shit?'

'She went on my advice,' Rosling said. 'The psychiatrist confirmed that she's predisposed to depression and shouldn't be left alone in a cell.'

'Thanks,' Bülow cut in, waving the papers. 'I'll use this in court. So why's Lund telling us she's crazy?'

'Because she wants help!' the lawyer said. 'Is this your attitude towards the health of your officers? I'll use that in court too. Let us take care of her. Then you've got some time to reconsider these ridiculous accusations which frankly I will tear to shreds if you're ever stupid enough to proceed with them. Before launching a civil suit for punitive damages.'

'You're bluffing,' Bülow grunted.

'Try me.'

Thirty minutes later Lund picked up her things. Put the white and black jumper back on, her jeans, her boots.

She signed the release paper, watched by Brix.

'You're suspended,' he said. 'Your statement's being investigated. You need to surrender your passport. Your flat's being searched.'

She went through the contents of her handbag. Found the Nicotinell, popped a piece in her mouth.

'I had some cigarettes in here.'

'No one's touched your cigarettes. Report here immediately if we ask you.'

She tied up her uncombed hair, put on the elastic band.

'I need to see the storage box.'

Brix stared at her.

'Goodbye, Lund,' he said and made for the door.

'Give me a list of the contents, Brix. Give me something. You're not dumb. You know I didn't shoot Meyer. You know Leon Frevert didn't kill Nanna.'

He stopped.

'I know your case doesn't look good.'

'A list of the contents. That's all.'

He hesitated. Then he said, 'Bengt Rosling's waiting for you outside the building.'

He was in a silver rented Renault on a meter close to the front arcade.

Lund got in, didn't look at him.

'Did you talk to the pathologist like I asked?'

'If Bülow gets to hear of this—'

'He won't.'

She went through the autopsy report on Leon Frevert. Chipped tooth, injured mouth.

'It looks as if the injuries were caused by a gun barrel,' he said.

'Some suicide.'

'Forget about Frevert. It won't take them long to find out that file I gave them's a forgery. I put it in the name of a colleague I know. Magnus. He's away at a conference in Oslo right now. But maybe they'll contact him. That Bülow guy is out to get you.'

'Bülow's a moron.'

There was a knock on the door. Jansen, the helpful ginger-haired forensic officer.

'You wanted this,' he said and gave Lund a sheet of paper. 'Good luck.'

He was gone before she had the chance to say thanks.

'What's that?' Rosling asked.

'A list of the contents of Mette Hauge's storage box from the warehouse.' She went through it. 'He must have known Mette somehow. There was something there that linked him to her. He took it.'

Rosling looked at his watch.

She got out her notepad.

'We've an address for where Mette went to. It was a house share for students near Christiania. If I can find out who lived there twenty years ago . . .'

He didn't take the papers when she tried to hand them over. Just looked out of the window. Not at her.

'I'm sorry,' he said. 'I can't . . .'

She waited. Such a nice, weak man. He couldn't even bring himself to say it.

'You wrote that fake report very quickly, Bengt.'

'It wasn't hard. Most of it's true. You need help, Sarah. I can suggest someone.'

'I don't need that kind.'

'That's just the kind. This impulsive behaviour. The way you relate to distant people but not those close to you. Go off on your own with no regard to the consequences—'

'Enough, Bengt! What was I? Your lover or your patient?'

No answer.

'It's OK,' she said, and pulled on her seat belt.

'I'll call you from Sweden,' he said.

'If you like.'

She started the car. He got out. Lund drove off alone into the pale day.

They took the boys round to Humleby. Almost all the men were working there, painting, plastering, labouring round the clock.

No one had found anything. Not a passport. Not a thing that was out of place.

Anton stood near the door, eyes on the floor, miserable.

Vagn Skærbæk came in, crouched down, said, 'Happy birthday, buddy!'

Not a word.

'I had to tell them, Anton.'

Skærbæk glanced at Pernille.

'It was the right thing to do. Wasn't it, Mum?'

She was looking at the room. Not listening.

Anton shook his head.

'I've got a present for you, kid. You won't get it till tonight. OK?'

Punched him lightly on the shoulder. Still didn't get a smile.

'Dammit,' Birk Larsen said. 'Let's stop this now.'

He took Anton's hand, led him down to the basement with Pernille following. Fresh paint and plaster. New floorboards almost done.

'Where is it?'

'In the cupboard,' the boy said.

Birk Larsen pulled open the metal door.

No boiler. No pipes.

No passport.

Pernille ruffled his fair hair.

'Maybe it was something else. It was dark down here.'

He looked at his father and said, 'Can I go upstairs now?'

Birk Larsen leaned down, black jacket, black hat. Put his big face up to the boy's.

'Anton. Listen to me. I know it's hard moving house.' Narrow eyes open, straight at the child's. 'But you mustn't make up stories like this. Do you understand?'

The young head went down, rested, chin on chest.

'Do you?' Birk Larsen asked, voice rising. 'It upsets your mother. It upsets me. You can say whatever you want. But don't lie about Nanna. Don't ever—'

'That's enough, Theis,' Pernille broke in.

Anton was close to tears. She put a hand round his shoulder, led him upstairs.

Vagn Skærbæk stayed on the steps. When the two of them were gone he said, 'Was that really necessary?'

'What do you know about kids?'

'I used to be one. Did you find him a dog?'

'As if I've time for that—'

'I've got a friend who can't get rid of some puppies, Theis. Maybe . . .'

Birk Larsen stared at him.

'I don't want to interfere,' Skærbæk said quickly. 'Just if it helps.'

'I thought the boiler was supposed to be in by now.'

'No problem,' Vagn Skærbæk said. 'I'll fix that too.'

They were waiting vulture-like on the step of the Rådhus. Reporters, camera crews, sound men thrusting mikes at everyone who went inside.

Hartmann and Weber entered together, side by side.

The position was agreed. Hartmann stuck to it. In spite of all their differences, Bremer was a respected figure in Copenhagen politics. His sudden illness was a shock.

'The election, Hartmann!' someone yelled as he approached the door.

He turned, waited for the hubbub to fall silent.

'This is a time to wish Poul Bremer well. Not to try to take political advantage.'

'Convenient though, Troels!' cried a familiar voice in their midst.

Erik Salin elbowed his way through, bald head gleaming, cigarette dangling from his mouth. Voice recorder shoved out like a weapon.

'I don't think a stroke's convenient for anyone, is it?' Hartmann said.

Salin found the lights on him for a change.

'Bremer had proof that your office hindered the Nanna Birk Larsen murder investigation.'

'What proof?' Hartmann asked, hands in pockets, puzzled. 'I've received no proof at all.'

'Bremer has it.'

'I can't talk about what I've never seen.'

Be calm, be reasonable, Morten Weber said.

'But let me make this perfectly clear. I would never accept such behaviour from anyone on my team.'

He turned from Salin, found the TV cameras.

'It's against everything I believe and stand for.' Hand raised, finger to the sky, making a point. 'If ever I have proof that one of our people has stooped to something like that I assure you I will tell the world. And . . .' The slightest of self-deprecating smiles. 'I will seriously consider my own future in politics.'

He left it there, strode to his office. Threw his jacket on a chair.

Went to stand by the window.

'That was good,' Morten Weber said. 'Very.'

The Meyers' place was in Nørrebro, semi-detached, a little run-down. Basketball net in the yard along with a bird table, a Christmas tree, kids' scooters, a pram.

Lund parked the car in the street, stood in the drive for two long minutes. Asking herself why she was there. If it was the right thing.

She'd tried to get through to someone in the hospital. They were under orders not to talk to her. So, in all probability, was Hanne Meyer.

Shapes at the window. A blonde woman cuddling a crying child. An older girl, blonde hair too, staring mournfully from behind the glass.

Lund went and stood under the lean-to by the garage. The door was open. She could see more toys inside. A big motorbike. At the back a DJ's deck.

After a minute Hanne Meyer walked out leaving the kids behind, came and stood in front of her with arms folded, eyes still pink. Face lined.

'How is he?'

A stupid question. A necessary one.

Meyer's wife shrugged. There were tears not far off.

'Same as when he came out of the theatre. They say if things don't change . . .' A long look up at the grey sky. 'If things don't change soon we've got to talk about the life support. And . . . I don't know.'

She didn't cry. Lund had been close to situations like this so many times over the years. After a while a sense of the inevitable, of practicality, fell upon everyone.

'I didn't do what they say. I swear to you. When we got there . . .'

A sudden look of anger, of release.

'Why couldn't you leave him alone? You said the case was closed.'

'It wasn't. Jan knew it too.'

No response.

'It's not closed now,' Lund said.

'What's that to me? Tomorrow I might have to go there and watch him die. Do I hold his hand? What words do I use for that? Do you know?'

Lund shook her head.

'They told me he said something that sounded like Sarah.'

Hanne Meyer closed her eyes.

'Jan said your name. Not mine.'

'No he didn't. He never called me Sarah. Not once. It was always Lund. You heard him. Did he call me Sarah to you?'

Arms folded, eyes half closed.

'He was thinking of something else. Trying to say something important. Can you remember exactly what he said?'

'Why did you come here?'

'Because I want to find the man who shot him. The man who killed Nanna Birk Larsen. Other women too. I need your help. I want—'

'He said your name. Sarah. That's all.' Her eyes opened a little. 'And some numbers. I don't know—'

'What numbers?'

'I couldn't really hear.'

'What did it sound like?'

'Eight four.'

'Eighty-four?'

The door opened behind her. Two girls walked out. Tearful. Lost.

'Did he say anything else? Hanne?'

She stopped.

'No. He didn't. I don't even know if he knew I was there. OK?'

She kissed the youngest, put a hand to the hair of the older girl. Ushered them into the house.

Lund stood in the lean-to, next to the Christmas tree and the yellow motorbike she'd never seen Meyer ride.

Her phone rang.

'I made a call to a friend in Sweden,' Bengt Rosling said. 'They've got access to the Danish databases. I've got a name from the time Mette Hauge lived in that student house. A man called Paludan. He still lives at the same address.'

'That's good.'

'It's the only thing that is. Magnus called me. They tracked him down in Oslo. They know I lied about your file. Bülow has put out a call for you. The rental car's in my name. They won't have that. At least I don't think so.'

'Thanks,' she said, and looked out of the windscreen, out into the street.

Wondered what it would feel like to be on the other side. Hunted not hunter.

Troels Hartmann and Morten Weber caught Lennart Brix in his office going through records.

'I don't have time to deal with you right now,' Brix said, not looking up from the papers.

'We've got the press hounding us again,' Hartmann said. 'I think this comes from you. I want to talk to Lund.'

Brix looked up.

'Join the queue.'

Hartmann slammed his briefcase on the desk, glared at the tall cop.

'I'm at the end of my patience with you people. I want some answers.'

'You've already had them. If I could have pinned something on you I would have done. Instead you're out there on TV begging for votes. Don't play hurt with me. You're a consenting adult.'

Brix got up.

'Who sent Lund that tape?'

'I don't know. It's possible someone from your office took it. If I knew who it was I'd charge them. But I don't. I don't understand why they did that then waited until you were cleared. Frankly at the moment I don't much care. Do you think I should?'

'Is it important?' Weber asked.

Brix smiled.

'Who knows?'

He held out his hand.

'I assume you have votes to beg. Don't let me keep you.'

In the car on the way back Hartmann called the office. Rie Skovgaard answered. She'd turned up for work anyway, was going through his speech for the following day.

They talked as if nothing had happened.

'One of Bremer's people phoned from the hospital. He wants to see you.'

'Why? I thought he was supposed to be out of there by now.'

'Some kind of complications. They want to keep him in overnight.'

'What kind of complications?'

'I'm not a doctor. I said you didn't have time. What's wrong?'

'Nothing.'

Weber sat silent, listening.

Hartmann finished the call.

'When we get back I want you to find Rie's contract,' he said. 'I want to read it.'

It wasn't a student house any more. Mette Hauge's old block was neatly painted, converted into pricey apartments. Christiania trikes for the kids. Cobblestones and privacy.

Paludan was a lean, athletic-looking man who turned up on a racing bike while she was parking.

He didn't ask to see her police ID. He seemed more anxious that they talk outside, in the courtyard. Away from his wife.

Half a kilometre away was the so-called free state of Christiania. A kind of hippie commune gone bad. There'd been drug dealers in

639

the city for as long as Lund could remember. Half of them were in the gangs run by Danish biker groups. The rest were Turks and other foreigners. There was a constant war between the two. Sometimes people got caught in the crossfire.

She asked about Mette Hauge.

He shrugged.

'We shared the house. That was all. I didn't know her.'

Lund looked at him. His nervousness. The way he got more anxious when she wanted to go inside.

'You were students together. You must have talked. In the kitchen. At parties.'

'I told everyone this twenty years ago. We were studying. I was busy. Not doing dope and all the other shit like . . .'

He left it there.

'Did you sleep with her?' Lund asked.

Paludan didn't answer straight away.

Then, 'What?'

'Did you sleep with her?'

'No! What makes you ask that?'

'It's my job.'

'Is it? I want your name. Your department.'

'Listen to me. This case is open again and active. If you know something now's the time to say it.'

There were people coming and going in the courtyard.

'Can you keep your voice down? I don't know anything.' He was sweating. Patches on the arms of his biking gear. 'Everyone slept with her. OK?'

Lund listened.

'Me. Just once or twice. She probably never even noticed.'

Lund waited.

'We were young. Students. There were parties. You know what it's like.'

'Tell me.'

Footsteps across the courtyard. An old woman with a shopping cart. She called out a friendly hello.

When she was gone Paludan said, 'Mette was a lovely kid. But crazy. She'd do . . . anything. When they said she killed herself . . .'

He shook his head.

'It was ridiculous. Overdosed maybe—'

'She didn't overdose. Someone beat her to death. Why didn't you say any of this at the time?'

He leaned the bike against the wall.

'Because I was terrified.'

'Of what?'

His eyes drifted to the arch that led out from the cobbled courtyard.

'Of them. Mette used to hang round with some scary people. If you wanted dope she always had someone who could get it.'

'From Christiania?'

'I don't think so. We all knew those people. These were guys . . . like gypsies. They hung around with the gangs. Maybe were in the gangs. I don't know.'

'Any names?'

He laughed.

'I wouldn't have dared ask. I think one of them was her boyfriend. Maybe . . .' He coughed. 'Maybe more than one. Who knows? Mette was Mette. I wasn't telling anyone I'd slept with her.'

'You met some of them?'

'Years ago . . . I don't remember. I just—'

'We buried this case,' Lund said. 'We thought Mette was one more kid who'd gone missing. If you'd told us—'

'I'd just got married. My wife was pregnant at the time. Is that good enough for you?'

'I need a name.'

'I don't have one. They were serious guys. Someone was dead sweet on her.'

A memory.

'She came back one time with this ugly necklace. A black heart on it. I guess the bikers like that kind of thing.'

A tall young man was walking across the cobblestones. He looked at them, waved, smiled, said, 'Hi, Dad!'

Paludan tried to smile back.

'We were all stupid back then. Mette was a sweet kid. When I think back . . . in some ways she had it coming. Jesus . . .'

He stared at Lund.

'That's a terrible thing to say, isn't it?'

'I don't know. Is it?'

'What I mean is ... something was going to happen. I don't know what. But it was never going to be good.'

He bent down, lifted his bike onto the rack, chained it.

'That's why I never talked about it too, I guess. I could see it coming. And there was nothing I could do.'

Bülow was livid. He'd got the registration number for Bengt Rosling's rental car, put out a general call to bring Lund into headquarters. No bail this time. No chance of release.

Now he stood outside Brix's office, throwing out threats like a clown dispensing sweets at a birthday party.

'If I find out you knew about this—'

'I didn't know,' Brix said with a shrug. 'How could I?'

His phone rang. He looked at the ID.

'I've got to talk to my wife. We're supposed to be going out tonight.'

The phone rang again. Bülow didn't move.

'Do you like ballet?' Brix asked.

Bülow swore then strode down the black corridor.

When he was out of earshot Brix answered the call.

'The list of contents says there was a photo album in the box,' Lund said.

'What have you been up to?'

'Mette Hauge was a party girl. Sold dope. Had connections with gangs. Maybe in Christiania. Maybe not. One of the gang people was her boyfriend. Maybe more than one.'

'Lund, you need to come here immediately.'

'I need to see the photo album.'

'We've done that already. Wait ... I've got it here.'

He went back into his office, went through some of the material they'd recovered from the warehouse.

The album had a blue cover. School photos. Student shots. Trips to the beach. Parties.

'There's nothing in here.'

'It's either at the end or the beginning, Brix. That's how people file photos. Look for the pictures closest to Mette's disappearance.'

'We found Nanna's passport in Leon Frevert's back yard.'

'Where?'

'In the rubbish bin.'

'That doesn't add up. He'd have got rid of it two weeks ago. It wouldn't be in the bin any more. You need to find this photo, Brix.'

'Maybe he kept hold of it. Frevert had her passport. He was the last person to see Nanna Birk Larsen alive. Five minutes after he dropped her off he left a message on the Birk Larsen office phone. Vagn Skærbæk's confirmed to us he called in sick.'

She tried to think about this.

'Take me through that again—'

'Get the hell in here! Lund! *Lund!*'

Pernille Birk Larsen was in a flap. Anton's birthday. The last they'd ever celebrate in the cramped little apartment above the garage. The place was a mess. Packed bags everywhere, ready to move.

Anton was at a party with some school friends. Pernille would pick him up. No talk of passports. No talk of anything but birthdays.

'I need you to cook the roast, Theis,' she said, scrubbing the sink clean. 'I need you to hoover too.'

He was making some Nutella sandwiches for the kids.

'Anything else?'

'No.' She caught his eye. He was in a good mood. 'That'll do.'

'The place'll be a mess in five minutes anyway.'

He slapped some of the sticky spread on a couple of slices of bread.

'It's just family.'

'I want the place clean.'

He rubbed his forehead. She looked at him.

'So long as the boys have a good time . . .'

She had her hand over her mouth. Stifling a giggle.

'Oh. So I'm funny now, am I?'

Pernille walked up, ran a finger across his forehead. Picked up some of the spread he'd wiped there.

Showed him her finger.

'Oh shit.'

But he laughed.

Bags covered the kitchen table with its lacquered pictures and memories frozen in time. She wouldn't let them follow. The thing could go into storage. Maybe get looked at from time to time.

At some point they had to leave the past behind. She knew that now.

His big arm came round. He pulled her to him, kissed her cheek. Black leather and sweat, the rough touch of his beard.

She was still gazing round at the room, the walls that once bore photos, the missing plants, the blank, pale space that was the cork-board. Pernille Birk Larsen found herself crying and didn't know why. Only that these weren't bad tears, and they were temporary. The tight, cruel circle that had opened when Nanna died was beginning to close, hour by hour, day by day. It would always be there. But with time it would become a part of them, accepted, like a familiar scar, always acknowledged, no longer a source of constant hurt.

'Will you miss this place?' his low growl whispered in her ear.

'Only the happiness. And we can make all that again.'

He wiped her cheeks with his fat, scarred fingers.

She held him tight. He held her.

'I wish I could have made it better, sweetheart.'

'I know you do. I know.'

Twenty minutes later she picked up Anton from the party. He didn't look tired. He didn't look happy.

'Did you remember not to eat too much? Dad's cooking.'

'Didn't eat much.'

'Did you hand out the invitations to the house-warming next week?'

'Yes.'

She looked at him in the mirror, smiled.

'And the girls too?'

'And the girls,' he sighed.

He didn't want to talk. She did.

'They're fixing up the basement last,' Pernille said. 'The house is going to be really nice.'

His head went from side to side. He looked out at Vesterbrogade in the rain.

'Are you still mad at Uncle Vagn for telling us?'

For a second she turned and looked at him.

'Now we know there was no passport it makes everything better, doesn't it?'

'Somebody got it first,' he said in a sharp, young voice that took her breath away. 'Somebody.'

'No. They didn't! Lord . . . Anton. Why must you make up these things?'

He buried his arms in his jacket, said nothing.

'Nobody took it. Sometimes . . .' She looked in the mirror again. At least he was listening. 'Sometimes you see things that aren't really there.'

His eyes were on the mirror now, trying to find hers.

'That's true, isn't it? Anton?'

The boy sat in his safety seat, arms folded tight. Eyes on the mirror.

In a soft, scared voice she asked, 'Why would someone take it?'

'So you and Dad wouldn't get upset.'

He was still staring at her reflection.

'Who do you think took it?'

Silence.

'Who?'

'I don't tell on people. Don't ever tell.'

Face at the window, at the street again.

When they were home he ran straight upstairs. Pernille went to the office. Pulled out the schedules and the diaries. Found the work list for that weekend.

The name of the office company was there. And a number.

She called it, got voicemail.

'My name's Pernille Birk Larsen. We were meant to do a job for you. One of our employees cancelled it. Can you please call me back to discuss this? So we can clear up any misunderstanding? Thanks.'

Lund left the rental car two blocks from the Humleby house, down a dead-end alley, away from the street. Then she walked through the rain, hood up, to the narrow road. Birk Larsen's house was on the corner shrouded in plastic sheeting and scaffolding. A red company van was parked at the front. Lights were on inside.

The door was open. She walked in without knocking. There was no one on the ground floor. Just pots of paint, stepladders, sheets, paintbrushes.

A sound.

Someone walking up from the cellar.

Lund stood in the room and waited. It was Vagn Skærbæk. He stayed at the top by the shadowy stairwell. She could just make out the black hat, a sweatshirt jumper spattered with paint, a box of tools in his hands.

'I'm really sorry to bother you, Vagn . . .'

'Oh Christ. Not you again.'

He brushed past her, walked to the back of the room, didn't turn.

'It's about Leon Frevert. A couple of questions.'

'Make it quick. I'm going to a birthday party.'

'The message Leon left on the answering machine. Do you still have it?'

Skærbæk came and stood in the light, shaking his head.

'The other guy asked me the same thing. Don't you people talk to each other?'

'Tell me.'

'No. I deleted it. I didn't know it was important. It was just some guy cancelling.'

He tidied the tools, put each back into its slot in the box.

'What exactly did he say?'

'This was three weeks ago. Can you remember a ten-second message from—?'

'Bear with me.'

Skærbæk looked at the ceiling.

'It was something about being sick. He couldn't work that weekend.'

'Anything else?'

'No. And I didn't call him back. Pisses me off when people cut out of work like that. We were lucky the customer cancelled.'

Lund paced the floor, one half-painted wall to the other.

'How did he sound? Was he afraid? Did he sound strange? Did he say what—?'

'It was a message on the answering machine. It sounded like Leon.'

She looked at him. Lined face still babyish. Silver chain. Sad, pained eyes.

'Did he mention Nanna?'

'Don't you think I'd have mentioned that?'

He went and got a piece of rag, wiped his hands on it, looked at his watch, then a blue jacket thrown in the corner.

'Why did he call the company? Not you?'

'Everyone calls that line. If no one answers it redirects to me.'

'Right.'

Thinking.

Imagining.

'So Leon Frevert calls the company line thinking he's going to get Theis or Pernille. Instead he gets you.'

He'd stopped rubbing his hands. Stopped everything. Was still. Very still. Staring at her.

'No. He got my voicemail. I told you. I was with my uncle. I got the message the next morning when I went in to work.'

Thinking.

'Is that all?' Skærbæk asked. 'I'd like to turn off the lights. It's Anton's birthday. I'm going to be there. You're not stopping me.'

'I'm not.'

He ran downstairs. She followed him into the basement. The door there was old. A lock on it, and a key.

'Did Leon ever mention someone called Mette Hauge?' she asked.

He was taking down some temporary lamps, winding up the cabling.

'No.'

'Was he in the gangs?'

'I don't know! Listen. We're sick and tired of all your questions. OK?'

He walked to a stepladder, starting tying his shoes.

'We want to put this all behind us.'

Lund looked around at the basement.

'All that stuff about that bastard Frevert. What he did. We don't want to think about it.'

New timber boards across the floor. Springy and shiny. Quickly laid. Fresh chipboard covered the entire back wall, none of the other three.

'We're not taking this shit any more.'

He was near the steps, putting on his jacket, getting ready to leave.

'You've got to leave us alone. After what the family's been through . . .'

Sarah Lund was revolving slowly round the room, three hundred and sixty degrees.

'They need some peace.'

She stopped and looked at him.

Just the two of them there, in the empty house in Humleby. Something in Vagn Skærbæk's eyes she'd never seen before. A hint of recognition. Of knowledge.

In her face too she guessed.

'What's wrong?' Skærbæk asked.

All the tools, the hammers, the chisels, were near him.

She tried not to look. Not to seem scared.

'What's wrong?' he asked again.

He was a smart man. She'd known that all along. He looked at himself. At the jacket he'd just put on.

Old. Dark blue. The logo of the winter Olympics. And the words . . .

SARAJEVO 1984.

A car drove past outside. Dim street light through the stained-glass window. People walked down the street. She could hear the sound of pram wheels or maybe a Christiania trike. Laughter. A key in a lock. Steps on nearby stairs.

'Anything else?' Vagn Skærbæk asked.

It took a while but she said no in the end. Then walked towards the stairs and the hefty door with the lock and key.

Something was going on in his head. She didn't want to know.

He stood in her way.

Smart man. Maybe as scared as she was. His throat was moving. There was a glistening sheen of sweat on his brow.

'So we're agreed then?' Skærbæk asked. 'It's all done with. Finished.'

She couldn't take her eyes off his too-young face. A sense of grief, of shame was there. A recognition of who and what he was.

Lund looked around and said, 'I guess so, Vagn. You're right.'

Then slowly, very deliberately, he stepped to one side.

She was shaking by the time she got to the street. Crossed the road, found another house that was empty, being rebuilt, four doors away. Leaned against the grimy wall in the side alley, clutching herself, teeth chattering.

Waited three or four minutes then saw the last light go off. Skærbæk came out, looked up, looked down the street. Climbed into his scarlet van. Chucked a colourful bag of something in the driver's seat. Then left.

Lund looked at her phone. Thought better of it. Went back to the Birk Larsen house, found the back door.

She got a brick and broke the window. Removed the splinters and the shards piece by piece. Found the key in the other side and let herself in.

Lund called Jansen, the ginger-haired forensic officer Brix had entrusted with the Mette Hauge file.

A good man. Quiet to the point of taciturn. Told him to come in by the broken back door, and find her by the noise downstairs.

First she started on the wall. Chipboard. Easily removed with a pickaxe. If there was blood splatter she ought to see it. The floor was timber, nailed in tightly. She couldn't do that on her own.

A third of the chipboard was off by the time he arrived. Smashed and splintered wood was scattered across the floor. There seemed nothing behind except plain plaster. Recently washed by the look of it.

'I'm never inviting you to a DIY party,' Jansen said. 'They've got your registration plate. You're supposed to be taken into custody on sight. Go straight to those funny bastards across the building.'

It was probably the longest sentence she'd ever heard him speak.

'I'm having trouble with the floor,' she said, handing him a crowbar. 'Can you start there?'

Jansen had worked with her for years. He saw things. Like her.

'My,' he said, looking at the new timber boards. 'Someone was in a hurry here.'

'Did you tell anyone?'

'Yeah. I told them I was going home.'

'There are more tools upstairs if you need them.'

'They're going to find you, Lund.'

She tried to smile at him.

'Thanks. I need your phone.'

He handed it over.

'How much do you want me to remove?'

'Enough for us to find something,' she said, then walked upstairs to get a signal. 'We don't have a lot of time.'

*

Bülow was back in Brix's office, lost for a lead.

'If you know where Lund is I swear I'll bring you down with her.'

Brix shook his head.

'She phoned. She didn't say where from.'

'Did you trace the call?'

'Lund doesn't think Frevert killed the girl. Or shot Meyer.'

'She shot Meyer.'

Brix stared at him.

'It looks like Frevert was murdered.'

'I want Lund! Trace the call.'

'Her mobile's off. She's not stupid. She's the best officer in the building when it comes to tracing people.'

'She's forged evidence, Brix. She's gone missing. Gone crazy. And still . . .' He lost it. Yelled the last. 'Still someone here's helping her. If I find it's you—'

Brix's phone rang.

He looked at the number, put it straight to his ear.

'It's Lund here. Can you talk?'

'I don't think I'll make the concert. Give me a minute.'

'What do you think the Ministry of Justice is going to say about this?' Bülow barked at him.

Brix said nothing.

'You'll be watching ballet for the rest of your life,' the squat man said, then stomped out.

'Yes?' he said when Bülow had gone.

'Did you get the photo?' Lund asked.

'You've got to come in now.'

'I know who it is, Brix. I know where Nanna was taken after the flat. Where she was assaulted and beaten. Vagn Skærbæk. Send me a team from forensics.'

'We found the girl's passport—'

'Vagn planted it. We don't have time for this. Send someone.'

Brix looked outside the window. Bülow was still haranguing the men out there.

'Send him where?'

'Küchlersgade in Humleby.'

'That's Birk Larsen's house.'

'Yes. We need to move. Vagn knows I'm onto him.'

*

Among the plastic bags, the cases, the cardboard packing boxes, Anton was opening his presents. A fishing rod. A toy boat. A magic set and some pens and books for school. Lotte was back in their midst, helping with the table. Theis Birk Larsen wore his chef's apron, handed out drinks, wine for the adults, orange squash for the two boys.

Scalloped potatoes. An expensive joint of pork.

He took the meat out of the oven, put it on the side.

'I should let it rest.' He looked at her. 'Don't you think?'

She glanced at the pork, watched him reach for some foil, start to wrap it.

'I talked to Anton about the passport.'

His mood wavered.

'What? The passport wasn't there. We looked.'

'Anton thinks Vagn took it.'

Still messing with the pork.

'I thought we'd agreed not to talk about this nonsense.'

The boys were starting to squabble. Lotte tried to calm them down.

'I left a message with the people Vagn cancelled. The office. That Saturday.'

He smoothed down the edges of the foil, barely looked at her.

'Why would you do that? This is Anton's birthday . . .'

Her wide eyes flared. She came close and peered into his face.

'Because there's something wrong, Theis! Can't you feel it? Can't you . . . ?'

Quickly he kissed her.

Bristly cheeks. Beer on his breath. A lot, she thought.

Lotte was there asking if she could help. His phone rang.

'Take a look at the potatoes, Lotte,' she said.

He was laughing.

'Where the hell are you?' he asked.

Then listened, put a finger to his nose, said, 'Ssshhh.'

And went downstairs.

The kennel was by the garage door. Brand new. With a price tag on it which Vagn Skærbæk quickly snatched away as Theis Birk Larsen approached.

'What the hell are you doing?'

Skærbæk glared at him.

'Don't spoil it!'

He got a cover sheet, draped it over the kennel, grinned.

'I was coming past this shop. They had this outside.'

Birk Larsen peered under the drape.

'That must have cost a fortune.'

'The boys'll love a dog.' He was smiling. Smartly dressed in a black jacket and white shirt. Looked different. Older. More serious somehow. 'I always wanted one.'

An odd, uncharacteristic smile.

'You never really get what you want, do you?'

'For Christ's sake. We don't have a dog.'

'I got one from Poland.'

Birk Larsen stood in his blue apron and best shirt, starting to lose patience.

'You got a dog from Poland?'

'Yeah. I can get anything you want, Theis. Remember? I know a guy who imports them . . .'

'Vagn—'

'Don't get mad with me. It's a great dog. Pedigree and all. Nice surprise.'

'Big surprise,' Birk Larsen grumbled. He looked around the garage. 'So where the hell is it?'

'We can pick it up tonight. The two of us. After dinner.' He pointed to the kennel. 'Let's keep it covered up. Until we get the dog. OK?'

Birk Larsen shook his head. He thought he could hear something nearby, scratching. Time to put rat poison down again.

'It's like having another kid around here sometimes.'

'Kids are magic,' Skærbæk said. 'Kids are everything. I need to write the card.'

'And then they grow up. I've got to finish cooking.'

He looked at the office.

'I forgot to put the calls upstairs.'

'It's a birthday, Theis.'

'It's business.'

'I'll do it,' Skærbæk said. He waved the pen over the bright yellow birthday card. 'When I've written this. You go and see the boys.'

Vagn Skærbæk watched him go. Scrawled happy birthday on Anton's card.

Heard the familiar answering message greeting an incoming call on the speakerphone.

'This is Birk Larsen Removals. Please leave a message.'

A beep.

'Good evening,' said a stiff and tetchy male voice. 'Henrik Poulsen from HP Office Supplies.'

Skærbæk stopped writing, looked round, made sure he was alone, then walked into the office.

'You called about the move we ordered for the first weekend in November,' the voice said. 'To be honest we were very disappointed. We'd planned it for weeks. And suddenly your man cancels at the very last minute. It was very unfortunate. If you need more information you can call me at home. The number is . . .'

He let it run, took the tape out of the machine, placed it in his jacket pocket. Then switched the calls to upstairs.

Rie Skovgaard was bright and cheerful again, showing him the private polls. It was going the way Weber had predicted. A two-horse race with him in the lead. Bremer's illness provoked sympathy but not support. If anything it improved Hartmann's chances, not diminished them.

'I talked to a friend in the police,' Skovgaard said. 'There's something going on. It doesn't affect us.'

Hartmann got a decanter of brandy, poured himself a glass, said nothing.

'There's nothing to worry about. All this nonsense Erik Salin's been peddling. It's just . . .'

He was staring at her.

'Hot air,' she said in a voice close to a whisper. 'Should this be in private, Troels?'

Weber started to get up.

'Morten stays,' Hartmann said.

The brandy was old and expensive. A fire in the throat, in the head.

'I'm sorry,' she said, 'if you feel I let you down somehow.'

Hartmann sipped the strong liquor, thought of the night in Store

Kongensgade. Had felt much the same way then. As if nothing really mattered. As if he were hurtling towards a fate over which he had no control.

'I'll give you a choice, Rie. Either tell me the truth about the video, about the flat, and we go to the police. Or you take the consequences.'

Skovgaard stared at him, shook her head.

Morten Weber squirmed at the table, said, 'What the—?'

'I'll deal with this,' she broke in. 'What are you talking about, Troels?'

'Don't lie to me any more. I know. You went looking for me that night. You went to Store Kongensgade. When you saw the place you knew something was wrong. Come Monday when the police were sniffing around here you thought if you could keep people out of there for a few weeks it would all go away.'

She laughed.

'You're more ridiculous than that Lund woman. I was at the conference.'

'Not till ten o'clock.'

'If this is one more piece of shit from Bremer—'

'Was it someone from Parliament? Your father? Did he order you to step in and cover for your little puppet?'

Rie Skovgaard's mouth opened. No words.

'Or was this your own career move?'

Bright wide eyes filling with tears.

'How can you even think this?'

'There's a gross misconduct clause in your contract. Go home and read it. I want you out of here now. I don't want to see you again. In this office. Or anywhere else. Is that understood?'

He got up and went to the window. Took the brandy with him. Sipped it in the light of the blue neon sign.

She followed him.

'If I thought you'd killed that girl . . .'

Hartmann didn't turn to look at her.

'Do you think I'd have still stayed with you? I did this for us—'

Hartmann spun round, eyes wild, voice roaring.

'I know why you did it! I know what I was! A step on the ladder. A means to an end.'

'Troels—'

654

'Get out!'

Weber was behind her. An arm on her shoulder. Easing her towards the door.

'Get off me, Morten!' she yelled at him, and broke free.

Hartmann went back to the window. Looked at the city beyond the glass.

'They're the only people that matter,' Rie Skovgaard shot at him. 'Aren't they? You don't want love. You want adulation. You want—'

'Just go,' he said, not looking at her, waving with a single hand.

Not listening either to her curses and her screams.

And then she really was gone. Along with his only chance to seize Copenhagen for himself. A battle lost. The only victory that mattered put beyond reach.

When he went back to the brandy and poured another big glass, he thought he was alone.

Then a sound.

Morten Weber.

'Troels,' he said. 'We need to talk.'

'Call for the car,' Hartmann said. 'I want to see Bremer in the hospital.'

'We need to talk . . .'

There was a flame in his head and it wasn't the booze.

Hartmann turned on the little man screaming, high-pitched, like a lunatic, out of himself, out of the tidy, manicured, manufactured mannequin he'd become.

'Is there one fucking person in this office who will do as I say?'

He'd never seen Morten Weber look at him this way before.

'Of course, Troels. I just wanted to—'

Hartmann smashed the brandy glass against the window. It shattered a pane. Cold winter air came through, whipped round him, chilled his skin.

There was a release for everything somewhere. In booze. In action. In the physical rush of love. And still it led to the same bleak place, to nothing.

'I'm sorry,' he said in his old, quiet voice. 'I just thought she was . . .'

He kicked at the shards of broken glass with his shoe.

'I thought it was me she wanted. Not . . .' He looked at the poster, his face young and smiling from the wall. 'Not the other one.'

'He's the one they all want,' Weber said in a low, sad voice. 'This is politics. It's not for real people. They want figureheads. Icons they can watch rise and fall and say . . . Hey, they're all in it for themselves, aren't they? Just like us. Frail and human and venal. That's the game we're in.'

'Tell the police about the flat. About the video. We've been party to an obstruction of justice. Brix can work out what to do.'

'Now? It's late. And you're seeing Bremer. Why not . . . I don't know. Let me see if I can find some way we can make this work for all of us.'

'It can't work—'

'Troels, if we go to the police you're finished. It's too late to be the comeback kid again. You're dead.'

Hartmann glared at him.

'Call the police,' he ordered. 'You're not fixing this.'

Jansen had a third of the floorboards up. Lund was looking at the concrete floor beneath. The two of them were covered in sawdust, plaster, wood chips, broken board.

Lund got down on her knees, put her face against the cold floor below the boards.

'Give me the inspection lamp.'

She placed the bright bulb next to the joist and peered beneath the section leading back from the wall.

'I think they did this part first,' she said into the dead space. 'Where the hell's Brix and some help?'

Held out a hand.

'Hammer.'

Jansen put it in her fingers. She got the claw end lodged some way down the board, eased it up. He wound a crowbar in. Another line of Vagn Skærbæk's carefully laid, brand-new flooring rose from its fastenings.

'Can you see anything?' he asked.

'He won't have laid it straight over. He'll have cleaned the floor first. Bleach. I think it's on the walls too.'

She stood up. White and black sweater filthy with wood dust and dirt.

A light outside. Headlamps coming through the narrow blue window.

'About time,' Lund said. 'Pull up the rest and let's see what we've got.'

She walked upstairs. Brix was by his black Volvo.

'Have you picked up Skærbæk?' she asked.

'No.'

She put on her jacket. Looked round.

'Where's the new man?'

Bülow was walking towards her from the left. On the right Svendsen was getting out of his car. He looked happier than she'd ever seen him.

'You stupid bastard,' she hissed at Brix.

'He's doing his job,' Bülow said. 'You should have done yours.'

Brix looked at her, shrugged.

'There's nothing in the basement, Lund. We've been here before.'

'You were looking for Frevert before. Not Nanna.'

Svendsen came up, grabbed her arm and said, 'You're under arrest.'

She dragged herself free, stood in front of Brix.

'Frevert called Birk Larsen that night. He wanted to say he'd picked up Nanna and she was going somewhere. The call came through to Vagn Skærbæk instead.'

Svendsen began to grab at her arms.

'Don't touch me!' Lund shrieked at him. 'Brix! Listen. Skærbæk went to the flat. He took the keys to the car Hartmann used. He hid her in the basement here. If we look—'

'You can rant all you like in headquarters,' Bülow cut in.

She tried to dodge Svendsen's flying arms.

'Skærbæk shot Meyer. He didn't say Sarah. He said Sarajevo. Eighty-four. Look at Skærbæk's jacket. Shit!'

Svendsen had her arm in a lock, was twisting hard.

'Tell them about the missing picture, Brix. Tell them!'

She was caught then. Dragged towards the car.

'Skærbæk put in a new floor. Covered the walls. Check it out! Get him before he kills someone else . . .'

The cop's right hand grabbed her long hair, dragged her to the door. Pushed her down into the back.

Then he got in the front next to another man in the passenger seat. Rear doors secured.

Jansen came out of the house, walked up to Brix.

'Is there anything down there?'

'Nothing I can see,' the forensics man said. 'That doesn't mean—'

'Get out of there,' Bülow ordered. 'I'll send people to assess the damage Lund's done. We'll have to pay out for that too.'

He went back to his car.

'Wait.'

The squat man from prosecutions turned and scowled.

'It may be your job to prosecute Sarah Lund,' Brix said. 'But I run homicide.'

'Your case is solved. Cut yourself loose from that mad bitch while you can.'

He started walking again.

'Get a full lab team out here,' Brix said to Jansen. 'Everyone we have. I want the basement checked.'

Bülow turned, shook his head.

'We leave when I say so,' Brix insisted.

'Done,' Jansen said, reaching for his phone.

A birthday song. This is how we play the trumpets. Everyone standing round the table, making pretend instruments with their hands.

Party hats. Presents. Cake. Candles and little Danish flags.

A toast of wine and orange squash. Vagn Skærbæk in his smartest clothes, smiling like a proud uncle, beaming at the boys.

Pernille looked at him. So young sometimes, though there were bags beneath his eyes she hadn't noticed much before. And maybe he was starting to dye the grey flecks in his hair.

Vagn had been a part of them for so long she couldn't remember how it began. With Theis. Everything started with him. In that mad rush, when she was pregnant with Nanna, running away, getting married. Persuading him to give up the round of petty jobs and try to settle down. Start his own company.

The slight, diffident, sometimes frightened figure of Vagn was always there in the background. Always ready to help. To offer a kind word. To put the life of someone else before his own.

Now she watched him looking at the boys and felt with every passing second that something which once seemed so right, so natural, was deeply wrong. Not for any reason she could comprehend. Not through any single fact, more a line of circumstances and intuitions that still failed quite to connect.

'The boys are beautiful,' Vagn said, smiling in that unforced, genuine way she'd taken for granted.

Maybe he saw himself there. Or the boy he wished he'd been.

'The food was really delicious.'

'I'm glad, Vagn,' she said quietly.

And wanted to ask: why?

Was about to when Theis stood up, cleared his throat, announced he wanted to say a few words.

Were there any others, she thought. She loved this man but knew that, in some ways, he was as much a mystery to himself as he was to her.

'First of all,' Theis Birk Larsen declared in a voice that was mock-serious, though perhaps he didn't know it. 'I would like to say happy birthday to Anton. I hope it's been a nice day. A little bird told me . . .'

The man across the table put a hand over his mouth and giggled.

'That Uncle Vagn has another surprise for you later.'

He stood next to her like the rock, like the great tree in the forest he always was. Swaying a little now. Not the arrogant young tough of old.

Bowing down, his hand reached to the table and gently covered hers.

'Lotte,' he said, raising his glass. 'Anton. Emil. Vagn.'

He didn't cry. He never had. Not when she was looking. But it was close now.

'We couldn't have got through this time without you.'

He squeezed her fingers with his own.

'And I couldn't have got through anything . . .' Narrow eyes, impenetrable eyes, sly sometimes, fell on her. 'Not a thing without my Pernille. My sweet Pernille . . .'

The arm of Birk Larsen's clean shirt swept his face. No tears. Not quite.

'Soon we'll have a new house. And we'll welcome you all there. A new start. A new . . .'

The great tree wavered. The table was silent.

'Skål,' Pernille said, raising her glass.

'Skål,' said Lotte and Theis.

'Skål,' said the boys with their orange juice.

Vagn gulped at his beer and roared, 'Bunden i vejret eller resten i håret!'

The boys giggled. He put his hand over his mouth and blushed.

Bottoms up or the rest in your hair.

A drunken toast. Not for kids. But maybe Vagn didn't know that. Maybe there was a line between the boy he wanted to be and the adult he became. One, the imaginary child, happy and free, becoming real. The other, the adult, poor, careworn, solitary, turning into fantasy.

In the morning she'd call Lund. Would talk to her. Knew that the woman would listen. Till then . . .

She saw him smiling at Anton and Emil.

Till then she'd keep her family close, would not let them out of her keen and eager sight.

The phone rang.

Vagn Stærbæk got straight up from the table, went for the phone barely able to keep his eyes off the boys.

Off Pernille too. She looked so . . . intense. Happy in a way. As if something, some hidden mystery, was becoming clear.

'Hello?' he said. 'Birk Larsen residence.'

'It's Rudi. Is Theis there?'

Past the balloons, past the presents she was watching him.

Vagn Skærbæk smiled.

'Hi.'

Brightly.

'What's up?'

'I drove by the house. The police are there again.'

Still smiling.

'What do you mean?'

'They're in and out of the basement. Lots of them. Is that OK? I thought . . .'

'Well, yes,' he said. 'That's fine. We'll come right over. Thanks for calling. Bye.'

Sat down. Shrugged.

'Well,' he said, looking round the table. 'I think we have a change of plan.'

Birk Larsen's heavy brow furrowed

'The guy I told you about.' Vagn winked. 'You know? The one. He wants us to come out right now.'

'What plan?' Pernille asked, suddenly anxious. 'What plan's this?'

'Vagn's surprise,' Theis said.

He winked too. This annoyed her.

She got up, stood behind Anton and Emil.

'So how did he know to call here?'

'My phone's on the blink,' Vagn said. 'Didn't I mention it?'

He looked at the boys. At Lotte and Pernille.

'I don't want to break up the party, Theis. But if we're going to go we ought to get started. Sooner we leave the sooner we're back with . . .'

He looked at the ceiling, rolled his eyes.

'Can't we wait till after the cake?' Birk Larsen asked.

'No. We have to go now. Half an hour. That's all.'

A glance at the boys.

'Save me some,' he said, then got Birk Larsen's black leather jacket, held it for him.

Downstairs.

She heard the garage doors getting rolled up. Caught up with Theis as Skærbæk walked to his van.

'Don't go,' Pernille said.

'Come on.'

'Why can't Vagn go alone?'

'It's about the dog,' Birk Larsen whispered. 'We'll be back for cake. I promise.'

Then, a six-pack of Carlsberg in his hand, he walked outside.

She stood by the crates and the forklift. Cursing herself. Wondering why she let him ride over her this way.

A small, high voice from the shadows near the office said, 'Mum? Is this for me?'

Anton, searching round the place, looking where he shouldn't. He got that from Nanna.

'Let's go upstairs. Stop messing with things.'

'I'm not messing. It's got my name on it.'

She went over. A yellow envelope.

In Vagn's scrawl: *Anton.*

It sat on a tarpaulin over something that hadn't been there before. She dragged it off. There was a kennel underneath, shiny and new. And a cardboard box, old, half open, behind. A noise coming from it.

She pulled back the leaves of the lid.

Anton squealed. Shrieked. Screamed.

'He's cute, Mum! He's cute! He's mine.'

A black and white puppy.

Pernille looked, mind racing. Wondering.

Anton picked up the dog. Emil was running down the stairs.

Into the office, phone out. Called his number.

Waiting she heard an echo. Walked to the workbench, saw the red Nokia there, light flashing, tone trilling.

'What's his name, Mum?' Anton yelled, following the puppy round the vans. 'What's his name?'

'Lund,' Pernille murmured.

Anton looked at her.

'Lund?' the small voice said.

Svendsen was driving. Lund didn't know the other guy in the front. As they worked through the busy traffic in Vesterbrogade she said, 'Send someone for Skærbæk, for Christ's sake.'

'Why don't you shut up and enjoy the ride?'

'He killed Nanna. He killed Frevert. He shot Meyer.'

Svendsen took his hand off the wheel, wound a finger in the air, made a childish sound.

'Woo-woo-woo.'

Laughed.

'Maybe I'll come and visit you in the funny farm. Probably not though.'

'We need to bring in Skærbæk—'

'Tell Brix about it. You're boring the living shit out of me.'

The radio snapped into life.

'Twelve twenty-four, call in.'

Picked up the mike.

'Twelve twenty-four. Over.'

'Twelve twenty-four. Nanna's mother called. She insists on talking to Lund.'

'Lund's in a straitjacket howling at the moon. What's the problem?'

She wanted to shriek at him. Rip the mike from his hands. But she waited.

'She wants us to track down her husband.'

'Are we lost and found now?'

'Dammit, Svendsen,' Lund yelled.

'Yeah, yeah.' He waved. 'What's it about?'

'He left with an employee. She doesn't know where. She's worried.'

'What employee?' Lund said. 'Ask him that. Gimme the damned mike.'

As she reached over the one in the passenger seat slapped her hard in the face with the back of his fist.

'Come on, Svendsen!' she yelled. 'Bring that lonely brain cell into action for once in your life. Ask who it was? Humour me.'

He looked at her in the driving mirror, shook his head, asked the question anyway.

A pause.

'He went off with someone called Vagn Skærbæk. They were supposed to pick up a puppy. The wife says it's not true.'

Lund leaned over the seat. The other one kept watching her.

'We need to send a patrol car over there. Get the number of Skærbæk's van.'

'Copied that,' Svendsen said and put down the mike.

She blinked, bright eyes gleaming.

'What in God's name are you doing? Put out a call on Skærbæk. He's killed two people already. Svendsen!'

His big bull head rolled in anger.

'You don't know that, Lund! I can't put out a call because someone's gone out for a drive. It's Friday night. They're probably on the piss and don't want the old woman to know.'

'Skærbæk isn't going for a drive. Do your job.'

He looked at her again.

'My job's to take you back to headquarters and throw you in a cell. You've no idea how pleasant this is going to be.'

Lund sat back on the hard seat. Lights flashing past in the black night. Time running out.

Two men from homicide. Typical male detectives. Glocks on their belts always, like a piece of jewellery, an icon of their manhood.

She looked towards the dashboard, then lower. Svendsen was right-handed. The other guy left. Their weapons sat between them. Grips out. Calling.

'I did ask nicely,' she whispered.

'I'm sure the only cell left is the shittiest one,' Svendsen began. 'I so regret that, I—'

Reached forward, both hands. Flicked up the leather catches in one, grabbed the grips, dropped one gun in the footwell, pulled the slide to load on the second.

Held the barrel against Svendsen's bull neck.

'What is this crap?'

He sounded scared.

'Pull in,' she said. 'Right now.'

'Lund . . .'

She took the weapon away from his skin, edged it round his face, then for the first time outside the range fired.

The side window shattered in crazed glass. The car skidded and wheeled on the dark wet road.

By then Svendsen was on the brakes and the other guy was screaming. They came to a halt outside a gift shop. Red brick. Christmas trees in the window and decorations.

'Get out of the car,' Lund said. 'Both of you. Stand against the window. Don't piss me off.'

She watched them. Climbed over the seat, gun in one hand, eyes on Svendsen all the time.

Then turned the unmarked police car round in the broad road, back to Vesterbro.

Bülow refused to leave Humleby. He stood and watched as Brix's men tried to find some logical way to examine the mess that was now the basement.

Two senior forensic officers in white suits and mob caps were spraying for bloodstains. Brix stood with Jansen by the stairs, Bülow baiting them all the time.

'This isn't easy,' one of the men in white moaned. 'All this saw-dust and shit—'

'You're wasting police resources,' Bülow cut in. 'That's an offence in itself, Brix.'

The men were using luminol. Any trace of blood would shine bright yellow under the ultra violet lights they'd brought.

'Seen a single thing?' Bülow asked.

'Well, no,' the forensic officer answered carefully. 'That's often the case before you look.'

'Are all the people you employ smart-arses, Brix? Tell me. Truly. I'd like to know.'

'We need to turn off the lights,' Jansen said. 'See if we've got any traces.'

He glared at the man from prosecutions.

'Careful you don't trip.'

Then it went dark.

The two men in white suits picked up a pair of long fluorescent tubes.

Blue.

They ran them up and down the stripped and sprayed walls.

'I'm not seeing anything, Brix,' Bülow crowed.

His phone rang.

They moved their lights to the skirting board, ran round every inch.

'Right,' Bülow said. 'I'm on my way. Track down the car. Warn everyone she's armed. Approach with caution.'

He cut the call, stood in front of Brix and Jansen.

'Your colleague has just threatened two officers with their own firearms and hijacked a patrol car.'

Brix said, 'What?'

'You heard. I'm getting you suspended, Brix. You've been standing in our way all along. When I'm finished—'

A long whistle from one of the men in white.

'And now,' said a voice ahead in the strange blue light, 'stand back in wonder.'

They looked at the floor. Bülow and Brix. Jansen and the men in white.

Between the centre set of floorboards patches of yellow had crept across the blue pool of light.

Puddles and splatters. Long running stains.

'Raise your eyes, gentlemen,' said the man from forensics. 'This is something else.'

A yellow handprint on the wall. Fingers scraping at the plaster, like the shadows left behind by a vanished ghost.

It was coming to life everywhere. Strips and smears, scrawls and pools.

Like a room in a sick nightclub.

In the strange light Jansen looked around.

'She was fighting for her life in here, Brix. This was a . . .'

Bülow's mouth was half open, flapping, wordless.

Brix was getting out his phone.

'Get me control,' he said.

There was a solitary nurse at the desk of the private hospital wing.

'Are you family or friends?' she said when he asked to see Poul Bremer.

'Neither.'

'Well then I'm sorry.'

'Tell him Hartmann's here. He asked to see me.'

'He needs rest.'

Hartmann leaned on the desk and waited.

She went off to a room a few doors down. Not long after four people came out. Hartmann recognized Bremer's wife and sister. Both were weeping. They walked past him, down the corridor, towards the waiting room.

The nurse came back.

'I don't want him excited. If he becomes sick or agitated you need to let us know. There's a bell push by the bed. We've just moved him into this room and we don't have all the monitors working yet.'

'Sure,' Hartmann said with a shrug. 'How is he?'

She didn't say a word. Then showed him to the room and left.

Just a lamp over the bed. Bremer in a white gown lying on a white sheet. Drip feed into his nostrils. No spectacles. Unshaven.

He seemed younger like this. As if the small, solitary room had removed the cares of the outside world, burdens Poul Bremer carried with him every moment of the working day.

The Lord Mayor of Copenhagen looked up at him, squinted, laughed.

'I would have beaten you easily on Tuesday, Troels,' he said in a weak, faint voice. 'You know that, don't you?'

Hartmann stood by the IV stand, hands in pockets.

'Maybe you still will.'

'If only.'

'You know maybe you should talk to the doctors, Poul. Your family. Not me.'

'You're my legacy,' Bremer said with a feeble scowl. 'You can damn well listen.'

There was a stool by the curtain. Hartmann pulled it to the side of the bed and sat down.

'Oh please, Troels. Don't look so sympathetic. It turns my stomach.' That faint laugh again. 'If I were you, thirty years ago, I'd be standing on that drip feed now. Sending me to hell and stealing the prize for myself.'

'I don't believe that for one moment,' Hartmann said, surprised to find he was smiling.

'No,' Bremer agreed. 'I liked to bluster back then. To threaten. That's all it was. I was a lot like you. Wore my heart on my sleeve. Then you get the thing you dream of. And it's . . .'

Hartmann saw the expression of disgust.

'It's a piece of shit. You don't change anything. You're lucky just to keep the wheels on the cart.'

'You're supposed to rest.'

'Rest?' The voice grew a little louder. 'Rest? How can you rest? How can you do anything . . . change anything . . . if you don't have the power?'

'Poul . . .'

The old man's eyes were glazed and unfocused. His breath came in shallow irregular wheezes.

Bremer's hand came out and gripped Hartmann's arm. It was the weak and trembling touch of a frail man.

The monitor by the bed bleeped and blinked.

'You think you're different,' the old man groaned. 'Maybe you are. Everything's changed these days. There's so much I don't understand any more.'

He coughed, winced in pain.

'Poul? What did you want to tell me?'

Bremer's eyes rolled, trying to focus.

'I know who's been protecting you.'

The nurse came in quickly, looked at the monitor, said, 'I've got to ask you to step outside now.'

Hartmann got up. Bremer's weak hand still gripped him.

'I thought it was Rie but it wasn't.'

The old man gulped. In pain again. The nurse felt his forehead, checked the monitor again.

'I sent something to your office. It's up to you . . .'

The woman was calling for a doctor. He could hear footsteps down the corridor.

'You have to leave now,' she said firmly, pointing at the door.

Still Bremer's arm held him, still there was the blank basilisk stare, eyes the colour of the bleak marble inside the Politigården.

'Do the right thing, Troels. You have to live with it. No one else.'

There were tears and a sudden look of terror.

'You think you're the captain of this ship,' Poul Bremer whispered. 'But really . . . it's the master of us all.'

Voice high, trembling, frail. Hand on his.

'Troels . . .'

White-clad figures raced around him, pushing Hartmann out of the way. The monitor started shrieking. Doctors, nurses talking anxiously.

The grey eyes opened in stark fear then closed and Hartmann was manhandled out of the door.

Down the corridor, down to the exit.

Someone was causing an argument.

Yelling, 'But he's an old friend! He asked . . .'

Troels Hartmann reached the desk. It was as far as they'd allowed Erik Salin.

The bald hack was on him straight away.

'Hartmann? What did Bremer say? Huh? Come on, Troels . . .'

He looked at the man in the black coat, smelled the tobacco on him and the anxiety.

'Bremer gave you the proof, didn't he? He wouldn't have called you here for nothing. He had it. He told me.'

Hartmann stopped.

'What do you want?'

'Bremer told me he had something,' Salin repeated. 'So . . . ?' A look of defeat, of desperation. 'What is it?'

He doesn't know, Troels Hartmann thought. Any more than I do.

'Goodnight, Erik,' he said.

Brix went straight to the Birk Larsen house, talked to Lotte, looked at the puppy.

'We tried to call them,' she said. 'Theis left his phone here. Vagn's not answering.'

'What did Sarah Lund say?'

'She just came along and picked up my sister.'

'Where were they going?'

'To look for Theis and Vagn.'

'Where?' Brix asked.

She looked at the officers searching the garage, the blue flashing lights outside.

'Lund's police, isn't she? Why the hell are you asking me?'

A familiar voice on the radio.

'They're in a red van with Birk Larsen on the side. Registration number UE 93 682.'

'Lund,' said a voice from control. 'You've no authority. Come in now.'

'Just put out a call, will you?'

Brix strode to the car.

'The van was last seen going east on Vesterbrogade,' Lund said.

'Come in!' control barked again.

He picked up the mike.

'Brix here,' he said. 'I'll deal with this.'

Back in the Rådhus Hartmann marched to his office. The broken window was taped up. On his desk was a Christmas bouquet, holly and poinsettias, with an envelope bearing his name.

Inside was a photo he struggled to recognize. From the summer maybe. It looked like a school party in a park. He was smiling among a group of older students. Next to him was a young blonde woman, arm linked through his, laughing as if he'd just made a joke.

Hartmann's blood froze.

Nanna Birk Larsen.

A sound from the back of the office. In the shadows by the sofa Morten Weber sat, coat over his arm, scarf in hand.

He got up, came to the desk, looked.

'I was about to leave when that turned up. I thought I'd got every copy. It seems Bremer found the last one. He must have been looking very hard. Even Erik Salin didn't get that I gather.'

Weber took the seat opposite Hartmann.

'It was last July. The Frederiksholm school fun run. Remember?'

Hartmann stared at the photo.

'Arm in arm. Eye to eye. She doesn't look like a schoolkid at all, does she? In a way I guess she wasn't.'

Weber got up, went round the back of Hartmann, took the picture.

'Thank God it was never published. Nanna won the bronze medal. You gave it to her. That could have killed us. And Bremer hands it away for nothing. There must be a God.'

He passed the photo back to Hartmann, returned to his seat.

'I just heard he had another stroke. It looks serious. If he can't take the job it's yours. We need to think about how you play this . . .'

Troels Hartmann stared at the pretty blonde girl then looked at the Christmas bouquet, thought of the old man fighting for breath in the hospital.

'What have you done to me? What in God's name . . . ?'

Weber shrugged, looked at him, asked, 'Are you serious?'

'I'm serious.'

'You really must try to see things from the point of view of others sometimes. You'd been in the flat. You were dead drunk. When I found you in the cottage you were a stupid, incoherent mess.'

He shook his head, wouldn't take his eyes off Hartmann.

'You'd tried to kill yourself. I remembered that girl. I remembered that photo the moment the police said who it was. I had her name, Troels. I work. I keep records.'

'You . . . knew?'

'What was I supposed to think?'

'I don't know her,' Hartmann insisted, putting the photo on the desk, refusing to look at it. 'I don't remember this . . .'

Weber leaned back on the sofa, closed his eyes and sighed.

'You thought me capable of—'

'I've worked for twenty years making you what you are!' Weber cried. 'Waiting for a chance to achieve something finally. I wasn't having that go to waste.'

Voice quieter. Hartmann's breath became shallow. The room swam.

'Oh for pity's sake, Troels. I went round to the flat that Sunday. The table was broken. I could see something had happened. The next day they say it's her . . .'

His face became stern.

'Of course I made sure they didn't find it. As best I could. I got the security tape too. I thought maybe we could give it to the police once the election was over. Let them into the flat. When it was safe. *If* it was safe . . .'

'If?'

'Don't push it. In principle I did nothing to interfere with the investigation. Just helped it—'

'In principle?'

Weber got the brandy decanter, poured himself a drink, stood over Hartmann. Like a boss.

'I'm sorry about Rie,' he said nonchalantly. 'But let's face it. She wasn't the right woman for you.'

'That's your decision, is it?'

Weber scowled at him.

'After all the sweat I've put in you think I don't deserve some say? You should have hooked up with that policewoman, Lund. More your type. I can see you now . . .'

He took a swig of the brandy.

'In bed. You thinking of your next speech. Lund with those big wide eyes, wondering what's in the room to look at, what's next door.'

'You disgust me . . .'

'That's fine, Troels. Be as disgusted as you want. Was I supposed to throw away two decades of my life just because somebody killed a girl from Vesterbro?'

Hartmann lost it, dashed the brandy glass from his hand, stood above him.

'Are you mad, Morten?'

Weber didn't retreat the way he used to do. He stayed there, defiant, smirking.

'No. Just efficient.'

'The police are going to find out. They're in Store Kongensgade now.'

'No, they're not. I never called them.'

He got himself a new glass. Poured himself a second brandy. Took Hartmann's seat. Looked up at him.

'Sit, Troels? Sit. We've things to discuss.'

Hartmann stayed by the window.

'Oh for pity's sake,' Weber groaned and got another glass, poured Hartmann a brandy. 'If it makes a difference . . .'

He took the chair on the other side of the desk. Waited for Hartmann to fall into his own.

'You've nothing to worry about. Nothing at all. This speech for tomorrow . . .'

He took some sheets from the desk.

'I need to make a few changes. We have to insert some references to Bremer. Expressions of admiration. I'll handle it.'

'There isn't going to be a speech tomorrow. When they find out what you've done . . .'

Weber laughed.

'Oh, right.'

'If not I'll tell them.'

'Is that what you want? Fine.'

He pushed the phone across the desk.

'Go ahead. Call them.' He tapped a finger on the photo again. 'We can show them this. You can tell them what happened when you met her. Last July. Rie was on holiday with her father in Spain. Remember?'

Hartmann said nothing.

'You do remember, don't you? Fun run.' Finger on the photo. 'I was there. That's me at the back of the group. Always at the back. I know my place and . . .'

He pointed to his eyes, grinned.

'I watch. I have to. Had a few beers, didn't you? Those wandering eyes. Lingered around afterwards. Tell me, Troels. I was never much good with women. Did you even remember her name? Does it matter?'

'What do you mean?' Hartmann murmured.

'The thing is . . .' Weber had dropped the picture of Nanna Birk

Larsen, was playing with the photo of JFK and Jackie. 'You just dream of the White House. And I know you. I see what you're like. The way you were before you married. *While* you were married. After.'

He leaned forward. Voice rising.

'I *know*. You dream of the White House. And I just see Chappaquiddick. Pretty girl. A few beers. I saw you give her your number. I couldn't work it out at the time. But, well . . .'

He shrugged.

'Turns out she was screwing Jens Holck, wasn't she? Maybe she wanted to try out someone new from the political classes. A different notch on her bedpost. I saw you—'

'Morten—'

'You gave her your number. You went round to Store Kongensgade. You waited. Got some good wine. Brought in some food. Was that how it worked?'

Hartmann was shaking his head.

'I don't remember . . .'

'I took the kid to one side after you left for the flat. I ripped up the phone number. I scared the living daylights out of her. That's why she never turned up. But I did. Just by accident. To make sure you really were on your own. Not screwing a schoolkid you bumped into at a prize-giving. Do you remember that?'

No answer.

'So you see. When she was dead I had to ask myself. Did she get your number some other way? The pretty schoolgirl who looked so much older?'

'I never killed that girl!'

'I know you didn't. Now. This is good. This we can live with. Had it been otherwise . . . I'd have faced some difficult decisions.'

He got up, put on his coat.

'Any questions, Troels?'

The black phone stayed untouched.

'Good. We have this conversation once only. Never again.'

Morten Weber looked at his watch.

'I'll see you in the morning,' he said. 'Don't be late.'

On the long road that led from the city, Pernille wide-eyed and scared in the passenger seat, Lund behind the wheel.

673

Blustery rain came in through the shattered side window. There was glass on the floor, on the dashboard.

'Can you think of any warehouses they might use?' Lund asked.

'We've got some in Sydhavnen.'

An industrial area, across the main road leading to the airport and Vestamager.

'Lund?' said the radio. 'It's Brix here.'

'And?'

'You were right about Skærbæk. The girl was held captive in the basement.'

Next to her Pernille Birk Larsen put a hand to her mouth.

'So let's find him,' Lund said.

'We will. You've got to come in.'

Straight away, 'Not a chance.'

'You don't know where they are, Lund! You're in the way of the operation. We're alerting the border patrols—'

'Vagn's not skipping the country. It's not about—'

'We found shotgun cartridges in Skærbæk's garage. He's armed. I don't want you out there. I don't want Pernille either. There's nothing you can do. Turn round and come back here.'

She looked at the woman next to her. Pernille shook her head.

'What about the woods?' Lund asked. 'Pinseskoven.'

The Pentecost Forest.

'Why the hell would he go there?' Brix asked. 'Middle of nowhere. A dead end.'

'It started there. Somehow. Maybe he wants to finish it there too.'

'Come in now. I'll deal with this.'

She put down the mike, drove on, took the turn for Vestamager.

'Why would they go to the woods?' Pernille asked.

The traffic grew lighter as the night darkened. Soon they were beyond the street lamps and the dual carriageway, heading down the long damp road that led to the forest.

After a while the road narrowed to a single carriageway, then little more than a lane.

Dead end, Brix said. There anyway he was right.

Theis Birk Larsen nursed his third can of beer, not taking any notice where they were going. He was a little drunk, a lot happy. Reminiscing.

674

'First dog I ever had was called Corfu. Remember that?'

'Yeah,' Vagn Skærbæk said, sounding bored.

'Smuggled it home from Greece in a backpack. We learned a few things then, huh?'

'I never knew a little dog could shit that much.'

Birk Larsen scowled at the beer.

'Maybe we'll be smuggling a few more things pretty soon. Got the house to pay for. If they put me inside for the damned teacher . . .'

He looked at the man at the wheel.

'You'll cope.' Birk Larsen slapped his shoulder. 'You'll manage.'

He grabbed the remaining cans.

'Want another beer?'

'Nah.'

'OK. I'll have yours.'

They were on a lane. The van bounced and lurched on the rough track.

'Where the hell are we going?'

'Not far.'

'Pernille's going to kill us if we're not back for cake.'

Birk Larsen raised his can.

'Here's to women.'

Then took a swig.

A distant roar above them. And lights. Birk Larsen watched as a passenger jet descended through the night sky.

'We're near the airport. What kind of idiot keeps dogs out here?'

'There's something I need to show you. It won't take long. And then we're done.'

'Pernille . . .'

The van bounced. He looked at the lane in the headlights. Gravel. What looked like ditches by the side. In the grey light cast by a moon behind clouds the outline of a wood.

A dim memory, fuddled by beer.

Vagn Skærbæk interrupted it.

'Do you remember when we used to go out fishing at night?'

'Fuck fishing, Vagn. Where's the damned dog?'

Trees now. Bare silver bark. Slender trunks rising like dead limbs from the earth.

'It was always freezing. We never caught a damned thing.'

The van had slowed almost to walking pace. It kept running in and out of black potholes.

Birk Larsen felt slow and drunk and stupid.

'You said Pernille would think we'd been drinking if we didn't come back with some eels. You should have seen your face when I got some. You never asked where they came from.'

'Vagn—'

'I just went and stole them from someone's trap.'

'So what?'

Skærbæk nodded.

'Yeah. So what? So long as things get fixed. Then they never come back to haunt you. What's it matter?'

He found the place he was looking for. Stopped the van. Pulled on the brake.

Silver peeling trunks in the faint moonlight. Deep ditches both sides of the road. No sign of life.

Skærbæk leapt out, went to the back of the van, opened the doors.

Birk Larsen sighed. Took a swig of the beer. Decided he wanted a piss anyway.

Climbed out of the passenger side, walked round the side.

Vagn Skærbæk had dressed. He stood there in full hunting gear. Long black galoshes, long khaki coat. Over his shoulder was a shotgun on a strap.

He pulled another pair of rubber boots out of the back.

'You need to put those on, Theis.'

'What is this?'

'Just put them on, will you?'

Then he picked up a heavy piece of timber, held it in both hands.

'Let's go home,' Birk Larsen sighed. 'Pernille . . .'

He didn't see it coming. The lump of wood struck him on the temple, bloodied his eyes, sent him reeling against the van door, stumbling down to the ground.

Skærbæk prodded him with the barrel of the shotgun.

'You're OK. Get up.'

He pulled a big electric lantern out of the back, turned on the light. Closed the van doors.

'Forget the boots,' Skærbæk said. 'Start moving.'

Then pushed him towards the trees.

Ten minutes later Lund parked by the bridge where Nanna's body was found, walked towards the forest down a long straight path, Pernille striding beside her. Some way behind there were flashing lights. The sound of radios and men. A helicopter was sweeping overhead, its bright beam penetrating the darkness of the Pentecost Forest.

All she had was a single, weak torch and the wan moonlight that seeped through the thin cloud.

The phone rang.

'I sent a couple of cars and a dog team from the airport,' Brix said. 'They've got the van. It's empty.'

She remembered the woods from before. A maze of paths and tracks, criss-crossed with ditches, patches of swampy marsh, and canals. Logging piles blocked some forest roads. Others would be a quagmire from the recent rain.

'The dogs . . .' Lund started.

'The dogs have got a scent. They're onto it.'

'How many people have you got?'

'Five patrols now. Where are you?'

'Inside the forest. Ahead of you I think. We need to hurry.'

She could hear the sound of barking. Make out torches. Waited. Saw a direction.

Pulled out the map she'd picked up from the boxes the nature reserve left everywhere.

Remembered Jan Meyer grinning with a dead animal beneath his arm, a wire round its neck and a cub scout scarf.

Lund walked.

Pernille followed.

Theis Birk Larsen stumbled.

Vagn Skærbæk, shotgun in hand, behind him.

'Come on,' he barked, watching the big man lurch against a silver trunk. 'Move it.'

The trees grew thicker, spindlier. They marched through bracken and rotten leaves.

The sound of dogs. Men's voices.

Birk Larsen lost his footing going over a puddle, fell to the wet earth, floundered in the mud.

'Vagn . . .'

Skærbæk looked at the puzzled, damaged face of the man on the ground.

'What is this, Vagn? What the fuck—?'

Skærbæk fired, put a shotgun blast into a bole of fungus and mildew a step from the hurt and wallowing figure in front of him, watched the yellow fire and flying mud.

Dogs barking. Voices getting louder, nearer.

'Get up. Keep walking,' he said. 'Don't stop now. Not far. Not long.'

Lund heard the shotgun. Pernille loosed a high, faint shriek.

No more shots.

'Where are they?' Pernille gasped. 'Theis . . .'

A voice in Lund's ear.

Brix said, 'What's going on?'

'I don't know.'

'How close are you?'

'I don't know. I—'

Jet engines drowned her words. Drowned her thoughts.

A ditch, green with algae. Birk Larsen stumbled, fell face in, got lifted by Skærbæk's hands.

Stumbled through dead branches, through the mire. Climbed out of the other side, panting. Bleeding.

The trees got thicker.

The trees thinned out.

Lights nearby. The staccato sound of dogs anxious to follow a scent. Shouts of their handlers, cries in the dark.

A patch of clear ground ahead. Tall grass. Broken branches. A circle amidst the silver trees.

In his green hunting coat, Skærbæk looked around, said, 'Stop here.'

Cast his eyes around the woods. The distant flicker of approaching torches.

Turned back to the big, stricken man with him. The blood ran down from Birk Larsen's left temple, around his eye, around his nose and stubbled cheek like a gory mask.

'Theis. In a while they'll tell you all sorts of things.'

Birk Larsen stood hunched and stupid.

'I want you to hear it from me.'

Torch in left hand, shotgun slung low in right, Vagn Skærbæk listened, again, shook his head, laughed for a moment.

'Things just happen sometimes. You never know. You never see them. Then they're there and nothing you can do can stop them. Nothing . . .'

The big man with the bloody face stared at him.

'Leon called to tell you he'd picked up Nanna, dropped her at this flat in Store Kongensgade. I knew she was up to something. I saw them at the station. She was going away with that raghead. The stupid little Indian kid.'

Skærbæk waved the gun at him.

'Going away. You get me?'

Birk Larsen grunted something wordless.

'I knew what you'd say. But you weren't there. So I went and found her.'

His voice rose.

'I'm a reasonable man! You know it! I went to talk her out of it. To make her see sense. But not Nanna.'

He ripped off his hat, looked at Birk Larsen with pleading eyes.

'Not Nanna. She's got your blood in her, huh? She wouldn't listen. She came at me screaming with her nails.'

Birk Larsen stood as still as any tree.

'You know what she was like. Your blood. Me?'

Skærbæk shone the torch on his own face.

'I thought about you and Pernille and the boys. What you'd think. How you'd feel. Abandoned like that.'

A part of the mask fell. His eyes began to water. Voice crack.

'We all loved her. But she didn't care. Not Nanna. Not about you. Not about me. You know that's right, don't you? You know, Theis. Yeah.'

No words from the shambling man, blood congealing on his rigid face.

'Theis . . .'

Voices getting closer. Flashing beams of torchlight on the silver tree trunks behind.

'Sometimes things just happen. You can't tell. You don't know where they come from. They just do.'

The shotgun waved, pointed.

'You know that. Don't you?'

He looked around.

'No explaining. No apologies. You just . . .' Vagn Skærbæk wiped something from his eyes. 'You just have to fix them. Do your best to make things right.'

He heaved the weapon to his shoulder, checked it had shells.

'You understand what I'm saying?'

No answer.

The shotgun came down, indicated the ground.

'We came here. This spot. She was scared. I knew you'd never understand.'

Young eyes, young voice, no silver chain, no red overalls any more.

'I couldn't kill her. I couldn't.'

He sniffed. Shrugged.

'So I carried her to the car and pushed it into the water.'

Gun up. Birk Larsen stared it.

'Here.'

Vagn Skærbæk threw it. Watched the long barrel twist in the air between them. The stock fell straight into Birk Larsen's massive hand. His fingers closed automatically around the wood.

The magic weapon. The gun that closed things.

Big man, black jacket, bleeding face.

'Come on, you dumb bastard. Go on. Get it over with.'

Racing footsteps. Voices.

'Do it!'

A woman's voice broke from the night.

'Theis Birk Larsen, put the weapon down.'

The two men turned and looked. Saw Sarah Lund beyond the tall dead grass. Weapon in hand. Ready. Next to her Pernille in her fawn coat.

Vagn Skærbæk opened his hands, smiled at the man with the shotgun.

The explosion tore through the dark. Lund firing into the sky.

'Walk away from Skærbæk now,' she ordered. 'We know what happened, Theis. Drop the gun. Walk away.'

Skærbæk was laughing.

'What happened?' he asked. 'You think they know, big man, huh? Or did I get it wrong?'

No words. Theis Birk Larsen was never good at those. But he could look.

'You'll never move into Humleby now,' Skærbæk threw at him with that same sarcastic smile. 'That's where I did it. Can you imagine?'

'Put down the weapon, Theis!' Lund shrieked

She was beyond the grass. They could both see the black Glock in her hands. More bodies too. Lights behind her. Dark figures sweeping through the silver trees with their peeling bark. Dogs and torches, gathering round, encircling the two men in the bare patch where they stood.

Birk Larsen held the gun at his waist. Forty-five degrees.

'Theis,' Lund cried. 'There's someone here who wants to talk to you.'

Fawn coat striding through into the clearing.

'It's finished now,' Pernille said. 'Theis . . .'

For a brief moment he shifted his attention away from the man in the green hunting coat, saw her.

'It's over now.'

'It's not over,' Skærbæk snarled. 'Not yet. Even a big stupid lunk like you knows that. Don't you? Come on. You'll be out in a couple of years at most. What's there to lose?'

A brief, hard laugh.

'You'll be a hero. Theis Birk Larsen. The avenging angel. You'll like that, won't you?'

From beyond the circle, fast approaching, Pernille's soft and frightened voice pleaded, 'Let's go home, Theis. Let's go home to the boys.'

The gun relaxed.

'The boys. Look at me. Look at me. Step away from him.'

Birk Larsen took a stride back, let his eyes roam round the small circle in the Pentecost Forest. Torches and men ringed them on every side like a crowd for a spectacle. Like an audience for the arena.

Getting closer.

Lund's hard, scared voice chanting, 'Drop the gun, Theis. Drop the—'

'I covered my ears,' Skærbæk said suddenly. 'Because I couldn't stand the way she screamed. Can you imagine?'

Birk Larsen glared at him, heard nothing else.

Skærbæk's face was different now. Scared and desperate. Still determined.

'When I pushed her in the water. On and on it went . . . Christ! She begged and screamed and . . .'

Skærbæk's high, weak voice broke. His head twisted from side to side, in fear, in agony.

'Nanna just kept pleading for me to get her out of there.'

Gun rising, Skærbæk's anxious eyes on the big man with the grizzled face.

'She called for you and Pernille. Pathetic. I can still hear it.'

A shrug of the shoulders of the green hunting jacket.

'But I mean really. It was too late then, wasn't it? She could scream all she liked but what the fuck could I do . . . where are your balls now, you cowardly jerk?'

The gun rose, yellow fire in the night, smoke and a high-pitched shriek.

The man in the long coat flew back. Clutched his chest. Fell on a hummock of low rushes. Face up to the night sky.

Up to Theis Birk Larsen, ignoring the calls around him. The woman, Lund. Pernille. Ignoring the black figures racing towards them.

Sees nothing but the man on the ground.

Gun to shoulder. Face set. Blinking into Skærbæk's scared eyes.

Someone screaming, not that it matters.

Blood on the green coat. Blood on Vagn Skærbæk's open, gasping mouth. Still breathing. Still alive.

'You owe me,' the stricken man says, the words coming with scarlet bubbles as he fights to speak. 'You owe me now, you big idiot—'

A second shot sends the night birds scuttling through the branches in the dark wood where the dead trees give no shelter.

Then Theis Birk Larsen stands back.

Throws the hunting gun on the ground. Stares at the broken, contorted shape at his feet.

Then retreats.

No words. No need for them.

Around him dark figures circling.

Barking orders. Holding steady weapons.

He rolls round his pained, confused head, like a cornered beast, looks about him and sees.

There is a woman in a black and white jumper and she's weeping.

A woman in a fawn coat. And she's not.

Thirteen

Friday, 21st November

Five in the morning. Brix was in his office.

Lund waited by a window in the circling corridor outside, staring down into the yard in front of the prison cells that now held Theis Birk Larsen on a charge of manslaughter.

Soon it would be daylight, and with it a need for explanations. Press conferences. The case of Nanna Birk Larsen would be closed for good.

Brix looked at the lonely woman by the glass, lost in her thoughts. Lost in everything except herself. He wished, against his own instincts, he'd got to work with her more. Not know her better. That was a challenge beyond him. Beyond most, he felt.

'Lund!' he called, and beckoned her in.

She was still in her blue anorak and woollen jumper, caked with mud from the Kalvebod Fælled.

'Did you find the photo?'

'No. Take a seat.'

'Leon Frevert . . .'

'Lund.'

He tried to smile.

'Forensics have matched residue on Skærbæk's sweatshirt. We know he was the one who shot Meyer.'

She stared at him with those large, all-seeing eyes.

'Bülow still wants your blood. He'll complete his report. You can expect consequences. Especially for what you did in the car.'

'Svendsen wouldn't listen.'

'You pulled a gun on him.'

She repeated, very slowly, 'He wouldn't listen.'

Brix waited for a moment.

'Bülow isn't the only one involved. I have some say. They'll take into consideration the nature of the case. And the investigation.'

She was looking round the office, eyeing the evidence bags.

'Your situation's very serious.'

He noticed the door was still ajar. Brix got up and closed it. Came and stood over her.

'I can present you with an opportunity. It won't stay open for long. You need to think about it.'

She stared at her filthy hands.

'This case has caused a lot of difficulties. Everyone wants them to go away. For good.'

Hands in pockets, speaking confidently.

'Certain aspects of the investigation will be omitted from the reports. Your allegation that someone was protecting figures in the Rådhus. The idea that there are other missing-person cases connected to Skærbæk.'

He sat down again.

'The Nanna Birk Larsen case is dead. It's going to stay that way.'

No answer.

'In my view this is a good solution for you. For all of us.'

Lund folded her arms, said nothing.

'I advise you to accept it.'

No answer.

'Sarah, you solved the case. That's the only thing that matters. If you agree you can get a job somewhere else. I can give you a reference. You can start—'

She got up, walked to the door, opened it.

'Lund?'

Carefully, slowly, she brushed some of the muck from the sleeve of her black and white jumper.

'The people upstairs are waiting for an answer.'

'Aren't we all?' she said, then walked down the black marble corridor, past the office with the toy police car and the basketball net, past Jansen, past the noisy room where the homicide men gathered to tell their dirty jokes.

Out into the dark, cold morning.

At six o'clock Troels Hartmann woke in his office. A winter wind was howling. The tape on the broken window had worked loose. The icy gale was working its way into the room.

Stinking head, stinking breath. The empty brandy decanter on the floor, along with the papers, the speeches, the posters. Pretty much everything he could throw around on that long and bitter night.

Crouched on the floor and aching he pulled out his phone, called Brix.

'I'm busy,' the cop said. 'I'll get back to you when I genuinely have nothing better to do.'

The tone of his voice rankled.

'This is important. Don't hang up on me!'

'Why not?'

'It's about the Nanna case. I tried to get you at home last night. You weren't there.'

'Working.'

'I've discovered something. You're going to have to look into it. The flat—'

'I'm pleased you're suddenly so cooperative, Hartmann. But you're too late. The case is closed. For good this time. We found him. Nothing to do with you or the Rådhus. This was a . . .' The cop paused, as he found what he was about to say distasteful. 'A family affair, you might say.'

Hartmann stopped and found himself staring in shame at the mess around him. The bottles. The rubbish on the floor.

Thick head, sore throat, he went to the desk, sat down.

'Who—?'

'You'll be hearing about it on the news soon enough.'

The photo Weber had found was still there. Nanna, smiling, arm through his. Looking up into his face.

He never did get her name.

'Hello?' Brix said.

'He's dead?'

'Didn't I just say that? Listen, Hartmann. I've got a lot to do—'

'There's something else.'

He could hear the tall cop sigh down the phone.

'Make it quick.'

The rich smell of mahogany. The gilt. The frescoes. The warm and comfortable cell that enclosed Troels Hartmann seemed to wrap itself around him, whisper like a seductive siren in his ear.

'It's just that . . .'

His croaky voice died. He couldn't speak.

'I'll send someone over later in the week if you want,' Brix broke in. 'Good luck with the election. And by the way. Don't ever think of trying to lean on us the way your predecessor did. That's not happening again.'

The line went dead. Hartmann found the remote control. Turned on the TV. Listened to the news.

'Poul Bremer had another stroke late last night. He's withdrawn from the election for the next city council. Bremer has been Lord Mayor of Copenhagen for twelve years. Our political editor says his decision to pull out of the race makes the election of Troels Hartmann a certainty . . .'

A knock on the door. A smiling blonde woman in a green dress came through. She had newspapers in her hand and said, cheerily, 'Good morning.'

Looked at the mess, the state of him, still smiling. The broken window.

'We'll clear this up,' she said. 'There'll be photos later. I'm sending in a man to fix the glass.'

Came to the desk, held out her hand. He took it. Warm and soft.

'Maja Randrup. I'm Rie Skovgaard's replacement. Morten asked me to step in.'

She placed some printouts in front of him.

'He gave me your speech to type up. I read it. Very good.'

With dainty steps she started picking up things from the floor. His jacket. The empty glass. The decanter and the folders. Still smiling.

'I suggested a few changes after I heard about Bremer,' she said, setting an overturned chair upright.

'Morten and I think they set the right tone. Sympathetic but determined to do right by the city. To take the good parts of Bremer's legacy, build on them, and add to them your own.'

A turn of the room, checking everything. A wave of her hand.

'There's a shower here, right? You've got shaving things. I'll bring in fresh clothes.'

Didn't wait for an answer.

'We need you fit for purpose in forty-five minutes.'

Grabbed the brandy decanter. Kept it.

'It's too bad you had to win this way. But let's face it, winning's winning. There'll be some free time in your calendar after the press conference. Morten says you should take it. Go home. Stay out of public view as much as you can for the next couple of days. The campaign's over. Now we just wait.'

She opened the windows. The cold November gale grew bolder, making him shiver, teeth chattering, mind locked in blunt, dumb pain.

Sounds of traffic. Still dark. The blue neon of the hotel.

He sat at the desk, head still swimming, looked at her. An attractive woman. Thirty or so. Tight green shiny shirt. Good figure. No ring on her finger. She knew he was checking.

Maja Randrup picked up the picture of him with Nanna.

'I'll take this now,' she said and left the room.

The lawyer met Pernille Birk Larsen in the circling corridor opposite the jail block.

'He'll be in court first thing. Afterwards they'll probably send him to Vestre prison. I won't waste your money trying to get bail.'

Lis Gamborg. The same woman who'd argued for Theis, for Vagn too when he demanded it. Pernille didn't know many lawyers. Didn't want to.

'I'm so sorry,' she said. 'I'll call when I have a time for the court appearance.'

Then she left.

Pernille stood in the narrow corridor, looked outside. Day was breaking. Bright and clear. In the yard below a group of prison officers marched a big man in a blue prison suit, handcuffed, a bandage on his temple, out towards a van.

She started to run.

Down the winding spiral stairs, feet flying. Pushing cops and guards, lawyers and stumbling drunks out of her way.

Two flights and she found herself in the grey concrete car park. Heads were turning, people starting to shout.

He was halfway across the yard, a uniformed officer on each arm, walking the way he always did. Head upright, eyes ahead. Mouth locked shut. Mute and waiting for whatever the day brought.

'Theis!'

They'd caught sight of her now.

'Theis!'

And so had he.

A policewoman raced to her, grabbed her arm.

Pernille fought free, arms flailing. Fought the next one.

Ran and ran.

Two guards holding him, reaching for their truncheons, looking round.

In the light of a rosy winter dawn Pernille Birk Larsen kicked and punched and screamed her away across the narrow yard, flung herself on him, arms round his neck, legs on the massive tree trunk of his frame.

Face against face. Smooth cheek against rough. Words she'd never remember, not that it mattered.

Her strength with his. His with hers.

Briefly locked together. A love unspoken. A commitment re-affirmed.

When they dragged her from him he stood there, too big to move easily.

She never knew what was in his eyes. Never would. Never wanted to. What mattered was in the heart, and there they were one.

Eight thirty. Fresh suit, fresh shirt. Fresh air in the office. An aerosol to mask the overnight stink of brandy. No papers on the floor.

Maja Randrup stood in front of him. Adjusted his tie. Checked his hair. His face.

'Don't sound victorious,' she said. 'The media may be calling the election. There's no one else to win it. But a little humility doesn't go amiss.'

She stood back to consider him, the way a window dresser might judge a mannequin.

Gave him the speech.

Troels Hartmann didn't look at it. Didn't need it. He knew every word.

Her smile dropped for a moment. He wondered if he'd disappointed her somehow.

Disappointing people was bad. They remembered. They held it against you.

This was politics. Satisfaction. Delivery. Image. Appearance. These were paramount.

The caustic glance was aimed at his desk, not him. She spoke of the coming photo shoot. Of the need for a visible, consistent personality.

'We don't need this,' Maja Randrup said and tucked the photo of Jack and Jackie beneath her arm. 'It's too . . .'

She screwed up her snub nose. A gesture he liked.

'Too old.'

In his clean shirt and fresh cologne, feeling light-hearted but not so bad, Troels Hartmann stood and waited. To be told.

A knock on the door. Morten Weber nodding. To her not to him.

'Is he ready?' Weber asked.

She speaks. Troels Hartmann doesn't listen. On Weber's cue, behind the little man with the wayward curly hair and cheap gold glasses, he walks out of the office, out through the Liberals' quarters, along the shining walkways, past doors opening, past curious faces.

Close to the great room Morten Weber starts to clap. Maja Randrup does the same. The applause catches like fire on a dry heath.

He walks on to the polished grandeur of the council chamber, a place so bright it dazzles his eyes.

Sees the doors. Halts. Steps through them.

Sees the cameras, the faces, the hands clapping, the hands clapping.

Stands on the podium by the great throne of Copenhagen.

Walks to the polished seat, places a firm hand on the old wood.

Turns to the crowd, the cameras, the expectant faces.

And smiles.

And smiles.

And smiles.

Fourteen

A bright day, painted in sparse colours. Winter was falling on Copenhagen, the salt air sharp and cold, the sun harsh and dazzling. Lund sat outside the hospital shivering in the thin blue cagoule. Her belongings were still in Vibeke's basement. Just a few clothes and a washbag had followed her to the hostel room she'd taken by Central Station, wondering what to do, where next to go.

She'd been about to go inside an hour earlier only to see Hanne Meyer and her children turn up in a cab as she approached the entrance. So Lund waited, hugging herself in the too-flimsy jacket, sitting on a wall, smoking, clutching the folder Jansen had smuggled to her that morning, running through the options in her overactive mind.

At a quarter to eleven they left, hunched against the cold.

Lund tucked the folder beneath her jacket, pulled the hood over her face, stayed where she was till they were out of sight.

Then she went to the hospital reception, pleaded for entry.

It took ten minutes. Finally she was led down a long white corridor to a private room at the end. The police would be paying. They had to in the circumstances.

She walked in, was briefly dazzled by the light from the long windows.

A shape by the glass. White hospital gown, blue pyjamas underneath, gleaming silver wheelchair.

Pale face, stubbly skin. Big ears. Pop eyes that seemed sadder than ever. A saline bag on a silver IV stand, a line running into the back of his left hand.

The television was on. Troels Hartmann's coronation as Lord

Mayor of Copenhagen. He was taking his seat in the council chamber, majestic as he waved to an audience on its feet, applauding enthusiastically, heralding the new master of the Rådhus.

Young and vigorous. Full of energy and hope.

Hope.

Meyer sat at a round table. He had a short knife in his hand and was peeling an apple very slowly, the line of the drip shifting up and down with each sluggish movement.

'I brought you something,' Lund said and pulled out two bananas from her pocket.

He looked at the yellow fruit, no expression on his face.

'I knew you'd beat it. I couldn't see your name on a wall in the Politigården.'

Pale blue pyjamas. White smock.

Hartmann was starting to make a speech on the TV.

'Bastard,' Meyer muttered.

Fine words. Noble aspirations. Poul Bremer's natural heir.

'He thinks . . .' Meyer struggled to find the right words. 'He thinks being not guilty's the same as being innocent. They all do. Just wash their hands . . .'

'I need—'

'They lied to us. The kids. The teacher. Those sons of bitches in the Rådhus.'

'You've got to—'

'Every last one of them. They didn't give a fuck about Nanna. It was all about them.'

He reached for the remote. Hartmann was getting into his stride. Talking about responsibility and social cohesion. Integration and sustainable development.

The Birk Larsen case was dead, gone for good. It hadn't been mentioned in the press at all that morning.

Meyer turned off the TV. The room became heavy with their silence.

Lund pulled Jansen's folder out of her jacket.

He stared as she emptied the contents onto the table next to the bananas.

Photos. New ones.

'What do you want?' he asked in a high, broken voice.

'There's something you need to know. Something . . .'

It was racing around her head, hadn't stopped since soon after Vagn Skærbæk died. Jansen's photos only made it run more quickly, like a movie looping through her imagination. There was evidence there. Dots screaming to be joined. If only someone would help. Someone who trusted her.

'Look,' she said. 'I can see it. So can you.'

Through the dark wood where the dead trees give no shelter Mette Hauge runs.

Breathless, shivering in her torn shirt and ragged jeans, bare feet stumbling in the clinging mud.

Cruel roots snag her ankles, snarling branches tear her strong and flailing arms. She falls, she clambers, she struggles out of vile dank gullies, trying to still her chattering teeth, to think, to hope, to hide.

Two bright beams follow, like hunters after a wounded deer. Moving in a slow approaching zigzag, marching through the Pinseskoven wasteland, through the Pentecost Forest.

Bare silver trunks rise from barren soil like limbs of ancient corpses frozen in their final throes.

Another fall, the worst. The ground beneath her vanishes and with it her legs. Hands windmilling, crying out in pain and despair she crashes into the filthy, ice-cold ditch, collides with rocks and logs, paddles through sharp and cutting gravel, feels her head and hands, her elbows, her knees, graze the hard invisible terrain that lurks below.

The chill water, the fear, their presence not so far away.

And a savage storm is raging through her head.

She thinks of her parents, alone in their distant farmhouse. A small, quiet world left behind.

Thinks of the day, the tiny pink tab they gave her. The rush, the glee, the promises. The demands.

A cheap gilt chain round her neck. A black heart made of glass. A half-finished tattoo on her ankle.

And then came the fury. The acid magic from Christiania working its livid sorcery. On her. On them

Out in the bleak lands beyond Kastrup. Hidden in the yellow grass, teeth chattering, blood racing.

An initiation she asked for. A ritual she cannot now reject.

Mette Hauge runs, knowing she is lost. Ahead of her lies nothing but the wasteland, and then the grey chill barrier that is the sea.

Still she flees, then falls.

Falls and waits, fists bunched and ready.

This Lund sees bright and clear in her restless head.

'The photos . . .'

Meyer wouldn't look at them.

'I got Jansen to go back and check things. Everything we had. What was left in the Merkur store.'

'I thought you were fired.'

'Mette's autopsy. The tape in the Rådhus garage. We never looked properly. You have to *look*.'

A picture passed across the table.

'On Mette's right ankle there are traces of a tattoo. A black heart. Half-finished. I think it happened the day she died. It was part of the . . . ritual.'

He stared out of the window, blinking at the brilliant winter's day.

'It wasn't done in a tattoo parlour. Not with professional needles. They did this themselves. It came with the ceremony. An ordeal you had to undergo to join.'

Meyer closed his big eyes, sighed.

'There was a gang called the Black Hearts. Small. They distributed dope and acid and cocaine from Christiania into Vesterbro.'

More papers.

'There's some intelligence in the files. They disbanded not long after Mette vanished.'

'What are you saying, Lund?'

'I'm saying Mette hung out with them. Wanted to join them. That's why they gave her the necklace. The tattoo. There was an initiation rite—'

'You said.'

'If she wanted to join she had to . . .'

It's coming clearer as she speaks. Makes her breath short. Makes her head spin.

'Had to what?'

'Let them do anything they wanted. Take whatever dope they

pushed on her. It was a biker gang, Meyer. You know what I'm talking about. What she had to pay . . .'

Pay the price.

Two men. One she liked. One she hated. Both the same now with the pink tab of acid running through their veins too. A lone beast, a single intent.

Trapped in the mud and the mire, half naked, screaming at the lowering sky, Mette Hauge sees them.

Feels them.

Hand on her, fingers ripping at her clothes.

Faces the decision.

Give in or fight.

A fist in her face. The crack of bone. The shriek of fear and pain.

A choice made. In the Pentecost Forest where none can hear.

'Here,' Lund said.

Another photo. Nanna in the Rådhus security office, talking to Jens Holck, asking for the keys to the flat in Store Kongensgade, telling him she's leaving.

The picture's blown up.

Around her throat, fuzzy from the magnification, sits what looks like the black heart necklace.

'She put it on when she changed after the Halloween party. Nanna had the necklace already.'

Pernille and Lotte both said . . . she was always going through drawers, looking where she shouldn't, borrowing things without asking.

'Nanna found that for herself.'

More pictures. A body floating face down in the water. The autopsy after. The shot marks of pellet wounds. A dead face. Grey moustache and scar. A fading mark on the arm.

Black heart.

'John Lynge. Picked out of the water near Dragør on Sunday. Shotgun wounds to the chest and head. He had the tattoo. I got out his files. When he attacked girls before he made them wash. He cut their fingernails.'

'We cleared the driver,' Meyer said with a pained, bored groan. 'He was in hospital.'

She hesitated. He seemed fragile. Upset by her presence.

'They let him out at seven the next morning. We've got the logs. Vagn called the agency that employed him not long after. Birk Larsen used them too. So we never thought much of it. The agency gave him Lynge's mobile. Vagn talked to him. He was trying to avoid trouble. For Nanna's sake—'

'But—'

'Vagn shot you. Vagn killed Leon Frevert. Killed John Lynge.'

This much was clear.

'You saw for yourself. He loved that family. Loved the boys. Loved . . .' Thinking, imagining. 'Loved what the Birk Larsens became. Something he could never find for himself.'

'Lund . . .'

She peeled the nearest banana, took a bite, liking the way the images formed in her head as she spoke.

'Vagn didn't have the black heart tattoo. That part of the wood he took Theis wasn't where Nanna was attacked. There's no evidence she was ever there. Vagn didn't know. Because he didn't kill her.'

Meyer had his head in his hands, looked ready to weep.

Saturday morning, the day after Halloween, outside the house in Humleby. Bright and sunny. Paper monster masks from the night before blowing up and down the street.

Vagn Skærbæk paced around the plastic sheets and scaffolding, turning to stop and yell at an angry face in the blue glass windows of the basement.

Someone was walking towards him from the green patch of Enghaven park. One day soon Anton and Emil would play there on the new bikes Skærbæk had reserved in the toy shop in Strøget, paying for them with some smuggled alcohol he'd got on the side. Soon . . .

The man who was approaching was tall and muscular. He stopped at the house, checked the number, looked at the Ford then said, 'Hi. I'm John. You called about the car.'

One more glance at the black vehicle.

'It doesn't look damaged.'

'It isn't. There's nothing wrong with it.'

A pause.

'Did you look inside?'

'It was a misunderstanding, OK? A mistake.'

The two men stood in silence for a moment, eyeing each other.

'Don't I know you?' Skærbæk asked, feeling a sudden and puzzling sense of recognition.

'If there's no damage . . .' the man began.

'I do know you.'

'What happened?'

'Does it matter? You've got it back. There's no damage. Can't we leave it there?'

Pasty face, sick maybe. Cheap clothes. Grey hippie moustache. Scar on right cheek. A memory swam through Skærbæk's head, teasing him, refusing to surface.

It had been a long and difficult night. The argument with Nanna at the flat where he found her after Frevert's call still rankled. Trying to find some truth among the lies she'd thrown at him, spitting, scratching with her nails.

'You're not going to the police, are you? She's a good kid really. She didn't steal it. There was an Indian boy who was messing with her. God, if I get my hands on him. I found your agency ID on the floor. Here . . .'

The man with the scar took the card and keys.

'I don't like the police,' he said. 'The car looks fine. Let's forget about it. No harm done.'

'I do know you,' Skærbæk said again. 'Maybe the agency. We use them sometimes . . .'

The bright morning felt confusing and strange. He'd scarcely slept in the Humleby house, listening to her cries and pleas locked in the basement, one floor below.

Now the young voice beyond the scaffolding and sheeting was back to high and shrill and getting louder.

Temper rising, Vagn Skærbæk went to the front door, bent down, looked at the blue glass and the shrieking face there.

'Nanna! For fuck's sake shut up! You're staying there till I get your dad. I'll be back here at twelve whatever. At least I'll know where you are.'

Eyes to the window, blonde hair bobbing, she yelled, 'Vagn, you creep—'

'Just wait, for God's sake! They're supposed to be on a break, you know. Having a weekend away. From you for one thing.'

She went silent then.

'Think about what your dad's going to say when he hears, huh? Jesus. Ripping off a car—'

'I didn't steal the fucking car!'

'Your raghead boyfriend then. Christ, you're Theis's daughter. Aren't you just?'

The man by the black Ford shifted on his big feet.

Skærbæk barely noticed. He was thinking about what Nanna was wearing.

'And take that bloody necklace off before your dad gets back. If he sees that . . .'

He left it there. Went to the road, to the man who was checking out the boot of the car.

'There's nothing missing, is there?' Skærbæk asked.

The lid went down quickly.

'Nothing.'

'Damned kids,' Vagn Skærbæk grumbled. 'She can stay in that hole and rot for all I care. If her old man hears . . .'

The stranger was listening.

'What did she do?'

'Never mind.' Skærbæk took out his phone. Tried to call again. Got voicemail. 'Come on, Theis. I've got work to do.'

'Best leave her there,' the stranger said. 'Kids need a lesson.'

A bleat from behind.

'She'd have to listen for that,' Skærbæk muttered, then yelled some more abuse at the blue window.

It was pointless. She'd never taken any notice of him. Of anyone really.

So he left the car with the man who looked vaguely familiar then stomped off back to the depot, cursing under his breath, juggling phone calls and schedules, callbacks and deliveries. Wondering how he might make everything fit, run along in one piece the way it should.

Twenty minutes later Vagn Skærbæk fell fast asleep on the chair in the office. Didn't stir for three hours. And then a sharp, cruel nightmare woke him with a startling memory. Too real, it felt. Too real.

A bright day. An empty day.

John Lynge looked at the black Ford. Couldn't stop listening to the high-pitched voice coming from the house, through the blue glass windows.

A girl's voice. Strong and weak at the same time. Young and knowing too.

A girl's voice.

He looked along the empty street of grey houses. Walked up to the window. Could see her through the stained glass. Bubbly hair. Beautiful face. Pleading eyes.

'Get me out of here, mister.'

One more careful sweep of the deserted road in Humleby. Up. Down.

'Get me out of here before that bastard comes back.'

Just after ten. A good hour to spare.

'Please. I'll give you something.' She paused. 'Some money.'

November. The month he always chose. He hadn't expected the opportunity to come so soon. The very first day. But it would come. It always had since that first time set the wheels in motion, turning like clockwork once a year.

'OK,' he said, then went back to the Ford and found the briefcase he had left in the boot the previous night.

Opened it.

Scissors and a bottle of ether. A gag. Two knives, two rolls of duct tape. A screwdriver and chisel. A bottle of liquid soap, a sponge and some medical wipes. Two packs of condoms and a tube of lubricating jelly. He was a careful man and always came prepared.

'Mister! Hey!' squealed the young voice from the basement.

Lynge closed the briefcase, walked to the door. They'd left their tools there anyway. A crowbar, waiting, begging.

That was easy.

At the foot of the stairs the door was locked and bolted. Her glittery handbag lay outside, left there he guessed for when she decided to be good.

He picked it up. Tissues, a purse, a phone. A pack of condoms with a happy couple on it. Naked. Smiling.

Lynge lifted it to his lips and kissed the picture there. Laughed to himself.

The girl called out through the door.

'I'm here,' he said. 'Don't worry.'

*

Lund fidgeted in her chair, blinking at the washed-out sun. There were more photos in Jansen's file. He'd done a good job. Risked a lot to help her.

'Vagn told Theis he got the call from Nanna. We'd worked that out. He locked her in the basement in Humleby overnight. But it was Lynge who attacked her there. Got her out the next morning. Took her somewhere else.'

'Why didn't Vagn go to the police?'

His voice was tetchy, hurt.

'He didn't realize who it was till Nanna was gone. He called the agency Birk Larsen used again. Vagn was checking. He'd remembered.'

'Remembered what?'

'Vagn loved Nanna. Loved them all—'

'Then why did he say he killed her? Why didn't he talk to us?'

She ate some more banana. Said nothing.

'You need help,' Meyer told her. 'You should be in here. Not me. You break lives, you know that?'

'Meyer—'

'You broke your own. You broke mine. You break everyone's and you don't even notice enough to care—'

'I care!'

A nurse appeared in the corridor, looking through the glass, checking out the sound of angry voices.

'I care,' she said more quietly.

'No. You just think you do. If you care you've got connections. Relationships. You depend on other people and other people depend on you. You don't connect, Lund. Not to me, not your mother, not your son. Any more than that bastard Hartmann connects. Or Brix . . .'

His eyes were shining. She thought he might cry.

'I've got a family. Theis and Pernille had one too until this black fucking thing came along and ripped them apart. With a little help from us. Don't forget that—'

'I care,' she whispered, feeling the tears begin to cloud her own eyes.

He wasn't a cruel man. A hard man even. She'd judged him badly at the start. Meyer didn't want to hurt her. He simply didn't understand.

'Vagn didn't do it. When you're feeling better. When you're out of here, back at work. You can go and find the records. I'm so close. For God's sake. You've got to help me—'

Jan Meyer threw back his head and howled.

Twenty years before, mobile phones cost a fortune so a run-down, near-bankrupt outfit like Merkur had just two. Aage Lonstrup was drunk in the office, no idea one of them was missing. No clue where the temps who made up the day's staff had gone. No work on the schedules. No future ahead.

Vagn Skærbæk went through the diary, trying to keep things afloat. Worrying. About money. About friendship. About the future.

The big black mobile on the desk rang. So crackly it was barely audible.

Skærbæk listened.

An inarticulate, scared plea for help.

Looked at Lonstrup snoring at his desk.

Took a Merkur van out to Vestamager, down the narrow roads, past the fencing that marked what would one day be new houses and a metro line running out into the wilds by the grey Øresund, past the warning signs of the dead firing range, into the wilderness.

Heart thumping, mind racing.

Found two motorbikes by the side of a black canal. One, the Triumph, he recognized. The other, a cheaper, smaller Honda, he didn't.

Thought for a moment. Opened the back doors, ran down the ramp, strained and heaved to get both machines inside.

November. Light falling. No sound except the jets going in and out of Kastrup.

He could have turned back. Gone home to his little flat. Taken out the books again, the training guides on becoming a teacher. Tried to pick up the threads of a life that had never truly started.

But debts were owed. Lives were saved. A conscience was like a wound. Once pricked it kept bleeding until something, some balancing deed, came along and staunched the flow.

So he took a torch out of the back and headed off into the wilderness, calling out one name over and over again.

*

'Thanks,' the girl said when Lynge broke open the downstairs door.

Pretty. Blonde. Tired. Angry.

Not frightened. Not yet.

He turned and closed the basement door behind him.

An hour and then they'd be somewhere else. Out in the wetlands. A hunter's hide. A log store. He knew the Pentecost Forest well. Could always find a place there. Could wash her in the cold black water, trim her nails, make her his.

'I'm going now,' she said.

He leaned against the wall. Looked.

Two decades, one girl each November, like a Christmas present come early. Hookers and drifters mainly. Dregs on the edge of the world, like him. So many over the years they all got blurred after a while.

But this one was different. This one was beautiful and young and pure.

He opened the case, retrieved the bottle of ether and the gag, placed them on the floor. Removed his belt, took out a roll of duct tape and ran out a length, cut it free.

Was on her the instant she started to scream. Strong arms round her golden head, strong fingers turning the tape around her pretty mouth, one hard blow to the skull dashing her to the floor.

Easy, he thought.

It was always easy. They begged for it anyway.

John Lynge checked his watch. Then began.

'Why would Vagn do that?'

'I need to be sure. I don't want to screw up again. To cause more pain.'

'Is that possible?'

'Yes. It is.'

He blinked. Picked up the knife, returned to peeling the apple, not noticing the exposed flesh had turned brown.

The transparent line in his arm bobbed up and down beneath the bag and the silver pole.

'You should go now,' he said.

She kept back the last picture. It wasn't the right time. Later. When he was better. When he came round.

'You'll be back in the Politigården before long. Once Brix realizes. Once you go through the files I tell you to—'

'Get out!' he yelled.

'I need you! I need your help!'

The nurse was through the door flapping, tugging at her arm.

'Meyer. When you're back at work . . .'

He held the knife upright, pushed it in front of her face.

The blade was so close. Lund went quiet. So did the nurse.

'What did you say?'

'When you're back at work,' she whispered, looking at him properly for the first time. Noting the strange, immobile way he sat. The force with which his left hand gripped the wheel of the chair.

There were no crutches in the room. None of the signs of recuperation she might have expected.

Jan Meyer waved the fruit knife in front of her then turned it, gripped the wooden handle hard in his fist, stabbed the sharp point through his blue pyjama leg with a vicious, deliberate force.

The nurse was screaming. Lund sat on her chair, stiff and cold and frightened.

He let go. The blade stood firm and upright in his thigh. Blood began to seep through the blue fabric. Meyer stared at her with his sad pop eyes.

No pain. No feeling at all. She saw this now and wondered why she'd never asked the simple, sensible question when she arrived.

How are you?

It wasn't because she didn't want to know. There were more pressing ones. That was all.

'Get out of here,' Meyer pleaded. 'For God's sake leave me alone.'

A doctor and a male nurse were there. Two of them dragging her to the door, one racing to Meyer, yanking the knife out of his flesh.

Dark blood staining the blue fabric. Spreading slowly. Not a sign of pain on his stubbly face. Not a hint he felt a thing.

They had Lund's arms, too strong for her.

There was something she wanted to say. But couldn't.

Something . . .

Three years was all Theis Birk Larsen would get. That was the betting in the Politigården.

Three years, half with parole. Out in eighteen months. Theis and

Pernille would survive, perhaps made stronger in some strange, cruel way.

Outside the sky was darkening. Rain on the way. Snow even.

Vibeke had taken back her green Beetle. So Lund walked to the station and bought a ticket to Vestamager, sat on the empty train, watched the city disappear out of the windows. After a while there was nothing left but a flat bleak wasteland speeding by as she headed towards the end of the line.

There were three of them in a shallow, muddy indentation hidden among the yellow grass, not far from a narrow canal. One, the smallest, a half-naked, bloody woman, not moving. The second, a man with a Zapata moustache and scarred cheek, tattoos and long black hair, wild-eyed and cackling, prodding at her from time to time. The other, the biggest, curled up in a foetal ball, eyes vacant and lost, a pool of vomit by his ginger head.

'Theis,' Skærbæk said.

The narrow slit eyes looked up at him. Pupils black and glassy, as blank and deep as the water in the canal.

'Jesus. What did you do this time?'

The guy with the stupid moustache stopped poking at the girl, pulled a bottle out of his pocket. Swilled some beer, passed it to Theis Birk Larsen.

Skærbæk grabbed the bottle, threw it away, screamed at them.

For no good reason. The girl was dead. These two were lost in an imaginary world of acid where nothing was real.

Forks in the road.

He wanted to turn back, leave them there.

Wanted to call the police for the first time in his small and irrelevant life.

But debts were owed. Consciences pricked. They were out on the Kalvebod Fælled, a wasteland no one visited. A place for hiding things. The harsh choice was made.

So he went to the Merkur van, climbed behind the Triumph and the Honda, took out plastic wrapping and strong tape, returned to the trio in the mud. Kicked the idiot with the moustache out of the way when he objected. Rolled the dead girl round and round, bound her tight like a carpet about to be moved.

Dumped her in the deep canal. Went back and yelled at them till they stumbled to the van.

The stranger was called John. He didn't want to leave at all. Looked ready to stay there, drag the dead body out of the water, unwrap her from the Merkur sheeting and start all over again.

By the time Skærbæk had got them out of there the night had turned pitch-black, damp and bitter.

He'd never forget this. Vagn Skærbæk knew that. Understood he'd joined himself to them. Was no different.

Where the public road started, and a few street lights marked the site of the coming metro station, he stopped the van, told them to get out. Made them empty all their pockets, the hash, the resin, the tabs and pills. Bellowed at them, made threats until it was gone.

Twenty minutes later he dumped John and his battered Honda on a back street near Christiania and thought: *I never saw your face before today and I pray I never will again.*

Drove back to Vesterbro, listening to the grunts of the big man in the passenger seat, huddled into a heap with his shame and his returning memories.

'I can't save you twice.'

There was puke in the footwell. He'd thrown up somewhere along the way.

'I mean that, Theis. You've got to cut this out. Leave the gang guys behind. Pick up with that nice girl again. The one who's sweet on you.'

No answer.

He pulled in by the side of the road not far from the Dybbølsbro bridge, looked at the early evening hookers out flashing their legs for the cars.

Turned to the slumped figure next to him.

'If you don't you're dead. Just one more piece of Vesterbro shit gone to waste.'

The sly, narrow eyes stared back at him.

Skærbæk never could read them.

He wound down the window, let the smell of puke drift out into the cold winter air.

Reached into his pocket, pulled out the thing he'd taken from the dead girl's neck.

'Here,' he said, and forced it into Birk Larsen's bloody hand.

A cheap necklace, a black heart made out of glass.

'It's yours now. I want you to remember. I want you to think of it and pray something like that never . . .'

He got mad. Had to scream.

'Never comes back and haunts you. I can't save you twice. Even if I wanted.'

There was a rap on the windscreen. A haggard skinny face, once pretty. A Vesterbro girl Vagn Skærbæk half recognized.

'Are you crying?' she asked, and seemed surprised.

He crunched the gears. Got the Merkur van out of there.

Next to him Theis Birk Larsen sat clutching the necklace. Staring at the black heart.

'Put it in your pocket,' Skærbæk told him and watched to see it was done. 'You keep that. You look at it the next time some moron comes along and puts some stupid idea in your stupid head. I want you to think . . .'

Debts owed, debts repaid. They were Vesterbro brats and they lived on the edge, always would. That made it all the more important to remember how easy it was to slip over and fall for good.

'I want you to think if you ever let go of that thing we'll end up back in this nightmare some day. Because you let the monster out again.'

No answer.

We're not like that, he thought. Not quite.

Vesterbro. Grubby streets. Cheap houses. Hookers and dope. The world as it was.

A black heart necklace. Like a Romany curse. Theis Birk Larsen could take it to his grave.

'You don't want that to happen,' Vagn Skærbæk said, driving over the bumpy cobbled road, staring into the drab distance. 'No one does.'

Lund got a bike from the study centre near the station, pedalled through the icy rain out to the marshland and the woods. Found the low metal bridge, sat on the concrete slabs that crossed it. Arms through the railings, feet dangling over the canal. The way Amir El' Namen was the week before with his sad bouquet of flowers behind him, tears falling down to the black water where Nanna died.

It was all in the photos and documents Jansen had found for her. Enough on its own. She didn't need Meyer really. That was cowardice on her part. Even Brix would listen if she made him.

If . . .

She put that decision to one side and counted what she knew.

Nanna was leaving, taking memories with her. A reminder of her father, who never rolled up his sleeve when he was working or washing the dishes, never showed his bare arms when the police were around.

But a child would see those old tattoos. A child would make the connection when she found a black heart necklace hidden away in a locked drawer. And a loving runaway daughter would want a memory to take with her for the journey.

Vagn did what he did because that was who he was. The man who fixed things, the one who kept the wheels turning.

Nanna was gone from Humleby. There was blood in the basement and it led all the way to the Pentecost Forest.

They were all gypsies. Lonstrup's daughter said that. Paths crossing constantly over the years, lugging furniture, cutting crooked deals. Theis and Vagn and the creature that was John Lynge, the first man they chased and then let go, trying to stay alive in the dismal underworld of Vesterbro.

She reached into the blue cagoule. The drizzle was pondering whether to turn to snow, settling on her, freezing her cheeks, making her simple ponytail hang icily against her neck.

Lund took out the last photo. The one she never showed Meyer.

Twenty-one years before. A fading Kodacolor snapshot. Outside a hippie house in Christiania, gaudy with peace and love signs. Three people. In the middle Mette Hauge, hair long and greasy, face blank and stoned. An innocent wandering from the straightforward pathway, out of curiosity and a childlike sense of excitement. As Pernille did once. As Nanna strayed too.

On Mette's left a long-haired man with a Zapata moustache, a furrowed forehead, dark, deep-set eyes, what looked like a fresh knife slash across his right cheek.

Take away the hair. Age the scar. Cut and grey the moustache. John Lynge.

On the other side the young Theis Birk Larsen, huge and brutally imposing. Ginger hair, ginger stubble. Grinning triumphantly at the camera, blue jeans, a denim waistcoat with gang colours. Possessive arm around her. King of the quarter. On his bulging right bicep, just visible, a line of tattoos. Among them what looked like – had to be – a small black heart.

There was only one answer to the riddle she'd refused to answer in the hospital. Racked by grief and guilt and shame, Vagn Skærbæk sacrificed his life to keep this other Theis hidden. Buried the truth about Nanna out of horror that a worse nightmare might rise from the bleak wasteland of the Kalvebod Fælled alongside John Lynge's black Ford dripping stagnant water and fresh blood. And take with it the secret miracle he cherished – envied – most of all, the precious bond of family, the ties that kept Pernille, Theis and the boys together in the face of a bleak, uncaring world.

All the lines were joined, in Lund's head if no one else's.

The wind murmured in the bare silver trees of the Pentecost Forest. She heard the soft hoots of owls, the pained screeches of a fox, the world breathing, rustling, moving. In her imagination she saw all the dead faces John Lynge had left rotting beneath the scummy water, watched their mouths open, heard them scream.

It was their shrieks with Nanna's that woke her that first morning, before the trip to Sweden, asleep in the arms of Bengt Rosling, a man she'd never see again.

Cries she'd never lose. A guilt she couldn't evade.

Seated on the hard ground, legs over the edge, Sarah Lund stared at the grainy snapshot leeching out its colour with age. Three faces, two dead, one living, trapped inside his own inarticulate guilt.

Eighteen months and Theis Birk Larsen would be back in the world, trying to rebuild his business, his family, to find the man he wanted to be, to lose the creature he once was.

Mette Hauge's murderer. The proof was in her hands.

Watching the icy rain fall on the old snapshot in her fingers, Sarah Lund leaned against the cold metal railings, wondering whether to let go.